Dear Readers,

Summer means only one thing to us: weddings! If you're in the mood for love, four fabulous new stories from Bouquet are sure to do the trick.

Award-winning author Vivian Lieber returns this month with the second installment of the Men of Sugar Mountain series, in which **Two Hearts** are re-united with sweet—if unexpected—results. Then Karen Drogin, praised by *Romantic Times* as a "rising star," offers **The Right Choice**—something one spirited advice columnist never thought she would need help making.

In **Love in Bloom**, from fabulous former Mira author Michaila Callan, a woman who ran away from a youthful passion finds herself all grown up . . . and ready for love. Finally, Kathryn Attalla wraps up the month with her second book for Zebra, **Worth the Wait**, in which a woman haunted by her past meets the man who promises her a future.

So hang up your bridesmaid's dress and relax with four terrific new Bouquet romances this month. True love never looked better.

Kate Duffy
Editorial Director

AN INNOCENT OUTING

"I love cotton candy." Taking a bite of the pink fluff, Carly closed her eyes and let the sugar dissolve in her mouth. "Heaven."

"Show me."

At the sound of Mike's deep voice, her eyes popped open wide.

"Just a little taste." The laugh lines crinkled around his eyes. "Please."

Before she could change her mind, she stuck one finger into the ball of pink fluff. "Open." She barely recognized her own voice.

Mike complied. She raised her sugar-laden finger and placed it into his waiting mouth, watching intently as his lips closed around her finger. Warm, wet, and welcoming. A rush of dizziness assaulted her, but that was like a small wave compared to the heady rush she received when he nibbled on her fingertip with his teeth. A tidal wave of sensations surged through her. Such a simple act threatened her very being.

She wanted what she'd never realized she was capable of wanting. What she'd never *allowed* herself to desire. She wanted passion. Wanted to soothe the ache that pounded in every part of her body. She wanted Mike.

And she couldn't allow it. . . .

THE
RIGHT
CHOICE

KAREN DROGIN

Zebra Books
Kensington Publishing Corp.
http://www.zebrabooks.com

ZEBRA BOOKS are published by

Kensington Publishing Corp.
850 Third Avenue
New York, NY 10022

First Printing: June, 2000
10 9 8 7 6 5 4 3 2 1

Printed in the United States of America

To Phil, who has always been the right choice for me, and to my special girls, Jaclyn and Jennifer, for making my life complete. I love you.

ONE

Carly Wexler stood back and admired the window display. Rays of sunlight streamed through the plate glass, illuminating an assortment of gold and diamond wedding bands. The enduring symbols of love and commitment caused her stomach to bunch into a tight knot. She closed her eyes, firmly convinced that a fresh glance at the sparkling rings would calm her nerves. After all, nothing could go wrong when a wedding had been planned as meticulously as hers.

She opened her eyes for another look. To her left, complementary wedding bands shimmered against a black velvet backdrop. His and hers. Carly and Peter. They were, as her fiancé reminded her, well-suited, sharing mutual friends and interests. A matched set, she thought, her gaze drifting over the glittering selections.

Every piece in the window had a partner . . . an apt description of her relationship with her fiancé. They didn't share a grand passion, but that was what made theirs a perfect union. In an ideal world, love and passion could coexist, making a couple a perfect fit, instead of merely offering them a perfect coexistence. But Carly no longer believed in fairy tales. Thanks to her father's destructive actions, she had seen the damage running on pure emotion could cause. Better to accept mutual respect and caring than to risk pain and disillusionment. She brushed at her newly cut bangs, paying little attention when they fell forward again.

A plain platinum and 18-karat gold set caught her eye. Though the criss-crossed bands were flanked on either side by more jeweled rings, Carly couldn't take her eyes off the simpler pair. "Perfect," she murmured. Too bad her fiancé would prefer a ring with more precious stones, one designed to impress.

"Like those." She tapped her finger against the window.

She understood Peter's need to make a statement, just as he understood her need for the perfect wedding with all the trimmings. Give and take, she reminded herself. Her finger traced a pattern on the cool glass.

"What woman wouldn't like all those glittering diamonds?" From directly behind her, a sexy yet unfamiliar voice vibrated in her ear.

The question intrigued her. "One with substance perhaps?" She answered without turning. Both her heart and her gaze had refocused on her ring of choice.

"And wit," the man added with obvious admiration.

She clasped her hands behind her back. "Good taste," she responded, enjoying the innocent game.

The answering chuckle, deep and resonant, captured her interest, diverting her from choosing the circular band that would forever bind her to her future husband.

"It takes brains to see beyond the dazzle of diamonds," the stranger said, approval marking his masculine drawl.

"I suppose." Curiosity aroused, she turned toward the voice, her long skirt floating around her bare legs as she moved.

The sensual voice tantalized but hadn't deceived. A ruggedly handsome man smiled at her. Her gaze locked with his. Hazel eyes flecked with gold shimmered beneath the afternoon sun and laugh lines bracketed a sensuous mouth.

Those mesmerizing eyes studied her intently. "Real beauty speaks for itself."

Her cheeks heated at the unexpected compliment. "Thank you," she murmured.

"Just stating the obvious."

Embarrassed, Carly acknowledged his words with a nod. She felt a connection with this stranger, one that defied logic. With long sandy hair streaked by the sun and the sexy way he rocked on the heels of worn hiking boots, he oozed wildness and danger, raw masculinity and cocky confidence. She brushed at her bangs with trembling hands. She preferred tame and safe. This man was anything but.

"So, what attracts *you*?" he asked. His gaze lingered on her an instant too long before darting to the jewel-filled window.

You do. The unbidden thought rocketed through her brain. "Those," she said in a hoarse croak. She pointed to the simple bands with a none too steady hand.

"Nice," he murmured in agreement. "So have we discovered what kind of woman prefers plain gold to diamonds?" His rich laugh hung in the air.

The sound warmed her, even as an unexpected chill dashed over her skin. She glanced up at the blue sky. A single puff of cloud covered the sun. Carly knew with complete certainty that this man, and not a passing feat of nature, caused her tremors and distinct sense of unease.

"Someone with more sense than to stand on a street corner in Manhattan and talk to a perfect stranger," she murmured. "Excuse me." She pivoted on her heel, intending to head inside the store, where safety in numbers awaited her.

"Carly, wait."

She froze in midflight, turning back toward that compelling voice. "Who are you?" she asked warily.

"Mike Novack, Peter's brother." He held a bronzed hand toward her.

She silently cursed her fiancé's lack of sentiment. The only picture she'd seen of Mike had been as a young boy. Certainly she'd have recalled seeing a current photo of the good-looking man standing before her.

"Brother." Even as she reached out her hand, dismay and self-loathing rippled through her. Flirting with a stranger while shopping for wedding bands had been bad enough, but flirting with Peter's errant brother showed a decided lack of judgment.

The type of judgment she'd expect from her father, not from herself.

"Last time I checked," Mike said.

His strong hand grasped hers and she lost any sense of equilibrium she might have felt. His calloused fingers wrapped around her skin, enclosing her hand in warmth.

Heat traveled from her fingers, up her arm and into her breasts before settling in the pit of her stomach. Through sheer force of will, she tried to ignore the new and unnerving sensations.

She wrenched her hand free from Mike's grasp and focused all her attention on the plate-glass window. Without the sun's rays, the rings had lost much of their sparkle and allure. She wrapped her arms across her chest in a futile attempt to warm herself inside and out.

"Carly?"

She grit her teeth against the sound of concern in his deep voice. "Obviously you've seen my picture."

Mike smiled. "The one on Peter's desk."

"I wish I could say the same of you."

"I'm the photographer in the family, not Pete."

"So I've heard. Are you also the family flirt?"

His eyes narrowed in confusion. "I know I've been out of the country for a while, but when did casual conversation become slang for come-on?"

She blew her bangs out of her eyes with a hard puff of air. "Okay, I overreacted." To a man who made her heart race and her palms sweat. As far as she was concerned, she'd definitely underreacted.

She really wanted to run and hide from Mike and from herself. "Truce?" she asked, holding out her hand. To prove she could handle physical contact, not because she craved the sensations his warm touch aroused.

"Truce." Mike grasped and released her hand in a quick movement. Not because he couldn't handle touching her soft skin, but because his mere presence had obviously left her shaken. He had no idea why.

"Where is Peter?" Carly asked.

"Work. He was on his way out the door when a last minute crisis hit. He sent me along with his apologies."

"Lawyers." The nonchalant shrug of her shoulders was at distinct odds with the disappointed look in her eyes. "At least this time he remembered to send someone to tell me." She smiled. "Thank you."

"My pleasure," he said. The woman standing before him was a definite surprise.

When Mike had asked about Carly, Peter had answered with a distracted, "We're two of a kind, a match made in professional heaven." To Mike the answer had been the equivalent of "She's got a good personality." Never a rave review for a woman. Mike had then sought answers in the framed picture on Peter's desk. The black-and-white photo hadn't done justice to this woman.

Perhaps she wasn't a knockout, but she definitely possessed a certain something that made a man look twice. An elusive quality he'd like to capture on film. Light brown hair with golden highlights framed her face and caressed her shoulders in soft waves. Wispy bangs fell just below her eyebrows—when she wasn't swiping at them with one hand. Mike suppressed the urge to brush them aside, just to see if her hair felt as soft as it looked. Her lips were a bit too full but glistened enticingly beneath a sheen of pink gloss.

His brother was one lucky SOB. Not that Mike would ever trade his freedom for the confines of marriage, but he intended to make sure Peter appreciated his good fortune.

"Mike?"

A tap on his shoulder took him by surprise and he flinched.

"Are you okay?" she asked.

"Fine." He rolled his shoulder in a circle, stretching the tight muscles. He wondered if the recent injury would ever heal, or if the ache along with the scars were meant as a permanent reminder of what he'd left behind and all he still had to go back to.

"I asked how much time we've got." She lifted one eyebrow in question.

"About . . ." He glanced at his watch. "Another five, ten minutes, depending on whether or not Pete gets sidetracked. If he's not here by a quarter after, he said to consider him a no-show and he'll call to reschedule." He grinned. "His words, not mine."

"Not a problem. It's nothing unusual anyway."

Awfully accepting for a woman waiting to pick wedding bands with her beloved fiancé, Mike thought. "I see Pete still treats his personal life like a business meeting."

"Don't judge him." Her eyes narrowed, flashing angry sparks.

Her defense of her fiancé was admirable if undeserved, Mike thought.

"Lawyers' hours are unpredictable. I understand."

"So do I." But if his driven, workaholic brother often ignored Carly in favor of legal briefs and pestering clients, he needed a libido transplant.

"He wanted to be here," she said.

"I never said otherwise. I just said he hasn't changed."

A muscle twitched in her cheek for a second before she gave in and smiled. "I guess you do know your brother well."

"You sound surprised."

"It's just that he's always concerned about you, but you're . . ." She trailed off. A slight flush stained her cheeks, painting them a rosy pink.

"Rarely in touch," he finished for her. "Comes with the territory. The places I travel lack the luxury of pay phones."

"But the two of you are close."

"We're brothers." For Mike, that said it all. But for each other, Mike and Peter had no one else in the world who cared. Except Carly. Peter now had his fiancée and Mike had to stop staring at her as if he'd discovered uncharted territory. Better to concentrate on the upcoming wedding and lifelong commitment between Carly and his brother.

"How long will you be in town?" she asked.

"At least the month until the wedding and probably awhile afterward. Then I hit the road again." He had no other choice. He'd left midassignment because he'd allowed personal demons to haunt him. He knew damn well he had to face them down if he wanted to look himself in the mirror every morning. Mike Novack never left a job undone, and the man he knew himself to be wouldn't let the past haunt him.

Once he returned to the rambling life he'd always loved, everything would get back to normal. Or so he hoped, glancing at the woman about to marry his brother.

"Ready to check out the rings inside?" Mike asked.

"Sure." But her gaze strayed to the jewel-filled window once again.

"Is there one you really like?" he asked.

"Those." She leaned forward and tapped lightly, indicating a set of simple two-toned rings.

A woman with substance. His mind ran through their earlier banter and he realized she'd meant every word. "They're beautiful," he said.

She turned to look at him. "But not Peter's taste." A frown touched her lips and a corresponding sadness flashed in her gentle brown eyes.

"You're right. They wouldn't stop traffic. Pete would prefer something a little more . . . noticeable."

She sighed.

"You obviously know him well, too," Mike said.

She smiled. "We understand each other."

Did they? Mike had spent but a few minutes with each and he'd already begun to wonder. Watching Carly stare longingly at the rings in the window, he grew concerned.

"It's getting late," she murmured. "I hope he realizes these things can't be rushed and we have to have them ordered, sized and engraved. Then there's the tuxedos, the final flower arrangements, the . . ."

"Relax. No list is set in stone. It'll all get done in time."

"Only if we follow my schedule."

Mike placed a comforting hand on her bare shoulder, realizing his mistake too late. Her skin felt like fine silk beneath his roughened fingers. He breathed in deeply. She looked like sunshine and smelled like vanilla. A potent combination, he discovered.

"What if we get a cup of coffee and go over this schedule of yours? I'm sure you'd relax once you see everything will fall into place."

Her frantic gaze darted from his hand, which remained on her shoulder, to the rings in the storefront window. "Coffee's not such a good idea."

He ought to let her go. After his overwhelming reaction to her, distance seemed the safest route. "We've got the time," he muttered instead.

"Pick up any magazine or newspaper. Caffeine's not good for you." She stepped toward the street. Before he realized her intent, a yellow taxi screeched to a halt.

"Thanks for meeting me. I'm sure with all the wedding things going on I'll be seeing a lot more of you." Her rambling clearly stated that she hoped that wouldn't be the case. Those huge brown eyes told another story.

"Count on it," he said with a smile.

No sooner had she darted into the waiting cab than the taxi pulled away from the curb.

"Ah, the joys of living in New York City." He watched as the brake lights disappeared into the maze of traffic, taking Carly farther away.

Carly stepped into the familiar lobby of Peter's building. The smell of fresh paint permeated the air. Clean white walls surrounded chrome and mirrors. She wasn't surprised. Thanks to the cost of the apartment and the condominium fees, the tenants in this Upper East Side luxury building demanded quality service and maintenance. Peter was no exception.

"Evening, Miss Wexler."

"Hi, George." Carly smiled at the gray-haired doorman she'd known as long as she'd known Peter. "Is he in?" she asked.

"Flew past me not ten minutes ago."

"Good. Do me a favor, don't announce me." She leaned closer to the small desk. "I want to surprise him."

The older man grinned. "Not a problem. You be good," he said with a laugh.

"I always am. Thanks, George. And you have a

nice night." With a wave, she headed for the bank of elevators at the far end of the hall.

In the normal course of events, Carly went out of her way *not* to surprise Peter, but his schedule had been decidedly uncooperative lately.

The elevator doors glided open and Carly stepped inside. Since her engagement, she'd given the wedding planning "experts" free rein. In her role as columnist and counselor, others relied on Carly for advice, but in her personal life she had no problem deferring to those more experienced than she . . . especially now. She'd made a commitment, and vows were something she intended to repeat only once in this lifetime.

She stepped out of the elevator and walked down the familiar hallway, pausing outside Peter's apartment. A rush of panic hit her and she wished she'd called first.

Too late. She rapped lightly on the door.

"Coming." The muffled voice was followed by heavy footsteps and the rattle of a chain lock.

"You guys are late and I'm starving." The door swung open wide. "You're not the pizza man."

Carly swallowed hard. "And you're not Peter." She hadn't expected to see Mike again without being forewarned. Nor had she expected the adrenaline rush to be quite so potent the second time.

"Thankfully, no. I'm much more laid-back and a heck of a lot better-looking."

"All ego," she said, suppressing a grin.

"Not enough substance?" Mike asked.

Too much, she thought, as they fell into the easy banter of earlier that afternoon.

He gestured her inside. Carly stepped past him. The warm aroma of spiced aftershave assaulted her senses, heightening her awareness of the man standing in the entryway. Behind her, the apartment door closed with a heavy thud. She turned to find Mike leaning, one shoulder propped against the wall. One bare muscular shoulder. A shudder rippled through her, catching her unaware.

"Did you decide to take me up on that cup of coffee?" he asked with a knowing grin.

She fingered her bangs. "I'd forgotten all about it." She hadn't forgotten him, though. In fact, she'd spent the rest of the day attempting to push all thoughts of Mike Novack out of her mind.

He walked toward her, forcing her to acknowledge that she'd been unsuccessful in her attempt. "I'm disappointed," he said. "But you can make up for your lack of concern by sharing my pizza." His gaze never wavered.

Golden eyes captured her, making her feel cornered. Light-headed. Excited. She anticipated the rush that came with their verbal sparring.

He tapped the tip of her nose with one finger. "I hate eating alone."

"I'll bet you rarely do," she muttered.

A cough jolted Carly into sudden awareness of her surroundings. She jerked away from Mike, feeling a mixture of guilt and lingering desire.

"This is a surprise," Peter said, watching them both from a few feet away.

"Not an unwelcome one, I'm sure." Mike walked past her and seated himself on the sleek leather couch in the living room. He propped his feet on a glass cocktail table and crossed his arms over his chest.

"Of course not," Peter said. He smiled and extended a hand toward Carly. She went to him, trying to ignore the feel of Mike's burning gaze. She brushed a kiss on Peter's damp cheek. Freshly showered, he smelled of familiar soap and shampoo. He drew her against him, resting his arm around her waist. "Carly's always welcome. This visit just wasn't planned."

Carly grinned and elbowed him in the ribs. "Since planning hasn't worked, I decided to ambush you instead. Look." She patted the bag that hung from her shoulder, bulging with lists and articles from the most recent wedding magazines.

Peter groaned. Looking thoroughly put out and grumbling about neurotic women, he allowed Carly to lead him to the couch and push him onto the cushion beside Mike. She knew better than to be insulted. Long before they'd gotten engaged, she and Peter had been friends. He understood her even when she drove him to sheer exasperation with her never-ending lists and articles. Besides, they shared the same goal—marriage and the perks that came with it.

For Carly those perks included stability and security. For Peter, she sensed their engagement had more to do with her solid support as he climbed the ladder toward partnership. When all was said and done, they wanted the same things, even if their dreams were a little different.

"Ready to get started?" She knelt down beside her fiancé.

"Go for it," Mike said.

She chuckled aloud, determined to ignore the feelings he aroused. Seated together, Carly noticed a slight resemblance between the brothers. Both had light brown hair, though Peter's had been recently cut and lacked the sun-kissed streaks of gold. They possessed similar profiles, but Mike's tanned skin glowed from time spent in the rugged outdoors. Peter possessed a refined polish, a veneer he'd worked hard to achieve. She appreciated both men's handsome looks . . . and refused to compare any further.

"Can we make it quick?" Peter asked. "I've got a brief to finish and file by nine tomorrow morning."

"Pete . . ."

"Sure," Carly said, cutting Mike off. He hadn't been around often enough to understand the demands of his brother's job. Having grown up the daughter of a prominent attorney, Carly did. "Humor me for a little while," she said and began to pull items from her bag

Calendar, lists and pictures soon decorated the table. Despite Peter's token protests, Carly knew he realized that a few hours tonight would save them both a lot of aggravation in the future.

"See what I have to put up with?" Peter asked. She recognized the tinge of humor in his voice.

Mike glanced at Carly. "Life's rough, Pete. Next

time a beautiful woman wants my undivided attention for a few hours, remind me to complain."

"Even if she wants to domesticate you?" Peter held up a glossy photo of a bride and groom.

The brothers shared a laugh, allowing Carly to see the bond that existed between them. One she hadn't truly believed in before now.

"In that case," Mike said, "I'd be on the first plane out of here."

Carly's stomach contracted painfully, a spasm she attributed to an aching emptiness and a sudden need . . . for food.

Mike yawned, glad the wedding plans were finally winding down.

"That's two P.M. Friday at the tuxedo place and ten A.M. Saturday at the florist?" Pete asked.

Carly glanced down at her appointment book and nodded. "No excuses, no delays." She pointedly raised her eyes and looked at her fiancé.

"As long as no surprises come up."

"They won't."

Mike closed the pizza box. Despite the presence of his brother and Carly, he'd eaten alone. For the better part of two hours, Carly and Peter had bargained their way through last minute wedding arrangements. If the couple sitting before him was to be believed, the perfect wedding involved little sentiment and a lot of details. The Carly Wexler he'd seen mooning over her favorite wedding band hours earlier had displayed more emotion than the one here tonight.

What had happened to the glimpse he'd gotten of the softhearted romantic? Around his brother, she was nowhere to be found.

"You'll be there or I'll compromise my principles and have my father cover your caseload himself." An angelic smile lit her features.

"Father?" Mike couldn't help but interrupt.

His brother glanced over. "Senior partner," he muttered. *A match made in professional heaven.* Mike nearly choked on a mouthful of soda.

Peter turned to Carly. "I'll be there," he promised.

"Then we're all set." She snapped her leather-bound diary closed.

"Definitely for the tuxedos, possibly for the flowers," Pete said in an obvious last-minute attempt to maneuver the plans to his advantage.

She lifted one eyebrow. Mike held his breath.

"Done," she said.

A woman who apparently knew when to accept compromise gracefully.

Peter stood. Carly followed, rising from her seat on the floor. She stretched her arms above her head. Her round breasts lifted enticingly beneath the body-hugging material of her tank top. Mike's groin hardened, thrusting against the rough denim of his jeans. He swallowed a groan. A long night was about to get much longer.

"Time to let you get back to your work," she said to Peter.

His brother smiled. "A woman after my own heart." He placed one hand on the small of her back.

To his shock, Mike bit back a protest at the intimate contact. Throughout the evening, other than to ask Mike an occasional wedding-related question, Carly had ignored him. Having been the sole focus of her attention twice today, he couldn't help feeling slighted.

"Good job, you two," Mike said.

Startled, she whirled around and met his gaze. She brushed at her bangs. Her wide-eyed vulnerability hit him hard.

"Mike."

His name on her lips sounded incredibly right . . . despite the fact that his brother stood by her side.

"Good night." She ducked her head, brushing past him without another glance.

The vanilla scent he'd noticed earlier wrapped around him like a warm friend. "See you."

While Peter walked Carly to the door, Mike flipped channels on the television with the remote control. Their muffled voices and Carly's soft laugh drifted inside, commanding his attention. He swore and raised the volume a notch higher. Whether or not Peter kissed Carly was none of his concern. What those full lips would feel like was also none of his business.

With a guttural curse he'd picked up abroad, Mike shut the television, rose and headed into the guest room. Better to face his nightmares than to eavesdrop on the two lovers saying good night.

TWO

Mike glanced around in disbelief. The tuxedo store couldn't possibly hold more than five people comfortably. Yet there had to be at least fifteen customers vying for the attention of two harassed salesmen. "I don't believe this," he muttered.

"I do."

Mike stood in the crowded store, too close to Carly, surrounded by her tantalizing scent. Whoever coined the term *best man* hadn't had him in mind. At this rate, his goal of getting in and out looked bleak. And though he'd enjoy a morning in her company, he didn't need the temptation. His brother wouldn't appreciate Mike's interest in his future wife.

"Looks like everyone wants to be a June bride," he said.

She rolled her eyes. "Did you get a good look around you? The girls can't be out of their teens and half of these guys have barely begun to shave. This is prom season, too." Folding her hands in her lap, she took a seat in a vacant chair in the corner.

Mike leaned against the wall beside her. "Since

Peter's meeting us and he's typically late, I guess we'll have to wait anyway."

"True."

"Would you really have pulled rank on him?" Mike asked, seeking to understand this unlikely twosome. He knew that only a threat to Peter's career would keep his single-minded brother from getting lost in work and forgetting an appointment. Even for his own wedding.

"We'll never know, will we?" She sighed and glanced at her watch.

"He isn't late yet."

"I never said he was. I'm the one on a tight schedule today."

"Business or pleasure?"

"Both. I've got a late-afternoon deadline for my column and a four o'clock meeting."

"Pete mentioned something about an advice column and some kind of counseling." Mike glanced in Carly's direction, more than a little curious about the many facets of Carly Wexler.

"Mmm. I write a magazine column for teens and I'm also a high-school guidance counselor."

"Social worker?" he asked.

"Psychologist."

"Sounds like you're busy."

She shrugged. "It's seasonal. The fall is pretty hectic, but the summers are my own."

"A job with perks. I like that."

"Considering you're a world traveler, I don't doubt it," she said with a grin.

From across the room a loud burst of male laughter was followed by distinctly feminine giggles. "What sort of advice do you give these kids?" Mike gestured in the direction of the carefree teens.

When was the last time he'd been *that* carefree? he wondered and immediately realized the incongruity of the question. He went out of his way to keep his life unencumbered by ties or commitments, yet lately he felt more burdened than ever before.

"They write in asking about how to deal with life. Friendship in some cases, love in others."

"And you answer with the voice of experience?"

"Hardly." She blushed a becoming shade of pink.

More like the voice of inexperience? Suddenly he wondered—about Carly, Pete, Carly and Pete— about a lot more than he had a right to know.

"I can't be late for that meeting." She not so subtly changed the topic.

"School appointment?" he asked.

She shook her head. "A publisher contacted me through the magazine. They'd like me to consider turning my columns into a self-help type of book."

"I'm impressed."

She waved away his compliment. "Good thing this shouldn't take long. Black double-breasted tuxedos, white shirt, wing-tipped shoes and black bow ties and cummerbunds. What could be simpler?"

"Or more boring."

She tilted her head backward and glared up at him. "What is that supposed to mean?" Fire flashed in her dark eyes, an unbelievable contrast to the controlled woman who'd sat with Peter and bartered over wedding arrangements.

The simmering passion intrigued him, made him want to dig deeper, beyond the exterior to the woman beneath. "Ever hear of color?" He deliberately baited her. "Or do you want the wedding party to resemble the Sunday *Times?*"

"Mike . . ."

"Sorry. Bridesmaids dresses bring in color, right? What would you pick? Pink?" He shook his head. "Too childish. There's yellow . . ."

"Mike."

"Peach."

"Mike."

"Or my personal favorite, purple." He eyed her intently. "Which is it?"

"White."

He groaned aloud. "Your choice?" he asked. *Not a chance in hell.* Behind those rigid lists and schedules lurked a woman brimming with passion and fire. He'd bet his favorite camera on it.

More than once he'd ignited sparks in those expressive brown eyes. Sparks he'd yet to notice between Carly and her fiancé. His brother, he harshly reminded himself. "White," he muttered, shaking his head.

"Not my choice exactly. I wasn't sure. Peter wanted elegant, my mother wanted formal, so we . . ."

"Compromised," he finished for her. "It's a good thing you're so compliant."

"You make me sound like a well-behaved pet. Are you looking to start trouble?"

Looking for trouble? No. Looking for a glimpse

of the untapped sensuality that sizzled beneath the conservative facade? Definitely. "Of course not," he said.

"Good. I just pick my battles carefully."

"I'll remember that. It's just . . ." He shook his head. "Never mind. None of my business."

Her eyes narrowed with distrust . . . and a slight spark? "What?" she asked through clenched teeth.

"This is your wedding, right?"

"Stupid question."

"Is it? For someone loaded down with wedding books and bridal pictures you're giving up control of some major issues." He reached for her, covering her ice-cold hand with his warmer one. He gazed into her eyes. The spark erupted into a flame of unchecked desire.

His thumb brushed over her third finger, avoiding the large diamond ring that looked so out of place on her delicate hand. Traitorous desires consumed his body while conflicting emotions swirled inside his head. The pad of his thumb traced a pattern just above her knuckle, where her wedding band would sit. "Think about it," he murmured.

She shot him a look that could freeze hot coffee and wrenched her hand free from his.

"Miss Wexler?" a salesman greeted her. The rush of high-school students disappeared out the door, taking the loud laughs and boisterous shouts along with them. "Sorry to keep you waiting."

"That's okay." She stood, obviously grateful for the interruption.

"If you and your fiancé are ready to get

started . . ." Mike remained standing against the wall and glanced at Carly.

She fingered her bangs, a nervous gesture he found awfully endearing. And sweet. The woman would never hold her own in a game of poker, but at least he'd never be left guessing about her true feelings.

"He's not my fiancé," she finally said.

"Future brother-in-law." The label grated. Mike forced a smile and shook the other man's hand.

"Are we waiting for the groom?"

"No. We can start with the best man. Peter will be here soon," Carly said.

Wisely, Mike didn't touch that statement. Ten minutes later he stood in front of a full-length mirror, decked out in formal attire. "Jacket's too tight," he said, rolling his bad shoulder to alleviate the discomfort. He'd deal with the bow-tie issue later.

"We have a tailor downstairs." The salesman brushed a hand across the back of the jacket.

Carly swallowed hard. The material rippled over Mike's broad shoulders. She clenched her hands into tight fists but the gesture didn't alleviate the need to touch him. Nor did it lessen the painful knot in her stomach.

The salesman continued to speak, drawing her attention back to tuxedos and tailoring. "Needs some alterations, but nothing major. If you folks will excuse me, I'll be right back."

Carly walked around Mike, scrutinizing the snug fit of the material and trying not to imagine the lean, hard body beneath the tailored clothing. "It suits you."

He shrugged. "I'm more comfortable in jeans and work boots."

He looked sexy in either. "More comfortable for the jungle, huh?"

She took two steps backward. "What would you change . . . presuming the choice was yours?"

"For starters, this would have to go." He reached up and untied the black bow tie, tossing it onto the nearest chair. "Then this." He unbuttoned the conservative jacket and flung it aside. The black cummerbund followed.

Carly barely had time to assimilate his intent when he began to unbutton his shirt. "Now hang on a second."

He grinned but didn't stop removing his clothes. "You asked."

She watched in silence as he shed the shirt, baring a tanned chest, muscular forearms and a flat stomach. Without warning a wave of desire overcame common sense and her body reacted. The knot in her stomach tightened almost painfully, making her more aware of him than she had been before. If such a thing was possible.

He stood in front of her clad only in black trousers while she did her best to remain composed despite the rapid beating of her heart. "What next?" she managed to ask.

An irreverent gleam sparkled in his eyes, which appeared more golden than hazel, and held her in thrall.

"Don't answer that," she muttered.

"Close your eyes."

Carly did as he asked, hoping to find a respite from the newly awakened sexual feelings this man aroused. But her imagination failed to cooperate. Mike's tanned chest, well-muscled arms and overall powerful physique had been forever imprinted in her mind.

She heard the rustle of clothing and a few colorful curses before he finally spoke. "Open those beautiful eyes and tell me what you think."

Looking every inch the rebel, Mike's new outfit blatantly defied convention. His black European tuxedo jacket sported a shawl collar. In place of the old tuxedo shirt he now wore a white collarless one, buttoned to the top. The lavender cummerbund distinguished him from the typical attorney look Carly was used to.

"I told you purple was my favorite." He grinned. "So what do you think?"

She opened her mouth to speak, but words wouldn't come. Considering the thoughts rampaging around her brain, perhaps that was just as well. A little wild, a little sexy and a lot she desired. Beyond that Carly couldn't think at all.

"Your shirt's crooked." She walked up to him and stood on tiptoe. Her fingers gripped the front of the shirt. She drew a deep breath, only to find she'd made another mistake. His cologne, an enticing scent she'd recently come to know, seeped inside her.

She'd dreamed of this scent. Of him.

"Carly."

She glanced up, meeting his gaze. Now darkened by unmistakable need, his eyes turned a deeper shade of gold, and she felt drawn into the compelling depths. Unnerved, her fingers began to tremble.

He rested his warm hand on her waist. If he'd meant to steady her, his touch had the opposite effect and a tremor shot through her. A soft sigh escaped her lips.

He drew her close. Their bodies never connected, but something else did. His fingers tightened around her waist and the heat of his body wrapped her in warmth. Passion flared to life inside her. As if she could feel the imprint of his arousal against her skin, she ached for fulfillment. For him. Her hips jerked forward without her permission.

"Easy," he whispered, but his hold on her waist tightened.

In the back of her mind she heard the gentle tinkling of bells. Is this what she'd always feared? What she'd been so ingrained to distrust? Her father's love affair had destroyed so many lives. Carly had learned early that protestations of love couldn't be trusted and passion could only lead to disaster. But with Mike's arms wrapped firmly around her waist, the lessons of her parents' past seemed far away.

"Sorry I'm late, but a client showed up unexpectedly from the West Coast."

"Peter." With a startled gasp, Carly wrenched herself from Mike's embrace and turned to face her fiancé. "I was just . . ." She groped for an explanation and settled on the truth. "Crooked shirt," she said, gesturing toward Mike. Even as she spoke, she struggled to get hold of her emotions.

"I'm glad you started without me, but . . ." Peter's gaze darted to Mike. Seconds passed during which she held her breath before Peter turned back to face her. "I thought we agreed on conventional."

She exhaled, relieved that all seemed normal. Although she wondered if anything would ever be right again. But for now, with Peter focused on getting the "right look" and then heading back to the office, Carly realized that everything was truly fine. She was safe. For now.

She glanced at her fiancé. He studied his brother and shook his head. "With all the business associates who will be there, this won't work."

For the first time since planning her wedding, Carly vacillated—between the old need to make Peter happy and a sudden desire to please Mike. Between her old, compliant self and this unfamiliar woman with desires she didn't recognize.

"This was a joke, Pete." Mike grinned and tugged at the purple cummerbund. "I was just killing time."

Stark relief etched Peter's face. Carly turned away and mouthed a silent "thank you" in Mike's direction. His mouth tightened, but he nodded imperceptibly.

She inhaled and forced much needed air back into her lungs. Crisis averted, she thought, as Mike scooped up the original clothing and ducked inside the dressing room to change.

She ought to have felt relieved. So why did she feel so empty instead?

"That's it." Carly reached for the purse she'd hung over the side of the full-length mirror. She desperately needed fresh air and time alone.

"Don't forget dinner tomorrow night with your parents," Peter reminded her. "Your father wants to meet my brother." He turned to Mike. "And with the way your plans change, this might be his last chance for a while."

Carly caught her breath and pivoted on her heel. "I thought you were staying the month until the wedding." To her dismay she hadn't kept the hint of panic from creeping into her voice.

Mike smiled, a warm, engaging smile, not the boyish grin he'd treated her to earlier. It was almost as if he knew she sought reassurance and wanted to relax her. But that was silly. "I am," he said with certainty. "I wouldn't miss this for anything."

"Oh." She swiped at her bangs. "Well then, I'd better get going. I can't afford to be late." She leaned forward and brushed a kiss on Peter's cheek.

She dared a brief glance at Mike. His penetrating gaze met hers. " 'Bye," she whispered before heading for the door.

The tinkling of bells echoed long after she'd left. "Well," Mike said, turning toward his brother. "This trip home has been extremely interesting."

"How so?"

"I never thought I'd see the day you'd trade your freedom for a white picket fence."

Peter opened the top button on his white, starched shirt and tucked his paisley tie into his jacket pocket. "People change."

"Not that much. I thought you had one thing in mind: the fast track toward partnership."

Pete grinned. "I'm doing just that."

Which is what had Mike worried. "You're sure about this marriage?"

"Absolutely. Look, sometimes in life you compromise to get what you want. Carly and I get along well. She understands that business is important to me."

"She's something, all right," Mike muttered. He'd touched her and she'd nearly come apart in his arms. The memory still lingered, teasing his tenuous restraint. Even in passion she radiated innocence, something lacking in his jaded life. "How'd you two meet?" he asked his brother.

"At a dinner honoring her father. She's been a good friend for the last few years."

Not an easy feat where his uptight, self-absorbed brother was concerned. "I know it's none of my business, but is that a reason to get married?"

Pete sighed. "She's looking for a little stability, a happy home life, kids and her career. She'll have those things with me."

Mike watched his kid brother fidget the way he'd done after accidentally breaking the porch light with his baseball. Looking to protect him from their uncle's wrath, Mike had taken the blame and the punishment. And Peter had let him. Mike had a hunch that given the chance, Pete would still take the easy way out. "And what are you getting out of this . . . arrangement?"

"She's a sweet woman, Mike."

Tell me something I don't know. "And would her father being senior partner have something to do with this sudden urge to say 'I do?' "

"Doesn't hurt," he admitted. "Lately new partnerships are rare. Even the most outstanding associates have been passed over. Things should return to normal with an economic upswing like this firm experienced this last year."

"So Carly's added insurance." Mike couldn't suppress a groan.

"It's not like that." Pete gestured toward the door, and Mike followed his brother out to the street. The summer heat drifted up from the pavement. Mike broke into a sweat before they'd reached the corner.

"Do you love her?"

"No." Pete didn't hesitate before answering. "Not like you mean. But she's not *in* love with me either." He shrugged. "We have a mutual respect for one another, though, and that's more than a lot of married couples can say. I do care about her, Mike."

Not liking the matter-of-fact way Pete laid out what should have been emotional feelings, Mike clenched his fists at his sides. "You're something else, Pete."

"We're both adults and we understand each other."

So Carly had said. Mike didn't like the picture

he'd gotten of this relationship, but their lives weren't his concern. As long as he repeated the mantra and believed it, he'd be fine. "Okay then, I'll drop the subject."

"I'll probably work late to make up for lost time this afternoon." Pete grinned. "So you're on your own for cold pizza. Unless . . ."

"I ate it this morning."

Pete groaned. Mike shrugged; he'd eaten a lot worse in much worse conditions. He pushed the encroaching memories aside. He glanced at his kid brother. "Hey, let me know how Carly's meeting with the publisher went."

Pete lifted an eyebrow. "What meeting?"

"Forget it. I must have misunderstood," Mike said, sensing that he'd understood perfectly. It was Carly and Pete who had yet to catch on.

"You'll be at dinner tomorrow?" his brother asked.

"To meet your boss?" His brother's future in-laws. Carly's parents. "Sure."

"Great. That means a lot." Peter turned toward the street and then back to Mike. "One more thing."

"What's that?"

"I'm training a new associate and my time is even more limited than before. If Carly needs any help planning or anything . . . would you be there?"

Mike hesitated, knowing time with Carly was dangerous for them both. Then again, his brother needed a favor, and Mike could use the distraction from dealing with his own unsettled life. Since his return, Mike had had too much free time to think. "No sweat."

"Thanks." Pete smiled and Mike knew he'd made the right decision. Time to discover whether these two were headed for disaster had nothing to do with his sudden agreement.

His brother hailed an empty cab. "I'm glad you're back."

"Me, too, Pete." But he hoped his brother didn't live to regret that sentiment.

However different Pete and Carly turned out to be, Mike had no right to interfere. The sooner Carly planned and executed this wedding, the better for everyone involved.

Especially Mike.

"A book contract. Carly Wexler, I am impressed."

"Glad you took a shot on a rookie?" Carly asked the editor of her column.

Juliette Parsons leaned forward in her seat, hands clasped in front of her on the age-worn desk. "I've been glad since day one."

"Me, too." And Carly wasn't just talking about her job. Since the day she'd hired on as an intern at the magazine, Juliette had taken her under her wing. Professionally she treated Carly to stern lectures on proper writing technique. And Carly had turned to Juliette for personal advice far more than she'd ever allowed herself to turn to her own mother.

She sat down on the futon couch in Juliette's office. Among her other qualities, Juliette was a bit of an eccentric. Juliette pressed the intercom on her phone. "Herbal tea, Stacey. Two, please." Then she joined Carly on the couch. "So tell me what Peter said."

Carly bit down on her lip. "About what?"

Her friend's blue eyes opened wide. "You haven't told him?"

"I thought I'd surprise him with the news."

"Ahh. He must be on pins and needles waiting to hear. If he can tear himself away from his office," Juliette muttered almost under her breath.

"I heard that."

"You were supposed to." She pulled her long hair back and twisted it into a bun at the base of her neck. "But he *is* waiting to hear?"

"Umm . . . I wanted to keep the news to myself in case it fell through."

"In that case, who would have comforted you if you were down?"

Mike. Carly pushed the traitorous thought aside. She had no business thinking of Peter's brother that way.

"I'd have confided in Peter." Eventually. If he had time. She shook her head, surprised at how disloyal she seemed to have become in such a short time. Peter deserved better from the woman he was going to marry.

"Good." Juliette patted her hand. "If you're look-ing to surprise him, I suppose he must be improving in the stuffy department."

Carly sighed. "Juliette, you know he has to work hard. He cares; he just doesn't show it the way Armando does." She paused, thinking about Juliette's ardent and amorous lover. "Come to think of it, no one shows it the way Armando does."

"It's the Latin in him." Juliette grinned. "Sexy men make sensual, lasting lovers. I should know. We've been together for ten years."

Carly rolled her eyes. They'd had this conversation too many times to count. "What a man's like in bed is no reflection on whether a couple has a lasting future."

Juliette raised a knowing eyebrow. "How would you know?"

Carly sighed. "So we haven't slept together . . . it doesn't mean we don't have staying power."

"What I don't get is the *why*. You're marrying him. Seems to me you ought to want him, too."

She twisted uncomfortably in her seat. Not from the topic of conversation, because she and Juliette could talk about anything, but because of the deadly accuracy of her friend's point. She cared about Peter, but she didn't much care that they hadn't consummated their relationship. The desire wasn't all-consuming and strong . . . which was a large part of the reason she wanted to marry him. He was safe. Safe from passion, safe from her family's past. And she loved him for that.

"There's time, Juliette."

Her friend leaned forward. "Not if you're marrying for the wrong reasons. Then you'll find out too late that you made a mistake."

"Are you saying my marriage to Peter is wrong?" Carly tensed, almost afraid to hear the answer.

"Of course not. Only you would know that. I just worry about you."

"Well, don't, because there's no problem." A knock on the door prevented Carly from following up on that statement. A good thing, since she didn't feel as secure as she sounded. After Juliette's assistant left the tea and two bone-china cups on a table, Juliette poured, then slid Carly's cup across the glass table.

"Chamomile?" Carly asked, glancing at the light amber-colored liquid.

"This week's blend is lavender and patchouli. It will soothe your nerves, and some believe it acts as an aphrodisiac. But only you will know whether that is true."

She eyed Juliette doubtfully.

The older woman shrugged. "What do you have to lose? Drink up and maybe you'll be the one surprised tonight."

"Anything is possible," Carly murmured. She lifted the cup and took a hefty sip.

Feeling light-headed and giddy, Carly packed the dinner she had ordered from Peter's favorite gourmet restaurant. She stopped at the liquor store across the street from his office. On a whim she splurged and bought the most expensive brand of champagne the small shop carried. Maybe Juliette was right and tonight would be a special one for her and Peter.

Clutching the bottle under her arm, she waved at

the same rotund security guard who'd held the night shift since she was in her teens. He'd seen her grow up and no longer required her to sign in or call after hours.

At eight P.M. the reception area was empty, and Carly wound her way back to the large conference room at the end of a long hall. Hushed voices and a feminine laugh rang out in the quiet office. She rounded the corner and stopped in the doorway. She'd expected to find Peter and one or more of his colleagues hard at work preparing for an important closing in the morning.

Instead she found Peter and a very feminine, very young associate sharing a laugh over a large pizza. The woman appeared relaxed, her stockinged feet perched on a chair beside Peter's. And Carly's meticulously neat fiancé had loosened his tie and tucked the end inside his shirt, presumably to avoid stains. He'd rolled up his sleeves and leaned back, feet propped, in a comfortable-looking chair. Unopened legal-size folders sat in a stack on the conference table. From the look of things, they'd remain unopened for a while.

Though she'd had second thoughts about stopping by unannounced, Carly was suddenly glad she had. Their relationship could obviously benefit from added spice and her surprise would be a great start.

"Excuse me." Carly cleared her throat. "I hope I'm not interrupting."

Startled, Peter's feet hit the floor with a thud. "Carly."

"Last time I looked."

He shot her a curious glance. The casual banter that came so naturally around Mike fell flat with Peter.

"This is a surprise," he said.

"Good or bad?"

His eyebrows creased in confusion. "Neither. It just is."

Carly forced herself to remain composed. Not an easy task while standing in the doorway holding a picnic basket in one hand and a bottle of bubbly in the other, spouting bad jokes and feeling ridiculously out of place.

Peter hadn't yet noticed her packages.

"Is this your fiancée?" The petite brunette rose from her seat, turning to face Carly.

"Yes. Roger's daughter." He gestured between the two women. "Carly Wexler, Regina Grey."

"Nice to meet you," Carly said.

"Same here. I've heard a lot about you."

I wish I could say the same. "All good, I hope."

"All fathers have nothing but wonderful things to say about their daughters." Regina smiled and took a long sip of bottled water. "And of course," she continued, "Peter speaks highly of you as well."

"Of course." Away from the office Peter was preoccupied with work. At the office he was preoccupied with Carly. Yeah, right. This pint-sized barracuda certainly didn't need any courtroom training in how to go for the jugular.

Peter wrapped one arm around Carly's shoulders. "You know I enjoy seeing you, but two surprises in one week?"

"Shocking, I know. Next time I'll call." She could no longer keep the hurt out of her voice.

"That's not what I meant, but this is unexpected. What are you doing here?"

The compulsion to share her news with Peter had evaporated as quickly as it had come. "Nothing important. I thought I'd bring dinner." She raised her arms to show him her bag of goodies.

"Oh. Well. Uh, we've already . . ." He stammered and flushed a deep crimson.

"Eaten. I can see that. Don't worry. You two are busy, so I'll be going."

Peter brushed a strand of hair off her cheek. "After the florist on Saturday we'll do wedding bands. How's that?"

She plastered a smile on her face. "Sounds great." But for some reason this didn't feel like a compromise she'd won. In fact, his gesture seemed out of place, like that of a man who'd bought his wife flowers to assuage his guilt over an affair. She ought to know. She'd seen her father exhibit those signs often enough, growing up.

With his hand on the small of her back, Peter guided her out and toward the bank of elevators. Not five minutes after she'd arrived, Carly took the same elevator down with the same full picnic basket and expensive bottle of champagne in her hands. Some surprises backfired, she thought. And this had been one of them.

THREE

With mellow jazz music playing on the stereo, Carly settled herself on a plush pillow in front of her cocktail table. She unpacked the gourmet meal and uncorked the bottle of champagne.

She poured champagne into a wineglass and lifted it in the air. "Congratulations," she muttered and downed the bubbly wine. She poured some more and enjoyed the bubbles as they tickled their way down her throat. No matter how lousy she felt, at least the expensive champagne wouldn't go to waste.

When the doorbell rang the first time, she ignored the sound. The second chime was a more prolonged spurt. "Go away. This isn't an open party."

At the sound of the third ring, she picked up a drumstick and padded barefoot across the hardwood floor. She peered through the peephole and cursed the heavens. How could she possibly forget about this man if he showed up on her doorstep uninvited?

Drawing a deep breath, she opened the door. "Did you smell the chicken all the way uptown?" she asked.

"Cute."

That crooked grin did funny things to her heart.

"Aren't you going to invite me in?" he asked.

She bowed and waved Mike into her small apartment. The haven where she was safe from everyone and everything. Including her own feelings. *But no more.*

She shut the door behind him and followed him inside. He glanced around the living room and frowned. "You shouldn't be drinking alone."

"I'm not, I'm celebrating."

"By yourself?"

"It doesn't take two to celebrate, Mike."

He grinned. "No, but it's a heck of a lot more fun."

At his deliberate innuendo, she felt the heat rise to her face.

"You made a deal with the publishers?" The genuine excitement in his voice brought her earlier rush of adrenaline back full force.

She nodded, pleased with herself, proud of what she'd accomplished and suddenly not ashamed to show it. "Yup. A good deal, too."

"Hey!" Before she knew what hit her, he'd swept her into his arms and twirled her around the floor. His body felt warm and hard against her breasts.

"That's great."

As he lowered her to the floor, the slight bulge in his pants caused a quickening in her stomach. Apparently Juliette's aphrodisiac worked all right . . . with the wrong brother. Carly stepped back to avoid further contact.

"How about another glass so I can share the celebration?"

Using the time to catch her breath, Carly walked into the kitchen and returned with a second wineglass. She grinned. "Only the finest."

"I'm used to drinking out of bottles and cans. Anything else is paradise."

"Peter said something about you being a photojournalist?"

"I was," Mike said.

"And now you're . . . ?"

"On vacation," he said smoothly. He glanced around the room and chose a reclining chair in the corner. It rocked slightly under his weight and he laughed. "I love these things."

She smiled. "Me, too."

"So much more comfortable than that hard leather thing Pete calls a couch."

Carly's smile faded and he regretted whatever he'd said to cause the change.

"I see. Talking about work is off-limits?" She pushed the topic away from herself and back to him.

"Not if there's something you really want to know."

"What subjects have you covered recently?"

"This and that," he said, unwilling to delve deeper into his most current assignment. Even for Carly.

"Can't you be more specific?"

I'd prefer not to. "I cover hard news. I don't

dig around in celebrity trash cans." He forced a grin.

She smiled in understanding. Her brown eyes met his. A man could drown in the compassion he saw there. "I'd like to see your work sometime," she said.

"My pleasure." That he wanted to share his private photos with Carly gave him some indication of his level of involvement. More than was prudent, he knew. For a man who avoided emotional entanglements, the revelation stunned him.

He forced himself to think of his brother and suppressed a groan. "After you left this afternoon I spoke with Pete."

"And?"

"Since he'll be busy training a new associate, I'm at your disposal for any wedding-related things you need." *Or anything else, for that matter.*

"Training. Is that what they call it these days?"

"What?"

"See this?" Her arm swept the table loaded with food that smelled amazing. Between the canned food he'd eaten overseas and the takeout he'd feasted on since his return, Carly's table looked like manna from heaven.

So did she. A silky lemon yellow pajama set—pants and a long-sleeved top—draped across her soft curves and smooth skin. The material rustled as she crossed the room.

"Chicken, gourmet salads, caviar and assorted desserts. All your brother's favorites."

He glanced from the food to her stricken expression. "He stood you up?" That thought was as sick-ening to him as the thought of Carly greeting his brother dressed for bed.

"No, that would have hurt," she admitted. "He wasn't at fault; I was. I broke the ultimate taboo."

Her cheeks burned with color and a range of emotion flared in her eyes. She was, Mike decided, either angry or on her way toward drunk. He couldn't determine which. He glanced at the bottle, but the deep green obscured the level of the liquid inside.

He turned back to Carly. "And what was that?" he asked.

"I showed up unexpectedly, dinner in hand for my overworked fiancé."

"He ignored you for *work?*" *The selfish bastard.* Mike stood, crossing the room until he was close enough to breathe the intoxicating scent of vanilla. Who needed champagne when a man could get drunk on this?

"Nope. Guess again."

He rubbed his forehead, wondering what his mo-ron brother, who cared about but didn't love Carly, had done now. "Was he angry you surprised him?"

"Nope. Guess again." A smile quirked around the edges of her mouth. "Three strikes and you're out."

Mike tossed his hands in the air in a gesture of defeat. "I give up. What happened?" If his brother had hurt her, Mike would ring his stuffy neck.

"He was already eating." She paced the floor. Her hips swayed beneath the opaque material.

He already knew he could span her waist with his bare hands. "And?"

"And laughing." She whirled around to face him. "Did you ever hear anything so ridiculous? Peter was laughing with that associate *in training*—who, by the way, needs as much training as Flipper."

Mike walked up beside her and placed a comforting hand on her shoulder. "Was he doing anything . . . wrong?"

She shook her head slowly from side to side.

"Anything . . . unethical maybe?"

Again, she shook her head. "But he laughed." She leaned against a pink marbleized wall and sighed. "He never laughs with me."

The admission cost her, Mike could tell. She looked up at him, her eyes bright with unshed tears. "And I can't remember the last time I laughed with him."

"Oh, sweetheart." *I could have told you that.*

He placed a hand around her waist, ignoring how easily she fit her body to his, how soft and right she felt in his arms, and led her to the oversized pillow on the floor.

Seating himself next to her, Mike took her hand in his. "If you think you're making a mistake, now's the time . . ."

"No!" Carly jerked her hand back and rubbed it against the silk pants. "I didn't say that. It's just that with planning the wedding, things have been tense. His work, my work . . . you know how it is."

Oh, yeah. He knew. And he had a strange feeling she did, too. So why push so hard for something that wasn't right? That would only make her un-happy for the next fifty or so years? And why didn't his intelligent brother, who'd attended college and law school on scholarships, see the truth?

Mike sighed, reminding himself that he'd be back touring the world in no time and Carly's pain would be a distant memory. Or would it?

"Okay, then. Let's eat and help you plan. After all, you've only got three weeks left until the big day."

"Later. Right now I just want to relax." She busied herself loading up two plates with food, setting one down in front of Mike and refilling the champagne glasses.

For the next hour, he amused her with tales about his less than glamorous assignments, some of the more squalid places he'd slept and the interesting people he'd met along the way. Though he hoped the stories would bring back a wave of nostalgia for the life he'd left behind, all he felt was an aching emptiness for all he lacked—and that, more than anything else, made him nervous.

He helped Carly clean up her living room and put the half-full bottle of champagne into the fridge. Since she'd had one glass and he'd shared a fair amount himself, he realized Carly's earlier fit hadn't been made while drunk. It had been made while hurt and angry at his insensitive brother. Mike's hands clenched into fists at his sides.

While she replaced what appeared to be volumes of magazines on top of her cocktail table, Mike in-dulged his curiosity. He examined the wall of bookshelves, astounded at the number of self-help books crammed into the narrow space. Then he appraised the apartment with a photographer's eye. Moonlight filtered in through a bay window, catching vibrant colors in its wayward beams. The oversized recliner matched the comfortable sofa and picked up the pale pink shade on the walls.

Organization offset by plush comfort. Everything said *touch me*. Nothing had the stark, hands-off feeling of Pete's apartment, a place where Mike slept but had yet to feel at home. That he did here didn't surprise him. Shook him up some, but what was one more punch in the gut when everything around him seemed to be falling apart?

His career—hell, his life for that matter—was in shambles. This engagement between two polar opposites shouldn't have any effect on him, yet he cared for both people involved . . . one of whom he'd known for one week. In three weeks he'd be her brother-in-law.

"Mike?"

Her light touch on his arm startled him. "Yeah?"

"Are you okay? You seem a little . . . I don't know. Out there."

He smiled. "I'm fine. And you ought to get some sleep."

She nodded, watching him with those deep brown eyes as he headed for the door. He turned back to find her close behind him. Her scented perfume drifted around him, causing his body to stir in an unbrotherly way. Captured in a sensual haze, he remembered the moment she'd fixed his cummerbund, when her body had jerked against him. His hands had itched to cup her breasts, to pull her close and bury himself deep inside her. If not for the fact that they'd been in a public place, he would have.

No such restraints bound him now . . . but too many others did. They'd come too damn close. "Hell," he muttered. He didn't need this aggravation. Whatever happened to brotherly devotion? To loyalty?

He thought of Pete, who counted on this woman for all the wrong reasons. The only right one was love, something his sibling had instantly discounted. This entire situation was a mess Mike could do without. If he was smart, he'd forget he'd ever met Carly Wexler.

He looked into those bottomless eyes. He could no more forget her than he could fail to respond to the innocence in her gaze. Without conscious thought, he fingered her bangs. The strands felt like fine silk. He bent down and brushed his mouth across hers.

She tasted unique, sweet with a hint of champagne. His lips lingered for a second, pulling back before he lost control. "Take care, Carly."

Forcing his feet to move, he turned and walked out without looking back.

With Mike gone, the apartment felt more like a lonely prison. She left the living room and headed for the safety of her bedroom. The one place in the small apartment Mike hadn't marked with his presence.

She paused at the foot of her bed and glanced at the newspaper article she'd been reading earlier. *Looking for Mr. Right. Is Your Man the Man for You?* She shouldn't have to wonder, and until the arrival of Peter's wandering brother, she never had.

With Peter she'd looked forward to an uncomplicated, comfortable relationship. *Comfortable* being the important word. They shared the same ideals. Marriage, family and career, if not necessarily in that order. They shared the same circle of friends, courtesy of his working for her father. And though he was an attorney like Roger Wexler, she'd trusted that when he said he had to work late, she'd find him at the office, not in another woman's bed.

Regina's face came to mind and Carly pushed it aside. People who worked together often bonded. How could they not, with the amount of hours they spent together? But she and Peter shared something more important. The comfort factor she found so important had always been there, and *that* was something she could count on, and so could he.

She closed her eyes, but instead of her fiancé, Mike's deep laugh, handsome face and well-honed body filled her mind. She touched her lips with her fingers. They tingled at the thought of Mike's mouth on hers. Disgust filled her.

She'd come so close . . .

Close to following in her father's footsteps.

How could she be so careless as to forget that passion destroys? She picked up the page and gazed at the article in her hand. No, Carly thought. She didn't need to find Mr. Right. She already had.

For a brief second the sparkling diamond ring caught her eye. She was engaged to the right man. She had to be. With a sigh, she crumpled the article into a ball and arced it toward the center of the room.

Life was filled with compromise. So Peter wasn't perfect. Neither was she. In an imperfect world, one made the best choices possible and honored one's commitments. Unlike her father, Carly intended to live by those rules. Intense passion burned itself out fast. It meant little when compared to a lifetime.

Putting Mike out of her mind wouldn't be easy, but it was necessary. Yet how could she do that with him helping her out at every turn, being so damn nice when Peter all but ignored her, and just being . . . Mike.

Mike stretched his arms over his head. He'd hit the sack early, but the hours he'd spent tossing and turning in bed didn't count. He hadn't slept much or well and all because of Carly. And that told him that he had too much free time on his hands. So he decided to make some inquiries.

By late afternoon, he'd not only called in a few favors and arranged a Saturday afternoon meeting with the editor of the local paper, but he'd also secured the job. The guy was impressed with Mike's credentials and portfolio of shots. He was as pleased to have Mike on board as Mike was to have a temporary job to occupy his free time.

Mike had never been one to sit idle while the rest of the world passed him by. On the plane ride home, he'd told himself that a temporary position would keep him from thinking too much, yet allow him time to sort out his future. His ultimate return had never been in question . . . he just wasn't ready. Now, with the unexpected Peter and Carly saga, Mike felt more compelled than ever to stick around. The thought of Carly and his brother together turned his usually strong stomach.

So he was staying at least for a while. He'd make his own hours, giving him time to learn more about his brother's soon-to-be wife. That thought alone should have sent him running for the first flight out of New York. Anywhere USA would work just fine. Unfortunately even the next town over would lack the presence of the bright lights and fast pace of New York. Lack the presence of one dark-eyed beauty who'd been haunting his dreams with more frequency than back-biting bullets and screaming children.

Carly approached the wedding band issue with bright-eyed optimism. After all, two people sharing a life together wanted to make each other happy. Standing in front of the jewelry store, it was hard not to remember her first meeting with Mike. But she pushed the memory aside. No point in looking to the past when she had a future to build.

She peeked into the window and the cramping in her stomach eased when she saw her favorite rings were still there. She placed a hand on Peter's elbow. "Look," she whispered, pointing to the simple wedding bands she'd chosen with Mike.

"They are nice," he said. It sounded like a reluctant concession drawn from deep inside him. "But how would a ring like that look?" he asked, and she knew she was right.

"Beautiful?"

"Anything would look lovely on you. But people would think I couldn't afford to get you something special."

"Those are special." She grit her teeth while she spoke. She knew she was being obtuse. For the first time she didn't care.

He sighed. "Perhaps I didn't explain that correctly." He paused. "I'd like something with more . . . presence." Silence followed while he perused the window display. He tapped the glass thoughtfully. "Something understated but designed to impress."

"Like those?" Her voice lost any enthusiasm at all, but her fiancé, too caught up in his own needs, failed to notice.

"No . . . like . . . those!"

Carly cringed at Peter's preference, a ring that glittered with diamonds and would overpower her small hand.

For someone loaded down with wedding books and bridal pictures, you're giving up control of some major issues. Had Mike been right? Was she too compliant?

She shook her head. No! Peter's reasons for wanting the more obvious rings had to do with his status and need to impress his colleagues. She understood. Mike didn't.

Besides, what did the world traveler, a man incapable of sticking around longer than the next assignment, know about commitment anyway?

But she and Peter did have conflicting desires. That much was true. She wanted the chance to convince Peter that commitment meant more to her than flashy rings and making a statement. That sentiment counted more than points scored with his colleagues.

As he grabbed her hand and pulled her into the store, Carly was determined to do just that.

"So did you two compromise on wedding bands today?" Mike took a sip of his Scotch and soda, ignoring Carly's furious glare. He wondered from which parent she'd inherited those expressive eyes, then realized he'd find out soon enough.

"We chose the perfect rings," his brother said, then turned toward the bar. "I'll have the same and a glass of white wine for the lady."

"Let me guess," Mike said. "Two-toned platinum and gold by chance?"

"Actually . . ." Peter began.

"I didn't like them as much once I saw them a second time. Peter picked out a pair that suited us much better," Carly said, a forced smile on her lips.

Sure he did, sweetheart. More likely her good nature

had gotten lost in his brother's well-meaning but overwhelming need to impress others. "Well, good. Because I'd hate to see a bride getting married with a wedding band she didn't love. One she'd have to wear the rest of her life. That she'd compromised on . . ."

"We get the picture," she said through clenched teeth. "If you'll both excuse me, I see some friends I'd like to say hello to." She gave Peter a brief kiss on the cheek. A chaste kiss more suited to a friend of the family than her fiancé. What was it with these two? Mike wondered, and not for the first time.

"We'll be here," Peter said.

Mike merely shook his head, watching as Carly wound her way through the crowded club. Her black dress was simple yet clung to every curve. He gulped a mouthful of Scotch.

Peter rested one elbow on the bar. "Thanks for making it tonight. Wexler and Greene is a large firm, but they make it a policy to get to know their associates well."

Mike suppressed a groan. "Marriage isn't the same as a merger, Pete. Work probably has nothing to do with this dinner. You're marrying the man's daughter, for heaven's sake."

"What? You think by meeting you he's checking me out?"

Mike shrugged. "Could be. Maybe he's checking out the family, making sure Carly's not getting stuck with the wrong sort of people." He slapped his brother on the back. "At least you're safe there. Two orphans with no family to speak of. I'd say the man doesn't have much to concern himself with. How 'bout you?"

A wry smile touched Peter's lips. "True. So long as you're on your best behavior, I'll have no problem. And maybe the partnership will follow."

"That's what I love about you, Pete."

"What's that?"

"Nothing gets in the way of work."

"Of course not."

The insult obviously went over his brother's head, but what could be expected from a man who took most things literally and only work seriously?

"Anyhow, I doubt Roger would check me out for Carly's sake. Those two aren't particularly close."

Mike grabbed a handful of peanuts from a dish on the bar. "Why not?"

"Who knows? They do the father-daughter thing, but it's mostly for show." Peter rubbed his forehead with one hand. Finally he lifted his shoulders. "If Roger has any interest in me at all, it must be professional."

Mike remained silent. The dynamics at work in these relationships went way beyond anything he'd seen before. He doubted things were as simple as Peter made them out to be. But he knew for sure Pete was oblivious to anything that concerned Carly and her family unless it affected his career.

If Mike was smart he'd take his cue from his self-centered brother. He downed the rest of his drink, knowing where Carly was concerned he was anything but smart.

* * *

A small band played in the corner of the darkened dining room. Mirrors lined the walls and reflected light gave the impression of a larger room than the otherwise intimate atmosphere implied. With Carly beside him, Mike found relaxing all but impossible. The sweet scent of her perfume had him on edge, shifting uncomfortably in his seat. More than once he'd jolted himself out of a sensual daydream that had her writhing with passion beneath him.

With her father on his left side and his brother seated to her right, fantasies involving Carly Wexler were not only disrespectful but downright wrong. Peter, oblivious to everything, had involved Anne Wexler in a discussion about attorneys and their wives.

Those beautiful brown eyes had come from Anne, Mike realized, but Carly possessed an inner warmth. She seemed almost to glow from within. Dressed in an ice blue chiffon gown, her mother appeared cool and aloof. Although friendly, she lacked her daughter's special sparkle, the elusive something that drew Mike so deeply.

"Mike," Roger said, "Peter tells me you've been out of the country on assignment until recently."

Mike nodded. "The Middle East," he said by way of clarification. A place and a subject he was in no mood to revisit. "But I wouldn't miss my brother's wedding," he said, returning to a topic he found more interesting.

"I can hardly believe it's almost time to walk my only daughter down the aisle."

Carly shifted, her bare leg brushing his for a split second before she realized and jerked away. Mike suppressed a grin and tried to concentrate on her father's musings.

Beside him, she lifted a glass of water and brought it to her lips.

"It seems like only yesterday she was a teenager, and now she's all grown up." The older man sighed wistfully.

"It happens, sir."

"I really miss those days."

The glass slipped from Carly's hand. Mike caught and steadied the crystal goblet before more than a few drops of water splattered onto the plate.

"Carly?"

"I'm fine."

He doubted it. "No harm done," he murmured. Beneath the table, he squeezed her hand in a token gesture of comfort before reaching to wipe the small mess.

"Thanks," she whispered. One look at her ashen face had him questioning the depth of this father-daughter relationship. She wrung the linen napkin between her hands. Peter had been mistaken. Carly cared . . . too much.

No one except Mike appeared to notice her discomfort. He waited until they'd all ordered before turning to his brother. "Do you mind if I dance with your future wife?" Before getting that close to Carly, Mike needed to cement their status in his mind.

Peter leaned back in his chair and smiled. "My pleasure. I'll just . . ."

"Spend time discussing business," Mike finished for him. As if there was any other ending to the sentence, Mike thought. "Okay, then." He pushed back his chair and rose from his seat.

"May I?" He extended his hand toward Carly.

If ever someone needed to get away from friends, family and all-around stress, Carly did. And he wanted to be her salvation, if only for the night. No one, including her parents or her fiancé, had realized how shaken she was. Another telling sign, he thought.

"I don't think a dance is such a good idea." She glanced around her for confirmation, but everyone else was already engrossed in conversation.

She looked at his outstretched hand. With the slightest hesitation, she put her napkin down on the table and rose from her seat, placing her warm hand in his.

Mike's insides did a one-eighty. For a man who faced danger daily while on assignment without flinching, this sudden kick of adrenaline was a warning. Sexual chemistry was one thing. Caring another.

Carly followed Mike, unable to understand how he'd read her so well. He'd sensed her discomfort and offered her a chance to compose herself away from prying eyes. She already knew a dangerous attraction raced between them. She didn't need or want an emotional connection with him as well.

As they approached the dance floor, Carly felt as though she were stepping over an imaginary boundary, crossing a path that would lead to nothing but disaster if she wasn't careful. Yet with each step away from the table and toward Mike, her mood lightened. His grip tightened on her hand, prompting hers to do the same.

The floor wasn't crowded, nor were they the only couple dancing. There was enough room for them to maneuver comfortably without feeling crushed, yet enough people surrounding them to offer her the illusion of being safe in Mike's arms. He drew her close, slipping his arm around her back while still keeping a respectable space between them. She appreciated his discretion, and yet there was nothing respectable about her feelings for Mike.

"Was my SOS that obvious?" she asked.

"Only to someone paying attention," he said, implying what she'd already realized on her own.

Though she ought to jump to her fiancé's defense, she was too tired to make the effort. She glanced at Mike and smiled. "Well, thank you, sir."

"No problem, ma'am," he drawled.

She tilted her head back in time to catch his lopsided grin and couldn't contain the impish smile he inspired in return. When silence descended, she let herself drift in time to the music. She laid one hand on his shoulder, idly moving her fingers along his jacket, feeling the broad planes of his chest and the ripple of muscle beneath the material. She heard his deep breath at the same time he captured her hand in his, intertwining their fingers.

Embarrassed, she searched for a neutral topic.

"After all your travels, family dinners must bore you to tears."

"You'd be surprised." His gaze roamed over her face before he captured the back of her head in his strong hand and settled her head against his chest. But he kept her wandering hand wrapped in his, close to his heart.

The song changed to a slow, romantic ballad. As the lights dimmed, more couples joined them on the dance floor, forcing Mike's body closer. The rasp of material as his jacket brushed her linen dress sounded unnaturally loud in her ears.

She glanced up to find his golden eyes smoldering with unspoken need. For Carly the world had shrunk in size, to two people dancing in near twilight, alone with each other.

When she drew a deep breath, she was enveloped by the essence of Mike. She closed her eyes and rested her head against his shoulder, feeling like she'd come home. Without warning, the music shifted again, this time to a 1970s' pop song. Carly was bumped from behind, pushed against Mike . . . and discovered he desired her much the same way she wanted him. The proof of something she'd spent the last week alternately denying and forcing out of her mind sent her reeling. She backed off immediately.

"Carly, wait."

She turned. "Please don't say anything."

"But . . ."

"Not a single word." She placed one finger over his lips, then jerked back as if she'd touched a live wire. With a single touch or a heated glance, the man caused her nerve endings to tingle and her entire body to vibrate in a way that was both new and familiar at the same time.

She clenched her fists to keep from trembling. "I'm going back to the table before anyone misses us."

He opened his mouth to speak.

"Now, please." She cut him off, the entreaty in her voice plain.

Mike, powerless to deny this woman anything, turned and followed her back to the table. His body still burned from a simple dance.

He held Carly's chair before lowering himself into his seat beside her. He had to bite back a curse as his brother covered her hand with his.

"That's the best news I've heard in months." Peter beamed with pleasure, more honest emotion than Mike had seen since his return.

"What's that?" Carly asked. She laid a hand on Peter's arm. Mike tensed but said nothing.

"Partnership decisions have been moved up," Roger said. "We've seen a boost in almost every department and want to make up for the last few years. We'll make final decisions in about a week and a half."

"That's great news, Pete." Mike knew his brother lived and breathed little else but work. This turn of events ought to make him ecstatic.

"Carly?" Anne looked at her daughter. Obviously she expected some reaction from the soon-to-be wife of an attorney and almost partner.

"Great," Carly echoed.

Sincere but flat. Anne didn't appear to notice. Mike did.

"Well, with that settled . . ." Anne smiled, then cleared her throat. "I mean almost settled. What's going on with the wedding details? Are you all set?"

Carly nodded. "Pretty much." She leaned closer to Mike to allow the waiter room to maneuver.

Caesar salad had always been Mike's favorite, and when everyone had been served, he picked up his fork.

"All that's left is the final fitting on my dress."

Mike's appetite disappeared. Watching as Carly moved one leaf around the plate, he surmised that she wasn't any more hungry than he.

"I'll be glad to go with you," Anne said, hope shining in her eyes. "After all, it isn't every day your daughter gets married."

Whatever Mike's first impressions of Anne Wexler, they were obviously as false as the shield she hid behind. It was obvious now that she loved her daughter but feared being rejected.

"No thanks, Mom. I don't need your help. I've got a million errands to run and last-minute appointments before the high school graduation."

"All of which have nothing to do with me. I want to be there. Just name the time."

Carly raised her eyes from her dish and glanced toward her mother. "I'll probably just drop by the bridal shop during lunch on Friday."

"Friday's the Bar Association luncheon honoring your father." Disappointment radiated from Anne in waves.

"I know, and I can handle this alone. After all, the dress is picked. It's just a final fitting."

"But every bride needs someone there for them." Anne paused. "Your bridesmaids?" she asked hopefully.

"Are coming from out of town, you know that. And Juliette has a business lunch."

Anne turned toward her husband, her intention clear.

"No! You belong with Dad. I can deal with this alone. I'm fine, Mom."

Mike couldn't take it anymore. For either of them. "If you need a second opinion, I could help out." He draped an arm over Carly's chair and leaned back. "I might enjoy it," he said with a grin.

Peter looked up from his conversation with Roger. "Not a bad idea, Carly. At least you'd have someone there . . . you know, for moral support."

"I don't need . . ."

"Sure you do," Pete insisted. "You've handled all this on your own, planned everything, picked everything."

She raised a napkin to those luscious lips. "Not quite everything," she muttered, then lowered the napkin back to her lap.

Mike shifted his wrist and tapped her on the shoulder. "I don't mind."

"We can't," she said. "It's bad luck or something."

He roared with laughter. "Why would you say that?"

"It's not like he's the groom," Pete said, joining Mike for a laugh.

Suddenly Mike didn't find the subject all that amusing. "If you want me, I'm available," he said, suppressing the nudging guilt that threatened whenever he even thought about Carly.

Mike loved his brother. For Peter, Mike felt a kinship born of childhood struggles. For Carly, Mike felt . . . something stronger than he could put into words. But regardless of Peter's faults or reasons for this engagement, Mike's interest in his brother's fiancé was low.

If he allowed Carly to come between them, he would lose the only family he had left. And so would Pete. For that reason alone, Mike was determined to keep a safe distance from Carly from here on in. With all the self-control that had gotten him the perfect picture numerous times, that shouldn't be too difficult. But his conflicting desires just might tear him apart.

"Carly?" Peter laid a hand on her bare arm. Mike clenched his teeth in response.

"Okay," she said, glancing at Mike. "I'd appreciate it."

"Mike?" Peter glanced at him, one eyebrow lifted, waiting for an answer.

"Sure." He'd help her. He'd help Pete. But at what cost? And to whom?

FOUR

Operating under the assumption that busy minds didn't have time to think, Carly awoke early and spent the morning tackling belated spring cleaning and ignoring the persistent ring of the telephone. Unfortunately she couldn't do the same thing with the doorbell.

She wiped her dusty hands on her jeans and brushed her bangs out of her eyes with the back of her hand. Whoever stood by the buzzer had more determination than she did. "Who is it?" she called out.

"Mike."

Her stomach flipped, but she grabbed for the doorknob before she could change her mind. "We've got to stop meeting like this."

"And we would if you'd answer your telephone." He grinned. "May I?" He gestured inside and, without waiting for an answer, slid past her into the apartment.

"Pushy," she muttered.

"So I've been told," he called over his shoulder.

"You weren't supposed to hear that." Despite her

late-night resolution to steer clear of Peter's brother, she couldn't deny she was glad to see him. She shut the door, turned and followed him inside.

"To what do I owe the pleasure?" she asked.

He stood by the window overlooking the small park. Wearing ragged denim shorts and a black T-shirt, his impact was as potent as ever.

"I thought we should talk." He crossed his muscular forearms over his chest.

Idly she wondered if he worked out and where. She'd love to watch him develop those biceps. She licked her suddenly dry lips. The Carly Wexler she knew never had such wayward thoughts about men.

He pushed himself off the wall and took two steps toward her. The sexy swagger and casual air that were so much a part of him never ceased to amaze her. Neither did the fact that he was related to Peter. And that was the thought that sobered her.

"Talk about what?" she asked warily.

"What happened last night."

She folded her arms across her chest. "Nothing happened."

His eyes narrowed, pinning her in place. "Funny, but you didn't strike me as a coward."

She ignored that comment. "We were on a crowded dance floor. Nothing happened." *If you don't acknowledge it, it can't hurt you.* Her mother's voice echoed inside her head. Tears she'd suppressed late in the night rushed forth, threatening to fall at the slightest provocation.

"Why did I know you'd say that?"

She swiped at her bangs, then tucked a stray strand of hair behind her ear. "Because it's true."

He held up his hands in a mock gesture of surrender. "You win. For now," he muttered. "It's a beautiful day. Too nice to spend inside." He glanced around, taking in the rags, cleaning solutions and Good Will boxes scattered around the room. "Definitely too nice to spend indoors cleaning."

"Got any better ideas?" Carly regretted the words the minute they left her mouth.

A knowing smirk formed on his lips. "I do. Do you like amusement parks?"

"Who doesn't?" Peter. The traitorous thought formed and she pushed it aside. If he'd returned her call before going to the office, maybe he'd be here now instead of Mike. Then again, knowing Peter, maybe not. Work came first, after all.

She forced a smile. "Disliking amusement parks and carnivals is un-American."

"So I don't have to pour on the charm to convince you." He grinned. "Well? What are you waiting for?" He prodded her gently on the back. "Go get changed, unless you don't mind roasting in those heavy jeans."

"You're serious." How could she go anywhere with him and keep a clear conscience?

"Of course. I rented a car. Playland is a short half-hour ride from here, or haven't you heard?"

The last good memory she had of her father was a Sunday when he'd taken her to Playland. "Have you been there before?" she asked, stalling for time.

"Grew up near there."

"That's right, I forgot."

"You're stalling," he said with dead-on accuracy. "Are you coming or not?" he asked.

Playland. She reached back into pleasant childhood memories and felt the beginning of a relaxed smile take hold, her first in a long while. Mike reached his bronzed hand toward her. She hesitated, and silence stretched taut between them.

Carly listened to the conflicting voices deep inside her before making a decision. Finally she placed her hand inside his. Just this once she'd follow her heart.

Carly looked down at her hand firmly enclosed in Mike's strong grasp. Crazy Glue couldn't bond more thoroughly than she and Mike had over the past few hours. Unable to resist the opportunity to spend time with him, she had broken her self-imposed promise to keep her distance. One time wouldn't hurt, she'd rationalized. She now wondered how much rationalizing her father had done during his affair with his twenty-five-year-old secretary.

She gazed around the park and listened to the shouts coming from the brazen riders of the Dragon Coaster, the Tilt-a-Whirl and the Spider. With the exception of the carousel, she had laid her head on Mike's chest and screamed through each ride. She had loved every heart-stopping minute spent in his arms.

Juggling her newly won stuffed animals, she gingerly tugged on Mike's sleeve. When he turned, she gestured toward the cotton candy concession stand.

"Two snow cones, one hot dog and a bag of popcorn weren't enough for you?" he asked with a grin.

She shrugged.

He pulled his wallet from his pants pocket. "I'll say one thing, you're not a cheap date."

"Maybe not, but I'm a fun one." She laughed. "And I'm not the one who wasted almost fifty dollars trying to win that oversized bear."

"No, but who was it who sighed and said 'Oh, he'd look so cute sitting in my living room'?"

"Guilty." She grinned. "And it was kind of you to accommodate me." She thought of the cuddly pink bear that now rested comfortably on the backseat of the rental car. "How's the pitching arm?" She gave his muscled biceps a playful squeeze, drawing her hand back before she succumbed to temptation and explored further.

He grunted and handed her the cloud of spun sugar.

"I love cotton candy." Taking a bite of the pink fluff, she closed her eyes and let the sugar dissolve in her mouth. "Heaven."

"Show me."

At the sound of his deep voice, her eyes popped open wide.

"Just a little taste." The laugh lines crinkled around his eyes. "Please."

Before she could change her mind, she stuck one finger into the ball of pink fluff. "Open." She barely recognized her own voice.

Mike complied. She raised her sugar-laden finger and placed it into his waiting mouth, watching intently as his lips closed around her finger. Warm, wet and welcoming. A rush of dizziness assaulted her, but that was like a small wave compared to the heady rush she received when he nibbled on her fingertip with his teeth. A tidal wave of sensations surged through her. Such a simple act threatened her very being.

She wanted what she'd never realized she was capable of wanting. What she'd never *allowed* herself to desire. She wanted passion. Wanted to soothe the ache that pounded in every part of her body. She wanted Mike.

And she couldn't allow it.

Slowly, she pulled back, wiping her now cool finger against her denim shorts. "Well," she murmured. Flustered and embarrassed, she turned away.

Mike cleared his throat. "You and Pete do this often?" he asked.

"What?" His question had her pivoting back to face him in an instant.

He smiled, the charming grin that came naturally but knocked the wind right out of her.

"Carnivals. Do you and Pete do this sort of thing often?" he asked.

"Oh." She exhaled a sigh of relief. "No." They talked, ate in fancy restaurants when he wasn't working, attended work-related functions. His and hers, but mostly his. Not once did they let loose and have fun.

Why had she allowed herself to believe that was

enough for her? Because safety and security were more important to her than a good time. Had her feelings changed so drastically in such a short period of time, or was Mike just the catalyst, forcing her to face things she'd buried for too long?

"I guess Peter doesn't relax often enough to enjoy something like this," Mike said.

"No, he doesn't."

"It's a shame. He used to love this place when we were kids."

"Did your parents take you?" She immediately placed a hand on his arm. "I'm sorry," she murmured. "That was thoughtless. I was comparing my own childhood to yours and spoke without thinking." How could she have been so careless?

He shrugged. "No problem. Pete and I were abandoned a long time ago. We made out okay."

His words startled her. He smiled, but she didn't buy the act. Orphaned wasn't the same as abandoned. She wondered if he recognized the distinction.

"What happened?" she asked.

"Pete never told you?"

She shook her head. "Not in detail." And she hadn't pushed. So why force Mike to talk now?

He exhaled a sigh. "My aunt and uncle weren't the best parents. Very little love and even less laughter." He spoke without rancor, but as he looked over the park, he clenched his jaw and donned a closed expression. The carefree man of earlier in the afternoon had disappeared.

Obviously he hadn't come to terms with his past

as completely as he'd have her believe. That was something she could relate to. "So that's why you two are so close, even when you're not on the same continent," she said.

"Yeah. We didn't choose the same paths, but we're close."

"Looks like the Novack brothers made good."

He shrugged. "One brother never stays in one place and the other looks for the easy way. I'm not sure I'd call that making good."

"Law school isn't taking the easy way," she reminded him. Neither was traveling the globe to the world's hot spots.

"No, but in Pete's mind, success in law school guaranteed money. Another thing in short supply growing up."

The sudden insight into her fiancé astounded her . . . not just because she had thought she understood Peter and didn't, but because her information came from Mike and not the man she was about to marry.

Mike glanced at her, a serious expression clouding his handsome features. "Pete's willing to sacrifice an awful lot to achieve his goals."

She pondered his words. "Life's full of sacrifices."

"Do you want to be one of them?" He waved away his words with a jerk of his hand. "What I meant was, sacrifice is fine as long as you don't give up what counts."

What counts for you, Mike? Though she wanted to know, she was more afraid of hearing his response.

So the question remained unasked—and unanswered.

"Hey. You up for one last ride before we go home?" He pointed toward the large Ferris wheel and all other thoughts fled.

"You bet." She turned and ran toward the ride. The fact that she was also running from her thoughts didn't escape her notice.

Mike followed a short distance behind Carly, admiring the sexy sway of her hips as she sprinted ahead. Until today, when he'd seen her in those brief cutoff shorts, he hadn't realized how long her legs actually were. Long enough for a good many things, he realized, halting his thoughts before he embarrassed himself in a public place.

She stopped at the entrance to the ride and swung around. "Hey, are you coming or am I riding this thing alone?"

He grinned and caught up with her. All afternoon her enthusiasm had been contagious, making him glad he'd stopped by Pete's apartment to retrieve his camera. Though he'd been unwilling to look at the damn thing up until now, an afternoon in the sunshine with Carly provided a not-to-be missed opportunity. He'd enjoyed today more than any other in recent memory. And he knew . . . the shots he'd taken today would have to last him a lifetime.

The day had been full of revelations, though. If he'd had an inkling before, he now realized how mismatched Carly and his brother actually were. Although he had no right to judge, no right to come between them, the idea of letting them end up together, making each other miserable, ate at his gut. So did the never-ending sense of guilt. Technically he'd done nothing wrong, yet he couldn't shake the nagging feeling that he was betraying his brother.

Stepping back, he allowed her to precede him onto the ride. He handed the operator the tickets and a tip, pointing to the top of the Ferris wheel. The teenager, obviously used to such requests, slapped Mike on the back and winked.

After taking his place next to Carly, Mike nudged her in the ribs. "Drop the loot. We'll scoop up the animals when the ride's over."

"Do I have to?" She looked like a child ordered to retire her favorite toy.

He nodded. "If I can drop the camera, you can drop the winnings."

"I get attached quickly," she said, obviously embarrassed. But she scattered them around the small area at their feet.

He wished she'd get attached to him that fast and immediately banished the thought.

"So what are your plans?" Carly asked on their third trip around.

"I got a temporary job working for a city paper."

"How temporary?"

He wondered that himself. A light breeze surrounded them, causing tendrils of hair to caress her face. The sounds of the park and the realities of life seemed far away. When the huge wheel stranded them at the summit, Carly hung her head over the side in an attempt to discern the problem.

With a gentle tug he pulled her back into the car. "Relax, it'll get started again soon."

She sat back in her seat and spoke so quietly he had to strain to hear. "You didn't answer me. How long before you're off and running to the next trouble spot in the world?" she asked, looking off into the clear blue sky.

"No specific date." And right now, leaving was the furthest thing from his mind. With Carly sitting beside him, nothing else seemed to matter. Not a good sign, he thought. "But when the call comes, I'll be ready."

He cleared his throat. "Why didn't you tell Pete about the book?" he asked, changing the subject.

She remained silent, refusing to acknowledge his question.

"What about the rings?"

"What about them?" she asked.

"You loved those other rings."

She didn't refute his statement and Mike wondered. If he kept pushing, would she realize that she and his brother were mismatched opposites? Would she call things off before two people got hurt? Did he want her to?

Hell, he didn't need that responsibility. He could walk her through this now, but he wouldn't be there for her in the long run. His lifestyle wasn't suited to the white picket fence and security she so obviously sought.

If he pushed, he could end up hurting her as

badly as his brother could. Helluva pair he and Pete made. He shook his head. "You really love him, don't you?" Mike asked.

"Who?"

He stared. "Peter. Who else?" He held his breath waiting for her answer. An answer that shouldn't matter to him, but dammit, it did.

"Oh. Yes. Of course." She answered without meeting his gaze, a sure indication that his gut instincts were on target.

Since those same instincts had saved his behind many times, he hadn't really been in doubt.

She turned her attention from the cloudless sky, fingering her bangs with trembling hands.

"You do that a lot."

"What?" she asked.

"This." With a slow but steady hand, he ran his fingers through her bangs. She swallowed, and his eyes were drawn to the slender column of her neck. In silence, she glanced up at him from beneath thick lashes before lowering her eyes. He had no doubt she hoped to hide the feelings he'd seen reflected there. She'd been unsuccessful.

He tried to speak but words wouldn't come. Instead, as the silky strands of hair grazed his hands, he ached with the intensity of his feelings for this woman he'd known such a short time.

He trailed one finger down the side of her face until his hand rested beneath her chin. He tilted her head upward. Acting on impulse and not common sense, he lowered his head until his lips brushed hers. Whisper soft and brief, but that light touch stirred his body to life.

She sucked in a deep breath but didn't attempt to break the tenuous connection between them. Mike did, drawing himself back with extreme difficulty.

Looking at her flushed face and full lips, he knew, without a doubt, she had never felt this way about his brother. Not in the past, not now and especially not in the future. He was certain, not because of conceit or arrogance, but because he'd never experienced anything like the magic of being with Carly. Something that powerful could not be one-sided.

He pushed aside the guilt that continued to plague him at the thought of Peter. His brother didn't care about this woman, not the way an engaged man ought to care about his fiancé.

And Mike couldn't offer her much better. But that didn't mean he could remain silent much longer. He cared about her too much to watch her throw her life away. "We need to talk," he said.

Her lower lip trembled and she shook her head.

"It can't wait, Carly. You've been so busy planning that you haven't dealt with . . . things. I don't want to see you or Peter hurt."

She turned wet, shadowed eyes toward him. "I would never hurt your brother."

At that moment the mechanism on the Ferris wheel kicked into gear and they began their descent. "Damn," he muttered. "That wasn't what I meant. You and I . . ."

"Forget it." Eyes wide, she spoke with something akin to fear in her voice.

"No. We're getting off this ride and sitting down someplace to talk."

She backed into the corner of the small car. "No. We're getting off this ride, collecting my animals and going home. We'll listen to the radio and talk about comfortable things but nothing remotely personal." Without looking in his direction, she scrambled to gather her prizes.

They reached the bottom. The ride's operator waited for Mike to exit before extending his hand and helping Carly from the car. He patted Mike on the back. "Enough time for you and your lady to enjoy?" he asked with a chuckle.

"Not nearly," he muttered. He had to sprint to keep up with Carly, who appeared to be running for her life.

Mike reached out and turned off the car radio. Carly felt his steady gaze. She clenched her jaw and flipped the stereo back on. Easy-listening music filled her ears but wasn't nearly loud or distracting enough. She fiddled with the dial until she found hard rock. His hand reached out and stilled her frantic movements.

"What's bothering you?" he asked.

"Nothing. We had a great time."

"Am I wrong in thinking there's a connection between us?"

She didn't want to hear this. She had kissed him

while engaged to another man. Kissed him while engaged to his brother, she amended. Worse, she had enjoyed it. Apparently her father's blood flowed through her veins after all. "Don't you love carnivals?" she asked, changing the subject.

"Carly, do you trust me?"

"Of course. That's a stupid question. How did you fit that bear in the backseat anyway?" She fidgeted uncomfortably, hoping he would take her not-too-subtle hint and drop the idea of discussing *them*.

"I stuffed it in headfirst." He muttered a curse and slammed his hand against the steering wheel.

Ignoring his agitation, she turned the radio louder. She replayed their first meeting and today's brief kiss in her mind. Her traitorous body responded to the mere thought of his lips on hers. Two men at the same time. Two brothers, no less. And she thought her father should be tarred and feathered? With a groan she laid her head against the car window.

He made a few more attempts to draw her into any kind of conversation, which she childishly ignored, pretending instead to be asleep. Finally he lapsed into blessed silence. She knew her behavior was infantile, but she couldn't help feeling relieved nevertheless.

Anything he might have said would only reinforce the fact that each time she let her guard down around Mike, she lost a little more self-control.

She and Mike were an explosion waiting to happen and Carly knew one thing for certain. Explosions, once they occurred, were impossible to control.

This afternoon Mike had visited heaven. Now he prepared himself for hell. Sure, Pete had asked him to watch out for Carly and help with last-minute wedding details. But he hadn't asked Mike to take his fiancée out for the day, nor had he asked him to kiss her . . . or enjoy the experience quite so much. Pete also hadn't asked Mike to push her into questioning her upcoming marriage.

Mike muttered a curse. He approached Pete's apartment with as much excitement as a man facing a firing squad. Turning the key in the lock, he silently prayed for the strength to do the right thing for everyone involved. Damned if he knew what that was.

He stepped into the dimly lit apartment. "Hey, Pete, you back yet?" Silence greeted him, granting him a temporary reprieve. He tossed the keys on a shelf near the door and walked inside unprepared for what he saw.

Pete and a young woman sat on the floor of the living room poring over files and legal briefs. They didn't glance up, obviously too engrossed in work to have heard him come in. Nothing unusual or untoward about that, Mike thought.

Unless you knew Peter. The last time Mike had seen Pete casually dressed, they'd been teenagers . . . and he'd asked Mike for pointers on how to dress to impress the opposite sex. Looking at his brother now, Mike suppressed a groan.

Dressed in one of Mike's Polo shirts, a pair of khaki chinos and Docksiders, his brother looked like he'd stepped out of a Ralph Lauren ad. The woman gave the appearance of a little pixie, but based on Carly's description, he'd guess barracuda would be more accurate.

Mike walked into the room and was about to say hello when Pete burst out laughing, prompting the attractive associate to place a manicured hand on his shoulder and laugh with him. Her bare feet nudged Peter's calf. Then, as if a silent under-standing had been reached, they returned to their respective files and work.

Innocent, and yet . . . Mike shook his head. He ought to throttle his brother, but even as the thought took hold, he felt the vise that had gripped his heart for the last few weeks lessen and ease, until breathing became effortless.

"Hi." Mike cleared his throat. "Sorry to inter-rupt."

His brother glanced up from his seat on the floor. "No big deal. We were just finishing up some work." Pete stood, then reached out a hand to help the woman up from the floor.

Was it Mike's imagination or did her fingers linger seconds too long before releasing Peter's hand?

"Regina Grey, this is my brother, Mike." Pete smiled. "Mike, Regina."

Mike shook the dainty hand she held out toward him. "Nice to meet you."

"Same here." Regina began collecting items off the floor. "I just want to go over some things at home and we can meet first thing Monday morning and discuss strategy," she said.

"I'll be there."

No haggling, no bargaining, no compromise. Interesting, Mike thought.

When Peter returned from escorting the pretty Miss Grey to her cab, Mike turned on his brother. "What the hell's with you?" Mike asked.

Pete bent to retrieve the documents Regina had left behind. "What? The air-conditioning broke in the office and we came back here to work."

Mike waved a dismissive hand in the air. "I don't mean that." But he didn't know how to approach the subject with his brother. He raked a hand through his hair. "What is it with you two?"

"Who?" Pete asked, his brows crinkling in confusion.

"You and Carly, that's who." After shoving his hands in the front pockets of his shorts, Mike began pacing the room. "You laugh with this Regina?" he asked finally.

"She's quick."

"And bright. And pretty . . ."

"So is Carly," Pete chimed in. Too late, Mike thought.

"And an attorney," Mike continued as if he hadn't heard his brother speak. "And you have a hell of a lot more in common with her than you do with your fiancée, if you don't mind my saying so."

"You've always spoken your mind before," Pete said. "But this is my life, Mike. We didn't have parents to meddle in our lives as kids. I sure as hell don't need you to do it now."

"You're going through with this marriage, then?"

"The end result was never in question." Pete groaned and sat down on the leather sofa. "What she doesn't know won't hurt her."

"You're dead wrong. You may not mean to, but you'll destroy Carly and suffocate yourself." Forget what this marriage would do to him, Mike thought. "Is that a way to live?"

His brother didn't answer.

"Pete, you're not . . ." Mike trailed off. As close as the brothers had always been, they'd never traded sexual exploits, and Mike had no desire to start now. Still, he couldn't protect Carly if he didn't know the truth.

And though no one had appointed him her keeper, he'd taken on the role as if it was meant for him alone. "You're not sleeping with Regina, are you?"

Pete stared from his seat on the couch. His silence pronounced him guilty.

Mike let out a groan. "For the love of . . ."

Pete had the grace to look ashamed. "I thought I could wait, but . . ."

Sweet and innocent. How the hell had she gotten involved with either one of the Novack brothers? Each had the power to break her heart.

Pete shrugged. "We've been engaged for the last five months and dated on and off for three before that. A guy certainly can't go that long without . . ."

"He damn well can," Mike shouted. "And if you loved her, you would have."

"If she loved me, I wouldn't have had to look somewhere else," Pete retorted.

Mike clenched his teeth. "And what does that tell you?"

"Go back to globe-trotting and let me handle my own life." Apparently Pete was about to dig in his heels as hard as Carly had. Neither wanted to face reality.

Considering Mike had abandoned his own reality, he had no right to force theirs on them. "Just don't be surprised when things backfire."

Peter glared at him through narrowed, suspicious eyes. "Mind your own business," he said, clearly warning Mike to keep his mouth shut.

"Because you think your partnership's at stake?"

"Possibly."

"Then why'd you bring Regina back here? You know I'm staying over. Or did you take that risk on purpose?"

He couldn't stomach being in this apartment for another minute. Mike turned, scooped his keys off the counter and grabbed his camera from the front hall closet.

"Don't tell her, Mike." Pete's words reverberated in his head as he walked out, slamming the door behind him.

Parents and children, men and their dates, guys and their dogs and one lone man with his camera romped in Central Park. Mike wandered around, snapping photos without paying much attention to the setup. Each shot captured life in a way he treasured. Each would have a spot in his private collection. A select few he'd bring downtown to his new editor. He wasn't used to soft pieces, but after the hard stories he'd covered until recently, he welcomed the reprieve.

Until today, he'd retired his camera to the depths of Peter's closet, hoping to banish the unpleasant memories that went with it. To his surprise, when he'd picked up the camera and snapped the first shot, the rush of adrenaline had been powerful and positive. Of course, it had helped that Carly was his first subject.

If only he could view his life the same upbeat way. During his last assignment, he'd hitched a ride home from the countryside. Close to civilization, mortar fire hit the back tires of a bus ahead of him, sending it careening down the side of a ravine. Nothing Mike hadn't seen hundreds of times before in cities with different names. By the time he'd reached the bus, the smell of gasoline permeated the air. He and his companion managed to get the survivors out before the explosion hit. Jagged metal ripped through the muscle in his right shoulder. Just the memory made him break into a sweat, and he wiped the back of his hand over his brow.

All those young kids abandoned because their mothers had sat in the front of the bus while they played in the back. The luck of the draw, something Mike had also seen too many times before. All the carnival food he'd eaten with Carly threatened to come back up.

Over the next few weeks he was sidelined with his injury. He'd used the time to help track down the kids' fathers or other living relatives. Most had already been killed. All those children, orphaned like Mike and Peter. And though his boss had ordered him back to the center of the conflict once the doctors gave him a clean bill of health, Mike had bailed out instead.

He'd left midassignment, hopping the first plane back to the States. Three weeks early for his brother's wedding . . . or just in time, depending on one's place in this awful triangle, he thought wryly.

He glanced down at the camera in his hand, a piece of equipment that felt as comfortable as his own skin. At that moment, Mike knew. No matter what memories or doubts haunted him, he'd be facing them sooner rather than later. When his boss called—and he would—Mike wouldn't hesitate. Though Dom had finally given in on the extended leave issue, he swore that the next hot story was Mike's. Mike trusted his boss and friend not only to give him the time he needed, but to drag his butt back out there as soon as he could afterward. It would be the push he needed to return.

He'd be going back to the only life he knew. Carly's face flashed in front of his eyes. But in facing his past, he'd be leaving her behind . . . and exchanging one set of painful memories for another.

FIVE

Five days and no word from Mike. With her wedding a little over a week away, Carly knew she ought to feel relieved. Life went on, and Peter had even managed to get out of work early one night and take her for dinner. A sure sign things were looking up. If one believed in signs. These days Carly took any good omen she could get.

She put the finishing touches on her last column before summer repeats began and hit the print button. She'd drop the printout at Juliette's later in the week. Glancing at her watch, she realized she couldn't put off the inevitable any longer and headed uptown for her fitting. Since she hadn't been in touch with Mike, she hoped she could safely assume she was on her own.

She entered the bridal showroom where she'd purchased her gown, grateful the place wasn't crowded. With a little luck, this would be over in no time. Minutes later, the salesgirl who had taken her name reappeared with a long garment bag draped over her arm. One glance at the zippered bag and Carly's stomach did a nervous flip. Before the salesgirl could lead Carly back to the fitting room, she was paged to the front of the store.

She smiled apologetically and hung the gown from a hook on the side wall. "I'll be right back."

"I'll be here." Alone, Carly stared at the white bag, her stomach fluttering nonstop. Inside was the dress she'd wear when she married Peter. When she became Mrs. Peter Novack. When her life changed forever.

She pushed aside the nagging knowledge that something was terribly wrong. Since the fateful day she'd met Mike on the street, a tiny seed of doubt had taken root. She'd denied it, starved it, but it wouldn't go away. Now wasn't the time to examine it too closely. Once Mike was gone, life would return to normal. Safe, calm and peaceful.

She fingered the engagement ring, thinking of the wedding bands they'd chosen. Make that the bands *Peter* had chosen. She'd explained her feelings, but Peter had held firm. Despite her protests and explanations that stopped short of outright pleading, he'd been adamant. Had she broken down and cried, Peter would have succumbed in an instant, but she refused to resort to feminine manipulation to get her way. Obviously Peter's reasons meant more to him than she'd realized. For the sake of peace and Peter's happiness, she'd compromised. Again.

The one thing about this wedding that hadn't been a compromise lay in that bag.

"Go ahead and take a peek."

Carly whirled around to face Mike. "You startled

me." She placed a hand over her chest in a futile effort to calm her rapidly beating heart. "What are you doing here?"

"We had a date." Mike lifted one eyebrow, as if daring her to dispute his statement.

"I didn't think you'd show up."

"I try to honor my commitments," he said with complete sincerity.

She chose to ignore that comment. "How'd you find me?"

He leaned against the wall and grinned. His smile had the ability to stop her heart each and every time. She ground her teeth hard. "Well?"

"One phone call and a very efficient secretary. Did you ever think of giving her a raise?"

"Don't look so smug."

"And don't you look so unhappy. You know you're glad to see me."

She couldn't hide her smile. "Your ego astounds me."

"Can I have a look?" he asked, walking over to the garment bag. He reached for the zipper.

She smacked his hand. "Let me." With Mike staring from behind, she felt shy about looking at the dress she'd be wearing to wed another man. She bit her lower lip and gingerly unzipped the bag.

Reaching inside, she withdrew the material, gaping at the gown in shock. "It's pink."

Mike stepped back to appraise the dress and let out a long, approving whistle. "Nice," he murmured his gaze taking in the scooped neckline and intricate beading.

"It's pink." Her hand gripped his arm and her fingernails dug into his skin.

"I admit it's a surprise." And not just for him, Mike thought, judging by the horrified look on Carly's face. "You ordered white." Not a difficult guess.

After his brother's slip a few days before, Mike realized Carly was truly innocent. Not that most brides didn't wear white regardless, but Carly had maintained the right. Forget what Peter's reaction would be to his bride walking down the aisle in anything but traditional white, she deserved to have her first choice. After all her compromising, she shouldn't have to give in on something as important as her wedding gown.

He turned toward her, startled to see tears running down her face. "Hey," he said, brushing at the drop of moisture with his thumb. "I'm sure this can be fixed." He hoped.

"It's an omen."

"Come on, you don't believe in that stuff." He, on the other hand, agreed wholeheartedly.

"I planned this wedding and nothing has gone as I wanted. . . . No one has given a single thought to my feelings, but this . . ." She lifted the lace edge of the gown. "This was mine." She groaned. "Or it was supposed to be."

"Carly," he began carefully, "think about what you just said."

"So much for the perfect wedding."

She wasn't listening. He grabbed her by both arms, as if he were grabbing his last chance to reach her. "The *perfect* wedding won't change the fact that both people involved are far from the *perfect* couple. All the planning in the world won't change that."

The look of pain on her face almost destroyed him.

"How dare you?"

He swore silently. "I dare because you don't. Listen to yourself. Nothing about this wedding has turned out the way you wanted it. No one, including my brother, who I love but who can also be an ass, has given a damn about your needs."

She tried to jerk her arms free, but he held on fast. "What does that tell you?" he asked.

"That this is none of your business." She wrenched free from his grasp.

"You're right, but I can't sit around and watch this farce any longer. If I don't point out what you can't face, what kind of friend am I?" He shoved his fingers through his hair. *What kind of brother am I?*

She cocked her head to one side. Though her eyes remained wet and her pain was almost tangible, he sensed she was listening. At last.

"Look, sweetheart, you're two different people with two different personalities. It doesn't make either of you wrong or a bad person. That's just the way it is and it's time you faced the truth."

"What gives you the right to pass judgment?" she asked.

"Not a damn thing. But I love my brother and I . . . care about you. Marriage is forever. Promise me you'll think about that."

"And do what? Break off my engagement a week before the wedding?" Her voice cracked under the strain.

"If that's what feels right, then yes."

"I made a *commitment.*" She paced the small area before turning on him. "Do you even know what the word means?"

"Carly . . ." he said, warning her with his tone. "Don't make this personal."

"And what is it but personal? How can someone like you give me advice? What do you know about the long haul? About sticking with someone, for better or for worse?" She paused for air. "When things get tough, there's always that first flight out, isn't there?"

"I'll ignore the insult. We're discussing you, remember? For better or worse doesn't apply yet, sweetheart. And I suggest you get the hell out before it does." He exhaled, unable to believe he'd said the words on his tongue since day one.

Her eyes narrowed. "You have no right."

"Maybe not, but if you marry my brother, you're running the same way you think I am. I haven't figured out why yet, but I recognize the signs. Only difference between you and me is, when you wake up one morning with your heart and soul in pieces, you and your so-called commitment are stuck for good."

He glanced at Carly, expecting her to come at him swinging. Instead she sat in a chair and wrapped her arms around herself like a lost child. The sight pierced his heart. Though he wanted to hold her, she probably wouldn't let him near.

Just as well, he told himself. Now that he'd had his say, the rest was up to her. "You've got some decisions to make before it's too late." He drew a deep breath. "You say you're tired of compromise? Prove it."

She raised her head from where her chin rested on her knees. Her eyes mirrored her soul. Pain, anger, hurt, anguish . . . and myriad other emotions Mike couldn't decipher melded in the dark depths.

"Do me a favor?" she asked in a soft voice.

"Anything." He took two steps toward her.

"Get the hell out and leave me alone."

Juliette slid into the seat across from Carly at a small restaurant on Madison Avenue. "You could have faxed your column in or dropped it off at the office." She glanced back at the cases of baked goods, muffins, breads and scones. "But I'd much rather meet for food. I'm starving."

She shook the green linen napkin out in front of her and placed it on her lap. "Orange pekoe tea, please," she said to a passing waitress.

The younger woman paused. "Anything for you?" she asked, turning to Carly.

"Coffee."

"Chamomile tea," Juliette said. She leaned closer to Carly. "Your hands are shaking. The last thing you need is caffeine."

Carly glanced at the waitress and shrugged.

"Chamomile's fine." She wasn't here for food, just motherly advice and maybe a hug.

The waitress replaced her pad and walked away.

Juliette narrowed her eyes. "What's going on? You gave in too easily."

"Why is it everyone thinks I'm a lapdog? I make my own decisions. I even put on a different shade of eyeshadow this morning," Carly said, defiance in her voice.

"I said you're *too* compliant, meaning *I've* never known you to back down from an argument with me in your life."

Carly sighed. "That's professional."

"And you're damn good at what you do. So while I was making an observation that something's wrong because you're not behaving like your confident self, *someone else* obviously sees you differently." Juliette leaned back for the waitress to set down their cups, choice of tea and hot water. "Who?"

Carly needed to unburden herself with a desperation she'd never known before. And she trusted Juliette to listen without passing judgment and to offer the comfort she needed. "His name is Mike," she said softly. "Mike Novack."

"Peter's . . ."

"Brother," Carly finished for her.

"Good Lord, when you dive in, you really do it with both feet."

"You don't know the half of it." She drew a deep breath. "Jules . . . I don't think I can marry Peter," Carly said in a whisper. Then, to keep busy, she unwrapped the tea bag with shaking hands and let it steep in the steaming water.

Her friend braced her chin in her hands. "Go on. I don't want to influence you one way or another until I hear what's going through your mind. Keep talking."

"It's hard to explain. It's like up until now I've gone through life in a fog and now the mist has cleared. I *feel.*"

Juliette nodded. "And it scares the living daylights out of you."

"That's putting it mildly." What Mike did for her, to her and with her, reminded her of everything she'd sworn off early in life. Her father had destroyed her illusions, her perfect family, and worse, another human being. If that was the result of so-called love and passion, Carly could live without it.

But she couldn't compromise herself to be Peter's perfect mate. Not anymore. In fact, she couldn't believe she'd convinced herself it was for the best. She'd observed her mother doing that kind of compliance, and for years, Carly had silently condemned her for it. Yet in an effort to break free of her father's actions, she'd somehow believed she would be happy with that kind of bland life.

Thanks to Mike's appearance, she now knew better. In that respect, his observations had been on target. "Mike scares me," she admitted. "But he isn't what this is about."

Juliette raised an eyebrow, looking skeptical. "Okay, then. Peter's brother arrives from . . ."

"Overseas."

"Overseas. Knocks you off your feet, makes you reconsider marrying Peter, thank the good Lord, but *he* isn't what this life-altering decision is about?"

"No." The excuse sounded lame to Carly, too. But no matter how much Mike Novack affected her, he was not a part of her future. "The man is sexy and sweet, but he's just passing through my life."

"What if he's not? Every person has that perfect mate out there, Carly. What if he's the one?"

She closed her eyes, wishing it was possible. But instead of happily ever after, all she saw were the pictures Mike had graphically described to her. War zones and traveling, danger and excitement. Those things appealed to Mike. He wasn't the kind of man who wanted a wife and kids back home, or people to answer to.

And she wasn't the kind of woman who would accept any less. Once he was gone, he was out of her life forever. They both knew it. "Even if he's the one, Jules, he's just not the staying kind of guy."

Now that the decision had been made, Carly needed to get it over with as soon as possible. She drew a deep breath and with a trembling hand let herself into Peter's office.

"Hi." For his sake, she forced a smile.

"Hello." He stood, then adjusted his tie. His gaze traveled over her, his brows crinkling with concern. "You look exhausted."

"I am. Can I sit?" she asked, avoiding the urge to wring her hands. She had too much nervous energy building up inside her. She wasn't sure she could get through telling him. Nor was she sure *how* to tell him without hurting him, something she did not want to do.

"Sure." He gestured to the chair across from his desk. Carly sat, feeling more like a client than his fiancée. The signs had been there all along. She had just chosen not to heed them.

"I've got just a few minutes before the department meeting, so . . ."

She clenched her jaw, which only added to the building headache she'd had for the past few days. Even before talking to Juliette, she'd agonized over Mike's blunt words in the bridal shop. Hearing her own fears verbalized by someone else, especially Mike, had sent her into a panic. Fight or flight, she now realized. She'd chosen first to fight Mike and then to run from the truth in his words. After two days locked in a battle with herself, she could now face the truth.

She fingered the strap on her purse and wondered how in the world to begin. "I know you hate unexpected surprises, but this is important." And that was but one problem. Each time Peter ignored her for work or squeezed her in as an inconvenience to be tolerated, he put a serious dent in not only their relationship but in her self-esteem.

She deserved better.

"Like I said, I've got a few minutes. What's wrong?" he asked.

"What isn't wrong?" She leaned forward. "I don't know how to say this except to just . . . say it. I

want . . . I need . . . that is, I don't think this marriage will work." She forced the words out, then exhaled in relief.

She dared a glance at Peter's face. Shock and disbelief crossed his features. "You what?"

She swallowed over the lump in her throat.
"We're different. It's so obvious you can't miss it . . .
unless, of course, you want to." Or aren't paying
attention, she thought sadly. "Take the wedding: I
compromised on every major issue. The caterers,
the color scheme, the rings . . ."

"If this is about those plain rings, we'll cancel the
original order and go back to buy those."

Too little, too late, she thought.

"You should have said something sooner."

"I did. Over and over." Not that it had made a
difference in their relationship. Wedding arrangements should have solidified the bond between
them, not driven them farther apart. Their relationship had disintegrated and neither one had acknowledged the warning signs in time to rectify the
problem. If Peter searched his heart as she had
searched her own, would he also discover that he
really hadn't cared enough to bother? They'd each
wanted something out of their relationship. Unfortunately they'd been two people with parallel goals.
Their needs and desires had never crossed.

She glanced up at him through watery eyes. "You
never wanted to hear."

"All couples go through last-minute jitters right
before the wedding. I'm sure we can work things
out. Compromise on some issues, things like that."

Laughter bubbled from within, threatening to erupt in tears or hysterics, she wasn't sure which. She shook her head. "No more, Peter." She'd made her decision and intended to stick with it. The determination in her voice took her by surprise.

Peter slammed his hand on the desk. "I knew I couldn't trust my do-gooder brother." Peter stood and walked around the desk, kneeling in front of her. "If this is about Regina, it's over. I swear she has nothing to do with us. She never did. From now on . . ."

Carly tried to absorb Peter's words and meaning, but her head whirled and she couldn't manage to think straight. Feelings, however, pulsed through her, their message clear. Betrayal, pain and anger. Every reason she'd picked Peter as her *safe* fiancé disintegrated in front of her eyes.

And as his excuses turned to pleading, she rose from her chair, obviously too fast because the room began to spin around her and she leaned against the wall for support. Somehow, she couldn't bring herself to believe the truth. "Are you telling me you cheated on me?" Carly needed to hear the words.

"You didn't know?"

"No." *But Mike did.* And that, Carly realized, hurt most of all.

She swallowed hard. "Well, I'm only sorry I lost so much sleep agonizing over how to tell you." She wrapped the remains of her tattered pride around her like a warm cloak, but nothing helped ease the chill inside her heart.

"Carly, please." He rose and stood beside her.

"Please what?" she asked. "Don't do this?" She shook her head. "It took everything inside me to do what's right for both of us, while you never once thought of me."

"That's not true." He placed his hand on her arm.

She shook off his grasp. "Don't touch me."

"I'm sorry."

A brief knock jolted Carly into sudden awareness of her surroundings. She might not agree with how her mother had lived her life, but one lesson Carly had learned well: Keep private things private and never wear your heart on your sleeve. Although she'd never agreed with her mother's refusal to discuss the pain that rocked their lives, Carly suddenly understood that defense mechanism better than ever before. A lawyer's office was no place for theatrics or confrontations, and her emotions were hers. Peter didn't deserve to know how badly his betrayal had hurt her.

The door behind her swung open wide. Mike stood in the door frame. In his standard denim jeans, black T-shirt and hiking boots, he looked sexy and masculine. A man confident in his own skin.

She shook her head. Her conservative ex-fiancé had never stood a chance. With a flash of insight, she realized that Mike appealed to her wilder side. The part she'd tried unsuccessfully to suffocate. To hide.

Seeking comfort from Peter's admission, and what she viewed as Mike's betrayal as well as her own, she wrapped her arms around her chest. "What a great time for a family reunion," she muttered.

"Okay, what the hell's going on?" Mike asked, his gaze darting between Carly and his brother.

She had no intention of explaining anything to the man who hadn't seen fit to tell her the truth. Even as he'd spouted all the reasons she shouldn't marry Peter, he hadn't revealed the most important one of all.

"Ask your two-timing brother." Suddenly exhausted, she leaned against the wall once more. "I'll handle notifying the guests and the caterers and returning gifts."

The small office felt suffocating. She walked around Mike, ignoring his burning gaze. She'd reached the door when she paused in midstride and glanced at Peter. He looked stricken, but at this moment Carly couldn't bring herself to care. Nor could she bring herself to reassure him about his partnership. Before finding out about his affair, she'd made sure her decision wouldn't affect her father's feelings about Peter.

"One more thing."

"Yes?" he asked warily.

"Take this." She twisted her engagement ring off her finger and smacked it into his hand before turning on her heel and storming out of the room.

Mike started to sprint after Carly, but Peter's strong grip on his arm halted his departure. He pivoted and came face-to-face with his brother.

"What?" Mike asked. He didn't want to waste time dealing with Pete.

"The truth. Did you tell her?" For the first time, his composed brother looked shaken.

Though Mike wished he could pity him, the one person he felt for was Carly. "I wish I'd had that honor. Not telling her is something I'll have to live with." He prayed it wasn't too late. "Obviously she's brighter than you thought."

Peter groaned, bracing a hand on the doorknob. "No, I'm just a hell of a lot dumber."

Mike shook his head. "When will you learn, Pete? Things have a way of coming back to haunt you."

But he needed to speak to Carly, and unless the elevators were slow, she'd had enough of a head start for her to disappear into the crowd. By the time he'd reached the street, the clouds that had looked threatening earlier had erupted in rain showers. In this weather, finding an empty taxi would be damn difficult if not impossible.

He glanced to his right and relief kicked into him. Carly stood on a corner flagging down a cab. He ran, reaching the taxi just as she pulled the car door shut. He rapped on the glass and called her name.

She rolled down the window. "Go away." Her face was wet with moisture, making it impossible for him to distinguish between raindrops and tears.

"No." He reached for the handle and opened the door.

She promptly slammed it closed again.

"Have a heart, Carly. It's wet out here."

She glared through the half-opened window.

"Have a heart? That's a joke coming from you." She smacked her hand down on the inside panel.

He reached for the handle before she could lock the cab door. This time he was prepared for her resistance. His strength was no match for hers and the door flew open wide.

Ignoring her murderous look, he flung his wet body into the seat, forcing her to move over or be crushed. She slid over quickly.

"Wise move," he said, shutting the door behind him.

Silence greeted him.

Leaning forward, he spoke to the driver. "Seventy-second and Second."

"Wait." She tapped the driver and the man turned to look over his shoulder.

"He's not going with me." Carly gestured toward Mike.

"The hell I'm not."

A wide grin encompassed the older man's face. "Me, I don't care where we go or how long we sit. The meter's running." He patted the metal box. As if on cue, the digital numbers increased.

"I'm in no rush." Mike shrugged and leaned back in his seat.

She groaned but remained silent. Raindrops pelted the windshield and the cabdriver began whistling.

Mike slicked back his hair with one hand. This was one battle of wills he couldn't afford to lose. He needed the chance to explain. More important, Carly needed to be with someone who cared.

He glanced at his watch. The meter ticked off another fare increase. The driver switched tunes. Over
the off-key whistling, Mike heard a clicking sound
and turned. Carly huddled in the corner, arms
wrapped around herself, shivering, her teeth chattering. She pushed her wet bangs out of her eyes
with one hand before wrapping her arms around
her wet body once more.

He muttered a harsh curse and repeated her address aloud.

The driver looked at Carly. "Miss?"

"Just go," Mike said through clenched teeth.

The man glanced over his shoulder at Carly again
and she nodded. He swiveled back in his seat and
placed the car in gear, jamming his foot down on
the accelerator.

Mike looked at Carly and held out his arms.

"Either you've lost your mind or your ego is bigger than I thought." She curled into a tighter ball.

He let out a groan, reached over and pulled her
into his embrace. She tried to squirm free, but he
held on tight. "Save your energy to argue with me
later," he said. "Right now we're both wet and freezing. If you don't want to come down with pneumonia, take advantage of my body heat."

Heaven knew he was taking advantage of hers.
Every breath brought with it her unique scent, and
her soft body had begun to relax, molding to his.

"I'm only doing this to keep warm," she mumbled.

He chuckled. "I know."

"I'm still angry."

He leaned his chin on the top of her head. "I know that, too." And a confrontation was sure to follow.

After towel-drying her hair, Carly wrapped herself in an ivory terry-cloth robe. The hot shower had warmed her body but not her heart. She felt ice cold inside. Ironically, heartache wasn't the problem.

She'd already broken up with Peter, already accepted that caring couldn't replace love when he'd blundered into his admission. And though he'd shocked her, Mike's silence hurt worse than anything Peter had done. Her ex-fiancé had merely wounded her pride and convinced her that she'd been going through life with blinders on, in more ways than one. She pulled the lapels of the lace collar together at her throat, drew a deep breath and stepped out of the bathroom.

Mike stood in front of the credenza that provided a makeshift bar. He'd changed out of his wet clothes. He wore the large gray sweats she'd lent him, a towel draped around his neck . . . and nothing else. Her gaze was drawn to the muscles in his back and upper arms.

The strength in his body seemed as prevalent as the strength in his character. Another misguided perception, she thought. He too had betrayed her.

The rational part of her rebelled at the notion. The emotional part, the part that had been humiliated tonight, clung to the possibility. A confrontation with Mike was inevitable. Today's encounters were like a flood after a lifetime drought.

He turned, drinks in hand. "Here." He held out a brandy snifter. "I think we could both use this to warm up."

After accepting the glass, she walked away from him. "You knew."

"Yes."

She admired his honesty. She just wished it had come sooner. Carly closed her eyes and inhaled deeply. How could the confirmation of something she'd already known hurt so much? She pushed up the sleeves of the oversized robe. "That's something, I suppose."

"What is?"

"At least you didn't lie this time."

He grasped her arm and swung her toward him. His eyes bore into hers. "I never lied to you."

The heat of his fingertips seared her skin, branding her and making it difficult to remain focused. "What would you call it?" she asked. "A tiny omission?"

"Yes." With a groan, he released her. "Put yourself in my position. Where would you find yourself?"

In the middle, she silently conceded.

"I did the only thing I could. I pushed with the knowledge you already had and hoped you'd come to the right decision."

"And if I hadn't?"

Guilt etched his features. "I hadn't thought that far. I guess I had faith in you. And besides . . . I couldn't bring myself to be the one to hurt you."

"And you didn't want to betray your brother." A tear trickled down her cheek. She wiped it away with the back of her hand.

"That, too."

She lifted her drink to her lips with trembling hands. "Where did you find this stuff?" Carly only used the credenza when she entertained or had friends over to hang out. Brandy wasn't a staple in her liquor cabinet. She stifled a laugh. She didn't have a liquor cabinet.

"I dug through your kitchen and managed to come up with something we could use. Drink up. It should help relax you."

She took a sip. The dark liquid burned a path down her chest yet centered her somehow. She crossed the room and stared out the window to the street below. Carly tried to hold on to her anger at Mike. She had to. Without it, she didn't have anyone to turn the brunt of her feelings upon. So he had been torn between her and his brother. His brother, his only family, or a woman he'd just met. Not much of a decision there, she thought bitterly.

He walked toward her and placed a hand on her arm. "Do you understand what I'm saying?" His intense gaze bore into hers, causing a pulse-pounding heaviness in her chest.

Afraid she understood him *too* well, Carly backed off, heading for the center of the room, searching for space.

SIX

Mike watched Carly's retreat. Somehow she seemed too composed for a woman who had not only broken her engagement but just discovered that her fiancé had been cheating on her as well. She set down her drink on the hardwood floor and turned her attention to a white wicker basket overflowing with magazines. She crouched down, knees resting on two over-sized throw pillows fringed in yellow.

As he watched, she began rummaging through the stack of magazines, tossing unwanted ones to the side. A huge pile formed beside her. Whether her task enabled her to ignore him or whether she was searching for something, he couldn't say. The relevance of her actions escaped him, but she seemed to need the distraction.

Her movements caused her robe to part, revealing a hint of cleavage and the round swell of one breast. Mike sucked in a deep breath but found it impossible to look away. He shifted positions and lowered himself onto the couch because if she looked up now, she'd run far and fast. The sweats she had lent him were too tight under ordinary circumstances. What he felt now went way beyond ordinary.

He glanced at her again. "What are you . . ."

"Aha. Found it." She rose, then ripped a page from the chosen magazine. "Did you know there's such a thing as wedding insurance? Damage control for a wedding canceled due to unforeseeable events. Let's see." She skimmed the article in her hand.

Mike narrowed his eyes and focused on her distracted behavior. He realized now that she was more affected than he'd originally thought. He fought the urge to ease her pain. To wrap her in his arms and never let go.

Just because she'd dumped his brother didn't make her ready for another relationship. Especially a short-term affair with a man who, as she'd so rightly said, was unable to commit. Whose career was destined to take him farther away at any time.

She'd had enough pain. He had no desire to add to it.

She raised her gaze from the magazine page. "Too bad," she murmured. "Weddings canceled because the bride wore blinders while the groom was a cheating son of a bitch aren't covered." Her voice broke over her words. As she lowered her arm to her side, the page drifted to the floor.

"Carly . . ." Mike stood.

"It'll cost every penny I have in savings and then some to cover the expense of ending this charade."

"Peter will pay his share," Mike muttered. He'd see to it. "Better now than after the ceremony."

She attempted to laugh but choked on a sob instead. She dropped to her knees and bowed her head. Her damp hair fell forward, obscuring her face from view. Without warning, her shoulders began to shake violently.

Something inside him shattered at the sight. Not since his parents' deaths had he allowed another person to get close. As tight as they were, not even his brother had breached the wall around his heart. Carly tapped into emotions he'd never experienced before, ones he didn't understand now. She'd reached the part of him that he'd protected for the better part of his life. Watching her, he had the unsettling notion that nothing would ever be the same again.

Mike crossed the room and crouched down beside her. He lifted his hand and then let it drop uselessly to his side. Never having received a warm or loving embrace as a child, he wasn't sure how to comfort her now. He only knew he had to try.

He wrapped his arms around her. Her body molded to his. She rocked back and forth in his embrace as he held on tight. The fragrant smell of her shampoo drifted around him, tickling his nose, tempting his restraint.

As need surfaced, comfort became a hazy notion. He coaxed her back until they lay side by side against the pillows on the floor. Mike cradled her head, running his fingers through her silken hair. Gradually her trembling subsided, but she didn't push him away. They lay together in silence. Her rapid breathing slowed. As she unconsciously matched her breaths to his, a feeling of contentment stole over him. It was as if he'd been running away and had finally found what he'd been searching for.

"Want to talk about it?"

"No." The muffled sound was almost lost. With one hand, he brushed the tangled hair off her face.

"I'm sure it hurts to be betrayed by someone you love."

She shook her head. "I wasn't."

Wasn't what? he wondered. Betrayed? Because if Peter had done nothing else, he had betrayed both her trust and her innocence. Mike hoped he hadn't destroyed them as well.

She drew an unsteady breath. A glassy sheen coated her eyes and her dark lashes were fringed with moisture. "I wasn't betrayed by someone I loved," she said, lowering her gaze. "I compromised until there was almost nothing left of me. In being so accepting, I gave him the freedom to cheat on me." She sighed. "In a way, I deserve *some* of what I got."

"How the hell can you think that?"

"I didn't say I deserved all of it, but there's no escaping the fact that I used him, too." Looking down, she stared at her hands. "I never loved Peter."

Mike exhaled long and slow. He hadn't known how badly he'd needed to have his suspicions confirmed until now.

"But at the very least I thought he was the kind of man to honor his commitments the way I'd planned to honor mine."

Mike wanted to defend his brother. To insist that he was sure Peter *meant* to be faithful. But the truth was, Peter looked out for Peter first. Carly had never factored into the equation. He hadn't intended to hurt her, but he hadn't stopped to think about her before jumping into bed with his new associate, either. "If it makes you feel any better, he took me by surprise, too."

Her smile seemed forced. "It doesn't matter. I was so wrong. As long as things seemed right on the surface, I convinced myself I was happy. But I wasn't." She shifted positions, rotating her legs until she sat Indian-style beside him. Her robe ended below her knees, revealing toned calves and long legs. "I was dead inside and just never knew it. Until you, Peter was safe."

"And I'm not." Mike raised his hand to the back of her neck and brushed aside her hair.

"No." Her lips parted. "You're not."

"Why?" He massaged her muscles that had worked themselves into tight knots. Her skin felt smooth and soft beneath his hands.

"There was no . . ." She spread her hands in front of her. "No . . ."

"Passion." He ventured an educated guess. One based on the fact that she hadn't slept with his brother, had never seemed to want more from Peter than a passing touch. But mostly he based his knowledge on instinct.

Startled, she jerked her head up. "How . . ."

"Did I know?"

She nodded.

He grinned at the shocked expression on her face as he completed her sentence for the second time.

"Because you couldn't feel an emotional pull toward my brother and respond to me like this."

He leaned over and brushed his lips over hers. His hand, already at her nape, dug farther into her hair as he shifted positions and slid his tongue across her lips. She sighed aloud.

He meant to coax her into understanding but there was no need. Instead of pulling away as he'd expected, she raised her hands to his face and opened her mouth beneath his.

The kiss was hot, intense and like nothing in his previous experience. Although he had intended to prove a point, he lost track of everything but Carly.

He lifted his head and looked into her soft brown eyes.

"Mike." His name was a plea he couldn't resist. He captured her lips again. Together they tumbled backward onto the floor. He trapped her slender body between his legs and shifted until the heat of his arousal was pressed firmly at the juncture of her thighs.

Pausing long enough to open his eyes, he watched her face as he further inflamed her senses. He ground his hips against hers.

Her eyes glazed over. "More."

He grit his teeth against the combination of pleasure and pain and thrust himself against her welcoming body. She uttered a sigh and rotated her hips, causing him to curse the barrier of clothing that separated them. Then he closed his eyes and pushed deeper.

His mouth never left hers, his tongue mimicking

the erotic motion of their bodies. She rocked beneath him and wrapped her arms around his waist, pulling him closer. Their bodies fit together as one.

Still separated by layers of clothing, they were both close to losing control. Mike hadn't touched an inch of her skin, yet he ached to lose himself inside her. The thought amazed him. After everything she'd been through, she still . . . His mind cleared in an instant. His body, however, refused to cooperate and throbbed with unsatisfied need.

He gentled his kiss in an effort to bring them down from the peak they'd almost reached. He wanted Carly, but on equal terms. With her needing him as much as he needed her. Giving and receiving comfort wasn't a solid basis for making love.

He allowed himself one last lingering kiss before pulling himself up and away from her soft, willing body.

Seconds passed before Carly's passion-fogged mind cleared. Two things became evident at once. She'd succumbed to the heat of desire, to the point of almost making love on her living-room floor. And she wasn't the one who'd called a halt.

Her entire body throbbed. Need pulsed through her, but she drew a ragged breath and forced herself to relax. She looked at Mike. His head rested on bended knee and he studied her with a pensive expression. His golden eyes betrayed none of his inner thoughts. She didn't have to be a mind reader to know them.

Carly recognized Mike's withdrawal for what it was—another rejection in a day fraught with them.

She might have been the one to break things off with Peter, but in admitting his affair, he'd all but rejected her, declaring her worthless in his eyes.

She had the sinking notion that no one would ever love her enough to put her first. Her father hadn't cared enough to put his family before his mistress. Her fiancé had always given his career and lover higher priority. And Mike, the one person with whom she'd felt a solid connection, had rejected her twice. First by keeping silent and again by pushing her away.

And she would have slept with him anyway. Embarrassment flooded her, cooling her passion faster than an icy shower. "I'm sorry," she said, standing as she spoke. "But congratulations. You proved your point. I couldn't have been in love with Peter and I have no self-restraint when it comes to you." A lot that said about her moral fiber, she thought.

Mike groaned. "That wasn't the point I was trying to prove." He leaned back, propping himself up on both elbows.

"Why else pull back? Heaven knows I wouldn't have stopped you." Self-loathing filled her voice, directed at both her actions and the question she'd just voiced. He didn't need to know that his rejection bothered her.

"What happened just now"—he gestured back and forth between them—"that was about you and me. No one else was in the room. No one else was between us."

"I know," she whispered, remembering the way

she had writhed beneath him. The shame of her wanton response burned inside her.

"Don't look at me like that," Mike said in a husky voice.

"Like what?" Turning from the heat of his stare, she attempted to straighten her rumpled robe.

"Like you're afraid of me."

"I'm not."

"Aren't you?"

She shook her head. "I'm afraid of what you make me feel," she admitted. *Afraid of who you make me become.*

"Don't be. Because the next time will make this one pale in comparison, I promise." His eyes raked over her body. Beneath his heated gaze she felt naked and exposed.

He rose at a leisurely pace, a man comfortable with himself and his sexuality.

"There won't be a next time." She tightened the sash around her waist, turned and stepped back before he could crowd her personal space.

But he anticipated her reaction and grabbed for the material of her robe. He pulled her backward until she leaned against the hard contours of his body. "Yes, there will. But next time you'll want *me*, not just comfort." His warm breath fanned her ear.

If he only knew how much she wanted him . . . even more than she'd sought solace in his arms. But she closed her eyes and let his words sink in.

He assumed there'd be a next time. Because she'd been eager and willing, despite his betrayal, he'd assumed all was forgiven. Carly didn't know who she was more furious with, Mike or herself.

Because she wanted to believe in him. Wanted to trust that he desired more from her than just hot sex. Though it couldn't change things between them, she needed to believe they shared more than just passion. Because when that passion flared, a living, breathing monster came alive. It brought the past to life and caused her to doubt the present.

He pressed a gentle kiss against her neck. She trembled against the feather-light touch. "Just go, Mike."

"Will you be all right?" he asked, obviously resigned.

She nodded.

"I thought so." He gathered his damp clothing from the floor. "You're strong, Carly Wexler," he said before disappearing into her bathroom.

"But not strong enough to resist you," she murmured to the empty room. She leaned against the nearest wall, closed her eyes and forced air into her lungs. She couldn't resist the man whose omission had hurt her more than her fiancé's affair. She shook her head and breathed in deeply once more. No sooner had she drawn another breath than the bathroom door swung wide open.

"What are your plans now that you're officially unengaged?" he asked. He'd changed back into his damp jeans and working boots. His black T-shirt clung to his broad shoulders and back.

"Are you sure you want to go home like that?"

He grinned. "It's either the wet look or I leave half-naked and barefoot. Your choice."

When he focused his smile on her, nothing else in the world mattered. She could almost forgive him anything. "Go with the wet look. The neighbors don't need a free show." But *go*, she thought silently.

"Well?" he asked.

"What?"

"Your plans."

Obviously she couldn't get rid of him easily. If he sensed her need to be alone, he didn't show it. She hadn't had a chance to give her future much thought. But perhaps now that she had the time as well as her freedom, she ought to try. "I really don't know. I need to get away." The truth surprised her, as much as the fact that she'd spoken the words aloud.

"Anyplace special?"

No place she'd share with him, but she had an idea in mind. Someplace where she could be alone to learn about herself and what *she* wanted out of life. A place far from Mike and his charismatic influence, she thought. "No destination in mind," she said, forcing a smile.

"One minute you're planning a wedding, the next a vacation. You go with the flow. I like that in a woman."

She couldn't see pointing out that until now her rigid schedules and plans had ruled her life and kept her sane. She was on a wild free fall now and had no idea where she would land. The thought frightened her. He might like that carefree way of life, but she didn't.

He closed the gap between them and reached out a hand to touch her shoulder. She shook her head. "I'm okay." His touch would be her undoing. Both emotionally and physically she wasn't strong enough to resist him right now. She needed to keep her distance.

"I know." He lowered his hand to the side. "How will you keep busy?" he asked, as if understanding that she needed a mundane subject change.

"School is out, my column is in reruns and I'd planned on using the summer to write my book. I can work anywhere with a computer." She fingered her still damp bangs.

"Maybe someplace with a beach," she said, thinking aloud.

"Sounds therapeutic." He spoke as though his mind had escaped elsewhere.

"True. My life has just been thrown a curve. A vacation might get it back on track."

"Makes sense."

She nodded.

He offered no response.

An uncomfortable silence surrounded them. She glanced at him, her gaze drawn to the taut muscles in his arm, then the wide expanse of his chest. In her mind, she was back on the floor, Mike's firm body pressed against hers. This time, her lips tasted bare skin.

He cleared his throat.

She blinked and her eyes met his. Amusement

etched his features. A wide smile told her she'd been caught. She raised her hands to her flaming cheeks.

The safest move would be to get him out of her apartment. Once he left, he'd be out of her life. And she refused to analyze her feelings on *that* subject just yet.

She walked past him and headed toward the door. His footsteps sounded behind her. She placed her hand on the doorknob and turned.

"I can take a hint, however subtle."

She turned toward him. "Good. Then no hard feelings and good night."

"Get some rest and try not to dwell on anything too upsetting." He grasped her hand in his, entwined their fingers and caressed her palm with his thumb.

What should have been a casual gesture heated her senses. A flicker of warmth began deep inside and radiated throughout her body. Through sheer force of will, she didn't pull away.

He brushed her knuckles with his lips. " 'Night, Carly. Sleep tight."

He might as well have said *dream of me,* since she doubted she'd do anything else. " 'Night, Mike."

She shut the door behind him, knowing in her heart that it was for the last time.

Mike knew he was taking unfair advantage. He knew Carly wanted to be alone. Yet he sensed deep pain beneath the surface, hurt that went way beyond a broken engagement. And he believed that pain could be traced back in time. Although he couldn't be the man in her future—he had too many scars of his own and a lifestyle she couldn't understand or accept—he wanted to be the one to help her heal and move on.

He'd deal with his own pain of losing her later, when he'd pulled his life together and was back wandering the globe on assignment. He knocked and let himself into her father's office. Roger Wexler rose from his desk. "Good to see you, Mike."

"I appreciate you fitting me in, Mr. Wexler." He shook the older man's hand.

"Roger. And it's no problem. What can I do for you?" He gestured to the chair in front of his desk and waited for Mike to sit before lowering himself back into his own seat.

"Carly mentioned she was going on vacation. The beach sounds like a good place to recuperate." Mike was acting on a hunch, but he had no other leads.

Roger nodded and leaned forward on his elbows. "Sure is. We've spent a month at that beach house every summer for the past twelve years or so." The man's eyes narrowed, his curiosity evident. "Why?"

Mike wondered how much to reveal. Gazing into the older man's eyes, he opted for the truth. Too much in the way of lies had passed between this man and Mike's family. "One reason is a photo layout I'm doing for a local paper. I need a place to stay while I research the area and take some pictures."

"And the other reason?"

Mike cleared his throat. "Your daughter." Uncomfortable with the topic of conversation, he pushed himself up from his chair. He paced the plush office, admiring the view and the furnishings.

Despite the fact that this man was a lawyer, his office held a warmth that surprised him. The place reminded Mike of Carly. She obviously had more in common with her father than he'd realized. More than she wanted to admit.

"I see," Roger said.

Did he? Did the older man understand how Mike felt about his daughter, or did he put him in the same category as his brother? Mike shoved a hand beneath his blazer, into the back pocket of his jeans.

"Mr. Wexler . . ." Mike paused. How did one overcome the sins of one's brother? And did he have that right, considering his intentions were good but not long-term?

Roger rose and met him in the center of the large room. "I'm not going to judge you based on Peter. And in case he didn't tell you, I'm not going to judge his work based on his action toward Carly."

"I haven't spoken to Pete." Mike had left the apartment early each morning and returned late at night. Until he'd come to terms with what his brother had become, he wasn't ready to deal with him. At least not yet.

"Well, I was all set to toss him the hell out. Until Carly begged me not to mix business with her personal life."

Mike should have been surprised, but he wasn't. Carly was too sweet for her own good. He met Roger's assessing stare. Brown eyes, the same warm eyes he'd looked into last night, stared back at him.

THE PUBLISHERS OF ZEBRA BOUQUET

are making this special offer to lovers of contemporary romances to introduce this exciting new line of novels. Zebra's Bouquet Romances have been praised by critics and authors alike as being of the highest quality and best written romantic fiction available today.

EACH FULL-LENGTH NOVEL

has been written by authors you know and love as well as by up and coming writers that you'll only find with Zebra Bouquet. We'll bring you the newest novels by world famous authors like Vanessa Grant, Judy Gill Ann Josephson and award winning Suzanne Barrett and Leigh Greenwood—to name just a few. Zebra Bouquet's editors have selected only the very best and highest quality romances for up-and-coming publications under the Bouquet banner.

YOU'LL BE TREATED

to tales of star-crossed lovers in glamourous settings that are sure to captivate you. These stories will keep you enthralled to the very happy end.

4 FREE NOVELS As a way to introduce you to these terrific romances, the publishers of Bouquet are offering Zebra Romance readers Four Free Bouquet novels. They are yours for the asking with no obligation to buy a single book. Read them at your leisure. We are sure that after you've read these introductory books you'll want more! (If you do not wish to receive any further Bouquet novels, simply write "cancel" on the invoice and return to us within 10 days.)

SAVE 20% WITH HOME DELIVERY

Each month you'll receive four just-published Bouquet romances. We'll ship them to you as soon as they are printed (you may even get them before the bookstores). You'll have 10 days to preview these exciting novels for Free. If you decide to keep them, you'll be billed the special preferred home subscription price of just $3.20 per book; a total of just $12.80 — that's a savings of 20% off the publisher's price. If for any reason you are not satisfied simply return the novels for full credit, no questions asked. You'll never have to purchase a minimum number of books and you may cancel your subscription at any time.

If this response card is missing,
call us at 1-888-345-BOOK.

Be sure to visit our website at
www.kensingtonbooks.com

BOUQUET ROMANCES
Zebra Home Subscription Service, Inc.
P.O. Box 5214
Clifton NJ 07015-5214

"He'll have to work hard to keep his partnership. And right or wrong, I'll be watching him. One slip and I'll do everything in my power to have his partnership revoked."

The older man let out a sigh, one that seemed old and overdue in years. "Whatever else I may have done, I do love my daughter."

"I believe that, sir."

Roger nodded. "Back to you. You went after her last night. Is she okay?"

He obviously hadn't heard anything personal from Carly. The thought saddened Mike. And something in Roger's tone caught Mike's attention. Called to him, in fact. He'd bet the question hadn't been an easy one for the older man to ask.

"As well as can be expected," Mike said. "She's hurt. Feels betrayed." He shook his head.

"She's known too much of that."

"I wouldn't know, sir." Mike thought the older man deserved to know that Carly had kept family secrets buried.

Her father walked over to a group of framed photos on his desk. Picking up one in a small silver frame, he frowned. "Too damn much," he muttered.

Mike didn't know what else to say. Asking for an explanation felt like prying. Although he now realized the person who hadn't put Carly's needs first was her father.

"May I?" Mike reached out a hand.

Roger nodded. Enclosed in the small frame was a family photo of a younger Carly and her parents. Mike placed her age somewhere in her early teens.

Since he hadn't come from a typical family unit, family dynamics was unfamiliar terrain. But his years as a photographer had taught him to judge a picture by the body language of the subjects. Against the backdrop of a beach house and the ocean behind it, Roger stood, his hands at his sides. His wife leaned away from him, one hand around his waist, the other on her daughter's shoulder. Carly smiled for the camera, but her expressive eyes betrayed an inner unhappiness. This photo displayed the family Mike had seen at dinner the other night. Had things once been different?

"Nice," he said, handing the picture back to the older man.

Roger shook his head. "Some things in life you can't undo," he murmured, obviously caught in another time. He cleared his throat. "Well. You said you need a place to stay in the Hamptons."

Bingo. "Yes. I figured you're familiar with the area. Hotel, motel, whatever. Nothing fancy."

In silence, Roger studied him through narrowed eyes. Finally he spoke. "Okay." He walked over to his desk, pulled a sheet of paper from a Lucite tray before grabbing a pen and beginning to scribble. "Here's a list of decently priced hotels and motels near the beach."

Grateful, Mike reached across the desk and accepted the paper, fingering it between his thumb and forefinger. "I appreciate it."

"Good. There's something you can do for me in return."

"Name it."

"Don't hurt my daughter." Rounding the corner of the desk, Roger eased himself into his chair.

Uneasy, Mike shifted his stance. "We're friends and I think she could use one right about now." Mike didn't want the older man misinterpreting his long-term intentions toward Carly. He was only around to help her through a rough patch in her life, not to be a part of it later on. His gut twisted painfully.

"I think you're right. And she won't take comfort from me or her mother. I'm glad someone else cares enough to give it to her."

After he and Roger talked a little longer and the older man had given him additional beach information, Mike rose from his seat. He shook Roger's hand and walked into the hall.

He paused, debating the merits of speaking with his brother. His own anger hadn't yet subsided. Any discussion would only widen the rift between them. He'd deal with Pete before he left the States, but not now.

As he headed for the bank of elevators, the burden of Roger's words weighed heavily. The older man trusted him despite the actions of his brother. He trusted him with his only daughter.

But Mike couldn't live up to that trust. Not completely. Because though Mike wanted to be with Carly, to help her through the rough times, he knew he couldn't, wouldn't be there for the long haul.

SEVEN

Carly let herself in to the meticulously clean beach house. Nothing had changed since her parents first bought the place over ten years ago. The white cabinets and Wedgwood blue trim gave the illusion of a cheerful home. Growing up, knowing the farce her parents lived, Carly had found this room depressing.

Not so today. The house hadn't changed. Had she? Since the purpose of this vacation was self-discovery, she was about to find out. She'd taken care of ending her engagement, returning gifts and notifying friends and family before arriving, enabling her to come with an upbeat attitude. The airy kitchen, skylights and bright decor genuinely pleased her. The ringing of the phone brought her out of her musings.

Her mother's voice greeted her. "I just wanted to make sure you got there okay."

"I'm fine, Mom. I just walked in a little while ago."

The phone call shouldn't have surprised her, but it did. A while had passed since she'd turned to her mother for anything. Only now did Carly realize that her mother hadn't stopped trying. Carly had stopped accepting anything from Anne. Another thing she'd have to try and resolve on this solitary trip.

"I'm sure. I'm fine. Yes, he offered to pay for all the wedding expenses, but I broke things off and I want to cover my share." She and Peter had conversed via answering machine and somehow managed to undo all the arrangements.

As her mother spoke, Carly got yet another glimpse into Anne Wexler's way of dealing with life: grin and bear it. "Yes, I know people are talking at Dad's office. I assumed they would. Gossip's gossip. But I really don't care and you shouldn't either. Would you prefer I'd have gone through with it and been miserable for the rest of my life?" *Like you?*

"I'm sorry, Mom. Really. Can we just drop the whole thing? I appreciate you checking on me and I'll call you in a few days."

The doorbell rang. "Got to run. Talk to you soon. 'Bye."

Only after she'd hung up did Carly realize that her head had begun to pound. "Be right there," she called toward the front door."

She grabbed for two aspirin in her bag and a glass of water before answering the door. Just because her mother had opted to continue in her marriage didn't mean Carly wanted to deal with things the same way. Her entire life she'd walked a fine line, fearful of repeating both of her parents' mistakes— her father's search for more love and passion and her mother's blasé acceptance of all obstacles thrown in her way. Because her father's errors were so much more damaging, she'd unbelievably come within weeks of turning into a replica of her mother.

She was still petrified of becoming her father's daughter—the last interlude with Mike proved she was on the brink—but still, at some point she'd lost track of Carly and what *she* wanted out of life. And that was something else she'd have to look into. With her seniors' graduation behind her and the whole summer ahead of her, she could focus on herself.

The doorbell rang again. She headed into the hall. A door led to a small entryway and landing where a long staircase connected the upstairs and downstairs portions of the house. She swung the door open wide.

"Can I borrow a cup of sugar? I'm all out."

"Oh, no."

Mike grinned. "Yup. So how about that sugar, Sugar?"

"Couldn't you think of something more original?" she asked.

"Avon calling?" He advanced two steps.

Carly forced herself to remain in place. Any retreat would give him too much information about how much he affected her. Like he needed anything more than her overly enthusiastic response the last time they were together, she thought, her cheeks burning at the memory.

She shook her head. "Try again."

"How about this?" He took another two steps forward and met her lips with his in a scorching kiss. His mouth moved over hers with such skill and perfection, she was surprised her legs still supported her. All she could do was reach for his shoulders and hold on.

The kiss was all she'd dreamed about and everything she'd missed. It was also too short. He freed her with an agonized groan, but his golden eyes still glittered with desire.

She pushed her bangs out of her eyes and exhaled. A frustrated sigh escaped instead. Apparently her plans for solitude and self-learning were about to be drastically altered. "What are you doing here?" she asked. Forget about how he'd found her. She wasn't sure she wanted to know.

Mike shrugged and walked past her into the foyer. "Well?"

"I've got two answers to that. Work and you."

She narrowed her eyes. "Explain the work part."

Once in the kitchen, he turned a chair around and straddled it with his legs. Muscular legs, she noted before shifting her gaze to his face. She chose a chair opposite him.

"I'm doing a layout for a special on summer vacation spots," he said.

"Right. The man who loves travel and danger suddenly chooses the Hamptons. Hoping to expose the ever-present beach pickpockets?"

"Watch the sarcasm," he said with a grin.

"Then try the truth." She stood and walked to the refrigerator. She pulled out a can of soda and popped the top. "Cola?" She offered the can to him, hating the ingrained politeness that governed her actions. She wanted to toss him out before she could succumb again. The good girl in her didn't know how.

He shook his head.

She downed a large sip of soda herself.

"I'm here to work. And to see you," he said.

The bubbles burned her throat, causing her eyes to water.

"To make sure you have a friend if you need one, or a shoulder to cry on if it comes to that."

She coughed, wiping tears from her eyes. Damn his sense of chivalry, anyway. It made turning him away that much more difficult. "Well, I appreciate the sentiment, but there's no need." She slammed the soda can on the table for emphasis. The liquid popped up, splashing over the oak surface. She shot him a frustrated glance and grabbed for a towel to wipe up the mess.

Propping his elbows on the table, he sat in silence.

"What, nothing to say?"

"Why should I bother? Obviously you believe what you're saying, or you're trying to convince yourself." He shrugged. "I happen to know better."

"You're certainly full of yourself today."

He grinned. "It's part of my charm."

"I'm serious, Mike."

"So am I. I know you want to believe you don't need anyone, but it isn't true. No man . . . er, woman, is an island," he said with a grin.

She narrowed her eyes. "I see. So last time you ran into trouble, you turned to . . . who?"

"The psychologist in you," he muttered. "I respect that even if it makes my life more difficult. This isn't about me."

She shrugged. "Maybe it should be."

"Stalemate, sweetheart." Rising from the chair, he reversed positions and slid it under the table before starting across the kitchen.

"Where are you going?"

He turned. "I made this my first stop. I have to find a hotel."

"You mean you don't have a reservation?" she asked warily.

"Not yet. This assignment came up at the last minute."

"I'll just bet it did." She forced a grin. "Good luck." And he'd need it. A sunny weekend at the Hamptons. Just where did the man think he was going to find a hotel with a vacancy? Or a motel? Or even a rat-trap dive?

Carly swallowed a rising tide of anxiety. Maybe he'd get lucky. He'd better . . . or she'd find herself in deeper trouble than she'd ever imagined.

Hours later, Carly sat on the deck watching dusk fall. Dark clouds had rolled in over the horizon and thunder rumbled in the distance. She curled up her knees and wrapped her arms around her legs, letting the beauty and anger of nature rise around her. Despite the pending storm, she felt a measure of peace. By this time, Mike had to have found a room or he'd have returned. Though she knew he wouldn't make himself scarce for however long he planned to stay, at least she still had a measure of time to herself.

A cool breeze slid over her skin as the wind picked up in intensity. She shut her eyes and sighed with contentment. This trip away from home and her problems had been the perfect solution. Surely here she'd find the missing pieces in her life, the reasons she'd nearly married a man she knew she didn't love. The reasons she'd turned a blind eye to what she now viewed as his obvious betrayal. And the reasons she was so drawn to Mike, the antithesis of everything she'd ever believed she wanted in a man.

A lone drop of rain fell onto her arm. She wouldn't be able to sit here much longer. The storm would drive her in.

"I should have known stupidity ran in my family."

Carly opened her eyes. Mike stood before her, frustration evident in both his voice and the aggravation marring his expression.

"Not a hotel room to be found?" she asked in a sugary sweet voice.

"You knew."

She sighed. "Let's just say I figured."

"And I should have, too." He glanced at the sky. "Want to go in?"

A fine mist had begun to rain down, but Carly wasn't ready to head inside yet. Not when it meant she'd be enclosed in the small, cozy house with Mike.

She shook her head. "The drive back shouldn't be too bad. It's against traffic."

He raised an eyebrow. "No can do. I told you, I'm here to work."

"So you plan to stay where? In your car?" She fingered her bangs. They weren't soaking wet, but they were on their way.

"I'll make do." He studied her with those mesmerizing eyes until she felt he could read her mind and decipher her heart's desire. No, she didn't want him in her house. No, she didn't want him sleeping in the next room. How could she, when she'd proven she couldn't trust herself around him? Couldn't trust the wanton person she became?

"Make do how?" she asked.

Mike didn't answer. He wasn't sure where he was headed. But no way could he stay and torture her any more than she was torturing herself. He hadn't thought beyond renting a car and driving out to find her. Roger hadn't mentioned the booked hotel rooms. If Mike had been thinking, he would have realized it himself. But that was the problem. With Carly occupying his mind, other thoughts didn't exist.

He reached out and grabbed for her hand. "You take care of yourself, okay?" He squeezed once and let go, then made for the steps leading to the beach.

"Mike, wait."

He turned. "What?"

"Come back. Please. You deserve an explanation."

He walked toward her. His sneakers squeaked against the wooden planks. "You sure you don't want to take this inside?"

"Not yet. Just sit, okay?"

He joined her near a lounge chair and waited.

"I'm . . . afraid," she admitted softly.

Mike knelt down next to her and reached for her hand. Her skin felt cold and clammy and he realized she wasn't exaggerating. "You don't have a monopoly on fear, Carly."

He looked into her eyes. The emotions churning inside her caused her brown eyes to appear darker than usual. "How can you talk about fear? You drop into danger-filled situations for a photograph. What can possibly frighten you?"

"More than you can imagine." He'd witnessed children being orphaned like himself. He'd left in midassignment and violated every professional code by which he lived. Those realities were hard enough, but the fears he had been referring to had nothing to do with his past or his career. They had everything to do with Carly.

He traced the veins in her slender wrist with his thumb. She dropped her gaze. The wildly erratic beat of her pulse moved him in ways he failed to comprehend. And therein lay the source of his fear.

"I'm afraid you'll throw me out without us ever having had the chance to explore what's between us." Raising her hand, he kissed the throbbing pulse point in her wrist. "And I'm afraid you'll let me stay and I'll lose part of myself to you." Worse, he knew. Even if he stuck around now, he'd take off when the call came, leaving her stranded and alone. Hurt again. No matter how good his personal reasons, he'd create a mess he had no idea how to undo.

Startled eyes met his and he laughed. "Welcome to the club," she said.

"What frightens you?" he asked.

"The feelings between us."

He nodded in silent acknowledgment. Until recently he'd believed her fear was grounded in guilt over Peter. Without a ring binding her to another man that theory no longer applied. Which meant something more was at work, something more held her back from Mike.

"And," she continued, "the fact that no matter how torn you were, you betrayed me. You spent days on end with me, knowing Peter was cheating. Knowing I was sacrificing to make him happy when he wasn't doing nearly the same thing for me. I trusted him. I trusted you. And I'm not sure what that says about my judgment, all things considered."

"I tried every which way short of outright betraying my brother to let you know you were making a mistake. When you're ready, you'll know that's true. But since you're not, I'll be going."

She rolled her eyes. "Where? To sleep in your car, or were you planning to pitch a tent?"

"I've made do in worse and you know it."

"But not while I was consumed with guilt. There's a guest room," she muttered, just as the skies seemed to open wide and a torrential downpour began.

She ran for the house and Mike followed, ducking under the rolltop awning and through the sliding glass doors. Once inside, she grabbed for two towels in a hall closet and tossed one his way. They dried off in silence, Mike refusing to glance at her wet T-shirt or tousled hair, tossed by the wind.

He also refused to contemplate his motives. He could have gotten into his car and driven the long ride home. Instead he'd checked out the last motel and U-turned it back here. He glanced over.

"I'll take you up on that room," he said at last. He purposely didn't say for how long. Both knew he couldn't stay.

Carly nodded. So he was staying. It wouldn't be for long, she knew. She raised her gaze. "I'll make up the room."

"I'd appreciate that."

"I hope you realize you won," she said, unable to control her words. She couldn't help feeling as if she'd been set up with this trip of his.

"No, Carly. *We* win," he said quietly. "We share something special, and no matter how temporary my stay is, we're good for each other."

Unexpected tears filled her eyes as he spoke. Swallowing over the lump in her throat, she forced out equal amounts of honesty. "There's something you should know."

"I intend to know everything about you."

He retrieved her hand and she trembled under the heat of his strong touch.

"You're an experiment for me," she said.

He looked amused. "How's that?"

"I need to see if I can resist this pull between us."

"Why would you want to?" Lines creased his forehead in confusion. She resisted the urge to reassure him by smoothing them with her fingertips.

"Do you think there's such a thing as too much passion?" she asked instead, ignoring his question. "Feeling things too deeply?" She nibbled on her lower lip and watched him.

His face grew serious as he pondered her question. "Not unless the passion controls you," he said at last.

She clutched his hand tighter. "Explain that." She desperately needed to understand.

He was right. They were good for each other in many ways. But it was that sexual pull she couldn't understand. Her views in life were skewed by what she'd seen growing up. So much that she wondered if she'd ever get past it.

He lifted his free hand to twirl a stray lock of her hair between his thumb and forefinger. "In a healthy situation, passion may overwhelm you, but you know when and how to hold it in check." He treated her to a sexy grin. "And when to let go."

"And in an unhealthy situation?"

"It takes over areas of your life where it doesn't belong. Passion becomes a destructive force." He wiggled her fingers until she'd released her death grip on his hand.

She glanced down at the deep grooves her fingernails had etched in his skin. "Sorry," she murmured, running her hands over his bruised flesh.

"What's this all about?" he asked.

She shrugged, unable and unwilling to answer.

"Okay. But I've got a question of my own."

"What?" she asked.

"Did you get engaged to Peter because there was no passion or in spite of it?"

Without looking at him, she answered, "I think you know."

"Carly." He lifted her chin. His hazel eyes glittered with gold flecks and banked desire. When he spoke, he never took his gaze from hers. "Passion and love are healthy human emotions." He ran the pad of his thumb over her lower lip.

The pull reached down to her inner core, the words *passion* and *love* colliding in her brain.

"Whoever taught you differently?" he asked.

Two tears ran down her cheeks. "When you're ready to talk about it, I hope you'll come to me." Leaning toward her, he kissed the teardrops away.

Mike walked the stretch of private beach behind the Cape house. Barefoot, the sand felt cool beneath his feet. With the sun barely up over the horizon, the ground hadn't yet warmed and was still brisk from the evening chill.

He asked himself again what he was doing here. The question had haunted him for the past three days. Three days in which Carly had treated him like a guest she either ran into or didn't. He'd allowed her the privacy, ignoring the closeness of the small house even as he'd listened to her toss and turn in the next room at night. During the day he used the time to roam the public beaches and capture tourist shots for the newspaper. At night he paced the floors, wondering how much longer the reprieve would last.

He owed his colleagues more than a wave good-bye and a simple "see you later," and his boss wouldn't put up with much more of Mike's silent routine. Beyond calling with a phone number, Mike had deliberately stayed out of touch. Because once he had to return abroad, he would hurt Carly as badly if not worse than his brother had. Not that she'd asked a damn thing from him. She didn't have to. One glance at those bottomless eyes accomplished the same thing. He'd do anything for her.

Except leave her alone. If he left without testing those powerful feelings, he'd lose something precious. A less selfish man would walk away before she got hurt.

"Hi."

Startled, he turned. "I didn't hear you." But he was glad she'd sought him out on her own.

"Not too tough to sneak up on someone on the beach." She held her sandals over one shoulder. "Bare feet." She wiggled her toes for emphasis. Her pink nails stood out in sharp contrast to the beige sand.

"Someone's in a good mood this morning," he noted and wondered why. "Have you changed your mind about letting me hang around?"

She shook her head. "Hit the kitchen around seven. I'll treat you to a real feast."

She'd managed to shock him. "What did you have in mind?"

"It's a surprise." With that, she whirled and ran toward the house.

Mike took off after her. Catching up with her was easy, wrapping his arms around her waist and bringing her down on top of him easier still. To his neverending surprise, she didn't resist or try to pull away. She lay in the *V* of his legs, breathing hard from her run and laughing at the same time. Her face was flushed pink and her carefree smile told him that she'd left her problems behind, at least for now.

Lying beneath her sent a jolt of awareness through his system. Her soft laughter caused her body to move against him and he couldn't hide his instant reaction. He wanted her.

He knew the exact moment she realized their intimate position and his state of arousal. The joyful laughter ended and her expression clouded. She braced her arms and rolled off to the side.

As difficult as it was, he let her go. There was much he still didn't understand, but he recognized her fear. For whatever reason, the intense attraction between them caused her to pull back. He sensed the only way to reassure her was to prove they could control the passion. Easier said than done, he thought. He drew deep breaths, trying to concentrate on the waves crashing against the shore instead of Carly's ragged breathing. Proof she wanted him, too.

In silence they lay on their backs and stared at the wide expanse of sky. White puffy clouds dotted an otherwise clear blue backdrop.

"Beautiful," she murmured.

He glanced over at her. "Sure is."

"Mike?"

"Hmm?"

"What's it like dropping into the world's hot spots?"

He stiffened. Her choice of topic surprised him, but he couldn't bring himself to be anything but honest with her. "Exciting."

"Dangerous?" Carly asked. Because the thought of Mike in the center of some war-torn country or worse sent goose bumps chasing along her skin.

"Sometimes."

She wondered how she'd feel, knowing he was putting himself in danger, not knowing if he'd make it back home alive and in one piece. She shivered from the sudden chill. He drew her close, probably mistaking the impact of her turbulent emotions for a reaction to the cool ocean breeze.

Her head lay in the crook of his shoulder and she savored the closeness they'd found on an emotional level. "Why do it?" she asked.

"It's not for the glory or the thrill of cheating death, though there are some guys who feel that way." His warm breath fanned her hair. "I'm not sure exactly, but I like knowing I've made a difference. That maybe one picture prevented someone somewhere from starving to death or being killed."

Aid those in need. Did he realize how similar his goals were to her own? "Sort of like the reason for my column."

"How so?"

She didn't realize she'd spoken aloud. "So many

kids have no one to talk to. I hope at least one person is able to make a tough choice because someone cared enough to listen."

During the worst period of her life, no one had been there for her. No one had listened. Her mother had refused to discuss the tragedy or the impact on their lives, leaving a teenager to cope alone. She couldn't turn to her obviously grieving father, and besides, her anger at him wouldn't allow her to. She hoped some teenager used her column to vent feelings he didn't feel free to express at home.

"We're some pair." He chuckled aloud. "We sound like avenging angels."

"I'm no angel. I'm just making sure no kid thinks he has to go it alone."

"Like you did?"

Carly pushed herself to a sitting position and stared. She wanted to lash out, to shout at him. *Stop finishing my sentences. Stop reading my mind.* He was getting too close and it frightened her. "How . . ."

"Educated guess."

Obviously she was easy to read. Mike brushed the grains of sand from her back. After this roll in the sand, she'd need another shower. Unwilling to drop the subject at least until she learned what she wanted from him, Carly glanced over. "So what are your reasons for playing the Good Samaritan role?" Some deep, dark secret like her own? she wondered.

"Nothing I haven't already told you. When you grow up without, you tend to overcompensate. This latest escapade with Pete drove that point home."

At the mention of her ex-fiancé's name, she waited for the pain of betrayal to surface. It never came. Relief, pure and sweet, flooded her. "How so?" she asked Mike.

"He thinks money and power will make up for all he missed. He doesn't realize that material wealth won't replace love."

Why had he chosen that particular word? She whipped her head around expecting to meet his potent gaze. Instead, Mike was staring out at the ocean, one hand rubbing his right shoulder hard.

She studied him. His muscled physique created waves of longing, but what did she feel for this man that was so different than anything she'd ever experienced? Was it to be savored as something special or feared as an extension of her father's legacy? It was about time she found out.

Her future was at stake.

"So Peter's looking for money and power to make him happy." Which cemented what she'd already known—the reasons why he'd gotten and remained engaged to her. "But what are you looking for?" she asked Mike. "All the travel, the danger—are you running?" she asked softly.

He didn't respond.

She placed a hand on his arm. "I think you are." Which made them very much the same, Carly thought sadly. "The question is, when will you stop?" When would she?

He remained silent. The answer was locked inside him, she thought. And like her, he'd have to face his private demons. Sooner or later.

* * *

Mike stood in the entryway to Carly's kitchen, eavesdropping on his chef for the evening. She stood, hands on her hips, staring into an oversized lobster pot.

"Call me a coward, but I can't do it." She brushed her bangs off her forehead with her fingers.

He grinned as she glanced from the wriggling lobster on the counter to the boiling pot on the stove. "Can't do what?" he asked.

"Drop live lobsters in there. I thought I could, but I can't."

Mike glanced at the counter where two lobsters moved languidly in plastic bags. "Dinner?"

"Only if we boil them alive."

He chuckled. "Why don't you go outside for a while? I can handle things in here."

She glanced into the steaming pot. "They scream."

"What?"

"When I was younger I went to a friend's house for dinner. Her older brother took a lot of pleasure in informing us that if you listen carefully you can hear their high-pitched screams before they die." She shuddered.

"You don't believe that."

"Not anymore, but I did. I was ten. I had nightmares for weeks."

"Boys can be cruel."

"Yeah. So can men," she said.

"I'll give you that." He leaned over and kissed

her soft cheek, then gave her a playful swat on the behind. "I'll handle this."

"I owe you one."

He met her gaze. "And I fully intend to collect."

She turned for one last look into the lobster pot. Mike snuck up behind her, wrapping his arms around her waist and burying his face in the expanse of skin at her neck. Her vanillalike scent was permanently etched in his dreams. Reality was much sweeter.

She stiffened at his initial touch but relaxed against his insistent nuzzling at her ear. His hands splayed across her stomach. Every ounce of willpower he possessed went into keeping them below the round swell of her breasts. He pressed his lower body into her back and was greeted by her soft moan of pleasure in response.

He wanted to turn her around and bury himself inside her. He wanted to see her face when he entered her heat for the first time. He wanted all those things and more. But he didn't deserve them. Not when he couldn't give her all she so obviously needed.

He wanted to step back but needed her warmth and closeness for a minute more. Then he'd let her go. A yellow gauze dress ended above her knees and her bare back had turned a deep bronze courtesy of the sun. Her skin felt warm and welcoming to his touch.

He steeled himself to back off, but she turned. Any progress he'd made dissolved like a sand castle under a crushing wave. Eyes glazed and face flushed with desire, she looked disoriented and unsteady. He reached out a hand to support her and immediately noticed that her nipples were drawn tight beneath the flimsy fabric.

Without conscious thought he brushed one distended peak with his thumb. She swayed toward him, and damned if her knees didn't almost buckle. Control deserted him, and all good intentions along with it. Any thoughts he'd had of restraint vanished. He knelt down and replaced his hand with his mouth, suckling her through the material of her dress. She braced herself by grasping the handle of the stove.

He bit down lightly. She murmured his name at the same time her legs gave out completely. Mike reached for her, supporting her until she was able to stand on her own.

"You're a hazard in the kitchen," she said in a husky voice.

"Look who's talking. Dress like that and expect results." He laughed and she joined him. For the first time she didn't pull back or appear to mentally berate herself for her desire. Progress? A start? Or just an aberration? he wondered.

She pointed to the large metal pot. "You have lobsters to cook," she said in an unsteady voice.

"Then get going . . . before I get distracted again."

Carly didn't miss the desire in his gaze and opted to bolt for the deck. She kept herself busy setting the table, opening a bottle of wine and contemplating the wisdom of inviting Mike for dinner. She'd convinced herself she could get to know him without any complications. He'd been in the kitchen all of thirty seconds and common sense had deserted her.

The last time in her apartment, she'd been devastated by the fact that when she should have been seeking comfort, she'd only felt desire. Now while seeking to prove to herself that she could exert self-control, it all but deserted her.

What would happen if she gave in? a little voice in her head asked. Gave herself over to Mike, to passion, to all the emotions she'd taught herself to fear? The answer came easily and without thought. She'd fall in love . . . if she hadn't already. And then what?

The man had a penchant for travel and danger. He wasn't the type to settle down, and even if she could get past the fear of their explosive chemistry, she wanted someone who would put her first. How could she love a man who might never make it home? How could she have the safe family she wanted, or subject children to his kind of unstable life? No, she thought sadly, their future just didn't exist.

She deliberately ignored the shaft of pain the thought caused, attributing it to hunger. "How long does it take to boil the damn lobsters anyway?" she muttered aloud.

Carly picked up the nutcracker and attempted to tackle a large lobster claw. The shell cracked. Mike's startled laugh surprised her, and she looked up to find him wiping water from his face with a paper napkin.

"You squirted me." He grinned.

"Sorry." She licked freshly drawn butter off her fingers and stared at the large claw on her plate. "I forgot lobster's like spaghetti. It's a no-no on the first date."

"So is corn on the cob." With a grin, he took a large bite. "So it's a good thing this isn't a first date." He waved the corn in the air as he spoke. "We're way beyond first impressions, remember?"

She leaned back in her chair and swirled the wine in her goblet. "What were your first impressions, anyway?"

He rested on one elbow and turned to study her. "I thought you were sexy as hell and I wanted you," he said in a low, steady voice.

"Oh." She felt her lips move, heard her response, but her brain had ceased to function. Her body, on the other hand, leapt to life. Every nerve ending tingled in delicious anticipation of his touch. Even her breasts felt unnaturally heavy. She waited for him to reach for her.

Instead he asked, "What were your first impressions?" The gold flecks in his eyes danced with delight, in obvious anticipation of her response.

"I thought the police ought to do a better job of patrolling the city streets," she said, treating him to one of her sweetest smiles. After all, his rugged charm *had* nearly sent her running in the opposite direction.

Before she could gloat over her comeback, his

arm reached out and his hand grasped her wrist, pulling her close. The warmth of his touch seared her skin. "Didn't anyone ever teach you what happens to women with smart mouths?" His face was inches from hers.

"No. Why don't you show me?" The wine had dulled her more rational self and replaced it with a courage she didn't ordinarily possess. Nothing else explained such bold, wanton behavior, especially in light of her self-revelations earlier. But those revelations had served another purpose besides shedding light on the future. They'd made her realize she couldn't give up the present. It was all they had.

Her eyelids fluttered closed and he slanted his mouth across hers. He kissed her softly, gently. She had expected the hot intensity of their past encounters. His tenderness caught her off guard.

Nothing could have surprised her more than the reverent way he caressed her mouth. He wet her lips with his tongue, then rubbed his own against hers, soaking up the moisture. He created a damp path down the side of her neck and up to her ear, where he paused and nibbled the lobe with his teeth. As if from a distance, she heard her own satisfied moan.

The cool ocean air hit wet areas of skin and she shivered. His thumb traveled the same path as his lips, drying the moisture and warming her at the same time. The gentleness of the gesture shocked her, causing a lump to form deep in her throat.

She drew a deep breath and waited for the sensual onslaught to continue. His fingers merely traced the outline of her mouth. She opened her eyes to find herself staring into his. Her body felt alive with need. She ached for him, yet a part of her knew she should call a halt to this now. It wasn't too late.

Nervously she ran her tongue over her lips, coming into contact with the rough pad of his thumb. His skin tasted salty and warm, making her wonder what other tastes and textures awaited her. She wanted Mike with a depth of feeling that surpassed mere passion. As she contemplated those rampant emotions, she feared she had been wrong. Perhaps it was too late. For a lot of things.

Slowly, he removed his hand from her soft lips. "When you said feast, you weren't kidding." He pointed to the table. With difficulty, Mike changed the topic to more mundane issues. Like food.

Her forehead creased in confusion and she fingered her bangs in the nervous gesture he'd come to anticipate and enjoy at the same time. Mike stilled her hand with his and groaned. He'd had no choice but to stop. Every time he kissed her, her honest, open response startled him. When they made love—and he didn't kid himself that it might not happen—he wanted her acceptance to be made knowingly. Not in the throes of passion. After his glimpse into her innermost fears, he owed her at least that.

"You liked the dinner?" she finally asked, regaining her composure.

"Loved it. I can't remember the last time someone cooked for me."

"As it turned out, you did the cooking."

"Yeah, but only because their screams of pain didn't bother me."

He winked and she tossed a paper napkin at him. "Chicken," he teased.

"Maybe." She shrugged and began clearing the table. With his help, Carly collected the plates and extra food and carried everything into the kitchen. She looked at the pile of dishes in the sink and sighed. "The perils of eating in."

"Now that everything's inside, can cleanup wait?" he asked.

"I guess so. Why?"

"You up for a walk on the beach?" Mike extended one hand, silently asking her to meet him halfway. They might take that stroll on the beach, but he wanted much more. He had little doubt she knew exactly how much.

Her brown eyes narrowed. He hoped she was searching her heart.

"As long as I don't end up rolling in sand again." Her full lips turned upward in a provocative grin. "It took me forever to get the sand out of my shorts."

"Okay. I promise you won't roll around in the sand." He met her gentle gaze. "But I can't promise you won't be rolling around somewhere . . . more comfortable."

He scanned her face for some positive sign. She smiled and placed her hand in his.

"I always had doubts about that beach scene in *From Here to Eternity.*" She gave an exaggerated shudder. "All that sand and water. Hard to imagine how they maneuvered." She wrapped her fingers around his. "I'll bet there are plenty of rooms in this house that can accommodate us."

"Are you sure?" he asked.

She nodded. "I'm sure." From the hungry look in her eyes, he knew the walk on the beach would have to wait.

EIGHT

With her nerves stretched to the breaking point, Carly followed him into the bedroom in the back of the house. She gazed at the king-sized water bed in awe and trepidation. "This is incredible."

"Next best thing to the beach." Mike released her hand long enough to shut the bedside lamp.

With the shades open and the sun still in the process of setting, the room was cast into a dusky glow. Her gaze took in the unfamiliar space. Suddenly she was all too aware of the large bed.

"Did I give you too much time to think?" he asked, approaching her from behind. His hands brushed her hair off her shoulders as he placed a soft kiss on her neck.

She trembled and closed her eyes, heightening the pleasurable sensation. "Maybe."

The sound of his retreating footsteps was followed by the crush of leather as he sunk into the beanbag chair in the corner. Silence surrounded them, but she wasn't inclined to break it, not yet. She needed these precious minutes and he seemed to understand. She pushed back the hair from her face.

If she hadn't slept with her fiancé, why would she contemplate making love with Mike? She thought of his laugh, his smile, and the way he knew how to listen, then retreat without saying too much. He seemed to respect her feelings, even if he didn't comprehend the reasons behind them.

In the ensuing silence, she forced her mind to function, and the conclusions she reached were staggering. If she wasn't in love with him, she was well on her way. She knew the damage emotional involvement could cause, had avoided it this long. Especially with a man like him. So what now?

She swallowed hard and turned. In the shadows, she made out his masculine form reclining on the floor. A seagull screeched in the distance. Mike reached one hand toward her and waited.

She padded across the hardwood floor and stopped in front of him.

"I want you to know what you're getting into," he said.

Somewhere during the past few minutes her decision had been made. "I do," she whispered. They'd been moving toward this moment from the beginning. The outcome was as inevitable as the changing tide. She only hoped they didn't destroy each other in the process.

"I can't make any prom . . ."

She covered his lips with one finger. "I know."

Looking into her dark eyes, Mike believed her. The knowledge should have lifted an otherwise heavy burden. It didn't. What did he want from her?

he wondered. Better yet, what could she expect from him? He hoped it wasn't more than he could give.

"Carly?"

She wet her lips. "Have you ever made love on a water bed before?" she asked in a husky voice.

Her velvety words wrapped themselves around him. She had apparently made peace with herself, leaving her reservations along with her inhibitions behind.

He shook his head in response.

"A first for both of us, then." She smiled and placed her hand in his. "I'm glad." After shifting her skirt, she knelt beside him and pulled him up from his seat on the floor.

He allowed himself to be led, only until he'd reached a standing position. Then he backed her toward the large bed that beckoned to them. When her calves reached the platform, he stopped and encircled her waist with his hands.

She smiled and lifted his shirt, her soft hands linking behind his back. He dipped his head toward her, but she caught him off guard. In one smooth motion she wrapped one leg around his and pulled him toward her so they tumbled backward onto the bed together. The mattress rocked beneath them in undulating waves. Carly landed beneath him, laughing with delight.

The tinkling sound and the light in her eyes removed whatever reservations had remained in his mind. "Think you're so clever?" he asked, brushing his lips over hers.

"Nope. I *know* I am." She smiled and laughed some more.

He kissed her again, letting her unique scent fill the empty spaces inside him. To keep from crushing her, he rolled to his side and propped himself up on one elbow. Sealing his mouth over hers, he entwined his tongue and feasted until he could barely breath.

They'd never done much more than this, yet each kiss contained more power than the last. He marveled at her ability to reach inside him with nothing more than a touch. What would happen when they came together? The conflagration would probably consume them both.

He wondered if that was the source of her fear, but before he could analyze further, her hand came between them and caressed his arousal through the rough denim of his jeans. His body jerked involuntarily at her touch and the bed swirled beneath them.

"When did you get so bold?" he asked.

"Only with you." Her hand cupped him tighter.

"Not yet." He removed her hand and grasped her fingers with his own. "Not if you want this to last."

"I want," she murmured. From beneath heavy lids, her eyes fastened on his face. He removed a strand of blond hair from her cheek and kissed her lips.

"So do I." Reaching behind her neck, he opened the two buttons that held the top of her dress in place. He watched, mesmerized, as he drew the top down, inch by tantalizing inch. Since he'd been given a brief sample before dinner, he knew what lay beneath the light material.

The dress fell to her waist and he sucked in a deep breath. Carly, however, closed her eyes. A rosy color tinged her cheeks. He raised one hand to cup her face. "Hell of a time to get shy, sweetheart."

Personally she couldn't think of a better one. "Takes an awful long time for the sun to go down, doesn't it?" she asked, while silently praying for darkness. She raised her arms to cover herself, but he stopped her by grabbing hold of her wrists and pulling them down gently.

"Don't. I've been waiting too long." His voice sounded rough to her ears.

She allowed him to draw her arms to her sides, but kept her eyes tightly shut. Whatever she had anticipated, it wasn't this slow perusal. She no longer felt capable of lighthearted banter, not when she felt so vulnerable and exposed.

"Beautiful," he murmured, just before she felt wet heat on one breast. In shock, she opened her eyes to see him leaning over her, lavishing undivided attention on her hardened nipple. She gasped at the utter intimacy of the act. He suckled her, nipping and soothing with alternate breaths. Heat, which had begun in her chest, traveled with lightning speed to the juncture of her thighs.

Were these wonderful sensations the same ones she had feared hours earlier? Right now, she couldn't imagine why. She ran her fingers through his thick hair, enjoying the rasp of his day-old beard against the sensitive skin on her chest.

He lifted his head long enough to turn to the other breast, giving it equal attention. She felt only a moment of cool air on the spot his mouth had abandoned, before his hand began equally skillful maneuvers. Muscles in her stomach clenched as he rolled one nipple between his thumb and forefinger, while working the other with his mouth.

Unable to think, let alone feel embarrassment, she lay her head back on the pillow and gave herself up to sensation. She was only dimly aware when he lifted her up to release the back zipper of her dress, of when she raised her hips to help him remove the barrier between them. The bed shifted and swirled beneath them, causing her to giggle at more than one inopportune moment.

At some point, and she couldn't remember when, he'd shed his shirt, because her hands now buried themselves in the hair on his chest. He groaned as she worked her way outward. She smiled and licked each nipple in turn.

"Carly." He gasped her name, warning in his voice.

She blew cool air on his wet skin in response. With another groan, he grabbed her wrists and pinned her backward. The bed rocked beneath them. "You don't play fair."

She bat her eyelashes at him. "Was I supposed to?"

"Not if you don't mind my returning the favor." He paused for a hot, wet kiss, then made brief work of removing her lace panties. Together they got rid of his jeans and briefs. The bed wasn't nearly as cooperative, however, and he stood to complete the task.

Laughing, Carly grasped the purple cotton from his hands and dangled the briefs from her fingers. "I'd never figured you for plain white, but this?"

"I told you purple was my favorite." He bounced down next to her. "But I am glad you gave it some thought," he said with a grin.

She tossed them aside. "More than a little." Her hand circled his pulsing length. His sheer size stunned her and she gasped aloud.

"I would never hurt you."

She lowered her gaze. "I know. It's just that I've never . . ."

"I know." He silenced her and eased her embarrassment with a kiss before reaching for the night-table drawer. "Help me," he said, handing her the foil packet.

With shaking hands, she complied. Never had she thought of protection as an erotic act. In the future, she'd never think of it as anything else.

Her fears had long since evaporated under his gentleness. He'd touched a place deep inside her. More than her body was involved in the act that was to come. Much more.

He straddled her with muscular legs. His erection nudged at her, barely easing the throbbing ache of desire. She lifted her hips and he eased into her slowly at first and then harder, pushing inside with one hard thrust. She gasped at the initial shock of pain.

"I'm sorry."

She shook her head. He had nothing to be sorry for. He waited, poised above her. She felt him deep inside her. Mike filled her body but also her heart. She knew it the same way she knew nothing in her life would ever be the same. He paused to kiss her, working his tongue in her mouth as if searching for something greater than both of them.

He began to move inside her, and soon his gentle movements weren't enough. She wanted him deeper, wanted more from him than she'd ever dreamed possible.

The bed rocked in time with their movements, making it difficult for Mike to take things slowly. Enclosed in Carly's warmth, he fought against feelings so intense he thought they might drown him. She murmured his name and wrapped her long legs around his waist, forcing him as hard and as deep as he could reach.

He felt her contract around him, heard her cry out, and any control he had maintained shattered along with her. Surging into her, he drove higher. Mike let go, losing himself inside her the way he had always known—and feared—he would.

Carly lay in Mike's arms but sleep eluded her. She listened to his deep breathing and cuddled closer to his warmth. She tried not to think about anything but the miracle of them being together, but reality intruded. Eventually she would have to deal with their parting. She pressed a kiss against the back of his warm hand and tried to sleep.

She came awake with a start. Mike's body had stiffened and his arms tightened around her until breathing became next to impossible. His own breaths came in short gulps and he groaned. She felt the sheen of perspiration covering his body and realized he was in the throes of a violent nightmare. Should she wake him, or let the dream run its course?

"Mike?" She tried to turn, but his arms constricted her movement. "Mike?" she said, louder this time.

Abruptly he released her. With difficulty, she drew deep breaths and rolled toward him. He looked in her direction and turned away.

Her heart thudded painfully in her chest as she realized that he intended to shut her out. "I can't help if you won't talk to me," she said, drawing the sheet up over her bare chest. "Trust me." She placed a hand on his still clammy skin.

"Seems to me I told you the same thing a little while ago. You didn't open up." With his back to her, his words sounded all the more harsh and accusing.

"My mistake," she admitted.

He seemed not to hear. "You don't trust me, why shouldn't I return the favor?"

His words hit her like a blast of cold air, but she forced herself to remain rational, to let the professional part of her look in. She recognized his pain and as a trained psychologist realized he was lashing out at the only available person. It didn't make his accusations hurt less, but she cared enough to take the brunt of his anger and direct it toward helping him heal.

"You're wrong, Mike. If I didn't trust you, we wouldn't be here now."

He ran shaking fingers through his already disheveled hair. "It's not something you want to know." He swung his legs over the bed and stood, oblivious to his state of undress.

She allowed herself a moment to drink in the sight of his naked body before grounding her thoughts. "If it affects you, I need to know. But I'm not what's important now. You are, and you need to talk. Whatever it is, I can handle it."

He stood at the window, gazing into the darkness. "My last assignment," he said at last. "Rather, my last uncompleted assignment."

"I don't understand."

"I'd hitched a ride back from the countryside with a guy in a Jeep. For a while we were the only ones on the road, but as we neared civilization, a bus pulled in front of us." His hands gripped the windowsill. "Must have made for a bigger target than a small Jeep, because mortar fire hit the back tires and sent the damn thing careening down the side of a ravine."

He paused, and Carly waited for him to continue. "I jumped out of my seat before the guy could stop. By the time I reached the bus, I heard the screams and smelled gas." His hand went to his shoulder and he worked the muscles with his fingers. Even from her distance on the bed, she could see how brutally he clutched at his arm.

She gripped the bedsheet, watching as he wrestled with the demons that plagued him.

"We knew we didn't have much time, but we had to get as many out as we could before the tank exploded. We pried open the bus door. Most of the people up front had taken a direct hit. They didn't make it." His voice shook, but he continued. "Most were women. In the end, we managed to pull a bunch of young kids from the bus and get them up the hill. When the explosion hit, I had one kid hanging from my neck screaming for his mother."

She swallowed, but the lump in her throat remained. And no matter how much she wanted to comfort Mike, the right words wouldn't come.

"I spent the next few weeks trying to track down this kid's father. Turns out he'd already been killed. The crash orphaned most of those kids."

Just like Mike. Oh, God. In a daze, she rose and walked up behind him, placing a hand on the shoulder he'd been abusing. "And this?" she asked softly. She stilled his hand beneath hers.

"Ripped open some muscle getting to the back of the bus."

She dropped a kiss on his shoulder, her lips coming in contact with new scar tissue. Why hadn't she noticed it earlier? "It must have been awful."

"Want to know the worst part? My damned boss was furious that I hadn't taken pictures. These kids just had their worlds ripped apart and he wanted exclusive photos." He shook his head in disgust. "Abandoned children and he wanted headlines."

"Mike . . ."

"But you know what? He was right. It was my job and I didn't do it. I couldn't. Any more than I could go back afterward." He dropped his head lower, leaning against the window. "All those kids . . ."

No wonder he was back in the States covering fluff topics like summer hot spots.

"Mike." She turned him toward her. In his tortured face she saw how difficult the telling had been. Even worse was that he had lived alone with the pain all these months.

"Orphaned isn't the same as abandoned," she whispered. "There's a difference. Not much, I'll admit, but there is a difference."

"Tell that to those kids whose parents are gone." He paused. "Forever."

Her heart broke for the little boy he had been. "Those parents didn't walk out on their kids. They were taken by a cruel twist of fate. That may not seem to make a difference now, but in the long run, the knowledge will ease the pain."

As she said the words, she recognized the irony. In the long run, for Mike, the distinction had meant little. "How long have you had these dreams?" she asked.

He shrugged. "Since the accident."

"I see." A period of hell, of equating his own situation with those of the children, of beating himself up for not getting hit instead, for not doing his job. What would it take to vanquish his demons?

The answer, she knew, lay in their parting. He had to return to the profession he loved and prove to himself that he could face his past and his present.

She didn't fit into the equation. Knowing Mike's strength of character, the separation would come much sooner than she had anticipated. He'd be doing her a favor, but right now it didn't feel like one.

"Running isn't the answer. You have to fight this." Even as she said the words, she knew she was pushing him away. Tears threatened and she closed her eyes against them.

"I know. I just don't know if I'm ready."

"You'll know when the time's right."

He nodded.

His hands cupped her face and he brought their lips together. He kissed her deeply, drawing from her both physically and emotionally until she was drained. She leaned into him, brushing her breasts against the hard planes of his chest.

"Carly." He groaned her name, then lifted her into his arms and carried her back to the bed. "Make me forget," he said as he entered her.

This time they came together in an explosive combination of want and need. He climaxed first and she followed. Their bodies entwined, Mike still inside her, she rested her head against his cheek.

When he whispered, "Don't leave me," she refused to believe the words, choosing instead to reassure him with a kiss.

The summer sun shining through the window woke Mike first. In the harsh light of day, last night's dreams were but distant shadows. Carly's long legs were entangled around his, reminding him that there was beauty in this harsh world.

She had been there for him, offering herself when he needed her. He had taken much more than he had been able to give. No one in his life had ever given of themselves, given at their own expense for his benefit. His good mood this morning reflected the genuine concern he'd received during the night.

He stretched his arms over his head, letting his hand come to rest on her bare breast. It had been a long time since he'd felt so at peace. Perhaps he never had. And though reality tried to intrude, he forced it aside. He'd had little peace in his life. He wanted to enjoy it while he could.

Her brown eyes opened and she smiled.

"Morning." He placed a light kiss on her lips.

"Already?" She yawned. "Seems like we just went to sleep."

"I think we did, but there's always a way to make up for lack of sleep."

"How?"

Reaching for her, he said, "Spending the rest of the day in bed."

He wanted her again . . . as much as he wanted to avoid rehashing last night's nightmare. Whether she understood his dual need or not, he couldn't say. But she didn't argue. Instead she leaned over and kissed his lips, then playfully smacked at his wandering hand.

"Bed sounds good, but I can't put off my work any longer," she said.

"How much do you need to do today?"

"Well, I need to begin some sort of organizing for the book. And I need to sort through the letters that my editor forwarded for one or two new summer columns. I think one month of reruns is enough, don't you?"

"Not really. I could rerun last night with you over and over and never get bored." He brushed his fingers over her breast in a lazy circular motion. "What about you?"

Was it his imagination or did she stiffen at his touch. "I think we shouldn't go overboard." She grinned, but the smile seemed forced. "The work won't disappear, so I'm kicking you out."

Her backing off didn't surprise him and he decided to tread carefully. "Can't kick me out when I have nowhere to go," he reminded her, deliberately playing on her good nature.

"True. But I can bribe you to disappear for a while."

Her attempt at easy banter relaxed him somewhat, but he couldn't ignore the fact that she obviously needed to escape. And given her admitted fears, that need probably had more to do with their newly discovered intimacy and passion than with her need to work. Since making love had cemented an already strong bond, one *he'd* be forced to break, he decided to let her have her way.

"I'm a man easily bribed. What did you have in mind?"

"I'll make you breakfast and then you disappear for a few hours. Get lost. Go take pictures somewhere."

"Pancakes?" he asked. "You know you can't get pancakes in the places I've been hanging out lately."

"I think I can handle that," she said wryly.

"Bacon?"

"Okay."

"Fresh-squeezed orange juice?"

She grinned and poked him in the chest. "Now you're pushing your luck."

"Deal, then." With the subject off sex and onto food, Carly seemed completely at ease. Or did she just have him fooled? Before he left, the one thing he wanted more than anything was to help her get on with her life and put her painful past behind her.

"I'll get things started. Meet me in the kitchen in a few." She tossed off the covers and started to rise.

He reached for her, then changed his mind and let her go. Mike knew avoidance when he saw it. Hell, he was an expert on that subject. She'd helped draw him out last night. He owed her the same. Just because Carly had escaped his bed this morning didn't mean he'd let her elude her demons as well.

Carly removed the necessary breakfast ingredients from the refrigerator. She didn't want to analyze how much she'd enjoyed waking up with Mike beside her, or how relaxing she found making breakfast and knowing he'd be there to share it. Neither one could last.

More than once she stopped to pull down the blue oxford she had pilfered from Mike's closet. He had wrestled her for it, and of course he had won. Which was why she now wore nothing beneath the denim shirt. She yanked at the hem, but it still only reached as far as midthigh.

Once she began the pancakes, she was grateful for the activity that took her mind off last night. Not only making love but the revelations. Everything about the dark night had inadvertently served to strengthen the emotional bond between them.

She cared for him deeply. When he left her, she would be hurt in a way she hadn't believed possible. As much as she tried to convince herself that his departure was necessary for them both, the more time they spent together, the harder it was to believe.

Mike entered the kitchen to the delicious aroma of home cooking. The places he normally frequented lacked such a treat. Not only did the kitchen smell good but it felt good, too. Too good, too comfortable. "I guess you can cook."

"You were worried? I should be insulted. Sit." she waved a spatula in his direction.

"Yes, ma'am." He grinned.

"Mike?"

"What?"

She glanced in his direction, a serious glint in her eyes. "You told me why you're in the Hamptons, but how'd you end up here? At the house?"

"On a hunch, I went to see your father at the office. I asked him for motel names."

"I see."

"He showed me a picture of your family. Taken here, I think."

She turned her head. Her expression was unreadable.

Mike pushed on. "He keeps it on his desk." The sound of oil in the frying pan drew their attention to the stove, and Carly turned to work on breakfast.

"Nice of him," she said. "I wonder if it reminds him of happier times." Sarcasm was evident in her voice. So was the hurt. Hurt he'd also seen in her father's eyes.

He recalled the photo and the pained look in Carly's young eyes. Happier times? He doubted it. He wanted to broach the subject without her declaring it off-limits. And maybe help her, as she'd helped him, to at least discuss the source of her fear. "He asked about you."

"What did you tell him?" She flipped three pancakes over and transferred them to a dish beside the stove.

"Nothing. But he was concerned."

Her snort of laughter seemed forced. "He'll get over it. He's still got his top associate, even if Peter won't be his son-in-law."

"Unfair, Carly. He told me he wanted to dump Peter on his partner-climbing ass. *You* talked him out of it. He seemed genuinely concerned about you, not Pete."

She had finished the pancakes and added bacon to the frying pan. Her jerky motions were at odds with the casual air of indifference she tried to maintain.

"Tell me about it," he urged.

Silence reigned until finally she spoke. "Remember what it was like being a kid?" she asked. "When life was one big illusion?"

"After my parents died, reality killed any hopes of that. Do you?" he asked.

"Yes. One day we were a happy family, no major problems that I knew of. The next we're front-page news. Scandal of the year." She plucked the half-cooked bacon off the pan and stacked it next to the pancakes. He didn't see any reason to point that out. "Breakfast is served." She executed a mock curtsy and placed his dish before him.

"Thanks."

She smiled. "No problem. And because I like you, I caved in." Opening the refrigerator, she pulled out a large pitcher. "Freshly squeezed. Never say I don't accommodate you."

"Who me?" he asked. "Never."

He waited until she had seated herself across from him before continuing his questioning. "What kind of scandal?"

Her dark eyes met his, and though they beseeched him to drop the subject, he wanted her to unburden herself, to trust him enough to share her pain. "Well?"

"You should have been a cop," she muttered. "You never give up."

"I'm the next best thing to a journalist. What did you expect?"

She groaned and paused to eat something before beginning. "We lived in a small town in upstate New York. Everyone knew everyone else and gossip ran rampant. So when Roger Wexler, district attorney with political aspirations, hit the news he did it in style."

She flicked her bangs out of her eyes and looked at him. He waited for her to continue in silence. "Want to take a guess?" she asked.

He shook his head.

"My dad carried on an affair with his secretary for one year. Until the woman forced him to choose between her and his family. In political terms, that's your lover or your career. Take your pick." She toyed with her pancakes, staring at the now cold stack.

"He chose your mother?" Mike asked.

"Yes, but that doesn't make the man a saint. I have no illusions that his decision was politically motivated. And I guess he thought his choice was the end of it."

"But it wasn't."

She shook her head, her pained gaze meeting his. "The woman killed herself, Mike. But not before leaving a suicide note and mailing it to the local paper. She was pregnant."

Mike sucked in a breath, wishing he had never forced Carly to resurrect these memories. But he had . . . "Then what?" he asked, knowing he had to hear the end.

"Life went on. Dad's political career was in ruins, but he never let it get him down. After a while we packed up and moved to the city. Dad hooked up with some old law school buddies and started his own firm."

"What about you?"

"What about me?"

"How did all of this affect you?" he asked.

"I was fifteen. Your friends are your friends so long as there's nothing to laugh at. I went to school surrounded by gossip and laughter. I got used to it."

"I doubt that."

She shrugged. "Eventually we moved and I finished up in private school."

"But how'd you survive? Being a teenager is tough by definition. Add your problems . . ."

"I kept busy. Joined the teen crisis hot line. It kept me out of the house after school so I didn't have to go home where talk of our family problems was prohibited. I couldn't watch my mother pretend life was fine."

Bingo, Mike thought. Carly's problems weren't with her father alone. She resented her mother's behavior as well, and she'd closed them both out of her life. "So that's how you got started helping teenagers," Mike said.

She nodded. "I did similar work in college, majored in psychology, and eventually it translated into my column. End of boring story."

"You never forgave him, did you?" he asked, thinking of the distraught older man he had seen days earlier.

"Not in here." She placed a hand over her heart.

"Your mother did . . . or appears to."

"That's debatable. Mom's tough. She believes in handling your private pain in private. I got no support from her because she refused to admit we . . ." She gestured around the room, the house she'd visited as a child. "We as a family had a problem. I don't agree with how she chose to live her life, but I can't fault her for her coping mechanisms."

Mike disagreed. Carly blamed her mother every bit as much as her father but hadn't come to terms with her relationship with either one of them. But now wasn't the time to push her further.

"I'm not as big a person as my mother . . . you've seen that. She stuck by her man. I didn't stick with Peter. But my parents taught me one important lesson in life."

"And what's that?" he asked, sensing this was the key.

"I discovered firsthand what a destructive force passion can be and I'll never allow it to rule my life," she said with a vehemence that would have once shocked him.

But after experiencing her extreme reactions to their intense physical attraction, he now understood. She obviously believed she could separate their physical relationship from the emotional and thereby never repeat her father's mistakes.

He glanced across the table. Carly had begun clearing their half-eaten meal. When he had arrived in the Hamptons, Mike had feared he needed the safety Carly represented and not the woman herself. As he watched her clatter the plates into the sink, he realized how very wrong he had been. And how very much a part of him she had become. The truth frightened him almost as much as it obviously frightened her.

Carly turned from the sink with tears in her eyes.

THE RIGHT CHOICE

He held out his arms and she sank into them. Burying his face in her hair, he comforted her the best he could and pushed aside all questions about the future.

NINE

After their emotional discussion, Carly tossed Mike out. Pushing the morning's events out of her mind, she set about organizing her columns into broad topics. Family, Friendships and Male-Female Relationships seemed like perfect headings, and hours later she had three distinct piles.

Family was a logical starting point but not a topic she was anxious to delve into yet. The same could be said of Male-Female Relationships, she thought, recalling her night with Mike. She set those piles aside. Friendship seemed like a safe place to begin. From there she would progress to Male-Female Relationships and ultimately Family Relations. The last two topics caused a distinct and unwelcome freezing in the region of her heart.

She sighed. How could she give advice when those areas of her own life were so complicated and unsettled? For years she'd walled off her emotions for fear of facing them. Thanks to Mike, she couldn't put off facing her personal life much longer. But first she had a deadline to meet. As a professional she had learned to separate her personal feelings from her career. Anything less now and she would lose all objectivity.

She stood and stretched, each cramped muscle protesting her prolonged period of sitting in one position. The rumbling sounds of her stomach echoed in the empty room. This morning's breakfast had filled the garbage disposal more than it had her stomach. A late lunch would help, she decided, and headed for the kitchen.

The light tap on the side door startled her. This exit led not to the main drive but to the beach. She wasn't expecting company, and Mike wouldn't be so formal as to knock before announcing his presence. Pulling back the curtains, she found herself face-to-face with her ex-fiancé. He'd given her no warning and she found herself unprepared for any sort of confrontation.

"It was a long drive, Carly. Will you let me in?"

Stunned, she stared through the glass. "Sure." She opened the door and Peter walked into the kitchen. Dark circles surrounded his eyes and razor stubble covered his normally clean-shaven cheeks. He looked tired, she realized. And a lot more casual than the formality she'd grown accustomed to seeing. She took in his rumpled khaki chinos and a burgundy T-shirt and shook her head. She barely recognized him.

"This *was* a long drive." And he could have just used the telephone. "What are you doing here?" she asked.

He ran a hand through his neatly trimmed hair.

"I needed to straighten out a few things." His gaze traveled the length of her body.

Too late she remembered that she wore nothing but the blue oxford shirt and a pair of satin bikinis. After her shower, the button-down had seemed like the most comfortable item of clothing to work in. And, she grudgingly admitted, after the morning's painful revelations, she took comfort in something that smelled so much like Mike.

Embarrassed by her lack of clothing, she retreated behind the center island and immediately felt more protected. "Everything already makes sense to me, so you wasted the trip." She didn't want to get into a discussion of why he'd felt the need to cheat on her with Regina. She already knew and didn't need to hear how she'd fallen short with him in the romance department.

Peter cleared his throat. "I think you have the wrong impression." He shook his head. "No, you probably have the right impression." He let out a groan.

"Let's make this easy. I've done a lot of thinking since I've been here," Carly said. "We're both at fault. I certainly shouldn't have given in at every turn or let you think I was happy when I wasn't."

"And I shouldn't have . . ." He flushed, a deep red against pale skin.

"No, you shouldn't have." But she couldn't suppress a laugh. She much preferred being around Peter now that they were no longer engaged.

"I wanted to apologize in person. We were good friends once."

"I know." Her voice softened. "And I hope we will be again. We lost that somewhere along the line."

He shoved a hand into his front pocket and started across the kitchen. "We were good together for a while, and then . . . I stopped thinking about you and took advantage. Thanks for sticking up for me with Roger."

At least he'd admitted his mistakes. And maybe even learned from them. He deserved to be happy and she wished him the best, as long as it wasn't with her. "You're a good attorney. You never needed me as leverage."

He stepped up beside her.

"Nothing's happened to change your position . . . has it?" she asked, wondering if her father had acted out of belated parental concern.

"Actually, yes."

"I'm sorry. My father promised he'd be fair."

Peter grinned. "He was. You're looking at the newest litigation partner."

She breathed a sigh of relief. "That's great news."

His smile never reached his eyes. Instead he brushed a strand of hair off her cheek. "I never meant to hurt you." His hand came to rest on her shoulder.

She'd liked Peter, and he wasn't the only one who'd made mistakes. "I know that."

"Work time's over, Carly. Time for a little fun." Mike's deep chuckle and footsteps reverberated throughout the small house.

The sounds stopped abruptly. "I had no idea we had company."

"Mike . . ."

"I know you're my brother and she's your ex, but I'd appreciate it if you'd take your hands off her." The cool control in Mike's voice startled her.

Peter obeyed his command, releasing her immediately. No doubt it was the shock of Mike's sudden appearance that had him responding so quickly. Taking advantage, she took a few steps backward.

Peter's gaze ping-ponged from Carly to his brother. Mike stood, arms crossed over his bare chest. Fresh from a shower, his hair was damp and his jeans were zipped but unbuttoned. He looked settled and comfortable, a man who had a rightful place in her home.

The intimacy of the situation couldn't have escaped Peter. "Well," he said, "I see I'm not the only one who was fooled." The hurt in his voice was unmistakable. "While I was working, giving you free rein over my fiancée, you took advantage." He glared at his brother.

"It wasn't like that," Carly said, hoping to prevent irreparable harm between Mike and Peter.

"Are you telling me looks are deceiving?" He pinned her in place with a narrow stare.

"Yes." Carly glanced down at her bare legs. "I mean no." She threw up her hands in despair. "Nothing happened until after I got up here."

Peter laughed aloud. "I'm not that big a fool. At least you could have been honest about why you broke up with me." He turned toward Mike. "And you . . ."

Mike stepped toward his brother. "She's telling the truth."

"And why should I believe you?"

Mike groaned.

"Because he's your brother," Carly said. "And the only real family you have."

"Which is why he should have kept his damn hands to himself."

Carly drew a controlling breath. Until Mike, she had thought the devastating results of her father's affair spoiled the possibility of her enjoying a passionate, emotional relationship. He'd begun to make her believe otherwise, but she saw now that she had been right all along.

She had succumbed to her feelings for Mike. They had crossed the line, and if he had jeopardized his fraternal relationship as a result she would never forgive herself.

"Talk," she pleaded, attempting to reach both brothers. "You're family. Nothing is more important than that. Especially not me." She gave Mike a lingering glance before walking out the door.

Mike watched Carly's retreating form. He was glad she had the sense to leave before that shirt lifted any higher. With one hand, he gave his brother a shove between the shoulder blades and pointed toward the kitchen table and chairs. "Sit."

Peter glared before answering. "I'm going. Relax," he muttered.

Mike settled himself in a chair and waited for Peter to join him, using the time to pull himself together. His brother had every right to feel angry, hurt and betrayed.

Mike's irrational jealousy the moment he'd seen Peter's hand on Carly's shoulder had only made a bad situation worse. He glanced at his brother. "She's right, you know."

"About what?"

"We're brothers," Mike said.

"That sure as hell didn't stop you from making a move," Peter said.

Mike slammed his hand on the table. "It sure as hell did!"

Stunned silence followed Mike's statement. He cursed his lack of tact, knowing he'd given his brother more information than he was probably ready to handle. Having an affair with another woman or not, ego was involved here as well as trust.

"You said you came up here on assignment." Peter waited.

Mike assumed his brother expected him to dispute that fact. "I am on assignment. Finished this morning." But Mike wasn't about to admit he'd handpicked the location of the assignment or the reason for his choice. "Look, Pete . . ."

"Forget it. From where I sit, things are pretty damn obvious. I'm just amazed I didn't see it sooner." Pete leaned back in his seat, not defeated but accepting.

"See what?"

"You really care for her." He shook his head, his expression one of pure amazement. "And all this time I thought you were doing me a favor by hanging around her and helping her out."

"Of course I care about her, Pete." But he wasn't surprised that his brother hadn't known it. "You have tunnel vision. What's important to you and nothing else."

Pete had the grace to look ashamed. "I need to work on that."

Mike burst out laughing. He was surprised that his brother had bothered to drive up here, or to look deeper than his ego now. "Don't worry. There's hope for you."

Pete shot him a nasty glare. "Well, at least she's got you."

Mike didn't touch that statement because it would open up a discussion he didn't want to have with his brother. Whatever he felt for Carly, the emotion didn't change the course of his future. He couldn't expect her to rely on him if he couldn't rely on himself or the abilities he'd always trusted until recently. Nor could he expect her to accept a man who lived a transient life, one at odds with the stability she so obviously craved.

He looked at Peter. "If you'd really loved her or were marrying her for the right reasons, I'd never have . . . Hell, I should never have gotten involved anyway," he muttered.

Pete's smile was grim. "Neither one of us ever claimed to be a saint."

"But I should have come clean with you once she broke things off." But how could Mike have explained something to his brother that he hadn't understood himself? Things he still didn't have a firm grip on understanding.

"You know, I had a lot on my mind . . . the partnership decision, Regina, the ending of the engagement . . ."

Mike didn't miss the order of those things but chose to remain silent.

"You're right. You should have come clean. But you know something? It wouldn't have changed a damn thing. You'd have done what you wanted anyway. You always do." Pete laughed, breaking any lingering tension.

Mike relaxed. He and Pete would be fine. Carly was another story.

Mike jogged down to the beach and watched as Carly sat on the sand, gazing out at the waves crashing against the sandy shore. A light breeze blew her hair around her face. She had attempted to tie it back with a bandanna, but the wind had destroyed the effort. As he neared the water, the smell of salt air tickled his nose. He'd miss the beach, he realized with a pang of regret.

He'd miss a lot of things. "Carly."

She turned at the sound of her name. "Hi."

"Hi."

She didn't smile. "Well, how'd it go?"

"Everything's fine. Back to normal."

She let out a sigh of obvious relief. "He came to apologize, and you know, I believe he meant it."

Mike sat down next to her.

"So you're on speaking terms again. I'd never forgive myself for coming between brothers."

"You are something special, sweetheart."

She blushed. Her face turned a shade deeper than the lobsters they'd shared. "Did I ever mention how much I like it when you blush?"

She laid her chin on bent knees. "You have a way of doing that to me."

"If you're talking about last night, I'd love to do it again." His hand came to rest on the back of her neck and he massaged the back of her skull with his thumb. But instead of relaxing, she grew stiff and unyielding beneath the innocent touch.

He swallowed a groan. He had an uphill battle ahead of him and he refused to draw back. Not because he wanted to sleep with her again, but because she had to learn that passion between two people could be a wonderful thing.

"So he really forgave us?" she asked.

"After cheating on you, he really can't pass judgment. And you two are over, remember? You didn't do anything wrong."

"Depends on your perspective. I can't believe we jumped into bed without ever considering the consequences. We should have given some thought to Peter's reaction before we jeopardized your relationship by getting involved. And the fact that we didn't is telling."

It sure was. Mike had no illusions. Carly's emotional withdrawal now wasn't aimed at protecting Peter, but herself. "Getting involved. Is that what you'd call it?"

"Yes. Wouldn't you?"

"Hell, no. We had sex. Isn't that what you're trying to say? A purely physical relationship, no strings, no ties, no caring involved."

She winced at his blunt description of what they'd shared, and at that moment Mike hated himself for hurting her. But he knew damn well what she was thinking. That by keeping their relationship on a purely sexual plane, she could equate it to her father's affair . . . and all the subsequent pain it had caused. Instead of facing what she felt for him, she'd run far and fast.

A part of him didn't blame her. He was no safer than his brother for her sense of security. He couldn't be the hearth-and-home kind of man she needed, yet he couldn't leave things alone. "Just sex," he said again. "Am I right?"

Carly licked at her dry lips. "Sounds reasonable to me." But it didn't. Hearing Mike's passionless, uncaring description of what they'd shared cut deep. Yet his words stated what she had forced herself to believe was the proper way to categorize their relationship. The safest way to avoid complications like this afternoon. The easiest way to let him go when he decided it was time to return to his nomadic, dangerous way of life. It was her heart that refused to cooperate and believe.

"Very generous of you." He leaned back on his elbows. "You know, Carly, you aren't fooling me."

"That's good, because I wasn't trying to."

"You're afraid to let yourself feel. So you label us with the one thing that scares you above all else, you beat yourself up for acting selfishly like your father and you run. Far and fast instead of facing the truth."

"Which is?" she asked, with pure sarcasm lacing her voice. "Since you know so much about running, you'd have to be right. So what truth is it that you think I'm afraid of?"

His hand cupped her chin and he met her gaze. "That if you look *us* in the eye, you'll see a lot more than just sex . . . and that scares you a hell of a lot more than a lust-filled relationship you can walk away from unscathed."

She jerked her face out of his grasp. "You're damn right it does. You're out of here at the first phone call, so why the hell should I look deeper? Why the hell should I let myself care?" Without waiting for an answer, she jumped to her feet.

Mike rose but remained silent. Obviously he knew he couldn't fight the truth.

With her vision blurred, Carly ran for the house. More than once she stumbled on the sand and rocks in her path, but she kept going. She flung open the door to the house. Feeling out of breath and desperate for peace from her rampaging emotions, she sought the security of home.

Instead she ran into Peter. "Just what I needed," she muttered under her breath. They might have resolved their issues, but he was the last person she wanted to see right then.

She wiped the tears still running down her cheeks with the back of her hand.

"Carly . . ."

"Not now, Peter. You apologized, I apologized. Now let it be."

"I was just leaving." He glanced at her face and his brow furrowed. "You've been crying."

"It's been known to happen."

"Has it ever happened over me?" he asked.

She rolled her eyes. "For crying out loud, can we just . . ."

"I'll take that as a no. Whatever Mike said, just forgive him. It's obvious you care about each other."

She narrowed her eyes. "You figured that out based on the five minutes we all spent together in the kitchen?"

"We were friends before we made the mistake of getting engaged. I'd like to think I knew you pretty well. And I know that even though you broke up with me, what I did hurt you. Just remember one thing."

She swallowed hard. "What's that?"

"Mike isn't me."

"Thanks," she murmured, then attempted to duck around him.

"Carly, wait."

She sighed. "Make it quick."

His lips formed a wry smile. "I know my brother better than anyone. Everything he's done since he's been back proves one thing to me."

"What's that?" she asked, truly curious.

"He loves you. Think about that." Peter opened

the side door leading to the beach and slipped out, shutting it behind him.

Carly stood in mute silence, Peter's words wrapping around her heart. Even if he was right, it couldn't make one bit of difference.

Carly spent the rest of the day in her room sorting through mail sent by her editor. Periodically she would glance out the window only to discover Peter's rental car still parked on the street out front. Though she wondered when he would leave, she was glad Mike had time alone with his brother. As for her conversation with Mike, she preferred not to dwell on it for now.

She slit open a purple envelope and read the contents. The letter was brief and to the point.

I'm sixteen and pregnant. I haven't told anyone. I can't decide what to do and the problem is affecting every part of my life. I can't sleep, can't study for summer school, and no one has patience with my mood swings. Help.

Carly's answer was easy to formulate, but as this young girl would find out, even harder to carry through.

The first thing to do is seek medical attention, as prenatal care is of paramount importance. The next is to tell the people closest to you. Perhaps your parents, the baby's father, a teacher or local clergyman. If you

*don't talk, you can't expect to come to any meaningful
decisions. Only after you face your fears will they seem
less overwhelming. Then you can make the right decisions for yourself and your baby. Good luck.*

Carly realized the irony in her answer. Talk out
your answers. Face your fears. The one thing she
advocated for this young girl was the one thing she
hadn't been permitted to do. Talk. Perhaps if she
had, she wouldn't be in such a sorry state now.

She finished punching the keys in the computer
just as she heard a knock. After saving her document,
she opened the door and glanced down the empty
hall. But at her feet, she found a fast-food restaurant
bag with a note taped to the brown parcel. "Be angry
with me later. For now take the time to eat."

How could she be angry with Mike when he put
her feelings first, always? She knew she had overreacted earlier, but with his leaving imminent, and his
return as uncertain as their future, her nerves were
on edge.

Inside the bag she discovered a large vanilla
shake, a burger and fries. Apparently Mike had re-
worked the old adage, the way to a man's heart is
through his stomach. He had certainly reached this
woman's heart with his kind gesture.

Actually he had reached hers long before this. She
munched on a french fry, pausing to lick the salt
and grease off her fingers. She had decided not to
fight the attraction for the short time they had left.

"Coast is clear." Mike's voice sounded through
the bedroom door along with a loud knock. Startled,

she glanced at her watch. Hours had passed. It was half past seven.

"Come in," she called without looking up.

"I thought Pete would never leave," Mike said. And if he hadn't threatened bodily harm, he might still be hanging around.

Carly didn't answer. She had changed into a flowered dress that wrapped around her body and reminded him of sunshine and happiness. Her head bent, she tapped away on her laptop computer keys. "I wasn't hiding out," she said at last, still without looking up.

"Could have fooled me." A quick glance around the room revealed piles of documents, reference books and the crumpled brown lunch bag. "You get a lot done today?" he asked.

She glanced up. "Pretty much." Her gaze darted around the room, but she had yet to look him in the eye.

"Maybe I should have Pete come by more often. His presence seems to stimulate you."

"What?" Her startled gaze met his.

"Your mind," he said with a grin. "Stimulate your mind." He tapped his head and laughed. At least she'd finally looked him straight on.

"Oh."

She flushed, a reaction that inevitably reminded him of their first meeting. And their first kiss. Which led to even more intimate memories. "How was the burger?" he asked, more to distract himself than anything else.

"Greasy." Her face turned a darker shade of pink. "I mean good. Thanks for thinking of me."

He shrugged. "Not a problem. I'm always thinking of you." He crossed the room until he stood next to her.

Her eyes locked with his. Every time he looked into that brown-eyed gaze, her vulnerability hit him hard.

"I'm sorry about what happened earlier," she said. "I have no excuse and I apologize. We both know where things stand. I have no right to toss it back in your face."

He crouched down and took her hand in his. "Our first fight is nothing to apologize for." His thumb methodically worked the pulse point in her wrist, massaging in slow but deliberate circles. When her pulse rate jumped, he smiled in satisfaction.

"Why not?"

"An occasional argument is a healthy sign. Any good psychologist knows that."

He raised his eyes in time to catch her grin and flick her tongue over her lips. Nervous energy radiated from her and he waited for the gesture he associated with Carly. Any minute now, he thought. She brushed her bangs out of her eyes. Bingo. He suppressed a laugh. Never having had such an emotional connection before, it still amazed him that he could read another person so well.

"Is that the only reason?" she asked.

"No."

"What's the other?" Her voice sounded unusually husky and he guessed she had figured out reason number two.

Their mental connection amazed him. "I'm not above relying on old standbys. Making up is half the fun." He tugged on her arm and yanked her toward him. She came forward fast, and together they toppled to the floor.

Carly landed on top of him in an indelicate sprawl. He brushed his mouth over hers.

"Mike." Her breath was as moist and sweet as his name on her lips.

"What?" he asked, trailing kisses along her jawline.

"Have you given any thought to when you'll . . ." Before she could voice the question that had been plaguing him, he silenced her with his lips. His tongue plunged into her warm mouth and he savored the heated sensation.

But even their intimate joining couldn't stop the remnants of her question from nagging at him. *Have you given any thought to when you'll be leaving?* The notion was almost more than he could bear. He would go because he had to . . . but not without leaving a part of himself behind.

Surprising him, she took an aggressive role, her tongue slipping between his lips. She greedily drew from him as much as she gave. His lower body responded in kind. Given their positions, she had to notice. Apparently she did. She wriggled off him and began unfastening his jeans with trembling hands.

Mike took a moment to study her. Her face was flushed and her lips glistened with moisture. His gaze slid lower. Her nipples puckered against the light flowered fabric. The evidence of her desire fueled his own.

"I never thought I'd agree to this again," she murmured.

"Oh, sweetheart, we're inevitable."

Her slender fingers shook as they grasped his zipper. That small involuntary movement hit him like a body blow. She was frantic, yes, but something more was involved. Something she'd been reluctant to admit.

He realized that he'd been more on target than he thought that afternoon. Like him, she too cared more than she wanted to. More than she was even conscious of.

He covered her fingers with his own, steadying the tremors in her hand. Together they made quick work of his jeans and briefs, sending them to a pile on the floor.

Mike didn't kid himself. His self-control had deserted him long ago. Only one thought occupied his mind—burying himself so deep inside her, he wouldn't know where he left off and she began. He lifted her dress and yanked the small scrap of lace down around her legs.

She gasped and Mike forced himself to stop. Their eyes met. If he'd frightened her, he'd pull back now. Somehow.

"I . . ." She hesitated.

"You what?" His words sounded more like a groan. If she wanted to stop, now was the time. A few seconds more and he doubted he'd be capable. "Say it."

She wrapped her arms around his neck. "I want you," she whispered. "Now."

After that there was no need for words. He rolled on his back, pulling her on top of him. Though he lacked the restraint necessary to move to a bed, he'd be damned if he'd bruise her soft body against the hard floor.

She raised herself upward and lifted her hips, lowering herself onto him in an excruciatingly drawn-out motion. The moment their bodies met, she uttered a soft moan. Her feminine noises coupled with her tempting heat had him gasping for breath.

She closed her eyes. He watched as myriad emotions shifted across her face. At that moment, he understood that he would never get enough of her, not ever.

With one smooth thrust, he entered her fully and filled her completely. Carly had never dreamed such a wash of emotions could accompany a physical act. Each time they came together was more explosive than the last.

She wondered if he felt it, too. She opened her eyes. As she gazed into the face she adored, she ran her fingers through his thick hair. In his golden eyes, she read every unspoken feeling she, herself, possessed. Words she'd never admit to aloud. He was right. She feared all they could have . . . feared having it and losing it at the same time.

This man reached inside her. He understood her without the need for words. He was her other half. And he would leave her soon. Because she loved him more than life itself, she would let him go. She

pushed aside the doubt that assailed her, the nig-
gling feeling that maybe they *could* work together
toward a future.

Instead she draped herself across his chest, burying
her face in the strong column of his neck. She
wouldn't let him see her cry. His slight growth of beard
scraped the skin on her face. Cheek to cheek, she
nestled closer. He smelled of the ocean and of Mike.
With a cough, she managed to choke back a sob.

He began to move beneath her. Each upward
thrust was an expression of love, one she felt in
every part of her body. She matched his motions
until their surroundings faded and only they remained.

As he shuddered beneath her, she held him close.
She kissed him as her own world erupted in a too
brief but brilliant mixture of passion and love.

Carly's head rested on Mike's chest. Her hair tickled his nose and each breath he took was scented
with vanilla.

"Let's go out for a late-night snack," Mike suggested.

"Don't you think we're a little underdressed?"
Carly asked wryly.

He glanced down and grimaced. Her dress was
hiked to midthigh and her bare legs were entwined
with his. He was stark naked. For the first time he
realized how little thought he had given to Carly.
He hadn't bothered to undress her, let alone spared
a moment to see if she'd been truly ready.

His only excuse was his driving need to block out her question. The time was fast approaching when he'd have to make a decision, whether his boss called or not. He couldn't keep running. Unmet obligations awaited him and the longer he stayed here, the longer he allowed himself the luxury of being with Carly, the harder it was to go back.

"Mike, that was a joke. What's wrong?" she asked, propping herself up on one elbow to look at him.

"Nothing." *Everything.* "Let's get out of here for a while. We've spent too much damn time in the house."

"Cabin fever already?" She drew herself to a sitting position and smoothed her skirt over her thighs.

"Not at all. But I thought you might like to go out. Like a real couple." A dangerous dream, he thought. One that had but a slight chance of coming true.

"Oh. Sure." Her words were right, but they lacked feeling. She pushed her bangs off her forehead, a sure sign of trouble ahead.

He couldn't pinpoint the source of her anxiety, but he sensed it anyway.

"If we're going, I'd better shower." Bracing her hands against the floor, she started to rise.

"Hold it."

"What?"

"You tell me. One minute everything's fine and the next you've turned back into the old compliant Carly. What's bugging you?"

She turned, her normally expressive eyes blank. A haunted look shadowed her features. "Not a thing. Just tell me when you're ready to go," she said with patently false cheer and a forced smile.

Why did he suspect she was referring to a lot more than dinner?

TEN

Dinner was a strained event that Carly could have done without. Even the casual intimacy of the Mexican restaurant hadn't relaxed the tension. After her initial hesitation, she no longer doubted Mike's sincerity. She believed he genuinely wanted to spend an evening out rather than needing an escape from the restlessness she feared he'd begun to feel. But regardless of his reasons, she sensed their relationship inching toward its inevitable conclusion.

Though she understood Mike's inability to stick around, and though she'd expected it, waves of panic rippled through her anyway.

She clutched her water glass in an effort to stop the trembling in her hands. Thoughts of their earlier lovemaking did nothing to soothe her. Each of them had been frantic, as if they'd sensed that this time might be the last. For all she knew, it might have been.

"Dessert?" His deep voice intruded on her unpleasant thoughts. He held out a large plastic menu.

Like a peace offering, she accepted it and vowed to appreciate whatever time they had left. "After that

vanilla shake you expect me to eat dessert?" She
scanned the back page. "Fried ice cream sounds
good," she said to the waiter, and licked her lips in
anticipation.

Mike's burst of laughter broke the simmering tension that had surrounded them all evening. "I'm
still hungry," she admitted sheepishly.

"Guess you worked up an appetite." His eyes
gleamed with unchecked desire.

"Guess so." She swallowed hard. "Which means
I'll just have to work it off later."

He treated her to a sexy grin. "You bet you will."

So she still had more time. How much? she wondered.

She felt like she was in possession of a time bomb,
with the detonator ready to go off at any minute.
Yes, she feared the moment in which he walked out
of her life for good. But Mike was right. She also
feared the consequences if they stayed together,
feared he'd lose interest—or worse, that she would
betray him. Although, looking at this man seated
across from her, she doubted she'd ever be tempted
to search elsewhere. What more could she possibly
want?

So where did all her uncertainty leave her? she
wondered. She glanced up. With a bowl of fried ice
cream. The waiter cleared his throat and Carly
moved her arm to make room for the luscious dessert. Caramel dripped over the sides. She cracked
into the hard outer shell with a spoon, digging deep
for the vanilla inside. Concentrating on her dish en-

abled her to escape reality and she took full advantage.

She placed the spoon between her lips, closed her eyes and savored the flavor. "Mmm."

Just like the cotton candy at Playland, Mike thought. "Do you make eating food an erotic experience on purpose?" he asked. "Or does it just come naturally?"

A rosy blush colored her cheeks. "For a minute I forgot I wasn't alone." Clearly embarrassed, she pushed the plate toward the center of the table.

He nudged it back. "Don't mind me, I enjoy watching." He adored her feminine curves and ability to enjoy life without censoring it, calories included.

She shrugged and dug the spoon back into the caramel for another bite.

"How's the column coming?"

"Not bad. I finished next month's questions and answers and faxed them over to the magazine."

"What about the book?"

"Format's done." She paused for a sip of water. "Three distinct segments should work."

"What are the topics?" He leaned back in his chair and eyed her intently.

"You're really interested?"

"Of course. Why wouldn't I be?"

She bit down on her lower lip. "You could be just being polite."

Beneath the table, he clenched his hands into tight fists. "I don't do polite. Not for the hell of it, anyway."

She nodded. Blond strands of hair fell free from her loose braid and framed her face before she tucked them behind one ear. "I knew that."

Did she? He silently cursed his brother's reappearance since it had obviously brought back insecurities he thought she had let go. "But maybe I was just humoring you."

"Were you?"

This time he cursed aloud. "Let's get something straight. I don't humor any more than I do polite. It's condescending to us both."

Her gaze dropped to her plate. The ice cream, he noticed, had begun to melt. "If I wasn't interested, I wouldn't have asked," he said in a harsh voice meant to capture her attention.

It did. Her eyelids fluttered upward, and startled, her gaze met his. "Fine," she said in just as clipped a tone as he'd used on her.

At least she was on the offensive, he thought. "And while we're at it, I'd appreciate it if you'd remember one thing: I'm not Peter. I don't act like him and I sure as hell don't think like him." His hand came down hard on the table, causing the water in both their glasses to slosh over the top.

She grinned. "Personally, I agree with you. And believe it or not, I appreciate the reminder."

He let out a deep breath. The strain of this meal had begun to wear on him. Every possible emotion had passed between them and he was exhausted. He signaled for the check.

"Just one more bite." Taking advantage of her last spoonful, Mike watched as she licked the utensil clean, running her tongue over the sticky caramel coating to remove every remaining bit.

Desire hit him hard. His exhaustion disappeared in the wake of physical need. As he shamelessly followed every movement, he wondered if he was destined to be in her spell forever. Every damn thing she made him feel was good. Even when there was trouble hovering between them, she made him feel alive. But so did taking pictures and capturing the world on film. At least it always had before. Why was the thought so much less appealing now? Mike sensed the answer had less to do with the painful episode in the Middle East and more to do with Carly.

Get out, he thought.

While he still could.

He forced his gaze upward. Her beautiful brown eyes shimmered with amusement. "Want some?" she asked and dipped the spoon back into the half-melted ice cream.

He opened his mouth to answer and she hand-fed him the dessert. He wasn't sure if the sweetness came from the gooey dish or the woman who gave it to him. "Incredible," he said. His gaze locked with hers.

Reaching over, she wiped what must have been a trace of ice cream or caramel from his bottom lip. Her gentle touch finished him off.

He tossed his napkin down onto the table. "Let's go." With a glance at the check the waiter had placed on the edge of the table, he shoved his hand into his pocket and retrieved his wallet. He peeled off the bills and tossed them down.

The moment he stood, he was grateful for the dark lighting. His jeans were way too tight. Grasping her hand, he tugged and led her out of the restaurant and into the dark night.

The car was parked behind the restaurant, and thanks to the late hour that area of the parking lot had all but emptied out. Mike didn't know how it happened. One minute he'd been leading her toward the car, the next he'd bracketed her body between the himself and the metal door.

Carly gazed up at him, hope and expectancy warring in her heart. She'd been sending out mixed signals all evening, she knew. But she wasn't mixed up anymore. She wanted him for the time they had left. She licked at her dry lips.

And he wanted her. The hard erection pressed against her told her that.

He reached out and traced her moist lower lip with the pad of his finger. With his gaze never leaving hers, he placed his finger in his own mouth. "Sweet," he whispered.

"It's the caramel." She gripped his waist with both hands. He was her anchor in so many different ways.

"No," he said, shaking his head. "It's you. You always taste sweet to me."

A strange sensation gripped her chest. More emotional than physical, tears threatened to fall but she pushed them back. "You don't do polite and you don't humor me, but I do think you're just saying that so you can get lucky."

"Did it work?" Something about the hesitancy in his voice spoke to her. They'd been dancing around each other all night and for what? They understood each other too well, knew each other's deepest fears.

They knew the end was coming.

"It would have worked without the sweet talk," she murmured, grasping his face in both hands.

The kiss that came next was anything but sweet; in fact, *hot* was the only word that came to Carly's mind before she became so engulfed with Mike that she didn't want to think at all. She locked her leg around his ankle, securing him against her. The ridge of his arousal was firm and hard against her stomach and his warm breath fanned her neck as he trailed wet, seductive kisses down her collarbone. Cool air drifted over her damp skin, increasing the power of her desire.

He dipped the strap of her dress down over one shoulder and edged a fingertip above the swell of her breast. She exhaled, but a slow moan escaped instead. She anticipated his hot mouth on her breast, wanted his heated touch more than she wanted her next breath. And if the glazed but intense look in his eyes was any indication, she'd have it too. Carly closed her eyes, waiting, wanting . . .

A car horn honked and loud laughter sounded behind them. "Go for it, man." A group of rowdy teenagers waved and gunned the engine, leaving dust in their wake.

"You sure you want to keep giving kids like that a helping hand?" Mike muttered. He leaned his head against hers, his breathing coming in harsh, labored gasps.

Carly wanted to be mortified, but she couldn't suppress a laugh instead. "It's either that or let them out on their own . . ."

He shook his head. "Carly . . ." His husky voice held promise.

The dead silence of the night surrounded them. Her pulse beat faster as she answered his unspoken question by placing her hand inside his. "Let's go home."

Minutes later they entered the house. By unspoken agreement, she followed him toward his room. The blinking light on the answering machine in the family room stopped her and she paused. Carly hit the play button.

She didn't recognize the voice. She knew she wouldn't. Yet as soon as the deep baritone sounded in the empty room, she wished she could hit rewind, or turn back the clock. Somehow, she knew.

And when Mike's hand went to his bad shoulder, her fears were confirmed. Pain sliced through her as the message wound its way to completion. "Relaxation time's over. We could use you on assignment. Same place, different setup. Pack your bags and get the first flight out, buddy. It's time to move on."

Carly stood behind him. Bracing himself, Mike turned to face her. Moonlight filtered in through an open window, illuminating an otherwise dark room. Her eyes had taken on the bleak, haunted look he had seen earlier. To her credit, though, her shoulders were squared as she tried to look unaffected. Too bad he wasn't buying the act.

The time had come sooner than he had planned. Leaving her would be next to impossible, but he had no choice. He wondered if she would beg him to stay. Part of him longed for that security while another dreaded the confrontation.

He almost laughed aloud. For a moment he had forgotten her feelings about their relationship. She might just welcome his departure. His entire body turned cold at the thought.

"Mike?" she asked in an unsteady voice.

"What?"

"I have one favor to ask."

"Okay, but I can't promise anything." No matter how much he wanted to.

"This you can."

"What is it?"

Tears shimmered in her dark eyes. "Don't wake me to say good-bye."

She should have begged him to stay. That and a body blow would have been less painful than the plaintive but resigned note in Carly's voice. She was going to let him go. Mike thought he had been prepared.

He had been wrong. "Sit down." Pausing to flick on a lamp, he prodded her toward the living room couch.

He dropped onto the soft cushion and patted the

empty space next to him. She sat. But her silence unnerved him more than any hysterical scene.

"Tell me about the sections of your book," he said.

"What?" Startled, she looked up at him.

He cupped her chin in his hand and stared into her eyes. "We have tonight."

"And you want to spend it talking about my book?" She blinked and a lone teardrop leaked down her cheek. He caught it with his thumb, pausing to lick the salt off his finger.

"I want to spend it with you. In case you don't realize it, sex isn't the only thing between us." He couldn't leave letting her believe he cared only for the good time they'd had in bed. Given her inherent fear, the possibility shook him to the core. So he would spend what little time they had left condensing a few more weeks of intimate discussion into one night.

He drew a deep breath. "I care about *you*. All of you."

"You do?"

He slanted her a look meant to chastise.

"Sorry," she murmured.

"You should be." He let his hand come to rest on her shoulder. "Why do you keep doubting me?"

She flicked her bangs out of her eyes. A gesture that had become second nature to her and so familiar to Mike that it caused a warmth in the region of his heart . . . because she used it whenever he touched hers.

"I can't remember the last person who cared enough about me to ask something so . . . trivial."

"Since when is your career trivial?"

She shook her head. "To me it's not. But to other people . . ." Her shoulders lifted and fell.

"Hey."

Raising her long lashes, she looked at him with wide eyes.

"Don't I deserve a label a little more personal than *other people*?"

"Yeah, I guess you do." She laughed, a light-hearted sound that despite the tense and somber circumstances sounded natural, not forced. A sound Mike knew he would carry with him wherever he went.

"Progress." Releasing an exaggerated groan, he propped his feet up on the couch, prompting her to shift and join him laying down or be dislodged.

"So. How do you go about solving the problems of the American teenager?"

Carly leaned her head against his chest and snuggled closer so she wouldn't topple onto the floor. Enjoying his warmth and needing his strength had nothing to do with her actions. "Name your biggest problem as a teen," she said.

"Family," he said without hesitation.

Thinking about his parents' deaths and his disinterested aunt and uncle, she could only imagine the depth of the dysfunction he'd lived. "And after family?" she asked.

"Sex."

She nudged him in the side with her elbow.

He groaned. "Direct hit," he muttered. "I meant girls."

"Relationships," she clarified. "And from a teen-age girls' perspective, it was probably friends and then relationships," she said in a purely authoritative tone.

"I like this take-charge side of you," he said, wrapping his arms around her waist and resting his chin on her shoulder.

She laughed. "Normally I handle myself pretty well. You just came into my life at . . . a crossroads."

"You'll get through it. I have faith. So tell me, how far have you gotten on each section?" he asked, then listened intently as she filled him in on her progress—or lack thereof.

His interest warmed her. He obviously cared for her, for more than just the physical relationship they'd shared. And despite his imminent departure, he'd proven the kind of man he really was. The kind who wouldn't be content to leave friends and responsibilities hanging. The kind who would face his fears and move on, leaving her behind.

She snuggled closer into his embrace. Letting him go would be harder than she had thought, but he'd never expressed an interest in anything long-term, never even indicated he'd want to stay. She ignored the little voice reminding her that she hadn't exactly encouraged him, either.

Lacing his fingers through hers, he rested their hands together on her stomach. "I know you'll finish that book and make me proud."

He laughed, and the deep rumble passed right

through her. "If I can get past my own family history, maybe."

"I have faith, but we'll see, won't we?"

No, we won't. Because he wouldn't be around. "Will you be okay?" she asked, hating her unsteady voice and the trembling in her body.

"I'll be fine. I promise." He pressed a gentle kiss against her cheek.

Carly closed her eyes, fighting the tears his touch inspired. She knew his promise wasn't within his power to keep, but she let the words lie. She needed to hear them, to keep them close to her heart.

"You can handle this, Mike." Bolstering his confidence, even when her own was flagging, was the least she could do for the man she loved. And she did love him. No sense in denying the truth to herself. Not now. "And once you go back, you'll understand that. Everything you love is waiting for you."

"Not everything." His arms grasped her tighter, making it difficult to draw a breath.

She didn't care. For tonight, his embrace was the only thing that mattered.

They lay in silence. The clock in the hallway mocked them as it loudly ticked away the moments of the night. With each passing minute, dawn came closer.

Carly didn't realize she had dozed off. When she awoke, she had a stiff neck from her position on the couch. She knew without looking around.

Mike was gone.

He had kept his promise. He hadn't woken her to say good-bye.

And they hadn't made love, either.

For the next month, Carly indulged her need to mourn a relationship that was over before it had begun. She hadn't mourned the loss of her fiancé, but Mike's departure affected her in a much more profound way. He wasn't just a man who'd passed through her life. He'd touched her life and made it better. He'd made *her* better.

She found it difficult to touch food; even yogurt and liquid wouldn't pass the lump in her throat. She puttered around the bright kitchen and attempted to block out the memories of love, laughter and lobsters, without any success. So she turned her attention to her work, finding not solace but refuge from the painful truths that surrounded her.

But she couldn't hide out forever. When she couldn't stand the bright sunshine beating down on the beach since her own mood was so gray, she decided the time had come for change. Self-absorption and wallowing in pity wouldn't solve anything. Like Mike, she needed to reclaim her life. As fast as she had packed up and traveled to the Hamptons, she repacked and headed for the city.

Once back in familiar surroundings, she pulled herself together. She contacted the school and put herself on call for students who needed summer counseling. She worked on both her book and some new column ideas until she was so exhausted that she fell into bed each night both mentally and physically drained. She met Juliette for dinner and drinks, some of her friends for lunch, and tried to resume her life.

But she still dreamed of Mike. His laugh, his sexy swagger, his lips on hers. Nothing distracted her and nothing came easily. Not even the book. Looking back on all the work she'd done over the summer, she found length but not depth. Oh, the friendship section had fared well enough, but not the relationship or family portions. She hadn't expected them to be simple. But carrying Mike's faith deep inside her heart, she'd managed to put together a rough draft of both. Though she wanted to be pleased, she couldn't because the effort lacked heart. Perhaps because her own was so badly damaged.

With Mike gone and too many hours to fill, soul-searching became her favorite pastime. She needed to heal. Until she dealt with her irrational fears, she would never be free to commit to anyone or anything else. She couldn't change how things had ended with Mike. She hadn't asked him to stay because she knew how badly he'd needed to face his past, and how much he loved his career.

And because she hadn't had the guts.

Despite the fact that she'd turned off the air-conditioner in her apartment, she shivered and wrapped herself in a blanket to ward off the chill. She rose and headed for the kitchen. A hot cup of tea would warm her inside and out. After fumbling around, she resettled herself on the couch.

The teddy bear Mike had won in Playland stared

at her with large, accusing eyes. The beautiful
memories paraded through her mind and settled in
her heart.

So did the guilt. She'd allowed Mike to enter a
dangerous situation without telling him the truth.
She loved him. Whether or not she was capable of
committing to that love, regardless of the fact that
he *hadn't* been, he'd deserved to know.

What if something terrible happened again, only
this time he didn't make it? Then he would never
know someone in his life truly loved him.

Loved him and essentially abandoned him, just as
he believed his parents had. Laying her head in her
hands, Carly wept. For Mike and for herself.

There was no way she would let her past control
her future. Carly drew a deep breath and followed
her father into his study. The decision to come here
hadn't been easy, but it had been inevitable. She
couldn't find herself as a person or have a life if she
was still mired in her adolescent pain.

She knew without asking that she and her father
would have the opportunity to talk in private. Her
mother hadn't missed a weekly card game in fifteen
years. Carly glanced around at the rich mahogany
bookshelves her father had had installed when he'd
moved out of the city to Westchester County.
Though he still kept his apartment in Manhattan, it
was more a place for weekend stays and work emer-
gencies than his home.

She glanced around. Nothing in this room had

changed since she was a teenager. Nothing and everything, just like her life. She clenched her fists. Her father stood across the room, obviously waiting for her to speak. When it became clear she didn't know where to start, he cleared his throat. "I was surprised when you called and *asked* if you could come. Most daughters don't need permission to visit their fathers."

She turned to face him. "I'm not most daughters . . . and you're not most fathers."

"No, I'm not." His easy agreement surprised her, and she studied him more closely. His light hair was now more silver than tawny in color, and the dark circles beneath his eyes were a bit more prominent. But overall he looked well.

She couldn't have this conversation standing up, so she gestured toward the couch and chairs in the center of the room. She chose her favorite seat as a child, an oversized, beat-up leather club chair and ottoman. Her father sat on the matching chair beside her.

"So . . ." She curled her feet beneath her.

"So. If you're here, there's a reason. What can I do to make it better?" he asked.

"What do you mean?"

"I'm assuming you need something. Or *someone* to talk to, and picked me."

"Why would you think that?" Her relationship with Mike, such as it was, and her fear of passion and commitment weren't things she'd expect her father to be aware of. Funny how she'd accused Mike of being incapable of commitment when she suffered from the same thing herself. She just hadn't known it at the time. Commitment to Peter wasn't the same as commitment to someone she loved with her whole heart and soul. That frightened her to death.

Roger cleared his throat. "We had a company cocktail party a few nights ago. Peter mentioned that his brother was back overseas."

Carly tensed. "So?"

"So, I met with Mike. He's nothing like his brother."

She smiled. "I know."

"Judging by that glowing look on your face, I'd say that's a good thing. You can't be happy he's gone."

"And you think I'm here to talk about my love life?"

He shifted uncomfortably in his seat and a sheepish look crossed his face. "When you called, I didn't know what to think. But I knew if I didn't push, we wouldn't make any progress. I'm sorry if I'm prying." Apparently after all this time, father-daughter talks didn't come easy for him either.

She sighed. "You're not. I'm here, so we might as well say what's on our minds."

"Well, Pete seems to think you sent Mike away because of the pain he had caused you. He tends to ramble on when he has my ear, but I wondered."

Laughter bubbled inside her, breaking some of her inner tension. Startled, her father's shocked gaze met hers. "Who else but Peter would think so highly of himself?" she asked. "As if my whole life was affected by what *he* did."

Her father chuckled but sobered fast. "I know better than to think that. Your whole life was affected by what *I* did. And I wish it was ego talking, but it isn't."

Leave it to her father, the straight-talking attorney, to force the issue and conversation to the real reason she'd come. "Well, knowing Peter, he probably believes I lost endless nights of sleep mourning him."

Roger smiled back at her. "In his favor, I think he was trying to make amends between us by feeding me information I could use to approach you."

"Always look for an ulterior motive," she cautioned, still smiling. To her surprise, she and Roger were sharing an honest, father-daughter moment. A rarity in her life. "I'll bet he even thinks I turned to Mike on the rebound."

"You didn't." More statement than question, Roger looked Carly in the eye.

"No," she whispered. But she'd turned him away, and her father's indiscretion had been the catalyst. She'd been afraid to commit to Mike. Not because she feared repeating Roger's affair, but because, as Mike had once said, she was afraid of repeating Roger's mistakes in his marriage.

So she'd come to face her father's past in order to move forward with her own. "Why didn't you? Approach me, I mean? When Peter gave you all that information, why didn't you come talk to me?"

He had the grace to look ashamed. "Because I

knew you would turn me away. At least I feared you would."

Her hand rested on the armrest of the brown leather chair, and her father covered her hand with his own. The comforting touch soothed her, making her wonder why she'd waited so long to come to the one man she'd needed so badly in her life.

That was one mistake she didn't want to repeat again with Mike . . . if he ever returned to the States.

"He was much more than rebound, wasn't he?" Roger asked quietly.

"He was. I mean, he is."

"So what are you going to do about it?"

Carly bit back a sigh. It was one thing to talk about their family, another to discuss her relationship with Mike. It felt awkward and uncomfortable, but she should have known her father would be persistent. He was a trial lawyer, after all.

"You know, this all strikes me as hypocritical. You weren't willing to talk when I needed you. Why should I open up to you now?"

"Because after all these years, you came to me. And because after all these years, you deserve an explanation. Whether your mother approves or not."

"I'm not sure if I do or not, but it needs to be said," Anne said as she walked into the room. The three of them faced each other—three individuals who hadn't been a family for too long.

Anne's early return caught Carly by surprise, and she glanced at her father's guilty face. He'd called her mother home for this meeting. Well, better all at once than one at a time, she supposed. Still, her stomach churned in nervous anticipation.

Anne sat on the couch and Roger joined her, clasping her hand in his. Carly narrowed her eyes, seeing reality as if for the first time. Had her parents done more than made peace with their lives? Had they truly come together after all this time? Carly shook her head. They'd obviously done more than made peace, but it hadn't happened overnight. She'd just closed them out of her life and shut her eyes to the progress they'd made in the years following the scandal and her lonely childhood.

Carly sat alone. She faced her parents, who now sat together on the sofa, united in a way she hadn't understood until now.

"We didn't talk about things because *I* insisted. I thought if we just put it behind us, it would go away." Anne fiddled with a ring on her hand, twisting it in a nervous gesture.

"If you don't acknowledge things, they can't hurt you," Carly murmured in repetition of the phrase her mother had ingrained in her over the years. Only now did Carly realize that that philosophy had taught her to avoid personal confrontation and dealing with reality.

"And I went along," her father continued. "I'd promised. The only way your mother would take me back was to pretend it never happened. After all I'd put her though, that one request wasn't too much to ask." He met Carly's gaze. "I see now I was wrong.

We were wrong. In saving our marriage, we made you the victim."

His words were so on target that a lump rose to Carly's throat and remained there.

"But not on purpose." Anne came up beside Carly and knelt down beside her. "I thought I was protecting you. Honest to goodness, I believed I was doing the right thing for us all."

Carly blinked back tears. "I know you did." Although nothing could change the past, at least they were talking now. "But I have to know something."

Anne swallowed hard. "Anything," she said, and Carly understood for the first time how difficult that word was for her mother to say.

"Did you love each other once?" she asked in a small voice that sounded so childlike, it was pitiful. But she knew for certain she'd walk out of this room a much stronger person than she had been coming in.

"I always loved your father," Anne said slowly. "And he loved me."

Carly cleared her throat and turned to her father. "Then . . . why?" Why have an affair? Why go looking outside his marriage for something they'd started out with from the beginning?

Her father nodded, seeming to understand without hearing the rest of the words. "I can answer that."

"No. I will. Because I didn't know how to show that love and I drove him away with silence and lack of communication."

"But I shouldn't have strayed. I should have tried

harder to make things work. Spent more time at home and less time focusing on my career. It shouldn't have taken an affair and a tragedy to set us on the right course."

They each accepted blame. They'd each come to terms with their lives. It seemed only Carly continued to live in past shadows. "And you are? On the right course, I mean?" Carly asked.

Her mother had reseated herself on the couch and her father grabbed for Anne's hand. "We've been in counseling for years. Each time we tried to make an overture, you turned us away. We didn't blame you, but we couldn't figure out a way to make things right for you either."

Carly smiled. "Because it wasn't your job. I'm a grown-up, and I chose to be ruled by the past." But not anymore.

"We're so sorry. *I'm* so sorry."

She shook her head, then wiped the tears that dripped down her face. "You know, we're all to blame in a way. But . . ."

"I want to start over," Anne said. "I know it's too late to be the mother you should have had, but I want more than we've had lately. It's selfish, but . . ."

Carly didn't wait for her to finish. Without thinking, she joined her parents on the couch . . . and became part of her family once more.

ELEVEN

"Hi. I'd like to cancel my subscription to your paper." Carly spoke to the faceless telephone operator.

"You can't shut your eyes, Carly." Juliette kicked her feet out onto the cocktail table across from the couch. "It's on television and radio too. Do you have the name of his boss? Or maybe Peter has news . . ."

Ignoring her friend, Carly repeated the newspaper operator's question aloud. "Why cancel?" Because she hadn't been able to face her morning coffee and the news of the day without reading about the war torn country where Mike had gone. The news was never good and the result was too many nightmares and not enough sleep.

She sighed. "My schedule just doesn't work and I haven't been reading. I'm sorry." She juggled the phone. "No, I don't even want tomorrow's paper. Thanks." She hung up and stared at the months' worth of papers on the table.

"The recycling dump is going to love you," Juliette said.

Since Carly had forgotten to cancel her subscription before leaving for the summer, her considerate neighbor had taken in her back copies of the *Times* while she was away, keeping them for her return. Stacks of papers would have blatantly advertised an apartment ripe for theft, and Carly was grateful that a friend had been aware. She hadn't thought beyond getting away.

And she hadn't known what awaited her once she got back.

She lifted the top paper and the headlines jumped out at her, taking on a life of their own. Another small, war-torn country. More injured . . . She tossed the paper aside. She closed her eyes but couldn't escape the harrowing visions that plagued her.

Juliette draped a soft arm around her shoulders and gave Carly a friendly squeeze. "These aren't helping." She scooped up the remainder of the newspapers and headed for the disposal in the hall.

"You're a good friend," Carly said when the older woman returned.

"So are you. Now, what do you say we go for a walk? Clear your head and maybe you can figure out a way to contact that man and . . ."

"No!"

"Why not? You love him; you've admitted as much."

"Because how *I* feel isn't what matters. He left, Jules. I didn't ask him to stay, but it doesn't matter. If he wanted to be in the States, he'd be here regardless of me. I have no right to interfere in a life he loves. He isn't one for commitment. I always knew that."

This wasn't a case of accepting and avoiding, it was one of understanding the man she loved and moving on. A loud rapping sound caused her to jump. She rubbed her damp hands on her jeans and headed for the door. She peered through the peephole and her stomach did an involuntary flip.

She hadn't seen Peter since the Hamptons. His appearance now couldn't be good news. Carly flung the door open wide. "What's wrong?" she asked before she said hello. "Is he . . ."

"He's alive," he said in a reassuring voice. He placed a hand on her arm. "But . . ."

She glanced at his drawn face. He didn't look as if he'd had much sleep the night before. "He's alive *but*? What is it? You're scaring me."

She grabbed his wrist and pulled him into the apartment. She felt Juliette's hand on her shoulder for support and her heart swelled inside her chest. "Out with it, Peter."

He let out a deep breath. "Mike's back, but he's in the hospital."

The next hour passed in a foggy haze. Carly barely recalled the taxi ride to the hospital. Only the fact that Juliette had begged her to call with news and Peter had shoved her into the backseat registered in her memory.

She ran down a long corridor and stopped short

before the door indicated by the hall nurse. "You go on. You're his brother."

"Now's not the time to argue over who's more important," Peter said and gave her a nudge in the ribs.

"Ouch." She shot him a dirty look. "Watch it before you do some permanent damage."

"Quit stalling." He drew his arm back as if to give her a second push.

"Okay," she muttered, mentally acknowledging that fear held her back. She let out a deep breath and opened the door.

The room was small and antiseptic in appearance as well as smell. Beige walls and white bedsheets did little to add cheer to an otherwise bland atmosphere. Her heart thudded against her ribs and she glanced toward the bed where Mike lay, apparently asleep.

Quietly, so as not to disturb him, she tiptoed into the room and pulled out the chair next to the bed. She sat, then lifted his warm hand and clutched it between her own. Love rose deep within her and filled the emptiness that his departure had created. The need to throw herself into his arms and stay there forever grew with each passing second.

The panic that used to automatically follow her intense feelings for Mike didn't surface this time because thanks to her parents, she'd learned a lot. Like the fact that the father she'd accused of not honoring his commitments had done just that. By returning to his marriage and making it work, he wasn't the man of disgrace she'd believed, but a man of conscience.

Like Mike. Another man she'd accused of not knowing the first thing about keeping promises. His return abroad was proof. . . . She'd been wrong again.

She let her gaze rake over him, and she took in the fact that he was home and safe. Carly gave a silent prayer of thanks that he would be okay. It wasn't nearly enough. Peter had reassured her many times on the ride over that Mike wasn't injured, merely out of commission. Never before had her ex-fiancé's words given her so much comfort.

Mike stirred in his sleep and her gaze focused again on his face. Though he had only been gone a month, his hair was noticeably longer. He hadn't shaved at all during his stint abroad and his almost full beard did little to dim his sexy good looks. Despite the gray pallor beneath the tanned skin, he possessed that *give 'em hell* look she'd come to associate with Mike.

With care, she pushed a stray lock of hair off his forehead. When his golden eyes opened, relief washed through her and she smiled. "You're the only man I know who can spend a month in a war-torn country and come home unharmed only to get blindsided by appendicitis."

He grinned, but she could see the gesture took a great deal of effort. "You always knew I was unique." He motioned toward the plastic water jug.

She poured for him and he gulped the entire cup. "Better?" she asked.

"Much."

Silence filled the small room. Carly glanced over her shoulder and realized that Peter had sent her in alone. She turned back to Mike. "I was worried," she said in a whisper.

"I wanted to come back sooner."

"You did what you needed to. I understood that." She fingered her bangs. The desire to admit her feelings was overwhelming, but his weakened state stopped her. So did the fact that she had no idea how he felt in return.

Yes, he was back, but for how long this time, she wondered. And even if he was to stay, what kind of future could they have? What was she capable of giving to him, and he to her?

"Can I get you anything else?" she asked instead.

He shook his head.

"Now that I know you're okay, Peter's waiting in the hall." She rose, carefully releasing her grip on his hand. Before she could take a step, he caught her arm in a surprisingly strong grip for a man just out of surgery.

"Wait."

Carly swallowed hard and tried to keep her inner panic from showing on her face. Deep, cleansing breaths, she silently ordered. When dizziness assaulted her, she knew she'd been unsuccessful.

"I'm not running anymore," he said, in a voice still rough from medication but also tight with emotion.

"I know. You're flat on your back," she quipped with more lightness than she felt.

"You can't joke your way out of this. We need to talk."

"And you need to rest."

Mike closed his eyes. Apparently she was right. The exhaustion was evident on his face and every forced word he spoke.

"You're right," he said finally.

"I usually am." She smiled.

"Am I interrupting?" His brother pushed open the door to the hospital room.

Mike leaned his head back against the stack of hospital pillows and groaned. "Come on in," Carly called out, saving him the effort. She turned to Peter. "I was just leaving." She squeezed Mike's hand once and headed for the door without meeting his gaze.

Mike leaned back against the uncomfortable pillow and waited while Carly slipped out the door. A floor nurse walked in behind Peter. "Hey, Pete."

His brother grinned. "Looking better. I have to admit you scared the living daylights out of me."

"Doubling over in the airport wasn't my idea of a good time either." He waited while the nurse did her thing—temperature and blood pressure.

"All set, Mr. Novack." She jotted notes in his chart and walked out.

"If I had known about those good-looking nurses, I would have checked myself in here," Pete said, his eyes following the attractive nurse's departure.

"You're one of a kind, little brother." Mike eased

himself higher in the bed, ignoring the pain as well as the painkiller the nurse had tried to force on him. He preferred having a clear head.

"I am, aren't I?" Pete chuckled. "When are they releasing you?"

"Not soon enough," Mike muttered.

"What's your hurry?" His brother glanced back toward the closed door, but no voluptuous blond nurse answered his silent plea.

Mike laughed, then clenched his teeth at the accompanying pain in his side. "I can't get my life together from a hospital bed."

Carly had visited him twice yesterday and once already today. Each time she had stayed longer but left as soon as the questions turned personal.

"She playing hard to get?" Pete asked.

"She just needs some coaxing," Mike said, deliberately vague. He had no intention of discussing his relationship, or lack thereof, with Pete.

His brother paced the room. "I know she's worth the effort," he said at last.

"Having second thoughts?"

"Hell no." Pete laughed. "She's all yours. Carly and I wouldn't make each other happy," he said.

Mike raised his eyebrows in surprise. "Since when does happiness count?" he asked his work-devoted brother.

Pete sat himself on the chair next to Mike's bed. "Since I nearly destroyed someone who was nothing but good to me. And since Regina expected to marry the newest litigation partner on *her* way up the corporate ladder."

"Didn't like being on the other end of things, huh? There might be hope for you yet, little brother."

"Don't get carried away," Pete muttered.

Mike laughed. "Well, you did good letting Carly know after the hospital notified you."

He shrugged uncomfortably. "It was the least I could do. You're my brother, after all."

Mike nodded. It was something Carly had reminded him of time and again. He needed his brother, something he wouldn't have been able to admit prior to his return to the Middle East. He could face that truth now.

Along with many others. He only hoped it wasn't too late.

Carly stepped out of the bathroom to the sound of an insistent ring. "I'm coming," she called to her impatient visitor. She'd just gotten out of the shower and finished blow-drying her hair, probably missing the first couple of rings. Whoever was out there had his finger permanently attached to her doorbell. She opened the door a crack and glanced beyond the chain lock.

"Mike?" She closed the door to unlatch the lock. "What are you doing here?" He wasn't due to be released from the hospital until the next day.

"I couldn't take that place another minute." He smiled and headed straight for *his* chair. Holding his right side, he lowered himself slowly and dropped a duffel bag onto the floor. "I'll never take being mobile for granted again."

Carly stopped in the kitchen for a glass of ice water and tried to calm the pounding of her heart. She wasn't ready for this conversation, not without warning. Apparently, though, Mike had set the timetable. She'd just have to listen . . . and hope he hadn't come to tell her he was leaving again as soon as he was able.

"You checked out against doctor's orders, I'll bet." She handed him the glass and sat down on the couch.

He shrugged. "Another day or night wasn't going to make a difference."

"I'm sure your doctor had other ideas." She chewed on her lower lip. Finally curiosity got the better of her. "Where are you staying?" Until he was healed, she didn't have to worry about him hopping on the nearest airplane out of the country. At least not yet. She fingered her bangs. Her hand trembled and she shoved it beneath her leg.

"I'll stay with Pete for a week or so." Mike deliberately paused for a sip of water and watched her reaction.

She nodded slowly. "And then?" Her lips, which had been damp before, had lost their luster as she nibbled on her lower lip with her teeth.

"What do you expect me to do?"

Startled, she met his gaze. Her brown eyes reflected confusion and something else. What, he didn't know. Since his return he hadn't been able to read her as easily as before.

"Do you expect me to head overseas?"

"I . . . I don't know what to expect."

He placed his glass down, rose carefully and re-settled himself next to her on the couch. "There was a time when I didn't either."

"And now you do?"

He nodded. "You accused me of not understanding the concept of commitment once, and as much as that hurt, it was the truth."

She shook her head. "I was wrong. You've always been committed to your job, to your brother. To me, when you set your mind to proving certain points," she said with a grin.

He placed his hand beneath her chin, turning her so their eyes locked. "Committed to running away. It's not the same thing."

"Maybe not," she murmured.

"Definitely not. Until you damn near married my brother I didn't realize what a mess I'd made of my life. That was a wake-up call if I'd ever gotten one."

"I thought you provided me with the wake-up call." She smiled, the gesture so warm and open, he nearly forgot the last month of deprivation.

"We're good for each other." If her appearance was any indication, she'd missed him as much as he'd ached for her. She'd lost weight in the time they'd been apart. Slender legs were encased in tight leggings and suede boots. Her damp hair trailed over an oversized white sweater that hugged her thighs. And shadows lurked in her dark eyes. Shadows he'd do his damndest to remove, if she'd let him.

He touched her soft cheek with one knuckle. "In your own quiet way, you showed me all I was missing."

She shook her head. "I abandoned you." She didn't meet his gaze.

"No." Pulling her against him, he buried his face in her hair and inhaled the scent he'd only had the luxury of dreaming of. "You cared enough to let me go when I needed to."

In a move that stunned him, she jerked backward, removing herself from his arms and distancing herself from his touch. She stood. Tears ran unchecked down her cheeks.

"Don't give me so much credit." She shook her head and laughed, a harsh sound that tore at his heart. "I let you go because it was easier than walking away myself. But if you hadn't gotten that call, don't think for a minute I wouldn't have found an excuse to pull away."

He stood and remained silent. Nothing she said came as a shock to him, nor did it bother him the way she obviously thought it should. "And?"

"Don't you get it? I wanted you to go." She obviously felt she owed him the truth.

He respected her for that, he thought, watching her sink back into the couch. "And you wanted me to come back, just as much as I wanted to come back to you." He stayed silent until she looked at him. "I went because I had to and came back for the same reasons."

"I don't understand."

Or she didn't want to. The glimmer Mike saw in

her eyes wasn't happiness, it was uncertainty, and his heart clenched with the same emotion. Because for the first time he acknowledged that he might actually lose her.

"Commitment," he explained. "I had to complete one before I could make another." He leaned over. Lowering his head to hers, he tasted her lips, reveling in the sweetness that was uniquely Carly. His mouth moved over hers, coaxing and teasing, seeking acceptance. Her resistance fled in seconds, with a soft sigh and an intimate greeting. Her tongue met his and Mike's self-control went into remaining gentle but insistent. He couldn't, wouldn't lose her now.

She raked her fingers through his hair as she allowed him to draw her closer. He brushed feather-light kisses on the tip of her nose and across her jaw. He sat beside her and drew her close. She didn't pull away and that gave him hope.

Now he owed her honesty. "Orphaned isn't abandoned. Do you remember telling me that?" He separated them so he could look into her brown eyes.

She nodded.

"I didn't understand then. Until I spent time with those kids from the accident, I couldn't. But I realize now that I was still feeling like a lost kid . . . and pushing away any chance of ever settling down. Running from one job to the next without any long-term commitment, not letting anyone close to me . . . because I didn't want to give anyone the chance to leave me again."

"Including me?"

"Especially you. Because you meant more to me than anyone else. So I left you first."

She shook her head and laughed, but it wasn't a pleasant sound. "Some pair we are."

"But I came back. The appendicitis hit once I'd already landed, but I came back. Do you understand now?" he asked.

She pressed a kiss to his neck but remained silent, causing his heart to thud painfully against his chest. Mike grasped her arms in front of her, holding her before him, begging her to listen and understand. "We both had things to deal with, things to face. There's no shame in that."

"I know. I wasn't any better at dealing with the past than you were. But that's changed. While you were gone, I made peace with my parents."

Pride swelled inside him and her words gave him hope. "I know what that took for you."

She nodded. "And I learned something."

"What was that?"

"That my perception of safety was as false as my perception of life. *Nothing* about Peter was safe."

Mike reached for the duffel bag he'd dropped earlier and pulled out a stack of photos. "Look."

Carly accepted the pile and flipped through the pictures. "Rye Playland," she said, feeling the smile on her lips.

"Take a look at yourself."

She did and was surprised by what she saw. Wide smiles, huge laughing eyes . . . and they were hers. "I was happy," she whispered.

"We were happy."

"What are you saying?"

"Just what I said in the hospital. I'm not running anymore. I'm back."

"For . . . ?"

"For good."

"And your career?"

He exhaled. "I'm not saying I won't miss the travel, but I figure we can do that together. And I'm sure I can get a job with a national . . ."

"What about the danger? Won't you miss the danger? The excitement? The making a difference?" Afraid to hope, yet unable to prevent herself, Carly waited for his answer.

"I think you provide enough excitement, sweetheart."

Her heart pounded hard inside her chest. "You won't get bored? Miss your old way of life?"

He rubbed his thumb over the pulse point in her wrist. "You are my life. Together we can do things we've never dreamed of alone."

That much was true. It was Mike's strength and belief in her that had gotten her through the last month, even though he wasn't there. She rose and went into the bedroom. When she returned to face Mike, she held out a white box that contained her heart, all wrapped in one package.

He opened the box and pulled out her manuscript, handling it as if it was fragile glass. "You did it."

She nodded, watching from a few feet away as he began turning the pages. On page two, she held her breath.

The dedication was burned in her heart and soul. *To the man who told me that passion and love are healthy human emotions. And then set out to prove it.*

Slowly he raised his gaze to meet hers. The golden flecks danced in his eyes. "Thank you," he said softly.

"You're welcome. I couldn't have done it without you. You were right about me . . . about a lot of things. This is my way of saying thanks." She pointed to the stack of white pages in his hands.

He placed the manuscript back in the box.

"That copy is for you. I hoped . . . well, if you came back, I wanted you to have it. You can read it if you want," she said, suddenly feeling embarrassed. "There's a lot of me in there."

After meeting with her parents, she'd spent the next two weeks in front of the computer. The heart of the manuscript, the elusive something that had been missing, had miraculously found its way onto the screen. The results had been therapeutic.

"I'll read it because I want to. I already know you."

Afraid to speak because of the lump forming in her throat, and because she was afraid she'd break down, she merely nodded. He had always known her, even when she hadn't known herself.

Taking a deep breath, she gathered her courage and left her past behind. She looked the man she loved in the eye. "I'm not running anymore either," she whispered.

A harsh groan echoed from deep inside him as he reached for her, pulling her down to the couch with him. He winced but wrapped his arms around her anyway. Lowering his head, his lips met hers. His kiss was wet, hot, everything she remembered and more. Her heart kicked into high gear under the intensity of his kiss.

She lay back on the couch and he followed, bracing his arms on either side of her head. She could see the exertion it took for him to move. "Now tell me," he said, his voice hoarse and disbelieving.

"I love you, Mike. I always have."

"God, I love you too."

Carly grinned. "Good. Now get up slowly and march into that bedroom. I'm taking care of you."

He groaned.

"Someone has to make sure you don't do too much too fast."

He cupped her chin in his hand. "I'm glad that someone is you. Tell me something: When did you realize passion and love were good things?"

"It's silly, really. The night you left and we didn't make love. It just took me a long time to understand what you'd taught me."

He nibbled on her lower lip. "I'm glad it worked, because it was hell being with you, so close to losing you and walking away without . . ." He trailed off.

"I understand. When Peter said you were in the hospital and I didn't know what was wrong . . . I thought I'd lost you without ever having had the chance to tell you that I love you."

"You can't get rid of me that easily. I'm like a bad penny."

She brushed a kiss over his lips. "As long as you

keep turning up, my life is complete." Carly paused. "The question is, is yours? I don't want to wake up one day to find you resent me, that you gave up your career because you thought it was what I wanted . . . the kind of life Peter would have given me."

He shook his head. "Look at those pictures. You wouldn't have been happy with Peter's kind of staid life. As for me, I lost my parents, remember? Do you really think I'd want my kids to suffer the same fate?"

She blinked and tears rippled down her cheeks. "Kids," she said softly.

"And a dog, and a white picket fence if you want one." He brushed a lone tear aside with his thumb. "I'm through running, sweetheart."

She held her arms open wide. "Unless it's *toward* me."

EPILOGUE

"Life doesn't come with any guarantees. You just put your best foot . . . I mean paw forward and hope for the best." Mike knelt down and patted the head of the mutt he'd recently rescued from the ASPCA. He'd been covering a story for the local paper about animals that had survived a fire that had taken the lives of their owners.

Surprisingly, he enjoyed the lighter pieces as much as he enjoyed covering harder news. He appreciated the opportunity to do both. But he hadn't expected to get earmarked as a sucker by the first pooch he laid eyes on. He'd been a goner from the minute he'd taken a look at those big brown eyes.

"So there's the paper. Think you can remember that?" Mike asked.

The dog thumped its black tail enthusiastically against the wood floor.

"Good. Now let's hope Carly likes surprises," he said.

He'd left a message for her to meet him here with good news. Mutt, as he'd come to call him, had accompanied him on his daily run and his easier assignments. So here they were.

Despite the peace and quiet, or perhaps because of it, Mike knew he'd made the right decision. He glanced around at the rambling house that needed as much time and love as this pathetic new pet. He'd have time for both these days. The wandering and danger didn't suit him anymore. The restlessness had begun long before he'd gotten injured on assignment. He just hadn't known the longing was for permanent roots. Who'd have guessed?

Not Carly. She still seemed to be in a daze, as if happiness and security couldn't possibly go hand in hand. As if she was looking for it all to fall apart at any moment.

Mike refilled the mutt's water bowl and placed it on the floor. He understood the source of her fear. Time . . . and this surprise would prove that they shared something lasting.

The doorbell took him out of his musings and he was grateful for the interruption. The dog didn't react, but then he still hadn't learned to associate the doorbell with human company. Mike headed for the door but didn't miss seeing the dog walk up to the paper and use the floor anyway. He groaned and turned the doorknob, wondering who would ultimately win this battle, him or the pooch.

"Hi."

"Carly."

She smiled, radiating a glow in her cheeks he hadn't seen since . . . well, never. Talk about progress, he thought.

"Come in," he said.

Carly followed him inside and down a short hall. She'd taken two steps inside the living room when Mike barked out the command. "Stop." She did and looked down, grateful she hadn't gone a step farther. Meeting his gaze, she burst out laughing and stepped around the mess, the paper, but not the dog. How could she, when he insisted on nuzzling her leg with his nose?

She knelt down to give him the attention he craved. "He's cute," she said, tilting her head upward. "And so are you."

He frowned at her description. He'd shaved off the beard weeks ago, but he was still the rebel in attitude and look. He still favored worn jeans that hugged his lean hips and muscled thighs and a black T-shirt that accentuated his biceps.

He was still the man she loved beyond reason. The man she'd marry in a few weeks, in a private, family-only ceremony.

Tearing her gaze from him, she asked, "Okay, what's up? What is this place?" she asked, gesturing around the rambling farmhouse.

He let out a deep breath. "This . . . is home." He grabbed her hand and led her outside, down a small path to the edge of the property. He patted a peeling post. "And this is your white picket fence."

A smile twitched at the corners of her mouth. "And this is my dog?"

He grinned. "It's the American dream, sweetheart. The house, the dog, the white picket fence . . ."

"What about the two-point-five kids?" she asked, her eyes dancing with delight.

He leaned forward for a brief but satisfying kiss. "I was hoping one was on its way," he said in a voice he barely recognized.

"If not, I'm sure we can work on it."

Her light, tinkling laughter warmed him. To Mike, it was the sound of promise, of his future. He splayed his hand over her flat stomach. Her hand covered his and the dog nudged at her leg. She laughed again. He wanted to grow old listening to that sound, and he would.

"I like your thinking, and that might take care of one of those kids . . . but I had something else in mind." She was teasing him and he knew it.

"And here I thought I had all the surprises for today."

She waved papers in front of him. "I did some research, and there's an adoption agency placing orphans from war-ravaged countries. Now I know it's a big responsibility, and I know many of these kids come with problems, but *we* can handle it. I mean, if you want to."

Did he want to? Give a home to kids who'd lost parents as he had? Only this time, these kids would know love and happiness . . . and security . . . Mike glanced back at the old house, and the woman with whom he would make this place a home. He didn't know what he'd done in this life to get so lucky, but he intended to enjoy it.

He took Carly's hand. "I said it from day one: You're something else, sweetheart."

Her eyes glistened with sheer happiness. "So tell me—what's the dog's name?"

Mike paused in thought. "How about Lucky?"

She leaned down to scratch the dog's head. "It sure fits."

Mike grunted and pulled her close. "What do we do with him while we're on our honeymoon?" he murmured in her ear. "He's not paper trained yet, remember?"

Carly smiled.

Mike grinned.

"Peter," they both choked out, laughing at the thought.

ABOUT THE AUTHOR

Karen Drogin lives in Purchase, NY, with her husband and two young daughters. A former practicing
attorney, Karen is more at home writing romances
than legal briefs. She loves to read as much as she
loves to write and would enjoy hearing from those
who feel the same! Write to Karen at P.O. Box 483,
Purchase, NY 10577, or E-mail her at
Carlyphil@aol.com.

You can check out Karen's Web site at:
http://www.eclectics.com/carlyphillips.

BOOK YOUR PLACE ON OUR WEBSITE
AND MAKE THE
READING CONNECTION!

We've created a customized website just for our very special readers, where you can get the inside scoop on everything that's going on with Zebra, Pinnacle and Kensington books.

When you come online, you'll have the exciting opportunity to:

- View covers of upcoming books
- Read sample chapters
- Learn about our future publishing schedule (listed by publication month *and author*)
- Find out when your favorite authors will be visiting a city near you
- Search for and order backlist books from our online catalog
- Check out author bios and background information
- Send e-mail to your favorite authors
- Meet the Kensington staff online
- Join us in weekly chats with authors, readers and other guests
- Get writing guidelines
- AND MUCH MORE!

**Visit our website at
http://www.zebrabooks.com**

COMING IN JULY FROM
ZEBRA BOUQUET ROMANCES

#53 WILD IRISH ROGUE by Suzanne Barrett
_(0-8217-6649-X, $3.99) Justine Farris would do absolutely anything for her dotty old aunt—but marrying Declan Walsh seems just plain crazy. Although the handsome Irishman might be deported unless they pretend to tie the knot, how can Justine say "I do" when they can't agree on anything—even a wedding date? But where there's a will, there's a way . . .

#54 THE BRIDE'S BEST MAN by Laura Phillips
_(0-8217-6650-3, $3.99) Marcy Winters isn't going to marry Jack Rathert, her old fishing buddy. She's merely chosen him to be her honor attendant when she weds Roger Ashforth III. The trouble is, anyone can see that Marcy's marrying the wrong guy. She needs someone who will be her best friend as well as her lover . . . someone, well, someone like *Jack*.

#55 FALLING FOR GRACE by Maddie James
_(0-8217-6651-1 $3.99) Having once loved and lost, Gracie Hart has no intention of ever falling in love again—no matter how loudly her biological clock is ticking. But when her new tenants, Carson Price and his little daughter, arrive on the scene they proceed to wreak havoc in her life—and in her heart!

#56 STOLEN KISSES by Kate Donovan
_(0-8217-6652-X, $3.99) When an FBI agent interrogates tough defense attorney Josie Galloway's frail grandmother about a decades-old jewel heist, Josie is ready to nail the infuriating man to the wall. Then she discovers that her granny's been playing Cupid again and irresistibly handsome agent Locke Harper is her latest target!

Call toll free **1-888-345-BOOK** to order by phone or use this coupon to order by mail.

Name _____

Address _____

City _____ State _____ Zip _____

Please send me the books I have checked above.

I am enclosing	$_____
Plus postage and handling*	$_____
Sales tax (in NY and TN)	$_____
Total amount enclosed	$_____

*Add $2.50 for the first book and $.50 for each additional book.

Send check or money order (no cash or CODs) to:
Kensington Publishing Corp., Dept. C.O., 850 Third Avenue, New York, NY 10022

Prices and numbers subject to change without notice. Valid only in the U.S.
All books will be available 7/1/00. All orders subject to availability.

Visit our website at **www.kensingtonbooks.com**

Put a Little Romance in Your Life With
Fern Michaels

W9-AVS-249

Electrifying Praise for the Novels of

DAVID POYER

THE THREAT

"Plenty of action, plot twists. . . . frenetically paced . . . [an] engaging pot boiler." —*The Virginian-Pilot*

"Poyer remains the most thoughtful of the military-thriller set and a master of authentic detail." —*Kirkus Reviews*

"Poyer's forte is storytelling, and *The Threat* delivers a masterful tale that leaves the reader dazzled." —Steve Berry, *New York Times* bestselling author of *The Third Secret, The Templar Legacy,* and *The Romanov Prophecy*

"[Fans] of *The West Wing* . . . and political novels will enjoy the author's revealing portrayal of the backroom goings-on at the White House. . . . Recommended especially for fans of Robert Ludlum's political thrillers (although Poyer is a superior writer)." —*Booklist*

"Terrific suspense . . . perfect authenticity . . . powerful storytelling and compelling characters . . . David Poyer is our finest military novelist and *The Threat* is simply superb." —Ralph Peters, author of *New Glory* and *Never Quit the Fight*

"There's plenty of danger and gripping action to satisfy his legion of fans." —*Military.com*

MORE . . .

THE COMMAND

"[An] explosive climax . . . the reader takes a well-informed cruise on a U.S. destroyer. Poyer knows the ship intimately. Vivid descriptions cover everything from knee knockers to combat information center, radar to computers, wardroom to enlisted quarters. Battle scenes in particular come alive with authenticity . . . and all that, and more, is in this latest chapter of Commander Daniel Lenson's contentious career."
—Proceedings

"Poyer packs the story with both dense technical info and welcome local color. Unique Aisha merits a spinoff series."
—Kirkus Reviews

"Plows fearlessly—though with hair-raising effect on occasion—through today's stormy international and social seas... the salvos of nautical expertise also lend flavor and authenticity... the author provides believable insights into Muslim thinking... Poyer's genius for description impresses on page after page. The vividness of his scene-setting grabs you."
—Virginian-Pilot

"Lovers of procedural military fiction wait for David Poyer's next installment of the career of Dan Lenson."
—Roanoke Times

BLACK STORM

"No one writes gritty, realistic military fiction better than David Poyer. No one."
—Stephen Coonts

"A gripping, gritty novel that reads like the real thing. You're with the marines every step of the way. Poyer knows his stuff."
—Vince Flynn

"Exceptional . . . A straight-ahead adventure yarn, a frontal assault on the bestseller lists."   *—Boston Globe*

"A must-read . . . not since James Jones's *Thin Red Line* have readers experienced the gripping fear of what it's like to fight an enemy at close quarters . . . Poyer's research is impeccable, his characterization compelling, and the Iraqi Desert Storm scenario all too believable."
     —John J. Gobbell, author of *When Duty Whispers Low*

"I've been a David Poyer fan for over a decade, and his storytelling abilities—always first-rate—just get better and better. *Black Storm* is a timely, gripping, compelling yarn told by a master."   —Ralph Peters

"Absolutely riveting. David Poyer has captured the essence of what it is like on long-range patrols. His book is distinguished by quick action and continuing suspense that will keep the reader on edge until the very end."
     —Maj. Gen. H. W. Jenkins, United States Marine Corps (Ret.), Commander of the Marine Amphibious Forces in the Gulf War

"One of the strongest books in an outstanding series . . . the remarkably vivid portraits he draws of the variety of men and women drawn to serve their country merit high praise."   *—Booklist*

"One of the best . . . action fans will be rewarded."
     —Publishers Weekly

"Poyer's close attention to military practice and jargon will…suit those looking for accurate detail."
     —Newport News Press

"A thrilling and suspenseful fictional piece . . . you won't be able to put the book down."   *—Roanoke Times*

CHINA SEA

"Poyer's characters are as good as ever, and the action scenes lively."
—*Library Journal*

"The battle scenes are scintillating and satisfying . . . Poyer displays a fine sense of pace and plot." —*Publishers Weekly*

"Action, realism, and exotic locales . . . an absorbing, exciting, and thought-provoking experience." —*Chesapeake Life*

"An exciting story . . . The author's vivid descriptions of life on a ship show us not only the 'Anchors Aweigh' honor and dedication, but also the boiler-room sweat and frustrations of naval life."
—*Virginia Times*

"Poyer springs plenty of action on us . . . his narration and dialogue ring true."
—*Jacksonville Times-Union*

"Poyer brings the courage, honor, and commitment of sea duty to life in this vivid portrayal of life aboard a Knox-class frigate . . . the details describing life at sea are captivating as the action is continually rolling along, and each page pulls a new twist into the architecture of the story. In the end, the reader is treated to a fantastic battle that pulls each of the story threads together as a tightly woven yarn…the scales of intrigue, from murder, piracy, and battle to international diplomacy, capture the imagination with lifelike characters of heroes and villains most naval readers can link to real people met during their own world travels… *China Sea* belongs in the library of avid fiction readers."
—*Shipmate*

TOMAHAWK

"There can be no better writer of modern sea adventure around today."
                                                    —Clive Cussler

"An absorbing narrative that whips along at the author's usual firecracker pace . . . *Tomahawk* is very much a book of today."
                                                    —*Norfolk Virginian-Pilot*

"Poyer's characters are well-developed and frequently complex. His description is vivid. And he certainly knows the navy."
                                                    —*Jacksonville Times-Union*

"Sharp-edged . . . [a] tense tale."   —*Florida Times-Union*

"*Tomahawk* is a book of many levels. On the surface, it is a book of suspense—spies, secret missile strikes, murder . . . Dig a little further, and there is an officer who is troubled deeply by the effects of the weapons that he is developing."
                                                    —*Proceedings*

"The intrigues of bureaucracy have a ring of authenticity... if you're into military thrillers, you'll like this book."
                                                    —*Wisconsin State Journal*

"A gritty thriller."   —Microsoft Network

KOREA
STRAIT

David Poyer

St. Martin's Paperbacks

This is a work of fiction. All of the characters, organizations, and events portrayed in this novel are either products of the author's imagination or are used fictitiously.

KOREA STRAIT

Copyright © 2007 by David Poyer.
Excerpt from *The Weapon* copyright © 2008 by David Poyer.

Map by Paul J. Pugliese

For information address St. Martin's Press, 175 Fifth Avenue, New York, NY 10010.

Library of Congress Catalog Card Number: 2007032497

ISBN: 0-312-38412-2
EAN: 978-0-312-38412-8

Printed in the United States of America

St. Martin's Press hardcover edition / December 2007
St. Martin's Paperbacks edition / December 2008

St. Martin's Paperbacks are published by St. Martin's Press, 175 Fifth Avenue, New York, NY 10010.

10 9 8 7 6 5 4 3 2 1

To those who return, but not whole

ACKNOWLEDGMENTS

Ex nihilo nihil fit. For this book I owe thanks to Keith Adams, Barbara Breeden, Kyung "KC" Choi, Dick Enderly, Sean Gillespie, Adam Goldberger, Young P. Hong, Bill Hunteman, Chong Su Lim, Bill McQuade, Charles L. Owens, Patti Patterson, Laura Plattner, Warren L. Potts, Daniela Rapp, Sally Richardson, Matt Shear, James P. "Phil" Wisecup, and many others who preferred anonymity. Thanks also to the Eastern Shore Public Library; the Joint Staff College Library; Commander, Naval Surface Forces Atlantic; the Maritime Museum of San Diego; the Nimitz Library at the U.S. Naval Academy; Commander, Naval Forces Korea; and the officers and crew of ROKS *Chung Nam*, my shipmates some years ago, who bear little or no resemblance to their fictional counterparts created here—though we did go through two typhoons together, *that* much is true. My most grateful thanks to George Witte, editor of long standing; and to Lenore Hart, best friend and reality check.

The specifics of personalities, locations, and procedures in Korea, Japan, and Washington, and the units and theaters of operations described, are employed as the settings and materials of *fiction*, not as reportage of historical events. Some details have been altered to protect classified procedures.

As always, all errors and deficiencies are my own.

In every battle, the eye must first be deceived.

—Flavius Vegetius Renatus,
Epitoma Rei Militaris

RUSSIA

HOKKAIDO

•Vladivostok
•Nachodka

•Sapporo

•Hakodate

Hirosaki• •Aomori

•Akita

Sea of Japan
(Eastern Sea)

Sakata
Tsuruoka•

•Sendai

Sado

Nagaoka•

Oki-Shotō

Kanazawa•

JAPAN

Pacific
Ocean

Matsue
•Izumo

HONSHŪ

•Tottori

•Tokyo
Kawasaki• •
Yokohama

•Hamada
•Hiroshima

Kōbe•

•Kyoto
•Nagoya
•Ōsaka

Shizuoka
Hamamatsu

•Wakayama

SHIKOKU

The Eastern Sea
(Sea of Japan)
And Korea Strait

miles
0   200
0   kilometers   200

I
ROKN

1

Seoul, South Korea

The tall American moved stiffly, but his gray, observant eyes never stopped as he came down the jetway. He wore civvies: slacks and sport shirt and light Windbreaker. He wore a stainless-steel diver's watch, a heavy gold ring, and a wedding band with the traditional star and anchor. He carried a black briefcase, and a notebook computer was slung over his shoulder.

The huge concourse murmured with coughing and talking, the despairing screams of children, the human zoo-noise of thousands of other journeyers inchworming through baggage-dragging lines or perusing flickering monitors. The summer sun blazed through acres of vertical glass. Dan Lenson blotted his stinging eyes with the back of his hand. Every Korean on the 747 from Chicago had chain-smoked through the thirteen-hour flight. The concourse too milled with a blue murk through which people pushed, making the smoke eddy and whirl like the wakes of small boats in a crowded basin.

The customs agent looked up from the inspection table. He pointed to the sealed manila envelope in Dan's briefcase. "Take out, please."

The outer envelope was unmarked. It enclosed another, wrapping the contents in two layers of kraft paper. Dan had kept the locked briefcase wedged under his knees all the way from Washington, DC.

"Open, please."

"Sorry, can't. Classified material."

He dug out the letter. Headed with the Department of Defense seal, it designated Commander Daniel V. Lenson, USN, a command courier, authorized to receipt for and carry classified material up to and including Top Secret to Pusan, Korea. He snapped his russet official passport, his orders, and his Navy ID on top of it. The agent examined the letter and the ID. He compared the photo with Dan's face. Then reached for a stamp and nailed the envelope.

"Your computer. It is classified too?"

"That's right." Dan unzipped the carry case, opened it, and turned it to face him.

The agent didn't ask him to turn it on. Maybe he saw shielded Compaqs with encrypted comm capabilities and classified hard drives every day. He just stamped a paper label and stuck it to the case beside the red-and-white Top Secret stickers. "One thousand Republic of Korea won for domestic air tax. Two thousand for terminal fee. Three thousand won, please."

Dan handed over the limp colorful notes they'd issued him along with his travel orders. He got a receipt, closed and stowed the computer, the envelope, and the letter. Then headed out with the ebbing tide of jostling, chattering Asians, looking for the taxi desk.

Dan had spent most of his career at sea. Except during the Gulf War, when he'd been part of a Marine Recon team. He'd come out of that with a medal some thought was the only reason he was still in the service at all. Since then he'd commanded a destroyer in the Red Sea, then served on the White House staff. He'd hoped for another command after that, but things hadn't gone well in the East Wing.

Sitting in the cab, watching the buildings go by, all concrete and glass and balconies and all exactly the same, he remembered his last talk with "Nick" Niles.

He and Admiral Niles went way back. But Niles was no admirer. Quite the opposite. He'd leaned back and gotten that look he always had when they butted heads. "Why is it that wherever you go, Lenson, things go to shit? Carrying the football for the president—even I thought there was no way you could screw that up."

"I think I did all right, sir. The assassination attempt failed."

The flag officer's expression made it clear what he thought about that outcome. No president in living memory was so loathed by the armed services as the one whose life Dan had managed, at the last moment, to save. But all Niles said was, "Who do you think was behind it?" Then swiveled his chair and looked out his window at tombstones on a green hillside.

Dan had no doubt Niles knew. The guy was too smart, too well connected, not to. No, what he wanted was to find out how much Dan knew.

So Dan told him.

When Niles swung back, his heavy face was blank as polished onyx. "I don't believe it. To think that . . . impossible. Not in this country."

"Then why'd General Stahl resign?"

"Health reasons. Like the press release said."

"I see. And the others?"

Niles waved it away. "Doesn't matter. That's all gonna get settled behind closed doors. Way above both our pay grades, Lenson.

"Question remains: What do we do with you? How about putting in your letter? That'd be the best thing. Like I been telling you for a while now. There's your spine—they tell me you fucked that up on *Horn*. And you didn't do it any favors jumpin' out of that chopper either. Medical retirement. Full base salary. I know a guy over at Battelle. You can double-dip, make a good living—"

"If the Navy wants to fire me, Admiral, so be it. But I'm not resigning."

"So we put you on the shelf. Then you go public about the stuff you've been involved in. . . ."

"I know how to keep quiet, sir. Most of it, no one'd believe, anyway."

"True . . . I guess." Niles sucked his teeth. Grimaced, in neither a smile nor a frown. Then leaned, and pushed the jar of Atomic Fireballs that was always on his desk forward an inch. "Want one?"

"No, thanks."

"How's Blair takin' all this?"

"She says however it turns out, she's on my side."

"Well, if you're so fucking determined to stay in, maybe the best thing's for you to drop out of sight. Submerge."

"You're punishing me. For what?"

Niles's glance met his. "We're not *punishing* you. We're trying to keep you alive," he said, very softly.

"What? I didn't—"

"I'm not gonna say it again, or address why. We're just gonna cut you orders someplace past the orbit of Pluto. And you're going to go, and I won't hear a peep until I ask for one."

"If you want me out of DC, send me back to sea. Give me another ship."

"*That* ain't gonna happen. Ever, if I have anything to say about it." They stared at each other, two wills locked. The admiral added at last, "But if you want to go back to sea— ever heard of TAG?"

Dan nodded. The Tactical Analysis Group was the Navy's think tank, gaming and testing the three-dimensional tactical doctrine the fleet needed to fight at sea. Every line officer studied the naval warfare publications it produced.

"I'm gonna batten you down there till this blows over. That's as far from the Pentagon as we can get you without getting NASA involved. Maybe you'll even do us some good this time."

Dan clenched his fists in his lap. Niles had been riding his ass for years. He was almost used to it. But at least he'd be back with the Navy. The blackshoes and the white hats, whose sacrifices hardly ever made the papers. Not Beltway Commandos like Niles and his ilk.

He was getting up when Niles added, "Just do me one fucking favor, Lenson. Wherever you go next?"

"What's that, sir?"

"Try to keep everybody *alive* this time. All right?"

Dan stopped cold. He couldn't help baring his teeth. "You bastard. Do you think I wanted that, I've *ever* wanted any of it?"

"But it keeps happening. Doesn't it? You're making a name, all right. As a dangerous guy to be around. Hear me? *Don't* let it happen again."

It had been all he could do to stand rigid until Niles had flicked his fingers, that familiar grimace of bored disgust printed across his broad dark face like a customs inspector's stamp that said: REJECTED. "Now get the hell out of my office. And if I ever see you again, Commander, believe me, it'll be too fucking soon."

The driver braked with a screech of worn linings. Koreans boiled solid in the crosswalks. Fuck Niles, Dan told himself. Fuck Washington and everything that had happened there, ever. It had all been total shit, except for Blair. The taxi jerked forward and nudged an old woman, who turned on them. The driver wound down his window and they began berating each other.

He remembered another ride in a backseat, through wartime central Europe. And what a young Croatian had told him before she was raped and murdered.

If you run, you hit the bullet.

If you walk, the bullet hits you.

He pushed memories away and stared out as another overpass darkened the sky. The capital of the fastest-growing country in Asia was cupped by rugged mountains black as oil-smoke. Seoul looked as if it had been built by concrete contractors with Xerox machines. The streets were fronted with computer and fast-food stores with Western trademarks, and utterly thronged. The old folks were small and slight, but the young grew like weeds. Tall pale girls in cork platform shoes carried lavender parasols against the glaring July sun. Office apparatchiks hurried between them in gray suits and cropped black hair. Street vendors hawked bananas and noodles.

The Seoul Plaza was gleaming new, on a wide, newly paved street. He checked in, and asked if they had a guest named Henrickson.

He found his guys in the bar, in slacks and sport shirts not too different from his own. "One of you Dr. Montgomery Henrickson?" Dan asked.

Slightly built, almost boy-sized, Henrickson had a high forehead, a dark saggy mustache like a Civil War colonel's, and hair too long to be regulation. Which computed, since he was one of TAG's civilian staff. A PhD in operations analysis, he'd be either Dan's boss or his second in command—what little instruction Dan had gotten hadn't been clear on the exact relationship. Dan introduced himself and they shook hands.

"Just call me Monty. Not 'Doctor,' okay? Good to see you, Commander. Fast flight?"

"It was okay."

The others had gotten to their feet, making it obvious they were either current or ex-military. Henrickson did the honors. "These are all the guys on Team Bravo, except for Captain O'Quinn. Rit Carpenter, our sonar guy. Ex-bubblehead—I mean, submariner."

"I know what 'bubblehead' means. Dan Lenson, Rit."

"Hiya, Commander." A balding, muscular, thirtysomething, stocky but not pudgy, hairy arms bulging under a Kirin T-shirt, a firm brisk grip.

"Let's just go by first names," Dan said. He was used to it from the White House staff, and since they were all sorts—active, retired, civilian—it'd work to build the team. "Call me Dan. At least out of the office."

Donnie Wenck was a communications technician, gangly, younger than the others, redheaded, shyly enthusiastic. His hand was soft and wet-cold from the beer he'd just set down. "South Carolina, right?" Dan asked, catching a familiar accent.

"Yes sir—I mean, Dan."

Henrickson pointed with his head. "And this is Teddy

Oberg. Teddy's kind of our all-around guy. Pretty much handles himself in just about any situation."

Oberg looked reasonably fit. His dirty-blond hair was tied back. His bleached blue eyes were steady on Dan's. He wore jeans and running shoes. "You a runner, Teddy?"

"Could say that, Dan."

"Well, maybe we'll get a jog in. Good to meet you all."

Henrickson snagged the waitress, a tired-looking woman with heavily made-up pockmarks, who asked if he wanted a beer. Dan ordered a Coke, then sat back and looked them over as he sipped it, fighting jet lag and the yearning for sleep. Counting his upbrief at TAG and then the flight, he hadn't slept for fifty hours.

They looked like average American guy types, but a TAG team was a highly skilled bag of active-duty officers, senior enlisted, civilian analysts, and the occasional reservist. Two teams, Alfa and Bravo, took turns deploying from the home base in Virginia.

Team Bravo was in Korea to conduct SATYRE 17—Surface Antisubmarine Tactical Readiness Evaluation, with the *Y* just to make a cool acronym. SATYREs were huge multinational exercises. Surface ships, subs, and maritime air from the U.S., the Republic of Korea, Japan, and Australia would be involved, operating first separately and then together. The first week would be individual exercises, tuning sonars and sharpening antisubmarine, maneuvering, and communications skills. The second week would build teams, several surface and air units combining against one submarine. Phase Three would be a full-scale coordinated exercise in the Sea of Japan, Red versus Blue. Team Bravo would manage and monitor the play, deconflict any dangerous situations, make sure tactical and environmental data got recorded throughout the exercise, and take the results home for evaluation.

Dan's new commanding officer back in Little Creek had made it clear none of them were to take sides or even express an opinion in the field. He'd said the ships they rode would perceive them as "graders." But they weren't, not really. No one could tell who'd "won" even the simplest ship-on-sub play until all the data was laid out on the big light tables. Even then, it would take months of analysis before useful guidance emerged.

"ASW's still an art, not a science," Captain Todd Mullaly had said. "Always has been, maybe always will be. Too many variables. What doesn't work will get them killed if there's a real torpedo in the water. What does work, we'll put out there for the COs to think about. Who 'wins' a SATYRE isn't important. The data is. That's your job, to make sure all your track information, bathymetry, and tactical decisions get into the logs and tapes. Aside from that, depend on your guys. If they weren't good, they wouldn't be at TAG."

Carpenter said, not meeting Dan's eyes, "So . . . somebody said you had *Horn*."

"That's right." He waited for the rest of the interrogation.

"With the girls on it?"

"That's right." Along with everything else, *Horn* had been the first male-female integrated warship.

They exchanged glances. Carpenter said, "So, you must have stories. Lot of hanky-panky going on, I bet."

"Some, yeah—but not as much as you'd think. One of those 'girls' died saving her shipmates. I took her Silver Star down to New Orleans and gave it to her three-year-old. It won't replace her mom . . . but it was all I could do for her."

They looked away, and he tried to relax. They hadn't meant anything by it. They were just old-line Navy and probably would never get used to women doing guys' jobs.

Wenck said, "Y'all hit some kind of old drifting mine, right?"

"Something like that." That was the cover story.

"Guess you did a lot of antisub ops."

"The usual. Predeployment workup. JTFEX. But then mostly MIO in the Red Sea and Gulf."

"Maritime intercept. Boarding and search." Henrickson sounded doubtful. "Any shallow-water ASW?"

"Not too much on that deployment. But I've done it on previous tours. The Arctic, North Atlantic, the Med, the Gulf."

"How about here in WestPac?"

"I've operated in the South China Sea. A multinational antipirate task force."

"Any ASW there?" Henrickson said casually.

"Look, I get the picture. You're asking if I've got the level of antisubmarine expertise you need in the guy who's basically going to be conducting the exercise."

"What? No, we weren't—"

"Sure you were. So I'll tell you. I've had a solid grounding in destroyer ASW. I know ops analysis. I'll learn what else I need to fast as I can. But yeah, this is my first time out with a TAG team, so let me know if I'm headed for shoal water. They tell me you're the best in the business or you wouldn't be where you are. So I'm going to count on that.

"But right now, I'm going to get my head down for a few hours."

Dan noticed Wenck glancing apprehensively behind and above him. He twisted to see a somber-looking, fiftyish white man with a nose like Richard Nixon's and a scowl not too different either standing behind him, arms folded, listening.

"And here's Captain Joe O'Quinn," Henricksen said.

"Mister," O'Quinn said, impassive. Correcting him, not angrily, just as a matter of fact.

"Joe, nice to meet you," Dan said. The older man tilted his head and smiled faintly, looking him up and down.

Henrickson cleared his throat and studied his watch. "Uh— Dan—well, I know you're short on sleep, but you might want to grab a quick shower instead. Maybe a shave. And get a uniform on. We've got the kickoff meeting over at CNFK at two."

CNFK—Commander, U.S. Naval Forces, Korea—was at Yongsan Army Garrison, surrounded by the city, like Central Park, Dan thought. A mix of brick two-stories dating from the Japanese occupation, according to Henrickson, and 1950s-era U.S. Army prefab housing and rusting Quonsets. The usual anchors, painted the usual gloss black, stood outside the naval headquarters, along with a bronze of a medieval

Korean warrior. The conference room was upstairs, through a combination-keyed door. As Dan's group trooped in, Asians and Americans were helping themselves to buns and coffee at a side table. Conversation buzzed in various languages. Dan, in short-sleeved khakis, laid his combination cap on a table that already held those of several services, of several nations.

"Commander Lenson? Hi, I'm Dick Shappell. Got the button for the SATYRE."

Shappell was in khakis like Dan, but with aviator's wings. His name tag had the COMUSFORKOREA staff insignia: the Korean flag, eagle, and crossed anchors, and his name was spelled out in Hangul under the Roman lettering. He blinked at the pale blue and white stars of Dan's topmost ribbon. When he spoke again his tone was less brash. "Oh—Lenson! It sounded familiar when I read the clearance message, but I only just now—hell, it's a real honor meeting you. Sir. Look"—he glanced at the wall clock—"I'm gonna kick off with the welcome, since the big boss is out of town just now, but I want you to meet a couple people first. Hey, Commodore!"

A stocky Korean in what looked very much like U.S. Navy khakis, but with different ribbons and rank insignia—three little silver flowers—turned from the side table. He was bigger than the other Koreans but still shorter than Dan. He wore heavy, square-framed, PhotoGray glasses. A black mole grew beside his left eye. A leather tag with crossed silver torches inside an anchor hung from his breast pocket. He had big hands, big fingers, which were just now turning a pack of cigarettes over and over.

"Commodore, Commander Lenson here's in charge of the Taggers. He'll be riding with you on the exercise. Dan, this is Commodore Jung—first name Min Jun—commander, Antisubmarine Squadron 51, Republic of Korea Navy."

One of the oversized hands mashed Dan's as heavy-lidded eyes noted everything about him. They too snagged on the Congressional. "Hi, fella," Jung said. He smelled of mentholated tobacco and English Leather.

"Commodore. An honor."

The Korean shook a cigarette out of the pack. They had silver filter tips. Dan said thanks, no.

"Ship driver," Jung noted, looking at him still as he fit the cigarette into an ivory-colored holder and lit it with a gold Zippo engraved with a seal Dan didn't recognize. "Annapolis ring. And some pretty impressive experience, if I'm reading your ribbon bar right." His English was almost perfect, with a touch, Dan guessed, of California casual.

"Guilty."

"First time on the peninsula? Or you been with us before?"

"First time here, sir."

"Well, we'll try to treat you right. Where are you in from, Dan?"

"Just joined the TAG group. Last assignment was in DC."

"Where?"

"Well . . . the White House military staff." He wondered if he should mention that, but no one had told him not to.

Jung smiled so radiantly that the mole almost vanished. "Excellent! They've sent us their best." He turned to a willowy younger man who'd come up quietly behind him, and spoke rapidly in Korean. The younger raised an eyebrow, blinking at Dan. Jung gestured to him. "Commander Hwang, my chief of staff. Commander Lenson."

They shook hands too, Hwang's palm lying limp in Dan's. The chief of staff smiled almost fawningly, but said only, "I am pleased to meet you, Commander."

The lights flickered off, then back on. Shappell turned from the switch. Conversations cut off in midsentence. Men replenished their coffee cups, headed for seats.

The first PowerPoint slide went up, a yeoman began doling out briefing packages, and Dan pulled his new PDA out and began trying to figure out how to make notes with it.

Shappell spoke more slowly than Pentagon briefing standard, Dan guessed to let the foreign participants keep up. After the usual cover slides, he got down to business. Dan checked that hard copies of the presentation were in the briefing package. That'd save a lot of note taking.

Shappell kicked off by defining SATYRE 17 as part of a joint ROK and U.S. command post exercise called Ulchi Focus Lens, an annual joint and combined simulation-supported CPX that, as he put it, "trained Combined Forces Command personnel and major component, subordinate, and augmenting staffs using state-of-the-art wargaming computer simulations and support infrastructures."

The participants were from four countries: ROKN, USN, the Royal Australian Navy, and the Japanese Maritime Self-Defense Force. The chain of command went from CFC—Combined Forces Command, successor to the old UN Command Korea—to CINCROKFLT. Thence to Fifth Flotilla, based in Chinhae, down to the exercise level. Dan noted that the overall OTC, officer in tactical command, would be Korean, the commodore of Antisubmarine Squadron 51. In other words, the three-flower he'd just met, Commodore Jung.

The next slide showed the units assigned:

COMDESRON 15 (US)—*McCain, Cushing, Vandegrift*
COMASWRON 51 (ROK),—*Kim Chon, Dae Jon,*
      Chung Nam, Mok Po
Darwin, Torrens (Australian)
Japanese ASW air
Salt Lake City, San Francisco (USN, subs)
Chang Bo Go (ROK 209, sub)

Dan leaned back and tuned out for a while. In fact he almost fell asleep. He roused himself when he heard weather mentioned, and a female lieutenant commander took the stand. "Oooh ah," Carpenter muttered, louder than he needed to. "Why don't you put some lipstick around my dipstick?"

Her slide showed an immense sea, six hundred miles across at its widest point. It was bounded on the west by Korea, on the east and south by the great embryo-curved main island of Japan, and on the north by North Korea and Russia. The south access was Tsushima Strait, where nearly a hundred years before, a Russian admiral had come to grief after sailing halfway round the world. The northern was remote, icy La Pérouse Strait. She said briskly, "Climatology. It's going to be iffy out there, more than usually unsettled. For Phase One, participants can expect wind from the south-southwest at six to ten knots, seas three to four feet, and about sixty percent overcast. Fog the majority of the time, with visibility less than four miles twenty-five percent of the time at sea level. Remember the current in the op area will be about one point five knots set to the northeast."

Dan looked at the faces listening, brown, white, and yellow. All looked attentive, but how many spoke enough English to follow this? All comms for SATYRE 17 would be in English. He'd have to make them as transparent as possible.

Next up was a Korean. He had charts and sound-propagation tracings. A sonar guy. Dan rubbed his face, fighting to focus. He'd have to know all this cold once things started rolling. But the accent was tough to get through, *r*'s instead of *l*'s, and he wasn't sure he was getting it all. Apparently passive sonar ranges—"passive" meant sophisticated and enhanced listening only, without sending out pings—were going to be less than a thousand yards for hull-mounted sonars, with less than three kiloyards for direct path. The man mumbled, speaking into his papers. Dan got something like "With the soft sand bottom, bottom bounce mode wir be unreriable. Bathythermograph shows a negative gradient and no rayer. There wir be much fishing activity."

A hefty, six-foot-plus American captain in trop whites with chubby cheeks and short blond hair broke into the presentation. His name tag read LEAKHAM. "How about biologics?"

"Biologics" were noise from biological sources, mainly shrimp, which made a hell of a racket for so small a creature. The Korean bobbed his head. "Very good question, sir. There wir be high biorogics and high revelberation."

Carpenter leaned and muttered, "Meaning: Conditions are gonna be shit."

Henrickson: "And if the wind kicks up it'll be even worse."

Dan nodded. Terrible conditions to hunt submarines in. On the other hand, if there was no layer, a sub couldn't hide under it. And high environmental noise tended to blind a submarine. Sound was their only window on their surroundings, unless they wanted to risk poking up a scope or radar head. The moment they did a hunter could pick them up, visually, by radar, or by electronic surveillance. "It might work to our advantage," he whispered.

"Yeah . . . or not."

Shappell took the floor again. "The officer in tactical command. Commodore Jung."

The stocky Korean stood fiddling with the ivory holder a moment, looking around. Then handed it to his chief of staff with a lordly gesture, and locked his fingers behind him.

"Welcome to Korea, those new to our waters. First let me say we value having you by our side, both to teach, and to learn. Korea is very grateful for her allies. If I can ever show how much in some way, please let me know."

Once again Dan noticed how colloquial his speech was. Jung wasn't speaking from notes. He was just winging it. The guy had to be thinking in English. The chief of staff handed the holder back reloaded with a fresh filter tip. Jung bent it to the lighter, took a reflective drag, spoke with exhaled smoke.

"You will learn many new things in what *others* call the Sea of Japan. To us it is our Tong Hae: the Eastern Sea. Our people have sailed it from time immemorial, and on it—a bit to the south, in the Korea Strait—our great admiral Yi Sun-shin defeated his country's invaders through boldness and innovation.

"Boldness and innovation—we too must discover these virtues within ourselves during the next few weeks.

"Three points I wish all to bear in mind. First, all maneuvers must be made safely. We will not lose or injure a single man. We will not risk damage to ships or aircraft. That is our primary operational concern.

"Second, recall that strategy is driven by water conditions. As Mr. Ku said, water and sonar conditions will be tough. In Phase One, all sensors and teams must be tuned to the maximum. Once we begin free play, all assets will have to be deployed with maximum efficiency.

"Third: We've found the progressive barrier strategy works best in the shallow, noisy Tong Hae, especially near the salient that thrusts out from the coast between Kangnung and Changgi-Ap. Therefore my intent at this moment is to implement a succession of barriers, once we have identified and localized the threat and the *Schwerpunkt.*"

"The guy reads Clausewitz," Henrickson whispered. Dan give him a lifted eyebrow, not sure who was surprising him more, Jung or his own second in command—if he *was* second in command. The Korean commodore seemed to be on the ball. Which would, if true, be a welcome change from the last foreign officer Dan had worked closely with, an arrogant and dangerous idiot from the Pakistani Navy.

"Our motto will be *katchi kapshida* . . . we march ahead together. All right, any other comments or questions?" Jung finished.

Dan jabbed up a hand and stood at Jung's smile. "Commodore, if I may . . . Dan Lenson, heading up the TAG team. I'd like to say a few words about the data-collection requirements of this exercise."

A rain-mist obscured the hills. Dan zipped up the complimentary black portfolio, etched with the ROKN insignia, that the chief of staff, Hwang, had handed him as the briefing broke up. "So, what about it?" he asked his guys. "Pretty standard?"

Wenck said, "Yep. Pretty standard, sir, I'd say."

"Anything I should have picked up on that I didn't?"

"The ass on that tea girl," Carpenter said, leering. Dan noticed Rit didn't let an opportunity pass to crack a suggestive remark. It wasn't PC, and it wasn't current Navy policy, either. But a good many sailors, particularly those with a certain number of years in, spoke the same way, at least in male company. What Dan found intriguing was the sideways glance O'Quinn gave him. Disgust? Interesting.

"Just that those sonar ranges are awful short," Henrickson said. "That's going to make this whole exercise tough. Maybe even dangerous."

Dan said, "How dangerous?"

"You'll see," Henrickson said.

O'Quinn said, not looking at either of them, "He means that as the ranges close down, the risk of collision goes up. Pretty much a reciprocal relationship."

An awkward silence. Dan wondered why. He was missing something. But what?

"And that weather briefing sucked," Wenck added.

"Yeah, I'd like to have her suck my—"

"Give it a rest, Rit," Dan told him. "Donnie, you were saying—"

"She didn't mention the tropical depressions. Maybe it's early in the season, but I've never been here when wasn't at least a couple storms hanging around the Philippines. If they power up and head west they'll hook right over where we're gonna be operating."

Dan nodded. "So what now?" he asked Henrickson.

But Carpenter answered. "What now? Shit, sir, we're all gonna head on over to Itaewon. Start at the Rambunctious and slam down some brewskis. Then, who knows. The night, she is young. Like those sweet little brown-sugar mamasans." He smacked his lips. "You comin' with us? What happens in Korea, stays in Korea."

"Thanks, but I'm going back to the hotel and crawl into this op order."

"Gotta break loose, Skipper. We're gonna be out at sea next three weeks. No beer, no nookie."

He was tempted, but grinned and shook his head. "Next time—okay? The newbie's got to study up. You guys have one for me. Let's get together at zero-eight for breakfast and talk over the ship assignments, and then—what time's the flight to Pusan?"

They said noon. He shook hands, slapped backs, and moved off.

Then he turned back and beckoned to Henrickson. The analyst peeled off, yelling to the others to wait. "Yeah?"

Dan lowered his voice and turned away from the street. "Two questions, Monty. One: who's in charge of this outfit?"

"Which outfit?"

"Us. TAG Bravo. Is it you or me?"

"You're the one with the silver oak leaves."

"You're the one with the doctorate."

Henrickson snapped his head back and forth. "Uh-uh. We're under orders. TAG works looser back in the building, more collegial, but when we're on the road, it's all military. Next question?"

"Okay, that clears things up. Next is, what's the story on this O'Quinn character? Why do Rit and Donnie call him 'Captain'?"

"Because he's a captain." He caught Dan's puzzled frown; if O'Quinn was a captain, why was a commander in charge of the team? "A *retired* captain."

"Oh. Okay . . . retired. I guess that makes sense. But why do I get the feeling . . . ?"

Henrickson lowered his voice. "I figured everybody knew."

"I just got here."

"Remember the *Buchanan*?"

He searched his memory. A guided-missile cruiser, the class before Aegis and the Ticonderogas. Hadn't there been an accident . . . ? "The collision. The guys who were below—"

"Right. The engine room, main space was flooding. Joe was in command. And he lost it. Ordered the hull techs to weld a hatch shut. Saved the ship, but . . . left six guys on the wrong side of the hatch. He wasn't going anyplace after that. Resigned after the court of inquiry. Lost his wife too. I don't know the story behind that part, but she's history."

"Holy smoke." Dan glanced O'Quinn's way. The man stood alone, hands in his pockets, cigarette dangling from his lip as he studied the mist-wreathed hills. "So what's he doing here?"

"Oh, he knows his stuff. Works for a civilian contractor now. But if we ever get in a tight spot . . ."

Dan could finish that sentence: don't trust him not to weld the hatch shut on you.

"Anyway, so long."

"So long, Monty. See you guys in the a.m."

The hotel phone's electronic cheep sounded so much like the one that had been in USS *Thomas W. Horn*'s at-sea cabin that in the split second before he was awake he relived the whole explosion, the damage, their daylong fight to keep her from going down that sunny afternoon off the Israeli coast. By the time he reoriented and got his eyes locked on the red light that was the only illumination in the darkened room, his heart was pounding and he was bathed in sweat. His upper spine felt as if someone had mauled a log splitter into it.

"Lenson," he snapped.

"Hey, Dan? Dick Shappell. With CNFK?" He sounded taken aback at Dan's tone. "Sorry to get you up."

"Yeah. No problem. What—what is it?"

"Like I said, sorry to wake you. But Fifth Flotilla, down in Chinhae, cornered something interesting. Thirty miles off Sokch'o. That's—you probably wouldn't know—that's south of the DMZ, on the east coast."

"Yeah? Sokch'o." He cleared his throat, straining to see what time it was. He couldn't make out his watch, but when he skated the drapes open it was dark outside except for the dirty rose sky, the endless blue-white glitter of city lights. "They cornered something interesting? What?"

Shappell hesitated, as if unsure what to say over an open line. "Something that doesn't belong there. For some reason—and believe me, doesn't happen often—our good buddies and bosom pals the Koreans want us around when they bring it up. Want to go? Captain Owens thought you might."

Dan didn't know who Captain Owens was, or why he thought he'd want to see whatever this was. But he was already turning on the light, reaching for his pants as he tucked the phone in the crook of his shoulder. "I guess. Okay. Khakis all right?"

"Khakis are fine. And you don't need to shave, just be down in front of the entrance in about a hundred and twenty seconds. Tell your guys you're with me. And if you've got a camera, bring it. On the off chance."

"Be right down," he said, sticking his feet into his Corfams and pulling on his shirt at the same time. Thirty seconds later the door closed behind him.

2

The smooth-surfaced sea heaved under a cloudless araman-
thine sky. It was just before dawn. There was no wind. Not
a ripple marred the ever-changing, everlasting interface
between water and air. But it rose slowly, then fell away
along the worn steel of the hull, all but imperceptibly, as if
the sea were breathing.

One to two-foot swells at most, Dan judged, leaning over
the side to gaze into bottomless turquoise. Every hundred
feet or so a wave broke with a quiet splatter. It left a patch of
ivory lace rocking, slowly melting, till the clear blue welled
up again. Small silvery fish hovered in the hull-shadow, fluid
rippling commas poised tensely between quiescence and
alarm.

Beside him Major Zach Carmichael, U.S. Army, who was
beyond any reasonable doubt Defense Intelligence, was
telling him about the Maritime Department of the North Korean Reconnaissance Bureau. "That's who's most likely running it. The most elite of all NK Special Forces. Disciplined.
Tough. Sworn never to surrender. They caught one before, in
a fishing net. When they got it to the surface they were all
dead."

"Drowned? Hull breach?"

"Shot each other, far as we can tell. Last one used a
grenade." Carmichael sounded as if he admired this.

On the flight out, on an ROK helo, he'd looked down to

see the lights of fishing boats setting out, nodding their way toward their salty crop-fields from the flickering yellow lights of hamlets that clung to blackened zinc cliffs. Rocky islets dotted the coast. As the sun rose the pilot pointed out North Korea in the distance. Dan gazed out on a hazy, featureless sweep that gave no hint that anything human had ever existed. Save, far away, the contrail of a MiG patrolling the Northern Limiting Line, the naval extension of the DMZ out to sea.

They'd droned out till the land fell back and vanished in a nebulous mercury blurring. Gradually a ship emerged from the rosy haze. From her anachronistic, towering masts, her dented gray sides, she'd slid down some stateside shipway during World War II. They'd circled, the copilot barking into his throat mike in abrupt Korean, then moved over the bluff bow. He'd dangled, rotating on a sling, till Koreans crouched against the rotorblast reached up, receiving them like gifts from heaven. First Dan, then Shappell, then Carmichael.

Now they stood aft on the main deck, looking out on a wide rounded counter. The flat stern was almost featureless except for two large centerline hatches, a towing chock, a stanchion with the stern light, and bitts spotted to port and starboard. The black steel underfoot was scarred and dented with decades of dragged chains and dropped shackles. So many layers of old paint scabbed it, it looked like the Black Hills seen from above. A canvas awning reminded Dan of *The Sand Pebbles*. But wherever she'd been built, she was Korean now. They swarmed over the fantail. The divers, just now lifting their helmets above a gently heaving froth of bubbles, slowly making their way to a rigged-out platform and boat-ladder, were Korean too. She was at diving stations, with hoses and lines flemished out across the deck. Tanks, weight belts, suits, regulators, were lashed to the gunwales or laid out on canvas. Beyond them, out on the horizon, prowled the low wolf-gray silhouette of a destroyer.

"She was once USS ship," a junior officer told them. "USS *Grasp*. Now *Chung Wan*."

"So what exactly you people got down there?" Carmichael asked him. He fiddled with the Nikon around his neck, glancing at the divers clambering up the ladder.

"Enemy submarine," the ensign said.

Shappell muttered, "Aha." Carmichael focused his telephoto and snapped a couple frames of the divers.

"How deep?" Dan asked. The guy cocked his head, considering, then called to a squat Korean in slacks and a blue Windbreaker. His face was leathery, like that of an old tortoise.

"Kim Baksa nim!"

"Ke miguk sa ram del yi yo? Yi chok ue ro de rigo o si yo."

Dan bowed and shook hands. The man in the Windbreaker said he was Dr. Kim, in charge of the salvage operation. Carmichael asked again what they had.

"It appears to be a Sang-o," Kim said, choosing each word. "Which means 'Shark.' It is most likely either embarking on or returning from a reconnaissance mission. They come out of Toejo-Dong, and transit south across the Tongjoson-man. Sometimes they attempt to land agents."

"How'd you find it?"

"It broached, we are not sure why. Perhaps an accident. We did not detect it until then. Our units fired on it. Then it either sank, or was scuttled when they realized we had detected them."

"Wicked," Carmichael said. He advanced the film and tried for a picture of the Korean, but at the last moment the doctor turned away.

Dan had memorized everything the U.S. Navy knew about the Sang-os, which wasn't much. The North Korean People's Navy operated three classes of submarines. Sharks were the middle rung, small diesel-electrics built in-country to a native design at the Nampo or Wonsan shipyards. Naval Intelligence estimated their operational depth between three hundred and four hundred feet. They carried a crew of twenty with torpedo and mining capabilities. Their max speed was about nine knots at snorkel depth. They came in two variants, attack and infiltration. Even that was a guess . . . which meant it would be a coup to get their hands on one, or even get a close look.

Carmichael said, "Is the crew aboard?"

Dan, at the same monent: "How deep is it?"

Kim shouted a question to the divers. One shouted up, his answer cut off by a sea that jostled him into the ladder. The doctor turned back. "The crew is dead. The sub is lying on the bottom of sand thirty-five meters down. The salvage divers have blown one compartment clear."

"About a hundred and ten feet," Dan said. "Air range."

Kim glanced at him. "You are a diver?"

"I sport dive. Scuba."

"You have done this in wrecks?"

"Wrecks? Sure. Now and then."

"Then, of course, you will want to see for yourself. If you are willing."

The Korean held his gaze, and Dan realized it wasn't an invitation; he was being dared. "Sure," he said. "Suit me up. I'll take a look."

Carmichael and Shappell traded glances. "Hey now," said the commander. "I don't think you need to go down there yourself—"

But the Korean was smiling, and Dan very much wanted to have the first U.S. look at a Sang-o class sub, if that was what it was. He glanced over the side again, then at the sun, then off to where the destroyer hovered. Storing the information, in case he should need it.

"All right then," said the Korean. He called to one of the tenders, who came over, running a critical eye up Dan's height. "He will help you suit up."

The water was very cold. The wet suit was heavy black rubber, the biggest they had aboard, but still too tight, which wasn't good; he'd take some serious heat loss by the end of the dive.

Twenty feet down, he clung to the thick yellowing braided nylon of the descent line, sucking gas with a hissing click. His mouth was already parched and the moistureless gas didn't help. What the fuck had he gotten into? He gazed up at the black wedge of the salvage ship's stern, the motionless, cruel-looking screws. Golden rays flickered around it. They slid through the blue down into an inky twilight that yawned beneath his slowly kicking fins. The fish he'd watched from above undulated slowly between him and the light.

Dropping his gaze, he finned himself horizontal and slowly pivoted around the line, searching the sea to the accelerated thud of his heart. He was encased in light-filled sapphire, surrounded by a circular wall of blue-gray haze. About thirty yards visibility. No sharks yet. Some yards away red and black hoses and safety lines dropped away into the black, losing their color as they receded from the sun. The helmet divers were working down there. His free hand roved over the regulator, checked his mask, tested the buckle of his weight belt. The gear wasn't that different from what he was used to. Solid quality, but not exactly the latest technology.

A plunge of bubbles, and his partner fell through the silvery rocking roof. A pudgy fellow who'd made comic faces when they told him Dan would be going down with him. He hovered, adjusting his buoyancy, then jackknifed and headed down, jabbing a questioning finger to his head.

Dan pointed to his own ears and nodded. He thumbed the exhaust button of his buoyancy compensator and felt himself go from weightless to heavy.

He kept his right hand out, letting the line drag through it as they dropped into steadily darkening blue. Flecks of organic matter drove past them like a slow snowstorm. Pain jabbed inside his head. He grabbed his nose through the mask and cleared his ears. Again.

He grinned around the regulator, remembering Shappell's warning that he shouldn't go. They were here to observe, not participate. And the naked envy on the intel officer's face.

But he'd never enjoyed standing around and watching. And the Koreans who suited him up had slapped his back, grinning and nodding. These people operated on face. And strapping on a tank with them had earned him some.

He checked the depth, then his Seiko. Sixty feet. The

light from above was dimming away. He looked down, but saw only blackness. His partner was swimming down the line headfirst, fins kicking turbulence toward him. A back-turned mask flashed the last of the sunlight. Dan was content to drop slowly, staying vertical. He'd check out the hull, maybe swim along it, then come up. Punch his ticket and surface.

Was he being foolish? Stepping beyond what a full commander ought to be doing? To hell with it. He could push paper anytime. Carmichael wanted a report, didn't he?

Eighty feet, and sinking faster as the pressure squeezed the buoyancy out of vest and suit. His stay time would be only fifteen minutes at 110 feet. Longer than that would require decompression stops. He'd have to pay attention. That deep you could get fuzzy, disoriented—the famous rapture of the deep. He reminded himself he was short on sleep, and the cold wouldn't help. He'd better stay on the conservative side of the dive tables.

When he looked down again the sub lay below him. It was obscured by the dim and the blowing silt, but the surprise stopped his breath for a moment before the hiss and click resumed. The descent line was gray now, all yellow sucked away in the dim light. It was tied off on what looked like a rudder pivot. The after body was smoothly curved. The craft lay stern, or perhaps bow—he couldn't quite tell yet—down in soft-looking brown muddy sand.

He dropped a few more feet in the bubbling silence and realized he was looking at the stern. Then the whole picture, dim and fragmentary as it was, snapped into place. The craft was much smaller than he'd expected. It was dead black, dotted here and there with the pale flakes of barnacles. The tail planes and rudder were rigged with struts. He wondered why. Then realized they were antifouling guards, to keep fishing nets or mine cables out of the prop.

A ridge ran the length of the hull, with port-and-starboard swellings that had to be sidesaddle ballast tanks. He couldn't see the bow, but a small sail, or conning tower, loomed dimly through the murk. It was denser down here, blowing past at the rate, he remembered from the briefing, of the knot and a half's worth of slow massive current that was hanging him out along the descent line like a slowly flapping flag. He noted carefully that the sub lay crosscurrent. He didn't want to let go of this line and not know which way led back.

His dive buddy had already released it. He was finning forward just above the hull, toward a silvery gush. The bubbles rushed wavering up like a silver escalator. Dan saw he was following the air hoses. He bled air into his compensator until he hovered. It was colder down here, as if they'd passed through some chill barrier that blocked any emanation of the sun. His hands and feet, even in gloves and booties, were going numb. He fumbled for his watch and ratcheted the elapsed-time bezel to fifteen. Then let go of the line.

His buddy eased over the hull and disappeared into the darkness below. Dan followed, clearing his ears again as he descended. Brown rippled sand rose up through the milling murk. The bow was clear of the bottom. The hoses led under it. He startled at a flicker in the obscurity, then realized that what looked like black flames was the flutter of fins, *under* the hull. He hung back, wary of overhanging steel. Then forced himself forward.

The other diver hung on what looked like a hatch-rim. Dan caught dark eyes studying him. A finger pointed up.

He nodded, and the Korean turtled his head and chinned himself up into what must be a lockout chamber. Fins kicked, then disappeared.

Dreading the mass looming above him, Dan herded himself farther under it. When he looked up he saw only a vibrating green-golden gleam, trickling and twisting like melted light.

He checked his watch. Three minutes. He got a grip on his breathing and finned slowly upward, arms raised, fingering along smooth cold metal for some handhold.

His head burst through into an echoing ullage crammed with darkness, splashing, a deafening hiss of releasing gas, hollow shouts. A flashlight strobed across a circular emptiness above that mirrored that below.

"You come up," a voice gonged. A pudgy figure filled his

sky. A gloved hand grabbed his wet suit. "Set tank in rack. Give me hand."

They were in what seemed to be the control compartment— or more accurately, a combined control, berthing, and torpedo area. The upper hemisphere of the lockout module took up most of the space. It left a short, extremely cramped tube twelve feet across, so crammed with equipment they had to worm their way through an aisle that touched Dan's shoulders on either side. Dive lights beamed glares that left most of it in shadow. A discarded glove huddled like a small dead animal. The cold air was thick, dense, humid. It stank of the heavy oil that coated every surface and a bleachy sting he realized must be chlorine from the flooded batteries. The incoming air hissed so loudly from its hose fitting, vised to one of the hull ribs with a red C clamp, that communication had to be in shouts.

Compressed air, he reminded himself. He looked at his Seiko again. So they were still building up bottom time, tak- ing on nitrogen, though he was out of the water. Seven min- utes gone; eight remained.

The Koreans glanced at him as they worked. Four occupied the space, three hose divers and the guy who'd come down with him on tanks. The chubby diver belted out aggressive- sounding Korean, gesturing at Dan. They reached through pip- ing to shake hands, grinning and nodding. "Welcome," one said. "Thank you," another. He waved and smiled, feeling he was intruding.

He stepped on something soft, and instinctively lifted his bootied foot. An oil-smeared, startled, wide-cheekboned face appeared. Its features were delicate. It looked up at the curved ribs of the inner hull. The left side of its skull was missing. Brain was visible, but no blood. Dan stared. Then made out a shoe nearby. It was oil-stained dark, but bore a familiar boomerang-shaped logo.

"Nikes."

"*Muarago?* What did you say?"

"I didn't know they had Nikes in North Korea."

He followed a flaccid leg to another corpse wedged facedown behind a motor-generator. The barrel of an AK-type rifle poked out. He couldn't tell what had killed this second man. He had on a red Windbreaker with a red-and-white patch. The Marlboro logo.

"Three dead," the pudgy diver said at his elbow.

"I only see two."

"Another there." He pointed into the shadows forward.

"Who are they?"

"North Korea, like commando. Like SEAL."

"Who shot them?"

"They shoot each other. Do not give up."

"Huh."

"*Yichoyero!* You come, see this," called one of the others. "See what we find."

He gave the bodies a last glance, and followed the beams of their lights.

A few feet aft the diver slapped what Dan recognized as a fairly unsophisticated-looking periscope stand, then pulled him to a little fold-down wooden table. Either a captain's station or a navigator's chart table. Dan blinked at it: cheap plywood, complete with knot holes. Everything in the space was crude, hastily finished and covered, where it was shielded at all, with flimsy metal banged together with machine screws. He bent closer as a paper caught his eye. Someone had unfolded it carefully, so as not to tear the sodden, oil-stained fibers.

It was a chart. Shivering as the cold crept deeper, he stripped off a glove and traced a coastline by the beam of a flash. Curving away, small islands . . . a larger island offshore. The Hangul characters conveyed nothing, but he gradually made out the Korea Strait, if the long island was Tsushima.

He dug in with the spot of light till the lens touched the cheap shoddy paper. Was that a pencil trace? A dead-reckoning line, an advanced course? He let the chart sag where it lay. Fished in what looked like a wire wine-rack and came out with another. This was in English. *Approaches to Pusan,* it read.

Next came a small book that hefted astonishingly massive. When he opened the lead covers each soaking page was filled with tiny handwritten characters.

An exclamation from the far end of the compartment brought him back. He squinted at his watch. Twelve minutes gone, out of fifteen. He had to get out. It'd take a few minutes to get back to the bow, no, the stern—anyway, back to the ascent line.

A louder gabble from the divers. He glanced their way, then back toward the black toothless maw of the chamber. A hatch at the top, another at the bottom. The inner hatch opened upward, the lower, downward. Obviously to lock out divers while still submerged.

Since it left no room for torpedo stowage, this must be the infiltration version of the sub. But what were they doing here? Trying to tap submerged cables? The U.S. Navy had pioneered it, but that didn't mean nobody else could try.

And they were almost to the DMZ. Why charts for Pusan, the southernmost port on the Eastern Sea? And why was the crew wearing clothes that must have been purchased in South Korea?

Maybe the logbook held an answer. He unzipped the top of his suit and tucked it inside, against his chest, figuring he'd turn it over to Dr. Kim when they surfaced.

The unmistakable clack of a pistol slide slamming forward snapped his attention up. He wriggled toward the others. As he reached them his pudgy friend held up a hand. His mouth hung open. They were as far aft in the compartment as they could get. His ear was pressed to the steel bulkhead beside a heavy watertight door.

"What is it?" Dan murmured.

The diver made walking legs with his fingers. Jerked his head at the bulkhead. At the closed door.

He sucked an astonished breath. Someone still alive? A flooded forward compartment this big would take them to the bottom. But if they'd sealed off the boat in time, they could still have a bubble in there. It was just barely possible.

Only . . . weren't they supposed to commit suicide?

One of the divers lifted a pistol. It gleamed darkly with grease. They'd come armed. Apparently not as paranoid a precaution as one might think. But now what?

He looked at his watch again and felt fear crawl over his skin like ticks. He was into decompression time. But he wasn't sure he had enough air in his tank to get through it.

His pudgy friend slammed a wrench on the bulkhead. *"Kechokye itneonjadeol. Tohanghameon sal su yitda!"*

The only answer was silence. His guy, who apparently had rank, pointed to the dogging wheel. Two divers seized it, one on either side. They braced themselves and threw it over.

"Shit," Dan muttered. He scrambled to where the corpses lay and fumbled the AK out from under a thin arm. Oily water pissed out of the action, draining from the barrel as he pointed it down and jerked the bolt back. A cartridge flipped out and pinged away. He let go and the bolt slammed closed. But he couldn't remember which way the safety lever worked, and it was too dark to see any markings.

"Yeolligoit seom ni da!" Pudgy shouted. He aimed at the door. The others were straining at the wheel, faces going dark. The dogs crept back from their locking lugs, screeching, as if under terrific strain.

He realized with horror that the reason might be a pressure differential. "Goddamn it, you're going to bend us," he shouted. "Or flood us, if that's water on the other side."

They didn't even turn their heads.

The door slammed open with a bang like a bank vault being dynamited. His ears popped violently.

An object flew in through the opening, trailing smoke. Before his stunned mind had time even to register what it was, Pudgy scooped the grenade up and threw it back in. It exploded almost as it left his hand. The blast was deafening in the steel-walled tunnel. Fragments clanged into equipment cabinets. Explosive fumes filled the air, then thinned, pushed by the steadily inrushing compressed air toward where the air bubbled out through the open lock.

Leaning into the hatchway, Pudgy emptied the pistol through it, firing as rapidly as he could, then dove in after the bullets.

A rapid, roaring clatter from the far side of the bulkhead. He had a bad feeling his stocky friend was history. The others cursed frantically. One pulled a dive knife from a thigh sheath. The other spun and jerked the AK out of Dan's hands.

A wiry, black-haired, lithe little figure in black shorts flew through the door headfirst, as if bounced off a trampoline on the far side. It hit the deck and rolled, agile as a gymnast, and came up holding a commando-type knife that it instantly backhanded across one diver's face. The South Korean staggered back, shouting and pawing at his eyes. The enemy crew member whipped the blade back to guard and faced Dan, not four feet distant. Dan's instinctive hesitation at what he saw was almost fatal. Held at arm's length and lunged with incredible quickness, the blade drove in straight as an arrow and slammed into his chest.

The North Korean gaped as the point slid off, gouging black rubber with a tearing sound. Deflected by the soft lead cover of the logbook tucked against Dan's chest under the wet suit top.

Dark eyes dropped to the AK's muzzle just as the other diver pulled the trigger.

The rifle blasted twice, then stopped, either jammed or out of ammunition. Both bullets struck the North Korean in the chest. The knife went flying. The small face contracted in pain and shock. An arm clutched small nude breasts, welling now with dark blood. She gasped, struggled to speak; then crumpled.

The diver worked the bolt frantically, watching the open hatch. He aimed the rifle at it and pulled the trigger again, but got only a dry click. No light on the other side. But when Dan aimed a flashlight, something fluid gleamed back.

The water licked at the lip of the hatch like a black cat tasting a treat. Then edged forward, elongated, and began pouring in. They must have cracked a valve, yielded their one

unflooded compartment to the sea, when they realized someone was aboard who shouldn't be, on the far side, in the
control compartment.

He couldn't fault them for guts. Or was it something
darker, not heroism, but the unconscious reactions of au-
tomatons? He started to shake. The wounded diver moaned,
holding his gory face in one piece with the pressure of both
hands. His buddy threw the rifle aside and grabbed him by
the shoulders, asking something in a concerned tone.

That was when the last North Korean slid through.

She was larger than the others, more muscular than wiry.
Short hair, matted with oil and sweat. Pistol in one hand, knife
in the other. Smooth thick arms. Panting, with a craving for
death lighting black eyes. She squinted past the flashlights.
They must have dazzled her after the utter dark. Maybe that
was why she didn't see Dan, standing to the side of the access.
Why she focused on the South Korean bending over his
wounded buddy.

Barking something hoarsely, she brought the pistol around.

Dan tripped the buckle on his weight belt. The heavy nylon
strap studded with cast lead slid off his hips, and he continued
and altered the motion and whipped it around into the side of
her head. Lead impacted bone like a sledgehammer hitting a
hollow log. She went down at once. The gun hit the deck with
a clattering splash. The others were on her in a moment, knee-
ing, shouting, kicking, punching, until he screamed at them
over and over to stop.

He hung on the line, checking his watch only when he
couldn't help it. Decomp time passed so slowly. Shudders
writhed through him. His suit leaked cold water through the
knife-rip. He yearned up at the surface. Only fifteen feet
away now, a silvery rolling through which now and then bled
a hot golden vein of sun. He'd spent an hour hanging on the
line. Two safety divers hovered near. They'd brought down
the extra air he needed.

They'd found eleven more bodies in the after compartment, all shot in the head at close range.

He twisted to look behind him. The last alive, the woman he'd knocked out. Her hands were wired behind her. The South Koreans gripped her by the arms. They'd bundled her into the suit Dan's buddy, the dead diver, didn't need anymore, and wired her ankles and wrists together. She'd regained consciousness dangling on the ascent line. Struggled, glaring at them through the helmet port, before accepting captivity. Now she sagged in the water, slowly turning in the tidal current.

What had the Sang-o been doing? Why were they carrying charts for the Strait? Why had they surfaced? According to Dr. Kim, they'd been almost to the DMZ and safety when it had broached.

Lots of questions. Maybe she'd have some answers. Which was part, at least, of why he'd stopped them from killing her.

He checked his watch one last time. Gave it a few more seconds, just to be sure. Then valved air into his vest.

Shivering, he lofted toward the shivering light. Contemplating the fact that had startled him so much, there in the sunken pressure hull, that it had almost cost him his life. That he'd only belatedly recognized, so strange it seemed to a Western eye.

Every one of the submarine's crew had been a woman.

3

Seoul

"You open wide now," his feeder giggled. He grinned uncomfortably and obeyed. The morsel approached on chopsticks, hovered, teasing him, then was plopped in with another musical laugh. Stir-fried pork, he guessed. But he'd decided early in the endless progression of spicy dishes, noodle dishes, kimchi, not to ask. Across the table, the others were laughing at him.

He wasn't used to being fed, much less by a woman in a flowered kimono. But their host had been insistent. And since he'd turned down the *soju,* the rice whiskey, he figured it'd be best to go along.

The rest of the TAG team, under Henrickson, had gone on to Pusan. Now five men and one woman sat in stocking feet around the low red-lacquered table high in the 63 Building, the loftiest skyscraper in Seoul. Commodore Jung sat beside Commander Hwang, backs to a charcoal-glowing fireplace. Dick Shappell, the heavyset blond captain named Harry Leakham—commander, Destroyer Squadron 15—and Captain Carol Owens, the U.S. naval attaché to the Republic of Korea, rounded out the guests. They were all in civvy slacks and open-necked shirts, except for Owens, who was graceful and diminutive in a pantsuit and blouse.

Beside each diner reclined a woman in a bright silk *hanbok.* The women's faces were powdered ghost white, lips tinted cherry red, hair glossy black as a lacquered generator winding. The one feeding him was named Mi Ra. She was pretty but when she leaned close he caught her scent, less inviting than alien, like an unfamiliar spice you wouldn't like if you tasted it. Being fed by hand was embarrassing. But a notch up, he told himself, from fighting it out hand to hand with a desperate female commando.

"You must have *soju* with us, Dan," Jung said again. Dan had refused twice before as politely as he could. Across from him Shappell squinted, silently urging him to accept.

"Again, Commodore, as I said, I'm going to pass on that. I just can't handle it the way you can. With thanks."

Jung rolled his eyes, pouting. "You won't drink with us. Really, a little will not hurt you."

"I'll stay with this wonderful green tea, Commodore. It has nothing to do with you, or this truly fine . . . meal experience . . . you're so generously treating us to." Though he figured it would no doubt be the Korean government actually picking up the tab.

Jung took off his PhotoGrays. His girl snatched them from his hands and polished them with a napkin, cooing as she did so. He ignored her, scratching his neck. "You have not told us how old you are, Dan."

"I'm thirty-nine, Commodore."

"And married? Certainly yes; I see a ring. Any children? Any boys?"

"Yes sir, I'm married. My wife works in Washington. I have a daughter. She goes to school in northern Virginia. And you, sir?"

Jung said smiling that he was forty-five, and very fortunate; he had two daughters and two sons. He didn't mention a wife. He turned to Leakham and put him through the same quiz. Shappell and Owens he ignored, either because he already knew them, or for some other reason, Dan couldn't guess. Layers beneath layers . . . He felt out of place, as uncomfortable probably as Owens's server, who stared at her, as if she'd never seen a female guest at this table before. Maybe she hadn't.

"You open now," his mother robin giggled, breath lickingwarm in the porches of his ear. Deftly chopsticking a morsel

from the brazier bubbling on the table, cupping her hand beneath, she fed him the delicious barbecued beef. He wished
she'd stop, felt like grabbing the chopsticks, but kept his
smile pasted on. Shappell had briefed him on the protocol.
Don't offer to pay; Jung had invited them and trying to do so
would insult his hospitality. Don't tip. Bow back whenever
anyone bows to you. Don't talk business while the food's on
the table. And never wipe your nose—it was an insult, though
they might let it pass if an ignorant Westerner did it.

He tried to relax, to enjoy what the Korean officer no
doubt intended as a treat and an honor. He'd been very lucky
yesterday. Not just in having nothing more than a bruise to
show from what should've been a knife in his heart, but
managing not to get bent too.

As soon as he'd stepped onto the salvage ship's fantail
they'd stripped him, bundled him into fleece-lined clothes,
and handed him a mug of scalding hot chai. Their captive
had disappeared. She'd be subjected, Dr. Kim said with a
face like cast concrete, to interrogation by ROK military
counterintelligence. Oh yes, he told Dan, it was well known
that some of the Reconnaissance Bureau infiltration teams
were made up entirely of women. Dan's shivering had gradually eased as he'd been checked over by the ship's medic,
then debriefed by the DIA major. Not too long after, the destroyer had closed up, to run Dan, Shappell, and Carmichael
back into port.

"So what's your take on how we're going to set up this
Phase Three play?" Leakham was asking Jung.

The commodore made a face. "Let's talk about that later.
For now let's enjoy to the full this delicious food. This lovely
company." He cuddled the kitten next to him, who giggled and
popped another morsel into his mouth. Dan wondered how far
this geisha routine was supposed to go. Jung's cheeks were
turning darker, flushing from the hot booze, of which he'd had
several cups, tossed back and then handed to his girl for
refilling. Dan couldn't watch, and the fumes turned his stomach. He'd had to quit years back.

When his legs cramped, he excused himself and found the restroom. Washed his hands, looking in the mirror. He looked haggard. Needed a haircut too. All night he'd kept seeing that knife coming at him. The woman's slim torso punctured with bullets, the terrible wounds in her back where they'd tumbled out.

Finally he'd gotten up and tried to call his daughter, figuring the time would be right for her to be getting up. He'd just missed her, her roommate said; she'd already left for class.

Shappell came in and used the traditional-style urinal, porcelain skis on either side of a hole in the floor. "How you holding up?" he said over his shoulder.

"Okay."

"Love that octopus stew?"

"*Don't* tell me what it is, all right? All that garlic and red pepper. I'm eating it, aren't I?"

Shappell laughed.

Dan lowered his voice. "Say, Dick . . . should we be discussing classified stuff here? I mean, this isn't exactly a secure location, and these geishas or whatever they are . . ."

"You don't think they check those girls out six ways from Sunday? These people are a lot more security-conscious than we are." Shappell laughed again, zipped, and held the door for him.

Back at the table the servers were whipping away the little tulip-shaped bowls, leaving slices of orange and lemon and dishes of multicolored molded rice balls. Mi Ra fed him one. Almondy, sweet, not bad at all. The next tasted like licorice, the third, like cinnamon. He decided to stop while he was ahead. There was another drink too, which smelled like sweet rice. He turned it down as politely as he could, though it was getting annoying having it pushed on him. Especially since he actually *wanted* a drink. After what he'd been through, didn't he deserve one? . . . He barricaded that off-ramp in his mind, knowing what lay at its end. Nothing good.

Jung laughed and said something to the girls. They rose swiftly, dipped to the guests, beaming and giggling, and vanished. The commodore stretched and burped. He smiled around. "That is good manners, in our country," he said.

"How about this?" Leakham said. He tilted on his cushion and let go a loud fart. Shappell winced, Owens rolled her eyes, but Jung roared and slapped the table. Pointed at Leakham, who was grinning like a ten-year-old, and roared again. Beside him Commander Hwang waited, hands cupped on his knees, smiling, but with a narrowed, cool, all-examining gaze.

They moved into a discussion of the barrier strategy. Dan was still uneasy talking about it in a restaurant, but hey, if Shappell was okay with it . . . Anyway, what they were discussing was more in the nature of tactical philosophy. What was really classified was the specifics: ranges, frequencies, detection probabilities. The unglamorous facts.

"The trouble is that the exercise area is so shallow," Hwang was saying primly. "The 'Red' submarines, it is true, will find that reduced depths will reduce our detection-range advantage. Perhaps to as little as a quarter the normal ranges. Which will either force us to commit four times as many forces, or to reduce the length of our barrier."

"Or use more sonobuoys," Leakham said.

"Our exercise budget is limited. We are not a wealthy country like America. And sonobuoys suffer reduced effectiveness in shallow water too. Passive localization will be very difficult."

They discussed figures of merit and transmission-loss rates. Jung emphasized again, waving a bottle of Korean beer, how important it was to thoroughly tune both sensors and sonar teams during Phase I. "I have operated in these waters for many years. At this season, in the center of the basin, every decibel we gain between thirty and one thousand hertz will give us another kilometer at ten kilometers, half a kilometer at fifty kilometers. The barrier can lengthen and our detection rate goes up. Especially significant if we see heavy mixing due to storms."

Dan caught Owens's eye. The attaché smiled at him. He half smiled back and looked at Jung again.

"We will play against both the American nuclear sub—which one is it—"

"San Francisco."

"Yes, *San Francisco,* and our new 209. We have just taken delivery of *Chang Bo Go.* The crew may not be thoroughly familiar. Which we can exploit."

The 209s were new German-built diesel submarines. Leakham said, "What's their snorkel interval?"

Jung cocked his head. He raised his eyebrows at Hwang, who blinked, caught off guard.

Dan cleared his throat. "We can calculate it."

They looked at him. He pulled out his PDA and called up the graphing calculator function. Most skippers and tactical action officers were content to use the tables in the NWPs, the naval warfare publications, that TAG put out. But he always liked to know the equations behind the tables. Sometimes you could find an edge around the margins. "It's a twelve-hundred-ton boat, right? A quarter of that'll be batteries. They'll run about twenty-three watt-hours per pound at a discharge rate of one hundred hours." He totaled that, subtracted what he figured the life-support systems would require, and set up an algorithm, glad now he'd skipped the *soju.* A curve floated up on the screen. He lowered his voice, making sure none of the servers were near. "The indiscretion rate—when the snorkel has to be up—will be around five percent at a speed of advance of five knots, fifteen percent at ten knots, and fifty percent at fifteen knots."

When he looked up he sensed he'd done something out of place. Made Jung and Hwang lose face? He hoped not. Chappell was intent on whatever he could discover in his martini glass. Owens blinked off into space. After a moment Leakham said, "Okay, I'm ready to share on tactics."

"Share?" Hwang repeated. "Not sure what you mean, Captain. I mean, Commodore. We use the standard tactics. Out of ATP 28."

"I mean some things we came up with out of JIMPAC." The joint U.S.-Japanese exercises a few months before. "I was in Sasebo for the hot washup, and it really opened my eyes. Some new ideas the Japs are coming up with. Special shallow-water tactics—"

"We know the Eastern Sea," Hwang said, and Dan saw that yes, despite the courteous tone he was annoyed. "We know what tactics work there. It's just a matter of adjusting to environmental conditions, sea state and so on. And guessing the intent of the enemy, of course."

"In this case, the Red side," Shappell put in.

"No, you need to think outside that box," Leakham said, reeling a little as he sat. Sweat ran down his face as he drained his beer. "You know Kasugata? Admiral Kasugata? The Japs are putting a lot of study into this. Getting really smart on it. He's got a new way to use towed arrays in shallow water. A hunting matrix, he calls it. Here's how they work."

He searched around for paper. But Jung said coldly, "I don't really care what Kasugata thinks. We know our seas better than any of the Japanese."

Dan remembered how much the Koreans hated the Japanese, who'd behaved with appalling brutality during the occupation. Obviously Leakham either didn't know or didn't care. Shappell was shifting on his cushion. He tried to break in, but Leakham interrupted. "There's never a point where you say, you know it all, Commodore. You go by ATP 28, you're back in the seventies as far as tactics go."

"We know our seas," Jung repeated stubbornly.

Leakham beamed, patting the air like a used-car salesman trying to close a stubborn customer. Sweat dripped from his chin. "Hey, that's why *we're* here, Commodore. We'll work with you, no problem. Get you some help, get you up on the step here—"

Jung said nothing; his eyes were slits. His chief of staff leaned forward and tapped a finger on lacquered wood. "That is not the point of this exercise, Commodore. *You're* here to learn from *us*. Our expertise, in our home waters. Who caught the Sang-o yesterday, after all? We did."

"Oh, like hell, man," Leakham blustered, a man-to-man tone that might have worked in a stateside golf club. "Let's not bullshit each other, okay? The USN's always been number one at this game. And the Japanese, they're a close second. That piece of junk broached and self-destructed. You guys had no idea she was there until she popped up. And *then* you let 'em scuttle." He glanced at Dan. "Right, Lenson? You were there, yes-no? Didn't I hear you went down to the wreck?"

Jung was struggling to his feet, scowling. Dan caught Owens's glance of alarm. Yet she was sitting still, saying absolutely nothing. . . . He realized why. She couldn't step into this; being rescued by a woman would lose Jung even more face.

He cleared his throat and said, "You're wrong, Commodore."

Leakham froze. "Huh?"

"—and you're right. Just as you, Commodore"—he turned to Jung—"are right, but also mistaken. We're doing SATYRE 17 to learn from each other, and bring new ideas to the table. No one country has a monopoly on seamanship. Neither the heroic Korean Navy nor the equally brave U.S. Navy."

Hwang put a hand on his boss's shoulder. Said something rapidly and low in his ear. Jung grunted, swayed, at last sank to his cushion again. But Dan caught Leakham's glare. He hoped he hadn't made himself an enemy.

The silence was interrupted by a thin wail that began outside the windows. It rose and strengthened, became a keening, discordant chorus. For a moment Dan couldn't place it. Then he did. He hadn't heard it for a long time. Since grade school, in fact.

Hwang and Jung were lurching to their feet. Dan got up, uncertain what to do. Owens took his arm. "It's the monthly civil-defense drill," she said.

"An air-raid drill?"

"Just follow them," she said, nodding at the Koreans.
Bending to slip their zoris on, they were already filing out.

They joined the swarm queuing at the elevators and thronging
the oversized staircases down. Dan found that Koreans neither
bowed and gave way in a crowd, nor apologized when they
slammed you into a wall. It was like trying to get to the bargain counter in Macy's basement. Only main strength and ag-
gressiveness got them down the stairs.

Outside the sirens wailed on, endless and scary in the
canyoned streets. The traffic lights pulsed red. Troops with
M16s, pot helmets, and armbands shouted M's at any slug-
gard. They followed the restaurant manager across the street.
All traffic had stopped, the drivers leaving their cars unlocked in the middle of the road. Large blue *M's* marked the
subway entrance.

"This looks like the DC metro," Dan said, gazing around
at white concrete, wide stretches of tiled pavement, fluores-
cents in long rows high on the curving overhead. The crowd
pushed and jostled as they reached the first landing, turned,
and kept going down.

"Except it's cleaner," Owens said behind him.

"Well, yeah . . ." A little man with a pinched face, baggy
clothes, and a black stovepipe hat backed into him, thrusting
a slung bundle of high-smelling twigs into his face. Dan
pushed back, then at the last minute pulled the shove, not
wanting to be too rough. Without even glancing back the old
guy gave him a practiced elbow to the gut that doubled him
over and left him wheezing.

"See, they can take care of themselves," Owens cracked.

"I guess so. . . . Where to now?" They'd come out on the
platform, maybe sixty feet belowground, he guessed. It was
packed solid with people. The tracks stretched off into the
distance.

"Here's fine. Just don't get too close to the edge. They
stop the trains during the drill, but you don't want to get
pushed off the platform."

Dan craned on tiptoe, looking for the others. He caught Jung and Hwang's military caps some meters away, but there was no chance of getting to them. Packed tight the Korean masses smelled like garlic and beans and ginseng, an exotic flavoring somewhere between body odor and the kitchen of a Chinese restaurant. Dan caught opaque glances, but no one spoke to them. Being foreigners didn't win them any extra space, that was for sure. Everybody looked grim, as if they didn't like thinking about why they were down here. He turned and was jostled chest to chest with the attaché, looking down on dark hair. She smelled a lot better than the old man had. "How long . . . sorry, they're pushing me . . . how long do these drills last? Captain?"

"Not that long. They'll check the buildings, make sure no one's lagging back. They get a nice stiff fine if they do."

"They take this seriously, huh?"

"There's a million enemy troops, three thousand tanks, and nine thousand artillery tubes thirty miles away," she told him. "They pretty much destroyed this city last time they invaded. In 1950. Yes, they take it very seriously."

The crowd surged, wedging them even more tightly together. Urbanites were still streaming down the staircases. Dan felt her breasts pressing against him. To his horror he realized he was getting a boner on for a senior officer. "Whoa, thirty miles!" he said, trying to get his mind off where his hips were rubbing.

"That's how far we are from the DMZ." She didn't lower her voice and Dan figured either she didn't expect the people crowded tight against them to understand English, or they knew all this already—probably why they looked so dour. "We don't realize it back in the States. But if they start firing, and use chemical weapons, half the population of this city will die in the first forty minutes."

"But they're not going to. We've got them deterred—"

"Oh, so far, yeah. If they thought they could win, they'd have been here long ago. But they came damn close the last time they tried it." She glanced up at him, and he thought for a horrible second she'd felt his erection and was going to remark on it. Instead she said, "You remember your history."

"Of the Korean War?" He cleared his throat, trying to get his mind off her groin locked to his. From the side of his sight he glimpsed the old man with the twigs eyeing them curiously. "Well, that they attacked—took Seoul—pushed the Army back all the way down the peninsula to Pusan. We held there, then MacArthur landed at Inchon and cut them off."

"But then the Chinese came in," she prompted. "And kicked our tails back south, and it took us two years to fight our way back to the starting line. What I'm afraid of is, CFC—that's the Combined Forces Command, combined U.S./ROK forces, headed by an Army four-star—they act like the other side's going to call the same play the next time. But it won't work twice."

"Nothing ever does," Dan said. "Boy, we're crowded pretty freakin' tight here—"

"Ten more minutes, they'll sound the all clear. I was up at the DMZ last week. You can feel the tension."

"I hear they're starving up north."

"That's when a dictatorial regime gets dangerous, Commander. When there's famine, and it's isolated . . . though I sometimes wonder if they're as isolated as we think."

"What do you mean?"

"I mean the Chinese use them to jerk us around. And they're making threatening noises now too . . . which is why I don't think the SecDef's decision to withdraw the Second Infantry was well timed." She nodded at the drawn faces around them. "I don't know how they stand it. They've been sitting on a major fault line for fifty years. And the earthquake could come any day."

"I hear the ROK Army's not so bad. And we're behind them, if the bad guys do attack."

"If the Air Force can interdict, and the Army can get reinforcements here in time." She wriggled her watch up, tilted a blue-veined wrist. He caught another hint of her scent. Jasmine? Something flowery. "Should be any minute now . . .

And if the Navy can protect the sea lanes, to supply those re-inforcements . . . which brings us to your SATYRE, which is more important than it looks."

"How's that?"

Owens pulled his head down. Her whispering into his ear didn't exactly reduce his arousal. "I mean, there's a lot riding on what you report about their readiness. As you know. The Navy's considering withdrawal from the western Pacific as part of our reduction of forces."

"Holy smoke," Dan said. "No—I hadn't heard that."

"Since Second Division left, the Navy's got to take a bullet too. If the Koreans look like they can take over the sea lanes, we'll lease them six destroyers from the Pacific Fleet, help them buy or build five more 209s, and basically pull out. There'll still be a U.S. naval command here, but it'll be a shell without a pea under it. The idea being the fewer American forces, the less irritating it'll be to Kim Jong Il. Which I think misreads the situation . . . but like I said, things look different up close than they do from inside the Beltway."

Dan said, "Surely he can't think he'll win. Kim, I mean. Even if we don't have the forces actually on station. We're getting good at rapid force deployment. And what we did to the Iraqis and the Serbians from the air—that should make the North think twice."

Owens looked as thoughtful as someone squeezed against him could. "The only way they could succeed is to stop the Air Force from striking from Japan. And at the same time, keep us from reinforcing through the southern ports."

"That's a tall order."

"Let's hope they reach the same conclusion."

Dan remembered the headlines in the *Korea English Times*. "But what I was reading this morning, about Pyongyang turning down the Japanese offer to build new reactors for them if they close down their old Chernobyl-type power plants—"

"Part of the picture. The crippled-tiger syndrome. You know? That's when they turn man-eater. And again, I don't think the North's in this alone."

"The Chinese?"

"They play five moves ahead. Sooner or later, they plan to either bully us out of East Asia, or bloody our nose till we back away. The flash point could be Korea, Taiwan—even Japan. That's why I don't like reducing our forces. It puts the smell of blood in the water. And that's just the wrong message, around these parts."

The wail of the all clear echoed down the stairwells. The PA system shouted out impatient-sounding Korean, adding, as if in afterthought, "All clear. All clear. All go now. Thank you for participate."

The press eased only by degrees, but he breathed easier once he got their groins unlocked. She must have felt him. But not a smile, not a wink. He hoped she took it as a compliment. As they ebbed toward the exit, he thought of one more thing. "Where's this spy sub come in? With the all-girl crew?"

"The Sang-o? I don't know, and it worries me. Hopefully they're just probing our defenses. As usual. If it's something else . . . well, let's just hope it isn't. Okay?"

He was nodding when he remembered the other thing he'd been meaning to ask her. "Uh, Captain—Dick Shappell mentioned, at one point, it was you who got me aboard that sub. Or suggested to him that I go along."

"That's right."

"Can I ask why?"

"Other than that you're an antisubmarine expert?"

"That's the only reason?"

"No. Since you ask. A friend from DC said you were headed out my way. That you were one of the good guys, and might need a hand now and then."

He got another inch of clear space between them. "Can I ask who?"

"Jennifer Roald ring a bell?"

"Oh sure. Captain Roald . . . in the Sit Room. Yeah, we worked together." He was impressed. There was a good old girl network now.

Owens stuck out her hand. "Okay? It's been great talking to you, Commander."

"Yeah, very . . . very interesting. Uh, Captain."

She tilted her head, then added, "Just try to sort of . . . *relax* around me, Commander. Can you do that?"

He felt his face burning. Cleared his throat, but couldn't think of one damned thing to say.

Fortunately just then he caught Commodore Jung's uplifted beckoning wave from beside the exit. Shappell and Hwang stood beside him. He raised his hand in reply, and pushed toward them through the relieved, chattering crowd.

PHASE I

4

Pusan, South Korea

Commander Hwang piloted the little tan Hyundai. Dan figured it was just as well, once he saw how Koreans drove. No rule was sacred and they took no prisoners. He didn't relax until they got out of Seoul onto the highway. The sky was clear and shining, the air warm, yet not so hot as to be oppressive. He shook out a map and ran a finger down a crease. Over plains, mountains, plains again. The embattled peninsula, a clubfooted version of the Italian boot, stretched south till it frayed away into the East China Sea.

He closed his eyes, frowning, not liking the memories that came with that body of water. Where in a ship without a name he'd crossed the shadow-line separating warship from pirate . . .

"The shape drives the history," Hwang said.

Dan opened his eyes to purple mountains, rice-terraced hillsides in greens so brilliant they hurt to look at long. The hills escalatored down to a valley so lovely it stopped his breath. It was instantly recognizable from a thousand painted screens. The road coiled along it, through minuscule hamlets with red-tiled roofs and walls of painted block. "Sorry," he said. "I missed that. What you said."

"You know our history?"

"Hardly any of it."

Hwang laughed. "Do Americans even know their own?"

"No argument here," Dan said. He groped under the seat

for the bottled water. Offered one, then cracked another for himself.

The willowy, pale chief of staff said, "For seven hundred years there were three kingdoms in Korea. The Chinese aided whichever gave them the most influence. At last the Silla Kingdom defeated the Koguryo and Paekche, with the help of a Chinese army. They ruled for many years and became prosperous. Only to grow self-indulgent and peace-loving . . . as has happened many times before."

As Dan puzzled over what he meant—that the Republic of Korea was self-indulgent and peace-loving? that the Chinese were the eternal enemy? or that prosperity itself was?—he was jostled forward as Hwang braked, muttering under his breath.

It was another hamlet. Brightly painted houses crowded a road thronged with running children, elders wobbling on warp-wheeled bikes, battered, smoke-snorting farm-trucks loaded with vegetables, goats, and pigs. Hwang leaned on the horn as he continued his fast-forward through Korean history. Through the Mongol conquest, the Yi dynasty, and the great admiral, Yi Sun-shin, whose bronze statue Dan had admired at Yongsan.

"His fleet was smaller than that of his enemy, but his mind was greater. He defeated the Japanese every time they met. You have heard of the turtle boats? The ironclad war-ship?" Hwang honked again, a viciously long blast, but not one hustling head so much as glanced back. "This could take some time," he muttered. The window was open and Dan caught the stench of village life: pig shit, diesel exhaust, rotting cabbage, cheap tobacco smoke.

"Ironclad? I thought—"

"That your *Monitor* and *Merrimack* were first? Admiral Yi put iron armor on his ships in 1592. Perhaps you can make a side trip to Hyongchungsan while you are with us. There is a turtle boat there we have rebuilt."

The truck ahead of them snorted, belched black smoke, and began to move at last, a thin stinking tide drooling out

the back. Hwang pulled out and passed it on the right on a
blind curve as Dan clutched the edges of his seat. As they
passed he locked eyes with one of the hogs through the slats
of the truck. I know my doom, its sad regard said. Do you
know yours? A tunnel entrance loomed. They plunged into
darkness and the tinny racketing echo of the little engine.

"This shape drives our strategy as well," Hwang said.
"As one trained in sea power, you will understand this. If
the Northerners attack again, the war will be won or lost by
the shape of our land."

An aperture of light grew ahead, became the end of the
tunnel. Dan examined the map again. "Meaning because it's
surrounded by water?"

"Meaning that to conquer us they must attack north to
south, while their flanks rest on the sea. So air interdiction
and ground reinforcement will decide the outcome."

Dan had figured out that much. If the FEBA—Forward
Edge of the Battle Area, the defensive line south of the
DMZ—broke, and the Communists flooded into South Korea, they'd be like the Iraqi Army on the Highway of Death.
They'd have to blitz their heavy armor fast to occupy the airfields and stop U.S. reinforcements arriving through the
southern ports. Meanwhile the U.S. and ROK air forces
would be attriting them with every kilometer they traveled.
The Joint Chiefs J-3 and Eighth Army had no doubt calculated, diagrammed, computed it all out with mathematical
precision, from M-day on. So many percent losses per day.
So many sorties to produce that percentage. It would be a
war of remorseless, slowly advancing reptiles, picked off
day by day by crows diving fiercely from above.

As if following that exact thought process Hwang said,
"A thousand sorties per day. That is the dividing point in our
staff studies. More than that and the enemy will be destroyed
north of Pusan. Less, and he will occupy all of our country
before your tanks and troops can arrive to reinforce."

"So the sortie rate's key. What about the weather? Surprise?"

"In our training we always assume a surprise attack in bad weather."

"So what's your take? *Will* they try again?"

"Oh yes, of course. They are devils in human shape, these people," Hwang said, thin face not quite as impassive. His fingers sank into the padding of the steering wheel. "They killed my uncles, aunts, grandparents in Tanyang. Lined them up and shot them. My mother got to Pusan as a refugee." He cleared his throat, and Dan saw what he might look like a day after he was dead. "Our country was not prepared. And America—you did not stand behind us until it was almost too late."

"I'm sorry to hear that. I know there was some question whether we were obligated to defend you. Back then, I mean—there's no question now."

Hwang frowned. "I don't tell you this to make you feel guilty. I tell you because the other Americans I meet don't seem to think it will happen again."

"The way I see it, nothing happens the same way twice."

"Really? You are an optimistic people. We would say: Everything returns. And again. And again." He peered ahead, not slowing for a hairpin curve. Cliffs fell away to vertiginous valleys. Dan gripped his seat, visioning the long careening tumble down that rocky fall, how their bones would smash and snap inside the car before it finally impacted. The tires shrieked. Hwang said, "I believe every day they ask themselves, Is this the hour to attack? All it requires is that we be isolated. That is why the North has such large special-purpose forces. Missiles to hit our air bases. Chemical weapons. They will lay mines at sea. And they will threaten Japan. If the Japanese close their bases to your air force, and the mines keep your carriers out of the battle, there's no way to reach that thousand sorties a day."

"It still sounds like a gamble," Dan said. "For them."

"It is. But if they think they can succeed—then yes, they will gamble. And it will be a terrible war. It will destroy everything we have built since the last one." Hwang leaned on the horn again, swerved around a bus. Fresh mountains grew in the distance.

"A terrible war," he whispered again.

They descended hours later into a metropolitan cauldron edged by the distant sea. Now there were clouds, as if generated by the miles of city, the sweating breathing humanity that stretched from one wall of mountain to the other. Hwang told him Pusan had been a fleet base for the Imperial Japanese Navy in World War II. Dan knew its more recent history. Pusan was where the United Nations had finished retreating. They'd finally held the North Koreans, who were by then exhausted and strung out along the roads, depleted by garrisoning after their long advance. Then Douglas MacArthur's marines and troops had landed at Inchon, to bar the door behind the invaders. Before the Chinese had turned the course of the war once more.

The Hotel Commodore was a scarlet and green and gold pagoda perched on a hill too steep to walk up comfortably. Its upper floors overlooked miles of snaky narrow streets and back alleys, every square inch lined with small homes and tiny shopfronts and teahouses and restaurants. The city fell away downhill to the waterfront, still a couple of miles distant. Pusan looked much older than Seoul. But then, it hadn't been shelled to rubble, the way Seoul had.

Hwang let him off at the ornate red-and-yellow entrance, shouting angrily at a stone-faced valet as the man heaved Dan's bag out of the trunk. He didn't see why, but decided against getting involved. This was Hwang's country. He gave the porter a couple hundred won, checked in, and asked for Dr. Henrickson's number.

When Monty let him in the TV was on so loud the little analyst had to shout over his shoulder, "Donnie! Turn that crap down! The commander's here."

The very small room was crammed with heavy, dark-lacquered furniture and the gray scuffed shockproof containers that held the classified gear. A nature show was on, narrated in Korean. Donnie Wenck sprawled on the floor like a kid watching cartoons. He was in his underwear, surrounded by crumpled balls of shiny foil. Chocolate wrappers. When he saw Dan he blushed. He groped for the control and rolled to his stockinged feet.

"Everything good in Seoul?" the analyst said, pumping Dan's hand as if he never wanted to stop. He looked as if he'd gotten some sun.

"That tan looks good on you, Monty. But I thought you guys'd be in Chinhae."

"We were. Stocked up on those greasy burgers at the bowling alley."

"That Korean food, that shit's not good for you," Wenck said, pulling on black jeans.

Henrickson added, serious now, "But there might not be a SATYRE after all."

"What are you talking about?"

The analyst held out a fax with the TAG letterhead. Dan read it and looked up. "They're thinking about pulling out?"

"Not them, Seventh Fleet. They're getting cold feet."

He wondered why, but of course the fax didn't say. "It won't be much of an exercise without U.S. participation."

Henrickson shrugged as elephants trumpeted. At low volume it sounded more plaintive than threatening. Wenck had drifted back to the screen, riveted again. Dan said, "Hey, Donnie, you mind? Where are the others, Monty? Rit, and Teddy, and Captain . . . I mean, Joe? I figured you'd be aboard ship getting things checked out. Getting those nineteens installed. If the exercise cancels, we can always pull them out again."

"Well, we need to talk about that."

"About which?"

"Joe." Henrickson looked upward without moving his head. "He's up in his room. Been there since we got here, actually."

Dan said, astonished, "O'Quinn didn't go to Chinhae with you?"

"Just stayed in his room. He pays extra to get a single."

Henrickson looked as if he expected Dan to do something about it. Wenck was still hypnotized by the nature show, scratching his butt crack through the jeans. Dan lowered his voice. "So you're saying—what? That he's drinking?"

"Well, oh no, I wouldn't say that. I didn't say that."

"Just that he stays in his room? Nothing wrong with that. As long as he comes out when we need him."

The analyst shrugged. "I'm just letting you know."

"Okay. Message received. How about Oberg? Carpenter? Where are they?"

A leopard coughed. Wenck, mesmerized, slowly unpeeled another Hershey's Kiss. Henrickson sighed. "Well, Teddy's over in Chinhae. He wanted to use the gym. But Rit—Donnie? *Donnie?*"

"What?"

"You were there. Tell the commander what happened."

The sound went down again. "Who? Rit? Oh yeah—we were at the train station, waiting for a taxi. And Rit, he sees this Korean girl. Oh, you've never seen anything that cute. In that little plaid skirt they wear to school. So before I know it, he's over there hitting on her."

"She's a *student?*"

"Yeah. Goes to Pusan Women's College. At least that's what she *said*. He got in the taxi. Checked in here with us. But then he took off. Never used his bed, far as Oberg says. Him and Oberg are in the other double."

Henrickson said, "He left a number, but when we call there's nobody there who speaks English. At least, that we can understand."

Dan ran his fingers through his hair. "He's *UA?* Is *that* what you're telling me?"

"Well—not exactly. But if he's not here, and we can't get hold of him—"

"How old is this girl?"

"He said eighteen," Wenck called from the television.

"Damn it! I want one of you to take that number down to the desk. Have them call and translate for you."

"You want him to come in?"

"Of course I do! He belongs here with us, not shacked up with some eighteen-year-old."

"Looked more like thirteen," Wenck mumbled over the throb of jungle drums.

Dan started to ask if he was serious. Then decided that was one of those questions he was better off not asking. "I want him here for dinner. Six o'clock, and we'll get organized."

In his own room, he stood at the window looking down at Pusan. The mountains, the city sprawled halfway up them, and in the distance the sea, gleaming like ironed foil. He did a couple of stretches, just to get the car trip out of his muscles. Then unzipped the computer case.

He spent the next hour setting up the notebook, then getting connectivity with TAG with the scrambler modem. It was slow work, and at first the system wouldn't take his password and user ID. It was case sensitive, though nobody had mentioned that. At last bytes started oozing through, but it was like sucking molasses through a drink stirrer. All the way around the world. Most of his in-box was routine unclassified but there was also a message explaining in more detail what the fax had said. Team Bravo was to stand easy on station until Commander, Seventh Fleet made up his mind about participating. He rogered for it, logged off, and shut down, then looked at his watch. Still an hour till dinner.

He wasn't looking forward to it. But it was time to check on Captain Joseph O'Quinn, U.S. Navy, Retired.

"Just a second," came a muffled voice when he knocked. Dan stood in the corridor as a middle-aged Japanese couple brushed by, bowing and smiling. He smiled back, wondering how they perceived Korea, how older Koreans reacted to them. Certainly Hwang didn't seem to cherish any good memory of Japanese occupation.

"Who is it?" Through the door, louder.

"Lenson."

"Yeah?" The chain rattled. "C'mon in."

O'Quinn was in the same white terry bathrobe with an embroidered dragon that Dan had seen hanging in his own bathroom. He held a can of Diet Pepsi in one hand and a paperback novel, finger thrust between the pages, in the other. Smoke curled from an ashtray. He was unshaven. Dan smelled liquor. He stepped in, checking for bottles, and caught one on the sideboard. Dark rum, a fifth, nearly empty.

"You doing okay all alone up here, Joe?"

"I always get a single on the road. I can't sleep with another guy snoring in my ear. I guess we're just waiting for the assholes in charge to make up their fucking minds, right? Want a drink? Oh, yeah—you don't touch it. Pepsi?"

Dan accepted one from an ice bucket by the bed. More paperbacks lay on the night table. They were all science fiction: Greg Bear, Alan Dean Foster, Larry Niven, Jerry Pournelle.

They stood awkwardly a moment before O'Quinn pointed to the chair. He took the bed himself, reached for the cigarette. Said around it, "So, you Naval Academy?"

"That's right."

"Worked my way up from the spaces myself. Worked for some ring knockers over the years. Nothing personal, but I found 'em pretty much obsessed with themselves. Thought they had some kind of inside track. But they weren't all that smart. Some of 'em, pretty damn dumb."

"Some can be that way."

O'Quinn scratched grizzled stubble and half grinned. "Like I said. No offense."

"None taken." But Dan didn't buy it. The guy either was deliberately being offensive, or had been hiding behind the door when they were passing out social skills. He'd met men like that. Some surprisingly senior. Either way, the only way to meet it was to be just as blunt as they were. "How about you, Joe? I heard what happened on *Buchanan*. A lot of guys would have just quietly slunk away after something like that. But here you are. Still on the government payroll—or wait, no, it's Titan, right?"

The older man stubbed the cigarette out. His face was controlled. "Joe O'Quinn never slunk away from anything," he said at last. "What'd they tell you happened?"

"Just that there was a collision. Guys died."

"Not in the collision. Which was the freighter's fault, by the way. Failure to keep a proper lookout. Henrickson say they died in the collision?"

"No."

"'Cause they didn't. They drowned because I locked down on them. The pumps were falling behind. Firemain pressure, zip. I had to keep her afloat. The sea was too cold and too rough and we were too far out, this was way down in the South Atlantic, even to think about abandoning."

O'Quinn was staring at the drapes. Dark plush maroon, they were drawn against the light, against the jagged mountain panorama Dan knew lay on this side of the hotel. He wondered what the older man saw against that screen. O'Quinn drank out of the can, hesitated, then added a solid slug from the bottle. Amber drops bounced on the carpet. "Unfortunately, I should have waited and seen if the flooding reports were right. Yeah, there was a court. And yeah, I ended up on the beach. You were a skipper. Ever had to make a call that turned out wrong?"

"Yeah. I have."

"And lost people 'cause of it?"

Dan nodded again. You could argue they'd had to die, it was just the mission. Or that it was the commander's lack of resourcefulness, seamanship, judgment, that had doomed them. You could talk about risk analysis too. The line was there. But sometimes it was buried in darkness, and all the analysis went to shit, and shit happened. And in the dead watches of the night, faces and screams drifted back and woke you, if you'd been able to close your eyes in the first place. Now he knew why O'Quinn slept alone. If he slept at all. He cleared his throat and scrubbed his hand back over his hair. "I know what you mean. It's not an easy row to hoe. So I might have a little more sympathy than—"

O'Quinn jumped off the bed and thrust his face into

Dan's. Pepsi and rum spattered brown foam on the bedspread. "I never asked for your fucking *sympathy,* Mister Annapolis. Mister fucking *hero.* How many lives did that Medal of Honor cost you?"

"You'd better shut up," Dan said. His hands were claws around the armrests. "And back off. Sit down, O'Quinn."

The older man laughed as if he didn't care anymore. "Fucking ay I will. Don't worry. I'll keep it shut around the boys. I just want you to know I see through the act. What's a fucking hero, anyway? Just whatever dickhead's at the right place at the right time."

"And makes the right decision."

"The decision that turns out later was right."

"I used to think that," Dan said. "Yeah. That how it turned out told you whether it was right or wrong. But I finally figured out how you can tell which decision's right earlier than that. You just subtract yourself from the equation. No matter how scared or tired you are, or how bad it might be for your career. You just do what used to be called your duty. Just do that—and no matter how it turns out, you can live with it."

But O'Quinn was wagging his head, sneering. "Sure, if you got the wife who's the fucking undersecretary of defense. I heard what happened to *Horn.* You lost more guys than I did. And you're still in. You're Annapolis, all right. Through and fucking through."

It was the ship's name that did it. His temper broke like chilled glass. He pushed himself to his feet. Barely in time, Dan reminded himself that the guy was hurting. Striking out at whoever happened to be in range. He crammed his fists into his pockets, feeling his long muscles tensed hard. It would be all too pleasant to start punching. "You're way out of line, O'Quinn. Drunk, too. I'm cutting you a break. Because I feel sorry for you."

"Don't fucking—"

"Shut up and listen. I know you're not in the Navy anymore. But, you want to keep working for TAG? Don't get in whatever this mood of yours is, again. Not with me. And not around our host-country nationals. Got it?"

O'Quinn didn't answer. His cheeks were the color of fresh liver. He fumbled on the night table, found the pack, shook out more cigarettes. They flicked out and hit the carpet, bounced high, as if they had no mass whatsoever. He lit one, and the flame shook, making the hollows of his dead-looking eyes shiver. "I know my way around," he said in a low voice as toneless as Dan's. "I know what this job takes. And I'll do it. I just want you to know you're not fooling anybody."

Turning away, he scooped up the bottle again. Cradling it, he muttered, to the draped and shadowed window and not to Dan: "Now get out of my fucking room."

5

ROKS *Chung Nam* (FF 953)

He paced the foredeck, feeling more like himself back in uniform than in the civilian suits he'd had to wear on the Eighteen Acres. He was glad that tour was over. TAG duty wasn't what he'd hoped for—another command—but at least he was back aboard ship.

Even if it didn't fly the U.S. ensign.

Shading his eyes beside the gray egg of a 75mm gun mount, he looked out across the harbor. He'd never seen ships rafted this deep, and yet more lay across the floating pier. Rank after rank of destroyers, frigates, low, fast-looking patrol craft. Or wait—yes, he had. In old photos, from wars that had strained every sinew of American industry.

The ROKN base at Chinhae had that wartime feel. Gate security had searched their car on the way in and examined the chassis with a mirror. They'd opened and inspected every box of gear and examined and photocopied their orders. Two helmeted guards patrolled the pier with M16s, and there was nothing perfunctory about the way other compact, dour-faced troops checked IDs. A quarter mile out a guard boat churned the gray-green chop of the fjord, or bay. It was walled by slate blue mountains that grew from stubby peninsulas poked out into the sea. Beneath him the deck vibrated. A thin wash of nearly invisible smoke pushed up from the stack.

The okay had come through at last. Seventh Fleet and the Japanese would both play in Exercise SATYRE 17. Now all he had to do was make it happen, deal with any problems that came up, get along with Jung, keep Carpenter and O'Quinn on the straight and narrow, organize the data collection. . . .

"Commander Lenson! *Kim tae wi*," said a high-cheekboned young man in khakis, saluting.

Dan returned the salute. "Sorry. I don't speak Korean."

"*Tae wi*—Lieutenant." His escort fingered his rank insignia. "My family name—Kim. Kim *tae wi*—Lieutenant Kim."

"I see. Kim *tae wi*." Were they *all* named Kim?

"Very good! I am show you ship, engines, cabin. Start at forward."

"That'll be fine," Dan told him, and followed him down a ladder.

ROKS *Chung Nam* was an Ulsan-class frigate. At first glance, as he came down the pier, she'd reminded him of the old Leahy-class guided-missile cruisers. Closer in, though, he'd seen the Korean was smaller. About the size of *Reynolds Ryan,* his own first ship—which would make her a bit over two thousand tons. She was flush-decked, with a towering superstructure, two pyramidal masts, and a single large stack aft. The gray paint job with low-contrast bow numerals were just like U.S. practice. She was much more heavily armed, though, than a NATO warship of comparable size. Two automatic cannons, where an American frigate carried one. Four antiaircraft guns, twenty- or thirty-millimeters in tubs; Perrys carried none. Crisscrossed gray tubes aft of the stack were Harpoon surface-to-surface missiles. She probably carried some sort of short-range antiair missile as well, for point defense.

On the other hand, he didn't see a helicopter hangar, nor was there anything like the Perrys' Mark 13 launcher, the "one-armed bandit," which reloaded automatically with a choice of several missiles from belowdecks. She sounded different too. Quieter than the constant whoosh and whine of a U.S. ship, though the familiar clatter of a chipping tool echoed from somewhere forward.

Now, following his escort down into the forepeak, he submerged into hot air and smells. The boatswain's locker reeked of paint and thinner. No surprise there. But the next compartment aft was packed with nylon bags bearing bright labels. Rice gritted underfoot in forward berthing too. As enlisted men came to attention he caught other odors. Close-packed men and damp bedding. The man-smell was like turpentine and radishes, sweat with an undertone of mold and the spoiled-milk odor of latex paint. He wondered what he smelled like to them. They were striking more rice below. A human chain swayed thirty-kilo sacks from one bent, nearly child-sized sailor to the next, between racked pipe bunks down to a storage area he glimpsed, leaning over a hatchway, on the next deck down.

Aft, to a compact wardroom. The table was covered with green baize just as it would be on an American ship. An ornate silver box squatted at its geometric center. Kim lifted the lid for a cigarette from the stock inside. As he lit it Dan saw a coffeemaker, but the burners were empty. "Hey, Kim *tae wi*. Any chance of some coffee before we see the rest of the ship?"

"Coffee? No coffee. Sorry."

"I see that, yeah. But maybe they could make some."

The lieutenant didn't seem to get the picture. Dan rapped on the galley door. The slider clacked open. A steward in a white smock peered out. He did a double take when he saw Dan. There followed some moments of low comedy as he tried to communicate what he wanted, while the steward tried to convey something else; exactly what wasn't clear, except it didn't seem to involve Dan getting what he wanted.

"Can I help?" said someone behind him.

"May I present Captain Yu," said his escort.

Dan shook hands with a grave, wizened little man in ironed khakis. He looked older than Jung, which Dan thought odd. He was smoking and at once offered a cigarette. Dan mustered his first try at Korean, a phrase he'd picked up from Hwang. *"Aniyo, kam sa ham ni da."* He hoped that came out somewhere in the vicinity of "No, thanks."

The Koreans oh'd in surprise. Yu's cheeks wrinkled in

what was either pleasure or an intestinal cramp. He clutched his middle as if adjusting a cummerbund. "Ah, you speak Korean. And so beautiful!"

"I've just used all I know."

"But you speak so great. You must have study very hard."

He had to grin. The Koreans were 180 degrees out from the French. Even a couple of words, no doubt grotesquely mispronounced, elicited delight. They also seemed to appreciate compliments, so he ladled on some honey. "It's a difficult language, but very beautiful. Perhaps I can master a few more words before I have to leave your ship. Which is very impressive. Very advanced."

Yu touched Dan's Command at Sea pin. "You too have commanded ships. Destroyers? Which ones?"

"Destroyers—yes. USS *Horn*." He tensed, waiting for the questions that usually followed, but Yu didn't seem to recognize the name. Instead he gestured around him. "What you think? Are ship well kept?"

No doubt about it, the skipper's English wasn't in the same league as Hwang's or Jung's. His accent was so thick Dan had to process for a second or two to get the gist. "Uh—yes, very well kept. Well painted, nice brightwork. The watertight doors seal very well." His own quick benchmark for how well the details that mattered at sea were attended to.

"And now you here from TAG. Run exercise."

"Uh—correct."

"Welcome to *Chung Nam*. So, what you think of Ulsan class? First destroyer ships build here in South Korea. Hyundai Shipyard. Like the car."

"A very powerful warship. You must be proud to be her captain."

They discussed the tactical data control system, which, Dan had read in *Proceedings,* had given trouble early on. Yu stubbed out his cigarette and took another from the box, which seemed to be open to all comers. The *tae wi* was there instantly with a gold-toned Zippo. The captain leaned into the flame and exhaled luxuriously. Then they both stared at him, holding their cigarettes in exactly the same manner, the

European style that looked fey to an American, between thumb and forefinger.

Dan broke the pause. "So, Captain—I was trying to see if I could get a cup of coffee."

"I don't permit my officers to have coffee."

"I'm sorry? I don't—"

"It's not good for them." The Korean leaned to flick ash off his butt, then took another deep drag. "Young men. Very bad healthwise. So I forbid. You understand?"

They regarded each other. A couple of possible retorts crossed Dan's mind, but he decided on diplomacy. "Well, Captain, we drink a lot of coffee in the U.S. Navy. And we plan to be up for long periods of time at night monitoring these exercises. We'll need to be alert. You understand? Any chance I could persuade you to bend your rule for us? For me, and my men?"

After a moment Yu shrugged. He said a few words to the steward, who bowed hastily several times before slamming the access shut. "He'll make some for you," he told Dan.

"Thank you."

Yu smiled coldly. He lifted an eyebrow at Kim, nodded to Dan, and left.

Kim took a last drag and ground out the butt in the silver ashtray, a little more violently, Dan thought, than was absolutely necessary. Tension between the junior officers and the captain? Well, there nearly always was. "Shall we continue? Your coffee—he will make it. We will come back when it is ready. By way: "captain" is *ham jung*. *Kam sa, ha mi da, Hang jung nim:* thank you, Captain sir. Since you are studying Korean."

Dan hadn't intended to study Korean, but it didn't seem he had any choice now. He'd outsmarted himself again. "Got it," he said reluctantly. "Thanks. I mean, *kam sa, ha mi da*."

Aft again, through a narrow passageway lined with doors. Another boyish figure bowed silently, toting the bag they'd insisted on taking from him on the pier. "Your room here," Kim said, cracking a joiner door. Dan glanced into a small cabin with a porthole, a tan plastic tatami on the floor, a single bunk spread with a bright red knit wool comforter. His Compaq was racked above a foldout desk. He reminded himself to check where the rest of the team was bunked, make sure they were comfortable and had what they needed.

They continued aft. Two General Electric LM-2500 gas turbines and two German-built diesels were shoehorned into the engine spaces. He'd read about this combination. It was called CODOG, combined diesel or gas. Both engines used JP-5, but you could loiter on the diesels for weeks at a low fuel consumption. Then light off the turbines and accelerate to thirty-four knots. Though not for long; they burned a torrent of fuel.

Up narrow ladders, forward again, and he was walled in by gray bulkheads, gray overheads, cable runs, gray diamond-checked floor mats over bare aluminum. He bent under shock-mounted panels hanging from the overhead, but still caught his scalp on the edge of an air duct. CIC, the combat information center, and a tight little one it was. The radar repeaters, consoles, sonar stacks, and plot tables were familiar makes, but crammed into half the cubic he was used to.

Up yet higher to the bridge. Again, the equipment was familiar, but wedged into half the width and height an American seaman would feel comfortable in. Monty Henrickson was out on the starboard wing, deep in discussion with a Korean. The junior officers and the enlisted bridge team were all slight and all smooth-shaven. Dan worried how he was going to tell these guys apart.

Captain Yu was sitting in a tall leather chair, still smoking. His hooded reticent gaze met Dan's, but flicked past without change or acknowledgment.

Henrickson came over. "The rest of the guys get off all right?" Dan asked, meaning Oberg and Carpenter and Wenck, who'd ride the other ships to observe and get the data.

"They're all installed. No problem."

"Carpenter too? Didn't decide he'd rather sit this one out with his mamasan?"

"I saw him humping his gear up the brow two ships over. He'll be there, Commander. Rit may push the envelope liberty-wise, but he does his job."

"By the way, how do we talk to our TAG riders, Marty? They're out twenty miles away, we're on the flagship here?"

"Basically we don't, not that much, anyway. There's PRCs—the handheld radios?—but the range isn't that great and they're not encrypted. There's an exercise coordination net monitored from CIC."

"Right, I saw that in the op order."

"We can pass direction via that, but to be perfectly frank, by the time it gets passed phonetically by people who don't speak English that well. . . ."

"I get the picture. What were you doing out on the wing?"

"Installing the nineteen. These little antennas, they won't work inside, but I don't want the box out in the rain."

"So?"

"So, I'm gonna need to put the antenna assembly out on the wing, or maybe up on the flying bridge. Run cable up to it. Not a permanent install, just clamps and a handful of monkey shit."

Dan acted as a go-between, relaying the request to the captain. Yu spoke magisterially, and the Korean Henrickson had been arguing with picked up a phone.

Suddenly one of the enlisted men wheeled and shouted. At once everyone popped to as rigid a brace as Dan had seen since plebe year. He turned to see Jung threading through the rigidly unmoving junior officers and phone talkers with the gravity of a battleship approaching its mooring buoy. He came to attention too. But the commodore greeted no one, did not even meet their eyes. His PhotoGrays had gone to full dark. He took the starboard chair, the one Yu had just slid down out of, settled himself, still without a word, and gazed forward, tapping out a cigarette that one of the junior officers immediately darted in to light for him.

They cast off an hour later, with less ceremony than an American or British warship. The deck gang took in lines, chanting and swaying in unison. Yu rapped out a couple of commands, the deck vibrated harder, and *Chung Nam* accelerated out of the nest. Looking back, Dan saw their inboard companion casting off, line handlers boiling about the forecastles of the rest of the flotilla. One by one, so smoothly it was clear they were well drilled, the patrol boats and frigates peeled off and came to a course for the harbor exit.

Chung Nam inclined into a roll, then picked up the rhythm of the sea. Looking back, Dan saw they led a line of gray elephants, white bones gripped in their teeth. They ran out past Kadokto, a low rocky shadow, and the Hungnam headland, out into the Korea Strait.

It was cooler out here. He leaned against a bearing transmitter on the port wing, enjoying the sun and wind. The bow wave broke with a roar like surf on a pebbly beach. The sea's hue deepened from coastal green to a light-filled blue that drew his eye down into it. Every so often a gust of stack gas whirled down, sulfurous, choking when it got dense, but at the same time comforting just for being what he'd smelled a thousand times. Sea sparrows dipped and swerved along the bow wave. From its height, and the way they cruised through the wave systems, he judged they were making in excess of fifteen knots.

The Form One—the line ahead formation—turned south a couple of miles out, the flagship leading, each ship pivoting precisely in the guacamole green rudderwash of its predecessor. Another island came into view far to port, backlit by the morning sun into a black line only faintly softened by a haze the color of barbecue sauce. He went inside and checked the chart. Tsushima, midway between the southeastern tip of the peninsula and the southern main island of Japan, Kyushu.

He went back out and stood for a long time, brain pleasantly vacant, before glancing down to see a head he recognized below him. Joe O'Quinn was standing on the main deck. The wind ruffled his thinning hair and showed his scalp. He was looking out across the sea the same way Dan was. He thought about calling down to him, seeing if his mood had improved. But didn't. Let O'Quinn make the first move. Or let him go to hell.

Instead he turned for the pilothouse. It was time to start SATYRE 17.

The first days' events, kicking off Phase I, were two to four hours long, and took place within four imaginary squares. Each square was thirty minutes of latitude or longitude, respectively, on a side. Their corners met sixty-eight miles due south of Cheju-Do, Cheju Island. The area was very shallow for antisubmarine work. According to the chart, the bottom sloped from 120 meters—all Korean charts were in meters, not fathoms—at the northeast corner to only 49 meters, about 160 feet, at the southwest. But since their main goal was to test littoral sensors and tactics, that made sense.

Dan, O'Quinn, Henrickson, Jung, and the shortest Lieutenant Kim put in an hour over the chart, talking out the concept of operations. They had to start with water conditions. Water conditions determined just about everything in ASW. And to play this game, you had to understand the nature of sound.

Underwater sound, such as machinery noise from a submarine, traveled, or "propagated," by three pathways: direct path, convergence zones, and deep sound channels.

"Direct path" meant sound coming straight from the source to the receiving hydrophone. Point to where you heard it from, and you were pointing at the sub. The trouble was, sound tended to curve upward over long ranges. It was a refraction effect, since water at depth, under pressure, conducted sound faster. Direct-path sound formed a curved funnel shape, seen from the side. If you were outside that funnel, you wouldn't hear the sub at all.

Complicating it even more were the "layers," surfaces at which the sea's temperature and salinity suddenly changed. They reflected sound, meaning you couldn't hear someone on the other side. The main layer, between the warmer, mixed water near the surface and the cold stillness of the depths, moved up and down between about 90 and 250 feet. Dan had felt the change on his skin during his dive on the Sang-o: an instantaneous transition between warmth and chill. If a sub hid under a layer, a ship could pass right over it and never know it was there. Like a child pulling a blanket over himself to hide from the monsters.

The tendency of sound to bend upward over long distances formed "convergence zones." After about thirty miles, it hit the surface and bounced. If you had sensitive equipment, and positioned yourself right, that meant you could hear your quarry thirty, or sixty, even ninety miles away.

The "deep channel" was just that—deep. So deep he wasn't even going to worry about it here.

A playground this shallow—a wading pool, in ASW terms—meant they couldn't depend on the deep channels and convergence zone paths that were the bread and meat of open-ocean surveillance. Here, they'd use either direct path or active sonar. But "going active," pinging and listening for the echo, gave away your own location. And the quieter a submerged sub could run, the shorter direct-path detection range became. Not only that, Op Area 25 was right on the highway for shipping transiting the Strait, adding to the ambient noise.

Everything out here loaded the dice in favor of their submerged adversaries. Unfortunately this was where, and how, the naval wars of the future would probably be fought.

"So," Jung said, "You know what ASW really stands for?"

Dan said no. "Awfully slow warfare," the commodore explained.

It was worth a chuckle. "So we are going to do some of that in the next few days," Jung went on, touching his mole lightly, maybe unconsciously, with the tip of his little finger. "Our passive ranges will be between one point five and perhaps four thousand yards, active direct path. There will be high biologics and fishing activity. We can also expect reverberation. So, let us turn to event 27003."

That afternoon's exercises were "structured," meaning both sides knew exactly what maneuvers the other would be making and when. USS *San Francisco,* an attack nuke, would meet the slowly steaming Korean line on a gradually converging course. Starting at a distance of twenty thousand yards, depth one hundred feet, she'd run past them at a range, at the closest point, of three thousand yards from each ship in turn. Her first run would be a fast pass with all machinery engaged. Subsequent runs would cycle various combinations of pumps, sonars, and other equipment at varying speeds and depths. The purpose was twofold: to accustom the sonar operators to the visual and auditory return from a submerged submarine, and to tune the equipment itself to maximum sharpness.

Dan looked at his watch. Time to start. Jung was back in his chair, flipping through messages. Should he do anything? Or let the squadron staff handle it? The frigate didn't have a separate flag bridge. The skipper and the commodore had to share the pilothouse, and he had to keep all these different Kims straight. At last he went up to the commodore and saluted.

"Yes, Dan?"

"Comex, sir. Time to begin."

"Commander Hwang, start the exercise."

Dan hadn't seen the chief of staff come on the bridge. Hwang said a few words to the lieutenant. "This is Sierra Two Lima," Kim said carefully into a microphone. "Startex. Startex. Startex. Event 27003. Sierra Two Lima. Out."

Dan paced the bridge, then found a place to park by the chart table. *Chung Nam* should be on 270 at ten knots for this event. The other Korean ships would follow astern of her. But he didn't see it happening yet. In fact, he didn't see *anything* happening.

He was clearing his throat when Hwang saluted Yu. He spoke apologetically. The captain frowned, and shot angry Korean at the officer of the deck. Who in his turn wheeled and spat abuse at the helmsman. The gyro spun slowly and settled on 270.

The exercise proceeded. He went out onto the bridge wing and checked the 19. Henrickson had lashed the black box to the deck gratings. A cable ran up to a stubby whip clamped above them. The 19 computed and recorded ship location five times a minute, accurate to within twenty feet. When the mainframe back at TAG digested its recordings, those from the other ships, and those from the submarine, they'd be able to watch the tactical picture develop in twenty-second increments. When the decisions in the logs and the reports of the ship riders were factored in, analysis would yield who'd sunk whom, who'd missed chances and made wrong decisions, which tactics worked and which didn't.

He went down to CIC and poked his head through the black curtains into the little corner sonar room. It always seemed hushed back there. A survival of the days when sonarmen had actually listened. Now they depended more on sight, interpreting the visual displays on their screens, than on their ears. Monty Henrickson and the three Korean techs were so intent they didn't notice him for a few minutes. When they did, the eldest smiled and bobbed his head. Dan nodded back. The supervisor reached up and turned a dial.

A distant throb filled the compartment, the muffled but still audible signature of a U.S. nuclear submarine. Mixed with it were subtexts, the clicks, whines, and buzzes of biologics, pulsing throbs he guessed were the other ships and maybe *Chung Nam*'s own self-noise.

They were in passive mode: listening only, not pinging. The chief pointed to a shimmering display of what Dan guessed were the screw tonals. Everything that went to sea had its fingerprint, from rotating machinery, screws, cavitation, hull noise. Even dead in the water a ship chanted a narrow-frequency counterpoint composed of discrete tones from air-conditioning, generators, cooling pumps. With practice a sonar team could identify class, nationality, often individual ships. He gave them an encouraging wink. Henrickson waved back with his clipboard, and Dan backed out.

In the far corner the plotting team huddled in busy absorption. The DRT, dead reckoning tracer, was the heart of antisubmarine operations. A lit circle showing own-ship position projected from beneath the glass-topped table onto a large sheet of paper. He perched for some time on a wobbly stool, nursing what he finally realized was a caffeine-deprivation headache. The plotters, headphones clamped to their ears, had no time to talk or even look up. They jotted down ranges and bearings from sonar, radar, and the lookouts, a complete round every fifteen seconds. Own ship was in black pencil; the submarine, red; coordinating ships, blue. The wandering snarled snail-traces recorded the intricate minuet that was antisubmarine maneuvering, the remorseless long-drawn-out struggle that in wartime would end with sudden detonations and violent death.

Leaning over their shoulders, Dan saw *San Francisco* was drawing aft. It had passed its closest point of approach to the flagship and was now abreast of *Kim Chon,* the next ship astern. *Dae Jon* brought up the end of the line.

He refreshed his memory from his PDA. He'd have to know this cold once the pace picked up. *Kim Chon* was a patrol corvette, Korean-built. Corvettes were smaller than frigates, but the ASW-heavy ones, like her, carried sonar, Mark 46 Honeywell acoustic homing torpedoes, and depth charges. The depth-charge suite was interesting; he wondered if they'd be more effective against a bottomed, waiting sub than torpedoes. *Dae Jon,* or *Taejon,* was an old ex–USS Gearing class, formerly USS *New,* DD-818. Her sonar suite wouldn't be up to current standards. The last ship in line, *Mok Po,* was another corvette, heavily gunned, but one of the non-antisubmarine-capable variants. She didn't even *have* a sonar; he didn't know why she was in this exercise at all.

The plotters' hands whispered across the paper, etching in the new positions. Dan noted that the third in line—that would be *Dae Jon*—was tracking north. It had swung out of line four minutes before; now it was diverging markedly. He tapped its track, catching the evaluator's attention. "She's leaving the line. Closing the range. Do you know why?"

The chief smiled with an expression Dan was beginning to recognize: eager to please, but uncomprehending. He tried a few more words, then gave up and waited for the next round of bearings. When they showed *Dae Jon* even farther off course he pulled himself up the ladder to the bridge again.

On the wing, glancing astern—just to make sure, before he kicked up a fuss—he saw that indeed the old Gearing was pulling out of line. He checked the wing gyro, borrowed the lookout's binoculars, and searched out along the sub's bearing. He was looking for a periscope feather, or the gulls that often followed one, but didn't see anything.

Jung wasn't in the pilothouse, but Hwang was. "Uh, see what's happening with *Dae Jon*?" Dan murmured. "He's pulling out of line. Closing the range to the sub."

"They report problems acquiring." The chief of staff shrugged as if it were no big deal. "Once they pick up the target, they'll resume station."

Dan glanced astern again. The old destroyer was far out of line by now. He noticed *Mok Po* was hauling out now too, following the ship ahead of her. "Uh, how close are they going to go?"

"As I said: till they pick up the contact."

Dan was about to ask what if they didn't, but at that moment the bow of the distant destroyer swung back, her starboard-side hull numbers coming back into view. A speaker above their heads sputtered Korean. "She has contact now," Hwang announced. "She is rejoining."

Dan said that was good. He was turning to go below again when a white-jacketed steward bowed. He offered a tray covered with a spotless embroidered warming-cloth. Lifting it, Dan found a silver serving pot, a cruet of white fluid, and a dish of pure white crystalline cubes, stacked into what he realized after a bemused moment was a small replica *Chung Nam*. The smell of fresh hot coffee was overpowering. When he looked up every man on the bridge was staring at him.

He stayed in CIC all afternoon, keeping an eye on things. Events 27005 through 27007 went off without incident, though he noted the Koreans still didn't pay overmuch attention to the assigned course. In almost every case, they closed the range to the sub more than the event called for. They crept in gradually, as if drawn by a magnet. He thought about asking Jung to caution them, but dismissed it. That was what the intro phase was for: so Jung, or Hwang, or the individual COs would correct shortcomings themselves. There was a limit to how much he could, or should, hold their hands.

When dark fell the events were still going, though *Chung Nam* was off line for the time being and had withdrawn to the west to practice antitorpedo maneuvering. At last he got up and stretched. His feet hurt and his neck didn't feel so great either. He hadn't gotten all that much sleep over the last few days, what with jet lag and being roused early for the Sang-o. When he went back up to the pilothouse Jung was a shadow in the dark.

"Commodore? Evening, sir. I'm going to turn in for a couple hours, if you don't need me."

"Mr. Lenson. I understand you had some problems with our stationkeeping. That you mentioned it to one of the ship's company."

The sonar evaluator. "Uh, yes sir, but Commander Hwang explained what was going on. With *Dae Jon*." He thought about mentioning the range issue, but decided again to let them fix it themselves.

"All right, Dan. But any other comment you may have, I'd appreciate your bringing it directly to me or Commander Hwang. Not to the ship's company."

That was fair; he was here to support Jung as officer in tactical command. "Aye aye, Commodore."

"Get some sleep. I'll keep an eye on things."

"Aye aye, sir," he said again, already looking forward to the narrow bunk with its knit comforter. He looked back once more, to see Jung's shadow still resting motionless against the black, the radio speaker frying quietly above, the only sign of life the hot red dot of a cigarette like a faraway flare in the dark. It brightened, faded, and then winked out.

6

The helicopter sketched a charcoal line across a rough gray paper overcast, aimed directly at him. Lenson slouched with thumbs in this belt loops, steel-toes braced wide, briefcase slung off his back. *Chung Nam* rolled with a slow nodding lean. Around him the crew shouted and rushed about. Looking flushed, Kim #3—there were so many he'd resorted to numbering them—swung his landing-signal paddles on the fantail like a jayvee cheerleader warming up her pompons. The helo banked and rapidly grew larger. Its clatter echoed across the choppy sea.

Two days had passed. Phase I was complete. Every sonar team had at least five hours' practice tracking *San Francisco* and four hours tracking the smaller, and therefore harder to acquire, *Chang Bo Go*. The Korean 209 had joined up the day before.

The helo landing team froze in their tracks, saluting him. Or rather—Dan turned his head—saluting Jung, who'd just stepped out on the frigate's tennis-court-sized helo deck. Dan didn't salute, since he was uncovered, but he bowed. The commodore nodded back, then turned his attention to the approaching aircraft.

Five minutes later they sat squashed together with five other passengers, gripping their briefcases as the quivering fuselage banked hard. The deck rolled up and hovered nearly above them. They grew suddenly heavy. The sea scrolled past. He looked across the fuselage to meet Jung's eyes. They stared at each other until Dan dropped his gaze.

USS *John S. McCain* was the Destroyer Squadron 15 flagship. Since Jung was OTC, he'd wanted to hold the pre–Phase II meeting aboard *Chung Nam*. But Leakham had argued *McCain* had better comms, a full flight deck, and spaces for a large meeting. As Dan followed Jung and the others through her centerline passageway he felt like Woody Allen unfrozen in the far future. The air was chill with air-conditioning, which *Chung Nam* didn't have. The wide passageways were lined with advanced equipment. The crew, of which there seemed to be very few, wore spotless dark blue coveralls and ball caps instead of denims and greasy tees. The cold air smelled strange. It took a while before he realized the "smell" was the absence of stale smoke.

"Good morning, good to see ya. Commodore Jung, what a pleasure." Leakham, bulky and blond and hearty, was working the arriving COs in the spacious immaculate wardroom. He pumped Jung's hand. "Bring any PowerPoint matter? We can upload and project it here. No? Well, come on in. Decaf, muffins, hot fresh tarts on the sideboard." Dan got only a nod. "Lenson. How you doing over there?"

"All right," he said, but Leakham was already greeting the next officer in line, gaunt, bronzed, and glorious in white shorts and gold-encrusted cap; one of the Australians, from *Darwin* or *Torrens*.

Dan got a blueberry pastry and coffee, marveling at how strange human beings of European descent looked now. At first all Koreans had seemed identical. All dark haired, and almost all (except Jung) fairly small. But with his eye meeting no one else for days on end, they'd become individuals, each unique.

Now, back among Americans, he saw their differences not as within the norm of accustomed variability but as grotesqueries. The varied hues of face and hair and shape seemed no longer commonplace, but shocking and freakish.

He finished the muffin, ravenous, and was tearing into a

flaky still-warm raspberry tart when a balding captain, probably Leakham's chief of staff, called for seats.

The meeting went fast. He made only a few notes. Two events on the third were being switched, to avoid carrying one, which depended on visibility, into darkness if it went late. The weather didn't look good, though. A tropical storm near Indonesia would bear watching, the met briefer said. They'd see increased overcast, rain activity, and wind speeds between fifteen and twenty knots. But unless it actually came their way, the landmasses of Japan would mask any marked long-period swell activity.

Jung called on Dan for remarks. He reminded the assembled COs to make sure the TAG reps riding their ships had full access to tactical decision making. They should discuss with those riders their rationale for any departure from standard operating procedures. "I want to emphasize again, we're not here to *grade* you," he said, looking each in the eye in turn. "We don't expect or require you to hew to existing tactical guidelines. We put those out as suggestions, based on what's worked in the past, or what theoretically should give you better detection ranges, higher detection rates, better probabilities of reacquisition on a lost contact. And in the end, a better probability of kill during the attack phase. But it's ultimately up to you which tactics you implement. SATYREs can be a fruitful source of future tactical improvements, but only if we understand what's going through your head. Your intent is just as important as the maneuver itself. We'll then evaluate that maneuver against its objective success. Eventually the result will show up in your publications. So keep a close eye on those data-keeping requirements, and assign people you know are on the ball." He asked for questions, got none, and sat down.

Jung made a few remarks. He finished, "As the British learned in the Falklands—the last time submarines were faced in a wartime resupply operation—ASW is a force-intensive activity. Even when it's successful, it usually results, not in a kill, but just in keeping the enemy at bay.

"Given that—and we do understand that, I assure you—

Korean Navy doctrine is still somewhat different from standard NATO doctrine. We believe the most effective means of keeping the threat at bay *is* the kill. A dead submarine will not reattack. We emphasize overwhelming force, and offensive action at all costs. I understand this is at variance with U.S. procedures. But the difference is only one of emphasis. I expect to work very closely together during the remainder of this exercise, and I hope it is as productive as Commander Lenson"—he reached out suddenly, and Dan flinched as he was patted on the shoulder, no, almost *caressed*—"seems to think it will be."

Fat and bluff, Leakham heaved himself up and smiled around. Muffin crumbs clung to the front of his shirt. "Well, that's about all Commodore Jung and I had. Anything more before we break?"

Dan lifted his hand. Leakham looked away, but at last had to nod, though he frowned as he did so. "Lenson."

"One thing I've noticed, sir."

Another frown. "Go ahead."

"I'm not sure we're where we ought to be as far as prearranged signals for disengagement. We had an incident in event 27005 where a ship was getting out of station. It didn't proceed to extremis, but if it had, how would we have stopped the exercise play and warned both sides to go to safety courses?"

Leakham chuckled. "I don't see that as a problem, Mr. Lenson. There are standard disengagement signals in ATP 28."

"Well, sir, those signals assume there's several thousand yards, even miles, between the engaged units. The predicted direct-path ranges over the next few days here are so close I don't feel entirely comfortable—"

"We'll stay with the usual signals," Leakham announced. "Red flares and the voice radio warning on VHF primary tactical. They're perfectly workable. Everyone's familiar with them. I don't want to introduce new signals just for this exercise."

Dan looked at Jung, who was sitting with legs crossed. The Korean was the OTC, not Leakham. But Jung wasn't objecting, or even, apparently, taking much interest. Dan tried one more time. "I see your point, sir. But I'm not sure why having another emergency disengage signal would be confusing. The sub has to surface to use VHF radio. And if there's patchy fog, or someone's not looking in the right direction, he might miss the flare."

The U.S. commodore was shaking his head before Dan was done speaking. "Matter closed," Leakham said. "Any other questions? *Substantive* questions? Yes, there in back."

"On the data-keeping requirements—we've only got the one rider. What happens when he's down for sleep?"

Dan rose, ready to explain once more it was ship's company's responsibility to keep the data, not the riders'. With only one TAG member aboard each unit, he couldn't be in four spaces—bridge, CIC, sonar, and underwater battery plot—the clock round. But before he could speak Leakham said pontifically, "Data keeping's essential, but it's more important to keep the exercise events moving ahead and on time. Especially if the weather degenerates. We can't let this stretch out or we won't get everything accomplished. Let that be your guide."

"Sir, excuse me—"

Leakham didn't even look his way. "Thanks for coming, good hunting, and there are still some muffins left," he told the room. Put his arm around Jung and ushered him out, up to the flag quarters.

Dan got back to *Chung Nam* well steamed. What the hell was up with Leakham? He'd blown him off in front of the entire group on the emergency disengage issue. Then given the skippers carte blanche to push data recording to the back burner. Certainly they wanted to complete all the events. But without seamless and trustworthy data, TAG couldn't evaluate the play later. The guy acted as if they had history. But Dan didn't remember any fat, arrogant assholes named Leakham.

The first thing he did was look for Henrickson. He found the analyst in the wardroom. "How'd the conference go?" the little analyst asked.

"It sucked, big time."

He explained. Henrickson looked disturbed too. "That's just fucking wrong."

"So how do we fix it?"

"Well, Leakham's not OTC for this exercise."

"He sure as shit acts like he thinks he is."

"Well, he's not. The host nation's officially in charge—we specifically write that into every SATYRE. Go through Jung. Draft a message from him outlining exactly how important getting the data is, and who's responsible for it. Then he puts it out to everybody, problem solved." Henrickson added, "I'll draft it if you want."

"That's great. Could you do that, Monty? Just make it short—people don't read long messages."

"Absolutely. Three paragraphs." The analyst pulled a pad of the pulp-paper ROKN message blanks out of his briefcase.

"You seen Cap—you seen Joe O'Quinn?" Dan asked, turning back at the door.

"Not today. He was pulling late hours on the last event. He's probably catching up on sack time."

Dan realized he hadn't seen O'Quinn since the exercise had started. Just that one glimpse of him pondering the sea as they got under way. "Why doesn't he eat in the wardroom? I haven't seen him around much."

"He hates Korean food. He brought a bunch of granola bars and stuff."

"Guess I can understand that." The same kimchi and pickled fish meal after meal was getting to him too. Unfortunately, as the ranking TAG guy, he felt bound to eat with the Koreans.

"They give you anything good on *McCain*?"

"Blueberry muffins."

"Bring me one?"

"Sorry," Dan said. "Guess I should have, huh? Next time."

He went up to check on the 19, made the rounds to encourage the data keepers, then went back to the bridge.

The afternoon sky was overcast. *Chung Nam* and *Dae Jon* charged along at fifteen knots through a three-foot chop kicked up by a slowly increasing wind. The chop wasn't good news, he thought. Waves generated low-coherence background noise. With the water as shallow as it was already, that would make a sub, especially a quiet one, that much harder to pick up.

Event 30001 kicked off Phase II. A step up in complexity, a barrier exercise with subsequent two-ship play. The Korean 209 was off line to the east, snorkeling—running submerged, but with an air intake the size of a wastebasket above the surface to run her diesels and charge her batteries. Hwang said it took her about forty minutes to do a full charge.

So *San Francisco* was playing target. The nuke boat would start at the northeast corner of the op area and head southwest. The barrier, consisting of *Chung Nam, Dae Jon, Cushing,* and *Vandegrift,* would align on a bearing of 300 degrees true and conduct an intercept search while steaming slowly northeast. They'd be preceded by *Cushing*'s helicopter, dropping sonobuoy patterns. *San Fran* would attempt to slip through. The surface units would use standard search procedures. Once they made contact, they'd separate into two teams, Yu in charge of one, *Cushing*'s CO honchoing the other, and take turns carrying out deliberate multiship attacks. Dan thought it should prove interesting. In water this shallow—only three hundred feet through most of the exercise area, heavy mixing and no layer—the sub would be very difficult to pick up.

Hwang was talking over the barrier intervals with Jung. Dan stood at the edge of that conversation, left out of the Korean, but tracking its drift as they did the math and

summarized in English for him from time to time. The
sticky wicket was that with passive detection ranges so low,
the ships would have more frontage to cover than they could
actually search. An interesting problem; he wondered if he
could write a program to generate the optimal tactic. It'd
have to have a graphical user interface, and maybe a menu,
and use regression analysis. . . . He got a couple of notes
down in his PDA.

Finally Jung decided to deploy SAU 1—Surface Action
Unit 1, *Chung Nam* and *Dae Jon*—to port, then leave a gap
between them and SAU 2, to starboard. Both SAUs would go
active, pinging hard, flooding the sea with noise and radar
too, just in case *San Francisco* popped her scope up. But
Cushing's helo, flying at two thousand feet, would drop six
sonobuoys, set to passive, into the gap. "The sub'll pick up
the gap and drive for the hole. Once the sonobuoys pick her
up, we wheel in and she is in the bag," Hwang said. "Is it a
good plan, do you think?"

They looked at him expectantly. Dan doubted it would be
that simple. U.S. nuclear submarines, which were both very
covert and capable of high submerged speeds, were notori-
ously slippery. He figured it was about the best they could do
given the wretched sound-propagation conditions. But he
couldn't say so. "I'm not actually supposed to, uh, vouchsafe a tactical input."

"Vouchsafe?" Hwang frowned.

"Sorry. It means advise. I can't comment on your plan.
Just record it."

Jung's face darkened. He opened his mouth, then closed
it and sat back instead. *"Ke ro ke ha ko, jeon mon bo nae,"*
he said to Hwang. He sounded angry, but then, Dan thought,
almost all Koreans sounded enraged. It was just how the in-
tonation struck an American ear.

"The commodore approves," the willowy Korean told
Dan. "We are ordering the units to their comex stations."

"Yes sir," Dan said to Jung, hoping he didn't get ticked
off that he hadn't signed off on his plan. He felt like he was

dancing on a tightrope. The Koreans seemed so concerned with face.

He went down at lunchtime and confronted the usual. Hot tea, fish, kimchi, cigarette smoke, ten guys chattering in Korean, or worse, trying to tell him jokes in their fractured English. Kim #2 got off a real roarer. "Once upon a time, Tarzan lived in jungle," he said. "Understand?"

"Yeah, I got that," Dan said.

"One day his wife was in adversity. Tarzan catched a vine and was flying. Suddenly he was crying. 'Ah! Ah!' Why?"

"Gee," Dan said. "I don't know. Did he hit a tree?"

"His wife catched his middle leg," #2 said, and waited for Dan to laugh.

He managed to smile. "That's a good one all right. A real knee-slapper."

"Knee-slapper." #2 slapped his knee and giggled. "Knee-slapper!" He said something to the others and they just totally broke down. Dan shook his head in disbelief. What an audience.

"You tell one. You tell funny story."

He didn't think of himself as a teller of tales, but in the course of almost twenty years in the Navy, he'd heard a few. Most of the really funny ones were too raunchy to be retold. "Okay," he said.

"One cold night in New Jersey this guy's car breaks down on a hill. It's a really foggy, drizzly night. He stands by the side of the road for a long time, but no cars go by.

"Then finally he sees a black limousine coming slowly through the fog. It comes right up to him and stops, and he realizes it's a hearse. He bends down but can't see anyone inside, the windows are tinted and it's dark, so he opens the door and gets in.

"But when he turns to thank the driver for stopping, there's nobody there. Nobody—except a big black coffin in the back.

"He's staring at the wheel, shocked, when suddenly the car starts moving again. It moves very quietly, up the hill,

then down, faster and faster. At the same time he hears
moaning coming from the coffin. He's paralyzed with terror.
A curve looms ahead, with a drop-off on the outside of the
curve, and he starts to pray. Just before they're about to go
off the side of the hill, a hand floats in through the window
and turns the wheel.

All the Koreans were staring at him now, eyes wide. "So
the next curve the same thing happens. The guy's petrified.
Like, turned to stone.

"Suddenly the car slows down, and he recovers enough
from his terror to pull the door open and tumble out on the
road. He rolls down the hillside and gets all torn up, but he's
just so glad to be out of that car he doesn't care. He comes
out on another road and runs down it till he comes to a
tavern. Like a bar—you know? All wet, still shaking, he orders a couple shots of whiskey and tells everybody what just
happened. The bar goes quiet as they realize he's crying, and
he isn't drunk.

"About fifteen minutes later two guys walk into the tavern, panting and sweating, and one says to the other, 'Hey,
Louie, there's that idiot who climbed into the car while we
were pushing it.' "

They stared. Finally they smiled politely. Kim chuckled
uncomfortably, glancing at his mates. But no one slapped his
knee. Maybe humor just didn't translate. Dan slurped the
last of his tea, making it noisy to be polite, and was about to
excuse himself when a voice crackled over the announcing
system. They jumped up and left, pausing only for a hasty
bow in his direction. Dan jumped up too. He didn't grok the
whole announcement, but he'd caught *"jam su ham"*—
submarine.

When he got to the bridge it was dark. He hadn't thought it
was that late. But part of the darkness was rain. The wing
doors were open, and cool freshness and wind filled the pilothouse. The little tight space was crowded with helmsman,
lee helmsman, Captain Yu, the officer and junior officer of
the deck, the rest of the watch, and the ASWRON 51 staff,

Jung's people, too. The disks set into the windshields hummed steadily, giving them three circles of visibility despite the rivers streaming down the windows. Jung wasn't in his chair. Dan decided it was just too crowded and went back down to CIC. You could get a better tactical picture there anyway.

An hour later *Cushing*'s SH-60 reported a contact on one of the sonobuoys in the gap. The tracking team was still plotting it as the frigate heeled, cutting through the seas to a new course. A vibration wormed through the ship's fabric, and a low whoosh built from aft.

"The turbines," one of the JOs told him. Dan nodded, though he was surprised; at high speed they'd lose any chance of gaining sonar contact. The boys must be confident they actually had a sub. He pulled out his PDA to get down a note. He saw from the little blue penciled circles tracking alongside theirs on the DRT that *Dae Jon* was out to port, lagging a bit. That made sense. She was steam powered and didn't have the frigate's acceleration. But both elements of SAU 1 were pelting hell-bent down an intercept course. He checked the range to the datum and calculated a torpedo danger circle. This was the range inside which the submarine, at bay, could strike back.

But they didn't reach it. Three minutes later, the sonobuoy lost contact. The plotters etched in the little kite-shaped datum symbol, marking last known location. Yes, there, they were drawing in the torpedo danger circle.

Dan gripped the edge of the DRT table as they leaned into a roll, then back the other way. The joiner bulkheads creaked. They were weaving at high speed. Presenting a more difficult target. The frigate's motion in a high-speed regime was unsettling. She didn't roll so much as abruptly lurch, as if she were balanced on her keel. The heat in the cramped close space didn't help. Nor did the radish-and-garlic breath of the plotters. He took deep breaths, loosened his belt surreptitiously, and tried to think about something else.

Just short of the dotted danger circle *Dae Jon* broke left

and *Chung Nam* right, wheeling in a yin-and-yang around the datum. The whoosh descended the scale. Dan felt deceleration tug him forward as they coasted out. It looked as if Captain Yu, who was the on-scene commander, was looking to hold contact with his own ship, and sending *Dae Jon* in for the initial attack.

He went into the sonar compartment for a while and discussed the search procedures with Henrickson. The ship leaned in a couple more tight turns while he was in there. He figured it was normal evasive maneuvering in the vicinity of a sub. He borrowed the sonarmen's tables and worked out the effective acoustic range of their torpedoes. They were homing torpedoes, of course, Mark 46s, using a small active sonar in the nose to pick up and then zero in on their target.

This triggered another thought, and he ran down his attack checklist and went out into CIC again and checked that their own antitorpedo countermeasures were streamed. The SLQ-25 was the same decoy the U.S. Navy employed. It howled the identical noise spectrum into the water as a ship's screw. A fish approaching from astern would home on it and explode, instead of going into the propeller.

He was occupied with this when he glanced at the DRT.

The green pencil trace—*Dae Jon*'s—was crossing almost directly over the datum.

He froze, not believing what he saw. His first thought was that the plotters had erred. He shoved between them and fingered the trace. "Is this good? Is this valid data?"

Even as he asked he knew it was. The track had diverged nine minutes earlier, about the time he'd gone into sonar. The evaluator gave him a blank look. Dan swore and wheeled, charging up the ladder to the bridge.

The pilothouse was absolutely dark and unfamiliar and he blundered into someone, who shot back abuse in Korean. Dan said the only phrase he could muster, "Sorry."

"Commander Lenson?"

It was Yu; of course if you were going to run into someone, it had to be the captain. On the other hand, Yu had tactical command of both ships. Dan said quickly, "Sorry, sir, but

I can't see yet. Captain: *Dae Jon* is very close to *San Francisco*'s safety zone. Maybe inside it by now."

"She is making attack."

"I understand that, but your plot shows her far too close in, sir." He peered out the windows, expecting any moment to see the red flare from the submarine that meant *danger, disengage*. But there was nothing but the black of midnight sea. The speed disks roared. Rain hammered on the windscreens. "I strongly advise you signal 'disengage' at once and withdraw to a safe distance."

"Commodore is not on the bridge—"

"Sir, he's not OTC for this event. *You* are." At that moment a distant red-orange spark caught Dan's eye out the starboard wing window. He swiveled instantly and pointed. "And the sub's at *periscope depth*. Sir, you have to disengage."

His eyes were adapting now and he could make out the men and equipment as black shapes against the faint luminescence from dials and indicator lamps. He left Yu standing and crossed the bridge and undogged the starboard door.

The warm rain cascaded down out of blackness. It smelled like a root cellar and like coal smoke and it soaked him within seconds. He ignored it. His face was welded to the little three-power scope on top of the pelorus stand. Through it he made out the orange wink of the strobe far away. He twisted the scope and made out the silhouette of a destroyer only a few degrees off it. Yeah. Showing a port running light. It was bearing down on the strobe, and by the distance intervals on the plot below, at flank speed.

It seemed like minutes as he fought his way through the door again, groped in the dark for the right microphone, and hit the button. Perhaps a tenth of second elapsed between pressing the button to speak and the red transmit light illuminating. In that instant his brain warned him he'd pay for this. But then he remembered the men in a fragile envelope not far below the surface. The knife-edged bow of the old destroyer, flank speed, bad visibility . . . an electric shock ran up the injured nerves of his spine. He couldn't wait for someone else to act.

"Buffalo, Buffalo," he said as clearly and slowly as he

could. "Event terminated. *Dae Jon, Dae Jon:* Speed zero, I say again, speed zero. Turn to safety course due north immediately. Acknowledge."

He wanted her dead in the water, *now.* An accented voice came back with a stilted interrogative. Dan repeated the order till he got a roger. Then said, "I say again, Buffalo, Buffalo. All units clear and disengage to safe standoff distance."

The Koreans were shouting at him. He felt a hand on his shoulder. He shoved it off and went through the litany again, slowly, precisely, sending in the clear so everyone could hear and not waste one precious second searching a signal book. He signed off, let up off the button. Took a deep breath. Then turned.

The bridge was emptying. He could only guess, but someone must have ordered it cleared.

The confrontation wasn't pleasant. Midway through it, with Yu spluttering in a spit-spattering froth of English and Korean, trying to tear him a new asshole without the vocabulary for it, *San Francisco* came up on the tactical coordination net. Laying it out in dry phrases, a midwestern voice from the American sub notified the overall exercise OTC— Commodore Jung, though Hwang had been the one who actually answered the radio—that *San Francisco* would no longer participate in exercise play. He was withdrawing to the east for the remainder of the dark hours and would report his pullout to SUBPAC. He requested that all Korean units stay well clear of him west of 127 degrees east longitude.

"May I talk to him?" Dan asked Hwang. He got a hesitation; then the handset.

"Romeo Kilo, this is TAG exercise coordinator. Request to speak to Romeo Kilo actual. Over."

"This is Romeo Kilo actual. Over." The sub's skipper, in person.

"This is TAG coordinator. Request to know reason for your dropping out of exercise. Over."

"This is Romeo Kilo. I can't play with these idiots. Over."

Dan cleared his throat, conscious of Hwang, and Yu, and the officer of the deck, Kim #2, he thought, listening to the exchange, which was being piped over the speaker as well as through his handset. Plus everybody in CIC as well, no doubt. "Uh, this is TAG coordinator. Understand there was a violation of standoff distance. Over."

"Romeo Kilo. You could call it that. I call it irresponsible maneuvering, too close at too high a speed. He missed me by less than two hundred yards. That's too dangerous for me to continue participation. Over."

Dan rubbed his forehead. Without the sub, they no longer had an event. "This is TAG coordinator. The signal for a dangerously close approach is a red flare. Over."

The sub skipper explained he'd tried to fire one, but it had hung up in the ejection tube. When the inner door had been opened to extract it, it had ignited and fallen out on the deck. Dan closed his eyes. No wonder the guy was pulling out. At periscope depth, with a destroyer charging down on him, and a fire aboard too. "Any casualties? Is the fire under control? Over."

"Romeo Kilo. Fire is out. A couple guys down with smoke. Over."

Dan eased off the button, trying to think. He thought he knew where the Koreans were coming from. They had the fighting spirit. He didn't want to discourage that. But he also understood the sub skipper's misgivings. Captaining a billion dollars' worth of nuclear submarine was as exacting a trade as there was. His job was to get everyone working together. That was the only way to keep the exercise going. But at the moment, it was falling apart.

"Commander Lenson?"

Hwang. The staff officer tugged at his sleeve. Past him, in the corner of the pilothouse, Dan saw Commodore Jung. His stocky shape stood square in the dimness, like a rock around which the surf seethed. Dan steeled himself and went over. "Commodore. Commander Lenson here."

"I understand you interfered in Captain Yu's conduct of this event."

"Sir, *Dae Jon* was within *San Francisco*'s standoff distance. The sub was at periscope depth. It was too dangerous to continue."

"Yu is the OTC. You could have advised him. Rather than causing him to . . . rather than assuming his responsibilities."

Jung's tone was iron, the silence in the pilothouse complete. Dan decided diplomacy might be in order. "Sir, it's U.S. Navy doctrine that anyone observing a hazard during an exercise may terminate the exercise. *Must* terminate the exercise. If that's not Korean procedure, I most humbly apologize. Both to you and to the captain." He bowed, both to Jung and Yu, to make it plain even to those who didn't follow English what he was doing.

Jung cleared his throat but didn't respond, so Dan pressed on. "Unfortunately we have a problem."

He explained about *San Francisco*'s onboard fire, her CO's reaction to the close pass, and his withdrawal from the exercise. Jung's shadow stroked its chin. Said slowly, "If they leave, the only submarine involved will be *Chang Bo Go*. That won't be sufficient?"

"Well, sir, no, it won't. The free play just won't work with only one sub."

Jung said angrily, "I'm not happy about this, Commander. Korean doctrine too emphasizes safety. But after all, we also train the way we fight. And I don't plan to admonish any of my skippers for being too combative. No. I will not do that."

"No, sir. I understand where you're coming from on that. And if I acted too hastily, I apologize once again."

"Very well; that is closed. But about the submarine . . . what can I do about that? Is she really going to withdraw?"

"They take safety very seriously, sir. And you can't blame them."

"Tell me what to do," Jung said.

Dan thought a moment. He didn't like the idea, but it was all he could think of. "Well, sir," he said slowly, "there might be one thing we can try."

7

The rain blew down in slanted ramps from colorless clouds as somewhere dawn broke. It sparkled on the gray decks and skipped along the coamings and whirled in the scuppers. Dan was soaked all over again as he climbed up into *Chung Nam*'s motor whaleboat. The boat swayed like a cradle as he stood clutching the dripping monkey lines, waiting to lower away. The deep flute-roar of the stack ten feet away vibrated his very bones. He'd left his wallet with Henrickson. He carried a handheld radio and was laden-wet in foul weather jacket, fore-and-aft cap, and a bright orange flotation vest. Which was too tight across his chest, but it reassured him. Considering he was facing a heavy chop, with a doubtful destination. He hitched his sagging trou and looked toward the bridge.

A face he hadn't seen much of late looked back. Joe O'Quinn, back among the living. As Dan looked up, the retired captain raised two fingers from the rail like a pickup driver on a country road. Taking that as a greeting, he nodded back.

The chief shouted and pointed and a seaman pushed over a controller. The davits rotated out and the boat began its descent. Dan crouched, gripping the line as the whaleboat metronomed. The wet-glazed gray of *Chung Nam*'s hull swung close, then far away. The boat crew was ragged, tentative, as if they didn't do this very often. It wasn't quite up to par with what he'd come to expect, which was a high

standard in seamanship and gunnery, somewhat lower in
communications and tactics. And of course near the bottom
of the stack when it came to chow, showers, and the other
habitability issues. Or maybe they liked their food that way
and didn't care about the rest.

The front tackle lurched. The chief screamed his head off
above them, and Dan came back to where he was. He glanced
down into the rain-spackled, greasy-surfaced sea. He tightened the life jacket straps, gauging his chances. If that forward hook let go it'd drop the bow into the water, flip the
boat, and drag it over top of them. A gray-green sea crested
and spray rattled over them. He licked it as it ran down his
face. It tasted like sweat.

The flagship had checked out of the exercise. They were
fifteen miles east of the op area, headed into the prevailing
seas. The submarine was a black nub only occasionally visible two thousand yards distant. Her CO had refused to allow
them closer. Dan didn't think that boded well for his mission, but this was all he could think of to do.

The keel hit the sea. The chief screamed again and gestured violently. The hooks released with a ragged double
clank barely audible through the wind and the breaking seas
and the snorting growl of the boat's diesel. The forward
hook swung back at them and everybody ducked as it went
through. He crouched, feeling better being unhooked and
seaborne. The coxswain put the wheel over slowly, so as not
to slam their stern into the hull, then gunned it.

The frigate receded into a gray shadow in the rain astern.
He found a seat on the thwarts as another mass of spray
boarded. Water rolled to and fro on the thwart. His pants and
underwear were already sodden. He wished he had another
pair of shoes. Corfam was never the same after salt water.

The sea seemed bigger and much rougher down here. Also
dirtier: a scattered litter of cardboard scraps, bits of styro-
foam, chunks of what looked like plastic packing material,
bobbed in the dimpling rain. The diesel growled and burbled
and roared. The helm groaned as the coxswain, the biggest

Korean Dan had yet seen, spun the wheel, searching out an approach to each oncoming wave. As they surged to a crest Dan shaded his eyes against the rain and spray. He clicked his gaze across the horizon but saw nothing. Looking back, he couldn't see the frigate anymore either. The coxwain had his head down; Dan saw he was checking the compass.

Ten or eleven minutes later *San Francisco*'s massive sail loomed above them like a black keep just emerged from the sea. Even ballasted up the submarine was being swept from one end to the other, rolling much more violently than the frigate had. Two seamen, safety lines dragging in a track, clung to the base of the sail. The coxswain eyed Dan, then the rolling, seaswept rounded hull. Lenson swallowed, re-signing himself to a swim at least, major damage at worst. This wasn't going to be pretty.

"*Gal ryeom ni ka?*" the coxswain yelled. "You go?"

"*Nay, nay,*" Dan said, wondering why the Korean and English were exact opposites. He made a get-the-hell-in-there gesture. The coxswain shrugged, gauged the roll, and whipped the wheel over as the sail rolled to port.

As the hulls collided with a head-jerking slam the other Koreans grabbed him bodily and pitched him out. Dan hit on his feet, but staggered as the roll came back at him. His shoes flew out from under him on slippery rubber tiles. He went down hard and started sliding back down into the sea.

The two submariners hurled themselves at him. One smashed him in the skull with a hard object. Dazed, still sliding backward, Dan sucked a breath, anticipating a long time underwater. The second man got a line around him. Dan got his hands on it and together, somehow, they dragged him up to the sail. A sea hit them there, smacking them into the wet rubber that coated the steel. When it receded he saw recessed rungs leading up the sail. The sailors gave him a boost. Clinging hard against the roll, the centrifugal force of which got wilder the higher he climbed, he reached the top at last and ducked through an access cutout and came up in a little semienclosed cockpit.

"Welcome to *San Francisco*," a jaygee in a green foul-weather jacket yelled. "Skipper's below. Let's get you down there and dried off."

The hatch led to a ladder trunk that went down like a deep well. Dan kept his mind on his hands. They were burned from the lines, stinging from the salt, but if he slipped he'd fall sixty feet, break his legs or worse. He went down and down.

At last he stepped off, sopping wet, into the control room. Everyone was in blue coveralls. A tall officer with close-cropped champagne hair and high cheekbones shook his hand. "Dan? Thought that was you on the horn. Andy Mangum. Sixth Company."

Mangum's cabin was half the size of Dan's on *Chung Nam,* about like four shower stalls put together. The overhead curved in: they were just beneath the top of the pressure hull. Mangum sat on the bunk. Dan got the single chair, with the little modular desk folded up.

"Thanks for the b-robe." He fingered Mangum's gold-piped blue Naval Academy bathrobe.

"We're running your uniform through the wash and dry. Have it back in half an hour." Mangum leaned back. They'd already gone through the usual drill of Annapolis classmates running into each other on active duty, who was where, who'd gotten out, who'd been passed over. "Okay, what can I do for you?"

"First off, have you sent that message yet?"

"What message?"

"The one to SUBPAC. Saying you weren't going to play with us anymore."

"I've got it drafted." Mangum didn't meet his eyes.

"But have you sent it?"

"I hope that isn't what you came all the way over here for. To get me not to. Because it's not gonna happen." He shook his head. "I can't gamble the boat and my guys' lives on a bunch of overzealous shiphandlers."

"That's got to be your call," Dan said.

"Oh, it will be. Believe me. And if I have to err, it's on the side of caution. You had command, right? A couple of them?"

"Officially just one."

"Surface type?"

"Destroyer. Yeah."

"So you know what I mean. But the margins are narrower with no reserve buoyancy. We operate in a zero-error environment down here."

Dan noticed for the first time there was no motion whatsover. "We're submerged?"

"Two hundred feet. Eight knots."

"Very smooth." He'd sniffed the air in the control room, expecting the afterwhiff of fire, of a burning flare. There'd been nothing; the air had been polished clean, sterile, bland.

"So, given that's not negotiable, I hope you didn't come just for that." Mangum waited, palms cupping his kneecaps. "So, why *did* you come?"

"Actually I had something to give you."

He'd had them wrap it in a waterproof chart pouch. He unsealed it and took out the paper. Held it out. "From the captain of the ship that did the drive-by on you."

Mangum took it, looking suspicious. He glanced down the message. "Boy," he said.

"Takes a while to get the gist of what he's trying to say."

"I guess he writes better English than I do Korean."

"It's an apology."

"I can see that."

Dan gave him the second sheet. "And here's another one, handwritten, from the ROK COMDESRON. Commodore Min Jun Jung. They take apologies seriously."

"I've worked with the Japanese. Same same."

"Then you know they won't be happy campers if we just blow these off." Not giving Mangum a chance to argue back, he went on, "I also want to tell you, why you're getting all this personal attention from our allies here. Why I came over in person. I didn't want this on the VHF, or in anybody's signal log. And I want your assurance you never heard it from me."

Mangum hesitated. At last he said, "Okay. What?"

"I got this from the naval attaché in Seoul. We're going to pull out of Korea. Part of the reduction of forces."

"*What?* Pull out?"

"That was my reaction. The administration's already downsized the Army; we've got to take a cut too. If the Koreans can take over the sea lanes, we'll lease them six destroyers, buy them four more diesel boats, and retrograde."

Mangum said anxiously, "Did he say anything about the forces out of Japan?"

"It was a she. Oh, you guys'll stay. But that's what this exercise is about. Whether they're good enough to deal with the North Koreans on their own."

"Are they? What do you think?"

Dan pondered that, finally decided the honest answer was "I haven't seen enough yet to make that call, Andy. But I think what it means in this context—bottom line is what we owe, actually what I owe, the Navy. And that's a bona fide, no-shit assessment of the ROK's antisubmarine abilities. The chain of command needs an objective reading. Without that, they can't vote yea or nay on the pullout. What I'm afraid of is that if they don't give a clear signal, this administration'll go for the low-cost option: get out. And in that case, if they're *not* ready—"

"We'd have a real bitch-up," Mangum supplied. "If the North decided to try again."

Dan was waiting for him to make the connection when someone tapped on the door. Mangum said, "Come in." A young man in the ubiquitous blue coveralls didn't actually enter—there was literally no room to—but slid a tray in. Mangum settled it on his lap. "Coffee?"

"Thanks."

"How's the commander's uniform doing, Cus?"

"Out of the wash, in the dry, Skip."

Mangum nodded and the crewman closed the door. He handed Dan a cup. "And this all relates to me, how?"

"If you don't play, there's no exercise."

"They have their own boat. The new one."

"It's too easy with just one targ—uh, with just one opponent."

"*We* are not the targets," Mangum observed mildly.

"I didn't say you were."

"We pull out of here, the U.S. I mean, there'll be tanks in Seoul a week later."

"That's my thought too, but it's not my call. My bailiwick's to do this exercise and give them a valid grade."

He sipped the coffee and waited. After a couple of seconds the submariner said, "When they see that periscope, visually I mean, they don't know the range. We've got some new features that disappear us from radar. I just can't have them charging in on me."

"It's a valid concern. I'm willing to give up realism for safety."

"What are you offering?"

"Guaranteed two-thousand-yard standoff, under no circumstances to be violated. That's double what's in the op order. Also a three-ping signal. We hear three pings active from you, the exercise is over."

"Safety courses?"

"Better than that. Everyone goes dead in the water until you redistance and put up a green flare."

"Fuck that. I'm not cycling that fucking flare ejector again till I have the shipyard look at it."

"Well then, till you get your comm mast up and give us a pritac all clear."

"If they see a scope at all, they're to turn and put it on their beam."

"If that's how you want it. Sure."

"How's the OTC gonna get this word out to his people?"

Dan held out the third piece of paper. "Actually it's in Korean, but it spells out exactly what happens to any CO who gets inside two thousand yards of you. Let's just say he retires with no legs, no balls, and one eye ripped out."

"Now we're talking," said Mangum. He fanned himself

with the papers, portraying Man in Deep Thought. "Well, I can't think of anything else I can get out of you. Except what really happened with the *Horn*."

Dan was continually surprised at how many people had heard about what was supposedly compartmented top secret. As far as rumor, gossip, and backstairs intrigue, the Navy was like a small-town church choir. "I can't tell you anything more than what you probably already heard. We figure it was a drifting mine. Just managed to save her."

"So why's there chain-link and guards around her at Portsmouth Naval Shipyard?"

"I lost some of my people. Some very good people. I hope that never happens to you, Andy."

Mangum regarded him for a moment more. "Well, guess what? There's things I can't tell you either. I guess we have to wait for our memoirs?"

"Yeah. Our memoirs. We're go, then? You're back in?"

"I guess so. But I want your TAG guys on the scope too, when they're working close in."

Another tap heralded Dan's uniform, cleaned, pressed, on a hanger. "We dried his shoes on low heat," the crewman said. "But he's just going to get them wet again."

"We got a pair of boots we can lose?"

"Size?"

"Ten," Dan said.

"Take a good look at this guy," Mangum said to the crewman. "This is the most decorated guy on active duty in the U.S. Navy. Commander Dan Lenson. But hardly anybody knows his name outside of it."

"It's a real honor, sir," the crewman said.

"You bilger," Dan muttered to his classmate.

"Hey, and maybe a worn-out set of rain gear, Cus?"

"We'll take a look, sir," the crewman said. "How worn-out's it got to be?"

"This dude holds the Medal of Honor. That give you a hint?"

"Message received, Captain," the crewman said. He looked at Dan as if he were a demigod, as if he wanted to touch him but was afraid to. Dan wished Mangum hadn't said all that.

Mangum reached for a phone on the bulkhead. "Captain. Return to pickup point and prepare to surface. Complete three-sixty sonar search. Course into prevailing sea." To Dan, "We'll be there in twenty minutes. Ever seen one of these?"

Dan said, "I'd be honored if you'd show me around, Andy. I'd like to see your—boat. But really, they don't need to know all that stuff you were telling him."

"I'll tell them whatever I goddamn well want to tell them. Who's the fucking CO here? You or me?" His classmate punched the phone again. "XO? Everybody off watch, in the crew's mess, ten minutes."

The whaleboat, which had stood off while Dan was below, took him loping back over the waves. The rain had eased off, the squall-clouds moved on. It was smoother headed downsea. Small brown birds soared and dipped, flinging their wings over at each crest as if they too were enjoying themselves. He wiggled his toes deliciously in dry socks, in the new boots. All he had to do now was make sure the Koreans restrained themselves, kept safety in mind, and this whole thing might yet work out.

It occurred to him that if it didn't—if anything *did* happen to one of the subs, even just a bent 'scope, anything at all from here on till the end of SATYRE 17—he could expect to be hammered, having coaxed the reluctant Mangum back into play.

But that didn't worry him. It was too nice a day. He even saw, gradually wearing its way through the gray denim of the departing squall, a bright patch he suspected might be the sun.

He ducked his head going into CIC, missing the air duct that'd creamed him before, and caught Henrickson's eye. The analyst looked unwontedly grim. He said a word to the sonarman he'd been talking to, patted his shoulder, and got up and came Dan's way, carrying a clipboard. "A word?"

"Hey, Monty."

"How'd it go? Heard you went over to *San Fran*."

"On the whole good, I think. She's back in the game, given some additional precautions. What is it? O'Quinn?"

"What? No."

Henrickson handed Dan the clipboard. He ran his finger down the message headers. It was from CTF 74—the U.S. task force assigned to the exercise, that would be Harry Fatass Leakham—to COMTAG, Commander, Tactical Analysis Group, Little Creek, Virginia.

4 (C) Safety is paramount in all exercise operations. It is the concern of this commander that the personal direction being exercised on COMASWRON 51 by the TAG representative is prejudicial to the safety of maneuvers. Numerous close passes at dangerously high speeds inside danger zones have been noted.

5 (C) It has also been observed that a close relationship seems to exist between the senior TAG team member, CDR. D. V. Lenson, USN, and COMASWRON 51, Commo. Jung Min Jun, ROKN. This unprofessional relationship operates to the detriment of the US components in the exercise.

6 (S) It is therefore proposed that CDR Lenson be immediately relieved as exercise director and replaced either by this commander's chief of staff or other TAG personnel now on scene.

The betrayal and outrage felt like incipient lightning. Like a day, out sailing, when he'd bent to run out more scope of anchor line as a thunderstorm came on, and felt the electrical charge thrilling up his fists from where they gripped the sea-soaked nylon. "Unprofessional relationship"? That could only mean one thing in this context. He'd suspected Leakham had a hard-on for him, but this was out of the ballpark. He looked up. "How'd we get this, Monty?"

"Came in while you were over there."

"Has Jung seen it? Yu?"

"No. At least, I don't think so. Their radio guys are supposed to bring our traffic right to us. And not keep any copies."

"Does this happen often?" Dan asked him. "The fucking U.S. commander tries to get you relieved?"

"There's friction, sure," the analyst said, not meeting his eye. "Shouting matches, even. Once, off Sardina . . . but this is the first time I've had anyone ask for the director's head. And you're right, this reads ugly."

"What is it with this idiot? You dealt with him before?"

"No, but you must've. Sounds like he's got it in for you, all right."

"I barely *know* the son of a bitch," Dan muttered. He reread the message, nauseated now. It wasn't often you got stabbed in the back like this in the Navy. Especially when you were actually doing your job reasonably well. As he'd thought he had.

"Political?" Henrickson prompted.

Dan was about to answer when he realized he didn't really know much about Henrickson either. He worked for TAG, of course, but who else? How plugged in was he to the rest of the Navy? And which Navy? The Vatican had no monopoly on heresy, schism, inquisitors, and Martin Luthers. He raised his eyes from the message to stare into his face. Henrickson looked evasive, but then he often did. Probably he was just what he said he was. Just another civ-mil contractor, though it was odd, now he thought about it, to see a full PhD out in the field.

Because just that one word, *political,* had bungee-corded him back to a mind-set he'd hoped to leave behind. With a pullout from Korea at stake, there might be forces at work beyond the usual multinational-exercise tiffs. Things that might go up the line. Things that his wife, Blair, part of the current administration, after all, might find not as puzzling as he did.

Or maybe he was being too suspicious. So in the end he didn't say anything. Just lowered his head slightly. Henrickson blinked, looking bewildered, as Dan folded the message twice, neatly, carefully, making his face noncommittal, unconcerned, and slipped it into his shirt pocket and buttoned the flap over it.

Sealing it in, as if against the possibility it might escape.

8

The commodore's cabin was furnished more spartanly than he'd expected. Jung was well connected, smart, obviously a comer. But his cabin contained only a desk, an office chair, a low table, on which they were now eating lunch, and a plain reed tatami. A framed family photo was taped down on the desk, next to a notebook Toshiba and an empty in-box. A leather sample case sat on the deck, and on the bulkhead hung a calendar with a reproduction of a temple scene somewhere in the mountains. It looked as if the task force commander could throw it all in the case in sixty seconds and be ready to walk off the ship.

The table was at an awkward height: too high to eat from sitting on the floor Asian-style, yet too low to be comfortable from a chair. The result was that Dan's back hurt as he hunched, hunting with his chopsticks for something edible.

It was two days after his jaunt over to *San Francisco*. The exercise had gone smoothly since. He'd heard nothing from TAG about Leakham's message. Or if there'd been a response, he, the on-scene director, hadn't been one of the addees. Which left him in a position that made him furious, but that he couldn't do anything about. Other than stew, so he tried not to think about it. Which of course meant he couldn't get it out of his head. Being isolated aboard *Chung Nam*, unable to talk to anybody except by official message, made it worse. He wished he could get Blair's take on it. That always seemed to put things in perspective. But he couldn't; they were as out of touch by phone as every other way.

He didn't even know, come to think of it, whether the man tucking into the noodles across from him knew his American adviser's own senior officer was trying to have him recalled. Even if he'd read the message, had it back-channeled to him out of the radio shack, the broad face across from him was well able to keep whatever secrets it concealed.

Lunch, like breakfast and dinner, came in tiny porcelain bowls. Each contained two or three tablespoons of . . . matter. Dan picked and dabbled, trying to feign interest, or at least conceal disgust. Pickled seaweed, pickled fish, pickled radishes sliced fine, pickled grated carrot with some spicy sauce. There were several varieties of kimchi—fermented cabbage—with chili peppers, turnips, and other, unidentifiable ingredients. He loaded up on the steamed rice, but you couldn't eat just rice. Not with Jung.

"Try some of this," the commodore said, dropping a wad of what looked like cow-cud on Dan's plate.

He chopsticked it up—every Academy grad knew how to use chopsticks; the dividers you practiced with in nav class operated the same exact way—dented it as little as possible with his teeth, and gulped it whole. If he was careful he could miss actually tasting it. "Uh—*interesting* flavor. What is it? Seems a little like—pork?"

"Very good! That is close to my own family kimchi. When I was a boy we'd work at it for weeks, in the fall. The mountains of cabbages in the kitchen were taller than I was. If we kids didn't peel fast enough, my grandmother would threaten to pickle us in the jars too."

Dan slurped soup, watching for bones. Too salty, but it was fresh. They'd hove to beside a fishing smack that morning and bought the catch. The ship rolled around them, making the liquids slosh in their various containers. He felt light-headed.

"I have eaten on many U.S. ships. And at your colleges. But it's always nice to get back to the food you're used to." Jung sucked air politely, or maybe the hot sauce was getting to him too. "No doubt you feel the same."

"No, this is good." He'd noticed how anxious they were that he liked their food. And Jung was obviously laying it on: so many choices, so carefully presented. He fished around, got what looked like a meat dumpling, and made himself eat it. It tasted so shit-rotten he thought: God, they can't be serious. It stank like tripe with sweet dough wrapped around it. The ship rolled again and he fought to swallow.

Once down, though, Korean food stayed with you. He hadn't shat once since he came aboard. What must be going on in his gut, he didn't like to think about.

"I can't believe you don't like *soju.*"

"It's not that I don't like it, Commodore."

"Oh, yes, you don't drink. Still, just a taste couldn't harm you. Really. Could it?"

Jung glanced to his side and the attendant poured him a small porcelain cup of the rice liquor. The commodore raised it, saluting him. Dan picked up his teacup and toasted him back. Then pointed to the *soju* cup and said to the attendant, *"Anyo. Kamsahamnida."*

The sailor widened his eyes and looked to Jung. The commodore looked annoyed and waved at him to take it away. "No, no, the man cannot taste it, even for a toast. But you and your men are getting your coffee all right?" he asked, with an edge of irony.

Apparently Yu had mentioned their little confrontation in the wardroom. "Yes, sir. We are," Dan told him. "Thank you."

"No, thank Yu." Jung chuckled at the pun. "The exercise this morning. Combined torpedo-attack countermeasures. You do not think we reacted too slowly? When *Chang Bo Go* fired at *Cushing*?"

Dan played for time. Unfortunately that meant eating more, and he got one of the pepper dishes. He coughed and ate rice and swallowed tea. "Well, sir—excuse me—as you know, I'm not supposed to comment on how well things go. I explained that—"

"This is not about the grade, Commander. I know there is no grade. I'm asking your professional opinion. Between us. Off the record."

"Commodore, your men are earning my professional respect. Beyond that, I just can't comment."

Jung's swarthy face went sour again. "They're the same tactics Leakham's using. On the whole."

They weren't. Leakham depended far more on his helicopters, but Dan wasn't going to let the guy sucker him into saying so. "Sir, as long as they're safely executed, all I'm here for is to record them, not judge them."

"I'll tell you what irritates me. That Leakham. He says he doesn't *get* my directives. He gets them, but ignores them. He issues orders as if he is in command."

Dan kept his mouth shut. A smart commander stayed out of commodore-to-commodore disputes. Jung said, "I am the OTC, that is clearly specified. I have tactical command of all ships in the exercise, of whatever nationality. The Australians understand this. Even the Japanese. Only the Americans don't."

"Sir, I'd say that's a Harry Leakham problem, not an American problem. I totally agree with you about the clarity of the relationship."

Jung was nodding, clearly less satisfied than momentarily mollified. He was starting to discuss airspace management when someone tapped on the door.

It was Captain Yu. He bowed and handed Jung a message. Bowed again, though perfunctorily, to Dan, who'd gotten to his feet as the CO entered. They waited as Jung read.

The commodore started in Korean, but switched to English. "This will most likely mean *Umigiri* will be leaving. Any indication of it yet?"

"Nothing, Commodore-*nim*. She still in barrier station."

"Uh, what's going on?" Dan asked them.

Jung waved the message. "The Japanese Maritime Self-Defense Force has gone to full alert. The Chinese have fired a test ballistic missile across the island of Hokkaido."

At last Dan said, "Well, that's pretty far away from our operating area."

Yu nodded. "That is true. Hokkaido is northernmost island in the Japanese chain."

Jung: "Nevertheless they have gone to full alert. Lodged a protest with the Chinese, and with the Security Council. Test or not, firing a missile over another country's territory is a clear provocation. A strong message."

"But what is the message?" Yu said.

Dan remembered the way Tomahawks had headed off on their own, early in the development of that missile. "It couldn't be an accident?"

"The message does not say, but I would doubt it. Not with a ballistic missile."

Dan wondered what the American involvement might be if there was a crisis between Japan and China. He cleared his throat. "I don't see this as impacting our exercise. Not yet. Do you?"

"No, I agree. The most that may happen is *Umigiri* detaches, and any other JMSDF units in the southern areas are called back to the home islands. We may lose their maritime patrol air as well." Jung paused, pulling at his lower lip and blinking through the PhotoGrays. "If that happens we'll have to redraw the plan for the free-play event."

"Since we won't be able to seal off the flanks against an end-around?"

"That's right. Perhaps we could . . . move it into a sea area more tightly bounded by surrounding land?"

Dan said that might work, though having fewer assets would hurt in other ways too. He and the chief of staff would study the problem and come up with recommendations. Fortunately they had a few days in port before the free-play phase would begin. So they wouldn't have to pull it out on the spur of the moment. But it provided a good excuse to cut lunch short. He bowed to Jung. "I will go and look over the charts. If you will excuse me."

Curtly, Jung gave him a dismissive nod.

Dan stopped on the main deck and rested his palms on the lifeline. A thrilling-faint vibration violined through it, a pulse picked up and transmitted and sung its length from the very life of the ship. The sea was more nearly smooth than it had been for the last few days, the wave heights one to two feet, no more. The sky shone the clearest blue he'd yet seen it in this patch of ocean. The sea was the deep blue of old velvet where some heavy precious object has lain for a long time and kept the cloth from fading. Bubbles rocked along its surface as the flagship leaned, so very gradually you could hardly call it a roll, under way on diesels alone at an easy eight knots. Far to the north fluffy white clouds hovered, their upperworks glowing like heated silver. If they marked land, as they often did, he guessed it'd be Cheju-Do, off the southern tip of Korea.

He shaded his eyes, searching for the rest of the exercise force. Miles off a containership was transiting southward, bound for Singapore or Hong Kong. Heavily laden, top-heavy, it had all the grace of a shoebox floating down a rain gutter. Beyond that he glimpsed the gray upperworks of a Spruance-class: *Cushing.*

Turning, shielding his gaze again to check out the flat sea astern, he picked up *Mok Po* far off. The afternoon's event was another barrier exercise, this one more narrowly focused. The two submarines, acting in tandem, would try to crash through a double screen.

They'd not really know till the analysis back at TAG, but as far as he could see, the subs were holding their own. The new-generation diesel-electric, *Chang Bo Go*, was very quiet, possibly even more covert submerged than *San Francisco.* The days of long-range detection by passive sonar were ending. In a few years the only way to pick up a sub would be massive pulses of active sonar. Flood the ocean with huge power levels of sound, and let the computers sort through the echoes. Where they drew a tiny bubble of steel-enclosed air, that would be the target.

The whales wouldn't like it, that was for sure. He stood by the rail, gnawing his lip, hunting the ramifications of that thought. Maybe the answer wasn't more powerful sonars on surface ships, but hundreds of small intelligent devices scattered by aircraft. When something reflected their low-powered pulses, they'd pop to the surface and signal a monitoring station. He tried to conceive of how to power such a disposable device, how to suspend it in the water. Or else . . . he reversed the question; Could they make the *submarine* easier to detect? A noisemaker, a cricket, dropped by the thousands to stick magnetically to the sub's hull? A robotic vehicle, set to pick it up as it left harbor, and track it no matter how quickly it maneuvered?

Certainly something had to be done. He'd seen in the past few days how hard a modern boat was to detect amid the traffic and noise of the coastal sea. They'd have to throw out a lot of what the Navy had depended on for decades. They'd need new technology, new tactics . . . or run the risk, in any future crisis, of heavy losses.

That made him think again of the Chinese provocation, and that nation's increasingly brazen disregard of its weaker neighbors' rights. The Chinese had even published their plans: dominate the inner island chain by 2010, the second chain by 2020, and be a worldwide naval power, deploying carrier battle groups, by 2050. A few years before, he'd tried to push back against their expansion into the oil- and gas-rich South China Sea. Maybe even slowed their timetable by a few years . . .

But to date, their expansionistic tendencies had been directed south. What could they accomplish by threatening the Japanese? Tokyo's constitution capped defense spending, and Japan's Self-Defense Forces were just that—they didn't even own offensive armament. Why conjure up the ghost of Japanese militarism? It just didn't make sense.

Someone coughed at his elbow. He turned to see the tall, reddish-elegant Hwang tapping a cigarette out of a pack. For a moment Dan wondered if he was gay. Was that what Leakham was so hot about? "Unprofessional relationship" had been the way his message had phrased it. Was *Jung* gay? Did Leakham think *he* was?

"It is so beautiful out here today," the staffie opened. "A change from the lousy weather."

"You can say that again."

Hwang smiled in that slightly superior way. "Did you hear about what's going on up north?"

"The missile overflight? Over Japan? I was with the commodore when the news came in."

"They have refused to apologize. The Chinese."

"That makes it much more serious, then."

"Oh, yes. No official regrets—that is very serious. Of course, the Japanese have never apologized either. And for much worse things."

Dan hesitated. "What's the Korean take on that? About China?"

"Our take?"

"Your opinion."

"Oh. Our opinion—our 'take.' Well. China we can live with. We have for many thousands of years, after all. Our king acknowledged fealty to the Manchu emperor until 1895, did you know that? Until the Treaty of Shimonoseki. There is a mutual respect there. An understanding—or at least there once was." Hwang frowned. "With Japan our relationship has been much more unpleasant."

"I guess I can understand that." From Washington Asia looked monolithic, but out here the strains and differences between peoples became plain. Still, Hwang didn't sound as if he stayed awake nights worrying about Beijing. Dan wondered if the whole model of rising-state threat the West had imposed on China was really accurate.

"Are you ready for another Korean lesson?"

Dan tried to switch his mind back. "Sure."

"Okay, some very useful phrases here. *Gae sae kee.*"

He repeated it dutifully. *"Gae sae kee."* A passing deckhand did a double take, then went eyes front again when he saw their khakis. "What does that mean?"

"A bad name. Means you are not a human being. Almost a son of a bitch."

"Uh, okay. Got it. I guess."

"Now you say *aie* when something happens. It is not such a bad word."

"Like saying 'hell' in English."

"Like saying 'hell.' Now, you want to say something bad, to a man: you say *see-pol.* Or *see-pol, nome.*"

"I'm afraid to ask."

"Oh, do not be afraid. Means, 'Go have sex with yourself, gutter trash.' Or to a woman, you say *na pen ya.*"

Dan nodded, not really trying to commit it all to memory, amusing as it might be. He was still trying to keep the terms for port and starboard straight. But it occurred to him that it might serve his purposes to probe. Jung was a locked vault, but maybe his aide wasn't. "So. Anything interesting in your message traffic these days?"

The commander, flipped a hand languidly. "We are all warned to be on the alert."

"What for?"

"That, they do not tell us. It is a difficult time just now. The Northerners are making their threats. 'Rattling their swords,' that is in English? It is the election, I think. Each time we have one they make themselves unpleasant. They are like hagglers in the market. No, like ruffians. Is that the word? They threaten, then they ask for gifts. Ruffians?"

"That's one word for it. Or extortionists," Dan said. He tried a closer pass to his subject. "Commodore Jung. How long have you been with him?"

"I have been his chief of staff two years now. Before that I was his operations officer aboard *Chonju.*"

"*Chonju.* Destroyer type?"

"One of your Gearings. They called her 'the Jolly Rogers,' someone told me once. We fought a surface action off the DMZ one night. Against the Northern torpedo craft. That is why the commodore wears the Order of Military Merit." Hwang hesitated, then laughed as if at himself. "Yes, I will say this: It is why he respects you, Dan. You too have the combat decorations. You too have hunted the tiger. Not like the other officers they send us. That is what he told me."

"Well, I respect him too. My impression of the commodore is good. He seems very knowledgeable."

"Yes, he is that." Hwang seemed prouder than the usual

chief of staff, most of whom saw their bosses too close up for hero worship. "I believe he will become our CNO."

"Really?"

"Yes, I do. He is well placed. His family is wealthy. His father knows the president. Yes, I would say he is very well placed."

"You're not so badly 'placed' yourself," Dan told him. "I can see how much he depends on you."

"Oh, I am just the staff officer," Hwang said modestly. "Do not embarrass me! What is your opinion of the exercise? How are our Korean ships doing?"

"I think your personnel and equipment are first rate. The Ulsans and the new 209s will make for a very powerful coastal defense capability."

"And our training? Our tactics?"

Dan said carefully, "You'll get your answer to that when TAG goes through the tapes. That's what the exercise is for, after all."

"I have heard a rumor," Hwang said, still casual, not even meeting Dan's gaze, "that the U.S. Navy plans to withdraw from the Republic of Korea. That cannot be true. Can it?"

Dan cursed himself. He'd found out absolutely nothing, and now it was Hwang's turn at the pumps. "You hear a ton of scuttlebutt at sea," he said. "*Aie!* Who knows where it all comes from. Anyway, that'd be between your government and ours. We'd be the last to hear about it." He hoped that was convincing.

Hwang said, watching him narrowly, "You have heard of this, then? That if this exercise goes well, if we show ourselves worthy allies, you will abandon us?"

"We'd never *abandon* you. If you were ever attacked, we'd be there. Out of Japan. Out of Okinawa. Out of Guam, if it came to that."

"You abandoned Vietnam."

"That was a long time ago. We stood by Kuwait, and we didn't even have a treaty there. Or defense plans, like we do with you."

"Kuwait has oil. We don't."

"Uh—yeah. Look, I'm not saying you're wrong, okay? You're probably right. At least about Kuwait. But we'd never just walk away from the Republic of Korea," Dan said again.

"I believe you. Yes. We have been allies for a long time. Your soldiers fought and died for our freedom. That is what makes us friends. Blood. Not a treaty." The chief of staff flicked his cigarette butt down into the water, where it floated for a moment. Then the bow wave roared over it, and it was gone. "But we learned a lesson in 1950. It is this: An ally is most useful when he stands beside you. If he comes too late, what was most worth saving may already be gone."

Dan didn't have an answer to that. Especially considering what Hwang had told him, on the drive to Pusan, about what had happened to his family when the Reds took over. He took a deep breath, looking out over the passing sea, trying to ignore Hwang's waiting silence. Till the chief of staff added, "But if that were so—that if we were judged good enough, strong enough, you would feel justified to withdraw—you would think then during this SATYRE we would take care not to look so very efficient. Would you not? But *Jeon dae jang* Jung would not do that. It would not strike him as honorable. To do less than his very best."

Hwang paused again, giving him a second chance to respond. Dan felt both angry at being cornered and, for some obscure reason, guilty. He stuck his hands in his pockets and stepped back from the lifelines.

The chief of staff nodded. "But as you say: it is all 'scuttlebutt.' So. We will see you at dinner?"

Dan nodded. "Sure. At dinner."

Hwang touched his shoulder, and a moment later Dan was alone again with the wind.

He was in CIC that night, long after dark, when the message came in via tactical voice. The coded groups arrived one by one in precise, Japanese-accented English. Even before he reached for the book, Dan knew what they said. He'd noticed one of the pips on the scope change course to the northeast. Beside him Kim #1 was breaking the message too. The lieutenant laid the penciled lines carefully by his hand.

JMSDFS Umigiri recalled by national authorities. Detached from SATYRE 17 immediately. Departing exercise op area effective upon receipt.

"Their maritime patrol air is late too," Kim said.

"I wouldn't hold my breath waiting," Dan said. "We'd better count on doing the rest of this exercise without the Japanese."

"We didn't need them," Kim said confidently. "So let them go. We will do fine without them. We Koreans, and our good friends, our very good friends, the Americans. And the Australians too."

Dan wondered what was happening behind the scenes. Which, since his White House duty, he knew was where things that mattered happened, not in public view. The Japanese might be confronting the Chinese in a few days. In that case, the Pacific Fleet would be in the middle of the action. And he'd be stuck in a sideshow, if that.

But he didn't share any of this. Just nodded, looking back at what he'd been examining before the detachment message came in.

The printout was black on white, chattered digital lines on crisp flimsy paper, but in his mind it translated into falling pressures, circular motions, ominous progress across lines of longitude and landmasses, across hot seas feeding energy into an unstable atmosphere. East of the Philippines another tropical low had decided to promote itself into something more menacing. "Bad weather on the way," he said to Kim.

"It is not worth the worry. By then we will be back in port."

He nodded. In another day they'd be moored in Pusan for the midexercise break. He stretched and pounded his fists into the small of his back. The Ulsans were Korean-designed, and it showed. Everything on the ship was set either too low or too high for a guy his height. He'd slammed his head so often that he moved in a permanent crouch. "Yeah, I'm definitely looking forward to stretching my legs again," he muttered.

Kim looked first astonished, then delighted. "Stretching your legs," he said, and chuckled madly. He jerked out a notebook. "Stretching your legs," he said again, scribbling.

"It's not *that* funny," Dan told him. But he couldn't help grinning too.

9

Pusan, South Korea

When the hot washup for the first half of the exercise broke, Dan went into the bathroom down the hall. A white-jacketed attendant bowed. He was checking his uniform in the mirror when Leakham pushed through the door. Their gazes met, but the commodore's slipped aside as if greased. Leakham cleared his throat and went into a stall.

Dan was waiting by the sink, arms crossed, when he came out again. "Commander," Leakham muttered, still not meeting his eyes as he washed his hands.

"What exactly is your problem with the Koreans, Commodore? Or is it a problem with me?"

The big man's cheeks flushed. He twisted the faucet savagely. "If you read your message traffic, you know the problem. Commander."

"Yes sir, I believe I do. The *problem* is your accusations are inaccurate. The ROKN needed a course correction on their safe distances. Commodore Jung and I applied it. Then smoothed things over with *San Francisco*'s CO. There was no reason to kick it upstairs. If you'd had the courtesy to ask me, I'd have been happy to set you straight. Without me you wouldn't have an exercise."

The fair face flamed. Dan guessed he hadn't heard that kind of language from an O-5 in a while. "Set me straight? Without you, Lenson, I'd have a *better* exercise. These people need a tight rein. They don't want to learn. Want to charge off on their own. No regard for safety."

"That's because sonar conditions out there suck. Mixing, no layer, heavy biologicals, a lot of reverberation. They had to get in close to get contact—"

"Don't tell me what sonar conditions are! If you want to disagree with my conclusions, take it up with your home command. With Todd Mullaly—a personal friend of mine, by the way. But I don't owe you any explanations. Or any apologies, Commander." Leakham flicked water off his fingers and looked past Dan, holding them up. The Korean attendant, carefully poker-faced, handed him a towel.

Dan stepped up close. Right in his face. "The thing is, Commodore, you do. There was no good reason for you to send that message. And there was *no reason at all* to throw mud about my relations with Jung. That's what really burns my ass! So: what was the *real* reason, Commodore? Or would you rather I just punched you in the fucking nose here and now?"

Leakham blinked at him, and for a moment Dan saw fear. But just then the door opened, and the other attendees streamed in. Hwang looked from Leakham to Dan with a curious expression. Leakham took advantage of the interruption to push past, throwing the used towel at the attendant.

Back in the conference room the last of the pastries were disappearing. Dan got himself a reheat on the coffee and stood scowling, waiting for it to cool enough to drink. He still hadn't heard back from TAG about Leakham's accusations. He still didn't know what kind of bug was up the guy's ass.

The exercise was half over, though, and so far he'd held it together. The data was going in the logs. As long as they had that, the tapes in the 19 boxes could re-create every rudder order, every search tactic, every constructive "torpedo firing." And now the safety rules were being observed. He tried to convince himself that none of the rest—U.S. politics, Korean politics, whatever the Chinese were up to, whatever Leakham was up to—was his concern.

The TAG guys had congregated by the sandwich buffet. Dan exchanged a few words with an Australian skipper, then drifted in their direction. He hadn't seen Carpenter or Wenck or Oberg since the exercise started, as they'd been aboard the other ships. "Hi Rit, Don. Everything okay on your end?"

"Data's going down. Yes, sir."

"Backups?"

"Yes sir, taped backups, Xeroxes on all the logs. We'll get them on their way back today."

"Good. Everything okay where you live, Teddy?"

Oberg stood like a bear on skates. He looked out of place with the blond ponytail, the startlingly blue eyes, more like a surfer or some kind of Hollywood producer than a military guy. His biceps didn't belong on a producer, though. He smiled dreamily, looking past Dan like some dangerous predator that avoided confrontation. "Yes sir, Commander. Everything's going real fine. Monty's already got my data package."

O'Quinn stood silent a few paces distant, nursing a soda. Dan nodded to him. "Joe. Feeling better now?"

"Sure," the retired captain said.

"Rit 'n' me are going downtown after this. Down to Texas Street," Wenck said eagerly. "Want to come?"

"I'd better touch base with the commodore. Jung, I mean." He looked around but didn't see the Korean.

Henrickson said, "He's having dinner with Leakham and that female captain."

Dan was confused, not recalling any female captain in the exercise, until the analyst added, "The little one with the black hair."

"Just the right size to—" Carpenter started, then fell silent as Dan turned his gaze to him.

"What's that, Rit?"

"Nothing, sir."

"Monty, you mean Captain Owens? Carol Owens. She's the naval attaché."

"Well, they're getting together for dinner."

Dan wondered if he should try to join them, then decided to let the four-stripers have their private party. Of the three, he was pretty sure Jung and Owens were on his side. If he had a side. He didn't as far as the political issue went, whether the U.S. should withdraw or not. He'd come to admire the hardworking, gung ho Koreans, but that didn't mean he'd slant the outcome of the SATRYE. He didn't believe in abandoning an ally. But the U.S. couldn't do everything. At some point, its friends had to shoulder their own burden. Whether this was the time or not he was willing to leave to those who were getting paid to make those decisions. Like the civilian appointees he'd worked for back at the National Security Council.

Though their decisions had seemed to have more to do with domestic politics than anything resembling a national strategy.

He blinked, becoming aware they were waiting on his answer. "What?"

"Texas Street?" Henrickson prompted. "International Market? Whaddya say? Be nice to get out and walk."

Dan tilted his wrist, checked his Seiko, feeling the tension in his legs from too long cooped up aboard ship. "Oh—sure. Just give me a couple minutes to shower and change. No showers aboard *Chung Nam*."

Carpenter shuffled his feet. "I, uh, I got somebody to see. Maybe catch you guys down on the street."

"You still after that Korean girl, Rit?" Henrickson asked him.

"What if I am?"

"Better watch it," Henrickson warned him. Dan looked at the former submariner too. He considered taking him aside, then remembered: Carpenter wasn't in the military anymore. He didn't need a big-brother act. The contractor waved and faded.

"Meet you in the lobby, then? Sir?"

"You got it," Dan said. "And I told you: just call me Dan."

O'Quinn suggested a taxi, but Dan and the younger techs wanted to walk. O'Quinn grumbled and said he'd see them down there, he was taking a cab. "Come on, Joe, walk with us," Dan told him. "We've been cooped up for a week. Get

some fresh air." But O'Quinn shook his head and stayed behind, looking back and forth along the street in front of the
hotel.

Oberg said he wanted to get in a weight workout at the
hotel gym. So that left three of them. Dan, Wenck, and Henrickson rolled downhill through narrow streets that Henrickson seemed to know, though Dan lost his bearings quickly.

He thought again how Asian Pusan looked compared to
the capital. Tiny stores, tiny homes, warrens of walls behind
which invisible radios blared and invisible children shouted.
Street vendors hawked fresh fish, cooked fish, pickled fish,
salt fish, fish spitted on sharpened sticks. The Americans
didn't get a second glance from the swarms they moved
among.

The streets leveled and widened as they neared the water.
Past the train station the smell of the sea, or at least of the fish
market, grew stronger. Henrickson pointed out a sign that read
Texas Street. "Named after—you got it—USS *Texas*."

Down here the streets were for pedestrians only. They
looked into Chinese restaurants, companion bars, massage
parlors, questionable-looking "barbershops," *soju* joints.
Sweating little men in cheap rayon shirts piloted rattling
carts jammed with racks of clothing and boxes of micro-
wave ovens and toasters and fans and toys past them on the
asphalt, forcing them to step aside or be run down. A lot of
the neon was in English, but the newest signs were all in
Cyrillic.

Gradually Dan realized that the pasty, scruffy-looking Eu-
ropeans pushing carts, setting out displays, and calling to
them as they passed, trying to shill them into karaoke bars and
storefronts glittering with cheap jewelry, were Russians. The
pale women looking down from second-story windows in lin-
gerie or lopsided bridesmaid dresses, or parading the street
in skintight pants or leather slit skirts, bra tops, and fuck-me
shoes, were Slavic, not Asian. Dan swiveled, checking their
six, looking for MPs or the blue-and-gold armbands of the
shore patrol. Only a single black man in an NFL cap who
might or might not be military.

He blinked, trying to process it: American sleaze and decadence being replaced by Russian. Was that progress? Or some obscure form of conquest from below?

"Where are we meeting Joe?"

"Meet him?" Wenck drew his head back and bulged his eyes. "*Meet* him?"

"He said he was going to catch up with us."

They exchanged glances. "Old Joe doesn't go out steaming much," Monty said. "He just said that to get you off his back. He's back at the hotel, curled up with one of his science fiction books and a nice fifth of gin."

"Hey, you guys."

Dan and the others turned. It was Carpenter, accompanied by two girls. Beside Dan, Donnie Wenck breathed, "Oh, *man*."

Dan had to second that. The girl beside the stocky ex-submariner was slim and young, with legs so long under the midthigh skirt you couldn't look away, and flawless skin. Her eyes were bigger than they ought to be, like a manga heroine's. She couldn't be over eighteen, though on her cork-soled platforms she teetered above Carpenter.

"This here's the guy in charge," Carpenter told her, speaking loudly and spacing his words. "Dan Lenson. Dan, this is Lee Yung-Chul. Teaches English at Pusan U."

Dan doubted that. Henrickson's version, that she was a college student, rang truer. As he shook her limp cool fingers Carpenter reached behind her. He dragged another girl forward, neither as tall nor as impeccably beautiful, but sexy enough in her way. And even, Dan guessed, younger. "And this here's a friend of hers. Chang Joon-Yung."

"Wow," Wenck said again, flinching and jerking nervously. "Hi! I'm Donnie."

"Monty," said Henrickson. Both men smiled at her, but Chang wasn't looking at them. She was smiling through long lavender- and cherry-tinted hair, up at Dan.

"How do you do," she said in a soft voice that came clearly through the hubbub of Korean and Russian around them. Dan swallowed, looking at her pale slightly chubby

legs. The slit skirt wasn't as short as those of the hookers,
but it made her look more vulnerable and thus that much
more seductive. The freckles across the top of her breasts
looked strangely regular. He leaned in, trying not to stare but
failing. They weren't freckles. They were some sort of
decal, or maybe applied with a felt-tip marker. . . .

Four men chose that moment to push between them. They
were unshaven, sloppily dressed, so drunken they reeled. Too
unexpectedly for anyone to stop him, one made a sweeping
and regal flourish in the air that ended with his arm thrown
around Chang's shoulders. She pushed it off with a look of
disgust.

Henrickson shouted at them in a sudden torrent of Russian
so violent heads snapped their way all along the street. The
drunks hesitated. Then one said something in a low voice to
the others. They about-faced raggedly and lurched off.

"Well done, Monty," Dan told him. "Where'd you learn
to speak Russian like that?"

"Oh, you pick it up."

"Uh-uh. What'd you just tell them?"

"I said these girls were, uh, ours, and they'd do better
down at the Club Havana." Henrickson looked down the alley thoughtfully. "They're starting to call this Russian Street
now."

"I can see why. I thought we'd see more troops here.
Ours, I mean."

"They stay close to base these days. The girls won't have
much to do with them anymore. Rather snuggle up to the
rich Koreans, or even the Japanese."

The girls turned back to them, and Henrickson changed
tack instantly. "Where you guys headed? Want to get something to eat? Or go to a blowfish restaurant?" They made
faces, simultaneously, and Dan revised their ages downward
again. But Wenck joined in, he couldn't keep his eyes off
them, and they didn't seem to mind; Carpenter's girl clearly
loved the attention.

Finally they nodded reluctantly. Dan coughed into his fist
and said he needed to log on to TAG and get his traffic, make

sure everything was coming on okay on that end. Maybe he'd split early and catch them back at the hotel.

They didn't seem sorry to see him go.

When they were out of sight, instead of going back to the hotel he doubled back to the bazaar area and did some shopping. He found silk scarves for Blair. Got his daughter a lacquered box she might find a use for in her dorm room. He noticed the familiar logo of a Baskin-Robbins and stopped in for Rocky Road, but his stomach wasn't feeling that great and he threw it away unfinished. He felt bloated and uneasy. The uphill back to the hotel was steeper than he'd noticed coming down. He should get out and run a couple of miles before dark.

The thought of a workout improved his mood, which had grown dark after seeing the Korean girls and the available flesh all along the red-light street. And the whole inexplicable thing with Leakham. He was starting to put together what the guy had insinuated in his message, that he and Jung were getting it on together, with the fact that a couple of senior officers he knew were gay. One of them had once been his commanding officer. Cabals, countercabals. He'd hoped it wouldn't all follow him out here, but it looked like he'd hoped in vain.

He changed in his room and went out again. He warmed up and stretched in the parking circle, ignoring the looks of the valets and lobby staff, then shook the tension out of his shoulders and headed out.

He went uphill at first so it'd be easier to find his way back. The streets steepened till he was puffing. His wind wasn't as good as when he'd been able to run every day. Then the buildings ended. The hillside became a wooded park. He slowed at the top and jogged broad, quiet paths shaded by tall, perfectly straight trees he couldn't identify—their leaves looked like beeches' but their bark didn't—swerving to avoid elderly couples and strolling lovers. He got a pretty good run in, and when he got back as dusk fell he was sweating and felt less logy.

He was jogging in place in the lobby, waiting for the elevator, when someone plucked at his soaked shorts and giggled. He turned to see the younger girl smiling up through her ridiculously colored bangs.

"Uh—Hi! What are you doing here?"

"We all come back hotel."

"Uh-huh. Where's Rit? And Lee?"

"Lee up with Rit. Don-ee and Mont-ee are in the bar. Then I saw you." She rubbed the fabric of his shorts between thumb and forefinger and made a face. "Wet."

"I was out running. . . . You say your friend's with Rit?"

"They went to his room."

"I bet they did." Dan scrubbed a hand over his face, wondering exactly how old Lee was, what the legal age was in Korea, what would happen to Rit Carpenter if they got busted bare-ass in a hotel room. He regretted now he hadn't taken a more proactive role. He still wasn't sure how old these girls were. They could be fifteen. They could be *fourteen*. TAG was a military command, even if it was supported by contractor personnel. If Carpenter got himself in the papers, it'd embarrass the country just as much as if he were still in uniform.

Meanwhile Chang was running her hand down the inside of his leg. He was afraid he liked it. "I like practice English," she murmured. "You will talk to me? In your room?"

"No. Sorry. I don't really have time. Maybe Donnie could help you with that—"

"He sounds funny. Can't we talk?"

She smelled like candy. He swallowed and looked away. "I really need to do some things on the computer. Thanks, but I'd better not."

He craned toward the dining room, wishing Henrickson would come out looking for her, or better, Wenck would—the South Carolinian was closer to her age. Single, too. *Why* had she attached herself to him? He couldn't help looking down her blouse. No, they weren't freckles. Damn it! He suddenly realized his erection was clearly molded by the damp thin nylon shell of the shorts. And the hell of it was, she couldn't be any older than his own daughter.

She laughed, turned to put herself between him and the corridor, took a grip on his handle, and squeezed. "You are afraid of me? Why? I am just little girl."

"Let go of that! That's pretty much the problem. By the way—I'm married. So's Rit, actually." He glanced toward the elevator. Third floor and coming down. "Does your friend know that?"

"I don't think matters to her." She looked at the elevator too, and a mischievous smile tugged at her lips. She squeezed again, then bent him as if she were working a slot machine. It didn't feel too great, but the thought kept suggesting itself that it might be nice to teach her what did. "What floor your room is on?"

"Look, you seem like a nice person. A very beautiful girl. But I just can't," he told her in his firmest Dad voice. "Go find somebody your own age and have a good time." He patted her arm and got hold of her wrist and peeled her fingers off his dick.

The doors pinged and slid open at last. He got on quickly and jabbed the button with the "close" symbol on it. They slid shut on her pouting lips, her saucy ass as she whipped around and flounced off, flipping up her skirt behind her to show him peppermint-striped panties.

He was wondering if that had been the right decision, half sorry he'd turned her away, as he got his key out of where he'd tied it into his shoe and let himself into his room. Shit, if Leakham got wind of that, the bastard would *know* he was gay. His erection wasn't going away. He fingered it through the nylon as he kicked off his running shoes. Time for a shower, all right.

Then he noticed it was already running, a hollow roar behind the thin partition. He smelled the hot water.

He froze as the door clicked shut behind him. Was he in the wrong room? That was his hanging bag on the rack. His uniform cap on the side table. His case with the Compaq and power supply brick. This was his room.

So who was in the shower?

Just at that moment the water went off. He frowned. Tapped at the door, then tried the knob.

The air was opaque with steam. Suddenly he knew who it was. The other girl. Yung-Chul. They were double-teaming him. And he was giving way. Those legs. He couldn't resist those legs. He coughed into his fist, feeling his stomach go light, noting as if from far away as his last inhibition or scruple snapped from "on" to "off " like the last binary "fire inhibit" signal in a launching system. He was good to go.

"Uh—Miss Lee?" he said.

His wife slid open the frosted glass. She glanced up and started, then blinked back at him, her hair stuck wetly to her cheek, eyes slightly vague, slightly myopic without her contacts.

"Blair! What the hell are you doing here?"

She laughed. "What a great expression! You should see your face!"

"Well, I'm—I'm flabbergasted. You never said anything about coming to Korea."

"They needed an official body for the events tomorrow. Naturally I had to volunteer." She narrowed her eyes as she stepped carefully over the rim of the tub onto the wet slick tile, steadying herself on his shoulder. "Hand me that towel, will you? What was that you said?"

"When?"

"When you opened the door. What did you say?"

"What did I say? Uh—I forget. I just wondered who was in my shower. Events tomorrow? What events tomorrow?"

She gave him a hot damp kiss and told him the next day was the annual commemoration of the Korean War. "Nine a.m., at the International Cemetery. The ambassador will speak, and the Korean MOD. I'm representing DoD. Wear your uniform, you can represent the U.S. Navy."

"Sounds good to me. We're not getting under way till the day after. Last I heard, and considering the weather east of

Japan, it might be longer than that." He ran his lips along the side of her neck. Her damp short hair tickled his nose. His erection had shifted gears, but it was still on the same inter-state. His hand slid up under the towel, up smooth damp skin into an even smoother slickness that parted before a probing finger. "Good shower?"

"Great shower," she said. "Ow . . . *ow*. But do me a favor and just file those nails a little, okay? I'll give you an emery stick." She scrubbed at her face, then rummaged through the cabinet over the sink.

"What are you looking for?"

"Just seeing who else left her mascara. You know what they say about sailors in foreign ports."

He kept his face bland. "Sorry. One woman's all I can handle."

She loosened the towel, eyeing him. "Miss me?"

"Do you have to ask?"

"Just checking. The indicator pointer looks like the an-swer's yes, though."

"Come over here and I'll show you the reading up close."

"Oh, no," she said, and reached back to turn the shower on again. "You're all sweaty, and I am not going to rub up against that. Get over here. And let's see what a little soap and hot water can do."

With a whisper of cotton, the towel hit the floor.

She soaped him up thoroughly: chest, armpits, his neck, his hair. Her nipples were already erect and he ducked his head to kiss them, one after the other, nipping gently and cir-cling them with his tongue. Her fingers circled him and he closed his eyes. He pressed against her slick belly.

Her fingers went away and soaped down his back. They moved in slow circles. Then they came around his hips and met beneath his balls and slowly closed where another woman's had only minutes before.

He lost it. Cornered her against the tile, lifted her leg to curl around his back and he was in her, like that, starting to thrust, just gone. Just not really there anymore and at the same time never more there. *Out of fucking control* he thought vaguely, but actually he wasn't thinking at all. The shower drilled down into his skull and it was like fucking under a waterfall.

She said into his ear, the breath whuffing out of her as he drove in, "Well now. That little . . . *problem* we used to have . . . all gone away is it?"

He didn't answer. He didn't have enough computing capacity left to generate words and choose among them. He was all the way in and he came back out as slowly as he could. Then he went back in for more.

He felt like he was made out of cast iron still hot inside. There was a narrow place and he went all the way through it. He saw white thighs beneath a slit leather skirt. He saw calves swelling against the tightly laced straps of cork-soled platforms. Soap burned at the corners of his eyes. He came out as slowly as he could and went all the way in. The narrow place was parting. It tightened and then parted again.

A crack snapped through the universe and he went in again. There was nothing beyond it, no thought, no consciousness, no self, no existence. She put her head back against the green and white tile. She reached around him with both hands and pulled him into her. She had fingernails too. The shower roared on his skull like fuel-fed flames. The violet rubber mat with flowers molded into it squeaked and skidded down toward the foot of the tub as their feet thrust against it.

She almost always came before he did but this time it was an awfully close race.

They lay on the bed sweating with the air-conditioning on full and blowing over them. Her leg was thrown over him and she lay with her head on his chest. His hand moved over her hair, over and over. It was shorter than he remembered it. She looked bled out in the cruel light. Her eyes were closed tight as if she didn't want to see. They didn't say much, just little words that didn't have much meaning in them.

When he stirred against her again she gave a muffled chuckle. She breathed her warm breath down onto him again and then lowered her head and took him in, all the way.

The crack opened again and this time it was lined with livid lightning. The nothing wasn't waiting on the other side this time. Instead it was an all-obliterating something he couldn't look at directly because it was too hot and too bright. He went into it and became it for maybe a thousandth of a second. It was like being eaten by a nuclear fireball. And just for that moment he thought he glimpsed something. But after that thousandth of a second then another and maybe one more the white hotness bloomed out, cooling with expansion, fading to fiery yellow, orange, dull red, fading but still incredibly hot and powerful. The shock wave rolled out over his body. It hit the roof of his brain and his toes and rolled back. It gathered again at the center and pulsed one last time as she shifted her hips and sat up and wiped her lips with the back of her hand.

A frown gathered between her eyes. "What's wrong?"

"I thought I saw them." He rolled away from her, to the far side of the bed. "That must have been what they saw. Just as it hit."

"You're talking about the *Horn*?"

He took several deep breaths and didn't answer.

"What's wrong?" she said again. Then her voice came closer. He felt her fingers on his cheeks and turned his head away. "Are you crying? Damn. Don't be ashamed, Dan. I'd say it's long past time."

Later, after another shower, they dressed and went down for dinner. He kept an eye peeled for Asian Lolitas, but neither was in evidence. He didn't see the other Taggers either. Except O'Quinn, who was leaning against the desk, talking to the clerk. The bar was filled with Japanese businessmen. Their wives were in the gift shop bargaining shrilly over Korean vases painted with sunflowers and carved jade translucent as wax and delicate lacquered boxes full of nothing. He sat across from her in the restaurant, feeling like the boxes.

Blair looked more tired than he'd ever seen her. He didn't think it was the sex. She ate like a wolf, exclaiming over the Korean dishes Dan had gotten his fill of already. He had a steak. They caught up on the rezoning issue on the street in Arlington where they lived, and on the new front porch and renovations to the upstairs bathroom. She always had six projects going, along with the business of the assistant secretary of defense for manpower and personnel. Dan considered himself a hard worker, but he was in awe of how wide her span of control and attention extended.

"How's things working out at TAG?" she said, moving on from the renovations. "Is that far enough away from DC?"

"I was there a total of forty-eight hours. Met the CO. That's about it. He cut me orders and I was on my way." He cut the steak carefully. Took a bite. Not a trace of kimchi flavor. No radishes. He sighed. "Anybody miss me?"

"People call. Reporters. They leave numbers. I don't call back." She tried something Dan could have told her was loaded with enough garlic to clear out every vampire south of the DMZ, and closed her eyes in bliss. "Ooh, this is so good. And how about you? Are you happy with it . . . career-wise?"

"Well, it's not exactly the usual postcommand tour. The kind you want in your jacket when it's promotion-board time."

"It isn't? It's bad?"

"It's not *bad*. Just out of the . . . mainstream. For a surface-line type."

"Refining tactics is out of the mainstream?"

"It'd take too long to explain."

"Well, where should you be? At this point? I just wish you had a law degree. We'd get you in the secretary's office. I could get you taken on at Test and Evaluation. No, better yet, Modeling and Simulation. They're looking for operators, we're planning a huge effort there—"

"Where I should be as far as the Navy's concerned is on a headquarters staff. Maybe SURFLANT. Then a major command tour."

"Didn't the White House count for that? The staff thing."

"Some would say so," he said carefully. "Some wouldn't. As far as a promotion board goes, I'd say it'd hurt more than it'd help. With the way the president's cutting the active forces. It would've been better if I'd gone right to another command, I mean another ship command, instead of TAG. I'd be in the running for a squadron after that."

"Surely they can't blame you for that. Just for being on his staff."

"They can for being married to one of his appointees," Dan told her.

A dangerous storm-light glittered. "Well, anytime you don't want to be—"

"Take it easy! I'm teasing. You've always been more concerned about my career than I have, anyway. It'll take care of itself."

"A career never 'takes care of itself.' Yours especially." Her lips set. "All you've done for the Navy, all your decorations. Are you going to make O-6?"

"I don't really know. And frankly, Scarlett, I don't give a—"

"I'll ask some questions. Find out what's going on."

He sucked air. "Blair, *please* do not involve yourself in my career. The single worst thing you can do for me is start screwing around with that. No matter how subtle you think you are. And I never did things 'for the Navy.' If I ever did anything beyond the call, it was for the people who worked for me, or because somebody had to do it and I happened to have the watch. Anybody else in my shoes would have done exactly the same."

She shrugged. Was this his night for making women pout? He tried to change the subject. "Anything new from the investigation? The attempted assassination?"

"Actually that's getting to be old news. Attention moves on fast. . . . So, how's the SATYRE going? I don't hear much from Korea. That's the Far Eastern desk."

He'd thought about how to bring it up over the steak, and decided finally just to come right out with it. But first he looked around to make sure no one was listening at the other tables. They didn't seem to be. "Well, the word is the administration's considering more force reductions."

She didn't look up. "We're always looking at those. We BRAC'd the shit out of the stateside establishment. You remember I spent practically all year before last on that."

"Yeah."

"Now it's time to look overseas. We just spend way, far too much on these garrisons. We've got to transform. Having tens of thousands of guys sitting on their cans, basically stationary targets—that doesn't deter anymore. You know there's a hundred and five separate U.S. bases and installations in South Korea?"

"Huh. That many?"

"If we could get that down to twenty, we'd save serious money. Reduce our friction with the local population too. Whenever one of these kids goes apeshit—well, you just can't leave young troops in the middle of a population like this." She told him a horror story about a rape-murder the year before by a soldier from Camp Casey. "Every time that happens, the leftist students organize demonstrations. Sooner or later Seoul's going to do something about it. Then we won't have the choice. They'll hand us our walking papers. Just like the Japanese, in Okinawa. In some ways we're our own worst enemy."

"Guess we don't see much of that side of it in the Navy," he admitted.

"I guess you don't."

"Still, they've got to balance that against the threat. At least with that infrastructure, you've got surge capacity. You can ramp up, reinforce, mount a major counteroffensive."

"Oh, absolutely."

Maybe her answer wasn't meant to be dismissive but that's what he heard in her tone. Instead of reacting with his first impulse, he took the last bite of his steak and chewed. Remembering a dark, echoing, musty-smelling hull. The steady hiss of compressed air. The smells of burned powder and hot blood. And the contorted face of a fanatical believer.

"You know . . . these people are facing real enemies. I'm not sure they always remember that, back in DC."

She glanced up. "Which means what? The president's going to throw them to the wolves?"

"I doubt he'd do that. It's just that—"

"We're facing challenges all along the arc of crisis. If we try to maintain forces anywhere we can be attacked, guess what? We'll go as broke as the Soviet Union did. That's not a winning strategy." She dabbed at her lipstick with her napkin, and sketched a rapid end-around on the tablecloth with a fingernail. "A mobile force we can deploy where we need it, in days or hours—that's what we need to iterate toward. The Koreans have to understand that. The era of big forward-based divisions is over."

It made analytical sense. It made budgetary sense. But it also left him uneasy. He kept thinking of all those guns and tanks along the DMZ. How for forty years Kim Il Sung and now his weird son with the Eraserhead haircut had vowed to "reunite" Korea. Hwang's warning that an ally that came too late was no ally at all. A submarine that had no business where it'd been discovered. And the hatred he'd glimpsed in a human being's eyes moments before he'd slugged her.

He watched his wife sip wine and tried to let go of it. Not his decision. Not his watch.

But when he reflected on the people he'd worked with and for in the National Security Council, and the way policy got made in DC, his confidence factor in the right decision coming out the delivery end of that sausage grinder wasn't high. It wasn't absolutely accurate to say whoever came in with the highest payment bought the decision. But money talked and it talked loud. The special interests kept squeezing the toothpaste tube of the budget their way. And whatever didn't have a paying patron, no matter how important that issue was in and of itself, got left out.

And really, why should he have been surprised that in a country whose business was business, that everything, absolutely *everything,* should be for sale?

She put her hand on his. "Deep thoughts?"

He shook himself back to where he was: a nice hotel,

with his beautiful wife, whom he really didn't see that often, on a free night before he went back to sea. "Not really. How about it? Want to go out and paint the town?"

"I thought you'd never ask."

The next morning was cloudless and still. He stood at the base of a starkly modern tower built of what looked like concrete pipes. They emerged from the grass, bent upward, and met to support a great bronze globe. Around its perimeter the flags of many nations drooped in the breezeless heat. Beside him Blair stood in a white lace dress, adorned with one of the corsages a bowing official had distributed to the ladies in the official party.

Which was slowly breaking up, now that the final benediction had been said. The ceremony had been unmercifully long. One Korean had ranted for nearly forty minutes. Dozens of veterans, war widows, and their families had sat in the audience, many blotting away tears as generals and ambassadors from the coalition nations, in many different languages, had invoked the memories of the fallen. Then each had stepped forward to lay his or her wreath.

He felt out of place uniformwise. The other military were in whites. Gold braid and aiguillettes sparkled. All he'd brought, not expecting formal occasions, was khakis. But the Koreans were also in khakis, or a service dress green he thought was the equivalent. He'd cleaned up his shoes, gotten a close shave, and made sure his ribbons were straight. So far no one had said anything.

But now it was over, and the reception line on the carefully manicured grass was moving. He shook hands with an elderly American in a gray double-breasted suit. Blair said, "Ambassador, I'm Blair Titus."

"Of course, Blair. I know your boss very well." He turned his expressionless gaze to Dan and she introduced him. "My husband, who's currently serving with the ROK Navy."

"How interesting. Nice to meet you, Mr. Titus."

The ambassador looked past them and Dan pulled Blair

along, though she seemed to want to stay. "You could do his job," she told him under her breath.

"Me? His job?"

"In your sleep. What's one of these guys do anyway? Nothing I've ever been able to figure out."

Dan nodded to Carol Owens, in crisp whites. The attaché narrowed her eyes and looked closely at him, then at Blair, before nodding. She inclined her head to a U.S. Army general's at her side. Then brought him over, towing him through the throng. Dan caught the glare of four stars on his shoulders. The matching dazzle of shaven temples beneath his cap, a Ranger patch, and incongruous horn-rimmed glasses. Dan recognized him as one of the speakers—one of the brief ones.

"Dan."

"Captain. Blair, meet Captain Carol Owens, naval attaché to the Republic of Korea."

They shook hands. Owens introduced Mark Harlen, U.S. Army, Commander, Combined Forces Command, and Commander, U.S. Forces Korea. Which made him both the senior U.S. officer in theater and the representative of the UN Command. As a civilian appointee in the Department of Defense hierarchy, Blair was a four-star equivalent. She and the general were equals, but they were on Harlen's turf. It felt like the Field of Cloth of Gold, two high potentates, wary, surrounded by their subordinates.

"I know General Harlen," Blair said. "I think we met briefly last time you were in the building to brief the SecDef."

"And I know of the Honorable Ms. Titus." Harlen chuckled, but there was no humor in his eyes. He glanced at Dan, returned his salute, then stuck out a hand to him too. "And if this isn't your aide, it must be your husband."

Too late, Dan realized that if Nick Niles had sent him to TAG to get him out of the sights of the U.S. Army's senior commanders, this might not be the wisest venue to show himself off. Blair's warning glance told him she was thinking along the same lines. But he couldn't deny his identity when he was wearing his name tag. "Uh, pleased to meet you, General," he said, and caught himself just before he bowed.

"Take it easy, Commander," Harlen said, but he didn't say what Dan was to take it easy from. "Ms. Titus. Time for a quick tour of the DMZ? As long as you're on the peninsula?"

"I could check with my aide. The schedule's not all that flexible, though. I have to be back in DC Tuesday at 09."

"Three or four hours. An hour up from Pusan to Osan or K16 in Seoul, thirty minutes by helo to the DMZ, an hour on the ground, thirty minutes back. Most of our DVs leave from Osan. I'd like to bend your ear on a couple of personnel issues."

"I'd like very much to have your views."

"And perhaps we could discuss the transfer of wartime control of South Korean troops."

"That would be a Joint Staff issue, I believe." Blair deflected Harlen so smoothly Dan barely caught it. "I'm aware of the question, but we'd need to study it thoroughly before floating anything concrete. The United Nations would be involved too—your UN Command hat. But I'd be glad to discuss it with you, unofficially. If, as I say, we can make the time."

Dan felt left out, out of place. He glanced around and found himself face-to-face with Min Jun Jung. The commodore was in whites and it took a moment to recognize him. His PhotoGrays were black in the bright sunlight, and his eyes were totally invisible. They shook hands.

"Why, Dan. I didn't expect to run into you here. You do get around, don't you?"

"Good afternoon, Commodore. Nice to see you."

"Nice to see you too. This is your wife, I understand?"

"I'll introduce you as soon as she's done with General Harlen."

"I hadn't really understood. She is the secretary of defense?"

"No, no! Just the undersecretary for manpower and personnel."

"Still, that is news to me." Dan watched Jung mull it over, then look at him again. "I thought I'd ask you your opinion. On getting under way tomorrow."

"The typhoon?"

"Exactly. It's moving slowly just now, but the forecasts show it passing south of us."

"They're not always predictable," Dan said. "Or at least I've found it to be that way. Both typhoons and hurricanes. And they tend to turn north. This side of the equator, anyway."

"As we all know," Jung said drily.

"Sorry, sir."

"So you counsel caution?"

"Sir, in this case, I don't counsel anything. This really has nothing to do with conduct of the exercise. You're the OTC. You're the host country commander."

"The North takes advantage of heavy weather to slip their infiltration teams in. When we fought them, defending our fishing fleets, they attacked at night, in bad weather. I believe we need to be ready to fight in bad weather."

"I can't argue with that, sir. But you have to balance it against prudence."

"That's what the Australians said."

"Are they in?"

"They're out. Left last night."

"No guidance from Higher?"

Jung made an expression Dan couldn't interpret. "COM-ROKFLT left it up to me."

"Well then—that's good. If you're satisfied there's enough warning time to get into port, if it hooks toward us—"

Jung nodded, pursing his lips. He muttered, "And of course there is the question of what Commodore Leakham will decide. So far his cooperation is . . . spotty. If I order him to go out and resume exercise play—will he?"

"That's up to him," Dan told him. "Just do what you think is right. I don't have any fucking idea where Leakham's coming from on anything, if that's what you're asking me, though. Sir."

He looked toward Blair again. Her conversation with Harlen seemed to be winding down. He was moving up again, getting ready to introduce Jung, when a heavily bemedalled Korean Army aide pushed his way through the crowd toward them. Harlen bent to him, cupping his ear.

The general turned to Blair. "If you'd step this way, ma'am, I'll present you to the defense minister."

"Should I come?" Dan asked her. "Or wait here?"

"Sure, come on," she told him. "I want you to. Come on."

He smiled apologetically back at Jung. The commodore looked disappointed, but smiled back and shrugged.

The defense minister, a small man in a dark blue suit, turned out to be the guy who'd ranted for forty minutes. He was smiling and bowing to Blair. Dan and Harlen bowed back. They were exchanging stilted small talk about the ceremony, how pleasant the weather was, and so forth, when someone behind him clamped a hand on Dan's shoulder.

He turned to confront the tallest, strackest Korean he'd ever seen. The guy was in starched fatigues, gleaming black battle helmet, and gold armband. A lanyarded pistol was holstered at his belt, and his face was coldly, absolutely hostile. He jerked a thumb behind him. "Commander Lenson? Is this your man, sir?"

Dan leaned to see around him. To where, at some distance, Rit Carpenter, hands shackled behind him, was standing beside a jeep. Korean troops with unslung rifles surrounded him.

"Excuse me," he said, bowing first to the minister and then to Blair. She glanced from him to the jeep, and a line appeared between her brows, but only for a moment; she turned back to the politico, smiling and nodding, and moving ever so slightly—to mask what was going on from his view, Dan realized.

He followed the guy toward the vehicle. "What the hell's going on?" he snapped.

The military police officer said stiffly, "This man was found with a Korean woman. Among the gravestones."

"So what? They were walking among the—"

"They were not walking."

"Oh . . . shit," Dan muttered. Past Carpenter now, in the back of the vehicle, he saw Lee was huddled. The girl's dress was mussed. Her face was swollen with tears.

"Rit, god*damn* it. What the hell are you doing?"

"It's a tourist attraction. We heard there was some kind of celebration here—"

"So you came and—what've you gotten us into? In the *UN cemetery*? On their Memorial Day, or whatever the hell this is?"

"I'm sorry, damn it—I thought we were out of sight." It didn't look as if they'd hurt him, but Carpenter hung his head. "It's my fault. She didn't want to. I said, just for a minute—"

"What are the charges?" Dan asked the tall Korean.

The officer was deep in what seemed to be an English language phrase book. Finally he looked up. "Public fornication," he stated. "And—de-se-scra—?"

"Yes, *desecrating*," Dan helped him out.

"—*Desecrating* grave of British soldier. This is the charges. Very serious charges." He examined Dan's uniform, then Carpenter's slacks and striped shirt. Then, finally, accepted Carpenter's passport from one of the men guarding him. "This man is U.S. Navy?"

Dan thought quickly, trying to figure if there'd be an advantage either way. Then was disgusted with himself. Just stick with the truth! "Not exactly. He's a civilian, employed by the U.S. government."

"He is subject to Code of Military Justice?" the Korean said. "Covered, Status of Forces Agreement?"

"Actually probably not—I don't think so. It'd have to be a civilian trial."

The officer's face changed, and not favorably. Dan guessed he'd just tripled the paperwork and time involved. "But I'm his senior officer," he added.

"You are his senior officer?"

"That's what I said. I'll prefer charges against him in our system. If you'll give me a copy of your charge sheet."

The Korean wavered. He looked in at the sobbing girl. "What about her?"

"I think the shame is enough punishment," Dan told him. "Don't you?"

The Korean was thinking that over when Lee screamed out, *"Ke jag a na rel kan gan hat seo yo!"* The officer stiffened. He looked quickly in at her, then at Carpenter.

"What'd she say?"

"She accuses him of raping her."

They looked at each other. "This is much more serious," the Korean muttered. "What do you know about this woman? Have you seen her before? Who is she? Her identity documents say she is a student."

Dan rubbed sweat from his forehead. "She told us she was a teacher. At Pusan University."

"Your man here. *You!* Turn around. Let me see hands. He knew her? You see them together before?"

Dan felt they were getting deeper and deeper into something bad. He chose his words carefully, but spoke quickly; he saw Owens headed their way, a thunderhead riding over her. "Yes—I've seen them together before. I have witnesses who can testify she went to his room last night. At our hotel. Willingly. I can't swear as to what happened here today. I didn't see it. But to call it rape seems—unlikely."

The officer thought that over. He turned Carpenter's hands over, looking at the fingers. Then reached in and roughly pulled Lee's out of her lap and examined them too. The girl was sobbing noisily.

He straightened. "I will give you arrest report and remand custody. You will escort your man back to your ship. I do not believe her story, but that is not for me to decide. I will keep her for my superiors to interrogate."

"I'd rather take them both," Dan said, not liking the idea of leaving a teenager face-to-face with the military justice system.

"No, she is Korean citizen. Student. Some students join unwise associations."

Owens joined them, breathing hard. "What's going on here?"

"Let me handle this, Captain," Dan told her. "Believe me, it's better if we can keep it between the—arresting officer, here—and myself." He turned back to the Korean. "What kind of associations?"

"Leftist associations. Dangerous ones, that act as the Communists direct. I will take charge of her. We will find out the truth."

Carpenter licked his lips as if about to butt in. Dan hoped he had the good sense to keep his trap closed, and tried to get that across to him with a scowl. The submariner closed his mouth and looked at the grass, flexing his wrists, handcuffed once more, behind him.

Glancing back toward the official party, Dan saw Jung staring their way. Behind him, with a fast-sinking heart, he caught Blair's questioning glance too, and from beside her, the minister's. He had to wrap this up, now. "I will take both, or neither," he told the officer. "Look, Major: She's his girlfriend. They met a week ago. Things got out of hand. But there's no gain for any of us making an international incident out of this."

"I will keep the girl. This may be a plot. To make trouble."

"*You're* making it trouble, buddy. An ugly incident, at the Memorial Services, with the defense minister and the UN commander present. Wouldn't that be exactly what they want? If she *was* some kind of student radical?"

The Korean wavered, holding Dan's eye. At last he wheeled and spoke sharply. His troops sprang out of the jeep and pushed the girl out. She struggled, then stopped resisting. She stood with head drooping like the windless flags. Dan felt pity for her, whatever was in her heart. The officer scribbled on a pad. He tore a sheet off and handed it over, together with Carpenter's passport. He took a step back and saluted Dan smartly. Dan returned the salute, turned instantly on Carpenter, and started yelling. "You fool! Your punishment will be severe, you son of a dog. You have brought shame on us all! Get off the grounds this moment!" The Koreans looked more satisfied. They unlocked Carpenter's handcuffs. Dan kept shouting, whatever threats and abuse occurred to him. The officer waved, got in the jeep, and drove off.

As soon as they were out of earshot Dan took his hat off and wiped his forehead. "All right," he told Carpenter.

"Nice act, sir."

"It wasn't a fucking act! Well, maybe a little bit. But Jesus Christ, Rit! Couldn't you keep it in your pants, just during the ceremony? I don't know how you put somebody on report at TAG, but I'm going to find out. You're not skating on this one."

The contractor mumbled that he sure deserved it, that he was grateful not to be on his way to a Korean hoosegow. "You just remember that statement," Dan told him. He turned on Lee, but couldn't muster the same rage for that tear-smeared face. "I don't know what you tried to do just now. Or why. And I don't really care. I just want you to go home and not come back. Rit, give her cab fare. Good-bye."

Back with Blair he felt sweat trickling under his khakis. He eased the tucks of his blouse out, hoping he wasn't showing stains. The defense minister gazed up at him, a question in his eyes. But instead of asking it, he turned to speak to General Harlen.

"So what was *that* all about?" his wife muttered. "Who was that with the MPs?"

"One of my guys. And a local girl."

Her brows contracted. "Oh, no. Not . . . is it serious?"

"I defused it. At least I hope so."

"Rape?"

"Public sex. But apparently it was consensual."

"Sex *here*?"

Dan shook his head grimly. Blair blew out. "God, I hope you're right. We don't need any more bad press. Did you see any reporters?"

"Not a one."

"I can't believe you'd let this happen. Not here. Not now."

"It won't again. The guy's toast when I get his ass back to TAG."

She studied him; almost spoke; then seemed to dismiss whatever she'd been about to say.

"So what'd Harlen want?" Dan asked her.

"A lot of things are happening. A lot of other things might happen."

"That's cryptic."

"And that's how we'd better leave it. Considering tomorrow you'll be under way again." She glanced toward the reception tables, where aides were ushering the guests toward white-uniformed waiters, tables stacked with delicacies. "Hungry? Looks like they've really outdone themselves."

He wasn't, not really. Not for more kimchi and rice and the little sickly sweet pastries. In fact he felt slightly ill. But aloud he only said mildly, "Sure thing, honey. Sure thing."

III
PHASE II

10

The Eastern Sea

The wardroom lurched and heaved. The steward grabbed for a migrating bowl, but missed. Quickly accelerating, it lifted, took off from the table, and shattered, spattering kimchi across the bulkhead. Cups and plates slid one way, changed their minds, and slithered back. A junior officer jumped up, knocking his chair over, and rushed out holding his mouth.

Dan studied Hwang across the table. The chief of staff looked translucent. His head wobbled like a rear-deck toy as the bow crashed down. Dan didn't feel that great himself, but it wasn't the rolls that were the problem.

"You all right?" Monty Henrickson asked on the bridge later. The wind was moaning in every corner and crevice. The gray sky was darker than the hour called for. The bow lofted, then avalanched down into an oncoming sea. Green water geysered up through the hawseholes like a whale's spout. It turned into white spume, wheeled in the air, curved by the wind, and rained down across the black-gleaming anchor tackle. They huddled on the starboard wing, watching the every-twenty-seconds luminescent digital wink of the 19 as it tracked their progress out into the Korea Strait north of Tsushima, north of Honshu, where Phase II of SATYRE 17 would take place.

"Not exactly." Dan looked out at green-hearted swells tall as garages.

Henrickson looked at them too. "What do you call these? Ten, twelve feet?"

"Something like that." In the failing light they looked bigger and more threatening than that size sea should. But *Chung Nam*'s bridge was lower than *Horn*'s had been. "We're still on the coastal shelf, though. Sea state should drop farther out."

"It's gonna get worse, Brendan decides to head our way."

The typhoon's name was Brendan. Dan said, "The last plot from Met West shows it's still sitting over eastern Honshu."

"It's been stationary quite a while. Aren't they supposed to lose strength over land?"

"If it does start moving again, they think it'll head over southern Korea. South and west of us. The swells aren't the problem."

"Oh yeah. What's the problem?"

"Well—it's just that I haven't been able to take a crap for a week now."

"Ouch," the analyst said.

The officer of the deck looked out through the wing window. Dan beckoned. The Korean cracked the wing door a couple of inches. Dan pointed to the gray ovoid of the 75 mount, down on the forecastle. The tapered barrel was still pointed forward. "Don't you need to train that around? In case you take a really heavy one over the bow?" The officer looked down at it, at him, and said something in Korean. He slammed the door again.

"Well, you told him," Henrickson said. "Would Imodium help? I always bring some along on these things. Especially when we go to Turkey. I always get the shits with the Turks."

"That's for the opposite problem." Dan cradled his belly. It felt swollen, as if he were three months gone. He'd completely lost his appetite. Which presented a problem, since when he dined with the commodore politeness demanded he chow down.

Blair had left that morning, flying back to Washington via a short stop at the DMZ. The flagship had led the squadron out that afternoon past a conveyor belt of coasters and fishermen coming in. The high-prowed little trawlers had white hulls with a red stripe and red deckhouses. Their stumpy masts fore and aft seemed to be used mainly for drying nets. They reminded Dan of the dhows that had menaced *Horn* at her anchorage in Bahrain.

As one had swung out of line toward *Chung Nam* he'd tensed before reminding himself: this wasn't the Middle East. Except maybe for the student organizations, the population was friendly. A deep note had blared from the frigate's horn, repeated. The trawler had seemed to hesitate, then swung back into line and passed down their port side, the crew smiling and waving up, one holding up two small fish by their fins and dancing a jig, waving them about as his buddies doubled in glee.

Henrickson said, "Why's he taking us out in this, anyway? We're not going to get much done in mixing conditions like this."

"That's his point. We're talking the commodore, right? The way he gave it to me, the North Koreans take advantage of heavy weather to slip their infiltration teams in. When he was in that surface action, up along the DMZ, they attacked at night in bad weather. So he feels, he has to train his people to fight in heavy seas, bad viz, and less than optimal sonar conditions."

"Yeah, okay. But it's riskier. Collision, heavy weather damage—"

"I pointed that out. He understands. But I can't disagree with his reasoning. Anyway, like I told him, I can advise about the conduct of the exercise, but as to whether to put to sea—that was his call. And he made it."

"How about the other components?"

"Both the Australians pulled the pin yesterday. *Darwin* and *Torrens*."

"Leakham?"

"Haven't heard from him yet."

Henrickson shook his head and squatted to tweak the 19. "Well, we'll get location data, but that's about all. Sonar'll be shit."

Dan was shrugging when the wing door banged open again. It was Yu, *Chung Nam*'s little skipper, his dark aged face crinkled like a bad apple. He hissed at Henrickson, "I wish to speak alone to commander," squinting at Dan.

When the door slammed behind the analyst Yu raked Dan down pretty thoroughly. "Ship readiness is my concern. I understand you were captain once. This is good. You have my respect. But this is my ship. It is not place, is not *your* place, to tell officers what to do."

"I understand, Captain. But I've seen fiberglass mounts like that stove in by heavy seas. It wasn't an order. Just a suggestion—"

"It is *not your place*," Yu said again, his little wizened face crimping so hard Dan just muttered an apology and added nothing more. The small man stood breathing hard, obviously not done, but since he'd gotten a "sorry," forestalled in his anger. At last he grated out, "You are getting the coffee? All you want?"

"Yes. Thanks."

"I make special provision. Whenever you go into wardroom, coffee. For your men. Not mine." He was getting worked up again. His fists balled as a gust spattered down the first few heavy drops out of the now nearly dark sky. "My officers do not like this. But for you—coffee. It is so important to you."

Dan thought how the guy provided free cigarettes, smoked by one and all to the point it was like being teargassed. But obviously this wasn't the time to bring it up. Maybe changing the subject would help. "And I appreciate that, Captain Yu. It is very hospitable of you, to treat your guests so graciously. Now. This typhoon. Brendan. It's expected to head northwest, once it resumes its movement. We are turning north shortly, are we not? To head for the Phase II op area. What do you think is the commodore's plan, should it also turn to the north and catch us out here?"

Yu flipped a hand in contempt. "I have been through many typhoon. Typhoon is not a problem. If it come in Korea Peninsula, ROKN know early because of weather expectation and broadcasting." He patted his cheek, looking less furious now than just exhausted, or maybe depressed. "In worst case we go to the port in the east. Perhaps Donghae. Perhaps P'ohang. P'ohang is a commercial port but there is concrete mole. For protection. I have ridden storm in P'ohang before. Do you think we need the stabilizers now? I believe I will order them turned on."

Dan mollified him some more and at last got him back into the pilothouse as the running lights came on and the chart table light clicked to red. With the stabilizing planes on, the frigate rode differently. It didn't roll as far, but Dan wasn't sure he didn't prefer the rolls.

Yu bent over the chart. He showed Dan P'ohang, halfway up the east coast. Protected by a peninsula jutting up from the south, it looked deep and wide, a fine storm-hole. Unfortunately, there didn't seem to be any other good harbors or even sheltered anchorages near the operating area.

Dan studied it, pulling at his lip, trying to work out where the prevailing seas and winds would come from if the typhoon took this tack or that, which way would be best to run in each case. He wasn't as sanguine about conning a two-thousand-ton frigate through a typhoon as Yu seemed to be. A hell of a lot could go wrong, and if it happened when you were pinned against a rocky coast like Korea's, people could die.

However, he was not about to start lecturing Yu, not after the way he'd reacted on the suggestion to rotate the gun mount. So at last he just nodded to the little skipper and groped his way to the ladder and slid down it, pulling himself in chest-tight as the bulkheads leaned and the ship groaned around him and a spattering crash outside signaled a heavy sea coming over the splinter shields.

But she didn't go as far over as he'd braced himself for, and he remembered: the stabilizers. They were stubby fins below the waterline up forward. Computers and hydraulic rams automatically "flew" them to manage pitch and roll. They were supposed to make a ship a better seakeeper, reduce the wear and tear of violent motion on the crew, and improve sonar performance in heavy seas. With them on she didn't go over very far and she didn't stay very long.

But again, he wasn't sure he liked the effect. With the system off, *Chung Nam* had a short, snappy roll that cracked the whip when she came back, but signaled plenty of reserve buoyancy and a good righting arm. With it on the rolls were less extreme—that much was true—but she gave a disquieting impression of being artificially balanced, like an elephant teetering on a circus ball.

But she should be a good sea boat if they really got into something heavy. Though he still wouldn't want to venture out on deck without a good stout safety harness.

He wondered again what exactly Jung planned to do with them out here. Other than temper his men to heavy weather. They sure wouldn't be doing much exercise ASW. But they were at sea. You couldn't fault that.

Unless he pushed it past the point of safety.

CIC was dim and hot and man-humid and reeked with smoke. In one corner someone was recycling rice into a red plastic beach bucket. Dan rubbed his stubble, not looking forward to spending the night locked in here. But he had to recast the schedule to salvage as much training time as he could. According to the original program, free play was supposed to start twenty-four hours after the units reached their assigned positions. He decided to push that back a day, shorten the event, and do transmission runs tomorrow. He spread out his schedules and charts, then decided he needed help. He dialed. O'Quinn answered grumpily.

"Joe? Dan. I could use some help refiddling the schedule. Can you meet me in CIC?"

O'Quinn said unenthusiastically that he could.

When he slid into the chair Dan was startled to smell alcohol. He started to say something, then stopped. Then decided, no, he wouldn't overlook it anymore. "Joe, you been drinking?"

"They had *soju* in the wardroom."

"I'm trying to run an exercise. It'd be nice if my analysts were sober."

"Is that an order?" The older man was sneering now.

"We're not in uniform anymore, Commander. Show me where it says I can't have a beer, if I'm off duty and it's kosher with the host service. Know what? You won't find it."

Dan sighed. He just wasn't reaching the guy. He tried again to be reasonable. "It's a piece of advice. Lay off the booze till we're back ashore."

O'Quinn shrugged.

"What's that mean?" Dan said sharply.

"Sure, sure. You're the fucking boss. Whatever you say. What do you want me to do here? I see you're going to transmission runs. Across the prevailing seas, or with them?"

Around midnight he couldn't take it anymore. His eyes were blurry with tears. His gut felt like a cast lead lump, and he was desperately seasick. It didn't happen often, but heavy weather and tobacco smoke would eventually do in just about anyone. He found a weather door on the 01 level and groped outside, dogging it behind him.

The sea-night was utterly black, and much cooler than it had been during the day. The wind keened a higher note than it had piped at dusk. The deck bounded like the back of a galloping stallion, wet-slippery, the nonskid worn smooth by many feet. Spray slashed his face. His outstretched fingertips collided with a salt-greasy lifeline. He grabbed it with both hands and braced the boots Mangum had liberated for him aboard *San Francisco*.

It brought back a memory of a colder sea, an even darker night, a worn-out ship manned by a rebellious and disgruntled crew. Both *Reynolds Ryan* and her captain lay beneath the sullen rollers of the North Atlantic. But where were her other survivors now? His life had diverged from theirs long ago. But still he carried them with him. He'd never forget. Because they'd been shipmates.

He shook those memories off and clung blinking as more spray whipped out of the blackness. It stung his eyes but he didn't mind that. As he sucked deep long breaths of the clean night, his nausea ebbed. Far away a triangular constellation winked on and off amid passing swells. Two whites and a red. *Kim Chon,* port side to them. Making her way, with the rest of ASWRON 51, eastward.

The planned operating area for Phase II had been centered on 36° 30' N, 131° 20' E, between the Oki Shoto Islands and the Korean coast. It was deep water but Dan was starting to wonder if he should move the exercise north, past a couple of small and badly marked islands out to where there was more sea room. One good thing about this weather was that the fishermen had all gone in. Commercial traffic, freighters and tankers, would be rerouting too, or staying in port till the typhoon passed.

When he went back inside Jung was at the plot table, studying the new schedule. O'Quinn stood with arms folded, watching like a croupier in the shadowed light. The commodore nodded. "Dan. Feeling any better?"

What had O'Quinn told him? Dan shot him a glance. To Jung he said, "I'm fine, sir. We're trying to recast the order of events to salvage as much training time as we can. Both *San Francisco* and *Chang Bo Go* are standing by at their COMEX points. Here." He grabbed a pencil and ticked off their submerged positions. "Their next comm availability's 0200. So we need to have any sched changes out before then."

"The U.S. surface units are joining," O'Quinn said. "We have them about thirty miles northeast. Other side of Dogo Island."

Dan tried to recall a Dogo Island. O'Quinn must mean the Oki Shotos. "So, they're still in the exercise. That's good."

Jung said, "I just talked to Commodore Leakham. He's reserving the right to pull out and head for Yokosuka."

"He say anything else?"

Jung hesitated. "Nothing else, no. We're both just keeping an eye on the storm."

Hwang came over. The chief staff officer, shaky but unbowed, unrolled the latest weather fax, a warning plot dated midnight, from Met Center West in Guam. It showed Typhoon Brendan still stationary 160 miles away, over Kyushu. If it started moving again it would probably track up the central spine of the Korean Peninsula.

Dan studied this with growing doubt. *Still* stationary? He wished he had more data, references on how typhoons typically tracked at this latitude. Of course he didn't, or at least not here aboard *Chung Nam,* in any language he could read. To expect it to track straight, or nearly so, didn't seem realistic.

But the met weenies knew their job better than he did. He said that was fine, and they went over the revised schedule message. Jung changed the order of two events, then signed it. Dan handed it to Hwang and stretched. He wanted coffee, but still felt sick.

An hour later, as the swell and sea conditions stayed constant, or perhaps got slightly worse, confirmation came back from the American commodore. It gave away nothing in the closer: "CTF 74 will keep close eye on weather conditions and will terminate the exercise if conditions degenerate beyond prudent limits."

Which was, Dan reflected, pure Leakham. Only Jung could officially terminate the exercise. All Leakham could do was withdraw his own forces, as the Japanese and Australians had. But the guy just had to act, and talk, and write his messages, as if he was in charge.

At 0200 the subs erected their comm masts. When they'd rogered for the sched change, he went back to his stateroom, groping through the narrow, swaying passageways in the dim blackout lights. He stripped his damp salty clothes off and lay in his skivvies, arm angled around the bunk frame. He almost fell asleep a couple of times, but his reflexes didn't work the way they were supposed to. As space started to roll around him he gripped the frame in his half-sleep. But then the stabilizers came on, and instead of completing the roll the ship did a queer floating routine, as if it had somehow become lighter than air and soared up off the waves. It snapped him wide awake every time.

After it happened twenty or thirty times he got dressed again and went back up to the wardroom. True to Yu's promise, there was coffee on. It was boiled down to road tar, but he'd had worse. He drank a mug and got down a couple of the sugary sour Korean cookies from the sideboard. He was sorry as soon as he swallowed the last morsel, but by then it was too late.

On the bridge the rain came down in sheets. It drummed on the overhead and submerged the windshields. He went back down to CIC. He wedged himself into a corner of the sonar shack. He found a paperback copy of *Genesis* O'Quinn had left and tried to read. That didn't go too well either, but he didn't feel like trying his cabin again.

Jung came up at 0400. The men in CIC came to silent attention, as they did whenever he entered a space. He smelled as if he'd just had a shower and used plenty of his favorite cologne. He rubbed his eyes, ignoring the men, and after a moment a chief said something in a low voice and they went back to work, but without conversation now. "A lot of smoke in here," Jung said mildly, and lit a menthol to add to it. He peered around and saw Dan. "Has Commander Hwang been up?"

"Haven't seen him since midnight, Commodore."

Jung nodded. He checked the radar repeater, discussing each pip in a low voice with the chief. He paced back and forth, smoking with quick gestures, as if he couldn't sleep either. Then turned abruptly and took the door that led to the bridge ladder.

The chief of staff came in a few minutes later. "Looking for the commodore?" Dan asked him.

"Not really."

"Well, he was just in here asking where you were. I think he's up on the bridge."

Hwang sighed.

A radioman stopped at Hwang's elbow. The chief of staff took the clipboard with another sigh. He glanced down the message. Then reached out to steady himself as the ship took a lean.

When Dan looked back he'd paled. "What's wrong?"

"This is interesting." The chief of staff inhaled noisily through his teeth.

"Can I see?"

"It's in Korean. The English version went somewhere else." Hwang looked at the chart, then at the message again. He walked his fingers across the lat-long squares and went even whiter. As pale, in fact, as Dan had seen any of the Koreans get.

"What is it?" Dan asked again.

"There's been a slipup with the met reports."

"What kind of slipup?"

"They said the typhoon was stationary."

"It's started moving again?"

"Apparently it's been moving the whole time." Hwang snapped at the radioman, who responded with a subdued but voluble explanation. He turned back to Dan. "Unfortunately, someone made an error. For the last twenty-four hours they have been transmitting the same position data."

Dan felt the same spear-stab to the heart that the chief of staff had obviously taken. "They sent the six-hour updates. But they didn't change the position of the eye?"

"That is correct. We thought it would head northwest, once it began moving again. But someone made a mistake. The position was not updated. Even though the storm was moving. And yes, it moved northwest. Or northwest by north."

Dan eyed the chart too, dreading what was coming. He'd been through enough storms not to find the prospect of another exciting in the least. "Damn it. I had a bad feeling about this son of a bitch."

"It is the steel. The fishermen say the steel draws the storm."

He wasn't sure what the guy meant by that; maybe it was a proverb. "Uh-huh . . . I thought we were getting a lot of wind, a lot of precipitation, this far away. So what's the bad news?"

"That *is* the bad news."

"I mean, what's its current position?"

Hwang took a pencil. He checked the message again, then made a small ideograph on the chart. He lettered in a date-time group, referred to the chart again, and took hold of the jointed rule attached to the chart table. He swiveled it, set the degrees knob, and ran a pencil line out from the position. Then cleared his throat, looking unhappy. He reached up and unsnapped a phone. *"Hwang sareongkwan im ni da. Taepoong ae kwan hae an joe eon soshik yi it suem ni da."*

Dan figured he was reporting to the commodore. He leaned over the chart, feeling the dread, knowing before he looked what he'd see.

In the hours they'd lost track of Brendan it had hooked to the right, just as he'd feared. The ideograph—it must mean "typhoon"—lay between Tsushima Island and the Japanese mainland. Only seventy miles south of where the task force plunged and struggled in increasingly heavy rain and spray. The storm-track Hwang had laid out headed due north from there. It would go up the east coast of Korea, only a few miles offshore.

It wouldn't pass directly over them, but it'd be close. And it would block them from reaching either of their only two possible harbors of refuge.

11

The commodore's breath wasn't so sweet nor his canned-peaches-in-syrup cologne quite so effective as they all but snuggled on his stateroom settee. Koreans simply didn't have the same ideas about personal distance as Americans. Hwang and Yu sat across the coffee table from them. Jung offered cigarettes from a carved teakwood box. Hwang and Yu lit up. So did Jung. He didn't offer Dan any but said, "Would you like tea, Commander? I will order fresh tea."

"That sounds good. *Kam sa, ham ni da*—thanks."

Up here on the 02 level the wind was louder than in CIC, its shrill keen distinct against the creak and groan of flexing steel. And aluminum, Dan reminded himself—the Ulsan class used the light metal for its superstructures, a technique U.S. shipbuilders had abandoned after some horrific fires. In a storm, though, a lightweight top-hamper was a plus. The steward brought tea and laid out more of the rice cookies as well.

"We must make a decision quickly," Jung began. "First of all, I believe we cannot make P'ohang in time."

The chief of staff took that as his cue to unroll a chart. He'd drawn a track based on the storm's predicted speed of advance. He laid a pair of dividers on the table. Jung picked them up and measured. Dan called it at 130 nautical miles to P'ohang. No one said anything. A sea kettledrummed along the bulkheads. The ship started to roll, but the stabilizers caught it, and the tea sloshed in the cups, interrupted just as it had started to tilt. The wind rose to a whistle, then dropped back to the banshee keen.

They debated the situation, the little flag captain taking the lead while Jung listened. The discussion was in Korean, but Dan followed it; in this situation seamen of any nationality would be making the same points, pondering the same forces and gambits. If they tried for harbor, they'd be making downwind. An easier point of sailing, but they'd be cutting in front of the storm. Like a deer trying to get across a highway in front of a speeding truck. If they could sustain twenty knots, they'd probably make shelter ahead of the worst of the winds and seas. But they'd have no time to snug in pierside, and might also have to deal with mountainous seas at the harbor entrance. If any of the squadron lagged or had engine trouble, they'd have to leave her behind, T-boned in the path of the eye. . . .

"Your recommendation?" Jung asked him in English.

"I think you should make for a Japanese port, Commodore," Dan told him. "Forget P'ohang. If anything goes wrong, you're screwed. Stay out here, and you'll be in the dangerous semicircle. Japan's your safest option."

None of the Koreans looked pleased. "I don't like the idea of a Japanese harbor," Hwang said.

"Oh, for—haven't you ever heard 'any port in a storm'?" He tried to make a joke of it, but nobody laughed. He pulled the chart over and searched the coast of Honshu. It seemed to him that even if they could get close in to land, it would afford some lee from the worst of the seas, at least till the eye passed. "I don't know these ports the way you do— Matsue?"

"Sakaiminato," Yu corrected him disapprovingly. "Not a good harbor."

"Fukui?"

"That is not a port at all."

Jung muttered, "The ROKN does not seek shelter in Japan."

Dan sat forward on the settee. "Now wait. I understand you don't like the Japanese. That's fine. Personally, I wouldn't jump for joy about putting into Shanghai. But if it was a matter of ducking in from a typhoon, I'd do it. The safety of my ship, my crew, against a little embarrassment? I'd go in. Sure."

They looked to the commodore, but Jung shook his head. "The ports in western Honshu are not good ports. We will not go into Japan." He tapped the open sea north of Ullungdo and Tokto. "We will clear to the northeast, then ride it out in the open sea. That is the safest place for us now."

They scrutinized the chart again. Dan tried to envision how the wind would veer as the storm's eye advanced. Opening the range on a typhoon was always a good thing, especially when you were in the dangerous semicircle—that area, on the advancing eye's right hand in the Northern Hemisphere, where the winds were strongest, and also where those winds tended to blow you directly into the eye's path.

Steaming northeast, though, would put them in the trough of the waves. At some point, when it got too rough, they'd have to give up seeking northing and just aim their bows into the rollers and gut it out. If they could. If it lost power, a destroyer, with her low freeboard, tended to broach—put her beam to the seas, start rolling, and eventually capsize.

At that point the task force would cease to exist as an organized unit. It'd become isolated ships, each fighting for her life; struggling to keep power, keep steerageway, and stay afloat.

He couldn't exactly disagree with the commodore's decision. It wasn't the one he'd have made, but it was defensible. The proof of the pudding would be what happened. How fast the storm came on, how powerful the winds and seas became. And of course how long each ship, and each crew, and each commander, could take it.

"Any questions?" Jung said at last. "Then put that message out: course 045, away from the storm. Twenty knots."

Dan doubted they'd be able to make twenty for long in these seas, not without a hell of a pounding, but no one objected. Hwang rolled his chart and they rose.

"Perhaps that message should include an order to prepare

for heavy weather," Dan said. "Secure all equipment, prepare anchors for streaming, rig safety lines, ballast down—
the usual precautions. Just as a reminder?"

"We are already prepared for storm," Yu said with a
scowl. "All Korean commanders know this. Not your concern."

"Well, certainly *Chung Nam* probably is, but I wonder if
the other units in the squadron—"

"All my commanders know what to do," Jung agreed. He
threw a heavy arm over Dan's shoulders. Against his will,
Dan thought of Leakham's accusation. "We don't need to remind them. This force will do well in the open sea. That's
the place for us. I will of course leave Commodore Leakham
to his own decision, but I believe you'll see he too will not
trust the northern Honshu ports."

Dan wanted to say he hoped he was right. But he didn't,
just smiled and finished his tea.

Dawn, and the sea's former smile transformed into a leer of
rage. He crouched on the bridge, clutching a radar repeater
and watching the anemometer bump and lurch. The needle
edged 130 and went nearly to 150 on the gusts. That was in
kilometers per hour, of course. Translated into knots, he
made it around 75 steady, 90 on the gusts.

Brendan was a Class 3 typhoon. Only halfway up Nature's
scale of mindless violence. But at sea, with nothing to break
the wind, it pushed up green, shaggy, rippled mountains across
miles of fetch. On the radar a sparkling wash obscured everything within two miles, return from the wave-faces direct to the
antenna sentineling tirelessly above. Beyond that a straggling
line of pips flared and faded as TF 74 fought its way northeast.
The U.S. and ROKN ships were intermingled. The subs didn't
show, of course. At their last radio availability Jung had ordered them to go deep and shadow the surface units. Dan got
the impression that as soon as the eye passed he'd reconstitute
and resume the exercise. They'd be past the assigned dates by
then, but somebody else could worry about that.

He was impressed with how smoothly *Chung Nam* took

heavy seas. He'd never ridden a ship with active stabilizers before. The Korean frigate was traveling a little to port of cross-sea, at eighteen knots. With fifteen to twenty-foot seas coming from a little forward of the quarter, a ship this size would normally be rolling forty to fifty degrees.

He remembered the terror of forty-foot seas in the Arctic. How *Ryan* had gone damn near beam on more than once, leaving every man aboard walking on the bulkheads rather than the deck. The never-ending worry about whether they could keep the engines and bearings supplied with lube oil at a seventy-degree list.

He looked out to starboard as a foaming crest rose, seemed to hesitate, then toppled. A faint groan or hum came from forward. The fins turning, adjusting. Anticipating, then accepting the immense strain of thousands of tons of water bludgeoning their solid steel stocks. Instead of rolling, the frigate rode nearly upright, canting only a little, like a surfer, balanced, gliding down the wave. It passed and she rode up, but caught herself and only lurched the faintest bit, a slight jar, as she refused the roll back.

Impressive. But he wondered to what degree they'd work in really heavy seas, the chaotic fifty- or sixty-foot mountains that lurked at the sunlit heart of the typhoon. What he gazed on was nothing compared to that apocalyptic violence. What if the fins came out of the water? How would they respond then?

He didn't want to find out.

The hours dragged by. Lunchtime came, and an invitation from Jung. In CIC, folded and rammed into a corner, Dan couldn't face it. "Please convey my respects. I'm not feeling well enough for lunch," he told Kim #3.

"You are sick of the sea?"

"Something like that." Even coffee made him nauseated. His insides felt like a septic line backed up from a blocked drainfield. Sooner or later it was all going to let go. He didn't want it to be in front of the commodore. He sprawled in a stupor, only vaguely registering the whine of the wind, the

mumble of the diesels, the groan and hum of the stabilizers
conducted through the metal against which the bone of his
skull rested.

He dozed off, then came awake again, coughing. The low
space was the same, the hum of fans, the pall of smoke, the
fungoid faces dangling over the scopes. He hauled himself
to the nearest repeater. The green speckle of sea return pim-
pled the screen, but he made out a bowing in the line abreast
formation as the smaller units labored to keep pace.

He wondered dully where Andy Mangum was. Deep,
deep, was his guess, twisting in the oozy weeds, down where
the only witness of the tempest's rage was a conch-whisper
in the sonarman's cochlea. He bent over red polyethylene,
gut knotting, but all that came up was a sharp thin cough-
and-spit of acid.

On the bridge the stink of vomit and cigarettes was cut by
the iron smell of the heaters and the moldy aroma of standing
seawater. The doors were weeping through their gaskets. The
tile deck was plastered with transparent-wet paper towels. The
windshield disks squealed like tormented hamsters, whipping
off spray and rain.

Putting his face to one, he peered into a heaving waste.
Glanced at the anemometer and translated the reading labori-
ously into knots. He checked the heading and peered again,
trying to get a bearing on where the seas were coming from.
They seemed larger than before, but it was hard to tell, given
the mist and blowing spray. Another ten knots of wind and
visibility would vanish. They'd have to run on radar and faith.

He bent over, kneading his turgid gut and trying to deny
the nausea. He'd never felt quite this bad at sea before, though
he'd been more frightened. But he'd always had plenty to
do, watches to stand, a division or department to supervise.
Something to take his mind off his misery.

With the SATYRE at all stop, though, he and the rest of
the TAG team were excess cargo. He decided to try his bunk
again. Get his eyes shut for a few seconds. He was just so fucking *exhausted.* Maybe he was coming down with something.

He was making his way down the ladder when there was

a soft thud. The metal he gripped quivered. Not hard. Just a quiver. The same sort of tremor those aboard *Titanic* might have felt.

A second later all hell broke loose.

Chung Nam toppled fast and hard. She went so suddenly that the ladder jerked out of his hands. He floated up weightless in the narrow companionway. Only years of seagoing reflex snagged him the next rung. By then he was nearly perpendicular to the ladder, because it was on its side, whereas he'd dropped straight down.

With a boom that quaked through the hull, gravity returned. His knee slammed into a metal edge so hard he knew before sensation arrived that it would be bad. Pain shot through both wrists as they snatched his falling weight. Above him, below, men were shouting.

The ladderwell lay over at about seventy degrees, and the ship shook. Crashes shuddered aft. He scrambled to his feet and, bent over, scrabbled back up along the inclined bulkhead, boots shooting out from under him on the glossy paint, one hand on the ladder to steady himself.

He reached the top and pulled himself through the hatchway.

The pilothouse deck lay nearly vertical, a steep, wet-slick, tiled cliff no man could climb without pitons and a rock hammer. High above, the boatswain hung from the degaussing console, boots kicking desperately above a forty-foot drop. Others clung to repeaters, the helm console, the chart table. The officer of the deck was wedged behind the commodore's chair. A ruck of charts, clipboards, cuttlefish-flavored peanut snacks, containers of the barley water and orange pop the enlisted brought on watch, binoculars, and struggling men stirred at the base of the cliff. Even as he surveyed this the frigate heaved again, taking another sea from the beam, and an ominous grinding rumble came from below. It hammered again and the shock this time told him there was something down there, something hard, something *beneath the ship*. He couldn't imagine what it was. Ice? No, that was impossible. Not here, in summer.

The bulkhead he lay on shook again. He scrambled up, but his boot skidded away under the shattering porcelain of a teacup and he went down into the scrum. An elbow smashed his nose so hard he saw strobes going off. He fought back, got a knee on someone's chest. He had to get to the helm. No ship could live like this, broached to, battered by successive seas. But the helm was twenty feet above, and there was no way to climb that glassy inclined deck.

Above him he caught Kim #2's eye. Dan yelled above the scream of the wind, the batter and creak as another sea body-slammed them, shaking the frigate from end to end. "You've got to get her head into the seas!"

The lieutenant stared, then looked away through the windows. The wiper was still spinning, but nothing was visible outside but a hurtling gray. The world was dark, as if the sun was eclipsed.

Dan fought upright again, got to the after bulkhead, and started climbing it, hauling himself from hand- to foothold on junction boxes and cable brackets like a rock climber. He tasted salt. Above him the helmsman stared openmouthed, white as the paper towels that clung to the deck like taco wrappings in a parking lot. "Get your helm over! Right hard rudder!" he roared, but the seaman just blinked. He gave no sign of comprehending English, and Dan certainly didn't have the Korean. He couldn't even remember the word for "starboard." Where the hell was Yu? Hwang? Jung? Someone to take charge up here?

A seaman with a sound-powered headset, clinging above him, yelled something shrilly. Dan switched his gaze to Lieutenant Kim, who was struggling upright. "What?" he yelled.

"Taking water forward," the officer of the deck interpreted hoarsely.

"You've got to get her pointed into the seas. And secure the stabilizers. They're not working."

Kim screamed at the helmsman. After a second the man reacted, cranking the wheel over. Dan spotted a handhold above him. His foot slipped just then, though, leaving him dangling. The pain in his arm sliced right through the excitement. "Ah, fuck . . . that hurts. Full power! Use full power! You have to get her around, get out of the trough!"

But Kim was screaming just as loudly back at him. "Turn switch! Turn fucking switch!"

"*Which* fucking switch?"

"Blue switch! No! *Blue* switch!"

He got to it and snapped it over. Realized after a second it was the power to the stabilizers. Then got a boot-toe wedged into the cables. The helmsman had the wheel hard over now. The boatswain had joined him with a length of line, and was bighting him to the console.

The frigate sagged back upright, at first a little, then with more confidence. As soon as he could get traction on the deck Dan pushed himself uphill. Kim let go of the captain's chair and got to the engine control, which on *Chung Nam* wasn't part of the helm console, as on U.S. destroyers, but beneath the forward windows. He slammed the throttles forward and headed for the centerline gyrocompass. The boatswain started across to him, but lost his footing and slid, yelling, down the toboggan-slide of the still-canted deck, gathering wet paper as he tumbled, and slammed into the others struggling upright at the bottom. They went down in a discordant howl.

The rudder indicator was at hard right, gyro indicator passing 150. "Point into the seas," Dan screamed. The lieutenant stared back, gaze fixed, then whipped around and faced front, peering into the spinning circle of sight. He pointed to the right. Dan looked back at the console. The engine order indicator was labeled in Korean. It seemed to be coming up to full power, but he couldn't tell if it was full diesel or full turbine. Whichever, she seemed to be pointing up. Or so said the instrumentation, and he couldn't tell any other way.

He looked back up to see Kim glancing over his shoulder again. "Where's the water coming from?" Dan shouted.

"Water?"

"The goddamn report, *Tae wi!* Taking water forward! Where from?"

"Where from—from forward storage!"

"Port or starboard?"

"Port side. Port side." Kim shouted something long at the seaman with the headphones. "I am getting damage-control team there."

"Good, now you're thinking."

Where the fuck was the captain? Dan could get them out of a broach, but he didn't know the handling characteristics of an Ulsan-class frigate. The deck leveled, then fell off to starboard. He guessed the seas were from about 170 true, south by southeast. They were passing 180 and swinging right.

He put his finger on 170 on the compass and jabbed the helmsman in the ribs. The man flinched, and shifted his rudder to hard left. Dan looked up to see Kim cranking the telephone. "Keep pointing!" Dan screamed at him. Where the *fuck* was Yu?

On cue, the little captain reeled through the doorway. Dan glanced back. The door to the chartroom was open. He slid down the deck, grabbed the jamb, and spun inside in a figure skater's pirouette as Yu started shouting orders.

He grabbed a chart rack and eased the door shut with his other hand and then stood in the dark, not reaching for the light switch, catching his breath and listening to Yu screaming on the far side of the partition. The deck came back level, though it was pitching heavily, a long slow climb and then drop. This was good. It told him her bow was pointed where it had to go. If the power held, if the helmsman could keep her into the swell, they should be all right. If the storm didn't blow even harder, that is, and he didn't really see how it could, since its eye, by Buys Ballot's famous rule of thumb, should be behind them now and dropping farther astern each hour.

He gave it two or three minutes and then came out the port door. This made it look as if he'd just come up off the ladder. He picked his way through the bridge team, who were clearing up debris, restowing gear, and swabbing up various fluids, to stand beside Yu, who was belted into his chair. "Captain."

"Commander." The skipper scowled at him. Seated in the elevated chair, he was eye to eye with Dan.

"Stabilizers go out?"

"We hit thing," Yu said.

Kim made a report. Dan waited till he was done. "That's the flooding?" he said.

"Hole in port side, frame 15. That's where port stabilizer." Yu coughed into his fist. He had half a cigarette in his mouth, but it was soaking wet and bent at a right angle. "Your nose," the captain added.

When he touched it his fingers came away stained as if he'd been picking cherries. Yu sniffed and handed him a handkerchief.

"*Kam sa ham ni da.* We hit something? Is that what you said?"

"I think floating container. We see sometimes off Japan. Japanese very careless. Russians too. All is under control. Kim *tae wi* take proper action. We are repairing, patching hole. All under control."

Dan eyed Kim, who looked away. "Yeah, that'd do it," he told Yu. A washed-overboard container, steel, sharp-cornered, loaded with who knew what. Every seaman's nightmare. He peered through the blurred disk in front of Yu, but couldn't make out much. Judging from the jolting, the skipper had her about twenty degrees off the seas. She was riding rough and pitching hard, but it could be worse. "Have you heard from the commodore?"

"He's in his cabin. I advise him of the situation."

Dan offered the handkerchief back but Yu told him to keep it. The boatswain undogged the starboard door. The wind shrieked through it, and spray blew in as if pressurized. Yu cursed at him shrilly until he dogged it again.

"Are we on turbines?"

"Yes, turbines. Standard power."

"Standard?"

"Too much and she makes boom boom," Yu explained. He demonstrated with his hands. Dan guessed he meant slamming. "I will hold twenty degrees of the seas. Maybe try thirty."

Dan had no suggestions. Her skipper was the best judge of how much she'd take. The boatswain handed him a damp festoon of toilet paper. He stared at it a moment, then wadded a sheet up and packed his nostril with it.

The Pritac crackled. The voice was nearly blotted out by the whine of wind in the background. Yu stood in his chair to turn it up, riding the motion like a movie cowboy standing up in the saddle. Kim came over to listen. *"Dae Jon,"* he said.

"Mon jae ka sang keot seo."

Dan got the gist from their expressions: the message was from *Dae Jon*, and bad news. He wedged himself in front of Yu and plunged his face into the black rubber scope hood. It smelled like grease pencil, rubber, vomit. Jellyfish light ebbed and eddied, but he made out the smeared pip of the old destroyer. He ratcheted the knobs and got 275, about eleven thousand yards, if he had the right contact and the range wasn't in meters. He didn't think it was—the console looked like USN-issue.

"Eleven thousand yards, bearing two-seven-five," he said. "A little aft of our starboard beam. Five and a half miles. Uh . . . about nine kilometers."

"Eight point eight," Yu corrected him. He bent to squint out the whirling disk. A comber towered ahead. *Chung Nam* pitched to scoop it up. Her bullnose cut a wedge from the sea and skyrocketed it toward the clouds. It broke apart and crashed aft, boiling, creaming. The lifelines submerged, drawing momentary lines on the surface before the wind obliterated everything and plastered foam across the windows. Dan noticed someone had rotated the gun mount to point aft.

"What was that message, *Ham jung?*"

"Dae Jon is losing engine."

He squinted into the ambergris light. Losing power in seas like this . . . in a ship that old . . . He bent into the hood again and ratcheted like grinding coffee. Giving Yu time to come out with a decision. That next contact was *McCain*, he thought.

When he looked back the flag captain was on the phone. To Jung, probably. He spoke and listened. Frowned. Rapped out Korean too fast even for Dan to catch separate syllables, then handed, almost threw, the handset at the lieutenant.

"What's he say?"

"We go take look," Yu said. "But that is my decision, not commodore's."

He snapped an order. The bridge team took on a collective silence. The helm servos groaned as the wheel came over. The wind keened, dead on, then shifted, like some experiment in stereo listening, to port.

Dan waited, but Yu didn't add anything. Finally he cleared his throat. "Should we ask *McCain* to help out? Or at least let them know *Dae Jon*'s in trouble?"

Yu seemed displeased, a look Dan was getting familiar with. At last he gave a combined shrug and nod. "You do."

He got on the Pritac and passed that *Dae Jon* was reporting loss of power and *Chung Nam* was heading to assist. *McCain* rogered and asked if they needed help. Dan glanced at Yu, but the skipper gave him no clue. Dan said, "Mike Romeo, this is TAG coordinator: guess that's up to you. Over."

"Mike Romeo out."

They were coming around. He got in the hood again and switched the display to relative bearings. They weren't dead on *Dae Jon*, but they didn't want to be. At sea, the surest way never to get where you wanted to go was to aim right at it. He thought he saw the other contact moving downwind too. Engine trouble, that'd make sense.

He just hoped she had enough power left to keep bow to sea.

She emerged from the flying spray and heaving sea like a gull from a storm-cloud. Just a sketch at first. Then solidifying into the intimately known shape of a Gearing-class destroyer. He stared across from his crouch behind the splinter shield, keeping low to avoid the worst of the spray, deafened by the apocalyptic roar of the vortex. Watching her plunge and roll with a terrifying sense of déjà vu. The wind tore at his hair and buffeted in his ears. It was impossible to breathe when he faced it, an effect he'd never understood. You'd think it'd be hard to breathe out, not in, with the wind ramming itself into your teeth, but somehow you couldn't do either, just sort of suck vacuum.

This was what *Reynolds Ryan* had looked like in the Arctic, all those years ago. He hoped *Dae Jon,* ex–USS *New,* met a kinder fate. The two closed slowly, both pitching heavily head to sea, the frigate on a gradually converging course.

Yu came out, shielding his binoculars with his arm, and stared across. Dan made out a figure on the bridge opposite, in khakis. It started semaphoring, using its arms, no flags. Yu signaled back. The other figure kept sending. Yu gave him an acknowledgment and crouched to join Dan, who was tremendously impressed. He doubted one in a hundred U.S. naval officers could do semaphore. Fewer and fewer even knew Morse.

"He is still losing engine," Yu hollered.

"What's the problem?"

"He doesn't know. Just losing power."

He yelled, "How are your people doing with the leak forward?"

"It is down to ten liters a minute."

"The pumps can handle that."

Yu didn't respond, because just then a truly massive swell drove at them out of the fog and spray. No time to shift the rudder, though Dan had sensed the helmsman trying to judge the wave-periods. Putting the stem to each sea as it came, then swinging right to make up on the other destroyer. It was tricky and you couldn't do it every time.

It hit *Chung Nam,* blitzed down her forecastle, then hit *Dae Jon*. The older can's narrow prow went under. The breaking sea flooded all the way up to the 01 level, nearly submerging her boxy old-fashioned 5"/38 mount, and shoved her round bodily, till she was nearly bow on to the flagship.

She came back slowly, too slowly, to face the next. Dan saw she was just barely maintaining head to sea. Any fewer revolutions and she'd broach, as *Chung Nam* had for one or two seas. But if she didn't have reserve power, the old can couldn't recover. She dipped again, and this time he made out a black thread drawn down into the water from the far hawsehole. Her CO had deployed his anchor. It would never approach bottom, but its drag would help keep her head to the seas.

"I can think of nothing to help," Yu shouted, one hand clamping his cap to his head. "Can you?"

Dan yelled, "I dumped oil once."

"Yes?"

"It was in the Red Sea. A passenger ferry. I had a passing merchant dump lube oil upwind."

Yu cocked his head. Dan thought of adding, but didn't, that though the seas had been heavy, it hadn't been in a typhoon. Looking at how *Dae Jon* was pitching, he didn't think oil would make all that much difference here. "That was in typhoon?" the Korean yelled, paralleling his thought process.

"No. It wasn't in seas like this. And I don't know if we could fight our way upwind of her, either."

"If she broaches, she will capsize."

"Most likely."

"The crew will be trapped."

Dan tried to think of something more they could do. He couldn't come up with anything. If she capsized or went down, it would be impossible to lower boats in seas like this. In the end, the men on the ship opposite might as well be in another dimension. All they could offer was companionship amid the storm.

They stared across the boiling sea, and the man across from them gazed back.

They stayed in company until dark. Yu went in, but Dan stayed out, soaked through, but unwilling to go below. If you could put aside terror, the stormy sea was sublime. The voice of the whirlwind hypnotized the heart.

Just as the running lights snapped on, *McCain* emerged from the spray and mist as if procreated from them and took station half a mile on the other quarter of the laboring destroyer. As dark fell Yu sheered off, opening the distance to her imperiled sister. Dan lingered till he could make out only distant mist-haloed sparks, blotted out each time a comber roared past.

He went below reluctantly. Stripped his sodden clothes off and found dry skivvies. Then wrapped his arm around the frame again and lay curled tensely, shoes wedged where his feet would find them even if the lights failed. He kept trying to think of something they could do. But there was nothing.

That was his last conscious thought.

12

The phone was buzzing. He dredged himself up from confused dreams and groped. Jammed his finger into something sharp. "Fuck . . . Captain," he said. Then cleared his throat and corrected himself. He wasn't in command anymore. Just a foreign passenger, an alien body, a bacillus . . . "Uh, Lenson here."

"Commander?"

"Here. Yeah." His sea-tuned unconscious had registered that the surge and buck had eased, the wind no longer wailed to the crash of breaking seas. But his other hand, the one not on the phone, was still locked into the bar above the bunk.

It was Hwang. "The commodore was wondering where you were."

"Well, where's he?"

The chief of staff told him the bridge. He said he'd be right up. His watch, to his horror and shame, said 0912. He shaved quickly, brushed scum off his teeth, and climbed topside.

Light flooded the pilothouse. Every crumb of debris and evidence of struggle had been swept up, swabbed down, buffed away. The ship's bell shone with fresh polish. Circular gleams showed where the tile had been waxed, and he caught the bite of lemon oil and window cleaner. No one spoke. The only sound was the subdued moan of the servos as the helmsman corrected a degree this way, two degrees that. Past the polished Plexiglas the sun sparkled off five- to six-foot waves. He checked the gyrocompass and oriented himself. They were headed northeast again.

Jung was studying a clipboard in his elevated chair. Dan checked the chart. He went out on both wings and looked around. Dipped his face into the radarscope. One contact, ten miles at 120 degrees true, no indication who it was. Back in the picture, or so he hoped, he went up and saluted. *"An neong ha se yo, jeon dae jang nim."*

Jung returned the salute deadpan. *"An neong ha se yo,* Mr. Lenson."

Literally the phrase meant "hope you had pleasant dreams," but it was used for "good morning." He waited for the commodore to open, which he did with "Weather's better today."

"Yes sir. Typhoon still tracking north?"

"I'll let Pyongyang worry about it," Jung cracked. "It passed thirty-eight degrees north about 0500."

"Dae Jon?"

"Proceeding to Chinhae for repairs. She's only making ten knots, boiler trouble, but she's in no danger of sinking. We'll need to remove her from the order of exercise. And rewrite the schedule of events to reflect losing two days."

"Yes sir. I'll get on it. So you're resuming the SATYRE?"

"Well—we have another typhoon."

He did a double take. *"Another* typhoon? Are you serious?"

Jung flourished the clipboard. "Nowhere near impending, but it's spinning up down there. Callista."

"Jesus."

"My choices are to stay out here, or head into P'ohang. Or, I guess, just back to Pusan, and scrub the rest of the exercise." He studied the wavetops. "I thought I'd get your input before I make that decision."

Dan rubbed his face. "Well, sir—the most important part of the SATYRE's the free play. That's where we find out which tactics work and which don't. And it's unlikely we'd get two storms in a row tracking up the same coast. Isn't it?"

"So you'd like to continue?"

"If you feel it's at all possible. Yes sir."

Jung tapped the clipboard on the coaming. "Let me think

about it. Meanwhile, draft a restart message. Resume with event 0023 this afternoon. If we can achieve the geometry for a re-startex by then."

"Aye sir," Dan said. "Anything from COMDESRON 15?"

"I had a conversation with Commodore Leakham an hour ago. He'll conform to my decision."

"And the subs?"

"Also checked in. Commander Hwang has their posits on his plot. For your geometry. He asked if they had any damage to report. They said not." Jung looked out at the sea while Dan waited. Took off his PhotoGrays and rubbed them with a bit of lens paper from his shirt pocket. Then handed the used tissue to Dan. He hunted around for a wastebasket, slightly taken aback. The boatswain took it out of his hand without a word.

He was in CIC with Hwang and Henrickson working away at the restart message when O'Quinn came in. The front of his T-shirt was smudged with black grease. So was his forehead. "What's going on, Joe?" Dan asked him.

"Trying to get those stabilizers back on the line."

"Oh, you know stabilizers?"

"I know hydraulics. Was a chief engineer once. Don't worry. The crew's doing all the real work."

Dan frowned. "I didn't mean that. I meant—"

"Forget it, okay? I'm just helping them a little bit on where to put the chain hoists. To bend the splines back into true. Or close as we're gonna get, outside the yard."

"I was going to go down and check out the hull penetration."

"Don't bother. It's under control." O'Quinn looked away. "How's the gut doing?"

"I quit eating," Dan said.

"How long you gonna be able to keep that up?"

He made a production of his shrug.

Jung called him back to the bridge at 1130. He was still in his chair, looked as if he hadn't moved. His steward was clearing his tray. Hwang stood beside him, hands behind his back, rocking on his heels. The chief of staff looked grave. He had a bandage on his cheek.

The commodore waved another clipboard at him. "From CINCROKFLT. A Japanese air patrol's reporting a hot datum off Honshu."

"A hot datum. An intruder?"

"An unidentified submarine."

Jung swung down. "Let's get this on a geo plot," he said to Hwang. He glanced at the enlisted, whose attention seemed to be wholly on their jobs. To Dan he said, "Let's go out on the wing."

The wind was light and fresh, scrubbed by the storm. An occasional whiff of stack gas varied it. Dan took off his cap and let the sun iron his scalp. It felt good after days of overcast. The stocky Korean propped himself against the splinter shield. "Whatever it is, did you notice the course—no, you didn't, it's in Korean. Well. The unknown is roughly off the Northern Limiting Line and six hundred kilometers east."

Dan located this as on the Tokyo side of the Sea of Japan— then corrected himself: of the Eastern Sea. "Japanese territorial waters?"

"Not exactly, but it's within this new 'economic exclusion zone' they declared."

"You have a fisheries protection zone."

"Not the same thing at all," Jung said.

He started to ask the difference, but decided it wasn't worth the breath. "What about the course?"

Hwang came out with the chart. He folded down the little worktable on the wing and spread it out. He tapped the kite-symbol of the datum and ran his finger along the extended track. "Heading southwest," he said. They regarded it.

"What else?"

Hwang lifted his eyebrows. "That is about it, Dan. Unidentified submarine contact. Tracking on course two-three-zero true when detected. Speed ten knots."

"Initial detection by radar?"

"It says only, initial detection was by a Japanese SDF patrol aircraft."

"Then radar, most likely," Dan said. "Which means it was snorkeling when detected. Which at ten knots means a fairly large craft. A thousand tons or better."

The commodore looked thoughtful as Hwang walked dividers along the track. "If it holds that course, and the Japanese do not succeed in forcing it to surface, it will exit their exclusion zone at thirteen hundred," the chief of staff murmured.

"And enter ours when?" Jung asked.

Hwang explained, seeming uncomfortable, "The fisheries resources protection runs from a point on the Thirty-eighth Parallel at a longitude of one hundred thirty-two degrees fifty minutes east, past Tokto, down to Tsushima Island. So it looks to me like it could remain outside that zone all the way to the Strait. If, indeed, it is headed for the Korea Strait."

Dan said, "But it's international waters."

Any unidentified submarine in international waters was to a certain extent fair game. They couldn't attack it, but according to international convention they could track it, request it to identify itself, even harass it to some degree, though not to the extent of placing it in hazard.

"Yes, you are right. Very good. I will think out loud here a little," Hwang said. "It is not American; it would identify itself. Therefore it is either Chinese, or from the DPRK. The Chinese fired the missile over Japan. I believe this could be another provocation by the Chinese."

"That's the most likely explanation," the commodore said. "Not necessarily that it's a provocation—submarines have rights of peaceful transit. But that it is Chinese. Nonetheless—"

"Nonetheless, it might be DPRK," Hwang finished.

"Like the Sang-o off Sokch'o," Dan put in.

They both looked at him. "It might be," the tall Korean said mildly. "They also dispose of other types. As you know. Many minisubmarines . . . but I do not really think anyone would put one of them so far out to sea as this."

Dan wasn't so sure. Judging by the the way they scuttled their own subs and shot each other to avoid capture, he wouldn't put venturing that far offshore past the North Korean Special Forces. "These are the Yugos you're talking about? The minisubmarines?"

"I've heard them called that," Jung said, "but I don't think there's a Yugoslav connection. The North has about fifteen. They use them for penetrations and covert ops, along the coast."

Hwang said, "They have twenty-plus Romeos and a few Whiskeys. Either of those could be capable of operations that far out at sea. If it is the Northerners, I believe it would be one of these types."

"Whiskeys" were fairly large submarines, as diesel-electrics went; they were a Russian design about twice the displacement of a World War II U-boat. About equivalent to the Tangs and Barbels, the few U.S. diesels that had been lingering in the twilight of their service lives when Dan had joined the fleet. Romeos were a bit larger, a bit quieter, an improved design; both the Chinese and North Koreans had built copies. He said, "That'd make more sense. Again, based on the transit speed at detection."

Jung said, "Either of you see a reason why we shouldn't edge over there and see if we can pick it up?"

Dan said, taken aback, "Well, sir—I thought we were going to try to resume where we left off in the exercise. Proceed to the free-play phase."

"Can we free-play with an unidentified contact?"

Dan stood fidgeting, unsure how to answer. From the technical point of view, his response should be a flat no. They wouldn't know signal strength, or target geometry. They wouldn't have a 19 aboard their submerged quarry to pinpoint and record its location minute to minute. They wouldn't know its plans to evade, its attack tactics, or really anything else from its point of view.

True, in a general sense the best training was against a real opponent. But they weren't out here just to train. According to Owens, he was actually evaluating the ROKN's readiness for war.

In the end he decided the only truthful response was,

"No, sir, we can't. Not and fulfill the data-gathering requirements for a solid quantitative analysis."

The commodore considered, not looking happy. Finally he said, "It's a real-world submarine. Possibly an intruder."

"I understand that, sir. It doesn't change what I just told you. And we don't *know* it's an intruder. What the Japanese passed us was only his course on detection. He could be headed back to China now. Or even Russia—their Pacific Fleet's starting to revive a little."

"Let's do a message."

Hwang whipped out his notebook and prepared to copy. Jung went on, "To Fifth Flotilla, info First Fleet, CINCROK-FLT, COMNAVFORKOREA, and whoever you think needs to know —"

"Seventh Fleet, COMPACFLT. TAG as well," Dan put in.

"Of course. Propose we steam to intercept. Meanwhile we will move the comex of our first event thirty miles to the east. That will place us within two to three hours of the extended course of this contact." To Dan he added, "I know the SATYRE is a valuable exercise, but it is still only an exercise. If Seoul orders me to intercept, I'll have to obey. I'll try to position us so either option is possible."

Dan said reluctantly, "I guess I can't argue with that, Commodore."

Jung smiled, but it was a strange expression. He brushed at his lips as if ashamed of it, then made a shooing motion. The chief of staff bowed instantly and left. When he was gone the commodore said, "What is your agenda here, Mr. Lenson? Why is completing this exercise, getting your precious data, so very important to you?"

"I don't have an *agenda,* Commodore. It's just my assignment. That's all."

"But you seem so exceptionally—determined. No matter what. Typhoons. Mechanical failures. Putting up with our Korean food—"

"Your meals are delicious—"

"Embarrassments—such as your subordinate getting it on at the memorial ceremony. Oh, yes, I heard about what you said to the security officer. Very clever. But it makes me wonder, why? What is driving you so hard?"

Dan stuck his hands in his back pockets. Time to prevaricate for the Cause. "It's my job, sir, as I said. And I'm a stubborn guy."

"Obviously it's brought you far. So many decorations. Such a distinguished career." Dan couldn't tell if there was sarcasm there or not. So he didn't answer that one. After a moment Jung added, "And you're bending your efforts now to developing shallow-water tactics against diesel-electric submarines?"

"That's what TAG wants me to do. Sir."

"Hostile submarines? Or only friendly ones?"

When he didn't answer Jung went on. "Do you see why I ask?"

Dan said doggedly, "There're just too many ifs in your argument, Commodore. If we knew for sure it was headed our way—if we knew for sure it was Chinese or North Korean—then I'd say you had a point. Till then, as far as I can see, our mandate's to continue with the SATYRE. As close to the way it was originally planned as we can."

Jung looked toward the horizon. He tapped a cigarette out of the pack and lit it. A thin stream of smoke unreeled on the wind. He didn't say anything more. And after a while, realizing he wouldn't, Dan bowed and left him.

He was in CIC when a warning rumble sounded, so loud Henrickson looked over from the sonar console. "What the hell was that?"

"Uh—gangway," Dan said, lurching to his feet. Clinching desperately to hold in a sudden overwhelming spasm, he broken-fielded it for the little closet one deck down. He just made it when the world exploded.

An hour later, after repeated attempts to leave followed by decisions he'd better not, he reeled out and stacked himself against a bulkhead. He mopped his forehead with the last sheet from the last roll in the stall. It had been close. From not being able to shit at all, to not being able to stop.

He felt like a fired cartridge. His gut still cramped though there was nothing more to expel. He made it to his stateroom, chased out the steward, who was cleaning the sink, and rolled onto the bunk.

Cradling his stomach, he tried not to groan.

He spent the rest of the day in his bunk, in the head, or in rapid transit between the former and the latter. Toward late afternoon a double dose of Henrickson's Imodium locked the gates at last. He couldn't face dinner, though. An orange pop was all he could stomach.

Well after dark he ventured out, still shaky, to find no one he knew on the bridge. The chief in CIC avoided his eyes. But there was O'Quinn, unshaven, hunched morosely over a mug of coffee and smoking the free Korean cigarettes. Dan nodded warily. "Joe."

"Commander. Feelin' any better?"

"Some, I guess."

"See why I stick to food I bring with me?"

Dan didn't point out that he had to eat with the commodore, that part of the job here was to cement relationships with the host navy. If they could do that, everything else—data gathering, sharing tactical insights, accepting corrections and new initiatives when they were developed—got easier. But O'Quinn just didn't accept alternate points of view. So be it; he'd ask for someone else for his next team deployment. A wave of weakness hit, and he suddenly had to either sit or fall. He slid his chafed butt onto a stool and blotted cold sweat off his forehead.

"You look punk, Commander."

"I'll be all right. What's going on? Get the planes fixed?"

"They're back on line. Can't you tell? Noisier now, but they should work."

"Great. What happened? What'd we hit, anyway?"

"The hole's a perfect triangle. They've got a concrete patch on it. Should be good till we make port again. Only thing I can figure is the corner of a floating container. The planes were trying to correct for the impact when one of those big breakers hit from the other side. Bent the shafts, popped the splines, but the breakers blew before anything got really tore up."

"Uh-huh. Okay. How about the exercise?"

They spent the next few minutes going over the status of play. The transmission runs were over. A limited event was going on with *Chang Bo Go.* O'Quinn said he'd told Carpenter, over on *Dae Jon,* to run a systems test on his 19, make sure everything was good to go after taking so much spray and rain during the storm.

"Did we check ours?"

"Soon as the rain stopped."

"Good. Good."

O'Quinn's glance licked across his. "You don't expect too fucking much from me, do you, Lenson?"

"I expect the same effort I look for from the other folks on the team, Joe. But you don't make yourself the easiest guy in the world to work with."

"Would there be a point? A promotion, maybe?" He snickered. "I can just see it. Joseph Regale O'Quinn, head of tactics development at TAG. Head of personnel. Or maybe—how about—how about, accident prevention."

"Lay off it, Joe."

"Fuck it." O'Quinn wiped his mouth with the back of his hand and lit another free smoke. "Fuck it. Fuck it up, fuck it down, fuck it all, all around. . . . Okay, what's next?"

Dan asked if he'd heard anything more about the Japanese contact. O'Quinn reached for a clipboard. "Yeah, we got something on that. I plotted it. Here it is. The Japs are prosecuting. Holding it down. Got a destroyer out there, but it's mostly sonobuoy tracking by air, and some location data from this SOSUS network they've got in the Sea of Japan."

SOSUS was shorthand for undersea surveillance, arrays of fixed listening hydrophones and a shore-based computer to process their outputs into usable data. Dan went through the traffic, looking at O'Quinn's plot from time to time. "There's two of 'em out there," he said after a couple of minutes.

"That's what I thought too. Looking at it close."

Though the Japanese didn't say it in so many words, the location data jumped about so much there had to be two contacts, not one. It even appeared that at one point, one had popped up its snorkel to draw off a plane that was getting too aggressive on the other.

He frowned. Two submarines, apparently running in company. And though the reported courses varied—it looked like they were trying to evade their trackers—the overall course made good still looked generally southwest.

"They don't say whose they are. Or what class. Not in these messages."

"Right, just 'unidentified submarine.' And you know why," O'Quinn said.

"Why?"

"Because if they identify them, they have to do something about them. Call somebody down. And the fucking Japs just don't want to stick their dicks into that shithole."

Dan swallowed. His stomach, already tenuous, didn't care for that image. Nor for the stale smoke and old whiskey smell O'Quinn was putting out. He switched to a small-scale chart and tried to puzzle out where their trespassers could be headed. Once past Tsushima and the Strait, they'd be in the East China Sea. From there, he guessed, Tsingtao or Shanghai if they were Chinese; the fleet bases there. If they were North Korean, he had no idea where they were headed. Perhaps to the same ports—they were Beijing's clients, after all. If they were Russian, he guessed they'd make a hard port turn, through the Nansei Shoto and out into the Pacific.

"Hey, and you watch," the older man added. "Once they leave that exclusion zone of theirs, the Nips will drop them. No hot pursuit for them."

Dan's gut knotted painfully. He had only minutes before the white bus would leave again. "What's your call? On nationality?"

"I figure they're Russkis. Probably Kilos. Headed down past Taiwan on their way to a little R&R in Vietnam."

"Oh yeah?" Dan looked at the plot with new interest.

Kilos were old friends. Old enemies, actually. Running into a couple might yield useful data. "Let's go in the sonar shack."

They got down the classified references and read up on the Whiskey, Romeo, and Kilo classes. The sonarmen played comparison tapes as they all listened, noting the characteristic tonals both snorkeling and running silent, electric motors only, on the battery.

But then his gut twisted again, and he had more pressing things to think about. Such as whether he could get to the can before he wiped out another set of shorts.

He was in there when someone knocked on the door. "Occupied," he yelled.

They knocked again. "I'm fucking *in here*," he shouted.

"Is that Commander Lenson?"

"Yeah."

"It's Hwang Min Su, Dan. Just thought I'd let you know. We got a reply to the commodore's message asking for direction. COMROKFLT orders him to steam to intercept the contacts off Honshu. Try to pick up from the Japanese. If they continue toward the Strait. And if the Japanese have not lost them by then."

"Oh yeah?" A disappointment, but not unexpected. After the storm, the Japanese and Australian withdrawals, all the other problems, it was finally time to write SATYRE 17 off. He'd done all he could. Washington would just have to make its decision without his input. His disappointment was suddenly eclipsed by the sensation a sea anemone must feel when a little Greek boy pries it off its rock and sucks its guts out.

"Dan? Are you all right in there?"

He grunted through the closed door, "Yeah. So—the exercise is off."

"Well, officially just suspended. For forty-eight hours."

"Okay. Thanks for telling me." He raised his voice. "Oh—what's Leakham doing?"

"The U.S. contingent will stay in the op area. Do one-on-ones with *San Francisco*."

"Okay. So the plan is, we head on out and intercept these guy's extended track—"

"No. We will force them to surface and identify before they cross into our protection zone."

"The idea being . . ."

A pause before the reply. "To demonstrate we have control of our waters."

"Got it," Dan said. Seoul was playing the same games Washington did. Jerking the forces this way and that, cracking the whip. Not too concerned with what that meant to the guys out at the tip. He just hoped it didn't leave them out here for another typhoon. Callista, this time. Brendan had been about all he cared to take.

"Anything I can do for you? Heard you were feeling below the weather."

"Under the weather."

"What?"

"*Under* the weather," he shouted through the closed door as another spasm started. "I'm *fine*. I'm just taking a fucking *shit,* okay?"

He was back in his cabin, lying exhausted, when someone tapped on his door, then let himself in. It was a grinning little man who explained in broken English that he was "doctor." Dan figured him for a corpsman, but went through a point-and-grimace charade that ended with the guy motioning him to get out of bed and pull down his pants. The diagnosis seemed to consist mostly in the guy's smelling his butt, but at least he was up anyway when another paroxysm hit.

The door to the head didn't open to his frantic jerk. Someone was in there. He hammered frantically on it. "Fuck. Fuck," he muttered, to the compassionate gaze of the corpsman, who had come into the passageway after him and who stood now stroking his chin and tsking sadly. Then he turned and left. The door cracked and Dan practically knocked the sailor inside down, getting past him. "Sorry," he mumbled.

When he came out, though, the little guy was back, waiting

in his stateroom with a packet of white powder. No writing on it. Just a brown packet. He pointed to Dan's sink and mimed turning the faucet, mixing it into a glass, drinking it down. Dan nodded. When the "doctor" left he sniffed the powder. Then shuddered, and poured it down the sink.

He was on a train trying to sell Colin Powell a piece of veal for $6.98. The train was vibrating, about to go off the tracks. Powell kept insisting a four-star general should get his meat for less.

Then someone was shaking him. He threw his arm out, over his eyes. "The fuck."

"Hey. Dan?"

It was Henrickson. O'Quinn stood behind him in the passageway. Dan sat up, sensing how weak he was. Feeling, and hearing, the vibration all around him. *Chung Nam* was on turbines, and the sick floating feeling was her cutting through heavy seas on the stabilizers. He pulled an arm across his face, feeling grit at the corners of his mouth and eyes, hearing stubble rasp like a wire brush on rust. What he couldn't figure out was, why had Powell wanted the veal at all? "The fuck's going on?" he grunted.

"Got a little problem," O'Quinn drawled.

"What is it? A fire?"

"Not exactly," Henrickson said. "What it is, we've got to pack up to crossdeck."

"Crossdeck." He struggled to sit up. He must have a fever. Things were swimming, he felt chills. "You mean—*offload*?" The frigate leaned farther, and from down the passageway came a shout of excited Korean.

"Leakham says since the exercise is terminated they're detaching."

He played for time, trying to get his head in gear. But his transmission kept slipping and all he could do was repeat the last word he heard. "But—detaching?"

"Correct. Pulling out of the exercise. Whatever's left of it."

"Shit."

"Anyway, he's sending a chopper. Wants us packed and on deck an hour from now."

"*Leakham* wants us off?" Dan frowned.

Henrickson said patiently, "That's right. Chopper'll be here in an hour."

O'Quinn put in, "Oh—and there's now three probsubs headed our way."

The terminology was a little archaic, but Dan understood it. "Probsub" was "probable hostile submarine," the highest classification of contact unless someone had actually seen a periscope. *"Three?"*

"They're not sure, that's fixed-array sound-channel data. Passed by the Japanese."

Dan swung his feet to the deck and felt for his shoes. "Uh— here's what's wrong with that scenario. We don't take our direction from Harry Blowhard Leakham. Whatever the . . . whatever he thinks. In fact, whatever orders I get from that quarter, I'm going to do the exact opposite."

O'Quinn smiled darkly; Henrickson blinked. "Uh, my understanding, Dan, the SATYRE's been called off. Real-world operations. No point in us staying around."

"Jung put it on hold for forty-eight. Not shut it down."

"Well, technically you're right. But the Australians pulled out, the Japanese are gone, the U.S. squadron's on its way over the horizon, and the Koreans are steaming away from the op area at twenty-five knots. So you could argue pretty conclusively SATYRE 17 is in fact dead."

Dan was out of his bunk by now and trying to stuff his legs into his trou. They kept getting tangled up. Finally he realized he had one shoe on. That was why it was so hard to get his foot through the pants leg. He kicked it off savagely. "Uh, *technically,* Monty, if the South Korean Navy's on its way to intercept, force to the surface, and identify three unidentified submarines, most likely Russian Kilos, don't you think the U.S. Navy Tactical Analysis Group would like us to observe the action?"

"Uh . . . guess it could be tactically interesting . . ."

"Bet your ass. And it'd test pretty much exactly what this exercise is actually supposed to—" He bit his tongue; Owens hadn't cleared him to share their actual mission with the rest of the team.

Fortunately they didn't seem to notice his sudden self-censorship. "We could get some interesting recordings," O'Quinn put in. "I know we don't have much on these new diesels. Even less on the new torpedoes the Russkis are putting out. This new Shkval, now there's a—"

"See, Joe agrees with me." Sorry already for his tone, he slapped the little analyst on the shoulder. "Now help me get up to the bridge, Monty, okay?"

As Dan slid past, O'Quinn seized his shoulder. Said close to his ear, "You sure about this?"

"You can take off if you want, Joe." Dan raised his voice. "You too, Monty. Hear me? You guys want off? Helo's on its way."

"The team should stay together," Henrickson said.

"We don't all have to stay," Dan told him. "Joe? You want to go, go."

"Go where?" O'Quinn laughed, hoarsely, as if it didn't matter, as if nothing mattered. "There's nobody home waitin' dinner for me."

"If you stay, we all stay," Henrickson said, sounding more determined.

"You sure, Monty?"

"I'm sure. The team stays together."

He thought about ordering them to go, but that didn't seem right. If they wanted to stay, why not? It'd simplify their travel arrangements. And they could keep better track of the gear if they all went home together.

Topside it was night. The frigate heaved as she rushed through an immense darkness. Dan found Jung's chair empty, but Yu silent and motionless in his. He cleared his throat. "Skipper?"

"Commander Lenson. You have gear together? Are ready to be take off? We will come to course for helo approach when they notify us inbound."

"I've decided to stay aboard, Captain."

"You say, stay aboard?"

"That's right. We can't take off just when things might be getting interesting."

He expected questions, but Yu just sat silently. Finally Dan added, "With your permission, of course."

Yu still didn't answer. He just unsocketed the Pritac handset down off the overhead and handed it to him.

Dan checked the call-sign board behind him, dimly lit from behind and glowing ghostly in the black. CTG 75.1, Leakham, was Quebec Quebec tonight. "Quebec Quebec, this is TAG coordinator. Over."

The response was already distant, fading. VHF voice didn't have a very long range. "Quebec Quebec. Go ahead. Over."

He didn't recognize the voice. Not Leakham; one of his staff. "This is TAG coordinator, aboard Lima Alpha. My team is not debarking at this time. Thanks for your offer. You can scrub the helo. Over."

A short pause. Then, "This is Quebec Quebec. That was not an offer. That was an order. U.S. contingent has signaled finex and is proceeding outbound at this time. Stand by for helo at time four zero. Over."

"This is TAG coordinator. Quebec Quebec is not in our chain of command. Over."

"This is Quebec Quebec. Be advised, Quebec Quebec actual was acting on recommendation from Seventh Fleet that all national forces evacuate Korean waters at this time. Implementing that directive, he instructs you to crossdeck your personnel now aboard ROKN units at this time. Over."

Standing in the dark, knees shaking with weakness, he frowned, sensing a darkness that wasn't night. "This is TAG coordinator. Interrogative, why the evacuation order? Over."

"This is Quebec Quebec. Be advised: This is not a secure net. Stand by for helo at time four zero. Confirm wilco. Over."

"What the fuck?" somebody muttered behind him. Dan thought it was O'Quinn. "You hear this shit? Evacuating Korean waters? What the fuck is going on?"

Yu's profile was motionless, listening. Dan dragged a hand over his forehead. It came away dripping. Maybe he should have taken whatever the doc had tried to give him. He tried to discipline his thoughts. Get them in some kind of logical order.

U.S. forces were departing the theater. Obviously they knew something he didn't. Something the staffer couldn't even allude to over an uncovered circuit. So Leakham wanted them off. Wanted them back on a U.S. deck.

But something obdurate in his heart had no intention of leaving. Whatever Leakham said. The fat commodore had tried to dick with him ever since he got here. He had no idea why, but TAG had sent Team Bravo here to evaluate shallow-water antisubmarine tactics. The Joint Chiefs wanted a read-out on what league the South Koreans could play in. And it looked like some real-world ASW might be on its way. The Koreans were tough, smart, aggressive operators. Whatever was coming toward them, he wanted to find out what it was.

Unless he was very wrong, the Navy would appreciate having a professional observer on the scene.

But again, that didn't mean they all had to stay. And what he was hearing made him less certain they should. Leaving the transmit button up, he muttered, "Monty, Joe, I'm not sure what's going on. Some kind of recall message. Leakham thinks it applies to us."

Henrickson said, "Seventh Fleet's the theater commander—"

"So what?" O'Quinn broke in. "Not here. We're under CFC's Opcon."

Which was General Harlen. Dan gnawed his lip. The point could be argued, but he thought O'Quinn was closer to the truth. Especially as the threat became more dire. A TAG team was too small an element to be officially transferred to a combatant commander. But it seemed counterintuitive to pull his people back just when it looked like there could be action.

Or was he just being pigheaded? Mavericking it yet again? Letting himself be attracted to danger like some twentysomething jaygee? Looking at it as objectively as he could, he didn't think so. Tactics development was TAG's mission. And you never got the mission done by turning tail.

Probably the most accurate assessment would be that whatever he did, he'd have to justify it somewhere down the line. So finally he said, "Well—I don't think it applies to us. The recall, I mean. I'm going to stay.

"But, again: you're free to go. In fact, it'd be better—you're neither of you in an active-duty status. Pack up the nineteens. Get all the data back to TAG. I'll stay and see how this plays out."

They both muttered that they were staying too. Dan gave them a second or two to change their minds, wishing he could contact the guys on the other decks as well, Carpenter and Oberg. But he couldn't. There wasn't time. When they didn't, he keyed the handset again.

"Quebec Quebec, this is TAG coordinator. Belay the helo transfer. If you send it, we will not board. I say again, if you send it we will not board. Stand by to log this, and inform TAG and PACFLEET: Team Bravo is remaining with the ROKN aboard units of ASWRON 51 as observers, at the direction of the TAG coordinator. Over."

There. That'd cover his guys if things went wrong. Then there'd be only his ass to fry, if it all death-spiraled butt-ugly.

That was fair. More than fair.

The radio said, "This is Quebec Quebec. Be advised, I will advise Quebec Quebec actual and higher authority of this conversation. Over."

"This is TAG coordinator. Suggest you do exactly that. Over."

He listened for a moment more to the hiss of empty air, hoping he wasn't charging off over a cliff.

Utterly unforeseen, coming out of nowhere, in that fraction of a moment the sudden recognition hit that *he'd done this all before*. He'd stood on this bridge, in this darkness, committing these men and himself to an irreversible decision. It was utterly convincing. He *knew*. Beyond question or doubt.

But when he searched he couldn't recall *how*. Whether it'd been in a dream, a previous life . . . or if he'd just glimpsed this inevitable moment out of its ordained sequence, by some mysterious foreknowledge inexplicable by his culture's conventions of time and reality. He groped, bewildered, but found no explanation. Only a label—déjà vu—which explained nothing. Fancy? Delusion? No. It felt too meaningful, this unremitting moment. These waiting, expectant faces. He'd seen all this before. He'd *been here*.

But what good was a glimpse ahead if it couldn't tell him how the decision turned out? And if foreknowledge, what was that It, unbound by time and causality, that foreknew?

At a loss, appalled, he squeezed his eyes closed and asked whatever was behind the mystery, behind all the mysteries, that his decision be right.

Then added, "This is TAG coordinator. Out."

IV
CHONMYONJON

(the Typhoon)

13

"My officers tell me you're not feeling well," Jung said, sipping tea as he reclined. Dan was doubled over the table, unable to even think about eating. The commodore's stateroom reoriented itself slowly in space. The temple calendar shifted on the bulkhead. A golden slice of sun blazed through a porthole and sauntered across the tatami.

"It'll pass. Upset stomach, that's all."

"Korean food can seem strange to a Westerner."

"Oh, that's not it," he lied again. Or maybe it was the truth. "Just a bug. Some kind of intestinal flu or something."

"I asked my steward to prepare something special for you this morning. Something more like what you get at home."

Jung nodded, and with a flourish the white-coated server set the plate before him. Dan blinked at a folded yellow object, square, possibly incorporating egg.

"I gave him personal directions. Straight from Waffle King."

Dan cleared his throat. Hunger locked horns with nausea. It smelled okay. He picked up the fork. The steward hovered, wringing his hands like a newlywed serving her first meal.

The first bite of the omelet froze his mouth. He tried not to gag. Square-cut bits of carrot, green peas, spilled from the interior, hoary with frost. He chewed it grimly down to a cold paste, trying not to break a tooth on the frozen veggies. Swallowed, and set the fork carefully aside instead of driving it into Jung's expectant smile. "It's ... absolutely wonderful. How thoughtful of you."

"Is good?" The steward beamed.

"Just like Mom's! But I'm just not really up to it yet." He raised his cup to the commodore. "I'll stick with tea for now. *Salut.*"

"*Keon Bae*," said Jung, returning the toast with the beatific grin of a successful Samaritan.

The morning after the night before. He'd actually slept eventually, for a couple of hours. A pour-over and scrubdown, standing in one of the red plastic washtubs; a shaky shave. Then he'd stopped in CIC for an update from one of the Kims before responding to Jung's breakfast invite. The chart showed 1800 meters here, but to the south it started to shallow. First to 400, then another deep basin before the bottom rose again as you approached the Strait proper. He'd asked about sonar conditions. With the layer mixing from Brendan, they weren't good. Maybe 1200 meters direct path, though they might get convergence zone effects as the approaching contacts crossed the band.

Insofar as tactical disposition went, they were deploying out in a thirty-mile barrier oriented across the incomers' expected track, with the two ASW-capable ships' towed arrays streamed to try for long-range detection. Jung had them placed, from left to right, *Kim Chon, Chung Nam, Mok Po. Chang Bo Go* was thirty miles astern; even surfaced, the 209 was slower than the cans. She'd not yet deployed her own array, since that further reduced her speed of advance.

"We know anything else about these unidentifieds?" Dan had asked.

"We think there are four now," Kim had said.

Dan had checked the sea from the bridge wing. It stretched away, undulating like an antique mirror, prosaic, glossy, oilylooking. Bands of pewtery shadow crossed its gently bulging surface, narrowing as they neared the horizon. That watery margin where the sea shimmered into the sky, as if out there, at the edge of the world, it was boiling away with the heat.

Jung interrupted his musing. "You decided to stay."

"Yes, sir."

"May I ask why? Captain Yu tells me there was an exchange with Commodore Leakham."

"Not with him personally. I was speaking with his staffer." Dan explained the recall order. He wasn't sure if he should reveal that the whole U.S. Navy was pulling out, so he just said, "CTG 75.1's leaving the exercise. I guess, heading back to Yokosuka. He wanted us to crossdeck. I declined."

"Declined, or refused?"

It seemed like a good Korean-type answer, just to smile faintly. "I hope it is not out of place."

"So far you and I have been able to work together. Perhaps now exercise play has been suspended, I may call on you for tactical opinions now and then?"

"I'd be honored to help, if I can." He held out his cup and the steward refilled it.

"Then riddle me a riddle. Why has your navy suddenly pulled out of the Eastern Sea?"

So much for not telling him. "That I don't know, Commodore."

Jung's gaze was slicing-sharp as a wood chisel. "They didn't inform you? During this conversation in which you refused orders, and told them you would remain with us?"

"No sir. I asked more or less that same question, but they didn't have an answer."

Jung lowered his eyes and swirled his tea. "What do you know about this attack group—these unidentifieds—that would be useful to us?"

"Sir, I'm as much in the dark as you. It seems to me the Japanese, or whoever sent us that data, could have forwarded a lot more than just lat-long coordinates. Since they were tracking them for two days."

"The only conclusion I can draw is that they are Chinese. If they were Korean, or even Russian, the Japanese would have announced it and demanded an explanation."

Which was exactly what O'Quinn had said. Dan tipped in sugar and swirled his own tea while he contemplated the next step in the strange dance of a conversation every talk with this man seemed to become. "You think they're afraid of the Chinese."

Jung looked sleepy. "I'd say they are *wary* of them. The Japanese Maritime Self-Defense Force is very good. They are a first-class people, the Japanese. I will be the first to admit it, though Korea has suffered from their ambition. But their navy is small. And the Chinese buy many Japanese goods. I think the wariness may be as much economic as military." He sipped and added, "But it seems to me your country could be more helpful too. They must know more than we about these intruders. What precisely is your satellite detection capability in shallow seas? Synthetic aperture radar, temperature anomalies, internal wave effects?"

"Even if I knew that, Commodore, I couldn't tell you without specific clearance."

"Of course not," Jung said, but still he sounded disappointed, as if expecting Dan to pull some high-tech rabbit out of his cap. He waved at the tea things, signaling the steward to clear, and shook out one of his personal silver-tips. The Zippo clicked and flared. "Of course not. So. We are deploying to stop them. You know we think there are four now? At least that's what the Japanese have decided to give us. From their fixed array monitoring."

Dan decided to wet a hook of his own. "Does the Republic of Korea have fixed arrays in the Eastern Sea?"

"I could not tell you that without specific clearance. To use your words."

"If you did, you wouldn't have to depend on the Japanese. *Or* on us."

The commodore ignored that. "I'll tell you one other thing. Our Second Fleet has picked up another unidentified submarine contact in the Western Sea. Off Kunsan."

"*Another* unidentified?"

"It is so."

Dan rubbed his chin. "But only one?"

"So far."

"A diversion?"

"That was my thought too. You know the sonar conditions?"

"I saw the 0300 bathythermograph drop."

"They suck. If we get a thousand yards direct path we'll be lucky."

"I see you're planning a sonobuoy barrier to west and east. In case they try a runaround."

Jung said he didn't expect them to. "Not to the west, anyway. They're tracking down just off the boundary of the exclusion zone. My feeling is they won't cross it until they reach the Strait. And any easting they make, they'll attract the attention of the Japanese again. So I think they'll head right down our throats."

"Then what? They wouldn't identify for the Japanese."

"They'll identify for us," Jung said, and set his jaw like a lineman taking a grip on his mouthpiece. He turned his wrist to see his watch, and Dan realized their moment was over. "Now I'll go to the bridge. I enjoyed your company very much, and hope you feel better later in the day."

Dan wrote a message explaining his reasoning in keeping Team B with the Koreans. He addressed it to TAG, info CINCROKFLT, CINCPACFLT, and anyone else he thought might have an interest. As an afterthought he added COMDESRON 15. Not that he cared what Leakham thought; he just didn't want to be accused of going behind his back. He turned that in for Yu's countersign. Just like on a U.S. ship, nothing could go out without the skipper's chop. He chugged an orange pop to stay hydrated and went back to his stateroom to lie down.

At 1000 he was in CIC again, in the chair near the Harpoon console that had become the Americans' unofficial watch station. All battle stations were fully manned, compacting the limited space with unshowered bodies and tobacco smoke, but nobody spoke much. He watched green pips inchworm across radarscopes, aligning into the barrier, then begin their sweep northeast. At some point, the South Koreans and the oncoming group, whatever it was, would meet. Like a warm front and a cold. The result could well be thunderstorms.

Unless they missed each other. Which could happen in such wretched sonar conditions. The task force's biggest asset might well be radar. Diesel-electrics had to poke their snorkels up on a regular basis to vent the boats and recharge the batteries. To run at high speed, they had to keep those snorkel heads—larger than periscopes, and easier to catch on radar—above the waves full-time. In calm seas the SPS-10 *Chung Nam* carried should pick one up at fifteen thousand yards, seven and a half nautical miles.

Hwang came in. Dan watched him move from console to console like a bee making its rounds. When he got to Dan, Dan asked him, "Taking the duty?"

"From now on either the commodore or I will be in CIC. Or on the bridge." The chief of staff fingered a scroll under his arm. "What are your men doing now?"

"Not much. Securing the nineteen, boxing up the data forms from Phases I and II. What can we help you with?"

"The commodore would like to discuss a sort of . . . battle staff. Your people are deeply skilled in ASW. Would you be willing?"

This was an amazing honor, one he couldn't even imagine a U.S. task force commander extending to foreign riders. "We'd be happy to help. Sure! But . . . your crews are very good too."

"We are adequately trained on the ship-to-ship level. The commodore is thinking more broadly than that." Hwang pursed his lips. "He seems to believe you are well placed with the De Bari administration. Is that true, Dan?"

He almost rolled his eyes, before figuring that might be insulting. "Oh, jeez—only very indirectly. I know why he thinks that. He met my wife in Pusan. But I don't have any kind of political pull. No *influence,* if that's what he means."

"Would the president know your name?"

"I don't know. I went jogging with him. . . . Actually,

yeah, he might. Since I was one of his aides. But not necessarily in a good way."

"You are modest. The commodore said that about you. In
your situation a Korean would say he had great influence. He
would even boast of it."

"Believe me, it's not modesty," Dan told him. "Commander, please, *please* don't let him think I've got some kind of
clout in Washington. Through my wife or any other way. We
can advise on any tactical issues that come up. And we'll be
happy to do that. But that's all he should count on."

Hwang glanced toward the door, but lingered. "I should
also tell you this: ROK forces have gone to 'Fast Pace'
along the DMZ and elsewhere. *Jin do Kae*. As of 1030 this
morning."

"What's 'Fast Pace'? And this *Jin do*—"

"It's our highest readiness posture short of martial law
and a state of war. The same as Defcon Two in your vocabulary. Clear and immediate threat of an enemy attack. We are
mobilizing our reserves and going to intelligence Watchcon
One."

Dan nodded slowly. He understood the increased manning
in CIC now, and the lack of the usual hubbub and horseplay.
"That's serious, all right. What's the trigger? Not this intruder
group?"

. "They know in Seoul. We don't out here. I don't think it is
this group. At least not just them. There may be other intelligence indicators we don't know about." The chief of staff
looked toward the door again. "If I need to consult with you,
where will you be?"

"I'll set up a watch. Two of us on, one off. And set up my
notebook with our tactical tools. Is right here okay?"

"Right there will be fine," Hwang said.

He called O'Quinn and Henrickson and set up a rotation.
Twelve on, six off. They couldn't keep that up forever, but
it'd ensure someone was in CIC at all times while making
sure everybody got meals and at least some sleep.

Henrickson was beside him, trying to puzzle out the Korean intelligence summaries on the Whiskey-class boats, when the chief on duty came over. Dan wasn't sure whether he was the CIC officer, the evaluator, or just the watch supervisor, and they didn't have enough language in common for him to ask. He placed a handwritten note in front of them. It said *Barrer on Staion.*

"Barrier on station?" Henrickson asked after a moment. The chief nodded rapidly.

Dan said, "Thank you." The Korean bowed and went back to the plot.

"He's keeping us informed," Henrickson said. "In his shy way."

"This could be tricky, Monty. I always get the feeling Captain Yu would just as soon do without me. But Jung wants us around for advice. And we can't give it unless we know what's going on."

"It's psychological," Henrickson said.

"You think?"

"Sure. We're the only American faces left."

"So what? These guys don't need us."

"You know that. And I know that. But we also know it can get lonely at sea. Facing you don't know what, without anybody behind you."

Dan couldn't argue that point. If Jung wanted a backstop, a token, even a good-luck charm, he was willing enough to serve. "Okay. So. Let's think ahead a little bit. What's going to happen when we pick these boys up? The ones riding into town with masks over their faces?"

"They either surface and identify or they don't."

"And if they don't?"

"Jung says they will."

"He told me the same thing. But did he happen to mention exactly how he's going to make that happen?"

"That, he didn't say."

Dan nodded. He opened his notebook and turned it on. The battery indicator was low. He got down on the deck and crawled around till he found a vacant outlet. Fortunately

Korean ships were wired for 115 volts, sixty cycle, U.S. standard current. The computer beeped and powered up. He called up a spreadsheet and started entering variables.

At 1900 *Chang Bo Go* popped up a comm mast and reported in. Jung asked Dan where the best station for her would be. He and O'Quinn looked at the sonar conditions again. At last they recommended putting her at safety, ten thousand yards behind the line on the right flank, depth four hundred feet.

Mok Po reported first contact just before midnight. Radar contact, of course, since the PCC was non-ASW-capable, another reason Dan had suggested backstopping her with the Type 209. She reported a small intermittent blip at twenty-one thousand yards bearing 025. This was consistent with either a periscope or, more likely at that extreme detection range, a snorkel.

Dan joined the plotting team at the DRT as the commodore came down from the bridge. He told Jung, "That's farther east than the track the Japanese gave us, sir."

"They may have hoped to sidestep any patrols." Jung was freshly dressed, smelled of flowery cologne, carried a saucer with a steaming cup of tea. He patted his smoothly shaven cheeks absently, touched the mole lightly with the tip of his little finger. The enlisted men wove around him as they plotted four simultaneous tracks in black pencil, their ballet giving him a foot of clear air. Kim #1 was with him, his ASW staff officer. They all watched the new track, plotted in red, creep toward them.

Awfully slow warfare, Dan recalled. It was like a very deliberate game, played out above and below the surface of the sea. But with real ships for game pieces. Real lives for pawns and rooks. Its similarity to the exercise they'd just done didn't erase the tension. But he kept his expression detached. Jung fitted a cigarette into its holder. Charred its tip with the Zippo's wavering, almost invisible flame. Then spoke to the chief, who picked up a phone.

The general-quarters alarm began to bong. Dan's pulse

accelerated with the all-too-familiar electronic note. Running feet rumbled from outside the compartment, from above them and below. CIC was already crammed, but more men crowded in, sonarmen joining the team behind the black curtain, weapons console operators booting up system self-tests, phone talkers checking their circuits. Their babble filled the space.

A youngster on a radio headset exclaimed. He began to chant what Dan assumed were ranges and bearings. The chief pointed at another plotter.

A second red trail came into existence at the upper right of the chart paper. It too began tracking down toward them, about two miles west of the first contact.

At least two and possibly up to four diesel-electrics on snorkel were proceeding toward the Korea Strait. Dan scratched his head, frowning. Trying to figure out exactly what, the guys coming in on them were trying to do, and what Jung had in mind as a response.

Just seeing subs in company was creepy. Submariners were loners. Allergic to operating in close proximity. Only Doenitz's wolf packs in the North Atlantic had ever coordinated attacks successfully, along with, possibly, U.S. Pacific Fleet submarines against the Japanese; and both had kept in only loose contact by shortwave radio. He glanced at the ESM operators' stacks. If these guys were transmitting to each other, or to a shore station, the first warning would come from there. But the techs sat motionless, scrutinizing an empty screen.

"Do we want to sidestep the barrier to the eastward?" he asked Jung. "Or would it be better to switch *Kim Chon* out to the right flank?"

The Korean hesitated, eyeing the trace. Dan figured Jung was doing the same calculation as he was: how long it would take the ASW-capable PCC to switch flanks, versus when the oncoming subs would reach the barrier. Finally he nodded tightly to Kim. The staff officer pulled a phone off the overhead radio bank.

From one plot to the next the black line of *Kim Chon*'s

track altered. The gap between marks opened. She'd come to a southeasterly course and was racing across the back of the formation like a linebacker changing up. Dan hoped she was spitting sonobuoys on the way, to cover the hole where she'd been.

She was passing astern of *Chung Nam* when another contact came up. This time the notification came from one of their own radar consoles. Number three was *west* of the first two.

"Shee-it," O'Quinn muttered, and Dan shook his head. They'd just shot themselves in the foot, reoriented their screen assets to the wrong flank.

Seconds later the first radar contact vanished. Submerged, no doubt. The datum, their last positive fix on its position, was sixteen thousand yards out. Eight miles.

"Sorry about that," Dan said.

"Don't worry about it," Jung said imperturbably. He stubbed out a butt and took several small wrapped candies from his pocket and scattered them across the plotting surface. Dan tried one. It tasted like watermelon and ginseng. "She left sonobuoys. They'll pick up the track. But still I think I will begin moving *Chang Bo Go* west. She has a full charge in the can from her transit. She can move at high submerged speed."

The chief cleared his throat. "*Chang Bo Go* report passive contact. Bearing zero, zero, seven. Suspect snorkeling submarine." He glanced at Dan, probably to gauge the effect of his reporting in English.

"Excellent," Jung said.

The plotters got it down as an arrow pointing north from the 209's position. It matched the radar contacts, either the second or the third. "She's getting better transmission at depth," Kim said. "Too much surface mixing."

Some minutes passed. Then the second contact disappeared from the radar screen, as the first had. Seconds later, the third followed.

Now all the radar screens were empty, the beams sweeping futilely over the sea's surface. Dan visualized the approaching subs slipping through the depths. They'd retracted their snorkels, gone to electric propulsion, probably dropped to two or three hundred feet. Below the thermocline. But still headed inexorably for the waiting line. Head on. All together.

Creepy, he thought again, and a shiver wormed its way up his spine.

Jung turned aside to sneeze. He cleared his throat and announced, "I'm going to signal them to identify themselves now."

"I don't see why they should," Dan told him.

"International law. Submarines encountered on the high seas must respond when challenged."

"They didn't for the Japanese."

"That is what the *Japanese* say," Jung reminded him. "In fact they may very well have done so. But it was not revealed to us."

Dan hesitated, then nodded. Right. It was *possible.* But he didn't think this silently approaching formation would respond. It was unsettling. You just didn't see subs operating this way. It didn't compute tactically. That was what made it so ominous.

The eerie multitoned whalesong of an active sonar ping going out drilled through the frigate's metal. It prickled the hair on the back of his neck. Detection distances would be very short. Still, they might get something. The oncoming targets were slowly drawing into range.

Jung spoke sharply to Kim. The lieutenant nodded and picked up another handset. He spoke slowly, spacing his words. They went out in the haunted-house echo of an underwater voice transmission. It cut out in the middle, automatically silenced as the frigate's sonar pinged again. If it hadn't, the power they were pushing into the water would have burned the receiver out. He spoke in Korean, then in English, then in what Dan guessed was Chinese.

"*Chang Bo Go* will drop speed to bare steerageway in two minutes," Jung murmured. "She will have the best passive sonar conditions. She is beneath the mixing layer."

"Can she report in?"

"She's streamed an HF antenna. There is a slow data link

that should work as long as she's not too deep. We can't pick it up, but Seoul can. They will retransmit back to us over covered HF."

Complicated, but Dan didn't see why it wouldn't work. At least, as long as whoever was on the circuit back in Seoul was diligent about turning the reports around in a timely manner. In fact it was a pretty resourceful use of what limited comm channels they had, and his respect for Jung clicked up a notch.

"What I'm afraid of is they're going to envelop our line," O'Quinn muttered from across the light table. Dan started; he'd forgotten the retired captain was there. "Just keep coming and bop on by right under our keel."

"They can't pass us if we trail them," Jung pointed out. "If we keep their heads down until they're forced up to recharge."

"So what? They pop their snorkel up. They recharge and submerge again. And you're no wiser."

Jung didn't answer, and suddenly Dan suspected what he planned to do. "I hope there's no accident," he said, and both Jung and Kim glanced at him, startled. "They'd have to surface."

Jung waved the discussion away. He frowned at Kim, who was still holding the handset. *"Dap byeon up na?"*

"*Yeop sum ni da, jeon dae jang nim.* No response," Kim explained.

Over the next quarter hour Jung had him challenge twice more. They checked with the sonarmen on the effective range of the voice-phone. The consensus seemed to be that voice-phone range would be about twice active sonar detection range. Maybe a little less, but still close to a nautical mile in current conditions. Kim scribed range circles with a compass. Unless the contacts had altered course, at least one of them must have heard the demand for identification.

But they hadn't answered.

Dan wanted to ask "Okay, what now?" but didn't. They stood around the tracking table. Jung looked gloomy. Then a Teletype clattered into action on the far side of the space. A sailor ripped the paper off and brought it over.

It was the HF link from Seoul. Kim looked up. "*Chang Bo Go* reports: Passive sonar contact. Confirm Romeo-class submarine. Bearing two-seven-zero true. Time three-five. Shadowing."

Dan checked the bulkhead clock, then his watch. A firm identification at last, and ten minutes turnaround on the report. Not bad, but not terrific either. Assuming *Chang Bo Go* was where they thought she was, it meant the range was already opening, her contact already filtering through the screen. The target was most likely unaware of the new, quieter South Korean boat. "Shadowing," of course, meant the ROKN craft was now coming around to plod silently in its wake, directly astern. They looked at each other, stymied. "Any ideas here?" Jung said.

Henrickson had come in and stood listening. Now he said, "What's the procedure if a sub on the open sea fails to respond? The law, I mean?"

"You're allowed to force it to surface," Dan told him. "The question is, how? Used to be the Soviets, when they caught one of ours inside their limit, would drop depth charges. Not close enough to kill, but near enough to damage. We used small charges to do the same thing."

"We no longer carry depth charges," Kim said. "*Dae Jon* did, but she is—"

"No longer with us, right. And these guys aren't in your territorial waters either. We're still in the open sea out here."

Jung said, "So they are required to identify; but if they do not, we have no legal way to make them do so."

Dan hesitated, then nodded. Jung said to Kim, "Do we have comms back to *Chang Bo Go*?"

"I do, sir."

"Order them to force the contact to surface."

The door to the space undogged. It was Captain Yu. The flagship's skipper stood watching, but didn't approach. He shook a cigarette out. A sailor hurried to light it for him.

Dan tensed. He caught the others' alarmed glances too. He murmured, "Well, Commodore—that risks your own men as well. If you're thinking of forcing a collision."

"I was actually thinking of having her ram from astern. That would destroy either the screws or the prop. An accident, yes. Regrettable. But it would force them to surface."

A tactic Dan hadn't considered. He rubbed his mouth, considering the geometry of such a close pass, whether the 209's commander could actually localize the sub he was trailing well enough to put his bow in her screw. It sounded pretty fucking dangerous. What if the screw sliced through a ballast tank? He kept getting echoes of Nick Niles's valedictory injunction. "Try to keep everybody alive this time," his saturnine whatever-the-opposite-was-of-mentor had said.

Blood heated his cheeks at the memory. The imputation— that he was some kind of killer, some kind of Jonah—was grossly unfair. But somehow he'd internalized the mission. He was going to bend over backward to make sure no one got hurt.

This seemed like a good place to stick in his oar. "Well, sir—that *might* work. If he got lucky. But if he got unlucky, you could lose the boat. Both boats, actually. Is identifying them worth that kind of risk? I'm not sure it is."

"Those are my orders. Identify these craft. Your alternative?"

"Well, sir, if those are the orders—I'm not recommending this. But I'll raise it for discussion. If your orders *absolutely* are to make positive identification? You could ask Seoul for permission to attack instead."

Jung's eyelids drooped. "Why would I do that?"

"Because Higher obviously feels they're a threat."

"Why do you say that?"

Captain Yu drifted a couple of paces nearer.

"Because your national command authority's gone to a higher defense condition," Dan said. "Unless that has zip to do with what your task force is doing out here. Which I don't think it does."

Jung didn't meet his eyes. Finally he said, "It may. But then again it may not."

Dan had no idea what that was supposed to mean. They were both looking down, at a standstill, when the Teletype clattered again. Jung's head snapped around. The flimsy came sailing across the space in the sailor's hand. Kim studied it. He looked up.

"From *Chang Bo Go*. Outer torpedo doors opening on contact!"

At the same moment one of the sonarmen shouted behind the black curtain. Yu reacted instantly, lunging forward to slam the lever down on the intercom to the bridge and shout into it. The plotters burst into activity, drawing arrows across the paper and pressing their headphones to their skulls with the tips of their fingers. Jung took hold of the plotting table with both hands, lips compressing, eyebrows drawing together as his face turned to granite. After a moment he snapped an order. Kim passed it on instantly over the Pritac.

"What is it?" Dan said.

"From *Kim Chon:* torpedo in water," the chief said in a tense murmur. A moment later the sonarmen called out again from behind their curtains.

Just that suddenly, Dan realized, they were at war.

Jung muttered something in Korean. A curse, Dan suspected. Or maybe a prayer, to what deity in what tradition he didn't know. Maybe to the same titanic and dreaded presence sailors since before the Phoenicians had tried to propitiate. The great Mask Melville's mad captain had struck through to find eternal Truth, and met instead eternal Death.

The voracious, savage, and eternal Sea.

The frigate heeled, the noise level rising as the whooshing hum of the turbines spooled up from aft. He leaned over the table, gripping it with the same instinctive reaction as Jung, as if the ship were a horse they could urge to greater effort.

From *Kim Chon*, still on her crossfield sprint to the eastern side of the barrier, the arrow indicating torpedo effects pointed in front of the flagship. The plotter lifted his pencil from another arrow drawn out from *Chung Nam*'s own trace. The sound lines intersected six thousand yards ahead of the forward barrier edge. The flagship was at that moment at the rear of her assigned barrier box.

Dan grabbed Yu's shoulder. "Is your Nixie streamed? Turned on?"

"Of course. We practice evading torpedo. Not a problem." Yu frowned down at his fingers. Dan retrieved them, hoping the guy was right. He checked the heading indicator on the bulkhead. It marched steadily around as the ship shimmied, digging her butt into the turn at full power. Yu was putting his stern to the oncoming weapon, or weapons—there could be more than one, you couldn't tell from the reports. And he was speeding up.

Put the noisemaker out, aim your stern at the torpedo, and make tracks—that was about all they could do.

A minute passed. He stood clinging to an overhead handhold, still trying to wrap his head around the abrupt metamorphosis from peacetime steaming to mortal engagement. The first shot had been fired. No one *declared* war anymore. They hardly ever had, in Asian waters. But from now on, a state of war existed.

Only . . . whom was that war with? That was the puzzler.

The plotters leaned forward again. Dan's gaze moved from one hastily sketching pencil to the next.

Mok Po was turning left.

The second *X* they plotted made it perfectly plain. The non-ASW-capable patrol combatant, her easterly neighbor in the barrier, was cutting between the retreating flagship and the oncoming torpedo. As he leaned forward, horrified, the next *X* went down, at a noticeably greater interval from the first.

"She is at flank speed," Kim #1 said in an undertone. His eyes met Dan's. He was still holding the Pritac handset. The one he'd just transmitted on, passing on Jung's snapped-out command.

Dan blinked, trying to deny what he was seeing. "He ordered her across your front—?"

Kim sucked in his breath and nodded. He looked appalled.

Dan snapped to Henrickson, "Keep an eye on this." He caught the door before it dogged and followed the old skipper's double time up the narrow ladder.

It was full dark; no moon; he'd forgotten it was night. But as he stepped out onto the bridge wing after Yu, a light went on. It was off *Chung Nam*'s port quarter. The lit bubble slowly grew, turning from white to yellow to red. It went out for a second and dark fell again. Then the horizon lit from one hand to the other in a searing flash that tracered silent sparks, like ascending meteors, through a whole quadrant of the sky behind them.

A muffled thud rolled out of the dark. Then a ripple of detonations, both sharp and dull, drumming and popping like the finale of a fireworks display. Scarlet fire arched, then faded, leaving a dull red glow like the embers of a dying wood-fire. He stared, breath bated in utter horror, unable to accept what he'd just witnessed.

"Mok Po?" he breathed.

Yu said, voice grim, *"Mok Po."* Then spun, and shouted angrily at the officer of the deck.

Chung Nam tilted at the end of a roll, caught by the stabilizers. She began skating around, trembling with that strange dreamlike sensation of being balanced. Yu pulled himself in through the door and hiked to starboard, shouting with each step. Yells broke out all over the bridge, but it wasn't panic or disorganization, just a well-drilled crew responding to a rapid stream of terse orders.

Rushing out to the starboard wing, Dan looked down to see faintly, by a dim blue battle-light that had glowed to life directly above them, the triple tubes of the torpedo launcher swinging out to train abeam. Crew swarmed over it, then suddenly scrambled back as if from a live bomb.

The frigate steadied a point to the left of the drifting ember that as they ran through the blackness grew slowly, finally became recognizably a ship, adrift and aflame.

He ducked inside and grabbed a set of binoculars. Through them he made out she was listing, on fire, with an ominous darkness aft. Torpedoed, some hulls just broke apart. He could make out forms running about the deck but couldn't see what they were doing. He didn't see any water-spray, no hoses being employed, no evidence the fire was being fought.

The muffled bump of compressed air came from below him. One by one, three tubular masses extruded from the launcher. Each hovered for a moment over the racing sea, then arched over and dived splashlessly into the black. A green fire bloomed beneath the surface, wavering, formless, weird. Then swiftly dropped astern, pulsating and lengthening until the launcher coughed again and another weapon catapulted out.

Shouts, the groaning of the helm. Again *Chung Nam* banked and skated. He clutched the binoculars so hard his finger joints protested. He felt frustrated, nervous, charged; above all, *useless*. He slammed his fist on steel till pain informed him he was bruising bone.

He spun, hammered down the ladder again, and burst into CIC.

Jung, Kim, Henrickson, and O'Quinn stood where they had when he'd left. The plotters bent forward like rowers on the stroke. The red and blue and black traces were a little longer, that was all. *Mok Po*'s ended in a tiny stylized picture of a sinking ship. Five short neatly drawn lines. And the six-digit date/time group.

"You put her between you and the torpedo," he muttered.

The commodore eyed him. "She had no ASW capability," he said at last. "This ship does."

Dan gripped the table edge, fighting for control. He'd never witnessed a more cold-blooded act. Then, through the horror, protruded a reluctant edge of professional admiration. This son of a bitch was *stone*. *This* bastard didn't care who he killed.

He tried to speak and found he couldn't.

"Run time," said Kim. He held up a stopwatch. Dan lifted his head, giving up on words. There were no words. Not for this.

They listened, waiting for the detonations.

None came. The seconds stretched out. The Koreans looked ever grimmer. They probably knew men on the stricken ship.

"What happened?" Jung snapped. Kim shouted to the sonarmen. They yelled back, and Dan got the gist: nothing.

Not one of the three Mark 46s they'd fired had connected. He was surprised. The weapon had been in the inventory for many years; it was dependable. Still, misses happened.

"Very well," said Jung. He mopped his face with his palm, and Dan saw it was dripping when it came away. He felt shaky too. If he hadn't seen it before, in other situations, he wouldn't have believed how swiftly everything you thought and knew and assumed you were prepared for could come unglued. And all turn to utter shit.

Yet it just had. "Is *Kim Chon* launching too?" Dan asked the table in general.

"I've ordered her not to, unless she's fired on," Jung said. "In case this was the action of one hothead. But to remain in instant readiness to attack. By the way, she has active contact on one of the others." He placed his finger on a newly drawn dot. "She will maintain track and attack instantly if she suspects hostile intent.

"And now"—he switched his gaze to Kim—"we will call on them once more to identify. If they do not, we will destroy them all."

14

Topside again, he gripped the rail on the 01 level, looking down and out. The bow wave rolled out slowly into the black. Sailors talked excitedly beside him, pointing across the water.

Two hundred yards away *Mok Po* was burning. This close the firelight illuminated everything with terrible clarity. Everything aft of the patrol craft's aftermost mount was missing, gone, blown away. Fire roared amidships. Her bow was rising slowly as the stern section sank. And the men . . . some gathered on the bow, watching as the flagship approached. They didn't yell or wave, just stared. Another knot struggled around a boat, but even from this distance Dan could see they weren't making much progress. It looked like the davits were jammed.

But the inflatable rafts weren't going over. The fiberglass capsules that held them were still lined up neatly on the flying bridge. As he watched, a plume of white burst from amid a knot of men along the main deck. It wavered, sprayed straight up, then steadied and swung around to play into the flames.

He couldn't quite believe it, but it didn't look as if the CO had ordered abandon ship. He shook his head. It was both courageous and incredibly dangerous. Judging by how much of the stern was missing, they had to be taking at least some flooding in the engine spaces. If whatever bulkheads sealed off the remaining watertight compartments gave way, the craft could go under literally in seconds. She'd slide aft and down as the sea rammed into her like a crazed bull, killing anyone still belowdecks and sucking down those floundering in the water.

Not that he didn't understand how her skipper must feel. Exactly the same, probably, as he'd felt during *Horn*'s trial by nuclear fire.

The door behind him thumped open. O'Quinn said, "Jesus. Straight up the fucking ass. Didn't they have their Nixie streamed?"

"They probably did. These guys don't neglect countermeasures."

"Then it wasn't acoustic."

"Huh? Uh—no. Probably not."

"Sraight runner? Unlikely, from a submerged shot. Only one thing left."

Dan nodded, heart sinking. He should have come to the same conclusion. Wake-homing torpedoes were a Russian invention, dismissed as myth by the U.S. Navy for many years. But they were real. And the Chinese had them.

It looked like now they knew whom they were facing.

And with one less advantage the surface ships had counted on in case it came to an exchange of ordnance.

"They're gonna stick it out?"

"Looks like it." Dan figured he should get back to CIC, but couldn't tear himself from watching yet. They witnessed side by side as another hose cut on, as the bowless hulk rolled and a prolonged wailing protest of stressed steel and the cries of embattled seamen came plain across the dark sea.

But the men over there had firemain pressure. They still had power. If they could get the fire out before it set off the ready ordnance, get the engine room dewatered and the bulkheads shored up, they might have a chance of keeping her afloat.

Reluctantly, he turned away.

Back in CIC Yu and Jung were screaming at each other. Or at least the little skipper was screaming. Junior officers and men stood frozen, gazes averted from their seniors.

"What's going on?" he muttered to Hwang, who was standing as far from the altercation as he could get.

"Captain Yu wants to stop and lower the whaleboat. Take over firefighting supplies. Commodore has refused permission."

They didn't need him in that decision, but Dan hoped they got it settled soon. Dawdling around here, outlined by the flames, was as dangerous a position as he could well imagine if whoever had torpedoed the PCC was hanging around. But just then Yu swung away, face flushed nearly black. He shoved an enlisted man out of the way and stormed out.

Jung cleared his throat and passed a hand over his hair. He turned back to the plot. No one said anything, and after a moment he observed hoarsely, for some reason in English, "We cannot linger here. We will send a message to Seoul reporting the loss and requesting them to send assistance. Commander Hwang, see to that."

"Yae, jeon dae jang nim."

"We're too far out for helicopters. They will have to send fishing craft. Send the position twice. Make absolutely sure they record it correctly."

The chief of staff aye-aye'd again and Jung turned back to the DRT, eyes narrowed to X-Acto cuts. The turbines speeded up again. The heading indicator began to spin. Bending over the paper, Dan saw that *Kim Chon* was fifteen thousand yards distant and headed southwest. The trace showed she still held contact, though not with which sub.

The teleprinter chattered. Jung took the flimsy, lips compressed. Dan studied him, his emotions a mess. The guy had just sacrificed another ship to protect his flagship. Then left its men to the sea, and all without a word of regret or any indication, really, that he even rued having had to do it. Maybe it was tactically justified, but it took an iron will to condemn others to die. He'd had to, once or twice, and he still wondered, deep in the night, if he could've been smarter, have saved them somehow.

He looked across the space as O'Quinn came in. No

doubt he had nightmares too, about the guys he'd welded that hatch down on.

The trace showed *Chung Nam* steering southwest. At flank speed, judging by the vibration. He remembered the patched hull and hoped the concrete held. "Where's *Chang Bo Go*?" he asked the chief, who shrugged.

"Still at depth," Jung said.

"Unless she's been torpedoed too."

Dan took a deep breath, hoping not. But what he didn't understand was why the 209 hadn't taken out the hostile after it had fired on *Mok Po*. She'd been shadowing. She'd reported the outer doors opening. But hadn't fired. He wondered what the last teleprinter message said, and who it was from, but Jung had already folded it and stuck it into his breast pocket and buttoned it in, and it wasn't Dan's place to demand to see.

"We can't let these guys get away scot-free," he suggested.

"I'm warning them one last time to surface. Then I attack without making distinctions," Jung said. He spoke to Kim, and the lieutenant pulled down the handset.

They had it in hand, so Dan tried to back off. Look at it with some distance. This group, Chinese probably, had committed an act of war. Since they still weren't identifying, and were obviously operating together, Jung was fully justified in carrying out as savage an attack as he could with the remaining forces at his disposal.

Which over the next half hour he proceeded to do. With *Kim Chon* holding contact one thousand yards astern of her unknown, he assigned Captain Yu to conduct a deliberate attack from abeam. Dan cautioned that they might encounter wake homers. Jung said brusquely he'd reached that conclusion too. He sent a message to their own sub to stand clear. Kim called their target one last time on the underwater phone, but again, got not a syllable in response.

This time two torpedoes hit the water eight hundred yards to port of the contact. The shock when they went off, one after the other, rattled the frames.

"Target is breaking up," Hwang translated the sonarmen's report. "They're putting it on the loudspeaker."

The space went quiet. Men listened to the distant, reverberating crunch of imploding bulkheads. Then more explosions. And last, an eerie, ululating whine that faded slowly as the hulk sank away into eight hundred fathoms of dark sea.

The teleprinter broke the silence with its zipping rattle. This time Jung shared the message. "*Chang Bo Go* reports unable to fire torpedoes," he said. "Fault in the fire control system arming logic. They're trying to set up a manual workaround."

"So they tried to fire?"

"Apparently so."

Dan thought that over. Not encouraging. Understandable; after all, they were still on their delivery trials, not only of a new boat but of a new class. But still not good news, that a third of their remaining force, and the only sub, couldn't pull the trigger. "What about contacts? Do they have any?"

The commodore shook his head. This was bad too. It meant there were three subs down there slipping through the deep, aware now they were being hunted.

Jung slouched with hands in his pockets, looking into the trace as if into a screen that foretold the future. His face was like a sagging, blotchy rubber mask. Dan checked his watch. Nearly dawn. He needed coffee, but didn't dare leave. If they picked up another contact, or got another torpedo warning, things would move very fast indeed.

That was ASW; a game of slow hours and very fast seconds.

Henrickson pulled his sleeve. Dan turned, and got involved in a discussion of what the latest bathythermograph readings meant. The ship vibrated around them. In some corner of his mind he wondered what their fuel status was getting to be. They had to be burning a lot, running on the turbines for so many hours. There wasn't anything he could do about it, though, so he refocused his attention on the sound speed profile.

For the next two hours *Chung Nam* and *Kim Chon* executed a coordinated intercept search around the point where they'd destroyed the sub, gradually moving the pattern southwest at the estimated sustained speed of Romeos on battery. The son-armen reported only the amplified hiss-howl of the hollow sea. The remaining submarines had dissolved into it. They were still there somewhere, but passive conditions were too mushy and active ranges too short to comb them out of the vacant meaningless crackle, the furious emptiness of noise without signal.

Dan was pulling at his lip, pondering, when he saw Jung beckoning from the door. When he joined him the commodore led the way out into the ladderway. Gray vitiated light bled down from the half-open door at the top. Startled, he realized it was day again. "Yes, sir?"

"Seoul's informed us our contacts are North Korean."

"North Korean? Uh, sir, I don't think so—"

"I know. I thought they were Chinese too."

"I don't think that's possible. The North doesn't have wake homers, far as we know."

"If those were advanced torpedoes, the Chinese must have furnished them. But this is from intelligence. Very high confidence level, they say."

Which could mean anything, including a spy carrying Kim Jong Il's golf bag in Pyongyang. Dan pursed his lips, debating whether to accept it. He didn't really want to. He had no love for the Chinese. And whatever was going on, they were involved *somehow*. That was a given in this part of the world. But at last he nodded. "If they're sure. So it's the North. The offensive. At last."

"Or *part of* the offensive." Jung patted his breast pocket. "Also. The Chinese have issued a warning to the Japanese. They are not to interfere in the Eastern Sea."

Dan registered both pieces of information. Then multiplied them against each other. The product was appalling. "What do you mean, *part* of an offensive? There are other forces involved? And the Chinese are *protecting* them?"

"There's a surface amphibious group heading down the west coast. They used Brendan for cover from satellites and air reconnaissance."

He steadied his voice. No matter how bad the news, he

had to stay with the facts. Just as Jung was doing. "Intel says they're North Korean too?"

"Correct. Right now we don't know their intended landing point. It's unfortunate most of our maritime patrol aircraft were on the east coast for this exercise."

Dan nodded, feeling unreal. It was what they'd all waited for so long. Only the bad guys weren't coming over the DMZ, as everyone had expected for decades. The Germans hadn't come through the Maginot Line, either. Pyongyang was doing an end run.

But they didn't have that much amphibious shipping. From what he understood of their force levels, not even a division lift. Which wouldn't make much impact, no matter where it came ashore, not against ROK and U.S. air strikes, and behind that the combined armies.

So what was going on? It didn't make sense. Just as the phalanx of steadily advancing submarines had made no tactical sense.

"*Mok Po* reports she's still afloat," the commodore added. "They are very good people over there. I always was impressed on my inspections. She has a generator back. Captain Min sent down a diver. He reports the blades of both screws are blown away, though the shafts seem to be intact. She's even under way again. At three knots, under tow by her whaleboat."

"That's clever. The whaleboat, I mean."

"We Koreans are at our best in adversity. I told him to head for Ullungdo for now. If his after bulkhead suddenly gives way, the fishermen there can pick his men up."

Dan nodded. "Casualties?"

"A few. Yes."

He glanced at Jung, but apparently that was all he was going to say on the subject.

"So what's the idea?" Dan asked him. "These intruders, these Romeos are North Korean with Chinese torpedoes—fine, if Seoul says it's confirmed, I'll buy it. But this isn't falling into place for me as a cohesive operational picture. Where are they headed? What's their piece of this? Why did they attack—no, *one* of them attacked—then the others go into evasive mode, deep, quiet, gone? That's what doesn't jell here. If they'd done a coordinated attack they could really have screwed us up. With the advantage of surprise, like that."

"I hoped your people could tell me. Your skilled analysts. Your PhD's."

Dan sucked air through his teeth. "Well—we'll try to come up with something. Sir. But right now, I'm in the dark too. This just isn't how subs deploy, or operate."

"The Northerners seldom do anything the way the rest of the world does," Jung observed. "That's what they call *juche*."

"I thought *juche* meant 'independence.' "

"Only to an American."

Jung smiled. Dan hoped it was a joke. "Okay, so—what are your orders? I assume those were orders you got?"

"Correct. From CINCROKFLT. From now on we are to destroy all unidentified submarine contacts without warning."

Dan wondered if that mandate had been approved by General Harlen at CFC, whether U.S. Forces Korea was at Defcon One too, whether this was an ROK-only crisis or a combined-forces one. And whether the De Bari administration was standing behind its ally in what looked like the opening moves of a major war. At stake would be whether events were ramping up to an ROK-only fight, in which no ROK forces would come Opcon to CFC, or a combined fight, in which they all would.

But maybe he didn't want to hear the answer. It wouldn't make any difference to him or the other TAG riders, anyway.

The TAG riders . . . With a sense of falling he realized now what he'd dragged them into. Seventh Fleet had seen it coming. They'd directed them to get off Korean decks and out of the Eastern Sea. Leakham had tried to extract them.

But had Dan Lenson cooperated? Obeyed a perfectly rational order? Had he let his men leave an incipient war zone?

No. He remembered the radio conversation now with dismay. He'd done the opposite. Encouraged them to stay. Led them, by his own stubborn, self-righteous example, into the middle of a battle they had no business being in.

And they weren't even military, most of them. Civilians or retired, except for Oberg, who he suspected was a special ops type of some kind. He closed his eyes, feeling condemned. "Shoot on sight, then," he muttered.

"Those are our orders." Jung felt in his other pocket, got the holder out, and dropped it. One of the sailors was on the deck instantly, groping, holding it up. Jung fitted a cigarette to it without even looking at the kid. He leaned against the ladder and held the inhaled smoke longer than any human being should, squinting as if the light scorched his lids. Dan saw how worn-out he was. But if there was going to be a running fight, it could last for days. They'd all end up a lot more exhausted than this. If not dead.

He looked away from that very real possibility. "We need assets out here, Commodore. Romeos have to charge one in six, at least. We've got to have the hulls to give us radar coverage when they come up."

"There were no plans for action this far south. *Mesan* and *Cheju* are on their way to us out of Donghae. They will join in about"—the commodore squinted into his watch—"seven hours. Fleet at first thought they could assign me all of Squadron 11. But Seoul ordered them to keep the rest of the Eastern Fleet off the DMZ. For defensive operations, in case there is a second amphibious strike group.

"We should have maritime patrol air assets out of Chinhae, though. Whatever they give me, I will take tactical command and form an ASW strike group."

"Sounds like a plan. When's the air coming available?"

"That is on its way."

"And this second storm? 'Callista'?"

"We won't start to see increased winds for another twenty-four hours."

Dan thought it through as Jung smoked. Then cleared his throat. "Here's my recommendation, if you want it. I know you've probably already gotten started on most of it."

"I'd like to hear your ideas."

He took a deep breath. "First off, when your air assets report in, let them do the bulk of the radar flooding. Stand your gray-hulls off to the west, between this group and the coast. To kind of shepherd them away from it: if they get into shallow water, they'll be ten times harder to pick up." Jung nodded slightly, and Dan went on. "We've got what, two hundred miles till the Strait? Crank up to twenty-five knots and head south. Set up a fuel rendezvous. Get a tanker out there to get everybody topped off. Request resupply on your torpedos and sonobuoys. Get helo detachments out here, as many as you can find decks for. Then set up another barrier around thirty-six north."

But even as he spoke Dan became aware of a gap in his logic, a doughnut hole in what he was suggesting. They still didn't know where this group was heading, or what its tasking was.

There was only so much three diesel boats could do. The only plausible mission he could come up with for them in the Strait area was to interdict U.S. reinforcements coming into Pusan. But if that was the plan, the intruders wouldn't be in company, and they wouldn't have angled so far out to the east, all the way to Japanese waters, before zigging back toward land. They'd have slipped down the east coast one by one, hiding by day, snorkeling by night, and taken their positions silently and waited for the first MPS ship out of Guam to round Kyushu and heave over the horizon, wallowing-deep with vehicles and ammunition.

"But what are these guys trying to do?" Jung said, blinking reddened lids up at the growing radiance at the top of the ladderwell. "That's what's got me short-circuited."

"Same here. But if we don't know, we don't know. The point of ASW operations isn't to guess enemy intentions."

Actually, he thought, the point wasn't really to destroy subs either, though you didn't pass up the chance when you had it. It was to deny the enemy the use of them, to keep their heads down and so busy just surviving they couldn't act offensively.

If they could do that, and keep the southern ports open for the buildup and resupply, then no matter what the Communists did farther north, the Air Force would clobber the hell out of them on the way down the peninsula. Eventually they'd stop, be pushed back, and lose.

But this was the typhoon season, and it looked like an active one. What effect would that have on air support? And the carriers, the Air Force bomber squadrons from Okinawa, the long-planned U.S. surge—was it on its way? The massive artillery barrage everyone had always expected to signal Der Tag hadn't started. The tanks still hadn't crossed the line. The op plans had been written around those assumptions, and the planning and programming and budgeting and acquisition and time-phased force deployments and logistic arrangements had too.

But it wasn't playing out that way, and he found that far more ominous and sinister. It meant the other side had a strategy, a weapon, or an advantage that the Good Guys didn't know about; one the experts who'd gamed the Allied defense and counteroffensive didn't even suspect.

Jung climbed the ladder slowly, pulling himself up with muscular arms. Dan stayed at the bottom, relishing the steady cool current of relatively smoke-free air that streamed down it and at the same time worrying. He felt so fucking cut off out here. If he had just one comm channel that didn't run through the Koreans, he could at least ask what was going on. He didn't even have general news, to find out what the world reaction was. The Koreans, at least aboard Chung Nam, didn't publish anything like the daily bulletin a U.S. ship put out to keep the crew abreast of headlines and sports scores. It was a self-contained world, the way it must have been in the Pacific in World War II.

He looked up at the growing light, feeling alone. Feeling the sway and creak of the ship around him. A steel cocoon that protected him, but that for a couple of hours there had felt more like a magnet for torpedoes. He wondered how Mok Po's crew was doing. Creeping toward an island haven while war crescendoed around them. He hoped their bulkheads held, hoped they made it. He'd been in their shoes.

Now it was dawn, the break of another day that would

probably confirm war had come again. War with a savage enemy who'd planned and armed and trained for decades. He didn't feel ready. But probably not one of the hundreds of thousands of troops on both sides felt that way, not one of the thousands of sailors who must be putting to sea as news rippled across a stunned country. As the sirens wailed in Seoul, starting the evacuation.

He kneaded the back of his neck and yawned so hugely that his jawbone felt dislocated when it snapped closed.

Henrickson let himself out into the little enclosed space. "Dan? You okay?"

He tried to push the fear away. Tried to sound as if he weren't terrified. "Sure. Let's go see if Yu's boys are still honoring that coffee chit."

From the way Henrickson eyed him, he didn't think he was going to make it as an actor.

15

He sat behind the black curtain in Sonar, hands on knees and hunched like a supplicant. He felt so hollow that if someone dropped in a pea and shook him, he'd probably sound like a maraca. He stared at what O'Quinn had just plopped in front of him.

"Go ahead, take it."

"No, thanks, Joe; you need it more than I do."

But it was something familiar, a touch of home. Sugar and peanuts and chocolate . . .

"Brought a damn case of them," the older man said. "Never tell what kind of crap they're gonna dish up on these foreign deployments. Unbend a little, Commander. Have a Snickers."

Dan unwrapped it slowly, torn between hunger and nausea. Took a tentative bite, and chewed.

Across the closet-sized space two sonarmen stared with absolute concentration at endless, similar, but never completely identical amber lines that slowly precessed from the bottom to the top of their screens. Dan liked their concentration. An enemy more dangerous than a shark lurked within that arcane glow. He hoped they saw it before a warhead triggered beneath the hull. A little electric fan bolted to the tape rack went *wrow, wrow, wrow*. Something electronic clicked knitting needles behind him. The console plate read "Signaal," so it was part of the PHS-32 antisubmarine combat system. Dan wondered why they'd bought a Dutch sonar system. Then figured why not; Washington was weird about what it would or wouldn't sell its allies. While losing absolutely no sleep over what its enemies bought, extorted, or simply stole.

"So what've we got?" the older man prompted, lighting a cigarette.

Dan pushed himself upright in his chair, trying to center through fatigue and sugar buzz. "Uh, we're steaming southwest along the coast, thirty miles west of the attack group's presumed centroid."

"Thirty miles. Hunting a convergence zone?"

"Roger. This is where we figure the annulus ought to be. ROK MPA's over the group, radar flooding."

MPA was maritime patrol air, aircraft with sonobuoys and magnetic anomaly-detection gear—equipment that read the local magnetic field, which would be distorted by the presence of a mass of steel, such as a submarine. "They're armed, right?" O'Quinn asked.

"Correct. Lightweight torps. Now, these bogeys have absolutely got to vent boat and recharge soon. I don't know what they're breathing down there; the way I plot their cycle, they're way overdue." He woke up his notebook and brought up his calculations.

O'Quinn eyed the screen suspiciously. "I used a pencil and paper. Got the same answer." He looked toward the plotting team. They didn't seem to be doing much. "Well, nobody ever said the Reds weren't tough. Maybe their commissars just told 'em to hold their breath. What's Jung's scheme? He got one?"

"Refuel, rearm, pursue, and prosecute. Barrier ops in the Strait, backed up by whatever listening arrays they have on Tsushima. These guys are going to play hob with the reinforcement shipping if they get loose down in the East China Sea."

"They're not headed for the China Sea," O'Quinn said.

"What? That's where the heavy lift prepositioning has to come though. Equipment sets for two Marine brigades, heavy Army brigades—"

"I'd bet not. Know why? 'Cause they'll figure the same

way you just did. There's no way they're getting through the Strait, not with the defense the ROKs are gonna double-team down there. Maybe nukes could. Not diesels."

"Then where are they going?"

"My guess, wherever they can screw us up the worst, laying mines. Remember Wonsan?"

"Wonsan? No. What is it?"

The older man blinked. His cheeks were mottled red. "Up on the east coast, where we tried to land in the last war. After Inchon. They mined it, big-time. Took the sweepers weeks to clear it out. And that was when we still had a minesweeping capability. That's their game. Something sneaky like that. Not go through the Strait."

"I don't get the impression expected loss rates carry a lot of weight in the North Korean decision-making process," Dan told him. "If they can insert just one Romeo south of Tsushima, we'll have to scrub out every square before the MPS ships enter it. That'll take major forces. Slow our buildup. And maybe just lose us the war."

Dan explained what Hwang and Captain Owens had told him about the strategy for stopping an invasion. O'Quinn looked puzzled. "So what's the problem? If the Air Force is going to attrit the hell out of them?"

"Because most of the Air Force is based in Japan," Dan told him. "What if the Chinese say: Hey, Tokyo, we don't want the U.S. flying out of those bases. Remember those missiles they fired over them last week? That was a signal, Joe. A clear threat."

"You think so?"

"Absolutely. The Japanese already pulled their navy back to home waters. Think they'll risk a nuclear strike on the home islands, just to help the ROK? They probably care about as much for the Koreans as the Koreans care for them."

"Which isn't much."

"Exactly. Follow the logic. If the Air Force can't fly—and this new typhoon won't help—these people will get all the way down the peninsula before we can build up our heavy forces to stop them. And if they push us into the sea, it'd take a major amphibious landing to get back. Another D day. With casualties like D day."

"No way De Bari's gonna go for that," O'Quinn observed darkly. "That draft-dodging piece of shit. He'll just bitch to the UN. They should have impeached his ass years ago."

Dan reflected that a sizable segment of the senior military leadership felt the same way. But right now that was beside the point. "So the Republic goes under, the Chinese move another piece forward, and we lose whatever face we have left in Asia. We've got to finish this group off, Joe. We can't let a single boat get past the Strait and into open water."

"You told me why," O'Quinn said contemptuously. "All of which I knew. But you still haven't said how. Not with, what—four cans, and no helos? We'd have to get real lucky, real soon."

Dan rubbed his nose, wondering if he could reasonably bum another Snickers from a guy he'd never gotten along with. "Yeah. I guess."

"And, you know—I'm still wondering why it took two attacks to sink that one we got. Notice that?"

"Yeah. I did." He'd done more than wonder: he'd run the numbers. The P_k, probability of kill, for a Mark 46 on a Romeo-sized target, beam on, at four hundred feet was 0.62. Which meant it shouldn't have taken two attacks, expending six torpedoes, to destroy it.

"Want another Snickers?"

He looked at it. "Uh . . . no thanks. Joe."

"Go on. I got lots more." O'Quinn grinned and waved it, like a treat before a dog. "Got to keep that strength up." He laid it in Dan's lap, then sobered. As if remembering something less pleasant than ragging on his boss. "After all—we got a war to fight."

Dan expected Jung to send an invitation to lunch, but none came. Finally he went down to the wardroom. Plain rice didn't revolt him, so he ate a small bowl. Then went to his stateroom. But then the candy and rice filled him to the point he found it hard to move his arms and legs. Or maybe it was just so long since he'd slept. His bunk crooned a siren's song. He pushed his shoes off and after a moment lay back.

A clutter of images flickered behind his closed lids. Some were of events that had happened. Others, of things that might. He tried to ignore them. He concentrated on his toes. Then, his feet. Gradually he moved up his body, tensing and then relaxing each muscle.

He jerked fully awake, bathed in sweat, staring at the overhead and choking with terror.

He couldn't shake the image of the flames last night, of the men silhouetted against them. It took him back to things he'd rather not remember. The fire aboard *Reynolds Ryan,* before the blunt bow of a carrier smashed her under. The mine explosion aboard USS *Van Zandt.* The disaster aboard *Horn.*

He'd seen things he didn't like to remember. Ashore too, in Iraq and in Washington and on an island in the South China Sea. But in a way *Horn* had been the worst. Because he'd been the skipper. He, personally, had put her in harm's way. He, personally, had sent men and women to their deaths.

And yes, it filled him with terror.

Maybe Nick Niles was right. Maybe he was a magnet for trouble, a danger to the people around him. Second-guessing those who had the experience and the rank and the perspective and the intelligence sources to know better. Setting himself up as some kind of fucking moral paragon.

When all he was, was a jinx.

He lay rigid, shaking. A deep breath. Another. Oxygen in. Then fear out. Again. Trying to steer his rudderless, yawing mind somewhere productive.

Mok Po had been lucky to stay afloat. Whoever caught the next attack might not be. Not if their enemies carried wake-homing torpedoes, and their own weapons had some obscure flaw. It had happened in previous wars. Torpedoes were notorious for not performing in combat the way they'd worked in tests. And if they couldn't stop this wolf pack . . .

He blinked in the dim light at the life jacket someone had hung on his locker during the night. Not an inflatable, the kind you wore at general quarters in the U.S. Navy. These were the bright orange, high-collared, high-seas flotation devices that would keep an unconscious man's head out of the water.

At last the shaking eased. The fear stepped away. He just couldn't lie here, though. No matter how tired he was. He swung his feet down and slipped his shoes on. Searched his eyes in the mirror. Glanced again at the life jacket.

After a quick shave he went up to the bridge, leaving it hanging on the locker.

The sky had clouded over since the night before. The wind was stronger too, humming in antennas and lines, buffeting at the pilothouse windows as the frigate rolled, stabilizers off. He wondered if the concrete and timber bracing of their makeshift hull repair was up to another typhoon. The waves were the color of pneumonia victims. Their dull surfaces sucked in what light remained. He watched them, gripping the splinter shield. Down on the forecastle the deck gang was renewing the lashings on the ground tackle. Brass gleamed at the 40mm mount as the loaders wiped down ammunition. The .50 on the bridge wing was manned too. The wing gunners had on helmets and life jackets, and all three held binoculars. They were searching the horizon with the soul-riveting attention he recalled from old movies about convoys, about ravening U-boats and flaming tankers: the concentration of men whose lives hung on what they saw or failed to see.

He leaned on the shield, trying again to relax. The sky gave him back no assurance. It was dark as the sea, its dirty clouds warped into what looked like black corrugations, as if the world were ceilinged with scraps of cardboard box impregnated with roofing tar. Far to the west starless mountains rose like a rampart, keeping the Eastern Sea from pouring away over the edge of the world.

He was still trying to figure out what had gone wrong with the Mark 46s. They were the most common acoustic homing torpedoes used by U.S. and allied navies all over the world. They had a passive mode, but usually you set them to active search before firing. They didn't carry a huge warhead, but it was enough to rupture a pressure hull. The sea would do the rest. Tube-launched or air-dropped, they ran out to a preset range and bearing, then switched on their sonar and began a spiral search. You didn't have to know the target's exact depth; you simply preset the top and bottom of the search. The torpedo started at the upper limit, then spiraled downward, pointing its beam around in a 360-degree circle. When it got a return ping, it homed in.

His first suspicion was that someone had entered the presets wrong. If the torpedo started searching too deep, it'd miss a target running shallow. But he had to admit, that was just a guess. They might be defective. A crewman might have failed to arm the warheads. They might simply be old, with expired batteries and components—he didn't know what vintage the ones *Chung Nam* had fired were. The more he thought about it, the more likely an explanation that seemed. A programming error, an arming oversight, or ordnance beyond its shelf life.

What worried him more was what would happen the next time they attacked. If it was really a wake homer that had mutilated *Mok Po,* they'd have to reassess their tactics. But he couldn't think of any way of finding out what kind of torpedo the enemy was carrying, other than to go back in and make them fire more. Which would be a dangerous experiment.

He stared out at the leaden sea, the bizarre lightless light that seemed to hover over it and shine up through the waves. Somewhere past that horizon their quarry was slipping quietly south. Every mile gained brought them closer to their goal. Whatever that goal was. But they couldn't stay down forever. Very soon now, they'd have to at least poke up a periscope, take a tentative peek above, then send up the hydraulic mast with the snorkel. Crack the intake valves, start the diesels, and recharge.

When they did, Jung would have to move in, regardless

of what his casualties might be. Dan didn't think there was much chance of the guy hanging back. If the decorations Jung wore were real, if the scuttlebutt about him was true, the problem would be to keep him from charging in too fast, without doing his homework.

Which was what he and his guys could contribute. And about all they could do, as far as he could see. He rubbed his face, trying to pull his thoughts together. Trying to concentrate, as the gun crews were, on what was out there, and how they could stop it from killing them.

He was in Sonar, on the phone, trying to get production dates on the torpedoes from the ASW officer, when the radioman came in. "Commander Renson? Message."

It was in an envelope, which none of the others had been. He couldn't read the stamped red-inked Hangul. But beneath it, in carefully crafted block letters, someone had printed SECRET/RELEASABLE TO US/ROK ONLY.

It was addressed to him, or as close to a personal address as you could get in message traffic. "TAG Rep Embarked CTG 213.3." 213.3 was Jung's designation as commander of the new task group, reinforced by the additional pair of frigates from Squadron 11 out of Donghae.

Dan read it. Then dropped his feet to the deck and read it again, not believing what he saw.

"National technical intelligence sources" had identified what the message called the Whiskey/Romeo Group East, or WRGE for short, as a neutron emitter. In view of this, CFC and CNFK operations in the China Sea should be reevaluated. CTG 213.3 was directed to take appropriate action.

He felt as if the world had been taken apart and put back together again sideways. As if something in his inner ear, or maybe his brain, had diswired. If one of these subs was a neutron emitter, he had to revise everything. Starting with where they'd first been picked up: so far to the east the Japanese had first stumbled on them, not the Koreans. He'd puzzled about the dogleg so far out to sea, when the optimal tactic for a stealthy transit would have been to stick to the peninsular shelf, snorkel by night and lie low by day.

But if they were carrying a primitive nuclear device . . . something so massive and clumsy it had to be loaded, maybe even built into, a submarine . . .

Henrickson was on the starboard wing, boot propped on a cable run, scribbling in a wheelbook. Dan handed him the message, making sure Monty had it in his fingers before he let go; he didn't want the wind grabbing it away.

The analyst looked up, eyes blown wide. "Holy shit."

"My sentiments exactly."

"This means . . . shit. No way they're going to bring the carriers in with this thing out there."

He hadn't thought of that. A sizable amount of the scheduled air sortie generation was Navy, off the carriers. But then he remembered. "Uh, that'd make sense if these guys weren't still headed south, Monty. They're not out here to keep the carriers out."

"Unless there's more of them we don't know about." Henrickson read the message again, glancing at the .50 crew, but they were still intent on their search of the passing waves. "Why's it say, Whiskey/Romeo Group *East*? Unless there's another one on the west coast?"

"They don't mention one."

"Isn't there an amphib group coming down the west coast?"

"But no report of any subs with them. They might just be saying that in case another one comes on the screen."

Through the window Dan saw Hwang in the pilothouse. He noticed them and cracked the door. "Commander," he said. "Your presence—"

"Is requested in the commodore's cabin," Dan finished for him. "Monty, how about you come along too, and help me out on this."

Jung's cabin was pitch dark. Dan stood lost. Then a light clicked on by the desk.

The commodore had been sitting in the dark. He was in khaki trousers and zoris and a white V-necked undershirt. Dan noticed that it was monogrammed, and that dark sweat ringed his armpits. An identical buff envelope lay on his desk, opened.

"Seoul has ordered Watchcon I," he said. "A clear and immediate threat of attack. The first time it has ever been issued."

"That's not good news, sir."

"No, it is not. They are considering evacuating the capital. I am afraid there will be panic."

"I don't think your people will panic," Dan told him. "They seem very disciplined to me."

Jung tried to smile, but it wasn't convincing. "Thank you. You've seen the message?"

"Yes sir."

"How do you read it?"

"One of these transiters has nuclear material aboard. We have to assume, a nuclear device."

The chief of staff cleared his throat behind Dan. "Why just one, Commodore? The way I read the message, it is the group that's the emitter. It's not a . . . point source. So there could be two, or three. Or more, if we haven't detected all the intruders."

Dan nodded. "It's possible, sure. But I'd bet on just one. Kim Jong Il can't have that many of these things. What I've seen in our intelligence estimates, when I was at the White House"—he hesitated, then went ahead and told him—"no more than ten."

"The DPRK possesses six operational nuclear weapons," Jung said quietly.

Dan held his eyes. By his tone, it wasn't something he'd felt comfortable sharing either. So the South had an agent in place. Interesting. What else had the spy reported that Seoul hadn't passed on to Washington? And did the North have agents, moles, too?

"Still, that's not a lot. Not to fight a war against the U.S. They'll keep as many in reserve as they can. To deter us with. I think probably the neutron sensors on the satellite just can't localize it that closely. That's why they say the WRGE."

"There's another possibility," Henrickson said. All three looked at him. "That it's not a nuclear device they're picking up."

"What else emits neutrons?"

"A nuclear submarine."

Dan didn't think that was likely. Any nuke boat North Korea could buy or build would be much noisier submerged than anything they'd heard yet. And they'd already classed at least two of the boats as Romeos. Still, it was *possible*. Just another unknown to throw into what was getting to be a pretty goddamned murky stew.

Jung said, "What is the provenance of this data? You said satellites."

Dan took that one. "Most likely, sir."

"Can I trust it?"

Dan organized his thoughts. He'd had access to national technical means of verification, as the cant went, as a member of the National Security Council staff. But they were very highly classified. He was still bound by that. On the other hand, who had more need to know than this man, right now? Finally he said cautiously, "Sir, if they think it's worth sending you a heads-up, I'd say you can trust the data."

"Can they give me a location from these emissions?"

He thought again, trying to remember the briefings. "That'd take more than one satellite, several passes—no, sir. It's a good question, but I don't think you can plan on using it as a means of localization, to prosecute the contact. If that's what you're thinking."

"All right. We have three intruders. One carries a nuclear device. Your thoughts? Ideas? Any of you."

Dan said, "Well—other than prosecuting when they pop up to snorkel?"

Hwang said flatly, "Unfortunately, we can't just attack each snorkeler."

Henrickson frowned. "Why not?"

"Think about it. What will happen if we do?"

Dan saw it then. The chief of staff was right. It was like the old con game, where the grifter hides a pea under a walnut shell. But in this case, if they picked the one with the pea under it— "They'll set it off," he said.

"Exactly so." Hwang nodded. "Beneath the task force. We can attack the conventionally armed boats. But the minute the captain who is carrying the nuclear payload hears the incoming torpedo, and knows he cannot accomplish his primary mission—why should he *not* set it off? He and his crew are doomed in any case."

Henrickson said, "So what's he after? The carriers?"

Jung said heavily, "No. If that was their target, they wouldn't be heading south. They'd wait inshore of Ullungdo and let the Americans come to them. That leaves only one possibility. They're bound for Pusan."

Dan nodded slowly, the magnitude of it only now dawning. O'Quinn had glimpsed it. Only it wasn't mines, but something even more "sneaky," his word.

The only deepwater port in the South. The last-stand position for the Combined Forces. A light division could deploy by air, debark at airfields and airports carrying personal weapons. But heavy armored forces couldn't. Nor could you airlift hundreds of thousands of tons of fuel, food, ammunition, vehicles, bridging, field hospitals, everything the Army, Air Force, and Marines needed to fight a major war. In the last struggle the North had pushed them back into a fiercely contested toehold. But they'd held, reinforced, then fought their way back, not once, but twice: first against the Korean Communists, then against the Chinese.

But if a nuclear weapon went off in Pusan Harbor, there'd be no haven. No logistic support. No heavy armor. And knowing that, with their backs to the sea and no supply or reinforcement, how long could the ROK Army, and the already bare-bones U.S. contingent, continue to fight?

Jung cleared his throat with a grating, almost mechanical sound. "Here is what I want you to do. Commander Hwang, set up a voice link. Commander Lenson: You will call your wife, at the Pentagon."

Dan frowned. He hadn't expected this. "Commodore . . . with all due respect, that's not the road to take."

"She's high in the administration. You'll inform her of our situation—"

"No, sir. I won't."

Jung glared at him.

"Sir, that's not the appropriate channel for this pulse. The right one's General Harlen, to the chairman of the Joint Chiefs. The ambassador, to the secretary of state. Or your president direct to ours. Not two guys on a float in the Eastern Sea, to the deputy undersecretary for manpower and personnel. Believe me, that's not going to solve any of our problems."

"You will call your wife," Jung said again.

"No sir, I will not. But there's someone else I *can* talk to. Who might actually do us some good."

"Who's that?"

Dan told him. Jung thought it over. Then after a moment, nodded a reluctant assent.

He was in CIC again. This time Jung sat opposite. The commodore looked alternately glowering and scared. Dan liked the glower better. Fortunately, he'd remembered the phone number. He didn't know how the comm guys were making the connection. Probably HF to an international operator, in South Korea or Japan.

This call probably wouldn't do any good, and he was skipping at least four levels of command. But he couldn't just do nothing. As it rang he flashed back to a rosewood-furnished space in the West Wing basement. A small watch staff whose job was to keep the president informed, to staff out his communications, and on occasion, to advise him on the management of a military crisis. A glass-windowed booth, looking out over it.

"Situation Room. Director's station."

You never used your name answering a phone there.

Because you never knew whom you'd have to pass unpleasant news and unwelcome orders to. Generals and admirals had been known to shoot messengers. But he recognized this voice. It was a woman's, cool, self-possessed, brisk. Captain Jennifer—never "Jenny"—Roald, USN. He'd worked with her once to stop a terrorist strike. He figured that might have earned him two or three minutes of her time.

"Captain Roald?"

"Yes. Who's this?"

"Commander Dan Lenson. How are you, Jennifer?"

"Lenson—oh, *Dan.* Where are you? I heard you went back to the fleet."

"I did. Or at least to TAG."

"The Tactical Analysis Group, Team Charlie. That'd be a good fit for you."

"Actually it's Bravo. There's no Team Charlie."

"There isn't? Oh . . . that's right. Well, it's nice to hear from you, Dan. Things are pretty busy here, so—"

"Captain, right now I'm attached to the ROK Navy. Calling from the Sea of Japan."

Her voice sharpened. "You're in Korea?"

"Correct. We're aboard the ASW group bird-dogging this Whiskey slash Romeo formation that's tracking down the coast."

"The one on the east coast?"

Did that mean there were more? He started to ask, then didn't, since he didn't know how secure the line was. "Correct. Anyway, we just got the message, detailing what that group is—well, what makes that group so super special. Know what I mean?"

She didn't answer for a moment. Opposite him Jung leaned back, lighting a cigarette and looking dark. He was following the conversation on the overhead speaker.

Roald's voice went dry. "This is not a secure phone, Commander. Nice to hear from you, but what's the point of this call? That's so important you have to skip the whole chain of command?"

"Well, I'm sitting here with the commodore in charge of

the antisubmarine group. And I have to tell you the Koreans are starting to feel like we're leaving them twisting in the wind. Can I give them some good news?"

"I can't answer that. But the forces in support of Op Plan 5027 are being notified."

5027 was the plan for joint defense of Korea. "Well, that's good, Jennifer, but—has the heavy lift started to sail? The MPS lift?"

"I won't discuss that, Dan."

"Captain, here's the problem. We need more assets here in the Strait. To deal with what you're calling the WRGE. The ROKN's good but the environment's shit. They don't have the sonar ranges to stop these guys. We need augmentation out here. We've got surface forces and Korean patrol air. But the U.S. destroyer squadron hauled ass for Japan three days ago, and we just don't have the coverage."

He heard her go off-line, talking to someone else in the booth. Then she came back. "Dan, Korea's on the front burner here, if that's what you're asking me. We have activity along the DMZ. But we've got to manage the developing situation in Taiwan too. Forces are thin."

He swallowed. "Activity" along the DMZ. Which meant . . . shades of the crowded subway station, the monthly drills . . . did she mean artillery? Or just patrols? If the shells were falling, Seoul would already be evacuating. Millions of people—the old man who'd elbowed him, the elegant girls with the parasols, executives and store clerks and hotel staffs and mothers and grandmothers and kids, *everyone*—all streaming south in terror that what had happened to Hwang's family half a century before would happen to them. Then he tuned in to what else she'd said. "Taiwan? What's happening in Taiwan?"

"You're really out of touch out there, aren't you? The Chinese are threatening Taiwan."

"Forget that! It's a diversion. We need an ASW task group here. With helos. We've got to have helos."

"The *Enterprise* task group will be there in two days. Unless the president decides to divert to the Taiwan Strait."

"He can't send it to Taiwan! This is the hot button. Right here—"

Her tone was cool again. "This is not the proper line to discuss operational matters on, Commander. I suggest you devote your efforts on-scene, to helping the ROKN deal with its submarine threat. I'm going to hang up now."

"I know that, Captain, but this is the only line out I have. And what I've got to say is too important for you not to listen. Jennifer! Please!"

He wasn't proud of the pleading note, but it worked. She hesitated. Then said, "All right, Commander. Only because we've got history. Okay? Give it to me in three sentences or less."

"You got it. Executive summary. Don't get fixated on what's happening up along the DMZ. The target is Pusan. I say again, *Pusan*. Look at the op plan, the logistics situation, for what that means. This crisis will turn on what happens in the Strait. If we can stop this group, I don't think they'll come over the DMZ. And maybe we won't have to fight another Korean war."

"That's it?"

"That's all, Captain. Thanks for taking my call."

"Don't abuse the privilege again, Commander."

She hung up.

Jung was mining his eyes with his fingers. He seemed about to speak when one of the petty officers shouted across the space. "Radar contact. Small. Presume snorkel. Zero-nine-eight. Twenty-nine thousand yards. The aircraft is attacking with air-dropped torpedoes."

The team around the DRT scrambled up from squatting. Jung snapped orders. Kim repeated them over the air. The deckplates began to vibrate as fifty-four thousand horsepower brought *Chung Nam* up to flank speed again.

Dan pulled himself to his feet, with dread, with nausea, but at the same time too with a reluctant eagerness to get this over with one way or another.

The hunt was on again. But they were nearly blind and running out of fuel. Their quarry was forewarned. Their weapons didn't seem to work. Another typhoon was on its way. And somewhere below them was a weapon that, should they press whoever controlled it too hard, would destroy everything within ten miles' radius.

When he thought about it, this time they were as much the quarry as the hunter.

16

The plotting team worked with tight-lipped diligence, sketching gradually expanding circles around the now twenty-minute-old datum. *Chung Nam* steadied on a course of 100 true. The hull rumbled as the screws reached full power. She was already at general quarters, had been all night. Dan wondered how long the crew could stay sharp. After that many hours even trained men reacted slowly, or made stupid mistakes. He glanced at the clock; a little after 1500. Four hours of daylight left.

Opposite him Jung coughed as he chain-lit another silvertip. Then suddenly reached out, seized him by the shoulder, and gave him a one-armed hug. Dan tensed.

"Where's your life jacket?" the commodore muttered into his ear. He stank of tobacco and sweat.

"In my stateroom. Sir."

"We're going in to the attack. Get your life jacket on."

"You're not wearing one, Commodore."

"That does not inspire confidence, when I wear a life jacket."

"Does it inspire confidence when the American rider wears one?"

Jung's lips curled in mirthless acquiescence. "All right. I just hope neither of us needs it."

Dan just nodded, since his mouth had gone too dry to speak. It seemed like you'd get used to combat, but he was scared just as shitless as he always was. He swallowed and tried to relax. "So, what's our plan, sir?"

Jung said they'd have to accept the risk of the nuke going off. Dan nodded numbly; he'd expected nothing less. The commodore said he'd position TG 213.3 above where they guessed the intruders were and hold them down by brute presence, working with the patrol air and attacking each time they made sonar contact, caught a snorkel above water, or were fired on. At the very least that should hold the enemy to a low speed of advance. If they couldn't kill them all, they'd form a final barrier just north of Pusan.

"And if they do set off the bomb, it should at least destroy the remaining subs, as well as our forces," he finished.

"I guess it might at that," Dan said reluctantly. Not an elegant plan, either tactically or in terms of minimizing the risk to the prosecuting force. But he couldn't think of anything better.

"We'll head in at twenty knots. Then turn parallel to their line of advance and slow below sonar washout speed nine thousand yards from the farthest on circle," Jung said. "*Mesan* and *Cheju* are arriving from the south. They both have full torpedo loads. I'll use them for the first coordinated attack. Yu will stand off with his towed array streamed. It is possible we may pick something up."

Dan doubted it, not with sonar conditions the way they were and the sea state degenerating as the wind whipped up the waves. As the coasts of Korea and Honshu closed to form the Strait, the fetch, the distance across which that wind operated, was shrinking; but the bottom was shallowing, too. "What's this storm going to do to us?"

The chief had a weather fax ready. Dan examined it, hoping this time the weather guessers were keeping up with the clock. Typhoon Callista was rated as a Class 4, even more powerful than Brendan, but thank God, it was tracking much farther south. With any luck it would miss Korea and head past into the Yellow Sea. The forecast for the Strait area was thirty knots gusting to forty, ten- to twelve-foot seas.

"Could be worse," Hwang said over his shoulder.

"Could be better. For mixing conditions."

The air controller reported from his console, and Korean faces grew graver. "What's he saying?" Dan asked the chief of staff.

"The aircraft has expended both torpedoes on a magnetic anomaly contact two thousand yards south of the last datum."

"No hits?"

"No hits, no detonations. Also the aircraft are not sure how much longer they can maintain contact."

"Fuel state?"

"That's not the problem. It's winds at low altitudes, and sea state wiping out their sonobuoy returns."

"They've got to maintain contact. If they lose these guys, we'll never get them back."

Hwang looked grim too. "They know this is a high-priority mission. They'll stay out till they go down into the sea. It will be a useless sacrifice, I am afraid."

Jung came back down from the bridge, no doubt having passed on his orders, about paralleling and streaming the array, to Captain Yu personally. He looked haggard and moved slowly, and Dan realized the commodore hadn't slept any more than he had, maybe even less. He saw Henrickson leaning with arms folded near the vertical plot, watching the action, and gestured him over.

"Where's your life jacket, Monty?"

"Left it on my bunk."

"You should be wearing it."

"You're not wearing one."

"For Christ's sake, Henrickson, you're not even military. Get your fucking life jacket on."

"All the hatches are dogged. I can't get below." The analyst gnawed at his lip, glancing toward the plot table. "We just charging in? That's all we can think of?"

"We're gonna slow to sonar speed in a few minutes and parallel their track nine thousand yards out. The two new joins are going in for a coordinated attack."

"Did he say what speed?"

"No."

"I think their speed-noise curves are wrong. But I guess with this heavy a sea it doesn't matter. Anybody given any thought to anti-wake-homing tactics?"

Dan rubbed his cheeks hard. His mind kept slipping, as if gears weren't quite meshing. "Uh, I don't know much about them. Got any suggestions?"

"I ran some possibilities last night. Since I didn't have much else to do."

Henrickson pulled his own computer over on the desk and flipped up the screen. The notebook hummed as the hard drive powered up. "We don't know what they're carrying, but I'm assuming it's some version of the 53–65. Wake-homing, antiship, six-hundred-pound warhead. Range twenty thousand yards at full speed. The Russians sold them to the Chinese. This is a smart fish. It picks up wake turbulence and follows it to its source. You can't jam it or decoy it. And it runs out at fifty knots, so unless you have a long head start, you can't out-sprint it either."

"None of this sounds promising. You think that's what hit *Mok Po*? A wake homer?"

"That's consistent with the stern damage, and she had her Nixie streamed and turned on. So it was either a wake homer, or a real lucky shot with a straight runner."

Dan contemplated the screen, which now displayed the 53–65's wavy approach course as it acquired a wake. Henrickson went on, "This is really a good torpedo. Even if you spoof it, it presses on through the countermeasure and reenables on the other side. Team Charlie got their hands on three of them four years ago. We gave one to DARPA, one to DIA, and kept the one that had the fewest bullet holes in it. We took it apart, put it back together, and did fifteen instrument runs down at Tongue of the Ocean. There really isn't a soft kill possibility. The only way to evade it is the Dingo."

Dan had never heard of a Dingo, but this was the second time he'd heard a Team Charlie mentioned. He'd understood from the briefings back at TAG that there were only two teams, though. As for the other acronyms Henrickson had just used, DARPA was the Defense Advanced Research Projects Agency; DIA, the Defense Intelligence Agency. He filed it and pressed on with the immediate problem. "Dingo—what's that? An evasive tactic?"

"Yeah. As soon as you hear the thing coming, fire a Mark 46 on straight run, surface mode, shallow setting, off the side the detection's coming from. Simultaneously you go to all ahead flank and hard rudder and buttonhook back, just like a Williamson turn, as soon as the 46 clears the tube. With me so far?"

"I'm with you. Then—"

"Then, as soon as you pass about one twenty off your original track, you go to full-power reverse. If you do it right, you end up dead in the water, but with your bow headed back down your own track."

"Dead in the water, during a torpedo attack?"

"Just hear me out, okay? In our tests, the 65 either lost the ship's wake and reenabled on the Mark 46, if it was tracking near centerline, or followed the quarter-wave, if it was off-set."

He fingered the keyboard. The display changed, and Dan watched the tactic play out. The hostile torpedo bored in from astern. The target ship executed its turn. The torpedo overshot, carrying on along its original course, apparently following the original bow wave, which had been generated before the turn. It went into its sidewinder wriggle again as it reenabled and started searching again; then suddenly snapped back into homing mode and tracked steadily off the screen to the left.

Henrickson said, "A Mark 46 running shallow at top speed generates just enough turbulence to engage the seeker. Usually, that is . . . When it does, the 65 heads away after it. Eventually it overtakes, it's faster than the 46, but by then it's outside reacquisition parameters for its original target. It goes back into search mode and chases its tail till it exhausts its fuel, deactivates, and sinks."

"That's a complicated tactic," Dan said. "And isn't it suicide, if it's *not* a wake homer? Going to zero speed, backing down?"

"Yeah, that's your downside of Dingo. If it's not a wake homer they kicked out at you, if it's an acoustic homer, you just cut your Nixie cable during the buttonhook and walked right into the punch."

"And I suppose there's no way to tell which one's coming at you?"

"Not till two thousand yards out, when the acoustics turn on their active homer. And by then it's too late."

"Shit." Dan swiveled, blowing out, trying to pull his eyebrows down off the overhead. "This isn't an approved tactic, is it?"

"We put it out in a tacmemo last year. So it's not in ATP 28, no, but it's on the street."

"To the Koreans? Are they on distribution?"

"No. U.S. only."

He rubbed his mouth again, wishing he wasn't so dog-tired. He had the feeling he was missing something. This wasn't the way to do tactical development: on a notebook computer, at general quarters, charging in on a confirmed hostile at thirty-four knots. "What about our Mark 46s? There's something fucked there. The air-dropped ones didn't work any better than ours. We keep firing them but we don't get kills."

"We can hear them running. They're just not hard-locking, for some reason."

"Countermeasures? Jamming?"

"I'd guess some kind of new countermeasure. If I had to wing it." The analyst bared his teeth at his computer. "But I don't know what it is, so I can't tell you how to increase P sub K. Just keep throwing weapons in the water till one acquires. That's all Jung can do. And I'll tell you another thing."

"What?"

"This first contact might be bait. That's a tactic the DPRK uses a lot. Hang a fat, juicy target out there, wait till you go for it, then clobber you from ambush."

"We'd better tell the commodore about this. The whole

wake-homer thing, this Dingo business. You mind briefing him?"

Henrickson said he'd be happy to, as long as he could borrow the battery module to Dan's computer.

The heading indicator was spinning like a roulette wheel. Dan assumed they'd reached the nine-thousand-yard point and were coming to the parallel course. Nine thousand yards was inside torpedo range, of course, but it was far enough from the farthest on circle, the possible location of the sub given the elapsed time since detection, that they should have enough warning to turn away and outrun anything fired at them. Though at the cost, again, of burning more precious fuel.

Jung received Henrickson's briefing with a weary scowl. Before the analyst was done he snapped, "What you're saying is, there's no way to counter a wake homer without putting our own ships in just as much danger from the acoustic homers. So all the sub has to do is fire one of each, and you're nailed."

"Well, that's not quite true, sir—"

"You just said it was."

Dan stepped in. "Sir, what you haven't let us get to yet is the possibility of combining both tactics. It'll take close attention by the sonarmen, but it might work. We call it Dingo Plus."

"I'm waiting."

He explained. On a "torpedo in the water" warning—the sound of high-speed screws on a constant, incoming bearing—the target ship would execute Dingo. Or rather, start to. But instead of coming to the reciprocal of its original course, it would keep its rudder hard over, continue its turn, and steady up heading away from the original incoming bearing. By then its speed would have dropped below the turbulence-generation point, losing a wake homer.

At that point, the sonarmen would take another bearing on the sound of the incoming weapon. If they showed a drift in the direction of the ship's original direction of travel, then their pursuer was a wake homer; they had only to stand by till its fuel was exhausted. If there was no bearing drift, it was either a straight runner or an acoustic torpedo running passive, and odds were against a hit, since they'd altered their original course and with the engines stopped there was little machinery noise.

But if they heard active pulses, it was acoustic running active. They'd instantly flip the Nixie on, slam the throttles forward, and take off again, full turbine power, full speed.

Jung turned to Hwang. "Did you follow that, Commander?"

"I think so, *Jeon dae jang nim.*"

"Good, because I'm not sure I did. What if they do like I said? Fire both types at once?"

Dan cleared his throat. That was where Henrickson's model got wobbly. "Commodore, that solution seems to be sensitive to which one comes out of the tube first. If they fire the wake homer first, then the chances of evading are about fifty-fifty. The wake homer follows the wake away from the stopped ship, and the Nixie decoys the acoustic homer."

Hwang said, "Fifty-fifty each, or fifty-fifty for evading both?"

"Fifty percent probability of evading both shots."

"Well, that's better than nothing. What if they fire the acoustic torpedo first?"

"Then the chances of evasion drop to about ten percent," Henrickson said. "Of course, you multiply that by the reliability rate and the usual probability of kill for both types."

"The result then?"

"Maybe thirty percent."

"Kill, or survive?" Jung asked.

"Seventy percent kill," Henrickson said. "Thirty percent survive."

"These numbers suck," said Hwang.

"Maybe, but they're better than the tactics you have," Dan pointed out. "At least against the 53–65s."

"Not by much."

"It still gives your attacking ship a chance," Dan told him, suddenly exasperated. "If the target turns on him. You want tactical advice? That's our tactical advice. You can take it or leave it, but there it is."

Jung discussed it in Korean with Hwang. Lieutenant Kim, the ASW officer, listened respectfully. Once or twice he got asked a question, which he answered with an eager bob of the head. Finally Jung nodded to the Americans coldly. "Thank you for your suggestions, gentlemen. We'll take them under advisement."

Monty went back into Sonar. Leaning against the plot table, Dan watched Jung cough and wipe his mouth and and chain-light another cigarette. Fuel: that was what worried him now. He said in low voice to Lieutenant Kim, "How we doing on gas, anyway?"

The ASW officer looked grave. "Below thirty percent."

Dan sucked air. He'd known the high-speed regimes, running on the turbines, gulped enormous amounts of fuel. But he hadn't expect the tanks to be *that* low. U.S. Navy practice was to bunker up whenever you got below seventy. He thought of approaching the commodore about it, but one look at Jung brooding decided him against it. He'd bothered the man enough. Instead he drew a deep breath, coughing at the smoke, and went topside.

The wind had risen even more and the sky was black as a seam of Pennsylvania bituminous. A band of charcoal clouds dangled tendrils that occasionally twisted into spirals, like the business end of a corkscrew. They ran from one horizon to the other. He tensed with the primeval anxiety that wind and darkness, the oncoming storm, triggered in terrestrial animals. The seas, kicked steep by the shoaling shelf, were short and already breaking. *Chung Nam* surged through them, bulling up bursts of snowy spume that lofted on the windward side, hung in midair like loops of Christmas tinsel, then blew down and apart across the forecastle. Cables still snaked about from the system checks, but the crew had taken cover, except for two swarthy boatswains, older than the rest of the crew, who were frapping down the pelican hooks with bright yellow line. They wore blue coveralls and battle helmets and the bulky orange life jackets. A young officer watched them, arms akimbo. The forward gun was elevated as high as it would go. A black plastic trash bag flapped where it had been duct-taped over the tompion. Dan stood shivering. The wind was turning cool. He remembered when all he had to worry about was getting his division's tackle secured for sea. It felt like ages ago.

He shaded his eyes, then borrowed binoculars from the machine-gun crew. The gray upperworks and white sensor bubble of an Ulsan-class were just visible far out to port. Either *Mesan* or *Cheju*, one of the two new joins. The white sphere really stood out in the dimming light. He judged they were ten thousand yards distant.

He watched them for a few minutes, but they didn't turn or vary their speed, just steered a steady course. This wasn't good. Ten seconds' periscope exposure, and that great aiming point . . . He searched to right and left, but didn't see the other prosecutor, nor any of the patrol air, though they might be above the clouds, monitoring sonobuoys from there.

But at some point, as the wind rose, they'd have to leave. Then Jung would be nearly blind, like a man in a smoke-filled cave whose flashlight beam stops two feet from the lens.

He searched the rest of the way around the horizon, and was surprised when he saw another Ulsan-class pitching doggedly a thousand yards astern. He'd forgotten *Kim Chon* was still with them. A tiny figure on the port wing was waving. He lifted a hand in return, figuring it was Carpenter. At least out here Rit couldn't get in more girl trouble.

When he went back inside, Captain Yu gave him a dirty look from his perch in the skipper's chair. Dan saluted but Yu turned his nose away. Lenson rattled down the ladder to CIC again. Everyone was standing, leaning, sitting just as they had when he'd left, still as a Dutch painting, their attention on the plot table.

Henrickson told him in an off-line murmur that *Chang Bo Go* had reported in. The 209 was off the port of Ulsan; she'd transited back on a straight line from the original operating area. She too was getting low on fuel, but had been

opconned to 213.3. Jung had ordered her to take up an antisubmarine barrier position along the one-hundred-meter line
off Pusan Harbor.

"She won't use much fuel there," the analyst said. "Just
lie on the bottom and listen, probably. Play goalie, in case
we drop the ball."

"What sport exactly have you got in mind, Monty?"

"Ah, forget it. Forget it."

They talked one of the petty officers out of a large-scale
chart of Pusan Harbor and unrolled it on the Harpoon console. One of the other Koreans saw them with it, and brought
over a port guidebook that was printed in both Korean and
English.

Dan saw the good news at once. The harbor entrance was
narrow, just two kilometers wide, and only the main channel
would be deep enough for a submerged sub. That choke point
was six kilometers from the downtown area. The worst-case
scenario, a nuclear detonation in the center of the city basin,
seemed unlikely. One scuttled containership could block the
channel. The city's population would lose all their window
glass, and of course be subject to huge amounts of fallout
from a subsurface burst. But most of them would probably
survive the initial blast and flash of any weapon the North
could build.

The bad news was that the container piers—according
to the guidebook, Pusan handled 95 percent of Korea's
containerized cargo—were much closer to the harbor entrance. If the container cranes went, Pusan would be useless for Allied logistical purposes. Since there was no other
port with its capacity, all the North had to do was put it out
of action, break through the DMZ, and strategically the
war would be over. He found the one-hundred-meter line;
it ran eight miles offshore.

He rubbed his face. So they just had to stop that sub,
whichever one carried the warhead, from reaching Pusan.

At that moment a recently heard voice came over one of
the overhead speakers. Dan thought for a moment he was
hearing things. Jung and Hwang looked up, both frowning.

Lieutenant Kim reached up for the handset. He said tentatively, "This is *Chung Nam*. Go ahead. Over."

"Request to speak to Commander Lenson. The U.S. adviser."

Jung beckoned impatiently for the handset.

"Station calling *Chung Nam:* This is Commodore Jung Min Jun, Republic of Korea Navy. Lenson is a rider, not an adviser. Who is calling on this net? Over."

"Uh, I know who that is," Dan said, holding out his hand. Jung stared at him for a second, then handed over the phone.

"That is uncovered HF," Lieutenant Kim warned.

"Yes, I understand."

"*Chung Nam, Chung Nam,* over."

"This is ROKS *Chung Nam,* Dan Lenson here," he said into the handset. "Hello, Andy."

"Hello, Dan. How's those boots working out, classmate?"

It was Andy Mangum, *San Francisco*'s CO. Dan couldn't help smiling. "Breaking them in even as we speak. How you doing? Didn't expect to hear from you again so soon. Over."

"Well, somebody said you could use a hand. So we swapped ends and headed back. But we have to keep our name out of the papers. If you know what I mean. Over."

Dan struggled between delight and rage. Jennifer Roald had come through. Not with an antisubmarine squadron, but with something almost as good, maybe in some ways better; a primed and loaded U.S. attack boat. On the other hand, Mangum's hint at orders to stay covert didn't warm his cockles. It meant the administration was still scared of ticking off the Chinese. Which was not a good sign, if actual war came down.

But someone had pushed a chip onto the table—they weren't going to just fold. "Where the hell are you? Over."

Mangum gave him a lat-long position. Lieutenant Kim went to plot it, but it was off the paper, to the east. "We'll be with you pretty soon, though. We'd be breaking the speed limit on anything that wasn't an interstate. How's your situation? Over."

"Did they tell you what these guys are toting? Over."

"Yeah." The distant voice fell a note. "They told me. Haven't put the word out to my guys here yet . . . but I probably will. Anyway. How many bogeys on your tote board?"

"We've never had a hard count. Our best guess is three. Over."

"Whiskeys? Romeos?"

Dan looked at Jung. The commodore had lifted his chin, blinking tiredly as he listened to the exchange. "Romeos, we're pretty sure. Tagged by Seoul as North Korean assets. Over. Oh, wait one . . . what's your Opcon? Is it 213.3? Over."

"Negative. We're still chopped direct to Pearl."

He didn't meet the commodore's eye. *San Fran* would be with the task group, but not of it. Taking her orders from SUBLANT, not Jung. Awkward. But they'd just have to manage. "Ah, copy that. In case we need to call you, what's your handle? And what freq will you be monitoring and when?"

"This is . . . call us Shockwave. Like that? I just thought of it. Over."

"I like that a lot, Shockwave. Over."

"And as far as comm availability, I can make better speed with the comm head down, okay? We'll check in when we're in UHF range. Over."

"*Chung Nam,* out."

"Keep it in battery, classmate. Shockwave, out."

Dan smiled at Jung. The commodore looked pensive. Relieved, perhaps, but still thoughtful. "That was *San Francisco.* She's on her way back to us."

"Excellent," said Hwang, almost dancing. "I knew America would not abandon us."

Jung squinted, but said nothing. He seemed still to be considering how to react. Finally he too gave a faint smile.

Dan was putting the handset back when the deck under his feet heeled suddenly. Men grabbed consoles, tables, handholds. Loose gear slid and clattered. Phone talkers shouted. A moment later a thud bumped through the hull. It sounded as if something heavy, a sack of rice or maybe concrete mix, had been dropped somewhere aft.

Dan closed his eyes. In the flush of having one thing go

their way, he'd forgotten how many other cards were stacked against them.

He was pretty sure what it was. Not a sack of mix, a butterfingered sailor.

It was the detonation of a distant torpedo, transmitted through ocean, through steel, through air, to their ears.

17

The sea, the sky, were even darker now. The whirling tendrils reaching down were longer and more solid-looking. One dangled from a cloud's belly directly above the mast. It groped blindly, swaying, its wispy maw visibly spiraling. Dan barely glanced at it. His gaze followed a pointing finger from the 40mm crew.

Fine on the port bow, so far in the dimness it was all but lost, black smoke mushroomed against inky cloud. A red stream glimmered, then faded. Smoke rolled upward above a distant white bubble.

He cursed fate, cursed himself. If *San Francisco* had called in a few minutes earlier, he might have persuaded the commodore to pull his force off to let her make a pass. A Los Angeles–class had powerful active sonars, and they'd be below the mixing layer that was frustrating the surface units. She could've stood off, fired a spread of heavy Mark 48s into the wolf pack, and let them maraud. There was a good case for letting Mangum deal with the remaining North Koreans. Fewer lives would be at risk if the engagement went nuclear. They'd be American lives, not South Korean, but Dan didn't think he should be assigning them different values.

Instead, another ship had been hit. And now Jung was charging like a bull into the ring. He wasn't weaving, or zigzagging, or taking any other precautions. Yes, like a bull. But not into a ring. Into an abattoir.

With a droning roar a four-engined aircraft with an elongated tail like a dragonfly's emerged from the boiling clouds and banked toward the stricken frigate. It seemed to move more slowly than an aircraft should. It must be fighting a fierce headwind. One after the other, three specks fell seaward. Parachutes bloomed. The specks hit the sea and the chutes collapsed. Sonobuoys, going down in a line. With the rising seas Dan doubted they'd pick up much. The P-3 banked in the opposite direction and merged with the overcast once more.

Down on the forecastle the mount suddenly broke from its immobility. A clanking came from it as it trained left, trained right, elevated, depressed. The sea hollowed beneath the bow, then bulged like a tensed biceps and broke over the forecastle. The crew on the forward 40 ducked, gripping their helmets, as it rained down on them. Immediately two ran out and began frantically cleaning an optical sight.

He took a deep breath of the cool dark air, sucked it all the way down, trying to douse the tension in his gut. He didn't want more men to die. More ships to burn. There were those who loved war. He wasn't one of them. But it seemed the only thing that had ever extinguished its flames, once they started, was overwhelming force. He didn't see to the bottom of it. Sometimes he wondered if he was in the right profession. But maybe it was better to be reluctant than eager. Though sometimes there was no choice, when evil attacked those who just wanted to live in peace.

Just as there seemed to be no way out of mutual annihilation now.

He turned from the lightless sky, and went below.

CIC was a roaring babble, and desperately hot. The temperature in the packed space, with all the consoles operating, had to be over a hundred degrees. Transmissions were streaming in over the overhead speakers, reports from the other ships and probably, or so he guessed from the background noise, from the P-3s too—two or three nets were going at once. It was all in Korean so he got hardly any of it, just occasional prowords like "banjo" and "madman." He stood out of the way of the plotters' flying elbows, watching the attack develop on the flat white paper.

Henrickson, at his side. "Where you want me, boss?"

"Help the sonarmen if you can," Dan told him. "How about O'Quinn? Where the fuck's Joe?"

"UB plot, I think."

Mesan had gone dead in the water. A new datum symbol near her represented where the torpedo had been fired from. Some two thousand yards to the east, *Cheju,* the assisting ship during the last attack, had slewed around in a tight turn and was racing in. *Kim Chon,* the only PCC left in the task group, was following in *Chung Nam*'s wake as the flagship barreled into the attack.

Dan wondered exactly what Jung had ordered. It looked like an urgent attack, to divert the sub's attention from the ship she'd wounded. He really, really wished they had a helo. A dipping sonar could get them passive bearings without risking a hull and a crew. But there were no helos. And even if there had been, they couldn't have launched in this wind, with a landing platform going up and down the way *Chung Nam* was heaving. He clung to the table as the flagship lurched. A wave slammed against the bulkhead and roared down the port side, sounding just like a subway train.

Jung stood swaying to the lean, arms folded, mouth impassive. Lieutenant Kim stood to his left, Commander Hwang to his right. They stared at the lit tabletop. Dan noticed that the flagship was well inside the torpedo danger area, and approaching the optimal range to fire.

The gaps between successive one-minute positions seemed very long. He reached up and found a handhold on a bitch box and hung on, wondering when or even whether Jung planned to drop to a speed where the frigate's own sonar would be effective. She was rushing toward destruction, blind to what lay ahead. But just as he was opening his mouth the commodore snapped out an order in that harsh-sounding language that even when you were exchanging compliments sounded brusque. Now, giving mortal commands, it was even more peremptory.

A weak, distant voice, breaking up as it transmitted, came over the speaker. He caught the name *Mesan*. Still afloat, then. He glanced at the radar, trying to keep track of who was where. Fast as the plotters sketched, their trace would lag reality by a minute or two.

Jung snapped another order. The turbines wound down. The men around him swayed, and Dan tightened his hand-hold as the sea decelerated the rushing hull.

A cry came from the sonar cubicle. The contact light blinked on over the DRT. In midwriting the sub plotter switched to red pencil, whipped the protractor around, and jotted his first range and bearing to the new contact. The ASW officer was speaking into his sound-powered phones. A warning bell began shrilling, faint through the bulkhead, but perfectly audible.

Dan moved a step to the side, pushed past a phone talker, and pulled the curtain aside. Sonar control was also under-water battery plot; ordnance was controlled from here, as well as sensors. The petty officers didn't look up from their screens. O'Quinn, seated with them, was just as rapt. Dan said to the senior Korean, "How many torpedoes do we have left?"

"Sir?" He smiled, but obviously didn't understand.

Dan tried to communicate it by sign language but gave up halfway through. He switched to the American. "Joe? Do you know?"

"What?" O'Quinn jerked out of his hypnosis.

"Do you know? How many fish we've got left?"

He blinked. "How many fish? These Ulsans don't have a dedicated torpedo stowage space. I don't think they carry more than one reload."

Which meant the six rounds in the two triple tubes right now were all they had left. That wasn't good news.

On the other hand, they probably wouldn't get to make more than one more attack.

The turbines cut in again. The frigate lurched, with the same tormented groaning the stabilizers had made since their repairs. *Chung Nam* seemed to skate around, surfing on the crest of a swell. The heading indicator spun crazily, slowed, and eased to a stop at last thirty degrees to port of their last course.

He couldn't believe it. Jung was *increasing speed* as he attacked. Though he was zigzagging at last, probably not so much to evade a straight runner as to throw off the sub's target motion analysis.

But if their target got off a torpedo, they'd never hear it. At this speed, the sonarmen were totally deaf.

A speaker burst into life. Almost as if to himself, Hwang murmured a translation. "From aircraft tail number thirty-two. Passive sonar contact, bearing sixty-one thousand yards, zero three zero. Possible submarine. Proceeding to attack."

The team stared at the plot. For a moment Dan didn't understand either; then his whole body flinched, almost like a seizure. "No!" he shouted. "That's *San Francisco*. Call off the attack!"

Jung nodded and gave the order. The air coordinator repeated it, his tones urgent. Dan sucked one breath after another, dreadfully slowly, until an acknowledgment came back. He ran his hands over his face, cursing himself for a dangerous idiot. Too tired to think of it, he hadn't made sure the Korean P-3s knew about the incoming U.S. attack boat.

"They acknowledge, Commander," Hwang said. "I apologize. We overlooked passing that information to our MP air."

Jung nodded agreement, glanced at them, but didn't say anything. He seemed too absorbed in the unfolding attack even to speak. Which Dan understood. They were playing chess in three dimensions, at high speed, with sudden death as the penalty for a wrong move.

His skin crawled as he looked back at the range. Through the exchange with the aircraft they'd still been closing, and still at flank speed, pushing deeper and deeper into the zone of danger. The rudder shifted, and the heading indicator spun in the other direction, but the range still kept dropping.

He stopped breathing. They didn't fire, they *didn't* fire, they *still didn't fire*. They were abeam of the target, unless it had turned. This was the right target aspect for the Mark 46.

But they were too close now, the acquisition numbers degraded fast if the fish didn't have time to—

"Fire," barked Lieutenant Kim. A moment later the hissing clunk of an air slug pumping out a quarter-ton of metal, explosives, and electronics came through the bulkhead. Three long seconds followed. You had to separate homing torpedoes in salvo fire or their seekers would jam each other. Then another hiss and clunk shivered the frigate's frame.

Three more seconds, and the last pulse whunked and hissed. Kim barked again—the ASW officer controlled the ship and its weapons during an attack—and the rudder indicator reversed. The frigate leaned hard, still at speed, and pivoted her stern through the firing bearing. She was less than a thousand yards from the sub and now headed directly away.

Dan watched the sweep hand on his watch. They ran for a minute. Then another. Sweat trickled down his cheeks. He expected every second to die in nuclear flame. Actually it would happen so fast, at this range, he'd probably never know he was dead at all. Just phase shift instantly into superheated gas, carbon dioxide, and radioactive steam, along with the water and steel and other men around him.

Instead the seconds kept going by.

He sagged, unbelieving. Their torpedoes would have reached their target in about fifty seconds. He told himself they were activating, circling, they'd acquire and home and explode any moment. But still no thud of a hit came.

His gaze locked with Jung's. The older man's chin was stubbled gray. Sweat stood on his forehead too. His graying hair stuck up in spikes, and for the first time his uniform shirt looked rumpled. "What's wrong with our fucking torpedoes, Lenson? They're American. Do you have any idea?"

"You launched too close, I think. Time to acquire—"

"I don't buy that. Even if we fire too close, it should just circle once and reacquire. *One* should have worked. Out of three."

Dan thought so too. Their enemies had to have some kind of countermeasure. U.S. submarines did, though he didn't know much about them; the topic was highly classified. "If we hadn't attacked at such a high speed we might have heard something. Jamming. Ejecting some sort of countermeasure."

"The slower we go, the more vulnerable we are."

"It's a trade-off. Correct."

"Tell the captain we will reattack," Jung snapped to Kim in English. The junior officer swallowed, looking frightened, but spoke into his phones.

"What's our torpedo load?" Dan asked them.

Kim swallowed again. "We have three remaining."

"The three in the starboard tubes?"

"I am sorry. Three reloads, once those are fired. So six are left."

More than he'd expected. But now he wished they had something other than the Mark 46s. He'd always considered them good weapons. But for some reason they didn't seem to be cutting the mustard here in the Eastern Sea.

But there wasn't anything to be done about that, and Jung was barking orders again; the rudder-angle indicator was hard over again. Dan did some swallowing of his own. His mouth was so dry it seemed to close up. They were going in for another attack. This time, goddamn it, he'd have to make them do it at low speed. He cleared his throat. "How about the planes? Can we vector them in?"

"They've departed the area," Hwang said, remotely. "I forget you do not follow the radio comms. They have expended all torpedo and sonobuoy loadouts. They offered to stay and do passes until their fuel ran out but the commodore ordered them to return to base. There will be no reliefs; the crosswinds are too high on the runways for them to take off again."

This time Jung did something Dan should have expected, but hadn't; he sent both *Cheju* and *Kim Chon* in to the attack as well, all three converging, and sheered the flagship off at the last moment, as soon as they gained a solid active contact. Which was at only sixteen hundred yards. It was insanely dangerous, but with three attackers, on continuously altering courses and speeds, it would be nearly impossible for their target to build enough of a track on any one to shoot accurately.

Six torpedoes hit the water. The crunch of a hit tolled through the hull. The sonarmen shrieked. Another crunch, louder.

"Two hits," Henrickson yelled.

"Got it, great." He thought of the men who were dying below them, but couldn't spare compassion this time around. Right now, he just wanted them all dead. Like killing hornets as they tried to sting you. He stuck his head into Sonar. "Joe! Did you hear anything like jamming? Or something being ejected?"

O'Quinn pried an earphone off one temple. "No. But maybe they were out. They can't carry unlimited amounts, if it's some kind of mobile countermeasure."

That was true; if it was a swim-out decoy, each round would take the place of a torpedo. And such things were expensive and scarce. Jung's tactic might be the best they could do. Just get in there toe to toe and slug. Keep throwing ordnance until they got a hit. It was hell on the nerves, but eventually it should grind the other side down.

But how many subs were left? Did they have enough ordnance, and fuel, and sheer guts to outlast them?

And what if one of these shells had the pea under it?

His fingers danced over the keys of his Compaq. He could model fuel. He could model torpedoes per kill. He could simulate acoustic vertical beam width, and target doppler, and acquisition capability degradation.

But the biggest variables of all—storm and chance, Jung's dogged stubbornness, and his enemy's fanatical courage—he could put no numbers against at all.

The task group re-formed a search line and headed south. The cross seas made the deck lurch and sway, but no one seemed to mind. Rain roared against the bulkheads. The plotters and talkers were guzzling orange pops and smoking up a storm. Some looked dazed, others near manic, eyes glittering and movements badly controlled. They chattered in high-pitched voices and cackled at nothing Dan could see was funny. Jung slumped at one of the consoles, face gray. His hands shook as he lit up a silver-tip.

"You doing okay, sir?" Dan asked, slipping into the seat next to him.

"I had to leave *Mesan*."

With a surge of guilt he remembered the torpedoed frigate. "What's her damage?"

"Screws blown off. Rudders gone. Thirteen men dead or missing, five wounded. Taking water."

Two ROKN ships out of action; two North Korean subs sunk. The exchange rate was too even to be encouraging. "We're not that far from shore now. Maybe they can send somebody from P'ohang to help."

The Korean nodded somberly and sucked smoke. It trickled out of his nostrils. "They're getting a tug under way," he said. He squeezed his eyes closed and put his head back, rotated it as if his neck hurt.

Dan suddenly became conscious of his own fatigue, his aching feet, his own sore neck. He looked at his watch. Dinnertime, but he wasn't hungry. What he could use was strong and black. "Want some coffee?" he asked the commodore.

"Good idea . . . *Keopi jeom ka jeo o ji,*" Jung said to a passing petty officer.

Dan looked around the space. "And how about, uh—how about some for the rest of the boys?"

Jung looked taken aback. Suspicious. Then his face relaxed. He snapped out more Korean. Dan thought he caught Captain Yu's name. The man looked startled, then astonished. But still bowed quickly, then hurried off.

Dan was searching his mind for what he ought to be doing next when a bell shrilled. Jung came to his feet as if springloaded. Dan pivoted, looked through the parted curtain into Sonar. Saw all four men sardined in there staring at the screen with eyes wide. And heard, from the speaker, the band-saw whine of counterrotating screws singing through the deep.

Growing louder, closer, with each passing second.

"Where the hell'd *that* come from?" Henrickson breathed.

"Torpedo!" O'Quinn yelled. "Red Eighty!"

Dan had never heard of "Red Eighty" as a position indicator—it must date from before his time—but figured it meant from the port quarter. From a sub they'd never thought was there, never heard or suspected. "Is the Nixie streamed?" he shouted at Hwang.

"Yes."

But he wasn't looking at Dan. Nor was anyone else. They were all looking at Kim.

The *tae wi* stood with gaze unfocused, index finger on the Talk button of his mouthpiece, other hand on the plot table to steady himself. But he didn't speak.

Jung put out a hand as if to touch him. Then froze. Dan found himself starting forward too, orders jumping to his lips, wanting to tear the microphone out of the guy's hands. But the other stations on the phone circuit wouldn't understand him. Not in English. It was up to the ASW officer to respond. It took a physical effort to clamp his teeth together, and wait for him to act.

For an infinitely long second Kim did not. Then he jerked suddenly down on the button, and speech flooded from his lips.

The rudder slammed over. The turbines surged. *Chung Nam* heeled. To port, which meant a starboard turn. The first part of the Dingo maneuver.

Jung glanced his way, and their gazes locked. Then the commodore's moved on, to the rudder-angle indicator. Dan stared at it too, waiting for the reverse-rudder order, to come around hard to port, to snap out turbulence for the wake homer to follow away from the ship rather than toward it.

But it didn't reverse. Instead the angle steepened. The deck heeled, men slipped, the stabilizers groaned, pencils rolled. A reel of magnetic tape leaped out of its rack. It hit the sonar stack, then spun wildly out through the curtain into the main space, unwhipping yards of rust-colored ribbon that snagged instantly into a hopeless tangle. The shrill squeal kept getting louder, as did the turbine whoosh.

"What the fuck—," breathed Henrickson.

He was interrupted by a wave that felt like it hit broadside. It slammed into the frigate like a whole team of linemen crashing into a quarterback at once. She staggered again, and a sustained moaning shriek burst from the stabilizers as if each atom of hardened steel were being tormented into consciousness. Dan clutched the console, crouched, wishing right now above all else that he'd accepted Jung's offer, no, Jung's direct *order,* and gotten his life jacket.

The heading indicator hesitated. Then suddenly kicked around in heavy, ship-whipping jerks, ten, fifteen degrees at once. She rose high on a sea and then plunged, aiming it seemed nearly straight down.

"There's number two," O'Quinn shouted through the din, the whine, the clatter and roar. A thinner, more remote hornet-whine joined the first.

Dan stared at his computer screen. It was replaying the maneuver he'd just modeled. But *Chung Nam* wasn't. She was headed forty degrees to starboard of her original course. Directly away from the torps. Directly away . . . exposing her stern, her wake—

He let go of the console and staggered across the space between him and the DRT. Fetched up against it with a painful slam of the steel corner into his hip. "We have to come left," he shouted. "And fire a Mark 46, on 030!"

Jung shook his head.

"What're you doing? If it's a wake homer—"

"We don't have a torpedo to waste," Jung said.

Dan stared at him in utter horror. "To *waste*? If it's a wake homer—"

"What're the odds if it's wake first, then acoustic? You said fifty percent. But only ten percent if it's acoustic first, then wake. They're not stupid out there. They'll fire the wake homer second."

He opened his mouth to argue: the numbers were speculative; they didn't know the other side's loadout, analysis, training; then closed it. This was Jung's task group. His tactics. His enemy. Dan Lenson wasn't even an adviser. Just a rider.

The whine was deafening. Every man's face in the closed hot space was pale, averted, as if they were trying not to listen, as if not hearing might change the doom boring in on them at fifty knots. Dan's legs shook. He didn't want to go into the water. Not in seas like this. With the rest of the task group going on without them, sticking with the enemy, the way he had absolutely no doubt Jung would order them to with his last outgoing command.

A tremendous explosion jarred and whipped the frigate. It felt as if her stern were lifted, then dropped fifty feet onto solid stone. Lights burst with the spark-laced ping of shattering glass. Equipment snapped off the bulkhead and catapulted through the air. A fire extinguisher caught a man in the back, knocking him down.

Simultaneously with that image hitting his eyes, something nailed him in the back of the skull. White flame seared his retinas. He staggered and almost went down, but a hand, Henrickson's maybe, jerked him back up. His ears ululated. In the little sonar cubicle a short scream was cut off by the clap of a blow. Jung and Kim slammed together, recoiled, and grabbed, keeping each other on their feet. The commodore was shouting. Kim was nodding, then turning away, hunching his shoulders as he passed on whatever he'd been told into the sound-powered phone.

Dan clung to the table, blinking, feeling something wet and warm running down the back of his neck. He knew what it was before he lifted his hand. A seaman tossed him a folded handkerchief. Dan clamped it to his scalp, starting to nod his thanks, then caught sight of the heading indicator.

It was jerking right again, in great swoops as the bow labored through the seas. Each swoop was accompanied by a grating boom that set his teeth on edge. It seemed to be coming from astern, though he couldn't be sure; or maybe from below, the keel area. He tried to force his stunned brain into computing what that meant. The only thing that came didn't make sense. Or wait, maybe it did.

They were headed back toward the torpedo firing bearing. Meaning that if this next fish was an acoustic homer, they were running headlong into it.

He lurched forward and grabbed the chief of staff's shirt. "What the fuck's going on, Hwang?"

The tall pale officer lifted his head. "The first torpedo exploded close astern."

"On the Nixie?"

"How would I know?"

Dan nodded reluctantly; of course he couldn't. But despite the grinding of steel being gnawed apart, she seemed to be answering her rudder. So they were ahead of the game, compared to *Mok Po* and *Mesan*, anyway. "But what's he doing?"

"The maneuvering of the ship is not the commodore's responsibility. It is that of the captain."

"I don't see Yu down here."

"He is on the bridge."

The second hornet grew louder. Closer. *Chung Nam* rolled as another heavy sea plowed into her, or she into it. Her frame shuddered, flexing like a whip. But steel wasn't oiled leather. Stressed too hard, frame welds cracked. Ships broke up. He wished he could interpret the shouts and screams that came from talkers and petty officers around the space. Were they taking water? Reporting major damage? Was the hull patch holding?

Henrickson grabbed his biceps. He pointed to the computer, which he'd anchored to the tabletop with silvery strips of duct tape. "He's still coming around."

"I have no idea what these people are doing, if that's what you're asking me, Monty. They've still got their rudder hard a-starboard. Shit! I hate not knowing what's going on."

"You mean you hate not being the skipper," Henrickson said. "And you know what? I wish you were."

The rudder swung at last, but halted amidships. They stared at it. When it didn't budge, Henrickson rather reluctantly glanced down at the keyboard. He inputted numbers. "Son of a bitch. He's trying to do a Dingo in reverse. Head away first, from the acoustic, then cross back and do a wake knuckle to shake the wake homer—"

"Is it gonna work?"

The display changed. It now showed an elongated loop, an upside-down 6. Henrickson stared at it, then blinked up in disbelief.

"Only if he gets totally lucky on his timing. We never even heard that the fucker fired these. Not one peep. Nothing from the P-3s. He just bushwhacks us out of nowhere—"

The incoming screws grew louder, became a circular saw chewing its way into them. Dan clapped his hands over his ears.

Faintly, though his palms, he heard a *thunk-whisssh* of outgoing air. The torpedo tubes. They fired again. And three seconds later, again.

The enemy torpedo exploded.

This explosion, this shock, made the previous one seem like a mere tap. Instead of a dropping lurch, it jerked the deck out from under some men, sent others flying through the air. The bulkheads whipped so hard that the remaining lights fragmented instantly into an airy froth of glass. Henrickson's Compaq catapulted off the table, somersaulted through the slanting air, trailing duct tape like a comet's tail, and crashed into a tote board. The space went dark, succeeded a quarter second later by the rattle of tripping relays and the dim amber beams of the overhead-mounted battle lanterns. Dust and paint chips and fragments of overhead insulation blurred the already murky air. The DRT face cracked, and the lighted, projected tracking rosette within jarred and went dark. The noise was deafening. Stacks, consoles, repeaters, shrieked and bobbled as the heavy springs of their antishock mountings flexed. A warbling chorus of alarms and overspeeds triggered on. The rudder-angle indicator, heading indicator, and most of the other indicators and gauges either fell to zero registration or froze. The 1MC gave an expiring chirp and went dead.

The dim filled with shouting, the thunder of running

boots, and an ominous, gradually diminishing sequence of robust cracking sounds that seemed to come from below them. Dan pushed himself up off the rubber deck matting, not remembering exactly how he'd gotten down there. He felt no pain, but knew from experience that that had nothing whatever to do, at that moment, with whether and how badly he was hurt. He rubbed his neck. His hand came away bloody, but sticky; not fresh; he figured it was just seepage from the scalp wound.

Jung was sagged against one of the consoles. Dan hesitated, then pushed his way over. "You all right, sir?"

"I believe so. I believe so. But I don't think we are doing so well."

He nodded at the indicators. Dan became conscious then of the way she was rolling. Slow and heavy. No moan of the stabilizers, no engine-whoosh, either. "Engines tripped off? Maybe they can get them relit."

Kim said heavily, from the sound-powered circuit, "We are taking leak."

"Where? Aft?"

"Engine room."

Not good news. Especially since whoever'd just gunned them was still out there.

Wallowing, without power to train or fire weapons, *Chung Nam* was helpless in the face of another salvo. They didn't need homers now. One or two straight runners, the big idiotproof Type 53s the Russians had given all their third-world clients, would finish the job.

"What's going on?" O'Quinn, wearing a too-small battle helmet. "It's a spare. Want one?"

"No thanks."

"Time to go swimming?"

Dan cleared his throat. It was hard to formulate words, given that his paralyzed mind expected every moment to end in the final punctuation of an exploding torpedo. "I hope not," he got out at last.

O'Quinn, on the other hand, seemed buoyant, as cheerful as Dan had ever seen him. He glanced back at the dark stacks. "No power, no sonar, no point hanging around up here. What'd he say about the engine room?"

"Taking water."

"I'm gonna go down, see what needs doing."

"This crew knows how to do damage control, Joe."

"But they haven't been doing it as long as I have. You can always use another pair of hands on an eductor." The heavy-set retiree slapped him on the shoulder. "See ya."

"Better stay up here, Joe."

"You and Monty can handle it. Take care of yourself." He waved casually to Henrickson and exited by the after door.

"You too, Joe," Dan said softly, looking after him.

Dan caught up with Jung in the pilothouse, standing center-line with Captain Yu. They glanced at him as he came off the ladder, but didn't break their rapid conversation. He looked past them at the sea.

And all that was there was the sea. He caught one faint gray vertical on the horizon. Either *Kim Chon* or *Cheju,* but stern to, steaming away. He checked the magnetic compass to confirm: steaming to the south.

Jung had ordered them to leave the damaged flagship behind. And looking at a huge gray comber as it bore down, he doubted they'd live much longer, in this sea, without power, taking water.

"Just how bad are these leaks? Is it a split seam?"

Yu stared for a moment. "We are not actually hit. Very close blowup."

"A detonation close aboard," Jung interpreted. Dan caught the little skipper's poisonous glance, though it was behind Jung's back, and a light went on. His flag captain wasn't just worried. He hated the commodore. Resented him. Jung was younger, taller, better spoken, and if Hwang was right, better connected in the capital. Not a new situation at all, at all. But revealing.

"Anything I can do?" he asked them both.

"We have all in control," Yu snapped.

"Want me to take a look at the damage?"

"No, all in—"

"Yes, if you wouldn't mind," Jung interrupted smoothly. Yu fell silent, but the set of his shoulders told Dan he'd be just as happy if all the fucking foreigners, and his commodore too, jumped overboard.

He looked at the sea again, at the way the wind was blowing off the tops of the crests and smearing them across the hollowed craters of the combers. What was out there, under them, listening like a panther in the night for its wounded prey? At any moment another torpedo could crash into the hull. Send them to the bottom forever. His gut told him what it wanted very clearly. Go to his fucking stateroom, grab his fucking life jacket, and get as close to a fucking lifeboat as he could.

The rest wasn't his problem. He couldn't do anything more on the tactical level. But if *Chung Nam* went down, or caught fire, it *would* be his problem, in a very personal way.

He stood motionless, pulled in both directions. Wanting to run somewhere—where, he couldn't have said—and wanting to help. But how? He wasn't in the chain of command. He didn't have a job anymore, even in the most tenuous sense.

All he had to offer was his hands, his experience, his brain.

His body told him again to stay topside. But instead of listening he was remembering what someone had told him once deep in a forest in Bosnia. A woman who'd died seeking the truth.

If you run, you hit the bullet. If you walk, the bullet hits you.

That's what she'd said, before her bullet had hit her. It wasn't a bad motto. Not when danger was all around you, when there was no haven and no protection and nothing, really, you could do to affect what happened next. When all that mattered was what you could do for someone else.

He felt his teeth show in a sardonic smile. Try to keep everybody alive this time, Niles had said. Well, no chance of that. Not anymore.

But maybe he could still help out.

He saluted Jung and Yu, got preoccupied glances in return, and headed below.

The power was still out aft of the stack. Every door and hatch was dogged solid and had to be undogged and dogged again behind him. He was wheezing by the time he got to the interior passageway on the main deck. It was smoky with exhaust fumes, dark as a subway tunnel, and shot through with the random beams of battle lanterns. The deck was slick with water. Men were shouting, cursing, and the hammering clatter of dewatering pumps made it even harder to hear.

Immediately he felt at home. He pulled a breathing apparatus off a rack, donned it, popped the oxygen candle, and tailed on at the end of a hose team. Behind the mask he was just another guy. Tall for a Korean, but bent over as they edged through the door leading down into the engine spaces, even that probably didn't stand out.

He blinked ahead through the scratched lenses, his breathing loud and fast in his ears. The speaking diaphragm buzzed as he sucked air. The team caterpillared its way down a ladder into the dark. Steel gratings rang under his boots.

The biggest fear and greatest danger aboard ship was fire, so he was relieved not to see the hateful orange flicker. Just a white gush of foam below, the gleam of lanterns, a black slick and roil of water.

He was working his way after the team when the world toppled. The slick steel slanted suddenly beneath his boots. The men ahead of him reeled back, pinning him against the door, which slammed shut. He wheezed into the mask as the weight of five men drove the breath out of him. He tried to shove back, but the burden was too great.

Then the world toppled again, in the other direction, and the crush lifted and men flailed for handholds, going the other way. He grabbed a handrail just in time and clung like a frightened bonobo, staring down into a black gulf. If he lost his hold he'd shoot forward, over the railing and down into the mass of machinery below.

It had to be the stabilizers. Damaged already, they'd gone

out again, and no wonder—no electrical power, hence no hydraulics. The whipping action of the explosions couldn't
have done them any good either. Anyway, they were out, and
Chung Nam rolled in earnest now. At the mercy of the typhoon, powerless, unstabilized, defenseless; their enemy could
deliver the coup de grâce at any moment.

They might not even need to waste another torpedo.

The rolling became even more savage. He braced again,
one hand for himself, one hand for the hose, and to his surprise found a space had opened between himself and the #5
man. Despite everything, the team was still edging forward.
He panted, screwing up his courage to match theirs, and hauled
with all his strength, pulling the dead awkward water-filled
weight behind them another yard. Judging by its swollen stiff-
ness, the hose was charged. *Chung Nam* still had firemain pressure, then. Her inmost heart still beat.

A shout echoed back along the line. He didn't understand, but when the man ahead turned his face it was naked,
unmasked. Dan pushed his own up, sucking in air over and
over. When the guy ahead shucked his OBA he slipped out
of his too. They left them in a pile on one of the platforms
and moved on.

After some minutes of hauling and gripping, wrestling the
bulky weight of the hose along catwalks that were as much
handholds as walking surfaces, he crouched up to his waist in
water in a low-overheaded space that was totally black except
for shots of light from ahead. The hose writhed in his grip like
a drugged python. The main space was nowhere near as cav-
ernous as it would have been on a larger ship. But he was still
lost, in a dripping Escher universe of catwalks and accesses
meeting at impossible angles.

A flicker revealed faces upturned to where white water
jutted through a vertical seam. The inrush burst through hammered plugs and tore away patches men tried to jam into it.
Shouts echoed. Following pointing and gesticulations, Dan
and the #5 man wrestled the hose around a corner and lashed
it down. Another hose led up, toward an open scuttle where
faint light showed above. He jumped down to where more

figures struggled, and blundered into a body in the dark. The grunt sounded familiar. Dan grabbed an arm. "O'Quinn? That you? What're they trying to do?"

"Fuck you doing here, Commander?" O'Quinn shouted hoarsely.

"Trying to keep us afloat. Like you. What's going on?"

"Hold that, will you? We're riggin' this fuckin' eductor. Hold it *tight,* goddamn it." Dan got his hands where O'Quinn pointed. The other bent and he heard the clank of metal, then a scrape and clang as a wrench slipped and flew. The Koreans talked quickly, all together, and O'Quinn shouted, "Fuck. Fuck! No, let it go. Forget it! Just put a crimp in that fuckin' hose. Twist it and . . . okay, you guys know how to do that. Good. Just hold that for a second." Another grating squeak of metal on metal. "Okay. Let her go."

A hollow roar, a throb under his hands. It felt like the thing was working. He took his hands off gingerly and it held. "This the only penetration?" Dan yelled.

"It's a fucking parted seam. We got more leaks aft."

"Yu says they never hit us."

"Maybe not, but the fucking next goddamn thing to it. There's a lot of fumes back aft. I'm thinking flares or something, from the smell."

"Fire, you mean?"

"Not sure. I don't think fire, but I kept thinking I heard somebody yelling back there. I tried to get these assholes to go look, but they won't leave the main space."

"They're right, Joe. They've got to get a handle on the flooding. That's priority one."

"I know, I know, they're fucking right. But how about we go look? We're like fifth wheels down here anyway."

"Where are they? This way?"

"You're turned around, that's forward. No, aft somewhere—aft of the launcher—"

"Shaft alley? After steering?"

"Not that deep. Maybe some kind of deployment room for the towed array. All the way aft. I don't know exactly, but I can hear guys yelling back there."

"You can hear them? You sure?"

"That's what I said." O'Quinn jerked his head.

It sounded okay to go see if they could help. So he followed the older man through the darkness, past and nearly under a massive boxlike structure he recognized as one of the gas turbine enclosures.

The ship fell ominously silent once they left behind the clamor and clanging of the damage-control party. The whole aft section felt abandoned. They were climbing, not walking, going hand to hand along gratings and ladderways that tilted and shifted as the ship rolled. Dan wondered what was going on topside. If a torpedo hit now, they'd never make it out.

A grating suddenly gave way under their boots. O'Quinn slipped, slid, and went into the water. Dan grabbed his collar. When he came up he was spluttering. Laughing.

"Been fucking here before, boy."

"Yeah. Me too."

"PCF out of An Toi. Coastal Division 11. Hit a mine. Blew the bow off. Got her home though."

"Spruance class, in the Med."

"Did you get her home?"

He nodded in the dark, remembering the ones who hadn't made it. But the ship—yeah. He'd brought her back, and most of her people with her. Why couldn't he focus on that? On how many he'd brought back, not how many he hadn't?

He knew the answer. His own perfectionist self, his most persistent and merciless critic.

It wasn't that Niles had accused him that rankled. The admiral had only voiced the condemnation Dan Lenson himself had leveled long before.

"Asked you a question, Commander. Did you hear me?"

He bared his teeth in the dark. "I heard you—Captain. Yeah. We got her home."

"Let's get some of these Korean kids home too," O'Quinn rasped. Then slid, cursing, scrabbling, and went down again. Back here the water, the gratings, everything, was coated with oil. Dan hoped the stuff didn't catch fire. They'd be well and truly screwed.

Then he smelled it, what O'Quinn had told him about. A nitric burning stink, like the afterlingering of a fireworks show, or a burned-out roadside fusee. What the hell was it? It wasn't anything he'd ever smelled before aboard ship.

The ship rolled and something let go with a grinding clatter in the dark. Whatever it was, it sounded like it was right above them. Dan cowered, his arm whipping up in protective reflex. But nothing came down. Yet. He shouted, "Where the hell are they? You sure about this, Joe?"

O'Quinn was coughing, and Dan felt the tickle in his lungs too. The fumes, or smoke, or whatever it was, was getting thicker. "Just a couple more yards," he grunted between coughs. "Right under here. Duck under this thing."

When they finally reached the door, Dan saw the problem. One of the generators had come off its foundations, sheared its bolts, and been toppled by the sideways snap of explosive shock. A corner of its steel-I-beam base pinned the door closed.

He figured it was some sort of stern compartment, a Nixie handling room or the towed array deployment gear, like O'Quinn had said. The deepest, remotest manned station, all the way aft, all the way down. The door's dogs were turned to the open position. Whoever was inside must have done that. But they couldn't pop it against the weight.

They were both coughing now, unable to stop, the biting pungent fumes making it impossible to get a full breath. No wonder the others had stayed forward. He and O'Quinn leaned on the door, panting and bracing themselves against another heavy roll, another cacophony of terrifying sounds from above them. Something was hissing and bubbling not far away.

"They don't get power back pretty damn quick, she's going over," Dan gasped.

"Probably going anyway. With all this water."

O'Quinn's placid tone was so at variance with what he was saying that Dan glanced over in surprise. His face— what little of it was visible in the gleams from the lights far behind them—was smudged with oil, but the man was smiling. "Uh, you all right, Joe? Breathing this shit—"

"Huh? Never better." O'Quinn studied the fallen machinery. The frame pinned the hatch closed. The black water moved across its foot, a little higher each time the frigate rolled. He groped along the bulkhead and came up with a dogging wrench. He slammed it on the hatch, two, three times.

Dan listened but nothing came back. No answering concussions, no yells, nothing but the distant bubbling, the uneasy squeak of steel on steel. He coughed. Got out, "You heard somebody inside?"

"Yeah. Hear 'em shouting?"

"You sure, Joe?'

"Hell yeah, I'm fucking sure. There it is again. Say you didn't hear that?"

Dan hesitated, remembering what Henrickson had told him about O'Quinn. The *Buchanan* disaster. Hadn't his disgrace and dismissal been for leaving men trapped below? Was this some kind of flashback, some aural hallucination? He tried to catch O'Quinn's eye, but the man was already tugging at fallen metal. "Come on here, goddamn it. Put your back to it."

"Uh—I don't hear anything, Joe."

O'Quinn didn't answer and Dan gave up questioning. Maybe he *did* hear something—it was hard to tell with all the other noise around them. He got his back under a corner, where he could brace his legs. They grunted in unison a couple of times, then put all they had into it. The generator didn't move an inch, not a millimeter. There was no give to it at all.

The hull around him tilted farther, groaning. Black water bulged out of the dark and surged over the tops of his boots. He heard the damage-control parties shouting behind them, but they seemed more distant than before. Were they withdrawing? Called back out? Even . . . abandoning ship? He kept expecting another detonation, this one final: the flash, then the black end. He drew down acrid air, fighting an overpowering urge to bolt. "Joe, you really sure—I don't hear—"

"*I* fucking heard them, Lenson. We're all they got."
O'Quinn sounded frantic now. His oily hair stuck up in spikes.
He was bent, feeling around under the black water like a man
who's lost his keys. "You want to fucking get out, hey, go!
Save your own ass, all right?"

"I'm not going anywhere, I'm just asking—"

"Ask about the guys in that compartment. Figure how
they feel right now. Okay? Get on the other end of this thing.
Not that. The I beam there. Yeah, that one. That attached to
anything? See if we can get it over here."

The beam seemed to be part of a demounting kit, kept to
swap out the generator. In the dark it was hard to be sure, but
it appeared to be eight, nine feet long, a chunk of solid steel
with some machined fitting at the end Dan didn't recognize.
Halfway through getting it dragged over to the door Dan
grasped what the other had in mind. He sweated his end up
as O'Quinn, knee-deep in water now, fought to force the butt
end under the generator frame.

"Uh, hey—Joe? We actually get this hatch cracked, this
water's going to flood it. If it's not flooded already."

O'Quinn held up a thin snake Dan recognized after a moment as a hose. "What's that?" he muttered.

"Compressed air. What was hissing and bubbling, under
there."

"Uh-huh."

"Get it to 'em, maybe they can breathe."

"But if it's flooded—"

"If it was flooded, would we be hearing guys screaming
under there?"

"But I don't actually hear—"

"*I* heard 'em."

Dan muttered through gritted teeth, "I hear people
screaming sometimes too, Joe."

O'Quinn waited, not looking at him. At last he inclined
his head slightly, cocked, as if trying to identify distant music. "You hear them," he muttered.

"Yeah."

"And then what?"

"And you don't listen. You hear them but you don't listen. You can't. You just go on."

He straightened and sucked a breath so stacked deep with oil fumes and the choking smoke that his parched throat flamed. Circuits were snapping off in his brain. Red sparks arched and fell gracefully at the corners of his vision. "We're . . . losing the oxygen down here, Joe. Let's get serious. You really hear somebody? Or are you just remembering them from—before?"

O'Quinn bent him a look of the most complete hatred Dan had ever met. "Get the fuck out of here. No—wait. I need you. *They* need you. Or I'd tell you to go blow yourself! Now put your fuckin' weight on that thing!"

The beam took their weight, but instead of levering up the frame under their combined straining, it slowly bent. Nothing else moved, and Dan realized it was futile. Even if there were someone down there. Even if O'Quinn wasn't just hearing things, they were doomed.

But then the darkness rolled again. A wave crashed from outside, and somehow the added momentum or the cant added just enough to their grunting efforts that the lever came down a little more. Then even more.

The corner of the foundation pried slowly up. Maybe six inches. They worked the butt in farther, so it wouldn't slip, and tried desperately again to lever the generator up and off the hatch. But it didn't go. Just hung there, six inches of gap.

"Hold it there," O'Quinn grunted.

"Joe—"

To his astonishment and horror O'Quinn was on his hands and knees, then on his belly. In the water. Working hard with the dogging wrench.

A black crack showed. Dan groaned, trying to hold up the enormous weight of the frame single-handed. Cramps knotted his back. His arms were numb. He panted, but what his lungs sucked in wasn't air but some fiery gaseous acid. He watched for a hand to appear in the crack. For a flashlight to shine through, a face to appear, arms to push, a shout to echo.

Nothing. He said through teeth bared in effort, "There's nobody *there,* Joe."

"Yes, there is. Hold it up—"

"Maybe there was—"

"Get it *up,*" O'Quinn shouted. "*Now,*" and Dan gave a despairing heave and the older man did too, his back braced against the steel.

The whole great mass squealed upward another inch, another couple of inches. As it did the crack widened, and Dan was appalled to see O'Quinn stretch out around the frame and with a quick squirming motion thrust his hands, and head, and upper body inside the black gap.

"Joe!" Dan shouted, straining with desperate effort against the lever, praying it didn't slip. If it did it would close the door again, on O'Quinn's skull.

But the ship rolled, and he couldn't hold it. Slowly the generator began to descend. He heard a soft grunt from the man beneath it as the weight came down on him.

With a burst of dizzying effort that ripped something in his back he pulled the lever down, steel scraping against steel, getting just that much more lever arm on it, and put all he had, more than he had, into it. The descent halted. The generator hovered, poised, as he strained and panted, then came back up a little. "Get *out* of there," he squeezed through locked teeth. "I can't hold this. Joe! *Get out!*"

But O'Quinn either ignored him or didn't hear. He squirmed again, sending ripples across the water, and crawled forward even more.

Dan couldn't see his head now. Or his chest. O'Quinn's elbows worked at the edge of the door. His boots dragged, kicking, splashing, thrusting his body into the closing gap. Dragging the hose behind him.

Dan thought to grab for his leg, but that would mean slacking off on the lever. If that frame came down it'd crush him. "Joe. *Joe,*" he yelled, but got no more answer than before.

The boots gave a final kick and vanished at the same moment the generator began to descend again.

Dan was straining to hold it up, straining too to hear anything from below, when the ship went over.

She'd been rolling hard all the time, of course, but this was different. The swift jerk was like dropping the trap of a gallows. That steep, and that fast. Black water surged around his legs. From behind him came a prolonged, polyphonic chorus of ghastly screams. From above, what had a moment before been beside him but was now suspended terrifyingly came the shriek of ripping metal and the rushing hiss of a malevolent and powerful demon abruptly set free.

Its breath swept over him, icy, misting, and with it came a terrible aching emptiness in his head. Cylindrical tanks tumbled end over end in unnatural slow motion. They tolled and clanged like the iron bells of hell as they caromed and pinballed through the maze of rails and gratings, valves snapping off, spraying out whatever they were discharging. Some kind of gas—

He didn't see where the spark came from, only felt its instantaneous expansion into a bloom of yellow-white flame as overwhelming as the noon sun, ramming toward him through the beveled air. The shock blew him into a darkness as solid as if both his body and his instantly extinguished mind had been frozen now and forever into black everlasting ice.

18

He came to surrounded by creaking, whimpering, the crash and shush of seas going past. And the loveliest music ears could register: the faraway clatter of diesels, the muffled pulse of turning screws. He lay without moving, mind at first drifting, then as he returned sending queries to the outskirts. His arms and legs sent back the dull aches of bruises and sprains. His back hurt. His lungs burned. His worst fear was that his neck might've been injured again. The last time, he'd nearly been paralyzed. But when he wiggled his toes he could feel every itchy fiber of a cheap wool blanket.

He snapped his eyes open and half pushed, half rolled out of the bunk. Just as he started to fall his hand flew out, faster than thought, and snagged the bunk frame.

He was on a top bunk in the frigate's little sick bay. The whimpering came from a seaman whose ribs were being wound with yards of elastic bandage. Other Koreans sat about on the tile deck, nursing splinted arms, mashed fingers, bandaged heads.

The little corpsman who'd attended him before, the one they called "doctor," looked up at Dan's sudden near precipitation down out of the overhead. He smiled, cheeks wrinkling, and gave him a long, incomprehensible oration, complete with gestures. Dan could only nod and smile back. The tickle in his chest grew and he coughed and coughed. Then swung his legs over the edge and made as if to climb down. The other patients stared at him. Then, under the urging of the doctor, they stood—those who could—and helped ease him down, one with an unsplinted arm, another turning a bandaged shoulder away to let him lean on the other.

He teetered on the tilting deck, clinging to the bunk frame, and felt the world slip away again. The black loomed and wavered around him, shot through with golden lights.

The doctor waved something acrid under his nose. It stung like being teargassed, and he gasped and blinked. He pushed it away and staggered toward the door. Halfway there he realized he was still in his skivvies.

Henrickson did a double take when Dan wobbled into CIC. Dan had to admit that in the South Korean–issue coveralls, with most of his hair burned off, he must be a sight. "Commander. Uh, great to see you made it. They said you were hurt. Where'd you get the cool duds?"

"Sick bay."

"And the thong sandals? Which are cute, by the way. Specially with the white socks." The analyst steadied him as he winced his way down into a chair. "Sure you're okay? Looked like that hurt. That cough doesn't sound too good, either."

"They gave me some white pills."

"Hwang said you got knocked out."

"Yeah, but I'm okay." He blinked and got back a very bad image: a pair of boots disappearing into a black maw. "Joe! Where's O'Quinn? You seen Joe? He was down there too."

"Haven't seen him. Wasn't he with you?"

"For a while." O'Quinn hadn't been in sick bay, which probably meant nothing good. He tore his mind away from that hellish last image, tried to Velcro it again to the tactical situation. Which was still, as far as he knew, critical. "I see we're under way again."

"Diesels only. Turbines are out of alignment."

"Fuck. That limits us to—"

"About fifteen knots, yeah. But at least we're not pinned in the troughs. Like we were there for a couple of minutes. She damn near went over."

He'd definitely take the diesels over nothing. The rolling was still violent, though; gear and trash littered the deck, shifting underfoot with every roll; it was obvious without asking that the stabilizers were still down. He didn't mind. His inner ear seemed to prefer a rhythm, even if violent, to a motion it couldn't predict. He noted power was back, too. The radars were on, the lights were bright and steady, the overhead speakers hissed.

He kneaded his face. "Okay. What's happening with the task group?"

Monty laid it in in broad strokes. *Kim Chon* and *Cheju* were thirty miles ahead, following the predicted course of the remaining subs. The PCC was very low on fuel, as was the flagship herself. "Fifteen percent last I heard. Even if we had the turbines, we couldn't run them long."

"That's not very fucking much fuel. You can't go down to zero, not in heavy seas like this. Even in a new ship."

Henrickson frowned. "You can't?"

"Sludge, Monty. Especially for a diesel, you don't want to suck up whatever comes out of the tanks with those last few gallons."

"Huh. Then we got even less than I thought. Anyway, we're headed two one zero. That gives us all this motion, but Jung's determined to hang on. Just limping along after the other guys in the task group. If he could get a helo out here, I'm sure he'd have crossdecked long ago."

Dan was starting to ask about remaining weapons loadout when the commodore appeared at the doorway. He clung there through a roll, then came the rest of the way in. He stood swaying, glaring fixedly at the plot. Then saw Dan, and worked his way over, holding equipment as he progressed, as the space rolled and pitched and heaved and yawed around him. Dan noticed a slick of water sheening the deck. Where had that come from? CIC was many feet above the waterline. He tried to get to his feet but Jung's palms pressed his shoulders down. "Commodore," he said.

"Did the doctor release you, Commander?"

"Not exactly. Sir."

"I see."

Close up Jung was stubbled gray. His eyes looked like the flash hiders of overheated .50s. Dan thought about asking him about O'Quinn, but decided to keep the question for someone from ship's company. The commodore lowered his voice. He added, "A Romeo ran aground off Kanjolgap. North of Pusan."

"Trying to slip down the coast?" Henrickson said.

"Apparently. Very close inshore."

Dan deep-kneaded his neck, trying to corral his thoughts. "You think, another infiltration team? Trying to land near Pusan?"

"That I don't know." Jung thrust his hands into his pockets and came out with a crumpled pack. He fished one remaining silver-tip out and Bogarted it, blinking across the compartment. He seemed to lose the thread, then flinched and shook himself like a wet Labrador. "We're not getting much out of Seoul just now. I do have a channel to CNFK. An aide there. We're close enough I was able to get him on my cell."

"That's got to be one good cell phone," Dan said.

"We are actually not that far from the coast here. But it is a good phone, yes. Samsung—Korean-made." Jung smiled; then his eyes went dead again. "He told me ROK Marines stormed the sub. The crew fired back. The last few killed each other as they were boarded, rather than surrender. No one survived."

Dan found himself remembering the distorted face that had charged at him out of the darkness. "Yeah. They tend to do that. Was there anything—interesting—aboard?"

"Not in the sense you mean." Jung closed his eyes, swayed as they rolled; Henrickson reached to steady him. Dan realized the commodore was close to losing consciousness. He spoke like a player with dying batteries. "Nothing radioactive. Only small arms, light machine guns, supplies. Burst-transmission radios."

"An observation party," Henrickson said.

"You think so?" said Jung.

"That makes four," Dan said. His head was clearing a little. "One sub sunk the night *Mok Po* got torpedoed. The second, the one we destroyed yesterday. One aground at Kanjolgap. That leaves one boat out there."

"There could be more," Henrickson put in.

Jung seemed to remember the cigarette stuck to his lip. He lit it and gazed around the compartment before coming back to them.

"We've been tracking these guys for three days," Dan pointed out. "You're right, there could be more. But I think we'd have come up with them if they were there."

"We never detected the guy who shot us up last night," Henrickson pointed out.

"We've just been through a fucking typhoon, Monty. Sea state's been shit. He obviously snorkeled at the height of the storm, when we couldn't see squat on radar."

"It's hard to snorkel in heavy seas."

Dan couldn't help blinking at that statement. "These guys have been doing a lot of difficult things, Monty. Haven't you noticed? Including figuring out some way to reduce the probability of kill on our torpedoes to about a third of what it's supposed to be. And picking exactly the right weather and political conditions to stick it to us and snap it off." He lifted his head, making the connection. "Commodore—did the marines find any evidence of new countermeasures? When they searched this sub that beached?"

Jung said that was a good question; he'd have Hwang call back and ask. If necessary, they'd ask for a technical team to be dispatched.

"We could really use anything they can tell us," Dan told him. "But that's how he got past us, and how he almost clobbered us, too. We're so dependent on sonar and radar that when conditions deteriorate, we lose our ability to play. He was snorkeling and spotted us through his periscope. He pickled a couple off and got lucky. I think there's just the one guy left. But he's the one with the ball."

"The ball?" Jung said.

"The nuke," Henrickson interpreted.

"Oh." Jung closed his eyes and burned another half inch of the cigarette. He swayed, letting the smoke jet out through his nostrils, and sighed. "The ball," he muttered.

"Head for Pusan," Henrickson murmured.

Filled with sudden dread, Dan limped over and searched until he came up with a chart. "Where·are we now, sir?" he asked Jung. A nicotine-stained finger made a brown mark forty miles southeast of Ulsan.

Chill harrowed Dan's spine. Pusan was the next city down the coast.

"There are also—there are also reports of preparatory fires along the DMZ," Hwang said. "And aircraft flights."

Dan and Henrickson exchanged glances. "Artillery?" the analyst asked. The commodore nodded.

Dan rubbed his face hard, again. Whatever the doc had given him wasn't just aspirin. Not only were the aches and pains going away, he was starting to float. The golden cloud effect. But he had to stay centered. Artillery along the DMZ . . . which would be probing fires at first, to trigger the South Korean counterbattery radars and localize them for destruction. Same with the overflights, to pinpoint hidden radars and missile batteries so they could be targeted and destroyed.

It was the long-awaited run-up to war. The savage bloody tragedy of Korea was repeating itself. Driven by madmen, invited by weakness, facilitated by divided counsels and halfhearted attempts at appeasement. Even through the golden glow he felt sick. As soon as the glare of nuclear fission lit the hills of Pusan, the barrage would begin. Maybe the ROK Army and Air Force could still hold the enemy's armored thrusts. Maybe America could even muster its will, as it had before in the face of disaster, and stem the offensive. Develop alternate ports, reinvade, at what sacrifice of blood and treasure he could not even imagine.

No matter what the outcome, hundreds of thousands, possibly millions, would die.

If only they could have stopped this thing. And they almost had! They'd taken out half the group. The Korean marines had captured another. "There's only the one left," he muttered. But his lips felt like they weren't wired to his brain anymore.

"There's *Chang Bo Go,*" Henrickson offered. "She's still patrolling off the entrance."

"If we detect, I will go in," Jung said. His expression left no doubt what he meant. If he got the faintest sonar return, the vaguest hint of radar contact, he'd drive into the attack. And once engaged, prosecute to the finish.

But Dan had no doubt the men below them were just as determined. Corner them, and they'd trigger their weapon. Toss that ball they'd carried so far and so long, for the ultimate score.

They were all, all of them, locked into the game. There were no more options. Only the two stark, remaining consummations.

Pusan destroyed.

Or the last Romeo, and with it the whole task group, obliterated in one burst of nuclear light.

He scrubbed his face through the silken veil of the drug, trying desperately to drag something useful out of his woolly brain.

If only there were *some other possibility* . . .

A couple of hours later one of the Kims told him the aft repair party had found his man. Since "his man" could only be O'Quinn, Dan went to sick bay at once.

The retired captain was lying, eyes closed, in one of the lower bunks. They had an oxygen mask on him and an intravenous drip going. Beard stubble was black and gray against cyanotic skin. But he didn't seem to be wounded. At least, Dan didn't see any bandages. He bent to place his mouth beside the oil-smeared ear. "Joe, you okay?"

No answer, not even a flutter of the closed eyelids. He was breathing, with harsh ragged snores on the intake, but Dan didn't know what to make of the blue skin. Dan couldn't make out a lot of what the little doctor was trying to tell him, but the guy kept pointing to his chest and making mock coughs.

"Was there anyone with him?"

The medic smiled blankly. Dan tried to charade the question, but didn't get very far. Till one of the wounded sailors pointed to the bunk above O'Quinn. "He save that man," the Korean explained.

Dan was astonished to see that the guy in the upper bunk, also breathing oxygen with stertorous wheezes, was the steward from the wardroom, the one who'd refused to make coffee until Dan had argued Captain Yu into it. Then it made sense. U.S. ships, too, put messroom personnel at after steering stations, ammunition details, miscellaneous general-quarters assignments belowdecks.

"Saved him? Really?"

"Brought him air. I heard repair party chief say."

"Good work, Joe," he told the unconscious man. So there *had* been someone down there. He wanted to tell him he was sorry for doubting him. Sorry he'd given him such grief, when he'd been right. But O'Quinn couldn't hear him. Couldn't hear anyone right now. The oxygen hissed steadily, but his skin stayed dark. It wasn't getting to his bloodstream. His chest rattled. He sounded as if he was dying.

"Take good care of him," he told the medic. Then patted O'Quinn's shoulder, feeling helpless and guilty, and quickly turned away.

Back in CIC dawn arrived, along with cold rice and kimchi in a lacquered box. Dan washed a mouthful down with cold tea, so wrecked he could barely chew. He was thinking about heading for his stateroom when the comm lieutenant said he was being called on the task group covered net. Dan figured it'd be Mangum, or possibly even Captain Owens. But instead the comm officer said, "This is a secure over-the-horizon channel, sir. From something called Cement Mixer."

Dan blinked. For a second it didn't register.

Then it did.

Cement Mixer was the code phrase for the White House Situation Room.

He recognized Jennifer Roald's serene intonations even

distorted by hiss and distance, the through-a-tin-can hollowness of high frequency. "You're not easy to get hold of, Commander. Don't you have satellite comms out there?"

"Not in the ROK Navy, Captain. Over."

The lag before she answered told him there was a satellite uplink somewhere in their comm chain, even if he was getting the last jump by HF. Roald said, "Did you get my present?"

She meant *San Francisco*. "I sure did. Thanks, Jennifer. That's really upping the ante. Uh—over."

"Just keep its presence close hold. Since we had to keep certain people around here more or less in the dark about it."

Which probably meant the civilian defense staff. "Aye aye, ma'am. Will do. Over."

"Now listen carefully. This is not a secure conversation. Since we're using a non-US HF setup." Dan nodded, taking her meaning: the Koreans were probably listening in. "Where exactly are you, Commander?"

"We're about"—he craned to see the chart—"uh, about forty miles northeast of Tsushima. In the Korea Strait. Over."

"Have you got this thing localized?"

He pinched his cheeks, wishing they weren't so numb, that his tongue didn't feel twice as big as it ought to be. "Uh, thought we did. Then it got away from us again. The flagship took a torpedo last night. Still under way though. Max speed one five. Fuel state one five. Over."

"I'm going to read you something the Central News Agency just released. From Pyongyang, North Korea."

Dan pulled a pad toward him, clicked a ballpoint. "Go."

"I quote: 'Not content with escalating aggressive behavior in recent days, U.S. forces are now turning nuclear weapons over to the bandit dictator circles of South Korea. This is a clear violation of agreements denuclearizing the Korean Peninsula. The world knows that the Korean people demand the liquidation of the corrupt fascist "government" in Seoul. They steadfastly call for reunification under the fearless leadership of Secretary Kim Jong Il, Chairman of the DPRK National Defense Commission,

Supreme Commander of the North Korean People's Army, outstanding thinker and theoretician, prominent leader and the great sun of Asia. Washington must take full responsibility for the grave consequences reckless brandishing and unsafe handling of nuclear weapons on Korean soil will bring about.' Over."

Dan thought about it for all of three seconds. "They're setting up a cover story. For when this thing goes off."

"Exactly. It'll be our fault, and half the world will believe it. Over."

The air hissed for a moment. Until she resumed. "This is Cement Mixer. You should also know that Seoul has passed a short-fuze request to us. If they can give us a lat and long, will we put a missile into the water."

"A missile," Dan repeated. The concept bounced around inside a skull that felt stuffed with dandelion down. Then it connected and brought him bolt upright. "A *ballistic* missile?"

"Correct. Most likely a single-warhead Minuteman."

The hardened-silo buster, the biggest warhead in the strategic inventory. "What's, uh, what's the national security adviser say?"

"She saw Mustang twice. So far he's refused to commit himself."

This didn't surprise him. Before the assassination attempt, Dan had carried the Presidential Emergency Satched for "Mustang," Secret Service code for President "Bad Bob" De Bari. De Bari had some good points. Others, not so good. But even at the best of times, he liked to keep his options open. And when it came to military action, for good or ill, De Bari just didn't seem to believe in the concept that violence could produce peace.

Roald kept going when he didn't respond. "We ran the model here when the request came in. The kill radius in shallow water isn't actually that great. We'd have to have the target localized within a one-mile square. And NSC wants to preserve the nuclear firebreak. Especially since North Korea now has what amounts to a regional deterrent."

"So you're giving them first use?"

"Nuclear preemption doesn't generate much enthusiasm here." Roald added drily, "I don't mind telling you we could use some help with this. Over."

"I don't have much to offer, Captain. We already took out two of these things. If we could get a fix on this last boat, we could kill it ourselves. But it's just not that easy in this sea state and these shitty water conditions. That's what we've been fighting since day one. Uh, over."

"There's also the possibility of . . . premature detonation."

Very delicately put, he thought. Aloud he said tightly, "We understand that, Captain. Actually, consider it probable, once attack begins. But the task group commander here, uh, accepts that outcome. Over."

She didn't answer for a moment. "All right then . . . we weren't sure that point was clear. So what's his plan? I assume you're setting up a barrier operation?"

Dan said that was correct. The final barrier would be angled across the strait from Kanjolgap to the northern tip of Tsushima. The winds and seas were dropping and soon they'd have P-3Cs from ROKN Air Wing Six out of P'ohang. "That's only about forty miles up the coast from Pusan, so we'll have good availability on station. They won't tell me much about their underwater surveillance grid, but it may give us low-frequency cross bearings. One ROKN Type 209 is stationing off the harbor entrance. As a last line of defense. Over."

"This is Cement Mixer; copy all. So give me the bottom line. We have to make decisions here. About initiating the time-phased force deployment to support 5027. If Pusan's not going to be there when we arrive—"

"I just can't say which way it'll go, Captain," Dan told her. "If we can get a detection, we'll attack. Our torpedoes don't seem to be working too well, I'm not sure why, but we'll fix bayonets and charge in. What happens after that . . . I'm sorry, ma'am, that's the only input I can give from here. Over."

"Very well. If you can localize, call me," Roald said.

"Before the attack. Do you copy? The option's still on the table for the single-warhead strike. And on the rest of it . . . good luck, Commander. If this doesn't turn out well, I'll tell your wife we had this conversation."

He said he copied, and she signed off.

He replaced the handset, conscious of a new ache between his shoulder blades that cut through whatever the pills were doing. Fuck, fuck, fuck . . . He blinked at a chart labeled Korea Strait and Approaches to Pusan. It hadn't been there when he'd picked up. Someone had taped it in front of him and he hadn't even noticed.

He pulled the Compaq over and pulled up a Nuclear Effects program he'd seen listed in the program files. When he got it to execute it looked as if it had been written for the now-retired UUM-44A rocket-propelled nuclear depth charge. The old SUBROC warhead was rated at 250 kilotons equivalent, with a horizontal kill radius against a typical submarine hull, at optimal detonation depth, of eight kilometers.

So far, so good. But what the program rated as optimal burst depth was much deeper than two hundred meters. In fact, the menu didn't even let him enter a detonation depth of less than a hundred fathoms. He wasn't sure of the scaling effects, but when he reduced the "water depth" variable, the kill radius shrank drastically. Most of the energy went straight up into the air, not out into the water.

In the end, he guesstimated that a twenty-megaton warhead in such shallow seas would have a lethal radius of only around five miles. Captain Roald hadn't said what the retargeting time would be, but he figured it would be at least an hour. Add flight time to that, and even if they had it pinpointed, a sub stood a good chance of getting clear of the danger circle before the missile arrived.

He swiveled in the chair, wincing as the twist ratcheted up his aches, and checked the relative wind readout. The second problem was that a twenty-megaton burst in shallow water would blow thousands of tons of radioactive mud and sand into the atmosphere. Faced with that, he'd be hard put to say which would be worse for the prospect of using Pusan as a port, a North Korean bomb or the American Minuteman.

Along with the opprobrium of being the first to use nuclear weapons. For the North would instantly deny any such thing had been aboard, and probably even that there'd been a sub there at all. They were already laying the groundwork for accusing the U.S. of illegally smuggling warheads in through Pusan.

Not only would the crew of the last Romeo give up their lives, but they wouldn't even get credit for their sacrifice.

What could motivate such people? It couldn't be just ideology. Especially when that ideology denied immortality or posthumous reward. The only thing he could come up with was that the regime had to be holding their families hostage. If you knew your parents, brothers and sisters, children, would die if you didn't carry out orders—yeah, that'd put steel into your spine. He tried to imagine shirking an order if his daughter's life hung in the balance.

The frigate leaned and he braced himself without noticing. He rubbed his mouth, staring at the chart. It was out there somewhere, slipping through the storm-roiled sea. Its crew knowing they were nearing, mile by mile, the instant of their immolation.

There had to be some answer. Some way out. There were too many horrors bearing down on them. If they could just *stop* this thing . . .

He stared at nothing. His hand stopped moving. He blinked, trying to see whole what he'd just glimpsed.

It might be an alternative. It might not.

But there didn't seem to be any other road that didn't lead to the hell of nuclear war.

A torrent of excited words burst from the Pritac circuit. The plotting team sprang to their feet. Lieutenant Kim, shaken awake by the chief, shot groggily to his feet, glared around, then swung to focus on the speaker. Even though it was in

Korean, Dan understood. One of the ships ahead had made contact.

So it was time.

Time to see whether this last desperate scheme made any sense at all.

19

The wind still whistled through antennas and around the corners of the pilothouse. But it no longer screamed. Bursts of rain lashed the huddled .50 crews slickered on the wing, and a party on the forecastle retrieving a firehose trailing over the side. The dark sky was still turbulent, the sea still lumpy with gray boulders; but the worst had passed, unless the storm decided to loop back—which he'd seen them do before. After two typhoons and a torpedo detonation close aboard, belowdecks was a shambles. The compartments stank of damp and mold. They were cluttered with loose gear and the sodden grains from the burst rice sacks. The crew had tracked them all over the ship. White and swollen, they looked like maggot larvae on the tile decks. On the bridge the off watch lay wedged into the corners, snoring. The on watch clung to repeaters and chart tables, pale, unshaven, tottering, hollow-eyed.

Erect in his elevated chair, Yu didn't respond to Dan's salute. Lenson cleared his throat and tried again. "*An neong ha sim ni ka, Ham Jang nim.*"

"*An neong ha si yo, jung-ryung Renson.*" The little captain's voice was rusty, his slitted glance poisonous, but Dan noted he'd gained the honorific of being addressed by his Korean rank. "You survive injury. Congratulation."

"Thank you, sir. So has *Chung Nam.*"

"*Aniya*, she has."

They discussed the turbines for a few minutes. They

didn't share a technical vocabulary, but Dan gathered that
Yu didn't have much hope they'd be back on line before a
major yard availability. "Have you seen the commodore,
sir?"

"I believe he's in cabin."

"*Kam sa, ham ni da, Ham Jang nim.*"

The little skipper bowed gravely in his chair, then went
back to contemplating the onrushing sea.

Tapping at Jung's cabin, Dan caught a clicking from within.
But though he listened it wasn't repeated. A moment later
the door was opened by Jung's noiseless young steward. He
stared at Dan's coveralls, then bowed him in.

Jung lay prone on his bed, naked on a plastic sheet. The
steward resumed what he'd been doing, which was giving him
a massage. Brown skin gleamed with oil. Buttocks glowed
like pale moons in the dim room. Jung had moles elsewhere
than on his face, Dan noted. Bruises as well—he'd been
tossed around too in the last few days. The attendant began
slapping the commodore's back with cupped hands. That was
what he'd heard out in the passageway.

"Yeah," came a muffled voice, facedown in the mattress.

"Sir, it's Lenson."

"What do you have, Dan? We've got a detection. We'll be
going in to attack in about an hour." The steward/masseur
eyed Dan as he kneaded the senior officer's thighs. "I don't
expect we'll see our families again. But you have time to
send a message."

"Sir, I'd like to run an idea past you. Rather than just
charging in there and jumping on their . . . backs."

Jung didn't respond for a second. Then he rolled over
and sat up. Dan averted his gaze. The steward handed the
commodore a towel. Jung looked desperately fatigued as he
waved the man away. His voice dragged as he muttered, "I
know about the offer to preempt. I've advised Seoul against
it. We're too close to populated areas."

"It's not that, sir. Though I think that's the right decision.
Something else occurred to me."

Jung looked only faintly interested, as if he'd already re-signed himself to immolation. "Well, sit down, let's hear it."

Dan perched on the settee and tried to organize his thoughts. "Uh—okay. The crux here is that we seem to be able to detect and localize, even track this last guy without eliciting a reaction. Okay? We've done it, we've tracked him. He avoids us when he can. But when he can't, we can ping on him all we like. He'll maneuver to evade, if it doesn't take him too far off his base course, but he always keeps going. He took a potshot at us when he popped up his scope and there we were, but overall he's oriented to his mission, not to taking out naval units. With me so far?"

Jung nodded, looking annoyed, as if he'd been through all this and didn't need to be told again. Dan hurried on. "Now we'd have to coordinate pretty tightly to get this idea to work. It'd be risky too."

"There are no options left without risk."

"You've got that right, sir." But then he forgot what he was going to say and had to cough into his fist and search for it. They were all so fucking exhausted. . . . He coughed again and it came back to him. "Yeah. Anyway, we can't attack. If we do, the crew'll set the bomb off. They won't make Pusan, but they'll take us out, the task group, and hand Pyongyang a propaganda bonanza to boot. Bandit South Korea allows evil U.S. to import nukes, only somebody made a mistake and one went off."

"But we have to attack him," Jung pointed out, scratching a broad chest bare of hair. "There's no other choice. Other-wise he goes into the harbor and detonates. And even at that, they still can claim it was one of your nuclear weapons."

"With all due respect, sir, that's not precisely correct. About the propaganda thing—yeah. You're right. But about attacking—we don't have to fire on him. We don't have to sink this guy."

"What? Of course we do."

"No sir, actually, we don't. I thought so too, at first. But all we've really, absolutely got to do is keep him from reach-ing his target."

He gave Jung a beat to mull that over, then continued. "His mission's to destroy the port. Right? But if he—let's say for example, he can't make headway. What happens? The prevailing current in the Strait's northerly. So it carries him back north, away from Pusan. Not very fast, but that's what it'll do. Correct?"

"That's right. About the current." Jung frowned. "So you're proposing we . . . tell me again what you're proposing."

"Sir, I'm just tossing the idea out. I'm not sure how we'd go about implementing it. All I'm saying is, if we don't attack this guy, he might not. But if we blind him somehow, or cripple him so he can't make way, he can't accomplish his mission. What happens if they can't accomplish their mission, these special ops types? Do you have any insight into that?"

While Jung considered, Dan checked his watch. He'd used up six minutes so far of what otherwise would be his last hour alive. Once they got to the datum, Jung would unleash a coordinated attack. He'd use all his ships: the probability of kill was too low otherwise. And the sea would erupt, not with the mild detonations of Mark 46s, but with something only a few living had ever seen: the unimaginable rage of a nuclear detonation.

Somehow he'd survived one nuclear burst. He'd never make it through another. Not as close in as they'd have to be to attack. His own life—well, he didn't want to lose it, but after coming so close so many times, he didn't fear death as much as he once had. But the hundreds of young sailors in the task force—he wished he could find a way they didn't have to be vaporized, burned, torn apart, or to die of radiation or cancer.

"All right," Jung said at last. "I think I see where you're going. If we could disable this last Romeo, then you're saying, what? He might not detonate?"

"Well, he probably still would. But at the very least we could leave just one unit to track him, and clear the rest outside the danger area."

"Of course *Chung Nam* would be the one to remain," Jung said. "It is the flagship. It is also already damaged."

"I'd expect nothing less, yes sir," Dan said. Their gazes met.

"But how to cripple this submarine. Have you thought about that? Mark 46s, warheads set on safe?"

"No. They'd still think they were being attacked."

"Then how?"

Unfortunately this was where Dan had run out of bright ideas. "I'm not really clear on that point yet, Commodore. It'd have to happen so quickly they couldn't react. Or so quietly they wouldn't figure out what was going on until they were dead in the water."

Jung rubbed a trickle of oil, or maybe sweat, off his chin. Back in an adjoining room his attendant was crooning a Korean song. "Which would be—how?"

"Like I said, sir, not clear on that yet. I thought I'd ask one of my men who's an ex-submariner."

Jung stood. He grabbed the towel as it fell and started wiping off the oil. He snapped orders to the steward, and the shower came on. Jung padded toward it on fat bare feet, leaving oily prints on the carpet. Then turned back. "I will have Hwang convene my officers as well. I hope one of us will come up with something useful."

"Yes sir," Dan said. Looking past Jung into his bedroom, he saw, laid out ready to put on, a spotless white dress uniform. With medals, not ribbons. The kind of uniform you got married in. Or buried in, if you wanted a military funeral.

"Otherwise," said Jung, "I will attack as soon as we are in position."

On the bridge again, and still raining. No one in the pilothouse said anything. They looked lost in thought. Someone was praying or cursing under his breath in the chartroom. Dan pulled sweat off his forehead and gripped the Pritac handset tighter. Every second he had to wait seemed like an hour. But every time he looked at his watch, the minute hand had gone too far, too fast.

"Carpenter here, sir." The usually breezy voice sounded anxious.

"Rit, that you?"

"Mr. Lenson? Commander? Yes sir, I'm here."

Dan hadn't seen Carpenter since the incident at the cemetery. He'd been aboard *Mok Po* through the second storm and the running battle down the Strait. Despite everything that'd happened since, Dan still felt a snap of anger. He tried to keep it out of his tone. "Rit, you doing okay over there? How's the food?"

"Not bad, sir. Doing okay. Over." A pause, then he said, "I feel like I still owe you another apology, though."

"Not me, Rit. You didn't offend me. The insult was to the guys in that cemetery."

"Well, any of them'd probably have just cheered me on."

Dan thought that was probably both true and totally beside the point. He bit back at least three possible replies and said, "Never mind that now. Got a tactical question. Put on your bubblehead hat."

"Never took it off. Over."

He explained how he saw the situation, and what he and Jung wanted to do. When he finished, Carpenter didn't respond for a couple seconds. When he came back he sounded thoughtful. "I've done some figuring myself over the last couple days."

Dan coughed into his fist. Whatever he and O'Quinn had inhaled down there, his lungs didn't like it. "Anything useful?"

"Well, this last Romeo. You either want to blind him, which means take out the scope, or the sonar—right? Or better yet, both?"

"Yeah. I guess."

"Or else disable the motors. Let's take blinding him first. I don't see how you could do it without him sticking the scope up first. I don't see him doing that. Deafen him? Blow his sonar? No way I know of to do that."

"Roger that. Over," Dan said. He got a better grip on the handset. For some reason the plastic was slippery wet. "Okay, uh, so that's out. How about disabling his propulsion?"

"Uh, well, we're talking about pretty well-shielded electric motors. Some kind of really huge electromagnetic pulse might burn out the armature. I read something about that in *Popular Science* a couple years ago. But we don't have anything like that, that I know of."

"Me either, Rit." He felt his heart sinking. Well, he'd tried. "Just thought I'd raid your brain on it. See if I was missing anything. Over."

"Sorry I couldn't help. Or—wait a minute. Wait a *minute*."

He waited.

"Just occurred to me. Maybe it's stupid."

"Try me."

"It was back when I was on the . . . well, never mind that. We were up in Russian waters. Bird-dogging one of the new Alphas. Couple of hundred yards behind them, right in their baffles. They never knew we were there. But when we broke away a destroyer picked us up. They were holding us down. Anyway, they grabbed a trawler that was going by. Got them to try to drag their nets across us. Never got anywhere close, of course. Every time he stood on, the skipper'd nudge the rudder over a little and we'd sidestep out of the way. You could actually hear that net coming through the water at you. I was on the set at the time, that's how I know."

"They seriously think they could catch you in a net?"

"Well, it's happened before. Boats had to tow the fishermen around till the net broke. Just lucky it didn't wrap up in the screw."

Dan rubbed his mouth. The net idea obviously wouldn't work, but something in Carpenter's suggestion intrigued him. It brought to mind an Arctic night years before, when his very first ship had managed to hit a submerged sub with an experimental towed sonar.

He cleared his throat, trying to blank out what that recollection led to. "So what if a net, or something, *did* get fouled in the screw?"

"Well, I don't know, sir—most diesel boats have net cutters. Or used to."

"You think these guys would?"

"I honestly don't know that, Commander."

Dan tried to call to mind the Sang-o's stern, or what he'd glimpsed of it on the way forward from where he and his Korean diver buddy had caught their first look at it. He seemed to recall some sort of cagelike structure around the screw, but he didn't think it had been a cutter. And the Romeos were a different class, so their arrangements could be quite different from those of the smaller design.

Hwang came on the bridge, nodded to him. Dan ducked his head back. The chief of staff was in spotless pressed khakis. He looked shaken but resigned. Dan blocked him out and turned to look to starboard. The sea was rough and a strange color, a dismal, almost rusty gray. Far away, where the squall was wearing thin, he could just make out a flat shadow that might be land.

"Anyway," Carpenter's distant voice buzzed on, "what would you use out here? We don't have any nets. Or any trawlers."

Dan had been trying to think of something, but so far couldn't. Modern ships didn't carry much in the way of heavy line. Chain cable, anchor cable, was too heavy. Mooring line might do it, but generally you didn't haul around a heck of a lot even of that. If *Chung Nam* carried two hundred yards he'd be surprised. But to seriously try to foul the screw of a submerged submarine, they'd need more.

A *lot* more, trailed from every remaining ship in the task force. Crisscrossing their quarry's track till one happened to get sucked into the propeller. He pulled a sheet of used paper toward him and scribbled equations. The probabilities looked low. Too low. "Shit," he muttered, crumpling the paper and checking his watch again.

Twenty minutes left. "Well, thanks for the suggestion, Rit. It was just a thought. A coordinated attack looks like the best bet. Who knows, we might get lucky. If we don't see each other again—"

Carpenter said again that he was sorry about the girl. "But I gotta level with you, Commander, I never regretted a minute of it."

"I bet you didn't."

"See you on the flip side, boss. One way or the other."

Dan signed off and turned away. But the tile deck was slick with rice slurry and wet paper, and as the frigate rolled, his foot went the wrong way. He lurched for a handhold but just then something occurred to him. He missed his grab, and his head slammed into a repeater in a flash of pain.

"You all right?" said Hwang, helping him up. "You hit that thing pretty hard."

Dan didn't answer. He was still going over it—the thing that'd caught him, the image, just before he went down.

"We need to get hold of *San Francisco*," he told the chief of staff. "She's still in company, isn't she?"

"Far as I know."

"Get her on the horn. I need to talk to her captain."

20

He hated waiting more than anything. And they'd been waiting for two hours now, to learn whether they'd live or die. The first keenness had worn dull, reminding him of the old saying about hours of boredom and seconds of terror. You couldn't sustain mortal dread for long. On the other hand, you couldn't be bored when you didn't know which second would be your last. He flipped the pencil again, not caring when Henrickson, beside him, winced.

He was in the sonar shack, a spare set of headphones clamped to his temples. He'd talked to Mangum again on the Pritac, and explained their proposal. *San Francisco*'s skipper had thought it over. Then said, "We're quiet. But I'm not sure we're *that* quiet. Sounds high-risk to me, classmate."

"There isn't any other way, Andy. I know it's a gamble. But this isn't a peacetime operation anymore."

"Let me just shoot him. Get up so close he can't react and—no, fuck it, we've got that long run built in before the 48 arms."

"He'd hear it coming. And push the button."

"Right . . . Let me talk it over with my guys here. See what I haven't thought of."

Dan had waited some more, the seconds creeping like drugged snails, till the sub's CO came back on. "Consensus here's that if we close fast from his baffle area, then pull out, pass down his side at close range, and cross his bow, we might just manage to wrap our array around his screw."

Mangum didn't sound eager to try it, and Dan bared his teeth considering the maneuver. It was breathtaking, all right. It would take split-second timing.

Shadowing foreign submarines, getting their sonar signatures and observing their tactics, was one of the Silent Service's least-talked-about coups. But he hadn't considered the towed sonar array. The 688s deployed it from the tip of one of the stern planes, he couldn't recall which one, so it didn't foul the boat's own screw. The arrays were super durable. They had to be, to take the strain of being towed through the water. Getting one in a Romeo's blades would probably wreck not just the prop but whatever gearing was engaged too.

But passing down the other boat's side, then crossing in front of her to drag the array into her—that would take balls an order of magnitude bigger than he'd imagined his old classmate carried.

Mangum went on, "You might as well know we've been tracking him for the last day, by the way. Picking up what we can by listening. At the moment he's running shallow and noisy. We figure damage from snorkeling in those heavy seas. He's making about seven knots. So we're going to total quieting, and go in and give this a try."

"That's all we're asking here, Andy. One shot."

"Come in quiet from astern, then apply full power and blow by him."

"Got it."

"One thing, though: even if he snaps off a fish at us as we cross his bow, we're gonna need everybody else to hold fire. We can probably fox what he's carrying. But we absolutely cannot have you guys start splashing torpedoes while we're in the same cubic. Jung's got to promise us that. In writing, by message."

"Message will go out to you—"

"Not to me. Make it to SUBPAC. Just to cover us if this goes to shit and we don't come back."

Dan understood. Even if you didn't plan to come back from a mission, you got paper to cover it. At the very least you wouldn't go down in history as a total fuckup. Things like that were important to Annapolis guys. You could argue it as a plus or a minus. But when you looked at the record of the place over 150 years, you found a hell of a lot of heroes, not many incompetents, and no cowards or traitors at all. Not a bad record, all things considered.

And now he sat in Sonar, headphones tourniqueting his ears, trying to decode what sounded like a subway train running under miles of fiberglass insulation. Guided in on the contact by the detecting ship, the chief sonarman had managed to lock onto the Romeo. Dan had asked about *San Fran,* but got only a preoccupied shake of the head. This seemed like a good sign. The enemy sub was at 015 relative. Yu was keeping the contact on the frigate's bow, maintaining a constant bearing and range. *Cheju* was on the target's starboard quarter. *Kim Chon* lagged a mile astern, since her fuel state was even worse than the flagship's.

Which was bad enough; they were below 10 percent now. He expected any minute to hear the diesels falter as they sucked sludge. He just hoped whatever they had in the bunkers, it was high-quality stuff. Of course, if the engines failed, Jung couldn't attack. Which meant they might not die.

But at this point in the game, worrying about his own life seemed rather beside the point.

The sonarmen suddenly leaned into their displays. He frowned at them too, blinking through burning eyes. Nothing he could see, or hear. The subway clattered and roared in his ears. But the techs were pointing at spokes of light, talking a mile a minute. He pulled a hand down his face. It came off dripping. Surely they'd do more than murmur and point if it was a torpedo approaching.

But then he saw it: a momentarily brighter shimmer in the dance of light. *"Er rae da! Bhang hyang Kong Saet Da-sut!"* the chief shouted. "Torpedo! Bearing zero-three-five!"

Dan jumped up instantly and rushed through the curtain. He found the ASW officer bent over the relit and apparently repaired DRT, so intent he didn't react the first time he was addressed. When he looked up Dan grabbed his arm. "Remember, we don't fire. *We don't fire!* Those are the commodore's orders."

Kim's gaze slid past him, over his shoulder. "I take my orders from captain," the lieutenant muttered.

Dan turned, feeling suddenly threatened.

Yu stood in the doorway, for once without a cigarette. He looked wrecked and ghostly. Their eyes met, and Dan felt the world rock. His mind instantly outlined a whole downstream scenario from the captain countermanding Jung, ordering Kim to fire instead. But he couldn't let them put weapons in the water while Mangum was inside the kill envelope. A torpedo couldn't tell the difference between U.S. hull steel and North Korean.

But it wasn't his ship. Nor even his navy . . . still, he just couldn't . . . the conflicting demands shorted out his mind, leaving it null, like a sine wave canceled by a mirror-image signal. He wavered, one arm half raised.

Yu blinked at him, then came forward. He put his finger on the just-drawn noise spoke. *"Bhang hyang?"* he asked Kim.

"The direction? Not fired at us, Captain." The ASW officer must have been thinking along the same lines, because he cut his eyes at Dan and answered in English.

"Stand by to fire."

"We are standing by, Captain."

Yu met his eyes again. Dan said in a low voice, *"San Francisco* will pop up and radio when she's clear." Trying as unchallengingly as he could to remind the guy that the U.S. boat was still down there.

"That was Romeo firing on your submarine?"

Dan was about to answer when Korean spluttered like a lit fuze behind the curtain. Kim bent forward as the plotters lunged in, jotting like madmen.

"What is it?" he muttered. The lieutenant didn't answer. Dan felt like shaking it out of him, but got a grip and forced himself to step back. This was *their* action. *Their* ship. He had to let them handle it. The not-so-funny thing was that doing that was harder than anything he'd ever had to do as a skipper himself.

Henrickson, at his elbow. He said in a low voice, "Dan? Machinery noises."

"What kind of noises? From the Romeo, you mean?"

"We're not sure from who. Or what they are. Just . . . transients."

A "transient" was a onetime sound, rather than the tonals or continuing frequencies pumps or motors put in the water. A slamming hatch was a transient. Ejected garbage was a transient. But telling one from the other, or interpreting a particular burst of noise, took hundreds of hours of training. "So what is it?" Dan asked, knowing he probably wasn't going to get much of an answer. And he didn't; the analyst just shrugged.

The plot now showed a high-rpm contact headed east. Dan figured this was Mangum. The bearing of the torpedo sounds swung after it with each successive plot. And each successive plot showed more white space between the points. Andy was putting the pedal to the metal. Jamming every ounce of nuclear-generated steam he had into his turbines.

Dan gripped the DRT like a pinball wizard, praying they had enough of a head start. No matter what your top speed was, seven thousand tons of submarine took time to accelerate. He stepped back, tried to breathe out the tension, but it didn't ease, not even a little. He didn't want to think about how he'd feel if Andy and the men of SSN-711 didn't come back because of his harebrained idea.

On the other hand . . . the bomb hadn't gone off yet.

Of course it still could, any second. Looking at the plot, he saw no one had bothered to sketch in a danger circle for a nuclear burst. They were all inside it anyway. Though the way she was pushing it now, in excess of thirty-five knots, *San Fran* might be nearing its edge.

A shout from Sonar. Henrickson ducked out again. "Torpedo sounds ceased."

"Christ," Dan muttered, prying his fingers off the tracer. He caught Kim's tentative grin and tried to smile back. At least the eighty guys his classmate commanded were still safe. For now.

The next time he looked at the plot something seemed out of place. He had to lean closer, follow the plotter's tapping finger, before he saw it.

The red pencil-dots that denoted the Romeo were being drawn in at progressively closer intervals.

The plastic arm of the parallel rule reached out. Pencils flashed, and another dot lay even closer. Displaced slightly to port, as if their enemy had his rudder over. But at very low speed indeed.

Henrickson, reporting again. "No screw noises from contact. Mechanical transients continue."

Dan took a deep breath. Held it, and let it out. Waiting from breath to breath to be destroyed. Offering himself up to whatever had sustained him this long, brought him through so many trials. He'd never been able to define exactly what it was. Only that it was there. Because now and then, in the extremity of need, he'd felt it beside him, closer than any person could ever be.

The plotters leaned forward again.

And seconds later, again.

Now the red dots lay nearly atop each other. The transients kept coming. After a few minutes he moved unwilling limbs and went in to hear for himself. Even with headphones clamped tight and the gain all the way up, the sounds were very faint. Distant metallic scrapes. A dull recurrent pounding, like a cracked bell tolling deep underwater.

He went back out and stood beside Yu, hanging off a handhold on one of the intercoms like a brachiating chimp. Hwang had come in while Dan was behind the curtain. They stood together, not saying anything.

Yu asked the chief of staff something in a harsh voice. Hwang shook his head slowly. Dan could interpret that. The next order, to Kim, was easy to guess too. The plotters kept working, but traded uneasy looks. The *tae wi* spoke into his sound-powered mike as if sipping something bitter. Dan looked up to see the heading indicator start to spin.

Chung Nam was coming right. Headed for the motionless target. The beat of the diesels picked up through the steel around them.

They were going in for the kill.

Then another shout came from Sonar. Yu's head snapped up. He hesitated, then rapped out an order. The ASW officer instantly passed it on.

Dan couldn't take it anymore. He cleared his throat and when Yu looked up said, hearing his voice rasp higher-pitched than he'd expected, "What's going on, Captain?"

Yu let him hang for a second, then said, "It is sound of blowing tanks. Our dangerous friend has decided to surface."

Dan stood gripping the starboard splinter shield, staring across half a mile of crumpled sea the color of forged iron at a presence he'd never expected to even glimpse. The conning tower tolled in a pendulum–like roll. The sky was still threatening but it wasn't raining, at least at the moment. With the binoculars he'd snatched from the lookout he saw figures at the top of the sail, below the vertical cylinders of scopes and masts. They looked busy over there. As he watched, a large ensign unfurled, snapping in the wind. It was red and white and blue. It occurred to him only then that he didn't know what North Korean colors were. Shouldn't they be all red, like the Chinese? He set his elbows and tried to steady the field of view, but all he could say in the end was that they definitely weren't Chinese colors. A relief, after all, to finally be certain.

Jung stood contemplative beside him. Dan handed over the glasses without a word. The commodore balanced them on the tips of his fingers. Below, on the main deck, the torpedo tubes were trained outboard. The crewmen stood a few feet off, carefully clear of the firing bearing, staring in the same direction.

At last Jung said, "Well."

"Yes, sir."

"Now what?"

Dan looked across again. Yu was on a closing course, but at a low speed. *Chung Nam* barely had steerageway on. He craned aft; caught another escort on the horizon, gray as the clouds. And to the east, more visible now, the sooty bleak mountains of what the chart called the Kyongsangnam-Do. Not far past them the headlands of Pusan would reach seaward. It had been a damned close-run thing.

And it still wasn't over. A clacking from above reminded him of that. He looked up to see a signalman working a light. Jung handed a penciled note to Hwang, who wheeled and ran it up the ladder. He held it against the wind as the signalman looked it over, adjusting his signal lamp. Then swung it to point at the sub and grasped the handle. The shutter began batting rapidly, sounding like an old typewriter.

"No common frequency?" Dan asked Jung.

"We don't communicate. Or, I should say—the only way I've communicated with them up to now is with shells." Jung lowered the glasses and scowled. "I don't believe they are interested in talking. Perhaps not even capable of it anymore. These people are not quite human. They are robots, programmed with lies until their minds don't work in normal ways."

Dan thought about that. This wasn't the urbane, tolerant Jung he'd seen up to now. "So, uh—are these navy? Or special ops?"

"I don't believe there's much difference. To tell the truth."

Dan looked at the signalman, who'd abruptly stopped transmitting and was studying the conning tower through a massive pair of stand-mounted binoculars. "What are you sending?"

"A demand to surrender."

"Then what?"

"If they refuse, we destroy them."

Dan rubbed his face, trying to find something to say to that. Nothing came.

A dazzling pinprick ignited against black-painted steel, like a distant welding arc. He could read flashing light, not at a signalman's speed, but he could decipher it. But this was in Korean and he quickly gave up. Instead he accepted the binoculars one of the bridge crew handed him and leaned on the shield, checking the enemy out again as *Chung Nam* slowly closed over the ragged gray waves.

She didn't seem to have any way on at all. He didn't see the white kick of turbulence at her stern. The heavy, slow way she rolled, tilting drunkenly this way, then that, argued she'd lost power too. He saw no evidence of damage along the hull, though. It was smooth, both boxy and subtly streamlined, except for huge freeing ports. It looked very much like an old U.S. Guppy boat, except for a narrow upward projection of the periscope housing that he vaguely remembered was necessary because of the poor quality of Soviet optics. Another finned projection jutted from the bow; he called it as a sonar transducer.

Now he saw a second group busy on the after surface of the sail. They swung something up and steadied it. An automatic gun of some kind.

Jung looked up from the form the signalman's runner had brought down. Dan raised his eyebrows but the commodore didn't explain, just went into a long to-and-fro with Hwang. The chief of staff sounded agitated. Dan tried to leash his impatience. This was their enemy. And their lives at stake. Maybe the best thing for him to do was go below and turn in.

"Who the fuck are *you* kidding," he muttered to himself.

"Excuse me, Dan?"

"Nothing, sir."

The commodore squatted in the lee of the shield, his back to the wind, and shook out a silver-tip. The chief of staff bent to light it. Jung said around cupped palms, "They want *us* to surrender."

Dan whistled. "Pretty ballsy."

"Like I said: There's no way to talk to these people."

Dan said, trying to pitch it as an offhand comment: "Well, seems to me they're talking now. They just aren't saying what we want to hear yet."

Both Koreans regarded him. He pulled an arm across his forehead and tried to function. It was getting harder with each passing hour. "Uh, I was thinking. Usually the only way people act like this is if their families are threatened. Like, if they surrender, their relatives get shot. So how about something like this—you ask them again to give up. But say what you'll do is, put the word out that the sub and all aboard were destroyed in battle."

Jung stood expressionless, smoking hard, but listening.

"In battle," Hwang said, "or in a nuclear explosion?"

Dan saw an even better way to do it. "Yeah—or in some kind of low-order detonation. Hey—if it was a low-order det, that means it was the bomb design that was at fault."

"They would blame their scientific establishment," Hwang said, looking more interested. "And not the crew of the submarine."

Jung cocked his head, but didn't look like he was buying it. He studied the Romeo, about seven hundred yards off now. Dan saw the wan ovals of faces turned their way. The thin lines of gun barrels. He leaned over to look down on their own forecastle. *Chung Nam*'s stabilized 76mm returned the stare of the sub's machine guns, the long, tapered tube pointing easily up and down with the frigate's roll.

Finally the commodore nodded. Hwang already had a message started. Jung glanced at the pad when the commander was done. Nodded again.

A runner's boots banged on the ladder, and the shutter rattled again.

A staccato clatter from across the water echoed it. Binoculars up, Dan saw white water leap up beside the Romeo. A test, or a warning burst. Or both. He could hardly believe this. Torpedoes and guns pointed at them, powerless to move, and they were still defiant.

Of course, what they carried belowdecks might even the odds.

When the next reply came down the commodore and Hwang bent over it for some time. Their faces were a study in bafflement and rage. Dan tried not to look curious. He paced back and forth, the gratings clanging under his boots. The boots Mangum had given him aboard *San Francisco*. They fit better than he'd expected. He propped one on a stanchion base and examined it. Once you got salt into leather it kept coming to the surface. He'd rubbed it off a couple of times with a rag and fresh water, but there the ghost was again. He turned it to inspect the heel, then examined the other boot. He leaned against the shield and closed his eyes.

Jung said, louder than before, "Commander? Can I interrupt whatever it is you're doing over there?"

"Yes sir. Sorry, Commodore." Startled awake—he'd actually been out, leaning against the shield—Dan blinked at the paper. "Uh—so what's he say?"

They were both staring at him, almost sullenly, though it could simply be the same utter exhaustion he felt. Hwang said, "We don't really know."

"You don't know?"

"He won't communicate any further with us," Jung said. His lowered eyebrows looked threatening.

"Won't communicate, sir?"

"Do you have to repeat everything I say? He won't talk. Not with us. Not with the ROKN." After a moment the commodore added, frowning across the water at their nemesis, so long trailed, so suddenly revealed: "He will deal only with an American."

Gathered around Jung's chair in the pilothouse, Dan, Henrickson, Hwang, and the commodore debated it. As soon as he heard, Henrickson started shaking his head. "It's a trick. They want a hostage. Once they get their hands on an American, they've got a bargaining chip."

Hwang said mildly, "I don't know about that, Monty. This is part of their usual bargaining posture. To show contempt for us. They did this at Panmunjom. Did it in the Four Nation talks, too."

Dan looked on, arms folded, trying to figure it out. They could both be right. They could both be wrong.

The commodore cleared his throat and they fell silent. "Dan, what do you think?"

He rubbed his face. He didn't want to say it. He really, really didn't want to put himself in the situation. But he forced his mouth to make the words. "If there's half a chance to get our people out of this alive, Commodore . . . I'll go."

"It will be at grave risk to you."

He tried to muster some gallant rejoinder, but all his tired brain surfaced with was that great old all-purpose military response. "Yes, sir," he mumbled. "Just one thing—"

"Yes?"

"I'd better have some more coffee first. Or they're not going to get much useful out of me."

"Well, I don't like it," Henrickson mumbled. "Once they've got you over there, we have absolutely no way of getting you back. They can shoot you. Torture you. Submerge again, with you aboard—"

Jung sat with head cocked, eyes closed. He spoke to Hwang, who turned and relayed orders to one of the crewmen. The man came to attention, snapped out, *"Jal al get seum ni da,"* and disappeared below.

When the long-faced steward came up he carried a cloth-wrapped bundle. He handed it to Jung. The commodore unfolded it, revealing a holster. He took out the automatic, worked the slide, and put the safety on. He wiped oil off it with the cloth and handed it to Dan. "Take this."

Dan turned it over. An unfamiliar make, Korean, he guessed. He tried to hand it back, offering it butt first. "I don't think it's a good idea to go over there armed, sir."

"I didn't ask for your opinion, Commander."

That was pretty clear. Dan checked again that the magazine was seated and the safety was on, and tucked it into the small of his back, under his belt. When he'd carried the Presidential Emergency Satchel, and a sidearm to protect it, he'd found that was the only way he could carry a pistol and not have it come adrift on him.

Next up the ladder was the little guy from Yu's wardroom.

The steward O'Quinn had saved, Dan remembered. He lurched, he sniffled, but he was back in his white smock. Again he was carrying the silver coffee urn, the covered tray. Dan hoped they hadn't bothered with the sugar-cube ship this time. Seeing him, the server smiled and whipped off the napkin.

Dan closed his eyes. They had.

He took a big slug from the proffered steaming cup and almost choked: it was thick as syrup, boiled down nearly to solidity. They watched him gravely as he drank it off. It felt ominous, like a ceremonial send-off. It didn't help his already sizable reluctance. He shoved that cowardly, cringing Caliban back down into the shadows where it lived.

"So . . . shall I get going?"

Jung looked out at the waiting shadow. At last, he nodded.

A whaleboat had a mind of its own in seas like this. They were still eight, ten feet high, boiling in from every point of the compass. Dan crouched beside the helmsman as the latter wrestled the wheel. He felt like the Michelin Man in foul weather pants, foul weather jacket, then a life jacket over it all. Plus the pistol, and a portable radio in the pocket of the jacket. His boots were full of salt water again. When spray came over the bow he didn't bother to duck. Just bent his head and took the shower.

His neck ached, and he knew why. He kept expecting the black hull they steered toward, the sea, the air, to vanish in an incandescent flash. You won't feel a thing, he told himself. But the quickened corpse he rode kept flinching. His legs were rigid as iron and his breath came too fast. Now he wished he'd skipped the coffee. It sloshed sourly in a jittery gut, and the crazy seesaw of sea and sky didn't help.

They had four souls in the whaleboat: the big helmsman, a bowhook, another boatswain's mate type, and Dan. No visible weapons, and from the boat's staff flew not the ROK flag but a white one, made up at the last minute by Yu's guys from a bedsheet. This struck Dan as a cool touch. He'd never sailed under a flag of truce before.

He swung his gaze to the approaching conning tower, and the gun that tracked them from atop it. The sub was rolling violently. The gun crew were tethered by harnesses. One was just then being sick, trying to catch it in his palm till the outboard roll, but not having much success. That was the only sign of human weakness in the dour visages that glared down as they neared.

A door slammed open at the base of the tower. Two men peered out. They wore blue cotton uniforms, a lighter hue than that of the South Koreans. One fingered a coil of line. They pointed alongside, gesturing furiously. The coxswain blipped the horn to acknowledge and swung to parallel the sub's axis. Someone else was shouting down from the tower but the helmsman ignored him. He gunned the engine, then throttled back as a copper-green swell mounted, hung, then broke, gnashing and foaming down the Romeo's deck. When it smashed into the tower the spray leaped many fathoms into the air.

Dan flexed his fingers. He had to make it on the first jump. If he didn't he'd fall between the whaleboat and the hull, and most likely get something crushed—his leg if he was lucky, his head if he wasn't.

He nudged the coxswain. When he turned his head Dan shoved the pistol into the Korean's pocket. The sailor twisted to look down at it, then at Dan, gaping. "*Jeon dae jang,*" Dan yelled into his ear, slapping the bulge of the gun within wet cloth. Telling him it was the commodore's. The guy hesitated, then nodded. Boarding with a concealed weapon didn't seem like the way to build trust here. If any could be built, and he wasn't just setting himself up for a hostage situation.

The boatswain's bear-paw whammed down on his shoulder. Time to go. He unlocked his fingers and scuttled forward, then knelt in the bow. The boat zoomed dizzily, nearly level with the officers watching from the top of the tower, then sank away till the hull loomed over them. He examined green slime and razor-edged barnacles at close range.

"Yes, yes," yelled the coxswain in his high voice, and drove in as they soared once more. The bow slammed against

black steel so hard they all staggered. At that exact second
the linesman on the deck slung the bight. The wet heavy line
slammed Dan in the chest, almost knocking him down. But at
the same moment the boatswain grabbed it, slipped it under
his arms, picked him up, and threw him bodily over the bow.

He tried to get his legs around but instead took the impact
with his ribs. It felt like a truck crushing his chest, but he
clung to the line with both fists, hard as he could. The line
handlers braced their boots and got him in hand over hand.
He slammed his arm against the steel of the door coaming,
and couldn't suppress a groaned curse.

Then he was inside, his wheezing breath echoing in a
cramped, dripping, dark, reeling, sea-smelling space that ev-
idently flooded during submergence.

One of the guys who'd reeled him in threw him against
the bulkhead. The other began patting him down roughly,
grabbing his crotch hard, feeling behind his neck, the small
of his back. His breath smelled like radishes and rotten fish.
White sea-pimples circled his neck like a pearl necklace,
and his face was hard and flat as a mechanic's hammer. He
found the radio and shook it suspiciously, then handed it to
the other guy. When he came to the heavy bronze USS *Horn*
buckle he pulled it off, and Dan's belt with it. Dan grabbed
for his pants with one hand and braced against the next savage roll with the other.

They pushed him into the gloom. A coaming diked six
inches of rolling water on deck from a hatch leading down.
Dan leaned over it, breathing the reek of rotten rice and diesel
fuel and stinking bodies that flooded up from a region of
dim orange light.

A shout came up, and a totally enraged-looking scarlet
face followed it up the ladder. This character was shouting so
loud it was deafening in the closed space. He threw a canvas
bag at Dan's escorts. The next second it was being pulled
over his head.

The last time anyone had put a hood on him, it'd been
Saddam's Muhkbarat. Without even considering he yanked
it out of their hands and whipped it out the still-open door.

The sea heaved. The bag floated a moment, then was sucked
down. The face in the hatch opening went from scarlet to purple, screaming. The two guys beside Dan went stiff as posts.

One thing he'd learned on this float was that Koreans
feared rank and weren't afraid to pull it. Maybe the Northern
brand were the same. He rounded on Red Face and shook
his fist at him. "I'm not wearing that fucking hood!" he
screamed as loudly as he could. He grabbed his own collar,
the silver oak leaf insignia, and thrust it in the man's face.
"Get that through your thick fucking head, asshole! Now get
out of my fucking way!"

He stood in the little cramped messroom, the painted cork-
lined overhead low and curving, bracing himself with one
hand on an overboard discharge pipe. It was weepy with
condensation and rough with rust, but felt solid under his
weight at each roll. Down here the stink was close and choking, the air hot and thick with diesel fumes. All the lights were
twenty-watt incandescents. The bulkheads were wooden. The
equipment cabinets were pop riveted, with the round black
meter faces that had gone out of style in the West about 1949.
It was vintage technology, and he'd have been happy in a professional way, in different circumstances, to examine it more
closely.

It was also interesting to note several recent bullet-scars,
gleaming raw metal that marred the paneling in the dim light.
A dark red stain on the deck looked as if it had been hastily
blotted up with rags.

A harsh voice. "You are American officer?"

He was surrounded, hemmed in, by extremely hostile-
looking North Koreans. Two stood to either side, another behind him, between him and the access trunk. At a wooden
mess table with a stained tablecloth sat three men. The one
in the center, in his thirties, wore the light blue ship's coveralls. He had a hard, rawboned face, close-cropped hair, ears
that stuck out like propeller blades, and black, stabbing eyes.
His hands lay pressed flat on the tablecloth. The two who
flanked him looked younger. One was in the same powder

blue; the other wore a khaki uniform with red collar tabs. Dan did a double take when he saw their feet. They all wore white canvas slip-on tennis shoes, vintage surfer models, some very much the worse for wear.

His attention was redirected by Propeller Ears slamming his palm on the table. "I ask again! You are American officer?"

"Correct."

"Your name."

"Daniel V. Lenson. Commander, USN. You are the captain? *Hang-jung?*"

"I am Captain Im. Political Officer Park; my second in command, Lieutenant Won."

Dan nodded and looked around pointedly. "How about a chair?"

Won snapped an order, and a wooden one appeared. It looked handmade. Dan lowered himself, keeping his grip on the pipe. The rolling was so extreme that the chairs and the table kept grating this way and that. He felt light-headed, a prelude to seasickness, but kept his expression impassive. He'd just come through two typhoons, on the surface. This would be much worse for them. Submerged, they'd have experienced little motion, except when they snorkeled. The pervasive sour-vomit smell didn't help his stomach, though.

Time to establish some rapport, get this on a friendlier footing than what felt like an interrogation. "Any chance of tea?" he asked. "I very much enjoy Korean tea."

"No tea," Im snapped. "This is not party. Are you prepared to surrender all force under your command?"

"No. But I'm prepared to accept your capitulation."

Park and Won barked laughter; Im frowned. "That is not what you are here for. We have overwhelming force. Surrender, or we destroy all ships."

Dan said, as deadpan as he could, "What overwhelming force? I don't see such a force, Captain. Only one badly damaged submarine."

Im paused for dramatic effect. Then said gravely, tapping the table for emphasis, "We have *atomic weapon* aboard! *That* is overwhelming force."

"Is that right. May I see it?"

Consternation. They stared at each other. Then burst out arguing in Korean.

When Im turned back his frown plowed fresh grooves around his mouth. "We have nuclear weapon aboard. We will detonate it unless all South Korean bandit ships surrender to us and take measure to obey our command."

Despite queasiness and dread, Dan felt he was tuning in to what was going on. Im was starting out hard-line, the way North Koreans always did. He was convinced he held the top hand. And maybe he did, if he was willing to die. After a lifetime of regimentation, programming, indoctrination, he probably was.

All Dan had to do was convince the commander to ignore everything he'd ever been taught was right and honorable. Persuade him there was another way out than death and war.

Right, Lenson, he thought. How tough could it be? Persuading fanatical zealots, who believed their families would pay if they failed, to give up?

He folded his arms and put on the best command face he could muster. "Why should I believe you? Perhaps you are stinking Communist liars. I want to see this so-called weapon. It is probably nothing more than a fraud."

All three tensed. The word "fraud" meant something, then. Im barked at Won. The exec rose. When he beckoned impatiently Dan hauled himself up too.

They headed forward. At a small circular watertight door, the second in command swung himself through. Dan followed less gracefully, crouching, on all fours. There seemed to be only one deck, unlike *San Francisco*. More like World War II submarines: a single level, floored by a massive battery compartment. As they threaded a ballast control station Dan glimpsed scores of red-painted valve-wheels, a hull-penetration board glowing before a boyish crewman threw a blanket over it. The crewman's face was expressionless but his gaze followed Dan as he passed. Ahead along the passageway more blankets and sheets were being hastily pulled over what they obviously considered sensitive gear.

Forward of that was a berthing area, but all the bunks were
empty. Dan wondered where the crew was. Next came another watertight hatch, massive as the door of a bank vault.
Sacks of rice walled up the bulkhead around it. They were
working their way free with each roll; brittle grains grated
under his boots. He folded again and followed Won through,
grabbing a handhold, trying it feetfirst this time.

The next compartment looked like any torpedo room on
any submarine, though more cramped. The long fish lay
racked and strapped aft of the tubes and the maze of valves
and piping that wrapped them. But to port, as he straightened
from his crouch, was a large assembly that Dan saw at once
was no torpedo.

It was about twenty feet long and a yard in diameter. The
exterior looked like cast steel, painted gray. He saw instantly
from the shape alone that if it was indeed a nuclear weapon,
it must be a gun-type uranium bomb. Two crewmen stood at
attention in white paper suits, snoods, and booties. One held
a Geiger counter. Won took it from his hands and snapped a
switch. The clicks mounted to a roar as he passed it over the
massive tube.

Dan couldn't move. He couldn't even unlock his eyes
from the thing. He felt cold at the same instant sweat broke
all over his body.

He'd been close to them before, aboard carriers and
Tomahawk-armed cruisers. But never *this* close. *Touching*
close. The thing radiated, not just gamma and neutrons,
but pure, focused evil. He'd never believed *things* could be
malign, cross-grained with the universe, in and of themselves.

But intellectual conviction and this feeling of absolute
horror were two very different things.

"You are satisfied, then?" Won smiled, patting the massive
object as if it were a prizewinning hog he'd hand-fed from in-
fancy.

Dan nodded, taking a step back even as he tried to note
everything he could about it.

"You do not want us to open? We are much happy to open. Inspect."

He retreated another half step, till his back hit something hard behind him. If he was reading the scale on that counter right, he didn't want to spend a moment longer in this compartment than he had to. "No, no. I'm satisfied."

Won nodded again, looking pleased. He led them in a little reversed processional back to the messroom. Dan breathed easier when the massive door dogged behind them. Now he knew why the crew stayed aft. Why everything they owned was barricaded up against the bulkhead. He took his chair again opposite the trio, set his moves out in his mind, and began.

"Captain Im. I see you are well armed and bravely determined. You have fought very well. However, it is plain you can't achieve your mission. You cannot reach Pusan."

He paused, thinking they might confirm that *was* their mission. But all he got was Easter Island stone faces. He went on. "As you can't fulfill your orders, my commander, Commodore Jung, proposes the following. First, that you surrender your ship and your men."

"The People's forces do not surrender," the uniformed guy, Park, snapped.

"I understand. Their bravery is well known even in the United States." They seemed pleased when he complimented them; he decided to lay it on thicker. "You have sunk two ships and caused great damage to the ROK fleet. We never expected such seamanship and courage! The whole world is marveling at this moment. But even the bravest fighter must bow to inevitable defeat. The question then becomes, on what terms to surrender."

Park stirred again, but Dan hurried on. "Here is what I propose. We will announce that your submarine has been sunk and you all died heroically. You will receive Republic of Korea citizenship under new names. No one will ever know you surrendered. Your government, and your families at home, will remember you as heroes. As far as history will know, you will lie forever at the bottom of the Eastern Sea."

When he stopped speaking the exec began, apparently translating for those who didn't speak English, or speak it that well. Park burst out in a storm of protest. The others scowled at Dan, but he thought he saw interest in the captain's gaze. He looked at his watch, and turned the face toward them. "That is my proposal. You have one hour to make up your minds. After that, Commodore Jung will destroy your submarine."

"You are in us, Commander," Im pointed out.

"I came under a flag of truce. I will be back aboard *Chung Nam* before then."

"So *Chung Nam* is flagship?" Won wanted to know. Dan hesitated, then nodded. They'd showed him the bomb, after all.

They scowled. He stared back. He didn't want it to become a contest, so he added, "That is Commodore Jung's offer. Shall I tell him you accept?"

"It is *not* accepted. We will all die before surrendering," Im stated. The Party guy, or whatever he was, some kind of security or commissar type, and the exec both nodded vigorously. "We will never turn over our trust to Seoul bandit running dogs."

Dan thought about *San Francisco*. He hoped Mangum was far away by now, but maybe there was another possibility, if they hated the South so much they wouldn't even talk to them. Give them some choices, see if there was any flexibility. "Uh—then how about to Americans? Will you surrender to us?"

"Never to American imperialist pigs." They shook their heads and looked away.

The wallowing just didn't stop. She'd take four or five bad rolls, then the next one would wind up with her just about standing on her beam ends. The table slid sideways. The Koreans grabbed it, but slowly, uncoordinated; they were feeling it too. Park especially looked green. Dan swallowed a sudden spurt of saliva. Well, all they had to do was press a button and none of them would be seasick ever again.

To hell with this. If they wanted to die in proletarian glory, they could all fucking die. He pushed to his feet and stood riding with the motion. "Anyway, that's your choice. I'm going now. You have one hour to decide your fate."

The commissar type reached for something at his belt, but the captain's hand got to it first. He patted Park's hand reassuringly. "You are not leaving us," he told Dan.

"You're bound to release me. I came under a white flag."

Park chuckled. "That is bourgeois tradition. Not revolutionary tradition."

"Captain?" Dan addressed himself to Im, not the others.

The skipper hesitated, then waved at the chair. "Sit down. Sit down. We can talk a little more. You know, we are special trust, with what is up forward."

"I understand that, Captain. My proposal is designed to help you keep that trust."

Im frowned. "But how can that be? When you are enemy."

Dan considered. What did they have in common? Only one thing he could see. It might not be much. But it was the only card he held. He passed his hand over his hair and cleared his throat, hoping he got each word right.

"I may be your enemy, Captain, but we are both seamen. I too have commanded a ship. I know what it means, to care for your crew. To put the mission first, of course—but still, to consider what happens to your men. To do what is best for them. Not for yourself."

The dark eyes studied him. Dan hesitated, trying to piece together something convincing, then went on. "There are honorable ways to meet defeat. Without throwing away your men's lives. We are on opposite sides today, true. But I admire your bravery. You came very close to accomplishing your mission. And I can understand that you do not wish to turn such a powerful weapon over to your country's enemies. I wonder if you remember how the Germans disposed of their fleet after World War I."

All three looked bemused, so Dan abandoned the European history angle. "Look, we've destroyed or captured all the other subs in your task group. And now you're too damaged to make way. Your mission's over! The only thing you can do now is die. *Uselessly.* Condemning your men as well."

Park was frowning as Won translated. Dan let him catch up, then went on. "What if you scuttle instead? Sink your ship, with the weapon aboard it. You all live. You get citizenship and new names. As far as the People's Government will ever know, you were all killed in battle. That way your families will be safe as well. That is the wisest thing for you to do."

Park jerked to his feet, shouting. Not at Dan, but at his fellow officers, and at the crewmen who stood behind him. He pointed at Dan, screaming now. He jerked at his belt, and Dan saw the butt of the pistol.

With unhurried ease, the captain lifted a hand and laid it over the political officer's. Pulled the pistol from its holster himself, and handed it behind him to Won as he said a few words to the sailors.

Park looked astonished when they seized him. He stared down at Im incredulously. Then, abruptly, began to scream. The sound was high-pitched as a dentist's drill under the cupping steel. Dan couldn't make out words, though maybe there were words in it. If there were, the crewmen ignored them. Park struggled but the crew—the two beefeaters who'd dragged Dan aboard, he saw—were too brawny for him. They pushed his head down and forced him through the aft hatch, hands twisted behind him. The outraged, piping scream grew fainter, then cut off as the hatch sealed.

Im sighed, looking after him. No one spoke for a few seconds. Glancing forward, Dan saw sailors eyeing them around equipment cabinets, the jambs of joiner doors. They looked as shocked as Park had.

"They are truly all gone?" Im asked him.

"Who's that, Captain?"

"Our other submarines."

"That's correct."

"All four?"

"Three we sank. The other ran aground and was captured."

"Has the war begun?"

Dan looked him in the eye. "Not yet. Do you still want to start it?"

The captain rubbed his knees as he sat. His expression was growing closer to that of a human being. But he still didn't answer.

"Your mission was to destroy the harbor of Pusan," Dan said. "To prevent UN reinforcements and supply. But the American Army is sailing for Pusan now. Even if the People's Republic attacks, it cannot win. Hundreds of thousands will die. Hundreds of thousands of *Koreans*—from both sides of the DMZ. But victory for the North is impossible now."

He tried to catch Im's gaze, but it was not in the compartment with them. "Captain, do you really want your crew to die for nothing? Surely not, as brave as they've proven themselves. I see most are only boys. They have their whole lives ahead. They trust you. You are their captain. Are you going to condemn them to death? For nothing? I'm betting you don't."

Im looked away. Rubbed his face, looking at the bloodstain at his feet.

"It might be that enough have died," he said softly.

Dan breathed out. "I think so too, Captain."

"My men will be cared for? Protected?"

"I guarantee that personally."

"You will tell me how to do this thing, Captain?"

"I will—Captain."

Im looked at his commissar's pistol, then thrust it into his pocket. He glanced at Won, who was still staring, supporting himself on the table. He said a few words in a low voice. The second nodded hard, swallowing.

Won straightened suddenly, and gave his captain a rigid salute. Im returned it solemnly. Then turned to Dan, and gestured to the table.

"Let us discuss this thing a little more," he said.

Even without his Party guy around, Im drove a hard bargain. He wanted the sub sunk in his presence, now, as soon as the crew was taken off. He wanted a written guarantee that the device it carried would never be retrieved. His crew was to be rescued, given new names, and paid five thousand dollars U.S. apiece. Dan tried to disguise his relief. Rather than agree immediately—he had the feeling that might lead to fresh demands—he said he had to check the details with Jung.

The fresh air atop the sail felt like emerging from the seasick circle of Hell. *Chung Nam* stood off half a mile, bow on; the other frigate Dan couldn't pick up in the heavy seas. He tried not to look at the vomit staining the cockpit as he breathed deep. He keyed the VHF portable they'd given back to him. A lookout stared with an unreadable gaze. He was so drained he could barely stand.

"*Chung Nam,* this is—this is Lenson. Over."

"This is Hwang, Dan. Go ahead."

He reported the deal and asked for Jung's blessing on the terms. It came back within the minute. He acknowledged and signed off.

Then suddenly sagged against the steel, dizzy and all but unconscious. He felt like a capacitor suddenly discharged after holding too high a voltage for too long.

It was over. The mushroom cloud would not bloom over another city, nor destroy another ship. *Chung Nam* and her crew were safe. He didn't much care for the guys aboard this last Romeo—they'd tried their damnedest to kill him—but he couldn't deny they were brave too. And now they too would not have to die.

Pusan was saved. Which meant the war could be won. Or at least that the South had a fighting chance.

All in all, not a bad day's work.

Voices from below. He peered down the trunk, almost losing his balance and falling, but grabbing a handhold in time. Captain Im was down in the sail's interior, giving instructions, pointing out on deck. Won was nodding. They both looked grave. Im glanced up at him, looking distracted. Then grabbed the ladder and came up fast, boots ringing on the wet steel rungs.

They stood together, looking toward the whaleboat, which was approaching from the lee, where she'd apparently hove to while Dan had been below.

Dan didn't say anything. There was nothing left to say. He'd had bitter times, he'd lost men and seen ships go down in battle, but he'd never had to scuttle in defeat. He couldn't imagine how that might feel. Im didn't give him any clues. Unless he thought just saying nothing was all Dan needed to get it.

"You made the right decision," Dan told him in a low voice.

Im was considering that, maybe getting ready to answer, when shouts came from below. The captain frowned. He leaned over to look down the trunk.

Automatic fire chattered below them. Dan threw himself back as the bullets tore through Im's body. The captain rose up off the steel grating, then fell. He was crumpling into the hatchway when Dan got his hands on his shoulders.

When the Korean's legs came out of the well they were pumping bright blood. His stomach was torn open. Im's face wore the same shocked look his political officer's had when the crew grabbed him.

The firing stopped. Dan glanced down at the reeling deck. Five crewmen stood frozen in the act of rigging lifelines. They were staring up. The whaleboat was still three hundred yards off, and making heavy weather of it, pushing her bow toward the sky, then plunging as if she'd never come up. Making headway, but she wouldn't be alongside for a few minutes yet.

He leaned quickly over the trunk, just taking the briefest snap-glance down.

He glimpsed a khaki Soviet-style uniform, with red collar tabs. Park's wide scowling face turned to stare up at him. An AK muzzle whipped up.

He jerked back just as more bullets blasted past, clanging fragments off the steel lip of the hatch.

When he knelt by Im, the captain was dead. Dan shook him but he didn't respond. Fuck, fuck . . . fucking Park, the

Party guy, had gotten loose somehow. Threatened the crew until they let him go. Now he was trapped up here with a dead man. And in two or three minutes this political idiot would figure out he had to trigger the bomb *right now*. Before the guys he'd browbeaten back into line changed their minds again, and decided they'd just as soon live after all.

He looked over the cockpit coaming again. At the guys down on deck. Christ, how young they were, just boys most of them, still gazing up at him.

"Goddamn it," he muttered. "Shit. You *bastard*—"

He bent quickly and fumbled through Im's bloody bullet-ripped coveralls until he found Park's pistol. He wiped the captain's blood off on his jacket, racked the slide to make sure there was a round in the chamber, then stuck it under his belt and threw his leg over the coaming. Straddled it, looking down, trying to ignore the roaring sea. Just as he'd remembered, there were rungs down the side of the sail.

The deckhands below were still watching. He pointed to the approaching whaleboat and gave them as cheery a wave as he could muster. Could he get to it before things went to shit? He didn't know. Anyway, he had to get down to the main deck, whatever came next. Stay up here, and they had him cornered.

He threw his other leg over and started down.

The first couple rolls weren't too bad. Maybe fifteen, twenty degrees. But then came the hard ones, with a vicious snap at the end that came close to flicking him off the narrow, wet, rusty rungs into the boiling sea. They weren't really even rungs, just curved steel bars welded to the sail plating. He clung, feeling old injuries tear again in his neck and shoulders. The tea-green sea boiled beneath him as the swells broke over the lurching hull. Flung off into that foaming, swirling turmoil, he'd never make it back to the surface; air-filled water gave way beneath a swimmer, sucked him down.

Hugging the sail, he suddenly noticed something he hadn't before: the skin of the tower itself. He'd thought, from a distance, that it was steel. Then, that it was the radar-absorbing rubber compound U.S. subs were sheathed with.

But looking closely now, he saw it was neither. A rubber compound, yes. But embedded in it were hundreds of thin metal . . . *laminations*. Only slightly thicker than foil, they stuck up about a millimeter above the base material. Like the heat-radiating fins you saw on the outdoor side of air conditioners.

The sail rolled again, harder, and he had to grip with all his might to stay on it. Forget what the fucking sail's coated with, he told himself. Just concentrate on not dying here, okay?

It rolled twice more, harder each time, before he got to the main deck. By then his hands were streaked with blood, his own mixing with Im's, his skin grated off by the rusty rungs. He groped for footing, got it, slipped, and almost went overboard. At last he got his boot-toes locked to that narrow ledge between sail and deck edge, and eyed the door.

The door he'd leaped toward from the whaleboat, had been dragged through by two large Koreans. Now arguing shouts came from it, blown his way in snatches by the blustering wind.

Past the sail he caught the whaleboat coming up on the far side. The crew were waving to him. He measured the distance, looked again at the seas. Hope ignited. Rough, but not too heavy to swim in, if he could clear the frothy turbulence around the pitching hull itself. He was a strong swimmer. If he could jump clear, and no one started shooting at him, he might make it.

He sucked air, trying to pump himself up for the plunge. In the next few moments he might die. But at least he'd go out trying to escape.

But when he looked back the Koreans on deck were still watching him. Others were checking out the approaching boat, and the dark cloud of *Chung Nam* on their horizon. He could read no emotion on their faces. But neither was there the fanatic hatred with which the female commando had charged him, intent on his death.

These guys weren't special forces, as she'd been. Just plain navy. Did they even know what their savage state had done to them? Did they have any conception of freedom? He had no idea. But they were watching him. They looked so fucking *young*. They were watching *him*—

Im had surrendered to him, the Yankee officer. They knew that much. *He* was in charge now. That was what they were waiting for.

Not gladly—not at all—he put aside any thought of swimming for it. He might make it, but he'd be abandoning them. They weren't his people. Not exactly. But . . .

But he'd given their captain his word. His personal guarantee he'd take care of them. That Im was dead now, that the tables had turned against Dan, didn't alter that commitment.

"Try to keep everybody alive." Admiral Niles's words. He'd resented them. But that didn't mean they weren't true. They applied to everyone, didn't they? Even the enemy, when they weren't really your enemy anymore.

He hung there, knowing what he had to do but still not wanting to do it. Giving it another second. Then another.

A sea hit and exploded, spattering him with liquid salt. The sub rolled and his boots shot off the wet black tiles. He grabbed the last rung with his left hand, went for the pistol in his right, and hung grimly. She lay over, the sea boiling and snatching at him. He clung with his arm cramped closed, panting against the strain, counting the seconds till she came back. *Was* she coming back? It seemed dreadfully long.

But then she did, and he pushed aside hesitation and fear. He thumbed the hammer back on the automatic, scrambled around into the doorway, and leveled it.

Two sailors stood by the door. Past them, Park had his hands and one boot on the ladder up. An AK was slung over his back. The political officer met his eyes. Then, arms working frantically, he began unslinging his weapon.

Dan shot him three times in the chest from five feet away. The high-pitched cracks crammed the enclosed sail solid with sound. He expected with each shot that the men between whom he fired would knock the gun from his hands.

But they didn't. They didn't move as Park, hatred smeared across his face, struggled to get the sling untangled, to pull the assault rifle into position to fire.

He was still trying when Dan shot him once more. This bullet caught him in the throat. Park jerked his head back. He stopped struggling and relaxed. His eyes froze into an expression of incommunicable terror. He lay with arms thrust through the ladder, hanging from it by them and the rifle sling.

Suddenly the crewmen came to life. They seized Dan from both sides and jerked the pistol from his hands. His head rocked as one slapped his face. The men out on deck came boiling aft.

Then someone was shouting down below. Won stormed up from the control room, bellowing, cheeks flaming. The exec took the situation in with one glance. He kicked the body hanging on the ladder, shouting, waving his arms. He kicked the dead man again, spitting curses, and jabbed his finger at Dan.

The men hesitated, then released him and stepped back. The guy who'd slapped him grinned sweetly. He held his palms up, chuckling, as if it were all a game and he'd just scored a good one.

Dan looked past them at the two who still held AKs. Won stood directly in front of them, shouting at full pitch into their faces from six inches away. They looked confused, then just sullen.

The far side door, the port door into the sail, banged open. The exec turned his head and barked an order to the seamen who crowded in.

They jerked the rifles from the hands of those who held them and whipped them out into the sea. The weapons disappeared into the foam. Dan jerked the pistol away from the guy who'd grinned at him, and hurled it after them with all his strength.

When he wiped his shaking hands on his jacket they left sticky smears.

He suddenly folded, hands to his knees, and leaned in a

corner, shaking, fighting not to cry, not to vomit, not to
scream. His head felt separated from everything below it, as
if it were connected only by wireless. From outside, through
the crash and howl of wind and sea and a hollow clanking as
the crippled sub rolled, came the nasal staccato honks of the
whaleboat's monotonously insistent horn.

The Afterimage:
ROKS *Chung Nam*

Dan stood on the flagship's bridge wing two hours later, watching the somber shape that wallowed downwind and downsea a quarter mile off. Only two men were left aboard, and both were dead.

Won stood beside him, hunching his shoulders nervously and pondering his watch. The South Koreans had given the sub's Northern exec a wide berth when he'd stepped aboard a few minutes before—the last soul off the doomed boat. Captain Yu had ordered the master at arms to cuff him. Dan had thrust a protective arm in front of the North Korean, and said that wasn't part of the deal. The two Koreas were not yet at war. But even if they were, the Romeo's crew were *his* prisoners, not Yu's.

He had no illusions about how long he could keep the reins. Eventually he'd have to turn them over to military intelligence. Though even there, he'd do his best to get them into Combined Forces custody rather than Korean. He just didn't care for what he'd seen of that bunch.

Of course they had to be kept away from any weapons. But aside from that, he wanted them treated as guests, not prisoners. Especially the exec. His cooperation in the surrender aside, he could be an invaluable intelligence source down the road.

Won looked anxiously at his watch again. "How much longer?" Dan asked.

"It should happen now."

It didn't, though. Dan started to wonder if it was going to happen at all. So did Won, if his fidgeting was any guide. But at last a rippling thud drummed across the sea. It was so muffled that if they hadn't been facing it they might not have heard. A puff of thin black smoke whipped away off the top of the sail. It didn't seem like much. But the North Korean seemed to settle down.

Nothing changed for some minutes. Then, very gradually, Dan noticed that the sail's swings were growing less violent. Less of the hull showed aft, too. The seas swept over her whale's back, breaking into white foam, then hissing and swirling around her in shades of jade and emerald under the gradually lightening sky. The sun wasn't out yet, but at least now he could tell where it was. Before too long it might break free of the overcast.

Beside them Jung cleared his throat. The commodore tapped out a silver-tip and ducked into the lee to light it. He glanced at Dan, then at the Northerner. After a moment he held out the pack. Neither man's expression altered in the least, but Won took one. He borrowed Jung's lighter, too, and squatted in exactly the same way to touch flame to it.

When Dan looked back the hull was submerged. The last Romeo was taking her final dive. Her sail was nearly vertical; the battle flag, which Won had insisted remain hoisted, was still flying. Then she slowly tilted forward. Dan had never thought of submarines as graceful, as seacraft went. But it was with a surpassingly elegant inclination that the black fin glided slowly forward into a breaking wave. The wind-starched ensign of the People rose above it; dipped beneath another, and rose, yet not quite as high.

It nodded into a third swell, and did not emerge again.

The gray-green sea rolled empty of the least particle of debris or slick of oil. Barren of any sign of man. Save the unscrolling smoke trail of a low-flying patrol plane, making a last pass over the final datum of what Won told them had been submarine *S-13*.

Too late, Dan remembered it was taking something of his along in its plunge to the floor of the Eastern Sea: his USS

Horn belt buckle. He'd worn it to remember the men, and women, who'd died under his command. Without thought, he raised his hand in a curl-armed, bent-handed Navy salute.

Not to the Communist ensign, an emblem of tyranny and hatred. But to the brave man who'd captained her; to all the bold sailors, from whatever side and state, who carried out their duty, even for causes unworthy of their sacrifice. Sometimes orders were wrong, crusades misguided or even evil. But always there was duty.

Something like that must have been going through Won's mind too, because as Dan dropped his salute he saw the North Korean drop his too, and turn away, and cough, and under cover of the cough, rub his eyes. Jung seemed less affected. He was staring at the empty, heaving surface, eyes dull, jaw slack, exhaustion in every line of his body. He was just standing there smoking.

Hwang slammed the bridge door open, breaking the moment. He reported to Jung with a quick bow. With a side glance at Won, they conferred. Then moved off behind the .50 mount where they could not be heard.

Left alone with Dan, the North Korean looked nervous once again. "I should be with my men. "I must make sure they are treated well. What do you suggest I do?"

"They're having dinner now on the mess decks," Dan told him. "You're welcome to join them if you want. Actually that might be the best idea—I don't think Captain Yu'd react well to my inviting you into his wardroom."

"But what do *you* prefer me to do?"

"It's up to you," Dan told him, wondering if even a little liberty was going to be too much for this guy. Well, he'd just have to learn how to deal, like everybody else. "As far as I'm concerned, until we get back into Chinhae, you and your guys are on your own, as long as you stay out of trouble. Maybe I can get some of the ship's people to talk to your men. To sort of get them prepared. It's going to be different where you're going than where you came from."

Still looking uncertain, Won said all right; he'd be down on the mess decks if anyone needed him.

Dan lingered on the wing, looking down at the sea. It was slipping past more rapidly now, the diesels throbbing louder. *Chung Nam* was turning. Aiming her stem homeward.

If he'd left something of his own aboard *S-13*, he carried part of her with him too. Wrapped in a towel under the bunk pad in his stateroom was one of the laminated tiles from the sail. It had hung half torn off near where he'd waited for the whaleboat. He'd grabbed it while everyone's attention was on the approaching boat, and bent it back and forth and finally torn it free of whatever glued it to the steel.

He'd examined it in his cabin. The metal laminations were soft. He could bend them with his fingers. Aluminum? Lead? If used as deck coatings, you wouldn't be able to walk on them without deforming them—unless you wore something like . . . tennis shoes. The foils wouldn't last long in salt water either. They were already corroding. The system didn't look practical for long patrols. But he had a hunch that the precisely spaced laminations would trap and absorb the exact wavelength produced by the seeker head on the Mark 46 torpedo.

It wasn't anything he'd ever heard of before. But the tech guys back at TAG might be interested.

Come to think of it, they might want to sit down with Won, too. If, after getting acclimated, he was willing to talk.

Hwang came back. The chief of staff nodded to Dan. "We reported to Seoul."

"Reported destruction? Or capture?"

"The commodore gave me the exact wording. I think you'll be satisfied. Seoul will release the news immediately. They won't mention anything about the crew, or what was aboard."

Dan told him thanks. Hwang stood with him for a moment. Then said, "The commodore was quite angry with what you promised them."

"They wouldn't have surrendered otherwise."

"Oh, I know that. I pointed out how unreasonable he was being. And how this could have turned out much worse for everybody. I think he'll come around."

Dan nodded. Hwang waited a moment more, then left again.

He felt desperately tired, but still too wired even to think about sleeping. Instead he went down to sick bay. As the "doc" cleaned up the lacerations on his palms, and applied antibiotic salve and bandages, he sat watching O'Quinn breathe. The older man was still unconscious. He seemed no worse, though Dan had no medical qualifications. Beneath the oxygen mask he might even be regaining some color. But Dan couldn't tell if he truly was better. At least he was still breathing.

Without a word, Dan took the hand that lay on the bed. It was still stained with oil, and the fingernails were torn up pretty badly. O'Quinn must have literally clawed his way through to get to the man he'd saved.

"You did all right, Joe," Dan muttered. Not really to the man beneath the hissing mask, though he supposed it was possible O'Quinn might hear. It was to remind himself to never write a man off. Even the disgraced, the lost, the destroyed, still might find a way back. If they could find the courage; even if once, they hadn't displayed enough.

When his own hands were fixed up he went aft to the mess decks for rice and vegetables with the North Koreans. He drank tea afterward, saying little, just looking at them now and then with a strange feeling. Of something like wonder, or almost fondness—which felt weird. Most of the frigatesmen sat apart from them, scowling and muttering. But a few already hovered at nearby tables, leaving seats vacant between, but eyeing the strangers, curiosity plain even in their frowns. The Northerners were glancing their way too. He figured they'd all be slinging the bull together before the lines went over. Won seemed subdued, but forced a smile when Dan raised his cup to him.

Topside again, he stood on the main deck watching as dusk, then dark, came to the sea. The other frigate kept company astern. Distant lights glittered on the horizon, a wash of light that dimmed the emerging stars. A great city. Pusan. The lights rode slowly down their starboard side, then dropped astern and sank into the night. Not long after, he picked up the faraway on-and-off of the sea buoy marking the approach to Chinhae.

Henrickson found him there watching the passing waves. The analyst congratulated him, then passed on the latest news. Shelling along the DMZ had stopped. Air activity seemed to be lessening too. The stream of aggressive pronunciamentos from Radio Pyongyang had been replaced by optimistic crop bulletins.

"That's good," Dan told him. "Isn't it?"

"I'd say so, yeah. Maybe we put it off a few more years. The war, I mean."

"If we can keep on doing that long enough . . ."

"Yeah." The analyst didn't follow that line of thought out; maybe figured he didn't need to. Henrickson added, "There'll be an ambulance on the pier for Joe. They'll take him to the military hospital when we get in."

"Thanks for setting that up."

"I didn't. Yu did that. And the commodore wants to know about the rest of us. I figure he means, are we getting off in Chinhae."

"That's the plan, Monty." He roused himself; he'd better get something off to TAG, let them know his take on events, and that they were heading home. "I'll start getting an after-action report together. Can you start pulling data together, any observations you want in the message? And get our gear ready to go?"

"Already on it." Henrickson lingered, though. He scratched under his arms and added, after a moment, "I have to submit a report too."

"What report's that, Monty?"

"It's on you, Commander."

Dan turned to look at him, but it was too dark to see his expression. "Oh?"

"There's another team at TAG we were thinking about you for. One that does different things from the others. More of an operational-side group."

"And?"

"I'm going to say you need to be in it. If not in charge."

Dan said they could talk about that when they got back. For now, he just wanted to make sure they got the team back together, their gear broken down and backloaded, with as little fuss and trouble as possible. He wanted *S-13*'s crew properly handed off, with an official memo of the terms of their surrender, copies to TAG and Naval Intelligence and Combined Forces Korea. Meanwhile Henrickson could set up Team Bravo's transport back to the States.

And maybe after they got back he could put in for a few days' leave. See if Blair was home. He sucked a breath, feeling eager. Almost as eager as he was to get his head down. The hunger for sleep was overwhelming now that he'd eaten. He'd go below and snatch an hour before they pulled in. No, damn it—he had that fucking message to write—

Henrickson nodded and left. But instead of going below to work, Dan turned back to the darkening sea, the winking lights of the channel delineating the one proper and safe path.

If only there were something like that to guide a man's life. But it wasn't laid out that neatly. There were twists, and turns, and unmarked shoals. About all you could be sure of was that when it all looked clear ahead, that was when you'd better check your cross-bearings. Look astern, to make sure no one was coming up your ass. Calibrate your compass, and prepare for the heavy weather that was sure to come.

Because there were no guides, and no guarantees, and everyone made mistakes. If you just kept on, though, with faith, and the truth, and as much courage as you could muster, he was pretty sure it would turn out all right.

Hands in his pockets, to hold up his still-beltless trousers, he stood watching as the channel opened ahead.

Read on for an excerpt from
David Poyer's next book

THE WEAPON

Available in hardcover from St. Martin's Press

The main drag at Little Creek Naval Amphibious Base led from the gray behemoths at their piers east to what Dan remembered had once been the main exchange. It and the commissary had relocated to a new complex, but Headquarters, U.S. Navy Tactical Assessment Group, was near neither. It was down a side road that headed off into what years before had been scrub pines, dunes, sea oats, and sand fleas, a wind-whipped waste with verdigrised cartridges still littering the damp sand where draftees had trained before shipping out for Africa in 1942.

Now those bayfront dunes housed commands whose tenancy went unadvertised. TAG was housed in a low tan brick building that reminded him of a half-buried bunker. A Mark 48 torpedo and a Tomahawk missile pointed skyward on steel pylons before the entrance, and discreet bronze letters announced TACTICAL ASSESSMENT GROUP.

He and Henrickson showed their IDs at the front desk. The rest of the team had taken the weekend, and would be in on Monday. They clipped on their badges and headed to the back, down a hallway past the Game Room and the mainframe. The big IBM didn't get used much anymore; the crunchers used workstations that were faster and friendlier, but it was still there. It was Saturday but the offices were still full; a reserve unit came in on weekends. Dan punched numbers into the door lock and let himself into his office.

Home, or as close to it as shore duty Navy got. His office

was windowless and not much more luxurious than Schrade's, but it did have central air. He skated his duffel next to the plywood cruise box that held what uniforms he hadn't left at the house in Arlington. There was a bunk bed down the hall, but usually he stayed at the BOQ. He ought to get an apartment. But it didn't feel right, to set up housekeeping when he hoped to get back to Blair. The complexes he'd looked at in Ocean View and along Shore Drive had been too depressing to consider.

He slotted his cap into the rack and flipped on the coffeemaker. Unlocked his desk and checked that the Beretta Nine Mullaly had issued him when he reported aboard was still there. He booted up the terminal and went to the LAN.

Forty-six messages. Some were from the Surface Navy and the Alumni associations, others from friends, others relating to the operation they'd just finished off Korea, one from a former West Wing subordinate asking for a reference. He was working through them when the IM popped up with a request for him and Henrickson to report to Captain Mullaly.

Norman Todd Mullaly, TAG's CO, was heavyset and balding. When Dan closed the door, the commanding officer flicked his fingers at the chair and swivelled away the screen. He did it every time anyone came in. Monty was already there; the little analyst nodded to Dan.

"Dan. Siddown. How'd it go? GrayWolf trains rough, I hear."

"Yessir, I dropped a few pounds. I think they usually get younger people, trigger-pullers. Cops, Marines, the spec ops folks. They seemed a little uncertain what to do with us."

"Well, you can't tell everybody everything." Mullaly looked back at the computer. "By the way, word is, Dick O'Quinn? He's going to recover. Maybe not to a duty status, but he'll walk again. Figured you'd want to hear."

Dan nodded. In the operation in the Korea Strait in which Im's submarine had been sunk, O'Quinn—a retired captain—had nearly died trying to rescue a Korean sailor from a flooding compartment. It had been touch and go whether he'd regain consciousness. "That's good. I'll go by and see him, if he's still at Portsmouth."

Mullaly nodded. He cleared his throat, then carouseled the screen to face them.

Dan blinked. For a moment he couldn't guess what he was looking at. An oblately pointed cylinder rested base down on what looked like a black felt drop-cloth. The upper portion was cut away to show interior details. A pop-out fin stuck out from either side. A projectile of some sort? But at the bottom was a bell-shape that suggested a rocket engine.

"Some kind of terminal-guided munition?"

"Looks like it, doesn't it? But it's not. You fire this underwater."

"Underwater?" Dan leaned closer, trying to make out the lettering, but his eyes were giving him trouble. The call-outs wouldn't resolve into words. Then he realized why. They were in Cyrillic. "This is Russian?"

"You're looking at the VA-111 'Shkval' supercavitating projectile. It's not really a torpedo. Not really a rocket, either. But you could call it a rocket torpedo, and get the idea across." Mullaly keyed another window and brought up a document of which the image was apparently a part. "We don't have anything like it, which is maybe why the terminology difficulty. Thing's completely new to us."

"Well, Norm," Henrickson put in, folding his arms. Dan started before he remembered that a civilian analyst was perfectly correct calling their commanding officer by his first name. "Not *completely* new. I remember some work on cavitation envelopment back in the eighties. From NRL, I think."

"Monty, what we're hearing is pretty appalling," Mullaly said complacently, as if however appalling it was, it couldn't be that bad. "It uses a shaped noseplate to create cavitation— a bubble of water vapor—that's then fed with more gas to surround the body. Then the rocket motor kicks in, and it really accelerates. The Russians claim a top speed of two hundred knots."

No one spoke, as all three contemplated the tactical

advantages of a weapon that ran four times as fast as the U.S. Navy's fastest torpedo, and five times faster than its speediest submarine. Dan rubbed his face. He'd had torpedoes fired at him, and the ordinary versions had been terrifying enough. "Wait a minute. You said they're *claiming* this speed? You mean, like . . . *advertising* it?"

"Advertising it, exactly. For government-to-government sale." Mullaly tapped more keys and hit Enter. "I'm sending you the package on the secure LAN. A flyer from the 'Komponent' Scientific and Production Enterprise, Moscow. A Defense Intelligence Agency notice. Some open-source stuff from a Ukrainian scientific journal. And a classified evaluation from the Joint Chiefs of what a weapon like this means strategically."

"I thought the Russians were our buddies," Henrickson said.

"They're buddies to anyone with cash. And they're coming back as a problem set. They might see their national interest as to help out any of our regional challengers. North Korea, China, Iran, Syria—the usual suspects."

Henrickson said, "This is starting to sound familiar. The 53-65K. The wake-homer. They sold those to the Chinese."

Mullaly said, "That's right. And we sent Team Charlie after them. That was back when Christine was the CO, right?"

"We got three of them," Henrickson told Dan. "Gave one to DARPA, one to DIS, and kept the one with the fewest bullet holes. Did fifteen instrument runs down at Tongue of the Ocean."

Dan said, through dawning apprehension, "Are you saying, Captain—are you saying you want us to steal one of these? Is that the sense here?"

"Well, steal's a harsh word," Mullaly said. "But we have a tasking to get specs and if possible a working model, or best of all, one of the issue rounds and associated equipment—software and so forth. Because this is causing some stir up at J-3, and over at Sublant. The Russians have actually been carrying these around for some time. At least, an early model."

He explained that the sub community suspected Soviet

strategic ballistic missile submarines, like the Typhoons, had carried Shkvals as engagement breakers. As soon as they heard an incoming torpedo, they could fire into the noise spoke. If they could force the launching platform to turn away, that would break the guidance wire, after which both subs would be on equal ground, since the American would have lost the advantage of surprise.

"Uh, wait a minute, sir. This thing's surrounded by super-cavitation, and going two hundred plus? That's got to be way past the self-noise threshold for passive transducers."

"It is."

"So how's it guided?"

"You're right, it can't sonar-guide like a conventional homer. And it goes too fast and the turbulence trail's too violent to wire-guide or wake-home, either. The consensus is that up to now it's been a straight-run weapon. Like the old steam torpedoes, only a lot faster."

Henrickson said, "They just pick up a target bearing, and shoot down it? That's not going to give them much probability of a hit."

"With a nuke, you don't need a hit."

"A nuke?" Dan tried to keep his face from showing anything, though just the word brought back images of charred flesh, smashed metal, the ripping snarl of radiation meters. USS *Horn* was now a deserted, radioactive shell behind barbed wire at Norfolk Naval Shipyard. "What's the range, on this thing?"

"A couple thousand yards."

"With a *nuclear* warhead? That'd destroy both subs."

"Maybe they thought their double hulls would take it. Or didn't care, as long as they took down a *Los Angeles* class, too. But you're right—being unguided made it less dangerous. But now there's a twist. A kicker." He glanced at the screen, which was turned away from them again. "I'll summarize. Since this is beyond TS/SCI. There's a source—a spy—in the Russian Admiralty. According to this source, one of their designers has figured out a way around the homing problem."

TS/SCI stood for Top-Secret/Sensitive Compartmented

Information. Which Dan had been cleared for in the past, on the White House staff. But either Mullaly didn't know this, or his clearance had been revoked. He rubbed his chin, feeling as if he was being shadowed by something evil, like the Hound of the Baskervilles, or Hannibal Lector.

"What way?" Henrickson muttered.

"Our source doesn't know. Either that, or he's holding out for more money."

"Guided, that could be nasty," Dan said.

"It gets worse. This guided version—they call it the 'Shkval-K,' with the K for 'Komponent,' I guess—that's the name of the design bureau—the Iranians are looking at buying it. And that has *really* got some knickers kinked."

Dan said, "Because of the carriers?"

"Exactly," Mullaly told him. "Something this fast, and terminally guided, the Iranians could close the Gulf, cut off our oil. If the Chinese get it, they can take out our stalkers, use the Sea of Japan as a strategic haven—that would screw us up big time in Asia. We have to find out whether this thing works, and if so, how. That's the Chief of Naval Operation's tasking to us. Get our hands on a sample, so we can build countermeasures.

"Read up on it and we'll talk tomorrow about how you're going to go about it."

Henrickson nodded. He got up and left. But Dan stayed. When the door was closed, he cleared his throat. "Sir, we've got a slight problem."

"With Monty? Yeah, he can be kind of a know-it-all—"

"No, no. Monty and I get along fine. It's GrayWolf. I think the Army knows where I am."

"Well . . . it's not exactly a secret," Mullaly said cautiously. Dan frowned inside; he'd never really known how much his commanding officer knew about what had happened in the East Wing, and how convenient it might be for certain circles to be sure Dan Lenson would never give an interview or write a tell-all. "My understanding from Admiral Niles was, keep you outside the Beltway, and out of the country as much as possible. He even said to make sure you had a sidearm, which didn't make me popular with the base commander—his security people don't like firearms they don't control inside the gate. There more to it than that?"

Dan wondered if he, or maybe Niles, was being paranoid. Surely it was fantasy to think he might be in danger. This wasn't Byzantium or Florence. No matter how senior, military men weren't in service just for their own aggrandizement. He had to believe that, or he was in the wrong business and always had been. But he decided to push. "Has anyone asked? Any inquiries as to my whereabouts?"

Mullaly shook his head and looked back at the screen. Vertical lines appeared between his eyes. "No. But if Niles wants you out of the country, this tasking will require some travel. Like I said, look over the package, think about it, and we'll get together tomorrow. Let's say, zero-nine."

He read through the material, then searched the classified Internet, using key words like "high-speed," and "choke point," and "strategic threat." He found information on the State Scientific and Production Enterprise "Komponent" and on somebody named Yevgeny Dvorov, but very little detail. Which meant either this was all still below the radar, or else was classified tighter than Secret. He returned a call from Idaho, from the grandmother of a little girl whose mother had died helping to save *Horn* when Dan had been in command. The grandmother said the indemnity compensation checks had stopped. He made some calls to the VA. By the time he found the glitch and got a promise the checks would start again, it was time to knock off for the day.

Before he left, though, he punched in a Washington area code. Clarice, his wife's secretary, said she was on the phone, but if he'd hold, she'd see if she could free up. He listened to Pentagon elevator music.

"Dan. They let you out?"

"Hi, hon. Yeah. Back in the Navy, and glad to be here."

He was tempted to tell her about Schrade. She could give him chapter and verse about his backers, his contracts, but he didn't. The trouble with being married to an undersecretary of defense was that your wife was better plugged in than you were. Sometimes, even about things you thought you already knew. So much so that he found himself keeping things to himself. It wasn't that great for intimacy. But they'd managed to build a relationship, then a marriage, around not being together for long periods of time.

She sounded rushed, as usual. He checked his watch; she'd be there for two or three more hours. "You getting home anytime?" she asked.

"Uh, not really sure at this point. Just had a sit down with Mullaly. They might have something overseas for me."

"Can you make it this weekend?"

"I'll see. He didn't say when departure date would be. Or where we were going."

Her voice sharpened; he sensed the intense beam of her actual interest swinging his way for the first time in the conversation. "Something important?"

"Might be. I'll tell you about it if I can get back. How's everything going?"

"The bathroom's still a mess. The floor's gone, but I can't get a commitment from the tiling guys. You really think you might have to leave before this weekend?"

Her voice was softer now, as if it took a few minutes to melt her official persona. He knew the feeling, and suddenly missed her, and the quiet house in Arlington, and the new shelves he'd promised he'd build but hadn't gotten to yet. "Like I said, can't tell yet. But I miss you."

"I miss you, too."

"If I can get up even for a day, I'll be there."

"I'm looking at travel, too, but maybe we could get away. Go up to the Blue Ridge."

He jotted a note to himself to get the brakes checked on the Escort. Though if they went to the mountains they'd probably take her Lexus. She thought his car was too small to be safe. "That'd be nice. Oh, and Homecoming's coming up. Interested in that?"

"If I can go as your wife."

She meant, so she didn't have to talk to generals and admirals. "Absolutely. In a veil."

"That's more like it."

After some sappy endearments he hung up. He thought about calling his daughter, and at last he did. But the phone rang and rang in Nan's room and she didn't answer. She had a cell, too, but he didn't know its number. He left a message.

He changed in the locker room at the back of the building, broke out new shoes and fresh socks, a USNA tee laundered so many times the blue lettering was a shadow against the gray, and headed out for a run. The stored sun-energy blazed up off the pavement. A breeze tossed the treetops behind Rodriguez Range. Marines doubletimed past, chanting in unison. God, had he ever been that fresh-faced, that unreflectingly confident? Yeah, maybe he had. Back when he was an ensign, aboard *Reynolds Ryan* . . .

He jogged on, caught in memories that only after a time did he manage to wall off. He shook out his arms and shoulders, and picked up the pace.

When he slowed again, sweating in the heat, he was almost to the piers on the west bank of the inlet. He turned north, thinking to at least get a look—you couldn't jog down the piers anymore, a security fence cut them off from the rest of the base, but at least he could *look* at the ships—when a note caught his ear.

It was the slow tolling of braided wire clanging wind-driven against hollow aluminum. Masts loomed. He turned off the road and jogged past trailered powerboats waiting for the ramp. Then slowed to a walk as he reached the base marina. He hesitated, then headed past the OWNERS AND AUTHORIZED VISITORS ONLY sign, out onto the salt-weathered planks.

He was admiring a green-and-white sloop when a gray head popped out of the companionway. "Looking for me?"

"Uh, not really, sir. Just taking a break." He turned away.

"Just looking, eh? Come on aboard, then."

The owner's name was Adridge. He was retired, to judge by a paunch that wouldn't have passed the current fat standards. A captain or master chief, retired on thirty, Dan guessed. But he put on no airs. He showed Dan around, through main cabin to forward cabin, quarter berth, galley, head.

It wasn't new, but there was no scent of mold or rot, which was the smell of a badly kept boat. The bilges were dry and sweet. When Adridge unshipped the housing, the engine looked new. Even the fire extinguishers had inked tags with current inspection dates.

"Put a lot of elbow grease into her over the years," the owner mused, showing him the ball valves on the through-hulls. "All the electronics are up to date. But it's time to let somebody else enjoy her."

"Putting her on the market?"

"Yup. Just tinkering today, getting her ready for the broker to take pictures. Have to admit, though, I like the idea of another Navy guy sailing her."

Dan looked around the cabin again. He could change after work and jog to the marina. It wasn't an apartment, so he wouldn't be setting up separate housekeeping. And living on base meant that much added security, if Nick Niles was right and there really were people who'd just as soon keep him quiet.

"So . . . what're you asking?"

Adridge named a price. It was affordable; his car was paid off, his daughter's tuition was pretty much taken care of and she was even interning at a company in Springfield; he could do 10 percent down from his checking account, and USAA would be happy to loan him the rest. He asked about slip rental. Adridge said the slips went with the boat, not the owner, and the monthly fee sounded doable even with power and water included. Dan said he'd need a survey. Adridge said he wouldn't buy a boat without a survey, either. "Do you live around here, Dan?"

"Staying at the Q, right now. Share a suite with a guy from ATGLANT."

"Where you stationed? Aboard ship?"

"No, shore duty. Stationed over at—over at one of the tenant commands."

Adridge looked at the sky, then the channel. The basin was choppy with the wind coming over the dunes. "Well, what do you say we fire her up, see whether she likes you?"

The diesel stroked on the first press of the button, kicking out a gossamer blue smoke that vanished as it warmed up. Adridge backed out with one hand on the wheel—not a negligible performance, with one screw and an adverse wind—and headed out past the massive gray cliffs of the landing ships. Sailors shaded their eyes from the decks. Once past the jetty and in the Chesapeake, Adridge turned over the wheel. Moving about the deck stiffly but with perfect balance, reaching from shroud to shroud like a seagoing chimpanzee, the older man hoisted the main and set a roller-furled jib, then came aft to kill the engine as they accelerated, tilting on a starboard tack.

They sailed to Lynnhaven Roads and back, tacking through a stiff northeast breeze. She came about in her own length and cut through three-foot swells fast and clean as a sharp chisel through poplar. By the time they picked up the lines again Dan was sold, having remembered he'd promised to teach Nan to sail when she came East for college. He made an offer, conditional on the survey. Adridge held out his hand. "There were a couple of things I was going to do. Have the injectors checked. Replace the fore and aft stays—they've been up there a time. But if you wanted to take care of those, I could make your price."

"Injectors. Stays. Anything else I should keep an eye on?"

"There's a maintenance log in the navigator's desk. Oil change schedule and all the repair records and guarantees and so forth." Adridge looked up at the masthead. "We've had a lot of good times. Hope you have as much fun with her as we had, my wife and me." His eyes went far and Dan knew she wasn't with them anymore, that he was saying good-bye to a lot of memories with her in them. He blinked and lowered his gaze. " 'Course, it's your call. But I've heard it said, it's bad luck to change a boat's name."

"*Naiad*? It's a fine name," Dan said. "I'll keep it."

Adridge's weathered lips creased. "Grab that line then. Cross the stern lines—yeah. Like that. That way, she'll ride out anything that comes her way."